Darcy and Elizabeth
A Most Unlikely Couple

A Pride and Prejudice Adaptation

By
Brenda J. Webb

DARCY AND ELIZABETH – A MOST UNLIKELY COUPLE
Copyright November 14, 2014 by Brenda J. Webb
First Edition: November 2014
Front and back cover artist: Olga Dabrowska
Cover design by Wicked Covers
Formatted by IRONHORSE Formatting

All rights reserved. Without limiting the rights under copyright reserved above, no part of this publication may be reproduced, stored in or introduced into a retrieval system, or transmitted, in any form, or by any means (electronic, mechanical, photocopying, recording, or otherwise) without the prior written permission of both the copyright owner and the above publisher of this book.

Darcy and Elizabeth – A Most Unlikely Couple is a work of fiction. All characters are either from the author's imagination, or from Jane Austen's novel, Pride and Prejudice.

This e-book is licensed for your personal enjoyment only. This e-book may not be re-sold or given away to other people. If you would like to share this book with another person, please purchase an additional copy for each person you share it with. If you are reading this book and did not purchase it, or it was not purchased for your use only, then you should return to the publisher and purchase your own copy. Thank you for respecting the author's work.

DarcyandLizzy@earthlink.net
www.DarcyAndLizzy.com/forum

ISBN-10: 1496193113
ISBN-13: 978-1496193117

Dedication

To my editor, Debbie Styne, who keeps me focused on what is important and makes writing an adventure.

And to my team of betas: Kathryn Begley, Janet Foster, Wendy Delzell and Kimberley Kay, who brought their own special skills to the process. They worked tirelessly to correct my mistakes and to make this tale readable.

Without your help and support during the writing process, this book might never have been finished and I thank you so very much.

Other Books by Brenda J. Webb

Available on Amazon.com

※

Fitzwilliam Darcy An Honourable Man

※

Mr. Darcy's Forbidden Love

Chapter 1

Pemberley
April 1812

A light mist began to fall as Colonel Richard Fitzwilliam, sitting astride a newly purchased red stallion, galloped over a ridge and into the largest of Pemberley's meadows. If anyone had been watching, they might have thought him boyish despite his regimentals, for he was not very tall and only of average build; and having doffed his hat, his reddish blond hair was blowing about in the wind. Even so, one glance into his steel grey eyes would have put that notion to rest, for they held proof of what he had endured in service to his country.

Reining the horse to a stop in order to replace his hat, Richard looked up at the hills that bordered the field. This pasture happened to be situated just below his cousin's favourite haunt, and as he fixed his gaze on a particular ledge, he realised that the ridge was cosseted in a thick grey haze, obscuring his view. Looking skyward, his tired expression grew more serious as he noticed thickening clouds, which signified that a storm was not far off. He shivered from the dampness.

So much for seeing the magnificent view of Pemberley from this particular prospect!

Nonetheless, he had come this far and had no intention of turning back until he was certain that Darcy was not already there. Spurring Titan onward, he chuckled. Richard had been so confident of finding his cousin here that he had not bothered to stop at the manor house upon his arrival. Instead, he had urged his steed in this direction while simultaneously waving off the footmen who had rushed down the front steps to take his horse. At the time, he had found it amusing, but now that the rain and uncertainty was setting in, he feared that the joke had been on him. His cousin might have been at home, comfortable and dry, the entire time. And what was the use of gaining the hilltop if one could not see the view of the valley below?

Why did I bother trying to catch you here alone?

He knew the answer only too well. For several years now, whenever he and Darcy needed to discuss anything that they did not want Georgiana to hear, they rode out on horseback. She had developed an uncanny ability to know what was on their minds, and they were beginning to suspect that she had devised a way to listen to their conversations. Thus, when he received Darcy's letter requesting him to come as soon as possible, he assumed it important enough to necessitate confidentially. Well known for her propensity to sleep late, he was certain that when Georgiana got word that he had arrived, she would not rest until she located him—even if that meant riding out to find him. For that reason, he had departed Sheffield the day before and spent the night in an inn halfway to Lambton in a bid to be at Pemberley very early.

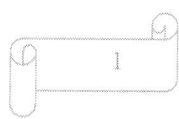

As these thoughts ran through his mind, Richard slowly worked his way up the trail that led to the top of the hill. Rounding the last bend, he was startled to hear a familiar voice greet him from somewhere in the haze.

"What took you so long? Has your stamina waned since you turned thirty?"

Glancing around, he could not see his cousin. Nevertheless, he answered, "It is barely daylight! And shall I remind you that you, too, are nearing that milestone, Darcy? I dare say that if you had trained raw recruits for the last month, sleeping in the fields like a nomad with rocks beneath your bedroll, you would not be nearly as hearty as I am this morning."

A deep, rumbling laugh echoed in the haze and made him smile. He enjoyed being able to lift his cousin's spirits. Waiting until a movement drew his eye in a certain direction, he watched as William stood from where he had been sitting undetected against the trunk of a huge tree. The branches had provided a canopy against the fine mist, so Richard kicked his mount in that direction.

Picking up his great coat, which had served as a seat, William brushed it off before answering, "No, I probably would not. Pray forgive me if I offended you."

"No offense taken."

When Richard came to halt beneath the tree, William examined his cousin's mount, sliding his hands down the beast's strong shoulder. "He is magnificent. I have not seen him before."

"Titan is the horse I spoke to you of last spring. I bought him when I was in York earlier this week. Lord Gordon had his man doing the training, so I waited until it was finished."

"Are you satisfied with him?"

"Yes. He is an excellent animal and readily obeys my commands."

"I am glad. I know that you wished for a horse to replace General, now that he is getting older."

"I am not sure that any horse could replace General, but I am grateful he is very content in your pastures. Thank you for taking him as I am not sure that father or Edgar would hesitate to put him down because of his age and infirmity. They were never fond of keeping an animal that was not pulling its weight and are not impressed with his bloodline. However, I shall never forget that that animal saw me through some rough campaigns."

"I, for one, appreciate that General has always brought you home in one piece. He can live here the rest of his days, and if he were to sire a few colts, all the better," Darcy replied.

"For him and for Pemberley!" Richard declared with a laugh. Quickly sobering as he took in his cousin's sombre mien, he brought up the motive for his summons. "The reason you sent for me must be quite serious, or we would not be engaging in pleasantries about my horses. Does it regard Andrew? Has that cad ruined another maiden?"

William stopped rubbing the horse's nose, and his expression darkened. "Not that I am aware of at present, thank God, though I do live in fear of hearing of another. In truth, I have not seen much of him since our last discussion regarding support of his illegitimate offspring."

"I wish I had been a fly on the wall when you informed him that you had the power to draw on his inheritance and that you had withdrawn a thousand pounds to establish a trust to provide income for the women who bore his children, as well as funds for the youngsters' educations."

"I would gladly have conceded the task to you. He can be quite irate where his funds are concerned, and he is livid that his monthly allowance has been cut in direct proportion to what I spent purchasing the land and constructing homes for his castoffs."

"Am I correct in thinking you bought land near Richmond?"

"Yes. The estate is called Eastbrooke and it is large enough to accommodate houses for both women and their children."

"Are you certain that Andrew is a Darcy? Could there have been some mistake?"

"Alas, I am afraid not. One has only to see him to ascertain that he is my cousin."

"Other than being about your height and colour, I do not see much resemblance, though, from the way Uncle George treated him, one would have believed him your brother!"

"I got the impression that Father always felt guilty that his brother Daniel became a vicar. After all Daniel was the rightful heir to Pemberley, but apparently he was drawn to the church and wanted no part of being the heir. Since Andrew's mother died shortly after his birth, when Daniel died unexpectedly, Father saw it as a chance to make amends by taking his son into our family."

"It is a shame his sympathy extended to everything that man did in conjunction with Wickham. How well I remember you being held accountable for things those two perpetrated!"

"I was the oldest and he expected me to keep them out of trouble."

"Something he himself was not willing to have a hand in!"

"That is true, but I cannot help but wonder if I could have done more to help Andrew. He was not such a bad fellow when he first came to live with us. Unfortunately, Mother was very ill at that time and I was—"

"No one could expect you to concern yourself with Andrew's feelings when your own dear mother was so ill! Besides, he never concerned himself with your feelings, as I recall."

"At any rate, I was preoccupied. But after Father sent him to Eton, he changed for the worse. You well know how the heirs like to torment the second sons, not to mention those like George, with no connections at all. There they became inseparable."

"Inseparable and indistinguishable," Richard growled. "How well I remember life at Eton, and still it did not make me a reprobate like Andrew or George Wickham! If anyone taunted me, I would just whip their snooty arses and go on about my business."

William smiled, though it quickly faded. "You had the fortitude. If only

Andrew could have been more—"

"How Andrew turned out was his own choice, Darcy!" Richard interrupted. "And what happened to those women was not your fault. Andrew thinks the world owes him a living because his father chose not to be the heir and he is not the Master of Pemberley! I will not stand here and listen to you take the blame for that sorry sot!"

"Perhaps you have the right of it," William said resignedly.

"I do! Fortunately, by the time Uncle George died, he had seen evidence of Andrew's dissipation and changed his will. Otherwise, you would have no leverage."

"Yes, he did leave me in control of the allowance allotted each year to keep Winfield Hall afloat and of the amount he will inherit in the next year if he has proven himself trustworthy. Unfortunately, he has shown no interest in running the estate left to him by Grandmother Darcy, preferring the vices of London to life as a gentleman farmer."

"He has never shown me anything but foolishness!" Richard declared. "In any event, your talk must have had some effect, for my spies report that he was last seen in London, charming the widows of the *ton*. I understand that a few of the handsomer blackguards earn a good living at that," he laughed aloud. "I can just picture Andrew as some old biddy's partner, bowing and scraping in order to acquire cash!"

"I cannot but pity anyone who takes up with him," William sighed.

"At least it keeps him away from shop girls, maids and tenant's daughters."

"Let us hope so. I suppose I will not hear from him until he causes more trouble." William's expression never lightened, so Richard probed further. "If this is not about Andrew, tell me why you have returned from Hertfordshire early? I thought you were to stay with Bingley for four weeks?"

"I left after two. I had done what I had set out to do, surveying the property, and there were circumstances that made an earlier departure necessary."

"Such as?"

"I have decided it is time that I marry."

Although the declaration caused Richard's heart to drum, he showed no emotion as he slid from the saddle and turned to secure Titan to a limb. *Has Darcy finally fallen in love, or has some woman trapped him into a marriage of convenience?* When he finally turned to confront William, all his reservations came spewing out.

"Just like that? Out of the blue? Only last month you spoke of the scarcity of women with good sense and character. Now, after spending two weeks in Hertfordshire, you have changed your mind? Sit back down and tell me what has happened or we shall stay here until you do."

"Do not be so dramatic," William replied, sitting down again. "It is not as if I never intended to marry. After all, you have heard me say often enough that I dearly love children, and I want an heir. It is just that I have found it almost impossible to meet the right woman."

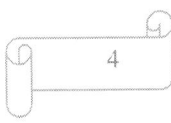

As Richard situated himself next to Darcy, he noted that his cousin did not look him in the eye.

"Evidently you met someone in Hertfordshire that has precipitated this change of heart." William's shoulders slumped and this spurred his cousin on. "Tell me about it, Darcy. You know I shall give you my honest opinion."

"That is what I fear. You may think me mad by the time I am finished."

Undaunted, Richard persevered. "I shall keep an open mind. Her name?"

"Is of no consequence, just as she is of no consequence. I shall just say that she is the sister of a woman who Bingley fancies himself in love with now."

"No consequence? What an odd way of describing the woman you aim to marry."

"You have misunderstood entirely! I could never marry *her*!"

Suddenly, it became clear to his best friend. "Now I understand. In essence, this mysterious creature has frightened you into doing your duty. You aim to secure a proper wife before you do something disastrous, like follow your heart?"

"In essence, yes."

"This should be interesting!" At William's scowl, Richard suppressed a laugh. "Please try to see my perspective, Cousin. Surely, you will not deny me the pleasure of hearing how some *nobody* stole the heart of one of the most sought-after men in England and perhaps the British Empire. Start at the beginning and tell me everything."

Resignedly, William began to relate how he met Elizabeth Bennet. "The first time I saw her it was… it was as though I suddenly entered another realm, perhaps between heaven and earth, I do not know."

Richard's jovial attitude vanished as his brow furrowed. *Heaven and earth?* Never had his logical cousin sounded more nonsensical.

"It was as though time was suspended for several seconds, and I could not move or speak." His expression grew more sombre. "Even now, I cannot adequately describe what transpired. It was remarkable to say the least."

"Good Lord, man! Was she real, or did you encounter a spectre?"

Shaking his head to remove the image of a slight woman with dark brown hair and sparkling eyes who had arrived unexpectedly at Charles' home, he replied, "She was definitely not a ghost, but I fear she may haunt me forever." A strong grip on William's shoulder reassured him. "She had walked more than three miles of muddy roads to attend her sister who had taken ill at Netherfield."

As William continued, it was not lost on Richard that his expression lightened, and a smile lifted the corner of his lips.

"Her hair was dark, almost black, and it hung down her back like a young girl's. Strong winds had tossed it about until it was a tangle of curls." Suddenly, his voice was wistful. "I remember wondering how long it would take her maid to brush it smooth."

William had stopped speaking and seemed to be lost in thought, so Richard coughed. Embarrassed, he schooled his features and began again.

"Her face fairly glowed—no doubt from the exertion of walking so long a distance—but it was her eyes that I recall most particularly. They were black as coal and flashed defiantly when Caroline Bingley made a derogatory comment about her having come so far on foot and another about all the mud she must have encountered." He added an explanation, "For the hem of her gown was six inches deep with mud."

Richard chuckled. "I can imagine that she did look a fright!"

"Actually, I thought she looked... *beautiful.*" The last was said almost too softly to be heard.

How strange that a man who has never approved of any display of impropriety would think a woman covered in mud is beautiful. "I could just imagine your reaction had that been Georgiana."

William dropped his head into his hands and rubbed his eyes wearily as he let out a deep groan. "All I know is that I was bewitched."

"If you truly care for her, Darcy—"

"I hardly know her!" William practically shouted as he took to his feet. "How could she wield such influence? And, to make matters worse, what little I do know of her makes a courtship impossible."

"Of course, it does," Richard said, pursing his lips in order not to smile. *Apparently Darcy has spent long hours considering the possibility.* "But, if you pursued her, what would be the impediment? Is she not the daughter of a gentleman?"

"Her father is a squire with a small estate, but the mother is of no consequence—the daughter of a country solicitor with a brother in trade."

"Still, that is not enough to—" He was quickly silenced.

"According to Bingley's sisters, the mother is vulgar, obnoxious and makes no secret of her intentions to marry her eldest to Bingley, though my friend has not declared himself. As a matter of fact, she has spread a rumour throughout the county that she expects Netherfield to be her daughter's home within mere months."

"That is appalling indeed, but is it any worse than the mothers of the *ton* who instruct their daughters in ways to compromise a man? Lady Clayton almost succeeded last year, if you remember—not to mention all who tried before her."

"I remember well enough, thank you. But it seems that this woman is especially coarse and, other than the sister who is Bingley's choice, the family has three more daughters as hopeless as the mother. One never takes her nose out of a book of sermons and the two youngest are extremely silly and chase after every red-coat who happens through Meryton!"

"And the father? If he is alive, why does he not rein them in?"

"I believe he is too lazy. Even Bingley expressed surprise that he does not try to regulate his family or worry about their future. Apparently, his daughters have little dowry to speak of, and the estate is entailed away from the female line."

"Yes, for all the good he does. Even Bingley expressed surprise that he does not try to regulate his family or worry about their future. Apparently, his daughters have little dowry to speak of, and the estate is entailed away from

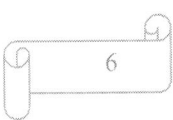

the female line."

"So upon his death, they will be out in the cold unless some generous man intervenes and provides for them all."

"Precisely! Whilst I sympathise with their plight, marrying into that family would be insupportable! And Charles' place in society will be irreparably harmed if he marries the eldest. I told him as much before I left."

"I must know, did Bingley agree?"

"He listened, but I was not able to extract a promise that he would not be so foolish as to make an offer without consulting me."

Richard smiled to himself. *Well, well. Perhaps the little puppy has grown up!* Seeing Darcy eyeing him strangely, he wiped the grin from his face, though he struggled to hold it at bay.

"What I do not understand is how you became enamoured of so unsuitable a woman, if you followed your usual method of keeping to yourself. I doubt anyone in the village knew you were visiting Bingley. So, pray tell, how was she in your company if you did not wish it?"

"As her sister's health improved, she began to come downstairs in the evenings. I could not be totally unsociable to Bingley or his family by hiding in my rooms just because she joined the party."

"I suppose she tried to impose herself on you by conversing?"

"Not in the least. She said very little, replying only to Charles' questions regarding her sister's health or to answer Miss Bingley's barbs. In truth, she and I read in silence whilst the others played cards."

"And, pray tell, does she prefer those romance novels that you complain so vehemently about, such as the one Georgiana showed me the last time I was here?"

"Georgiana showed you a—" William abruptly stopped at the knowing look on Richard's face. "You know that I do not purchase those things. I buy her books to improve her mind."

"And you have managed to change the subject. What of the mystery woman? What does she read?"

"Actually, she was reading ———" Under his cousin's steady gaze, he added reluctantly, "In Italian."

"So she is intelligent. That aspect of her character would certainly appeal to your sensibilities, even if you were not fully conscious of it. Perhaps that is the source of the bewitchment."

"Whatever the reason, I became aware of my vulnerability by the third evening."

"Did she try to sit next to you on the sofa?"

"No!" William said sharply. "I found myself looking forward to her company."

"Of course, *that* would never do!"

"Richard!" The tone of William's reprimand indicted that his patience was wearing thin. "You make it difficult to explain, when you so obviously take pleasure in hearing of my ordeal."

"I apologise." Richard did not look apologetic. "Is it correct to say that her only disadvantages are an atrocious family, no dowry and no connections? For you could always cut ties with the family, and heaven knows that you do not need her dowry or more connections."

"Regrettably, while she may read Italian, she decreed that she has never had a governess, lessons by the masters or a single season in Town. And she found great pleasure in declaring that she does not draw, paint tables, cover screens, sing or play the pianoforte well. I dare say she does little, other than read!"

"How abominable! Is there no end to her defects?" At William's scowl, he added, "Am I to assume that Miss Bingley managed to uncover all those lapses in her character?"

"You know her well. But, in this instance, I was glad for her prying. Can you imagine someone of her station hosting a dinner party or a ball for our circle of friends, or even attending one of your mother's soirées? And what about managing an estate the size of Pemberley?" William shivered. "She would be entirely lost."

"Her eyes must be truly mesmerizing to have caused such an extensive cataloguing of her faults."

"Please do not remind me," William groaned. "Until I met her, I prided myself on keeping my feelings under good regulation. This situation has shown me how weak I truly am."

"I do not consider falling for a lovely woman a weakness, Darcy, nor do I think marrying beneath your station would seriously affect you. After all, because of your disdain for the *ton*, you have never fully participated in society's traditions. You are as wealthy as sin and may marry as you wish. That is something *some* of us cannot even deliberate."

"Yes, but marrying below my station *would* greatly affect Georgiana's chance for a good match."

"Do you really believe that? After all she has a large dowry, is very pretty and her uncle is an earl, for heaven's sake. Even if you were not the richest man in England, I would say her prospects would still be good even if you married a chamber maid."

"I am NOT the richest man in England and I wish you would quit spreading that rumour! As far as Georgiana's prospects go, it would be nice if she did not have something else to throw in my face; nonetheless, to be truthful, after the drought's effect on crops the last two years, I cannot deny that Pemberley could use an infusion of money that a large dowry would provide."

"I dare say that you were not as badly affected by the reduction in crops as in the past. Since you have schooled yourself in the sciences of crop rotation, you have reaped greater yields than when your father was directing the planting."

"Still, we have suffered losses. Additionally, after the tantrum that Lady Catherine threw when I refused to marry Anne, can you imagine how she would react if I married someone not of our sphere, or your parent's reaction for that matter? Your father supported me then only because of Anne's

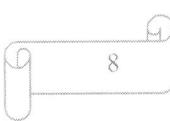

health."

"If you are determined not to care for this mystery woman, pray tell who *are* you determined to care for? Who is to be Mrs. Darcy?"

"Lady Susan."

William surreptitiously studied his cousin for a reaction. Richard's body went stiff, but he did not reply, so it prompted him to add, "Are you not going to argue with me?"

"Is it necessary to go over this again?" Richard snapped. "You know how I feel about Lady Susan. For heaven's sake she practically grew up alongside us at Pemberley! Did you not get enough of her intrigues and plotting back then?"

"She was a child then! Children do foolish things. Now that we are all adults, might not your opinion of her soften a bit?"

"Have you forgotten that, as she aged, she became more a confidant of Andrew and George Wickham than of you? I would think *that* would give you pause for concern."

"They were all closer in age, and as you and I paid her little mind, naturally, she gravitated towards them."

"Birds of a feather, I say."

"I believe that everything that has transpired in her life—her marriage, the birth of a child, Hartley's death— has matured her. Since she returned to Derbyshire, I have found her to be a different person."

"You conveniently forget the circumstances surrounding the marriage."

"To what are you referring?"

"Do not feign ignorance, Darcy. The summer you finished university she practically flung herself at you. When you toured Scotland in order to escape her barrage, she married one of your friends without a moment's hesitation."

"Obviously, they fell in love."

"But there was no courtship, just a marriage, and instantly she was with child! Did that not raise any questions in your mind?"

"I suppose I am not as suspicious as you."

"Lord Hartley was many things, but he was not in the least handsome or charismatic and certainly not the kind of man that the former Lady Susan Patton would have settled for... unless she was desperate."

"That is conjecture."

"I was not the only one who thought as much! And I am not surprised that his early death, which I also find puzzling, brings her right back to her father's estate as it is close by you."

"What is puzzling about his death?"

"The body was never recovered."

"There is no mystery. He drowned."

"I find it hard to believe that his body never surfaced."

"I fear that your work in intelligence for His Majesty has made you very cynical. At any rate, I think you will find that Lady Susan has changed for the better. Moreover, she shares a special bond with Georgiana, as they were always close, despite the difference in their ages. In fact, now that she is residing at Monthaven Manor, they spend a good bit of time together and it has made Georgiana a bit more amiable."

"I should have foreseen this. If Georgiana approves of her, then the biggest hurdle is eliminated."

"What hurdle?"

"You have tried to placate Georgiana since she got angry when you made Andrew reside at his own estate. I doubt you would make matters worse by marrying someone she dislikes."

"Be sensible!" William retorted. "What better candidate is there? She is adored by the *ton* and I am comfortable in her company. And, yes, Georgiana champions a match between us, though that is certainly NOT my priority. Most importantly, I can be certain that Lady Susan is not after my fortune. She is her father's heir, and I am sure that Hartley was generous with her. Besides, my father often expressed a wish that we marry in order to join our properties."

"Well, at least your tenants will be deliriously happy!"

"You are so entertaining, Richard."

"I try." He smirked. "May I be so ignoble as to ask, what will you find to do with her after you have satisfied your carnal appetite? Play charades?"

"You are being crude!"

"Afraid to imagine what your life will be like after the lust wears off?"

"While she may not be a great intellectual, she is not without her attributes."

Richard interjected, "Are you speaking of the two she displays most readily?"

"That is unfair! Her gowns are no different than those worn by other ladies. They simply reflect the current fashion, as you well know. Besides, beauty in itself does not impress me, for it shall eventually fade. She is almost as talented as Georgiana on the pianoforte, sings quite well and draws respectably, in addition to speaking some French. More importantly, she has managed Hartley Hall for the last four years, so I have no doubt that she can assume the role of mistress of Pemberley. Lastly, she has a child, so she is capable of bearing an heir."

"You have certainly given this ample thought."

"Surely you realise that Lady Susan has the right upbringing and connections so that when Georgiana is presented at court, she will be able to guide her through the steps and direct her first season—something my wife would be expected to do."

"There is only one thing missing from this lovely picture." William's brows knit as he awaited his cousin's point. "You are not in love with her. I know you too well, Darcy, and you will not be happy in a marriage of convenience."

"I... I have concluded that happiness in marriage is highly overrated," William declared, his stutter belying his bravado. "It is said that one comes to love one's partner over time."

"Who spouted that rubbish?"

"Your parents—when they were urging me to marry Anne."

"Do you not see that my parents' marriage is a testament to the error of that advice? Well, to be honest Mother does try, but Father is hopeless." Richard sighed wearily. "Darcy, in less than a month you have completely reversed yourself. All these years I have admired you, nay, practically worshipped you because you refused to settle for a marriage of convenience. I cheered you on, eager for you to defy the *ton* because I could not! And you held true until you met this seductress."

"I never asked you to put me on a pedestal! And Lady Susan is no seductress!"

"I was speaking of the one who stole your heart!" Richard threw up his hands. "Fine! I shall not try to talk you out of this madness, for I fear it will only serve to make you more resolute. But I plead with you! Wait at least a month or more before making an offer. Give me time to see this transformation in Lady Susan of which you speak, for I truly believe you are making the biggest mistake of your life."

"If I am, it is I who will have to live with it, not you."

"True. But you are like a brother to me, and I care deeply about your happiness. I do not think it lies with Lady Susan."

William slid an arm around Richard's shoulder, his features softening. "I care about you as well, and I trust your judgement like no other. And, if it will make you feel better, I will wait a month, maybe longer, to approach her. By then, hopefully, you will have gotten to know her better."

"I am relieved to hear it. I hope *my* getting to know her better changes *your* mind."

"Who knows? Perhaps it will." William smiled. "Meanwhile, may I make a request of you?"

"Are you going to tell me that she is to be at Pemberley today, so I should treat her kindly?"

"Actually, she left for Town yesterday."

"If it does not involve Lady Susan, I am your man."

"Our uncle and aunt have arrived from Ireland."

"Uncle Joseph and Aunt Olivia are here! You mentioned that they wished to visit Pemberley, but I do not remember your saying when they planned to come. Will I recognise them?"

"They arrived the same day that I returned from Netherfield. And I have to say that they are much as I remembered them—only with greyer hair. Uncle Joseph is still tall and regal looking and just as soft spoken and reserved—nothing like your father. Aunt Olivia seems to be much thinner but still lovely. Her comportment reminds me a lot of Mother. One would hardly realise they are in the house unless asked to stay for dinner."

"Then I am glad that I am always invited to dine, for I am anxious to see if I agree with your evaluation. Did Uncle retire as a captain?"

"Yes, though he was about to be promoted when he retired."

"I thought as much, but I have to wonder why he retired when he did. The retirement pay would have been so much more substantial had he gone up a rank. Perhaps we shall learn the reason while he is here without having to pry."

"Yes, please do not pry. I do not want them to be uncomfortable. In any event, Georgiana is not pleased with their visit. She has been feigning headaches to avoid them as much as possible. I have to leave for London tomorrow, and she insists that I take her."

"Why on earth do you have to return tomorrow? You just got back, for heaven's sake."

"I have to look over the second house I commissioned for the property. My solicitor is ready to pay the balance due on the construction; however, my foreman thinks there have been some irregularities and requests that I examine it personally."

"I see. So what are my cousin's plans for London?"

"She wishes to stay with your parents for the rest of the summer, and it may be for the best. I worry what she might say if I leave her here. I do not know what has gotten into her lately."

"Georgiana has spent too many hours with my family, listening to my father spouting nonsense over the dinner table! Make no mistake, once he learns they are at Pemberley, he will fill her head with more nonsense of how Uncle Joseph and Aunt Olivia are not worthy of the family's acknowledgment."

"Frankly, I do not care. I will not be gainsaid on this matter. I am the Master of Pemberley, not your father. My mother loved her brother and would be terribly hurt if he were not welcome here. Do you remember when you and I met him and Aunt Olivia the summer I was seven—before they left England? I recall that Uncle Joseph made my mother smile, and I was glad for it. She did not smile very often in those days, what with just losing another child."

"Yes, I was staying at Pemberley that summer. If I recall correctly, Uncle had joined the navy after marrying Olivia, and they were set to travel to Portsmouth after they departed Derbyshire. Years later, after he retired from the service, they moved to a small estate in Ireland that Grandmother Havilland left him in her will. I have to wonder why, after so many years, they would want to return to a country that holds such hurtful memories."

"In his letter, he mentioned that Aunt Olivia was born in Lambton and wished to see her relations before they were too old to travel. His request was to stay at Pemberley only until he could make arrangements to stay elsewhere; however, once they arrived, I was able to convince them to reside at Pemberley as long as they intend to stay in Derbyshire. I explained my current predicament, having to return to London, but assured them that I looked forward to visiting with them upon my return. Also, I offered the use of my townhouse should they ever wish to visit London."

"Bravo!" Richard howled. "It will chap my father's arse to find that they are staying on the next street if they go to Town!"

"Richard, really! Must you be so crude?"

"Blame it on service to my country, Cousin! Officers use more colourful language than the upper crust!" He smirked, causing William to shake his head in resignation.

"The point I was making is that I have no doubt that it will not sit well with your father, or Edgar, for that matter, when they learn that I have invited them to stay with me. As soon as Georgiana sets foot in Town, the cat will be out of the bag, if she has not written them already. I will be called upon to explain myself and you, by association, shall be called out."

"I am not afraid of my father. In fact, I rather enjoy watching him turn beet red! Fortunately, I have not listened to his advice since I quit short breeches, and I will be damned if I start now! Moreover, I relish anything that upsets my brother. My dear mother is the only reason I stop by the house when I am in Town."

William smiled and shook his head at Richard's bravado. "I appreciate your support, but I fear that sometimes you show too much contempt to those who can do you great harm. Edgar can make things very hard on you when your father passes, but still you refuse to call him Leighton."

"Oh and you show no contempt for those with whom you disagree? I do not hear you calling Edgar by his title either."

"Point taken."

"I refuse to bow to my brother. If he were to stop my allowance, I would just have to find another means of supplementing my income. As for siding with you, if it means enjoying the pleasures of Pemberley while I visit with Uncle Joseph and Aunt Olivia, then that is a sacrifice I am willing to make!"

William began to chuckle, which brought Richard great satisfaction. "Do you wish for company back to Town? I have papers to deliver to General Winthrop and I would dearly love to make the trip in one of your plush coaches."

"I was hoping you would accompany us. Georgiana is never as snippy when you are present, though I cannot fathom why. In any event, I do not think I could bear her company exclusively."

"She is pleased to see me because I spoil her. I let her think I do not always agree with you, which makes her trust me." At William's scowl he added, "Do not look so disturbed. Since we are both her guardians, I think it is to our advantage that she believes we do not see eye to eye."

"I suppose it is."

"Now, if we have settled all the world's problems, what say we hurry back to the house for some of Mrs. Lantrip's sweet rolls? Please say that she still makes them every morning, as I have dreamed of one of them and a steaming cup of coffee since I left Sheffield!"

"I think we might be able to oblige you," William said, stepping towards Zeus. Putting his foot in the stirrup and pulling himself effortlessly into the saddle, he added, "Perhaps we should see if your new purchase was worth the price!" With that, he kicked the black stallion and sped off down the trail.

"Darcy!" Richard yelled after him. "That is not fair."

Leaping upon Titan, he followed his cousin down the trail as fast as possible. Nonetheless, by the time he reached the meadow, Darcy was almost halfway across the expanse. Suddenly, the storm that had threatened earlier arrived with full force and rain began coming down in sheets.

Richard kicked his mount into a full gallop. "Next time, Titan, next time!"

Chapter 2

Pemberley

Though the table was set with the best linens, china, silverware and candles, the most exquisite vases of flowers and the finest food and wine, most of those gathered for dinner at Pemberley on this particular evening did not appear to be enjoying the occasion a great deal. Predictably, as they were not entertaining large numbers, the Darcys utilized the second dining room, which featured a more intimately-sized table. Everyone had already been seated when Georgiana hastily entered the room and sat in the chair opposite her brother, taking her place as hostess. Though Richard had informed his cousin that Georgiana had agreed to attend, neither had been certain she would follow through until that moment.

Having never met Georgiana before coming to Pemberley, the elder Fitzwilliams had been surprised to see that she had not taken after her father, as her brother had. Instead, she was her mother's mirror image—tall, with dark blond hair, deep-set green eyes and a dash of freckles across her nose. Moreover, she reminded them not only of Anne, but of their daughter Jenny, who would have been about her age had she not perished in an outbreak of influenza when she was five. Upon introduction, their niece had wilted under their looks of astonishment, and they were determined not to stare at her tonight. This dinner would mark only the second time they had been in her company for more than a few seconds, and they hoped to make her feel at ease in their presence.

As the meal progressed, the Fitzwilliams were cordial to her, but their every attempt to engage her in conversation was met with monosyllabic replies. Even Richard, whose levity had not induced a single smile from Georgiana, appeared to have given up, for it was obvious that she felt awkward amongst those she had spent days avoiding. The entire dinner hour she simply pushed the food about on her plate despite the fact that Mrs. Lantrip had prepared her favourites: a chicken dish and an apple tart for dessert.

Though she might have looked distracted, the object of the entire table's curiosity was actually studying them, noting that her aunt and uncle sat on either side of her brother, while Richard occupied the chair to her right. That left an empty chair between him and Aunt Olivia and meant that there were two empty chairs on her left. As she glanced to that side, her uncle caught her eye and smiled. It was a kindly smile, and it confused her.

Why would he be kind when I have shunned him? Quickly, she looked away.

Convinced that she did not wish to associate with people who the earl had referred to as *beneath our company*, Georgiana prayed that being subjected to them by her brother would be considered a valid excuse. After all, Lord Matlock would never expect her to defy her brother, even if they disagreed. This thought brought her some relief, and she relaxed enough to glance at Richard.

"Is something the matter, Pumpkin? I thought apple tart was your favourite dessert."

"Richard," she sighed, "must you address me in that manner?" Her disapproval caused him to laugh uproariously.

"I am sorry, Pumpkin, but old habits die hard! I have called you that since you were making mud pies."

"And I shall simply die if you call me that in public."

"Not to worry! I shall remember never to use that appellation in public, most especially in the company of the young bucks who will, no doubt, materialise out of thin air once we are in Town. Until then, you shall just have to forgive an *old man* his eccentricities."

"You are incorrigible!"

"That I am, Pumpkin! That I am!"

The others knew better than to join in the levity, for Georgiana would not forgive them as easily as she had her favourite cousin; thus, they exchanged wan smiles as they silently watched. Obviously humiliated by his sister's behaviour, William seemed eager to quit the table.

Looking directly at her, he challenged, "Since it seems we have all finished, I suggest we retire to the music room to have our coffee. Georgiana will, I am sure, be delighted to play a few selections on the pianoforte."

Georgiana was well acquainted with this look—the one that brooked no opposition. Consequently, despite the refusal on the tip of her tongue, she acquiesced, if somewhat begrudgingly. With that being the extent of her cooperation, she stalked from the room without waiting for her aunt to walk with her. Richard shook his head in disbelief at Georgiana's slight. William stood and offered Aunt Olivia his arm while Richard walked over to put an arm about his uncle's shoulder.

"Uncle Joseph, what do you say to Darcy opening a box of expensive cigars and a bottle of his best brandy? I know he would not do so for me, but he could never refuse you."

Joseph Fitzwilliam laughed. "I see that you are the same as the young boy I remember! You were always putting someone up to something, usually for your own entertainment or benefit."

Richard feigned shock, placing a hand over his heart. "Uncle, surely you are mistaken! I am as selfless as a cleric."

William and Olivia were not that far ahead of the two and, hearing the exchange, they laughed. William turned to say, "You have the right of it, Uncle! I was forever being punished for things that Richard instigated!"

For Georgiana, who had already taken her place at the pianoforte, the pleasant banter and laughter of the rest of the party entering the room caused her to act even more aloof. As she was less than eager to perform, she played three selections as quickly as possible before rising to her feet and stating that she was weary and, therefore, retiring. As she fled the room without waiting for proper replies, Joseph Fitzwilliam turned to his wife, tenderly feathering his fingers over her cheek.

"My dear, do you feel like exhibiting? You know how I love to hear you play, and this is such a fine instrument. No doubt it will sound far better than the one in our parlour."

Olivia returned his devotion with a loving smile, a gesture not lost on their nephews who were spellbound by the display of affection.

"I feel well enough, dear, though I dare say that I shall be a poor example after our niece."

Everyone refuted her statement simultaneously, urging her to play, and she consented. As Joseph escorted her to the instrument, Richard considered his cousin's earlier description of the couple. Joseph, indeed, was very much as he recalled—tall, with excellent posture, a stark contrast to his own father who was of medium height and slouched, in part due to a large belly. Olivia, on the other hand, was painfully thin. And while his uncle's dark hair had greyed around his face, Aunt Olivia's light brown was now largely white. Their eyes, too, told a story. His uncle's lively brown ones still occasionally lit with mischief, leaving no doubt that he was the uncle who had teased him mercilessly as a child, but his aunt's dark blue eyes reflected a kind but resigned acceptance.

While Richard pondered this, Joseph helped Olivia to the bench and then took the nearest chair. Playing from memory, in seconds she began a selection of songs that included Bach and Haydn. Afterward, an unfamiliar melody filled the room, and everyone sat transfixed throughout the piece. Complete silence followed the last notes until William began to applaud. The others swiftly joined him.

"Bravo!" he exclaimed, "just lovely. I cannot place that melody even though I purchase all the latest creations for Georgiana. What is the name of the piece and who wrote it? I must secure a copy."

Acknowledging their applause, Olivia turned to face them. At William's declaration, she blushed crimson. "I... I composed it, and I call it 'Joseph,' which is not very original, I suppose."

"Original enough for my taste," her husband declared. A wide smile could not be suppressed as he walked over and bent down to grasp her hand. "She wrote it for our twentieth anniversary and, as I told her then, I could not have asked for a lovelier gift." He placed a kiss on her palm before helping her to her feet. "I think it is time that we retired, dear. I do not want you to be overly tired tomorrow when we visit your cousins outside of Lambton."

"I apologise," William said, walking over to them. "I should not leave so soon after your arrival. I pray that you will continue with your visit in Derbyshire, making Pemberley your home while you are in this area. I shall return from London as soon as possible."

"We intend to stay until the end of summer, if you can tolerate us that long."

"That is indeed good news, as it shall afford us time to get reacquainted."

Their aunt and uncle exchanged glances, and their countenances grew solemn while Joseph addressed them.

"We are indebted to you, Fitzwilliam, for allowing us to stay here, but, primarily, Olivia and I appreciate your company." He turned to Richard. "And yours as well. It has been very hard not having our families near us for all these years. And I have no doubt it will not go well for either of you once news of our presence reaches my brother. It was not our intention to cause either of you difficulty."

"We are grown men, Uncle," Richard retorted. "We make up our own minds as to whom we shall associate. And I shall never regret our connection."

"Well said," William added. "You are family and nothing can change that. My mother loved you dearly, Uncle, and I hope to know you and Aunt Olivia better. Mother was an excellent judge of character."

"Anne was one of a kind, a truly gentle soul in a family more suited to bullies like Edward and Catherine," Joseph's eyes cut to Richard. "My apologies."

"Do not apologize, for I am inclined to agree with you."

"Well, I imagine that you both want to retire, since you are off to London early. Please do not worry about us. Mrs. Reynolds has been most welcoming and kind. She always prepares a picnic basket whenever we are to be gone all day. You have a rare jewel in that woman, Fitzwilliam."

"I am well aware of that, and, yes, we should retire."

Glancing between him and Richard, Aunt Olivia addressed them. "Would you mind too awfully if I kissed you both good night? I have missed having a son to kiss."

The mention of their son, killed in an accident while still a young man, did not surprise either man. News of Arthur's death had reached England too late for Darcy's parents to attend the funeral. Still, William remembered his mother's great sadness and how she often mentioned that he and Arthur were only a few years apart.

"Not at all," the nephews replied in chorus.

Timidly, Olivia stepped forward to place a kiss on first one dear face and then the other, patting their cheeks afterward in a motherly fashion. Then as they quit the room, an overwhelming sadness caused William to rub his cheek. Abruptly coming to his senses, he turned to find Richard smiling.

"What?"

"She reminds me of Aunt Anne—not so much in appearance, but in manner. I think you see the resemblance as well."

"I do, and I remember my mother kissing me in that manner before she retired each night."

"I think I am going to like having them at Pemberley. In fact, I fear that I shall want them to stay in England by the time they are ready to leave."

"I was thinking the same thing."

Nodding in agreement, they went out of the door and were soon crossing the marble floor of the foyer. Reaching the grand staircase, both stopped short and a flicker of mischievousness flashed simultaneously in both their eyes. Without warning, they raced up the stairs just as they had when they were boys. Reaching the landing at about the same time, both were shocked to find Mrs. Reynolds standing there. Her arms were crossed and a scowl marred her normally kind features.

The grin left Richard's face as he straightened to his full height and bowed toward the housekeeper. Then walking as quickly as possible, he went to his room, leaving William to deal with the woman who had chastised them for pulling this same folly when they were boys.

Assuming his best Master of Pemberley mien, William said, "My cousin and I are retiring for the night, Mrs. Reynolds. Please make sure that Mrs. Lantrip is aware that we will break our fast at daylight, as we wish to leave soon after."

"As you instructed this morning, I have already informed her," she answered dryly.

William bowed slightly and went past her, heaving a sigh. He was barely twenty feet down the hall, when he heard her add, "I am aware that you are fully grown, but I shall take this opportunity to quote your dear mother. 'You shall break your neck if you persist in that behaviour.'"

Having halted at the sound of her voice, William now continued without a reply. Nonetheless, he could not wipe the smile from his face. Had he turned, he would have seen a teary-eyed smile on Mrs. Reynolds' face as well, for his antics had awakened fond memories of the past.

Little boys never really grow up!

Still softly laughing to herself, Mrs. Reynolds made her way down the stairs to her own quarters.

Meryton
Netherfield
After the ball

As the Bennet family emerged from Netherfield to board their carriage, everything appeared to be clothed in a silvery light, the result of a full moon directly above the manor. Elizabeth thought it magical—right out of one of Grimm's fairy tales.

Perhaps it is only fitting, for I may have met Prince Charming tonight!

Jane had once more been singled out by Mr. Bingley, a genial man with a reported five thousand a year, and by chance, she herself had caught the eye of his well-to-do houseguest. Not used to such attention other than by the locals, Elizabeth was totally lost in contemplation of said gentleman by the time the carriage lurched forward. In her preoccupation, she did not see that all but her father and Jane had closed their eyes and were nodding off by the time they had travelled the first two miles. A sudden jolt caused by a hole in the road, brought her back to the present, and she turned to find Jane staring trancelike out the window. A fleeting look at her father proved that he was fully awake and watching her. As their eyes met, he winked.

Tilting his head towards those asleep, he whispered, "Kitty and Lydia are weary from dancing with every red-coat in attendance, and your mother is likely exhausted from deciding which men are in need of a wife." He chuckled softly. "And from where I stood, it appears that you are now on the same footing as Jane. In fact, I would dare say that you made your mother deliriously happy this evening."

The mention of her name caused Jane to turn, smile and then to resume looking out the window. As she was not one to readily divulge her feelings, Mr. Bennet was not surprised when his second daughter skirted the issue entirely and then changed the subject.

"My good fortune is easy to explain. With the militia attending, there were more men available to dance, though I have to wonder at Miss Bingley's demeanour tonight. She cooled the entire room with her icy stare, so I am convinced that, given the chance, she would not have attended at all."

Mr. Bennet chuckled a little too loudly, causing Lydia to stir. Then bringing a finger to his lips to signify his resolve to be quiet, he settled back into the seat and spoke no more. The next day would be soon enough to extract more information from his favourite daughter, for though he feigned indifference, he had been acutely aware of when Mr. Bingley's newest addition to Netherfield had asked Lizzy for a second dance.

Thus rendered speechless, Mr. Bennet began to compare the men likely to court his daughters. Bingley, whose lips seemed permanently parted in a good-humoured smile, was newly come to the neighbourhood. He had proven to be an amiable addition to Meryton and, most importantly, according to his wife, had taken a fancy to Jane. That was understandable, as Jane's beauty had always attracted the opposite sex. Moreover, the neighbourhood gossip was that he had an income of five thousand a year, which would place Jane in a very enviable position. While it circulated that Bingley's guest's fortune was twice that amount, Mr. Darcy's situation was only conjecture, so he refused to dwell on it. Obviously, the man was wealthy. Glancing first at Jane and then to Lizzy, their dreamy expressions left no doubt of what they would say should either man arrive on his doorstep requesting a meeting.

His heart lurched at the thought of losing Lizzy, and he studied her for a while longer. Mr. Bennet loved all his children, but she was definitely his pet, for she was the brightest of his offspring and shared his interests in languages, literature and the sciences, often spending hours with him, debating one author's view over another. Moreover, she alone understood his amusement in examining the idiosyncrasies of their friends and neighbours, often joining him in urging them to spout their nonsense, then surreptitiously winking at him after they had. No, he would not part with Lizzy lightly. Jane was meant to marry and have children, while Lizzy—well, she would make a wonderful mother, he was certain, but, most importantly, she needed to be valued for her intellect and encouraged to grow. If not, she would likely wither and die. Of that he was certain.

Can any man understand what a treasure he would have in my Lizzy? I think not!

Suddenly, the carriage leaned as it turned into the drive that led to the manor house, and Mr. Bennet pushed all thoughts of who might come to claim his daughters from his mind. For tonight, all he wished for was a warm bed to ease his aches and pains and a chance to sleep late in the morning.

I hope Hill has remembered to heat some stones for the foot of the bed.

Longbourn
Later that night

Save for Oscar, Mary's cat, which slept most of the day and prowled at night, the Bennet home had finally grown quiet. The sounds of Kitty and Lydia's laughter had died down along with Mrs. Bennet's threats of punishment if they did not hush. Now every creak of the stairs bespoke only of another servant retiring to their room after the fires had been banked, the doors and windows checked and secured, and preparations made for the morrow. Still, in a small bedroom at the far end of the hall, two of the Bennet sisters lay wide awake. Ensconced under the counterpane, they were discussing what had happened at the assembly.

"Lizzy, by the end of the evening you actually seemed fond of Mr. Darcy," Jane whispered. "I was astonished, given your opinion of his cousin, Fitzwilliam Darcy."

"I must confess to being astonished as well. You were so sick when we stayed at Netherfield that you had no chance to become acquainted with Fitzwilliam Darcy, and therefore could not come to your own conclusions, but I have no doubt that he thought me beneath his company and the Bingleys' as well. I am only surprised that he did not try to persuade his friend against you before he escaped from Meryton as fast as his horses could run!"

"You have a habit of painting everyone in the worst possible light."

"Really, Jane! Do you dispute the fact that he was in the neighbourhood for two weeks and, other than the Bingleys, not one soul knew? He did not participate in any of Meryton's society, and before I encountered him at Netherfield, I had no idea Mr. Darcy even existed. In addition, they must have sworn the servants to silence, for Charlotte said that her father had no knowledge of his being in town, and you know that their cook hears all the gossip. I would not be surprised to learn that he entered and left Meryton under cover of darkness."

"I admit that I find it odd that Mr. Bingley did not mention the fact that he had company, if for no other reason than to deflect criticism of his guest's reticent behaviour."

"Reticent behaviour?" Lizzy exclaimed before quieting again. "Fitzwilliam Darcy despises everyone he considers inferior in rank! The night before he quit Meryton, I thought he would strain his neck trying to see if the book I was reading was written in Italian. Then to prove that I could actually read in that language, he asked what I thought of certain portions. I imagine he thought I had unpacked my well-worn copy of **Paradiso** [1] as a ruse to impress him. After all, he and Caroline Bingley had waxed eloquent the night before about accomplished women. There was also the matter of my appearance under discussion."

"Your appearance?"

"Yes, the day I walked to Netherfield the rain had turned the road into mud." She giggled. "I probably wore most of it on the bottom of my gown by the time I got there—that is, if the look on Mr. Darcy's face was any indication."

Jane laughed. "Oh, my poor Lizzy! What lengths you went to in order to care for me."

"You would have done the same for me had I been ill." Jane nodded as Elizabeth continued. "In any event, I was outside the parlour when I heard a discussion of the impropriety of my muddy hem. They had a good laugh at my expense."

"Surely, Mr. Bingley did not laugh, and I cannot imagine any man joining in."

"Mr. Bingley was not in the room. As for Mr. Darcy, I cannot say that I heard him laughing, but he most stridently agreed that he would not want his sister behaving in such a manner."

"I think any man of his rank would have said the same."

"That is my point. His rank makes him feel superior!"

"And you do not think that Andrew Darcy feels the same?"

"No. He does not have his relation's awful prejudice." Lizzy grew silent for a moment as she searched for the right words. "I found that, other than a slight resemblance, they are nothing alike."

"I met Fitzwilliam Darcy only once, on the morning he left Netherfield, and I thought him the most extraordinarily handsome man I had ever seen. On the other hand, both Darcys are tall, similarly built and have dark hair, so I doubt that I could tell them apart if they turned their backs to me."

"Handsome is as handsome does! Give me an amiable man over a proud, taciturn one anytime!" Lizzy affirmed. "Besides, while Andrew Darcy may not be as handsome as his cousin, he is more attractive in other ways."

Jane noted Lizzy's offence. "I am sorry if I spoke amiss. I should never have mentioned that I found one more handsome than the other and certainly not the proud one."

"Do not fret over it, Jane, as I definitely will not." Lizzy turned on her back, studying the ceiling as she continued, "If anything, Fitzwilliam Darcy's behaviour simply reinforced what I have always believed."

"What is that?"

"That handsome features most often mask unpleasant attitudes. I suppose it is because such people have always gotten by on their looks." She glanced to Jane. "The exception being you, of course. You are as amiable as you are beautiful." Then she smiled at the ceiling again. "Good character is what is important, and Andrew Darcy was kind to one and all, danced with all the ladies and generally made himself a welcome addition to the neighbourhood—completely unlike his cousin."

"Though he chose to dance twice with you alone."

As her wont, Elizabeth redirected the conversation to Jane's beau. "And what of Mr. Bingley? Was he not just as obvious in his attention to you, for you were the only woman whom he danced with twice?"

Jane blushed. "Do you really think he likes me, Lizzy?"

"He danced with you twice tonight and then stared at you like a love-sick puppy for the rest of the evening. So I would say yes!"

Jane giggled, clamping her hand over her mouth in order not to be heard. When she recovered, she added, "Mr. Bingley is everything a young man ought to be—sensible, good-humoured, lively."

"And fine-looking!"

"I think him handsome, but I have always favoured ginger hair and blue eyes," Jane said dreamily. "By the by, he is to walk with us into Meryton in the morning."

"How would he know that we usually walk to Meryton in the morning?"

"Mr. Wickham mentioned it while we were all conversing before the dance began. You know that he talks to Lydia at Aunt Phillips' card games, and she tells him everything."

"I was just teasing. Besides, all of Meryton knows our habits, not just Mr. Wickham." Then she looked thoughtful. "I have to wonder, though, about his attentions towards Lydia. Do you not think him too old for her?"

"Mother promotes it as a good match, so any caution you and I might express would be ignored. Besides, he seems to be very pleasant and gentlemanly towards her—well, to all the ladies. He did not particularly single out Lydia at the dance tonight, instead dancing with our mother as well as Kitty, Charlotte, Mary King, Frances Gould and even you. So I cannot say that I find any fault with him."

"I suppose you are right. Perhaps I am borrowing trouble. Now, should we not try to get some sleep? I am sure that you wish to rise early tomorrow in order to have Sarah style your hair to impress your beau."

"He *is not* my beau," Jane protested weakly.

"Not yet perhaps, but I have a feeling he will be before long."

With that pronouncement, Jane and Lizzy both turned on their sides and quieted. For the present, they would both dream of the men who had invaded their world. And while Jane dreamed of a future that was previously unimaginable, Lizzy wondered if Andrew Darcy would accompany Mr. Bingley for their walk.

Oh, I do hope he comes!

Netherfield
The next day

The morning dawned cool and crisp, and a dense fog covered the ground as Charles Bingley stepped onto the portico of Netherfield. Though it was still quite dark, the sun was beginning to rise over the horizon, and he took a deep breath of fresh air. Other than Pemberley, he had never seen a house situated so agreeably amongst its surrounding park, and it pleased him. Moreover, the grey stone of the manor reminded him of his childhood home in York, though that modest abode bore little resemblance to this. Nonetheless, the memory of it caused an ache in his heart, for he was reminded of his father's goal for him—to be a gentleman.

As he reminisced, for the first time since Fitzwilliam Darcy had left Netherfield so abruptly, Bingley wondered if he would truly be happy amongst his friend's society. After all, the woman with whom he had fallen in love—a gentleman's daughter, for heaven's sake—was not good enough to suit the *ton*. At least, not according to Darcy! And though he wished to fulfil his father's expectations and to repay his best friend's faith and assistance, he wondered how far he was willing to go. Far enough to give up Jane Bennet?

Suddenly, a vision of her appeared before him as she had looked last night, in a blue gown trimmed in white lace, embroidered with roses and bluebells. Her sunny blond hair was piled atop her head and secured with combs of pearl, while several long curls hung down her back. The expression on her face was magical, the corners of her mouth lifting into a shy smile while her dark blue eyes sparkled with... dare he say, love?

Bingley smiled back, his question answered. *No! I shall not give you up, my dearest Jane! If Darcy abandons our friendship because I choose to marry you, then so be it!*

The sounds of footsteps broke his reverie, and he was not surprised to hear Mr. Mercer's voice. "The dining room is set, sir."

Charles' smile was genuine as he turned to answer. "Thank you, Mercer. Has Miss Bingley come down?"

"No, though I have heard footsteps overhead."

As they talked, Charles followed the butler back into the foyer where he looked up to find Caroline descending the grand staircase. "*Speak of the ⬛⬛⬛*," he said to himself, though it was loud enough for Mercer to hear.

The butler suppressed a smile and hurried to hold the dining room door open, while the master greeted his sister.

"What are you doing up so early, Caroline? I assumed you would sleep late today. After all, a woman needs her beauty rest."

"Do not make light of the seriousness of our problem, Charles. Surely you know we must do something about—" Suddenly she lowered her voice and glanced to the landing. "Mr. Darcy's attention to Eliza Bennet."

Charles walked towards the dining room. "I think whatever we have to discuss can best be said over a cup of coffee and a sweet roll."

Caroline hurried after him, whining, "How can you eat at a time like this? Our very standing in society is on shaky ground, and all you can think of is filling your stomach."

"We hardly have any standing with society now, so I fail to see how it could be affected by what Andrew does."

After they passed Mr. Mercer, he shut the door behind them, making sure that he stayed in the hallway. With a great sigh of relief, he motioned for the maids who were bringing still more trays from the kitchen to come ahead, while he escaped in the opposite direction.

Even though she criticised Charles for eating, Caroline immediately began to fill a plate full of food as she laid out the case against the Bennets.

"No doubt you know that Fitzwilliam Darcy left because of Eliza Bennet's attempts to secure him. Then as soon as he was gone and Andrew Darcy appeared, she saw another opportunity to… "

Charles paid little attention to Caroline's ranting. Instead, he steadily consumed the food on his plate.

Finally, her voice rose stridently as she concluded, "I do not see any other solution. You must write to Fitzwilliam Darcy this instant! Tell him that Eliza Bennet is trying to compromise his cousin, and he simply must intervene! Should we keep silent, he may hold it against us and our relationship could forever be strained, if not terminated."

"Andrew is his own man, and Darcy will not interfere. In truth, I think your problem stems from the fact that you are jealous of Miss Elizabeth." His eyes glinted with satisfaction as Caroline's flashed with anger. "She can attract both Darcys, while you cannot."

"You must be mad! I am not jealous of Eliza Bennet! I could have my choice of many gentlemen. I just need to be where they are—in London, not in the wilds of Hertfordshire!"

"Perhaps, then, it would be best if you return to London."

"You are absolutely right! We must close Netherfield and return!" Caroline cried, jumping up and heading towards the door. Charles' next words stopped her cold.

"You put words into my mouth, Caroline. I am NOT returning to London. I plan on staying and seeking permission to court Miss Bennet. It is you who may return to London."

Caroline whirled around. "You cannot be serious? I thought Mr. Darcy made his opinion on a match with the Bennets perfectly clear. Though she is a sweet girl, Jane Bennet will do nothing to further your acceptance by the *ton*!"

"Darcy is my friend, but he is not in charge of my life. What I need to be happy is to marry a woman I love and respect, not acceptance from the *ton*."

"It is always about you! Have you considered the effect your selfishness will have on my chances of marrying well?"

"Be serious! You are three and twenty and practically on the shelf because you would not let go of your dream of marrying Darcy. I have tried to arrange two fine matches for you, but you refused them both; thus, I am not inclined to worry about your future at this point. If you never marry, your inheritance will see you through life as a spinster, as long as you live with one of our elderly aunts."

"I shall NOT be a spinster! You shall see!"

"If you do not, it shall be because you made an effort to attract eligible men on your own. I am done worrying about you. Now, if you want to go back to London, simply say so, and I shall arrange a coach."

Quickly Caroline considered how little she could influence the outcome of the Bennet sisters' schemes if she were in London. And while she did not really wish to marry Andrew Darcy, his wealth paling in comparison to Fitzwilliam's, she certainly would as a second choice. "I shall stay."

"Then a word to the wise. Do not interfere with my plans—or Fitzwilliam's or Andrew's, either, for that matter."

With those words, Charles stood, tossed his serviette onto the table and stalked out of the room. His heavy boots marked his every step, resounding across the marble floors of the hall and then the foyer. As the sound grew more distant, Caroline Gertrude Bingley tossed a roll at the door, almost hitting a footman who had come to clear the table.

"Humph! We shall see about that!"

Chapter 3

Longbourn
The day after the ball

This morning the Bennet girls were taking far longer on their appearance than was common for a walk into Meryton. Well, at least the younger Miss Bennets were, for those two had cornered Sarah on first sight and pulled her into their bedroom. In anticipation of seeing the militia, they pleaded with the maid to design more intricate hairstyles for them in hopes of looking older. In addition, Kitty had purloined Jane's new bonnet, while Lydia had borrowed Jane's best day gown and the slippers purchased only last week for Lizzy. As she sat on the side of the bed, forcing her feet into the smaller shoes, their owner appeared in the doorway.

"Lydia, give them back this instant! Your feet are much too big and you shall ruin them as you have ruined all the others."

"Mama said I could borrow them!"

"I doubt that, and, in any case, they are not Mama's to lend. Papa bought them for me."

Lizzy's stern countenance and firm resolve convinced Lydia of the futility of complaining to their mother, for she was well aware that while her mother allowed her to borrow gowns, ribbons and bonnets with impunity, shoes were another matter entirely. In truth, she was the sole reason that Lizzy had to have a new pair.

"You are just selfish! That is all there is to it!" Lydia huffed as she tossed one shoe after another towards Lizzy. "Just see if I shall let you borrow my…" Unable to think of a single item that her sister had ever asked to borrow, she sniffed. "Just you wait until you want to borrow something of mine!"

Elizabeth frowned. *Surely there is not a more peevish girl in all of England. If Papa does not intervene soon, she will be hopeless.* Making a mental note to speak to him once more about Lydia, Elizabeth returned to the room she shared with Jane. There she found her eldest sister frantically searching the room.

"May I help you look for something?"

"Oh, Lizzy! I fear I may have lost my new bonnet. Mama shall be livid if I left it at Lucas Lodge yesterday."

Lizzy sighed. "Come with me."

Jane followed her to the other bedroom. Kitty sat in a chair facing the dresser while Sarah fixed her hair. On the dresser lay Jane's bonnet. Lizzy went over to pick it up.

"I think it is customary to ask when you want to borrow something."

Seeing Jane in the mirror, Kitty made a face as though she might cry. "I meant to ask, but you were not in your room." Then inspiration struck. "Please let me borrow it. You are so much prettier than I that you have no need of such beautiful things."

Lizzy groaned at Kitty's dramatics, knowing full well that Jane would take her seriously. Unsurprised when Jane replied that she was certainly not prettier and gave Kitty permission to borrow the bonnet, Elizabeth set it back on the dresser. She detected a small smirk on Kitty's face as their eyes met. Rolling her eyes, Elizabeth followed Jane into the hall.

"Lizzy, I know that I should be more like you and let Lydia and Kitty face the consequences of their actions, but I am not that strong."

Elizabeth hugged her. "We are who we are and I would not change anything about you. Come! Let me see what I can do with your hair. I fear that Sarah will still be working on Kitty when your Mr. Bingley arrives and I would think that he is on his way."

"He is not—"

"Your Mr. Bingley! I know!" With that, they broke into gales of laughter.

A knock on the front door signalled Charles Bingley's arrival. He wore a silly grin and held his hat in his hand, waiting for Mrs. Hill to acknowledge him.

"Welcome to Longbourn, Mr. Bingley. Come this way, sir."

The servant was forced to cover a smile when she showed Mr. Bingley into the parlour, for upon seeing him, Mrs. Bennet shrieked loud enough to be heard in Meryton.

"Mr. Bingley!" she howled, trying to rise gracefully from the soft cushions of the sofa. "How wonderful it is that you have decided to walk into Meryton with my girls! What a lovely gesture! Will you be staying for dinner after your return?"

Finally managing to get to her feet and without waiting for an answer, she waved her handkerchief at the housekeeper. "Hill, go and fetch Jane right this minute!" Then she addressed her guest again. "Jane is ready, I am sure, and should be down shortly! You have missed Mr. Bennet, as he just left for Purvis Lodge!" Then remembering her manners, she added, "Please be seated!"

Not used to every sentence being shouted, Bingley tried to think of a reply but could not. Luckily, Jane's mother did not seem to notice as she continued to chatter. Befuddled, he sat down.

"Would you like a cup of tea? Or perhaps a scone?" She rushed to the doorway to peer up the stairs that led to the bedrooms. "Hill?"

Sweeping back into the room, she ran the back of her hand over her forehead. "I have no idea what is taking her so long." Seeing the confusion on Bingley's face, she asked, "Have you found Netherfield to your liking? Of course, you have! It is the finest home in all of Hertfordshire, some say, and I would have to agree."

Charles was trying to form an answer when Jane rushed into the room followed by all of her sisters, except for Mary, each donning their bonnets and shawls. Lydia and Kitty were talking simultaneously, but Lizzy was uncharacteristically quiet as she looked about the room for another gentleman.

"See, I told you she would not be long," Mrs. Bennet crowed. Then her face fell. "But where is Mary?"

"Mary has decided to stay here and read," Lizzy offered.

"I shall have to talk to Mr. Bennet about that girl! She would stay in her room all the time if I let her." Quickly she changed the subject. "Come, Mr. Bingley! You had best be getting along while it is still cool. I shall not detain you."

As she shooed all the occupants of the room out the door, she pulled Elizabeth aside. "Be sure to walk far ahead of Jane and Mr. Bingley. After all, they have important things to discuss and do not need you listening to their every word."

"Mama, it would be improper to leave them alone."

"Leave what is proper to me. Do you hear?"

"Yes, Mama," Elizabeth said resignedly.

Meryton

As the sun rose higher, Meryton began to flood with people from every corner of the county. Overwhelming the boardwalks that led from store to store, they spilled into the dusty street. Occasionally crossing to the other side, people threaded between wagons, carriages and the occasional coach as they attempted to avoid the animals pulling the vehicles and their droppings.

Amongst the villagers, even the plainest girls caught the attentions of the redcoats who congregated on one end of the street nearest the public house. As usual, upon collecting their pay, the militia had rushed into town to enjoy a drink at the tavern and to get a peek at the local lasses. Occasionally a whistle would pierce the air, though the responsible party would quickly turn his head and feign innocence. This behaviour would result in respectable men and women looking about with furrowed brows, trying to discern the source of the offense. More often than not, the young lady being admired would blush and smile, often garnering a rebuke from her relations; however, it was never so severe as to deter her from glancing in the direction of the men again as she was dragged towards the shops.

Surrounded by the hodgepodge of humanity in Meryton this crisp morning, Lieutenant George Wickham appeared exceedingly unhappy as he leaned against a large oak tree next to the blacksmith's shop. Quite dapper in his regimentals and polished black boots, his dark brown hair and equally dark brown eyes only added to his appeal. This morning he shared an animated conversation with his childhood friend, Andrew Darcy. That gentleman was equally well dressed, and they both drew the scrutiny of the local women. Even as they conversed, George managed to nod and bestow a smile on every woman who deigned to look in his direction, though the smile quickly vanished afterward. After all, there could be a fortune to be had in one of those smiles, and, if so, he intended to find it.

"George, you are not listening," Andrew grumbled. "Can you not give me your undivided attention for one full minute?"

Wickham's eyes locked on him. "Satisfied? You have my attention, but you must be quick about it. If I can no longer rely on your help, I must make my fortune the old fashioned way—I must charm the ladies out of it!"

"I did not say I could not ever help you again," Andrew sighed. "I said that for now I have no extra funds. That idiot Fitz has cut my allowance again."

"You still call him that? He has always hated that appellation. I wonder that you get away with it."

"I have never called him anything else, so I suppose he must tolerate it from me."

"I see," Wickham said. "Not to change the subject, but I was under the impression that you had Lady Cowden under your sway. That old biddy is worth thousands of pounds if she is worth a farthing, but you say that you can only spare me ten pounds?"

"The situation is not quite that simple! Nonetheless, once I collect the payment for my latest drawing, I shall be happy to help you. After all, we are the best of friends, are we not?"

"I thought we were, but I am not so certain now. In Cambridge you promised that we would live extravagantly once you inherited your grandmother's estate, but that has not happened. As a result, I am still a slave to the militia, and you humiliate yourself entertaining ugly widows. If you can only spare me a few pounds, why did you bother to look me up?"

"I came to Meryton because of the letter you sent telling me of all the beautiful women you have met"

"Still, I expressly told you not to come if you were having success in Town, and I do not think my offer would have dislodged you from Lady Cowden's bed if you were still profiting from the arrangement. What it is that truly caused you to leave London?"

Andrew sighed. "If you must know, Lady Cowden found a nude I had drawn of Lady Marshall, her niece, and showed me the door. I am giving her time to reconsider her imprudence."

"You, an artist? Why have you not mentioned it before?"

"I have always drawn but never thought of it as a way to make a living until Lord Hepplewhite saw a nude I was doodling one day at White's. He remarked that it favoured Lady Norwood, whom he secretly admires. He offered to purchase it if I made it resemble her even more. An idea took root at that moment! Surely, I thought, there was money to be made by drawing nudes of unsuspecting ladies for lusty men, especially those who have ugly wives! And if word of mouth keeps steady, I may profit enough from the drawings to leave off the widows. Nevertheless, I must do everything clandestinely. If certain men—husbands, brothers or fathers—were to get wind of the drawings or how they came into being, I could find myself on the wrong end of a sword."

"And just how do you plan to keep it from becoming common knowledge? You know how men talk and if Darcy were to—"

"I will simply tell Fitz what I tell my customers—the drawings are done by a portrait artist who is down on his luck and wishes to remain anonymous. I will remind him that it is his fault that I must find other sources of income and that I am helping a starving artist, as well. He will not approve of the nudes, but he will never suspect me of drawing them. No one knows I can draw, save you."

"Then let us hope that your new adventure is profitable and you do not have to return to Lady Cowden. I do not think I could ever feign desire for her, much less perform."

"I had to keep the curtains drawn to bed her," Andrew said wearily. "But she is the wealthiest widow in Town." Slipping his thumbs beneath the lapels of his new blue jacket, he boasted, "And this is the outcome—the finest kerseymere [2] and I have three more in different colours, as well a new great coat and three pairs of boots that she purchased last month. With my meagre allowance, I can no longer afford such luxuries, so there is purpose to my madness."

"I see your point. But if you draw so well, why not become a legitimate portrait artist?"

"A gentleman does not work for a living! Can you imagine how the *ton* would react? Not to mention the censure of my cousin?" His expression sobered. "Besides, I do not want to be remembered as an artist! I want to be as revered as Fitz for his business acumen and wealth. One day I shall."

You are a fool if you think that will ever happen! Wickham mused. Aloud he asked, "Where do you find the room to paint? What few artists I know have canvases and paints spread throughout their quarters."

"At this point, I am doing mostly charcoals, which are not as untidy as oils. I have a workshop in a room above a tailor in London, Mr. Poindexter. It is a large area, enough to store my canvases and to draw. I keep the door locked so that he never sees me at work. He thinks I use it as a place to hide when I do not want my relations to find me.

"It worked out well until Lady Cowden started requiring that I spend more time with her, and I had to do the drawing of her niece in my bedroom." He chuckled mirthlessly. "I hid the results under a bed, but the maid found it and Lady Cowden was called. You should have seen the shock on her face!"

"Speaking of shock, I could scarcely keep from laughing aloud when I saw how you hovered over Elizabeth Bennet at the ball. Will she be your next conquest?"

"I am hesitant to say, as she has proven very elusive thus far. But after all the loathsome widows and simpering debutants of Town, I found it exhilarating to spar with someone both handsome and intelligent. At least there is a challenge involved. Miss Bennet will not go down easily."

"I would rather a woman be easy in every sense of the word."

"Luckily, you are still free to pursue such women, Wickham. Since Fitz has focused on me, I have to be more careful. I have assured him that I am done with compromising innocents and still I get nowhere with him regarding my additional inheritance, so I have decided to see things from his perspective."

"Will wonders never cease!"

"You jest, but I must think like him, if I wish to conquer him. What does

Fitz value? The answer is family. And to whom does he demonstrate the most sympathy? Children. He contends that I do not have the funds to marry and still care for those brats he claims are mine without a more profitable estate. And yet, he refuses to help me!"

"So, I have decided that perhaps I should marry. Once a child is born, his attitude shall soften, I just know it! After all, a man with a family to care for needs a thriving estate, and you know well how my cousin likes to orchestrate other people's lives."

"You will marry? The one who said he would rather die than take on a ball and chain?"

"Granted, it is not something I would wish on my worst enemy, but I could be persuaded if just to keep Fitz on the hook. He wants me to prove responsibility before he will release the additional inheritance. What better way than to take a wife? I can take the vows and then do as I please. After all, most men I know have wives that they barely acknowledge and mistresses who make them happy."

"This is insane! Despite your vaulted name and station, you are nearly insolvent! You cannot afford to regard Elizabeth Bennet as anything other than a bit of muslin!"

Andrew's voice lowered in warning. "That is enough, George."

"You are a Darcy, for heaven's sake! If you must marry, choose someone with a substantial dowry. Do not settle for a wench with so little. Besides, her wit will grow tiresome when she sees through your lies."

"I will be the judge of who I wish to pursue, thank you. And if I had wished to marry only a large dowry, I would not have wasted my time satisfying widows to pay my debts."

"If you follow this madness, do not call me when trouble follows, and it always does. I have discovered an ugly, freckled thing with red hair and a dowry of ten thousand pounds right under my nose. And unless I find a better mark, I intend to abscond with her dowry. Should that fail, I shall take the vows, loot her accounts and do as I please. I suggest that you do the same. Leave regard for those who can afford it—like Darcy."

Andrew shrugged, reluctant to dwell on George's advice. His growing fondness for Elizabeth Bennet had come as a complete surprise, and he was intrigued. Could he afford to marry her if he had the balance of the inheritance? What if he married and Fitz was not convinced that he should release it?

"Now who is not listening?"

Suddenly aware that he had been woolgathering, Andrew forced all those thoughts from his mind and turned to his childhood friend. "I am sorry. I was thinking of my last talk with Fitz."

"Better you than me. I hope never to talk to that killjoy again."

"Yes, well, I fear that we shall have to disparage him later. It must be near time for the Bennets to arrive in Meryton, if they left Longbourn when Miss Lydia said they would. My horse is tied at the end of the street, between the pub and the confectioners. From there, I have a clear view of the road, and as soon as I spy the Bennets, I plan to ride out to meet them. Women are intrigued by men in tight breeches who sit a horse well."

Wickham laughed out loud. "You have given it a lot of thought."

"Since women have been my means of survival lately, I have made a point of learning what appeals to them. For instance, they also like your hair to be long enough for them to run their fingers through it. Now, do you want to join me?"

"No, I shall be able to see them well enough from here, and I do not wish my pigeon to catch me flirting with Lydia Bennet. While I may have to court Mary King, I intend to keep the youngest Bennet sister under my spell. She seems eager to please me, and I most certainly want to encourage her."

"Then I shall see you later."

With those words Andrew donned his hat, gave it a pat and headed in the direction of his horse. As Wickham watched him go, his expression hardened.

It is too bad you did not listen to me and kill your sorry cousin years ago. Then we could have convinced Georgiana to marry me, and we would both be wealthy instead of scheming to survive.

Taking a deep breath and letting it go with a loud sigh, Wickham pushed away from the tree and looked for a place to sit. Spying a wooden bench near the shop door, he walked over to it and sat down to await the youngest Bennets.

Just as the Bennets and Charles Bingley reached the outskirts of Meryton, a commotion ensued. A man on horseback stopped as the two youngest sisters, who led the group, neared. The girls were making a spectacle of themselves by being too boisterous, whilst trying to convince the rider to dismount. Elizabeth's heart raced when she realised exactly who was riding the large grey stallion—none other than Andrew Darcy, looking striking in his tan riding breeches and blue coat, his black hair tousled by the wind.

As she, Jane and Bingley caught up with them, Charles stepped towards the rider, extending his hand. "I am sorry if I left you at Netherfield, Andrew. I did not think you would awaken this early."

Andrew laughed, not offended in the least as he shook Bingley's hand. "To tell the truth, I normally would not, as you well know." Then he caught Elizabeth's eye. "There is something about Meryton that makes me wish to know more about the area. Thus, I arose earlier today to explore and here I am!" Tipping his hat to her, he smiled beguilingly. "Miss Elizabeth."

Elizabeth's eyes fell to her feet. "Mr. Darcy."

Andrew threw a leg over the saddle, jumped from his horse, took a coin from his pocket and tossed the reins and the coin to one of the blacksmith's sons who had been watching everything and had come running.

"Come quickly, Kitty. I think I see Mr. Wickham." Lydia grabbed Kitty's arm, pulling her towards a group of redcoats now waiting near the oak tree.

While the youngest Bennets rushed to join the militia, the rest of the party made their way into the middle of town to frequent their favourite shops.

Much later, after leaving an order with the butcher to be picked up the next day, stopping in the confectioner's shop for some sweets and perusing new ribbons, lace and books, the Bennet party turned back towards Longbourn. Kitty and Lydia, who had rejoined their party after the militia gathered in the public house for ale, decided that they wished to call on Maria Lucas. Thus, a few hundred feet outside Meryton, they headed down the pathway to Lucas Lodge. Lost in conversation, Jane and Charles continued at their normal pace, while Elizabeth and Mr. Darcy got further behind as they slowed to a pace more conducive to conversation.

"I hope you do not mind that I was in Meryton when you arrived, Miss Elizabeth," Andrew said, attempting to appear insecure.

"I have no say about who may or may not go into Meryton, sir," Elizabeth teased.

"Do you always twist what a man says to mean something else entirely?" Andrew teased back. "For I know you are too intelligent to miss my meaning."

"My mother does say that I am too clever and that no man appreciates a clever woman."

"I assure you that your mother is wrong."

At his bold declaration, Elizabeth became self-conscious and began to walk faster. Andrew picked up his pace alongside her.

"What I meant to say is that many women are more educated these days. I am acquainted with a few who read books of a scientific nature in addition to poems and plays written in French, German and Italian. I even know of one who can read Latin, though I hardly know what good that will do her." He laughed, thinking he had made a good joke.

Elizabeth's brow knit, but he could not make out her expression. *Is she upset with what I said?*

"It is apparent that you, too, admire the accomplished women your cousin touts so highly!" Elizabeth declared sharply, stepping up her pace even more. Her ire at his cousin did not go unnoticed.

Ah! There is the rub! She has been exposed to Fitzwilliam's arrogance! How shall I handle this? How may I criticise that arse without seeming to disparage him intentionally?

"Ah yes, my dear cousin, Fitzwilliam. At the dance you alluded to having met him before, and I confess that I regret not asking your opinion of him then." As she glanced at him, he looked off into the distance, assuming a hurt expression that normally gained him sympathy from the ladies. "I suppose it is because I am not often compared favourably to him. After all, he is a very handsome fellow and extremely rich."

Elizabeth stopped walking, touching his arm and causing him to face her. "I can assure you that you have nothing to fear in that regard. Your cousin did not impress one single person in Meryton with his looks or his wealth while he was here. You, however, are highly regarded."

"I cannot feign surprise about their reaction to my cousin, but in his defence, I shall say that he has no idea how rude he appears to others. One can hardly fault the man. You see, he was very young when he was named guardian for his young sister and charged with the responsibility of Pemberley. Though he has done an excellent job in that regard and is respected by his servants and tenants, he no longer tries to be sociable in public. Frankly, I like to believe that he has been so occupied that he has forgotten how."

"I fear you are being much too kind in your defence of him."

Andrew's expression darkened. "It took me some time to think of him in that manner, especially after my uncle's death. His conduct since that day has been hard to explain or accept. It is as though he is a different man entirely."

"Whatever do you mean?"

Andrew looked around the countryside, and seeing no one, he whispered, "I shall tell you, but only because I trust it will go no further."

Elizabeth nodded, her dark eyes getting even darker. "It shall never pass my lips."

"I came to Meryton at the behest of a dear friend. I believe you know him, Lieutenant Wickham?"

"I do."

"He and I grew up at Pemberley, Fitz's estate. His father was Mr. Darcy's steward, so he lived on the grounds. We became good friends when I went there to live at age eleven, after my father's death."

"You had no other place to go?"

"No. My father was a vicar with a heart of gold, but not a farthing to his name. My mother died when I was born, and all the family I had left was Uncle George, Fitzwilliam and my cousin, Georgiana, Fitzwilliam's sister."

Seeing compassion in Elizabeth's face, he quickly continued. "So George and I became like brothers. I cannot say the same for Fitzwilliam, even if we are cousins."

"Was he unkind?"

"I would not say he was unkind. It is just that he was the heir and was raised to believe he was more important than the rest of us, so he kept his distance. At any rate, Wickham was a favourite of my Uncle George. So much so, that he bequeathed him three thousand pounds and the living at Kympton upon his death. But instead of honouring the will, Fitzwilliam gave him five hundred pounds and denied him the living."

"That is horrible! Why would he not honour his father's will?"

"You are as good a judge of that as I. However, I was treated just as unfairly when it came to my part."

Elizabeth gasped. "I shall not be upset if you feel it too personal to share."

"I trust you with all my secrets." The look of complete faith on Elizabeth's face inspired him to continue.

"George Darcy was like my own father, and he loved me like a son. In part, I think it was because I spent many hours with him, especially after he became ill. Fitzwilliam's hours were filled with duties, I suppose." He shrugged and was silent as though pondering the sad truth of his declaration.

"My uncle once told me that he would make sure that I continued to live in the manner to which I had become accustomed at Pemberley. Unfortunately, that has not been the case since his death—not in the least. I was informed that I had inherited a modest allowance which will end next year when I reach five and twenty; at that time I am to receive five thousand pounds. Only, Fitzwilliam claims that the five thousand pounds is conditional based entirely on the prerequisite that Winfield Hall, an estate I inherited, turns a profit before that date. I am confident that that was not my uncle's intent. So I can only conclude that my cousin has chosen not to follow his father's wishes regarding my inheritance any more than he did with George's."

"How selfish of him! Is there nothing you can do? Hire a solicitor or—"

"I have not the necessary funds to fight my cousin in court," Andrew cut in. "And I doubt that I would prevail if I did. After all, he has influential friends and I do not."

"That is so… so unfair!"

"Life is not always fair, Miss Elizabeth. Had my father been the heir instead of George Darcy," Andrew shrugged dramatically, "well, I hope that I would be more compassionate."

"I am sure you would!" Elizabeth stated earnestly.

"Thus, I find myself the owner of a neglected estate that belonged to my Grandmother Darcy." Andrew smiled. "Please do not get the impression that I do not appreciate her gift. It is only that the estate was neglected for so many years before it was passed to me at one and twenty. Presently, it does not earn enough to support the few servants and tenants who remain. The last few years I have used my small allowance to pay them and have not been able to invest in the estate as I would have liked."

"Where is your estate?"

"In Manchester."

"That is lovely country and good farming land, as I remember. Can you not convince a banker to loan you the funds to make it profitable?"

"Unfortunately, bankers only loan to those who are well off, and I am not in that category. I have been fortunate to receive loans from a few friends and most of the profit for some time will go to repay them. Suffice it to say, unless I make the acquaintance of a woman who does not care for the finer things in life, I am doomed to life as a bachelor!" Having said this, he laughed hollowly and then pretended to force a smile.

"Are there no debutants with large dowries this season?" Elizabeth teased. "Surely a Darcy would be able to marry his way out of this dilemma."

Andrew guffawed, "Only someone with your wit would say that after hearing my sad story." He caught Lizzy's hand and brought it to his lips, softly kissing the back of it though his eyes never left hers. "Alas, I always wished to marry for love, not convenience."

Elizabeth murmured, "How… how will you manage?"

Andrew had no reservations about stretching the truth to make his future look more promising, even to the point of resurrecting his long dead grandmother on his mother's side who never owned anything more than a cottage.

"For the present, I will continue to seek loans from my closest friends in order to bring in a harvest. And in the future, my maternal grandmother is still alive, though in ill health. I am her only heir, and she has a small estate that I shall dispose of after her death. The proceeds will go to improve Winfield Hall. God forbid that someone I love has to die, but she assures me that she wants me to use her bequest to improve my estate. And with a little luck and a great deal of hard work, Winfield may generate enough to support a wife and children. I fear that it may come too late to collect the sum Fitz owes me next year, though."

"I am sure there are many who wish to see you succeed."

"Yes, but it is not always easy to distinguish those who are truly my friends from those who tolerate me because Fitz is my cousin. Unfortunately, the ones I trust are not as wealthy as those in Fitz's circle. Even Mr. Bingley, whom I have known for years, is Fitz's friend, not mine. Of course, they attended university at the same time and it is only fitting. Still, I know that if I were of a mind to ask him for help, he would immediately tell my cousin. And Fitz would make sure no one loaned me a farthing."

"Why would he care if it would help keep your estate solvent?"

"If I cannot turn a profit this year, he will not have to part with the final five thousand pounds."

"Why you do not expose his dishonesty to Mr. Bingley?"

"Charles thinks well of my cousin, and I would not do anything to change that. You see, Fitz has few real friends and Bingley is one. I know that I can trust you not to say a word to him."

"I would never break a confidence, but I think you too kind," she said dryly. "I fear that I would tell any and all who would listen of his perfidy."

Andrew laughed aloud. "Then Fitz is lucky that I am his cousin and not you."

As they continued towards Longbourn, they talked of more pleasant subjects until they neared the house. Seeing the gate to the drive, Andrew stopped in his tracks.

"Unfortunately, Miss Bennet, I must return to Netherfield. I have neglected some business that must be handled today."

"Certainly, sir," she replied. "You must have great responsibilities."

He chuckled. "They often seem too great!" Then his expression changed to one of undisguised admiration. "Perhaps I shall see you tomorrow?"

"Perhaps," Lizzy said softly.

As she watched him easily mount his horse and spur the animal in the direction of Netherfield, Elizabeth realised that she had come to admire him even more, now that she knew of his circumstances. And when he looked over his shoulder and waved before he passed completely out of sight, her heart beat faster.

I am so glad that I gave him the benefit of the doubt that night at the ball. I would have missed knowing a wonderful man.

Chapter 4

London
Matlock House

As Darcy's coach pulled to a stop in front of his uncle's townhouse, both he and Richard glanced out the windows at the impressive red-brick facade that rose three stories into the London sky. Simultaneously, they shrugged at one another as a footman in fancy livery rushed to open the door. By the time they exited the vehicle, the large, intricately-carved front door was standing open, revealing the Matlocks' long-time butler, Mr. Soames. He smiled broadly, for he had recognised Darcy's coach. Richard, who had exited first, practically charged up the steps to greet the man he had known all his life, while William followed at a more sedate pace as he escorted Georgiana into the house.

"Colonel Fitzwilliam, sir, it is good to have you back in London! I hope you found the roads in good condition," the butler said, clearly delighted to see him once more.

"Thank you, Soames. My journey from Pemberley to London was excellent, given that I was riding in Darcy's coach," Richard declared as he reached the top step. "Oh, to have such luxury!"

"Your father's coaches are just as fine, if not finer, Cousin," Darcy pronounced solemnly as he and Georgiana reached the portico.

"Good morning, Mr. Darcy, Miss Darcy! It is a pleasure to have you at Matlock House once more," Soames said.

After they entered the foyer, he began to collect their coats, hats, bonnet and shawl, immediately passing them to a footman who appeared out of nowhere. All of a sudden, a loud exclamation caused all three guests to turn.

"My goodness! You are here at last!" Lady Matlock glided effortlessly across the marble floor, looking every inch a countess in her expensive gown and jewels. Still very attractive at four and fifty, she had hardly any grey in her dark brown hair and was as slim as a debutant. Clearly happy, she reached for her niece's hands.

"Georgiana, I have eagerly anticipated your visit. You and I shall have great fun shopping for clothes while you are here." She looked past Georgiana to her son and nephew. "And I am having a dinner party tonight honouring Lady Susan; both of you simply must attend."

"Oh, say you will, Brother!" Georgiana practically squealed as she turned back to him. "I told Lady Susan that we were coming, and I know she is expecting you."

William tried not to frown, though he detested being forced into obligations at a moment's notice. "I suppose I may be able to oblige, though I shall not stay long. After all, the trip from Pemberley was tiring, and I have much to do tomorrow."

"Excellent!" Lady Matlock proclaimed. "I know that Lady Susan will appreciate the effort. Lately, all she has talked about is the summers that she joined Richard and you at Pemberley between school terms." Then she awarded William a knowing wink.

Richard's brows shot up, and he gave his cousin a wry smile behind his mother's back. Oblivious to his antics, she continued cheerfully, "In addition, the earl and I are giving a ball to honour her in a sennight, and I wondered if you might be her escort that evening?"

Despite telling Richard of his plans to marry her, William did not want the rest of the family knowing his thoughts at this juncture and forcing his hand. Therefore, he replied nonchalantly, "We shall have to see. I had not planned to be in London that long."

"Oh, Brother, you do not have to hurry back to Pemberley to entertain those—"

"Georgiana," William scolded, his voice lowering in warning. "What I decide is not open for discussion." The smile fell from his sister's face.

Noting the coldness between her nephew and her niece, Lady Matlock instantly changed the subject. "Richard dear, I hope that this time you intend to stay with us while you are in Town."

Richard laughed mirthlessly. "No, Mother, I shall stay with Darcy, as usual. I would not want to disappoint Father. He so enjoys having something to disapprove of when it comes to me."

His glibness coaxed a frown from his mother, a sight rarely seen in public. As a result, the countess appealed to William.

"Please try to reason with him, Fitzwilliam. You know that the earl does not understand why Richard stays with you instead of with his own family."

"Richard is a grown man; I do not tell him what he should or should not do, and he returns the favour. Besides, I am family, too."

A disembodied voice roared, "If you are family, then why do you persist in going against my wishes?"

As everyone turned, the Earl of Matlock emerged from the shadows of the hallway leading to his study. His displeasure was apparent, and cringing, Georgiana moved behind her aunt.

Lady Matlock winced, knowing where this would lead. Noting, too, the number of servants who had stopped to listen, she ventured, "Dear, do you not think this is a matter for discussion in private—perhaps in your study?"

Allowing that the entire household was listening, Lord Matlock declared, "I shall see you in my study immediately, Fitzwilliam! I expect you as well, Richard!"

Without waiting for an answer, he turned and disappeared down the same hallway from which he had materialized. The countess tilted her head and lifted her shoulders as a sign of apology. Then smiling wanly, she turned her attention to Georgiana. As she guided her niece towards the grand staircase, she kept up a constant conversation in hopes of distracting her from the unpleasantness. As they ascended the stairs, she was heard saying, "You simply must have a new gown, a new pair of slippers and, of course, one of the lace shawls made fashionable by Lady... "

Meanwhile, Richard moved to stand next to William, whispering, "It seems that Lady Susan is as manipulative as ever! In addition to gaining Georgiana's support, it seems she has managed to make my mother think you are already a couple."

"You assume a great deal. Lady Susan may be the one being manipulated, not vice versa. You well know your mother's penchant for matching."

"No. I have seen this scenario too often in the past to miss the signs. My money is on Lady Susan!"

"Fine! Then you shall learn for yourself."

"I intend to, old man! Now, are you up for one of my father's lectures, or shall I inform him that you have departed for Darcy House and will speak to him later?"

"I will not cower, now or ever." With those words, he stalked towards the earl's study, leaving Richard to catch up.

The earl's study

As the cousins sat in matching upholstered chairs directly in front of the earl's oversized, mahogany desk, the drumming of Richard's fingers on the table between them was the only sound to be heard. William, his mind ever alert, twisted the insignia ring on his little finger, as he did whenever he was anxious.

Too upset to sit down, the earl had been standing behind his desk, howbeit facing the wall, since they entered. All the while, he kept his hands clasped behind his back, his pose reminding Richard of General Wade's description of Napoleon—short, portly, hands clasped behind his back.

Though his father was of medium height, the other adjectives fit, and the realisation made him stifle a laugh, drawing William's attention. Fortunately, the earl was too engrossed to notice. When the cousins' eyes met, Richard wagged his brows. Quickly covering a smile, William shook his head in warning and resumed staring blank-faced at his uncle.

Suddenly, the earl slammed his hands on the desk, startling them both. "What were you thinking, inviting my brother and that woman to stay at Pemberley, Fitzwilliam? You know the *ton* will have a grand time mocking me when this becomes common knowledge."

William's ire rose, but he was determined to stay calm. "*That woman* is his wife of over thirty years. Her name is Olivia. And I was not keeping anything secret. Uncle Joseph simply wrote to me, asking to visit Pemberley while—"

"He was disowned because he refused our father's command to do his duty! We needed him to marry a woman *of his station* with a substantial dowry to help the family. Instead, he married that lowly, shepherd's daughter!"

"Aunt Olivia's father was a gentleman, and though her dowry may have been modest, she is a rare jewel," Richard stated.

The earl skewered Richard with a glare. "Must you always argue your cousin's side?"

"Only if he is right."

Darcy explained. "He is my mother's brother, despite all that has happened. I was but a boy the last time he was at Pemberley, yet I do remember the affection they shared. She and Father kept up a correspondence with him and my aunt until my parents died. Uncle Joseph and I have corresponded since. Do you think I could be any less hospitable than my mother?"

"Of course, you would take his side! You have always been your mother's son."

"It is not a matter of choosing sides, Uncle. I would have done the same thing had you been in his place. And I do not agree that disowning him for choosing to marry for love was justified."

"That attitude is what led to my brother's ruin. He was deprived of his family and sentenced to a life at sea. Gone from England for years on end; all that awaited after the navy was a downtrodden estate in Ireland, and that only because of our grandmother's kindness. And now? Now, he is reduced to begging for accommodations because he wishes to visit his homeland. I doubt he has a farthing to pay for an inn if he wishes to stay in one. Let his situation be a forewarning to you both! Tread carefully when you ponder going against the dictates of your family and polite society. What seems the right course at the moment may actually be the road to your downfall."

"I have heard you out, Uncle, though I do not concur. We shall never agree on how Uncle Joseph and Aunt Olivia should be treated. Now I shall take my leave. Please excuse me."

As William headed towards the door, Richard quickly jumped up to follow.

"Just where do you think you are going?"

Richard turned, his usual smile replaced by aloofness. "I am going with Darcy. I find the atmosphere at his house less stifling."

"You try my patience, Richard. It is one thing to disagree with me, but quite another to flaunt it. Most of London is being entertained by news of our discord."

"If they are, it is because Edgar talks too much when he is in his cups. And rumour has it that he is especially verbose with his whores after bedding them."

Richard's statement hit the intended mark, and the earl said nothing in reply. Content with having silenced his father, the colonel exited the study to find his cousin in the foyer, donning his coat.

"Are you coming with me?"

"I would not stay here and suffer my father's contempt for all the brandy in France!"

༺༻

**Meryton
Longbourn
At Dinner**

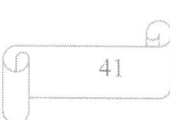

On this night, the dinner table was unusually quiet; the gaiety that most often surfaced when all five daughters talked at once was sadly lacking. On this particular day, the Bennets were joined by the one person capable of dampening any gathering—a distant cousin and their father's heir, Mr. William Collins.

Appearing at Longbourn concurrent with the letter announcing his intention to visit, the obsequious vicar blamed the gaffe on the fact that his noble patroness, Lady Catherine, had recommended the visit and then insisted that he leave at once.

Mr. Bennet had not been mollified. In fact, he had been so perturbed that he had considered telling Collins that it was an inopportune time to visit, and he would have, had his wife had not pushed him aside, gushing words of welcome. Being adept at matchmaking, she immediately grasped the import of the opportunity dropped into her lap, as it were. For if just one of her daughters pleased Mr. Bennet's heir, that would solve the problem of lodging in the hedgerows upon his death.

The vicar could not have been more revolting had he tried. Small in stature, his teeth were stained, his stomach protruded and his hair, what little there was of it, looked greasy. Nor did his clothes impress, for when he appeared at the door, they were wrinkled and smelled of sweat and cheap cologne. It was clear that he needed a bath, and dinner was postponed whilst he obliged. Nonetheless, when he joined the family at the table wearing the same coat and breeches, it was evident that a bath was no cure if one's clothes needed a good scrubbing too.

Taking his seat at the table, Mr. Collins did not detect the censure of those seated about him, likely because he was focused on a singular mission. Charged with returning to Hunsford with a bride, or at the least as an engaged man, he was determined not to disappoint his benefactress. Thus, beady little eyes began to examine one fair cousin after another, coming to a complete stop when they alighted on Jane, who sat to his right. Her fair countenance kept his interest until Mr. Bennet decided to have some sport.

"Mr. Collins, please tell us how you came to be the vicar of Hunsford."

The man's eyes lit up, and his chest swelled as he began to elaborate on the virtues of his patroness in between shovelling spoonfuls of food into his mouth; however, when he spoke, it became clear that he was not only unsightly, but simpleminded, as well.

"One could not hope to find a nobler benefactress among people of her rank. She is the mistress of Rosings, the most excellent estate in all of England. Lady Catherine is of the highest calibre, as is her lovely daughter, Miss Anne de Bourgh. They are the kindest, most gracious women of my acquaintance, as neither makes a distinction between my humble self and any gentleman. As to my position, I was amongst a group recommended to her ladyship by my superior. I was awarded the position after an interview, during which I was asked only one question."

Mr. Bennet pursed his lips to keep from smiling. "Pray, share with us the question."

Collins lifted his chin in an exaggerated manner. "She asked if I had any objections to having her plan my sermons."

Thomas Bennet caught Elizabeth's eye. The sparkle therein let him know that she agreed with his assessment of Collins' stupidity. "And your answer?"

"Naturally, I replied that I would be delighted to have her involvement. After all, she is highly esteemed by the entire county, if not the entirety of England. Who better to advise me of what should be addressed?"

"Who indeed?"

Lydia and Kitty giggled at his smugness, which Collins must have taken as esteem, since he nodded approvingly in their direction as he took another bite of potatoes and addressed his hostess. "This is a most delicious vegetable! Who am I to thank for this wonderful fare?"

Mrs. Bennet answered indignantly. "We are well able to afford a cook, Mr. Collins."

When his answer came, however, it only served to make her uneasy. "I am glad to hear that. Very glad indeed."

As he resumed eating, she became flustered at having given him more information regarding Longbourn's finances than she had planned.

Elizabeth ventured, "Is Miss de Bourgh very handsome? After all, she must be much sought after, with such an inheritance, and if she is beautiful as well, then that would attract even more suitors, I presume."

Collins shook his head sadly. "While she has handsome features that mark a young woman of distinguished birth, I am sad to say that her health prevents her appearance at court, and it is a deprivation indeed! The court is thus cheated of its most beautiful jewel, and she is deprived of the suitors her presence would no doubt attract. Nonetheless, I see her often as she drives past my humble abode in her small phaeton with matching ponies, and I make a point to be at the gate and wave whenever she passes."

"It must be the highlight of her day," Elizabeth teased, though Collins did not notice her sarcasm.

Actually blushing, he dropped his gaze. "You are too kind. But Lady Catherine tells me that her daughter often speaks of my devotion. In fact, only last week Miss de Bourgh remarked that she cannot fathom how I can perform my duties and still be at the gate whenever she passes."

"Remarkable! I confess that I find it hard to grasp as well," Mr. Bennet interjected flippantly.

Swallowing a mouthful of peas, Collins replied, "Oh, it is not too difficult. I repositioned my desk by the window that faces the road in order to watch for her phaeton. As soon as the ponies appear, I run from the house to the gate. Of course, I have often mistaken other vehicles for hers, but that is of no consequence. After all, the exercise is refreshing, even if it turns out to be someone else."

"It is clear that exercise has been a benefit," Elizabeth mocked, "and, of course, you must not disappoint Miss de Bourgh." Giggling, Lydia choked on her water, so Elizabeth patted her on the back.

As for Mr. Collins, he felt sure that he had impressed his relations, and, wanting to appear charitable, he made an announcement. "I thought I would entertain you by reading a selection of Fordyce's sermons after dinner."

Lydia leaned towards Kitty, making a groaning sound, which elicited a new round of giggles. Trying to cover for their impropriety, Jane said loudly, "I think that a lovely idea."

Mr. Collins' face lit up. "Oh, are you familiar with Fordyce's sermons, Miss Bennet?"

Jane was struck dumb as he had leaned closer, his eyes fastening on her bosom. "No, I… I…"

Mr. Bennet stood, his chair scraping the floor as he addressed the vicar. "Mr. Collins, if you will follow me to my study, we shall discuss the reason for your visit. You may entertain us with Fordyce afterward."

Reluctantly tearing his eyes from Jane's cleavage, Collins could do nothing but nod in agreement and follow his cousin from the room.

As Mrs. Bennet and her daughters reassembled in the parlour to await their cousin, Lydia began to complain. "I shall not sit and listen to sermons all night. I have a magazine that Aunt Gardiner sent me, and I wish to find a pattern for a new gown and ideas to trim my old bonnet."

"And I wish to help Lydia," Kitty whined.

"None of you shall leave this room until I say," their mother declared. "He is off to Brompton the day after tomorrow. One of you must catch his fancy to insure that he stops here on his way back to Kent!"

Elizabeth sighed. "Jane is practically engaged to Mr. Bingley. Surely you could not wish for her to catch his eye."

"This is true, although I have not been overly impressed with Mr. Bingley's devotion. Most men would have made her an offer by now; nonetheless, I shall dissuade Mr. Collins from pursuing Jane. You, however, are the next oldest and will do nicely!"

"Oh, but Mama!" Jane intervened. "Mr. Darcy has been paying Lizzy special attention of late, and he is reputed to have ten thousand a year, much more than Mr. Bingley. Surely, you would not wish her to settle for someone less wealthy."

"Mr. Darcy has been paying Lizzy attention? He has not called on your father or even bothered to dine with us like Mr. Bingley. Other than speaking with Lizzy at my sister's card parties and a few dances here and yon, he has shown her no favouritism of which I am aware. Is there something I should know?"

Jane cringed. Glancing at her sister's worried face, she stuttered, "I… I have seen no more favouritism than you, but in my opinion, he acts as though he is besotted."

"Besotted? Wealthy men do not marry girls as plain as Lizzy! Why should he? He can have any beautiful woman he fancies. And one with a large dowry." Then she chastised her second daughter. "Listen to me and stay clear of that man! Any attention he pays you cannot be credible, and if your good name is lost, it will bode ill for you and all your sisters!"

Jane started to object, but Lizzy intervened. "Whatever you say, Mama, but I shall not marry Mr. Collins, and I think Mary, Lydia and Kitty are all too young to marry anyone."

"You shall do as I say, and I shall determine at what age you all marry." With this pronouncement, Elizabeth hurried from the room to the sounds of her mother's shouts. "Come back here this instant! Do you hear me, Elizabeth Rose Bennet? You will suffer for your defiance!"

Mrs. Bennet did not go after her or ask Mr. Bennet to make her return when he and Collins entered the room later, for she was well aware that he coddled Lizzy and would not make her do anything she did not wish to do. However, if Mr. Collins should decide for Lizzy, she would force her second daughter to bend to her will. She was not above helping the man who would one day determine her future, compromise whichever of the girls he wanted, save Jane.

Later that night

A huge storm raged without, mirroring the tempest that Mr. Collins' presence had created within Longbourn's walls. Elizabeth's bedroom was pitch black due to the lack of moonlight; thus, as the door to the bedroom squeaked open, she strained to see who had entered. Holding her breath, she prayed that it was not her mother. When her eldest sister held up a small candle, illuminating her face, Elizabeth let go the breath she had been holding. Still, the diminutive candle gave little light and a muffled cry escaped as Jane stubbed her toe on a chair leg.

"Oh, blast!"

"Jane, do try not to fall with that candle."

"I am sorry if I awakened you. I thought Mr. Collins would never stop reading. Lydia and Kitty nodded off straightaway, and even Mama was snoring by the time he gave up."

Elizabeth could not help giggling. "What was Papa doing?"

"He was reading a book he brought from his library. Mr. Collins kept glancing over to him with an expression of displeasure, but you know how much good that did."

"That is one thing I love about our Papa—he does not hide his views. I have been praying that he will put an end to Mama's plan to marry us off to that horrible man."

"He is not so awful," Jane said. "Perhaps, under a woman's influence, he might be inclined to—"

"Clean his teeth? Bathe? Wash his clothes?" Lizzy retorted, causing Jane to collapse in giggles.

"Perhaps he would, though I should not like to be the one to influence him."

"Nor would I!" Lizzy added. "Now, let us try to sleep. Your beau will undoubtedly be here bright and early again tomorrow."

"But what of Mr. Darcy? Has he mentioned his plans? I know that you passed along Mama's invitation."

"I have no idea what his plans are. I issued the invitation, but thus far he claims that he has not had opportunity. He spends quite a bit of time travelling between here and London."

"Perhaps I shall ask Charles if he will invite him to come with him."

"That would be the perfect solution."

"Good. Then I shall do so tomorrow if Mr. Darcy is still missing."

"Thank you. Now sleep, fair maiden, for your knight shall be here ere you know it."

"Let us hope both knights appear tomorrow."

Darcy House
The next day

A constant banging brought Mr. Barnes to the front door to ascertain what could be so urgent that it was necessary to disturb the entire household. Anyone with proper manners knew that a door without a knocker meant that the owner was not at home or, at the least, did not wish to be disturbed. As it happened, Mr. Darcy had still not ordered the knocker replaced.

Shooing away a footman who started forward, Barnes cracked the heavy door a few inches. A gentleman of advanced age stood without. From his attire, his gold tipped cane, and the pocket watch that he consulted, it was clear that he was wealthy; thus, Barnes swung open the door.

"I beg your pardon, but I was told that Mr. Darcy is in town, and I wish an immediate audience with him."

The master and Colonel Fitzwilliam had left for an early ride in Hyde Park, hoping to be done before most of London decided to do likewise; however, Barnes was not about to share that information with a stranger.

"I am sorry, but Mr. Darcy is not here."

Snapping the watch case shut, the man asked, "But he is expected, is he not?"

"I am not at liberty to say, sir; however, if you will leave one of your cards, I shall inform him that you called when I see him next."

Obviously flustered, the white-haired man began to pat the inside pockets of his coat. "My sources are impeccable, so if he is not here, I believe he will be soon." Finally, he gave up the quest for a card, shaking his head in defeat. "I do not believe that I have a card, but I am Jameson Harrington of Marsden Park in Manchester. My estate is adjacent to Winfield Hall, Andrew Darcy's estate. I wish to speak to Mr. Darcy regarding his cousin."

The hair on the back of Barnes' neck stood up. As the senior servant at Darcy House, he was privy to private information and was aware of many of Andrew's failings. He was certain that Mr. Darcy would want to hear what the man had to say.

"Mr. Harrington of Marsden Park. I shall write that information down and see that he gets it."

"You do not understand! It is imperative that I talk with him as soon as possible. I am staying at Lord Warren's home, and he may contact me there. I know that he is familiar with Lord Warren." Then he pulled a small brown package from his pocket. "See that Mr. Darcy gets this when you give him my information."

The mention of Lord Warren's name brought Mr. Barnes even more unease. That gentlemen had been one of George Darcy's dearest friends and was still an occasional visitor to Darcy House. Taking the package, Barnes assured him, "You may rely on me, sir."

Watching as the man turned to leave, Barnes noted that he struggled for balance despite the cane. Reaching out to grasp his arm, the butler motioned to a footman who waited with the carriage on the street below.

"Thank you. I am afraid I forbade Jackson from seeing me to the door. Too proud, you see."

"Think nothing of it," Barnes replied warmly.

He watched until the carriage pulled away. Then taking a deep breath, he released a heavy sigh. *This cannot be good.*

Chapter 5

Hyde Park

When he and Richard entered the park at daybreak, William's favourite riding lane was unoccupied. It had been almost impossible to follow the trail as the sun had not risen sufficiently, and in some places the trees on either side of the lane obscured the view entirely. The steed that William rode whenever he was in London, Kronos, was used to Hyde Park and sped along as surefooted as ever.

"Slow down, Darcy! Titan is not familiar with this trail and I do not wish him to startle if a flock of birds takes flight."

William immediately pulled back on the reins, causing his stallion to fall into a trot. In a moment, Richard was alongside and a conversation that William had wished to avoid commenced.

"You seemed out of sorts last night, Cousin, especially when Lady Susan made a fuss over you at dinner. For a moment, I thought she was going to cut your roast into small pieces to prevent you from choking on it. No doubt that is something she learned after having a child. Very useful, very useful indeed."

"Humph!" William grumbled. Though he did not reply, he kicked Kronos back into a canter, leaving Richard behind once again. He had not been pleased with Susan's preoccupation with his every move, but he had hoped it had gone unnoticed by most of the party. Since Richard had not said a word when they returned to Darcy House last night, he assumed that he had been too busy arguing with Edgar to notice her fawning. Now it was plain that he had seen everything and meant to use it to annoy him. Bristling, he began to recall the humiliating experience.

Would you like another roll? Shall I signal the footman? Are you tired? Better a cup of coffee than another glass of wine. That will only make you sleepy.

And when the men joined the ladies in the music room, he noticed for the first time how closely her views mirrored women much younger than she, such as Georgiana.

All of you men smell of cigars! I think cigars are ghastly! They stain your teeth, and I have heard they contribute to colds.

Please do not tell me you like to hunt. Only barbarians hunt defenseless animals—foxes and such things as that.

Oh, please! Operas are so dull. I may speak Italian, but I do not wish to think too hard whilst I am being entertained.

I prefer the theatre as long as they are not performing one of those dreadfully boring plays about the monarchy. I had rather watch a comedy.

I may read a page or two from some boring book, but to be truthful I had rather peruse a magazine, especially one with illustrations of the latest fashions."

During the entire party, William had kept a serene expression, though inside he often cringed. Finally his patience had worn thin and he announced that he was leaving, much to Lady Susan's disappointment and Georgiana's annoyance.

While he was recalling all that had taken place, Richard overtook him once more, teasing, "I say, Darcy, I owe you an apology. I must admit that Lady Susan has certainly changed." William kept silent, for he knew that Richard was not serious. "Only, she has changed for the worse. I cannot believe you would voluntarily marry such a woman. How degrading to be spoken to like a child!"

William's temper flared. "I do not think Lady Susan worse than most women of the *ton*. She is young and will, no doubt, improve."

"She is four and twenty, yet I see no difference between her and Georgiana! Mark my words, Darcy, should you marry her, her stupidity will drive you stark raving mad!"

Having had his say, Richard turned Titan and kicked him into a gallop back toward Darcy House, leaving his cousin to ponder what he said. He had no way of knowing that William had suffered these same misgivings.

What choice is left to me if I do not marry Susan? I shall never settle for a mindless debutant, schooled to simper and bow to my every wish before I have any idea WHAT I wish!

He proclaimed aloud, "Since becoming of age, I have not met a single woman I find attractive who also possesses common sense!"

Instantly, the one lady he had no success banishing from his thoughts materialized—*Elizabeth Bennet.* Whenever the finality of marriage weighed on his mind, to his vexation she would appear.

Do not be a fool! It takes more than mesmerizing eyes to make a match, and she would never be accepted by your family or those in your circle! Besides, she has no knowledge of what it takes to run an estate such as Pemberley. She would be utterly destroyed by the gossip of your peers and overwhelmed by the responsibility of her position!

Disconcerted, he urged Kronos towards home with a swift kick of his heel.

Darcy House
Later that same evening

The rain that had begun at noon had not abated, but increased in amount and ferocity as the day dragged on. Now it was accompanied by loud claps of thunder and frequent lightning, both accurately reflecting William's present disposition. Safely ensconced in his carriage, he found it quite ironic that a day that had begun with such promise had darkened along with his mood.

Having read Mr. Harrington's note the moment he returned from his ride in the park, William immediately set out for Lord Warren's townhouse. Richard had offered to accompany him, but he thought it best not to bring someone the gentleman was not expecting. As it turned out, the news had been disappointing; thus, while the carriage slowly navigated the rain-swollen streets of London on the way back to Darcy House, he replayed in his head all that he had learnt. For despite any reservations Mr. Harrington might have, he intended to inform Richard.

Deep in reflection, his thoughts were suddenly interrupted as the carriage came to an abrupt halt. When the door flew open, a footman stood without, holding a large umbrella meant to shield him from the rain. Normally, in such a downpour, William would have jumped from the carriage and rushed to the door, but since the man had gone to the trouble, he took the umbrella and hurried up the steps. The front door swiftly opened and Mr. Barnes swept an arm across his body in a gesture of welcome. Tossing the wet umbrella to a footman who stood nearby, William walked inside.

"Mr. Darcy, you are soaked! Do you wish me to send Martin to your room to assist you in changing?" Barnes asked.

Mr. Martin, an older gentleman who was once his father's valet, resided at Darcy House, while Mr. Adams, William's valet, lived at Pemberley. William chose not to travel with a valet, so this arrangement suited, though he often took Adams if visiting elsewhere for very long. Being preoccupied with stamping his boots on the rug to remove much of the water, William did not answer right away. But as he turned to allow Barnes to remove his greatcoat, he replied, "No. While my coat is drenched, I am not. Is my cousin still here?"

"Colonel Fitzwilliam is in the library, I believe." The butler held out a letter. "This was delivered just moments ago, sir. It went to Pemberley before being forwarded here, so I thought you might want to read it straightaway."

William took the letter, his brows knitting as he broke the seal. It was from Bingley and had been sent by express to Pemberley in lieu of post. Examining the contents, he was surprised to find that it was actually from Caroline Bingley.

April 17, 1812
Mr. Darcy,
I pray that you excuse the deception, but my brother will not act, and I felt it imperative that you know of a new development.
Your cousin, Andrew Darcy, is currently our guest at Netherfield, having arrived on the heels of your departure. With your removal from Meryton, he has now become the focus of Miss Eliza Bennet's scheming.
I felt certain that you would want to know in order to put an end to her fortune hunting, for he seems quite taken with her, and I fear what may happen. Please come quickly."
Caroline Bingley

Giving no indication of what he had read, he addressed Barnes, "I shall join the colonel at once. Please see that we are not disturbed."

"Certainly, sir."

Barnes' unease increased as he watched his master walk towards the library. The set of William's shoulders and the heaviness of his step signified that either the interview with Mr. Harrington had gone poorly or the letter just received contained troubling news. Perhaps it was both.

Sighing, the butler turned to supervise the mopping up of the water, which was pooling on the marble floor where it dripped from William's coat. Spying his wife coming towards him, he implored, "A maid to clean this up, please, Mrs. Barnes, before someone takes a fall."

"Of course." She rushed back down the hall, calling for one of the downstairs maids who was just ahead of her.

The Library

For a brief moment after entering, William thought that his cousin had already quit the room. About to inform Barnes that he been mistaken as to Richard's whereabouts, he was turning to leave when he spied a hat lying atop a table near the wall of windows overlooking Hyde Park. The well-lit spot made an excellent place to read, but given today's cloudy skies, it made for an equally fine place to sleep.

As he approached, he noted that a sword was placed next to the hat. That, and his cousin's snores, left no doubt that Richard was still there. Peering over the couch just beyond the table, he spied the prone form of his cousin sound asleep, his boots dutifully removed. The sight caused William to smile, for he had chastised Richard often for not removing the boots when he napped. Sadly, what he had to relate came to mind, and his smile quickly vanished. Leaning over the sofa from behind, he shook his cousin's arm just as a loud clap of thunder vibrated the windows and echoed through the room.

"Richard."

"Wha... what?" Instantly Richard was on his feet, patting the place where his sword normally hung before grabbing one of his boots. Hopping on one foot, he demanded, "Where is my sword? Thaggart, find my sword!"

Regretting that he had startled him, William walked around the end of the sofa with his hands up in surrender. "Calm yourself, Richard. You are in Darcy House in London."

Richard was a little embarrassed, as well as annoyed. "Good heavens, Darcy! Could you not have awakened me a little less vigorously? I thought for a moment that Bonaparte... well, never mind what I thought."

"I apologize. I had no way of knowing that thunder would rattle the windows the moment I touched you." As if to validate his assertion, another round of thunder shook the entire room.

Richard sank down on the sofa, rubbing his eyes vigorously. "I only meant to close my eyes for a moment. How long was I asleep?"

"I imagine since I left for Lord Warren's residence, and there is no need to apologise, as you evidently needed the rest. After all, you were on the road constantly before you arrived at Pemberley, and then we left the next day for here."

"I am a little tired. Could you spare a poor soldier some coffee? I think I shall need it to help me think more clearly." Stopping to raise one brow as he got a good look at William, he added, "I assume, from that scowl on your face, that what you learned about Andrew was not welcome news."

William walked over to the bell pull and gave it a tug. "You assume correctly. Let us have our coffee before we begin. I think I need a clear head as well."

Several minutes later, they occupied comfortable chairs in front of the large marble-mantled hearth, neither speaking as they sipped hot coffee from china cups. Between them on a small table, Mrs. Barnes had placed a plate of various biscuits. At the sight of these delights, Richard had begun to whittle the number down, and it was only after his third helping that he decided he was sufficiently awake to listen.

"Tell me what that blackguard has done and leave nothing out."

⁘

A half-hour later, Richard let go a low whistle, shaking his head in disbelief. "I was not expecting that. Is there even a slight chance that Andrew has fallen prey to a fortune hunter? After all, by appearances he is a wealthy man, and his friends help him to sustain the illusion."

"Even if I were inclined to lean in Andrew's favour—and I am not—after meeting Mr. Harrington, I have no doubt as to the truth of the matter." William reached into his coat pocket and brought out an object that he tossed to Richard. "This settled it."

Examining the cameo, the colonel clucked his tongue. "So, Miss Harrington was the recipient of one of Andrew's calling cards. It matches those given to his other victims, so I would say that this brooch hammers the nails in his coffin."

"There were also several letters to Miss Harrington professing his undying love. I was allowed to read them, though her father insisted on keeping all but this one." William held up a folded paper. "I shall use it to force a confession, if necessary."

"I am surprised that he let even that one out of his sight." Richard scratched his chin. "Is he an imposing fellow? For, apparently, Andrew is not overly concerned. He put his promises in writing, for heaven's sake!"

"Truthfully, he is older than your father, I would guess, and does not appear in good health. When he walks, he relies heavily on a cane. Still, his comportment and determination are impressive. It is his intention to force Andrew do right by his daughter, regardless of the toll it may take on his health."

"He has no others he can rely on? No sons?"

"His only son died several years ago, and Effie, that is his daughter's name, is the only child left. I saw a small portrait of her, and though she is plain, she is not ugly. In thinking on the matter, I believe that Andrew may have been considering marrying her to combine their estates, since they are adjacent. According to Harrington, it is well known in Manchester that Marsden Park is profitable. What Andrew would not have known straight off is that the estate is entailed to the male line."

"And if he learned that Miss Harrington cannot inherit," Richard interjected, "he would cut and run!"

"This, according to the letters, seems to have been the case."

Richard examined the cameo, turning it over repeatedly. "I admit that this piece does impress. The border appears to be seed pearls and diamonds."

"It is a good reproduction. One would believe it authentic, especially if it was gifted with the same sad story."

"His dear departed mother's brooch? How despicable!" Richard exclaimed. "Are all women fools for a man who confesses to mourning his mother? And, naturally, the gift of a purported family heirloom makes his actions seem honourable!"

"It does," William sighed. "He promised he would dispose of the entire lot after our conversation regarding his children and his inheritance."

"How many brooches did he have at that time?"

"I found five in a box in his room, though it also contained a receipt for twenty. They could have been elsewhere."

Richard's curiosity grew as he watched William run his hand over his face nervously.

"However, there is another development that will make this affair much harder for Andrew to escape. After we finished our conversation, Lord Warren came into the room. He related that he is a distant cousin to Harrington, and now that he has been apprised of the situation, he has pledged his full support to Miss Harrington. He also made it plain that he expects me to use whatever pressure I must to make Andrew behave like a gentleman."

"That does not bode well. Lord Warren wields tremendous power in the House of Lords, in addition to being an expert shot and swordsman. As to making Andrew act like a gentleman, I do not know if that is possible."

"My cousin has no earthly idea what he has set in motion. If he does not marry Miss Harrington, regardless of anything I might do, there will be terrible repercussions."

"I apologise, Darcy. I have let you down and exposed you to Lord Warren's ire! I had no idea that Andrew was calling on Miss Harrington. The last report I received stated that he had been in London for the last eight months. When could he have returned to Manchester?"

"Heaven only knows, but please do not assume the blame. Your reports have helped me tremendously. I am at fault for believing he could change his ways. Not hearing from any enraged fathers in almost a year and a half gave me leave to think I had some influence on him."

"Do you regret not summoning Andrew to face Mr. Harrington with you?"

William stood, placing his empty cup on the coffee tray. "To be honest, I am grateful that Andrew is not aware of our meeting. I would not have wanted the distraction of hearing him interrupt to swear that he has done nothing wrong."

"That I can readily understand; in his eyes he is always blameless. Just remember, Andrew has plenty of ears and eyes in London and will know of your meeting ere long. You will have to locate the scoundrel soon or he shall vanish into thin air, just as he always does when he is caught in a scandal."

"Ironically, I received this mere minutes ago." He held up the express. "It went to Pemberley and my steward forwarded it here, per my instructions. I thought it was from Charles, but as it turns out, it is from Miss Bingley. She writes that Andrew is staying at Netherfield even as we speak."

"And her purpose in breaking with propriety and risking Charles' ire to write directly to you?"

"To warn me that Elizabeth Bennet has designs on Andrew, though I am inclined to believe it is the other way around."

"What shall you do? Surely you will not allow him to practice his trickery on that lady, even if she is not your choice?"

"I would never wish that on any woman. I leave for Netherfield tomorrow to inform Andrew of Mr. Harrington's connections to Lord Warren and the fact that he has stirred up a hornet's nest. Afterward, I shall insist he do the honourable thing and marry the woman."

"I am not sure that Miss Harrington would be better off married to that cad."

"Neither am I, but I have no choice. There is no other way to salvage her reputation, and her father insists. I cannot say I would act any differently."

"And should Andrew refuse?"

"If he refuses, he will not only face the wrath of her relations, he shall never receive another farthing from me—either in allowance or the inheritance left in my power. If he survives any challenges, he shall live on what his estate provides—less than three hundred pounds a year."

"I fear what he may do if you stand firm," Richard stated. "I have friends among some retired Bow Street Runners, and they would make excellent guards. Outfit them as footmen and station them on your vehicles. It would serve you to be better protected, at least for the present."

"I do not like his attitude, but I do not think Andrew capable of murder. He is simply lazy and self-indulgent."

"A lazy, self-indulgent man with no means of support is a threat. Mark my words. Let me arrange for at least two Runners to work for you until we are sure that your cousin will not try to retaliate."

"If it will ease your mind, I shall do as you ask, but only after I return from Netherfield. Dare I hope that you will come with me?"

"I would be delighted, but the general expects me to be in the office for the next three days."

"I understand. Will you reside here until I return?"

"Where else can I enjoy the best accommodations and food without being chastised for everything I say or do?"

"Then it is settled. You shall stay here, and I shall return as soon as possible. When I do, perhaps we can ride out to the estate I purchased for Andrew's castoffs to inspect the improvements. They are awaiting my approval to finish more renovations."

"That suits me," Richard replied, his mood lifting. "Now suppose we have a game of billiards to get your mind off all this unpleasantness?"

"I do not think I could—"

"Oh, come now, Cousin!" Richard chided. "You need something to

occupy you instead of brooding as you normally do."

William sighed. "If you insist, then what say we wager a pound a game to make it interesting?"

"That is just like you!" Richard said as he stood to place his empty cup on the tray and stretched, reaching towards the ceiling. "Feed me so many biscuits I cannot lean over a billiards table comfortably, then place bets on the game!"

"I did not tell you to eat all those biscuits! Besides, you have beaten me half-drunk before. A few biscuits should not spoil your game!"

As they departed the library, Richard put an arm around his cousin's shoulder as they continued down the hall. "Let us make it a crown for the first four games. And if I am not winning by then, we will dismiss with bets entirely."

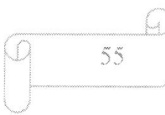

Pemberley

The noise from a team of horses and huge carriage circling the gravel on the drive in front of Pemberley drew Mrs. Reynolds' attention. Quickly leaving off her inspection of the library, she moved to a window to peek through the heavy, gold damask curtains. She was not surprised to see the carriage door swing open and Captain Fitzwilliam step down. She watched him carefully guide his wife to the ground. *He looks after her as though she were a delicate flower,* she thought.

Following their progress up the steps, something suddenly became obvious—Olivia Fitzwilliam looked completely exhausted even though the couple had slept late, and it was only early afternoon. A sudden realization came to the elderly housekeeper. She had seen this woman similarly affected numerous times since the Fitzwilliams had come to Pemberley. Rushing into the foyer, she managed to stop short and appear to have been standing there all along as they turned from giving Mr. Walker their coats.

"Mrs. Fitzwilliam," she began, "if you will forgive me, you do not look well. Should I send for Mr. Camryn? His office is in Lambton. In fact, you may have met him already. Mr. Darcy places great faith in his abilities."

Recalling the tall, slender, white-haired physician, her husband answered straightaway. "Indeed, we have had the pleasure of meeting him. He came by to care for Livy's aunt during our visit with her. And while we thank you for your concern, his help will not be necessary." He smiled. "I can assure you that all is well."

Though not convinced, Mrs. Reynolds knew that she could not force their guests to see a physician; however, she worried what Mr. Darcy would think if something happened to his aunt while in her care. "Perhaps a cup of tea or a scone, then? May I have Cook send you up a tray?"

Joseph shook his head, already helping his wife towards the staircase. "You are most kind, Mrs. Reynolds. But I think that what my wife needs most at this moment is a nap."

"Certainly! I shall send a maid up immediately to assist."

Her dark-blue eyes glowing with warmth, Olivia Fitzwilliam stopped walking to reply. "You are so kind. Please do not think I expect a lady's maid, though Mrs. Kelly is most accomplished. I fear it is too much for her to take me on, as I am only a visitor here."

"I assure you that Mrs. Kelly has expressed her joy in being asked. She was Lady Anne's lady's maid for many years and has missed the duties she performed."

"She does not attend Miss Georgiana?"

"Miss Darcy has her own lady's maid, who accompanied her to Town."

Olivia smiled gratefully. "Then I shall appreciate her help."

As soon as she finished speaking, the couple began to walk up the grand staircase. They were focused on that task and did not see Mrs. Reynolds' observation of their progress.

I wonder if Mr. Darcy suspects how ill Mrs. Fitzwilliam is. Is it my place to mention it?

In a guest room

Joseph Fitzwilliam watched as Olivia, sitting on a small settee, bent over to remove her short, brown walking boots. Instantly, he was on his knees in front of her, finishing the job.

"What have I asked you a thousand times, Livy? Let me help you! I thought you were going to wait for the maid."

"I only meant to remove my boots. My feet are aching."

As he pulled first one and then the other offending object off her feet, he noted that they were swollen, and he began to massage them gently. His actions caused her head to fall back against the cushions of the settee.

"Mmm. That feels so good."

"Olivia, are you sure you do not want Mr. Camryn summoned? After all, you have had more frequent episodes of breathlessness since we arrived."

"Joseph darling, no physician can help my fatigue. You know what Mr. O'Brien said when last I saw him in Dublin. The influenza I had as a child weakened my lungs, and now that I am older, I will simply have to rest more. The *episodes*, as you call them, are the result of all the travelling we have done lately. I should have taken your advice and rested for a few days after we arrived. Instead, I was so impatient to see everyone that I rushed headlong into making calls." She reached to cup his face before pulling him forward to plant a gentle kiss on his lips. When she pulled back, her blue eyes twinkled with mirth. "To ease your worries, I shall rest all day tomorrow. Will that make you happy?"

Smiling at the woman he loved more than life, he willed his eyes not to tear. "You make me happy, Livy, you alone." Sitting down next to her, he pulled her into a tight embrace and laid his head atop hers.

How shall I survive without her?

At Joseph's request, Mr. O'Brien had not told Olivia the truth of her situation. Her lungs were not the problem; it was her heart. The kindly, old physician had given her one year to live—perhaps two, if they were fortunate. Not wishing to burden his wife with that prospect, Joseph had requested that she be kept uninformed.

"Will you lie down, too, and hold me for a while?"

Her soft voice penetrated his thoughts, and he kissed her hair. Unable to be sure that his voice would not break, he nodded without speaking. At that very moment there was a knock on the door.

"Come," Olivia called.

The door opened and Mrs. Kelly stepped inside. Joseph managed to keep his voice steady. "I shall return in a few minutes, sweetheart."

Olivia smiled her agreement, while he left in order for the lady's maid to help her undress. Needless to say, he was grateful for the opportunity to gain control of his emotions. The last thing Joseph wished to do was break down in her presence. She might suspect that he was hiding something, and that would never do.

You are tenacious when you think I am not being totally honest. Would you hate me if you knew what I am hiding now?

Shaking his head as though to rid it of the spectre of her disappointment, he continued into the sitting room that adjoined the bedroom they shared. Seeing a book of poetry on the table, he sat down in the chair next to it and occupied himself by reading until the maid had finished. Hearing the door shut on her way out, he quietly walked back into the room.

Olivia was already in bed, her eyes closed. Taking off his coat, waistcoat and boots, he joined her, slipping behind her and pulling her tightly to his chest.

She sighed, murmuring, "There you are. I cannot sleep without you."

He kissed her hair. "Nor I you, my darling."

Forcing himself to think only of the present, Joseph fell asleep with her in his arms, just as he had every day that he was not at sea since the day they had wed.

Chapter 6

Meryton
Early Morning

As he rode into town, Charles Bingley was astonished to see his best friend's coach stopped in front of the blacksmith's shop. One horse was free of the traces and the smithy was working on that animal's shoe. Suddenly, he saw William round the corner from the main street.

"Darcy!" Bingley shouted, kicking his horse in that direction. When he reached his friend, he effortlessly dismounted the stallion and grabbed William's hand, pumping it with great enthusiasm.

"Darcy, old man! Good to see you again! What brings you back to Meryton? Did you forget your favourite hound? Seems I saw a few new dogs the last time I went shooting, though I have so many I can never be sure."

"I assure you that I have not lost any of my hounds."

"Then I am perplexed. I thought you were anxious to be rid of me and my problems when you left for Pemberley?"

"I was not eager to be rid of you," William said patiently. "I was eager to return to Pemberley. There were matters that required my attention, and I had done all that you asked. I felt there was no need to delay and thought you understood."

"That was what you said, but you and I both know that was not the only reason you departed like a man possessed," Bingley said with a chuckle. "I swear you were intrigued by Miss Bennet's sister and most likely intimidated, as well."

"I was certainly not intrigued by Elizabeth Bennet nor has any woman ever intimidated me!"

"Who said it was her sister Elizabeth?" Now Bingley smiled widely. "It could have been any of her sisters."

"If you would use your head, Charles, you would realise that I have never met any of Miss Bennet's sisters, save Miss Elizabeth."

Bingley rubbed his chin, looking thoughtful. "Well, I was correct when I said that you left Meryton as if your horse's tail was ablaze!"

William stiffened. "Whether you believe it or not, my explanation is the truth!"

"Have it your way," Bingley smirked, though he pursed his lips to keep from smiling outright. "So, tell me, why have you returned with no notice?"

"I returned in part because I received this," William pulled the letter from Caroline from the pocket of his coat, offering it to his friend. Bingley's brow furrowed as he took the proffered document, opened it and began to read.

"What in the ▮▮▮▮!" he exclaimed as his eyes flew to William's. "I had no idea she sent this! I told her I would not get involved in her scheme to call you back. Wait until I… "

William grasped his shoulder. "I believe you, but Caroline's impropriety is not the purpose of my visit."

Bingley's expression darkened. "Then why are you here?"

"Andrew."

"I see. And from your mood, it must involve another unpleasant situation."

"It does, and it is imperative that I find him before he realises I am here. Is he still at Netherfield?"

"At present he is, but he might as well be staying at an inn for all that I see of him. He comes and goes as he pleases—sometimes he is away overnight, other times he may be gone for days before he returns."

"I apologise for his behaviour. I know you only tolerate him for my sake."

"I hate to agree, but it is true. You know I have never been fond of him."

William reached to grasp Charles' shoulder. "You are a good friend."

"I am only repaying your kindness. Now, is there a way that I can help?" Charles tilted his head towards the horse being shoed. "It would seem that you are in need of transportation at the moment."

"Could I impose upon you to wait for the coach whilst I borrow your horse?"

Charles held out the reins. "Done! And, if you go straight to Netherfield, you should find Andrew still in bed. My butler informed me that he returned in the early morning hours. I imagine he will sleep until late this afternoon if no one wakes him."

"Oh, I shall wake him. Of that you can be certain."

"Are you sure you do not want to wait until we can go together?"

"There is no need. Andrew is not stupid enough to oppose me too strongly. After all, I control his living; but there is one more thing I would ask of you."

"Anything."

"First, I would like one of your men to follow Andrew the rest of the time he is in Meryton. I am convinced that he will see it is in his best interests to return to Manchester, but until he does, I want to know where he goes."

"I see no problem with that, and I know just the man. Tell Mercer that I wish for Starnes to follow Andrew. He will see to it."

"Good. I shall reimburse you for his wages whilst he follows my cousin. Now, I have one other request."

"You have only to ask."

"I would like to keep my presence at Netherfield a secret from Caroline for as long as possible. So if I finish with Andrew before she awakens, I will spend the rest of the day in my room. Other than visiting with you, should you wish it, I will read and rest."

"If you do not awaken Caroline when you and Andrew have your talk, I see no reason it will not work. When she comes down to break her fast, I shall send her and Louisa into Meryton to visit the seamstress in order to pick out materials for new curtains. She has asked me repeatedly to replace the ones downstairs, so that should keep her occupied most of the day. I have no doubt that Mr. Mercer and Mrs. Watkins will be happy to keep your secret. Just ring for a tray whenever you are ready."

"Thank you. I do not wish to listen to Caroline's prattling today."

"If you are certain you do not mind my company, I should like to join you in your room later." He looked towards the coach. "They will likely be done here in a half-hour, by the looks of it, so I shall see you in a while."

"I look forward to it."

Charles watched as William rode in the direction of his home, then he said a few words to the smithy and rounded the building towards the centre of town. If he hurried, there was time to check on the rifle he had ordered while they finished shoeing the horse.

Netherfield

"Mr. Darcy! How good to have you back, sir!" Mr. Mercer proclaimed as he crossed the foyer towards their guest. "The master is in Meryton, I am afraid, but I suspect he will return shortly."

"I met Bingley in town, as a matter of fact," William replied, nodding to the footman who had opened the door. "He will be returning in a short while with my coach. I borrowed his stallion in the hopes of catching my cousin here. Have I been successful?"

Mercer's smile faded. "Yes, sir. As far as I know, Mr. Darcy has been in his room since he wakened me in the middle of the night to let him into the house."

"That comes as no surprise. Allow me to apologise for his manners."

"No apology is necessary."

"If Andrew is still imbibing as much as ever, it is."

"Other than keeping odd hours, last night was the first time he came home in such a condition as to need help getting up the stairs."

"I do not know whether to be pleased or not." By this time, Mercer had relieved William of his great coat, hat and gloves, and he was headed towards the grand staircase. "Is everyone still asleep?"

"Yes, sir. Other than Mr. Bingley, it is unusual for the family to awaken until half past nine or later."

Staring at the landing at the top of the grand staircase, William appeared to be resigned to what lay ahead. "Good. I think it best they sleep through my conversation with my cousin. By the way, after I speak to Andrew, I am going to retire to my usual room. However, I want my cousin followed if he should leave Netherfield. I have Mr. Bingley's approval. He said to tell you that Starnes was to follow him until further notice."

"I shall see to it."

"In addition, I do not wish for the rest of the family to know that I am in residence for as long as possible. I would appreciate it if you would inform Mrs. Watkins."

"I will. And rest assured that you will have a pitcher of hot water waiting, so that you may wash off the dust of the road."

"Excellent. Now, may I have the key to Andrew's room?"

"I shall ask Mrs. Watkins for the key to the blue room—that is the one Mr.

Darcy is occupying presently. At his request, no maid has entered it in days, so please excuse any untidiness."

William nodded. "I shall wait in the upstairs hallway."

Mercer's expression darkened as he watched his master's good friend start up the staircase, his head down and his step heavy.

Quickly, he headed in the direction of Mrs. Watkins' office. He could easily let the housekeeper take the key to Mr. Darcy, but he would not. In the past, quite by chance, he had been witness to one of the cousins' arguments at a previous estate that Mr. Bingley rented and he did not want to subject her to that prospect. In fact, he planned to have two footmen stand by in case they were needed.

Would that Mr. Bingley was here in case tempers flared!

The blue guest room

Glancing about the thoroughly dishevelled room, William could not say he was surprised at the chaos. Andrew had never been one for keeping a room tidy, leaving it to servants to clean up after him. And since he had no money for a valet, he was entirely on his own in regards to the personal orderliness and clothes—the very clothes that were tossed over every available surface, though the open closet doors revealed that it was empty. Several pairs of boots and stockings were strewn in the middle of the floor, asking to be tripped over, while an empty tray with remnants of a meal, empty china cups and a cold pot of tea occupied a nearby dresser. On the table nearest the bed, a half-empty bottle of brandy and several glasses left room for little else.

Hearing snores, he approached the bed where his cousin lay hidden under a mountain of covers and pillows. Dreading what must be done, William reached out to shake his shoulder. There was no response, so he did it more forcefully the next time, calling his name simultaneously.

"I… I was not—" Andrew stuttered, sitting up in the bed as he wiped the sleep from his eyes, then looking about anxiously it dawned on him that William was the only one in the room. "For heaven's sake, Fitz! What in blazes are you doing here? And why have you come at this ungodly hour?"

"I am here because we have urgent things to discuss," William answered, his face emotionless.

Andrew rolled over in the bed. "Leave me alone! Let me rest and I will talk with you later. I did not get into bed until daylight." He concluded by pulling the counterpane over his head.

William reached for the counterpane, grasped it and jerked it completely off the bed. "That is no concern of mine. You will get up at once."

Andrew sat up now, his eyes shooting fiery darts at his tormentor. "What do you want this time? Have you not done enough by cutting my allowance to the bone? Must you make my life more miserable by harassing me in person?"

"Miss Effie Harrington."

For a brief moment, panic filled Andrew's eyes; however, he quickly recovered, wiping all emotion from his face. "What about Miss Harrington? Her father owns the estate next to Winfield Hall and I have known her for years."

"It seems that you know her too well. Her father paid me a visit whilst I was in Town. He is expecting you to make her an offer of marriage and, after listening to his story, I agree."

"An offer? Are you both daft?" Andrew sputtered, as he slid out of the bed and reached for his breeches. Pulling them on, he added, "Beyond exchanging greetings, I barely know the woman. And, have you seen her? She is certainly no beauty! Even you would concede that I would never have shown any interest in one so plain. I flirted with her, as I do all women. Anything else she maintains happened is a complete fabrication."

William pulled a letter from an inside pocket of his coat. "This letter proves otherwise."

Andrew grabbed the letter and glanced over it quickly before tossing it on the bed. "That is not my handwriting. You have been duped if you believe that it is."

Reaching into his coat pocket, William brought out the brooch. Tossing it to Andrew, he added, "I fear it is Miss Harrington who has been duped."

Taken aback, Andrew sat down on the side of the bed, his mind spinning with lies. "It is not what you think."

Forgetting his desire to let the rest of the house sleep, William lost his temper. "NOT ANOTHER WORD!" he commanded, pounding the bedside table. The brandy bottle sloshed from side to side, but held steady, while two glasses fell to the floor.

Andrew swallowed hard several times, as though attempting to keep from losing what little food occupied his stomach.

"Hear me, and hear me well," William demanded as he leaned down to look him in the eye. "I believe Miss Harrington's account of what happened and you WILL go to Marsden Park immediately and make her an offer of marriage."

"But... but I cannot possibly marry Miss Harrington. I care nothing for her! And if I were inclined to marry, it would certainly not be her. Besides, you have preached for years that I cannot afford a wife and I am in agreement."

"While it is true that your estate will barely support you, much less a wife or children, that is the least of your worries at this point. If you value your life, you will marry her."

"Have you sunk so low as to threaten to kill me if I do not obey your dictates?"

"It is not I who will be your executioner; it is Lord Warren."

Fear filled Andrew's eyes as his face went pale. William was glad for it. *Perhaps there is some sense left in him.*

William continued. "When I met with Mr. Harrington, it was at Lord Warren's townhouse. He informed me that he was the Harringtons' cousin and would champion Miss Harrington's side. If you have any intelligence, you will realise that you have no choice but to marry her. Otherwise, Lord Warren will likely call you out. If you face him on the field of honour, you will die."

"Duels are illegal! He would be a fool to chance being caught!"

"You are a fool if you think duels do not still occur frequently! The law will overlook anything Lord Warren does. But should he wish, he could make your existence pure hell without challenging you. With his contacts, he can see that no one will buy from or sell to you. Even the few goods Winfield Hall produces will find no takers. Nor will your so-called friends anger him by acknowledging you. You will be a social outcast among those you care for so dearly. Even Whites will be closed to you! It is as simple as that."

Andrew dropped his head in his hands. "How can this be? My sources never mentioned that Warren was their cousin."

"Your sources?" William chided. "The same sources that failed to tell you that Miss Harrington was not her father's heir until you carried your charade too far?"

Andrew reached for the shirt he had worn yesterday and pulled it over his head. "I shall make this right, Cousin. Just give me a few days and you will see that it was all a huge misunderstanding. She simply misconstrued my kindness."

Ignoring his words, William added, "You will leave for Manchester no later than tomorrow morning. I instructed Mr. Harrington to notify me immediately when the plans for the marriage are finalised."

"I assure you that after I have explained—"

William held up both hands. "Save your breath. Should you fail to satisfy the Harringtons, your allowance will be discontinued and any inheritance that was held in escrow for the slight chance that you would mature will be forfeited straightaway."

"You would really enjoy that!" Andrew sneered. "No more of your father's precious money being wasted on me."

William turned to leave, and Andrew grabbed his arm. "Wait!" He pasted on a smile. "Forgive me. I did not mean that. I am just upset that Mr. Harrington has involved you in a misunderstanding. Will you at least answer a question?"

"Ask."

"If Mr. Harrington writes to inform you that I am under no obligation to marry his daughter and all has been settled amicably, will my allowance and inheritance be restored to the former arrangement?"

"Though I find that highly unlikely, on the slight chance that you are successful in convincing the Harringtons, I will reconsider. But I would need to hear from Mr. Harrington and Lord Warren in person to believe it."

"Excellent! I shall be off to Manchester in the morning!" Andrew began rushing around the room, picking up his clothes. Shaking his head in disgust, William headed to the door.

Andrew suddenly seemed to remember something. "Wait!" William turned, his face set like stone. "In all the uproar, I forgot that my coach needs a wheel and as you have not paid my allowance for the month, I have no funds to fix it. It is presently at the smithy in Meryton. I have been forced to travel lately by horseback, but if I am to travel as far as Manchester, I shall need the coach."

William's eyes narrowed while he studied his cousin. Unable to tell if he were lying, he reached into his pocket for a few pounds. "Take this and have the wheel fixed, but do not loiter in town. I want you to have plenty of rest so that you are on the road to Manchester at daybreak."

Andrew ventured an insincere smile. "You have no worries on that account. I aim to do my duty, but might I ask when I can expect the rest of my allowance? What you have given me is but a pittance."

The smile faded with William's reply. "Due to your conduct, I am not in the mood to discuss it. Frankly, under the circumstances, I cannot believe you would mention it."

Having said that, he entered the hallway, pulling the door closed behind him. He had not taken ten steps when something hit the back of the door and curses filled the air. Normally, William might have shrugged off Andrew's ire, but this time he sighed in resignation. There was no pleasure to be found in coercing Andrew to marry a gentlewoman, even one so plain as Effie Harrington.

The sudden screech of Caroline's voice somewhere down the hall brought his thoughts back to the present. Picking up his pace, he hurried to the guest room he always occupied at Netherfield, rushed inside it and locked the door. Bone tired from his journey, he doffed his coat, waistcoat and cravat, all the while eyeing the large basin of steaming water fogging the dressing room mirror. Just the thought of the hot water on the back of his neck made the knot there relax a bit and he massaged it as he walked in that direction. In the years since his father's death, Andrew's troubles had taken a heavy toll and he yearned to be out from under that burden.

Is just a bit of peace, a touch of joy, too much to ask, Lord? A respectable wife to brighten my days and children to cherish? After all, Mother always said a good woman could make a man more than he would ever be on his own.

His thoughts flew to Andrew. *Perhaps if he married a decent woman, he would become a better man.* Stopping to examine that idea, William shook his head. *Even I cannot believe that.*

Aunt Phillips' House
That evening

Though not substantially larger than the abodes of many of the businessmen of Meryton, the Phillips' house appeared larger due to the sizeable portico that wrapped around three sides of it. It was this extra space that allowed most of the town's citizenry to attend the soirées given by John Phillips, a solicitor, and his wife, Agnes. In addition, it provided the young people with a ready excuse for slipping out of the oft-times airless parlour and, as they did so this evening, they were treated to a lovely view—the moon, full and luminescent. That sight, in addition to the romantic melodies wafting through the open windows, gave the night a magical quality, raising the expectations of the couples who fancied themselves in love.

This particular night a goodly number of militia were also in attendance, which added to the throng—and Lieutenant Wickham was among them. Lydia and Kitty had spied him straightaway and were now hanging on his every word in a far corner of the portico. Disappointing to Elizabeth, however, was the fact that Wickham's childhood friend, Andrew Darcy, was not with him. She particularly needed to speak to that gentleman before her father did. Ignoring the truth of the matter was no longer an option.

While she had been partial to Andrew Darcy from the start, his aim in lingering in Meryton was now troubling. After all, if he were unable to marry until after his grandmother's demise, then the proper course of action would have been to leave Meryton and return when his circumstances altered. Instead he had stayed, making a show of singling her out at every opportunity.

For a short time she had been flattered; now she was simply mortified. Summoned to her father's study that very day, he had demanded to know whether Mr. Darcy had been courting her without his permission, as the gossip indicated. Though she denied everything, upon reflection it was a logical assumption, and Elizabeth could not fault her neighbours for concluding as much. Instantly, everything was clear! Believing herself clever, she had tossed aside decorum for a game—a phantom courtship. Now, it was up to her to set the record straight.

"Lizzy, do you think Mr. Wickham will ask me to dance?"

Lydia's whining brought Elizabeth's thoughts back to the present and she turned to find her youngest sisters standing behind her. Their eyes, however, were still fixed on the spot where Wickham stood, now flirting with Mary King.

"I had his undivided attention until Mary arrived. Now he acts as though she is the only woman in the world. Why would he notice that freckled-face bore when I am here? I am a much prettier!"

"Lydia! How unkind you are," Elizabeth chided. "Mary King has always been a good friend to you and you should not disparage her appearance in that manner. If she has his attention, be glad for her. She is not used to being noticed."

"But why does she have to have my man's attention?" Lydia grumbled.

"Mr. Wickham is not yours, Lydia," Kitty giggled.

"Well, where is *your* favourite? Mr. Denny did not deign to come at all!" Kitty's face dropped, which was clearly Lydia's intention. "At least Mr. Wickham attended." Suddenly her face lit up. "Look! He is coming towards us now."

Lydia and Kitty turned to face him, while Elizabeth hurried in the opposite direction. She could not abide that gentleman's attempt to compliment her or the way he stared at her bosom all the while he spoke. Now on the side of the house, nearest the parlour, she glanced in through the window to see that a dance was beginning. Bingley was standing up with Jane and the sight made her smile with genuine happiness.

At least one of us has found a knight in shining armour!

"Miss Elizabeth!" She turned to find Andrew Darcy simultaneously bowing and removing his hat. "Forgive me, for I am late. My horse threw a shoe on my way back to Meryton and I was so late getting here that I slept most of the day."

What he did not say was that he had slipped out of Netherfield through a window to be there. He had no intention of missing this opportunity to see Elizabeth though his cousin would certainly not have approved. So when he paid the smithy for the coach wheel, he rigged a side door to the stable so that it would not close properly, knowing the hay in the loft would make an adequate bed and he would not have to risk sneaking back into Netherfield. At the crack of dawn, his driver and footmen were to bring the coach to the edge of Meryton where he would steal on board. Thus, Fitz would assume he had been in his room all night and, as ordered, had left for Manchester.

"You owe me no apologies, Mr. Darcy, for you are certainly under no obligation to inform me of your whereabouts."

"Nonetheless, I did not want you to think that I had not tried my best to get here on time, knowing that you would be in attendance."

"Actually, when last we talked, you said that you would return the day before yesterday."

"Hmmm, I do not remember saying that."

"I am surprised that you remembered this party, given that you travel so much."

"I remember everything that has to do with you."

Elizabeth was about to reply when a group of people tried to pass them, forcing both to stand aside to create a path. It was impossible to speak privately here so Andrew made a suggestion.

"Would you consider a walk in the moonlight?"

Several couples were already strolling the gravel path that circled behind the house, meandering through a small flower garden lit with lanterns, before winding to the front again.

"I consent to a very quick turn about the garden, as I do not wish to cause more gossip."

Unsettled by her matter-of-fact demeanour, Andrew drew her hand towards his lips and was offended when she pulled it away.

"Miss Elizabeth, I apologise if my actions have caused you to be the subject of gossip. I should have been more discreet, particularly in light of my present situation."

Ignoring his apology, Elizabeth answered, "Shall we begin our walk? Surely, there are enough witnesses tonight to suit the unkindest rumourmonger."

Leading her down the steps to the gravel path, Andrew placed his other hand over her petite one and gave it a squeeze. Elizabeth stiffened at the show of affection. Awkwardly, they made their way around the path, trying to keep several feet behind the couple ahead. Reaching the small gazebo in the middle of the rose garden, Andrew pulled Elizabeth up the steps, speaking quietly so as not to be heard.

"Miss Elizabeth, I have told you my circumstances—that I cannot ask permission to court you at present, so I have thought of a means to prove my sincerity." The lanterns illuminated a bejewelled cameo that he pulled from inside his coat. He was delighted at Elizabeth's quick intake of breath. "This was my mother's and I know that she would be pleased that you are in possession of it."

"I... I could not possibly accept this," Elizabeth stammered, staring at the brooch.

Another couple arrived at the gazebo and, seeing that it was occupied, walked on. Andrew waited until they were several yards away before resuming.

"Yes, you can! And you will, if you have any consideration for me. This is why I have been away. I returned to Manchester to fetch this from my family's jewels. Please say you will accept it as a token of my affection and a promise of what is to come."

Forcing her eyes from the exquisite piece, she looked up through her dark eyelashes. Andrew had assumed a pitiful expression and for a brief moment her resolve almost faltered.

"Mr. Darcy, do you realise what my father would do if he learnt of this? He would insist that we become engaged immediately, if not marry straightaway."

He smiled wryly. "I trust that you will not let him learn of it."

All of her doubts crumbled at his audacity. "It will not happen because my answer is NO."

"But you are the only woman I have ever considered courting! I cannot declare myself, but I hoped this brooch would prove my sincerity."

"You speak of sincerity, but if anything, this gift proves your faith in my gullibility. I fear that pride has been my Achilles heel, for I was flattered by your attention when, in truth, a gentleman would never court in secret."

Andrew stepped back as though he had been slapped. Shaking from the effort to control his temper, he took a deep breath and let it go noisily as he paced in front of her.

Then he stopped, asking brusquely, "How can you contend that asking you to wait for me is not gentlemanly? I know that it would be an unconventional engagement—"

"You have a habit of twisting words!" Elizabeth protested. "A secret engagement is no engagement. I will not agree to this madness!"

He stomped down the steps as if to depart. Proceeding several yards, he stopped short when she called, "You have left your brooch, sir!"

In a huff, he rushed back towards her. Unconsciously, Elizabeth stepped back at his angry demeanour, but that did not deter his plans. Grabbing her by the shoulders, he pulled her into an embrace that included a harsh kiss that was over before she had time to protest.

"At your wish I am leaving, however, the brooch stays. Let it be a reminder that I intend to return when my situation changes."

As he hurried back down the steps, she realised she had forgotten to warn him of her father. "Mr. Darcy, I must speak—"

Never slowing, he disappeared into the darkness. Debating going after him, disembodied voices from somewhere in the garden gave her pause. She waited, but no one rounded the gravel path in her direction. Glancing about nervously, she hurried back to the front.

Little did Elizabeth know that her life had just changed forever.

Mrs. Agatha Gould, the foremost gossip in Meryton, save Mrs. Bennet, could not suppress a wide smile as she followed Elizabeth back to the house at a safe distance. Only minutes before, she had been exceedingly upset, having spent the last quarter-hour searching for her headstrong daughter. She suspected that Gertrude had slipped off with the redcoat who had been paying her particular attention. After scouring every inch of the house and the huge portico with no success, she had entered the gardens in hopes of surprising her. She had no luck there, either—at least in regards to Gertrude; however, she had witnessed a most entertaining conversation that completely diverted her thoughts from her daughter.

It is true! Fanny's daughter is involved in a clandestine romance with a man who will not court her in public. I was right to have Walter inform her father of the rumours! I wonder what Thomas Bennet will do once he hears this! Or better still, what will Fanny do?

Mrs. Gould disliked Fanny Bennet immensely. Not only because she bragged of her eldest daughter's beauty, but because she talked endlessly of how Jane had little trouble luring the newest bachelor, Mr. Bingley, away from all the plain girls in town. Fanny seemed oblivious that her boast degraded her own daughter, Gertrude.

What I have witnessed will put an end to your braggadocio, Fanny! Perhaps it will even make you too ashamed to show your face in Meryton. She smirked. *How wonderful it would be to silence that hoyden forever!*

Quickly wiping the smile from her face as she entered the house, Mrs. Gould suppressed the urge to celebrate the twist of fate that would be the means of ruining her nemesis. Noting that her daughter was now dancing with another officer, she smiled as Gertrude waved from across the room. Nodding her approval, she made a mental note to address her disappearance when they got home. For now, there were more important things to consider.

Seeing Mrs. Hagood and Mrs. Long standing in one corner of the dining room, she nodded to catch their attention and hurried in that direction. Who better to begin the attack than those who loved a scandal as much as she? As she headed towards them, she assumed an expression of concern. *After all,* she mused, *I must not appear to be gloating.* Opening the fan that hung around her wrist, she fanned anxiously.

"Agatha! Are you well? You look as though you have seen a ghost," Bertha Hagood exclaimed. "Do you need some fresh air?"

"I was just in the garden, and believe me when I say I cannot afford more fresh air! A ghost would have been *preferable* to what I have just witnessed." Lowering her voice, she glanced nervously about. "I am so upset I can hardly speak."

Mrs. Hagood pulled Mrs. Long with her as she neared Mrs. Gould. "Pray, may we be of service? After all, it may help to discuss what has disturbed you so greatly."

"I know that I can rely on your confidence, but perhaps we should remove to a more private place. I would not want to be overheard."

"I agree!" Mrs. Hagood declared. "Let us go onto the front lawn where it is quiet. And you may rest assured that whatever you have to share with us will go no further."

"Absolutely, no further," Margaret Long echoed.

Mrs. Gould pursed her lips to keep from smiling. "I knew I could count on you."

Chapter 7

Netherfield
The next morning

Extreme exhaustion finally overtook Fitzwilliam in the early morning hours and he fell into a fitful sleep. But rest was not to be his, for he was roused from sleep for a *second* time. Not by Bingley's mellow baritone, but by a woman's high-pitched wails which sounded as though she stood right outside his bedroom door.

"We are ruined! Ruined, I tell you!"

In his stupor, William could not make sense of the screeches; however, the moment he opened his eyes, the disastrous express he had received last evening came to mind. His heart sank anew as he brought his hands to his face and rubbed his burning eyes.

Charles' interruption, shortly after dark, had been the result of an unexpected express from Lord Warren that Mrs. Barnes had forwarded from London. In it, he related that his cousin, Harrington, had returned to Manchester only to learn that his daughter had died. Apparently, she had drowned in the river that ran through their estate. Harrington was convinced that Effie had taken her life as a result of her disappointed hopes and the scandal that had ensued, for she could not swim and had no reason to be near the water. Lord Warren agreed.

Her death not only disturbed and saddened William, but also revived horrific memories from his eleventh summer. In that year, he and Richard had stumbled on a young girl who had hung herself from a tree in the woods behind the Matlock stables. It was a horrific sight, and only Richard's presence had kept him sensible. Sadly, she was barely seventeen and pregnant. Not from the area, it was surmised that she had travelled to Derbyshire in search of the father, with only the estate name to go by. Upon enquiring at the stables, she learned that, while the man had been employed there, he had left for parts unknown one month previously. After thanking the coachman, she had left the area, or so he thought.

As far back as he could remember, his father had lectured him on duty and honour. A man was expected to act like a gentleman and treat every woman with respect, just as he wished others to treat Georgiana. This tragedy had done more to sear those principals on his heart than all the lectures combined, as well as haunting his sleep for years afterward. Now the two incidences melded into one, bringing new depths of sleeplessness.

All at once another barrage of protests filled the hall outside his room, bringing his thoughts back to the present. This time the shrill voice of Caroline Bingley was impossible to dismiss. He forced himself to leave the warm bed. Splashing cold water on his face, William's stomach lurched as she mentioned the Darcy name in her tirade.

"Mr. Darcy stayed at Netherfield as our guest, and these country nobodies will never let us forget it! He is supposed to be a gentleman, for heaven's sake! Charles must be made to see reason and to break off his engagement with that horrible Bennet woman! If we vacate Netherfield this instant, we may escape being linked with the scandal."

The calmer voice of Louisa Hurst broke in. "Caroline, calm yourself before you have a paroxysm. Remember our Aunt Narcie!"

"A fit such as Aunt Narcie suffered would be preferable to being cast out of proper society! I told Charles that the Bennets were beneath us, but would he listen to me? No! He rushed headlong into an engagement with one of them. Now see what we suffer because of him? And that Eliza Bennet is nothing more than a hoyden and a fortune hunter, just as I said the first time I met her! Hurry, Louisa, we must see to the packing! There is nothing else to be done!"

By now, William was fully conscious. The mention of his name had gained his attention; however, it was Caroline's vilification of Elizabeth that really annoyed him. Angrily, he ran a hand through his hair and reached for his breeches. He stopped entirely, however, when he heard Charles enter the conversation.

"That is quite enough, Caroline! We are not departing Netherfield under any circumstances, so I suggest you calm yourself. Go downstairs and have something to eat while I talk with Darcy."

"HE IS HERE?" she shrieked. "It was my understanding that he left Meryton after that atrocious display of impropriety! What will the neighbours think if we let him stay here AFTER what he has done?"

"Not Andrew Darcy, Caroline. *Fitzwilliam* Darcy."

Caroline's hand flew to her hair and she patted it as she looked down at her gown. "He is back? Why did you not tell me sooner? I must look a fright. Come, Louisa, help me to find something to wear. I would ring for Marie, but she has left to break her fast, and that would take too long. I would not want Mr. Darcy to see me in this old gown with my hair in disarray."

Without awaiting an answer, Caroline rushed down the hall towards her bedroom. Louisa exchanged an exasperated look with Charles and, without a word, shrugged and followed Caroline.

William resumed pulling on his breeches, anticipating Charles's knock. Once dressed, he walked towards the door. Bingley was raising his hand just as he opened it and Charles' expression changed from a smile to a frown.

"Darcy? Good heavens, you look awful!" He walked into the room and closed the door. "I went to Longbourn and back believing you were getting some much needed rest, but it has not served you in the least!"

"If you had slept as little as I, you might look as bad."

"I am sorry for your trials, my friend. You have suffered more than your share and I despise adding to the burden. However, I have some bad news to report about Andrew. It explains why he was not in his room when I checked."

"What do you mean he is not in his room? That is impossible. A footman accompanied him to the blacksmith shop and back. Then when he retired for the night, I made certain that the door to his bedroom was locked from the outside!"

"Apparently he escaped the house by going out a window and climbing down a tree. There would have been no way for Starnes to know and follow him. In any event, he was a very busy man last night."

William's countenance darkened. "What more has he done?"

"In addition to spreading grief in Manchester, he has brought misery to Meryton. His actions have ruined Miss Elizabeth."

William's face crimsoned as he grabbed Charles's arm. "Are you telling me that he molest—"

"No! No! Not in that sense!" Bingley quickly explained. "But her reputation is ruined. And it shall affect all her family… all her sisters."

"Tell me everything."

"Last night a local woman, Mrs. Gould, happened upon Andrew and Miss Elizabeth in the gazebo located in the garden of Mrs. Phillips' house. Not only did she hear them speak of deceiving Mr. Bennet by means of a secret engagement, but she witnessed them kissing. And it was not an innocent kiss on the cheek!"

William slammed his fist on the dresser, causing everything atop it to rattle. "A secret engagement?! Only yesterday that cad swore to me that he would never marry!" William began to pace. "I should kill him myself!"

"Calm down, Darcy! He is no longer here. Apparently, directly after the incident, he left for Manchester, as you demanded. And from the express you received, Harrington is likely to shoot him on sight and solve that problem for you. However, if he survives the trip to Manchester, can you say with certainty that he will return to Meryton and make a proper offer for Miss Elizabeth?"

"With Andrew, nothing is certain. In the past, he has run from all responsibility. I have no hope that he will act any differently now."

Charles sighed. "Jane is disheartened. I found her staring out the window and weeping. It breaks my heart that all I can do is to assure her of my constancy. I do not know if she believes me." He walked over to a chair and sat down, worry etched on his face. "It was a desperate scene at Longbourn. Mr. Bennet was pacing about, shouting orders and placing blame, not caring who might hear, while Mrs. Bennet has taken to her bed. Her wails echo throughout the house, and I swear the sound of it makes me shiver. Forbidden to leave the house, the youngest girls are uncharacteristically silent."

William's heart was breaking for only one person. "Miss Elizabeth?"

"Jane told me that Miss Elizabeth and her father had an awful row first thing today. It was loud enough to be heard throughout the house. Jane was shocked at some of the terms he used, for Miss Elizabeth has always been his favourite. Afterward, she ran from the house in spite of her father's edict, which infuriated him all the more. Later, I heard him declare that he would send her to a nunnery in one breath and in the next, force her to marry some cousin, a vicar named Collins!"

"William Collins?"

"Yes, that was the name! Apparently he is Mr. Bennet's heir."

"That toady fool is my Aunt Catherine's vicar. He is senseless!"

"He may be senseless, but he is likely to be Miss Elizabeth's husband if her father has anything to say about it. Jane is beside herself, worrying for her sister's mental state. She talked Mr. Bennet into letting her go after Miss Elizabeth just before I left. I offered to assist but she contended that my presence might be a detriment, as her sister does not want to be seen by anyone. We can only pray that she does not do something foolish."

"Like Miss Harrington," William said woodenly.

"After hearing last night of what happened to her, I admit that the thought came to mind. A very similar situation, is it not?"

The thought of harm coming to the dark-eyed woman who still haunted his dreams, made William wince. "Perhaps I can reason with Mr. Bennet and together we can think of a solution."

"Are you sure? After all, you are a Darcy. He may not wish to see anyone with that name at this point."

"Andrew is my cousin and I feel responsible."

"You are a good man and I am glad to call you my friend, but you may be taking on too much."

"What if it were Georgiana? I have to try."

"If you insist on going, I am going with you. Surely, Mr. Bennet will not get as upset if I am present."

"Let us hope not," William said solemnly. "I shall finish dressing and meet you downstairs as soon as possible. If we are to prevent a disaster, we must act quickly."

Longbourn

By the time Caroline Bingley had dressed to impress Mr. Darcy, he and her brother were almost at Longbourn. As they rode in silence, Charles was beginning to question if this trip was prudent.

"Darcy, may I ask a favour of you?"

"Of course."

"Stay seated in the carriage until I send for you. As I said, Mr. Bennet was as angry this morning as I have ever seen any man and he might do something regrettable at the first glimpse of you. After all, you do favour Andrew quite a bit."

"You may be right. In matters of colour and height, Andrew and I are similar."

"Then you agree?"

"Yes."

By then the carriage had come to a halt in front of Longbourn and Charles opened the door and got out. Leaning back in the window, he said, "I appreciate that you are doing as I ask. I do not wish to upset the household further."

William merely nodded and watched as Charles disappeared inside the manor. Then he began to thoroughly examine the house and grounds, taking a measure of Longbourn. Unimpressed by the maintenance of the manor house, he focused on the grounds. Though there seemed to have once been a large rose garden on the left side, it had been sorely neglected. The roses needed pruning and the trellises and the stone wall surrounding them begged for repair.

Glancing to the right was another garden and William changed seats and opened the door to have a better view. This garden was populated with native plants and shrubs and he was inclined to favour it, for it did not require a great deal of care. Besides, from what he had seen, it was unlikely to receive any. Satisfied that this side of the house was the more presentable of the two, he was about to sit back and relax when he looked up. His gaze froze.

Elizabeth was standing on a small balcony on the third floor of the manor, almost invisible through the limbs of a large oak tree. Only the movement of a shawl slipping from her shoulders, exposing a bright yellow gown, had caught his eye. As William held his breath, she rose on her toes, leaned over the railing and looked to the ground. His pulse quickened.

Suddenly, Jane Bennet joined her sister on the balcony. She reached down to retrieve the shawl and place it around her sister's shoulders before pulling Elizabeth into an embrace. Even from where he sat, he could see both their bodies trembling as they cried. That was the moment he knew what he would do.

"DARCY!" Charles' voice penetrated his senses and he realised his friend was standing behind the open door. "Are you well? I called several times, but you paid me no mind."

"I... I apologise—"

"Never mind, we must hurry! Mr. Bennet has agreed to see you." As William stepped out of the carriage and they started towards the door, Bingley cautioned, "Please try not to upset him. Just remember that he has had a great shock and has a lot of things on his mind."

William stopped in his tracks. "Bingley, do you think me bereft of good manners?"

"No, not at all! Just try not to appear superior! I know that you do not think yourself superior, but those who are not acquainted with you have no way of knowing. From your manner—"

William broke in. "Thank you for the vote of confidence."

A housekeeper was already holding open the front door by then. She did not speak, nor did she meet their eyes as they entered the foyer. William glanced about, noting that the interior of the house was as neglected as the exterior. Suddenly, he noticed someone he assumed was the Master of Longbourn standing in the shadow of a doorway several feet ahead. Nodding in that direction, he was taken aback when the man stepped back into the room. A click signalled the door had closed.

Once Charles was alongside, the housekeeper led them to that very doorway. At her knock, a fatigued voice called, "Come!"

She opened the door and motioned for them to enter. William watched as Bingley stepped inside, then he steeled himself to follow. The room was dark, save for a place in front of a large window where the curtain was pulled back. It was in this light that Elizabeth's father stood, hands locked behind his back, staring woodenly into the distance. He did not bother to turn or otherwise acknowledge his guests. The friends exchanged pointed looks and Charles shrugged. Still, only a nudge from Darcy spurred him to speak.

"Ah, err, Mr. Bennet, sir. This is my good friend. The one I spoke to you about—Fitzwilliam Darcy of Pemberley in Derbyshire."

For a long while, Mr. Bennet was silent, and William became convinced that he was waiting for him to speak. He had just cleared his throat when their host deigned to reply.

"Mr. Bingley explained that *you* are the Darcy with *ten thousand a year*, while your cousin simply lets people assume that he is the one who is wealthy."

William, who preferred to keep his finances private, frowned at Charles as he replied, "I cannot control what people say or choose to believe."

"Nor, it seems, can you control the lies your cousin spews!" His bitterness silenced William and Mr. Bennet turned then to examine him. "You look remarkably alike. From my experience with the man, I think that must be a curse for you."

"Sir, I—"

A hand came up to silence him again. "Just looking at you, one would think you are a gentleman, but then your cousin looked the part as well." Mr. Bennet turned back to face the window. "Mr. Bingley puts great stock in your character, but he has not convinced me. So suppose you tell me why you are here? For seldom does one of your station deign to visit my humble estate. What can you possibly do to be of service now that that blackguard has compromised my daughter?"

William took a deep breath and slowly exhaled, gathering his courage. "I can marry her."

Mr. Bennet stiffened but otherwise did not react. Not so Charles! His head swung around and his mouth flew open, as he whispered anxiously, "Darcy, what are you saying?"

William gave Charles a sharp look, shaking his head in order to quiet him.

"As you say, Andrew and I look very similar. I have been told that he and your daughter were observed in the darkness of a gazebo; thus, it would seem a simple matter to convince your neighbours that I was the man with Miss Elizabeth. And if we were to marry as soon as possible, the matter could be easily forgotten—especially if no child follows in the next few months."

Mr. Bennet sneered. "Elizabeth has assured me that nothing happened between them other than a kiss that was forced upon her."

A load lifted from William's heart. "I am not surprised. Your daughter was always a lady whilst in my company."

"Would that she had shown such reserve last night! Still, you expect me to believe that you would marry my daughter just to right a wrong perpetrated by your cousin?"

"Yes."

Bennet turned to face him. "How noble! Why not force him to marry her and not muddle up your own life?"

"If you give me your word it will go no further, I shall explain."

"You have it."

"Besides the fact that he cannot support himself, much less a wife, he disdains the institution altogether. I have had to force him to support his two illegitimate children with two different women. And just this week I received news that he is likely responsible for another woman's early demise. Her father believes she drowned herself because Andrew had raised her hopes then fled when he learned she was not the heir to his estate. I would not discount that her family is searching for him as we speak."

"If all you tell me is true, he is not good enough for my Lizzy. But why do you think I should give you my consent?"

"I am in love with her."

Thomas Bennet barked a hollow laugh. "From what Lizzy said when she returned from Netherfield, you were anything BUT hospitable to her. And you left Meryton shortly afterward, so when did you find time to fall in love?"

"I believe I loved her from the beginning, but I convinced myself that it would not be to her advantage to make an offer."

"Not to her advantage or to yours?"

William looked sheepish. "Both, I fear. To be honest, I was impressed with her intelligence and liveliness from our first meeting, but those attributes do not necessarily translate into the skills needed for my wife. Being mistress of Pemberley is a daunting task in itself, but I also have homes in London and Brighton. In addition, my family will not readily accept a woman from outside our sphere and Miss Elizabeth could be subjected to contempt from many of my acquaintances. Frankly, I was not quite sure she could rise to the challenge or if it would be fair to ask it of her."

"How decent of you to consider Lizzy's feelings," he replied, though his voice challenged William's truthfulness. "Since we are being candid, having her marry you is not my only option."

Waiting for a reaction, Bennet was pleased when William's eyes narrowed. "I have a cousin who is a vicar, Mr. Collins, and he is currently seeking a wife. He was very enamoured of Lizzy when last he visited Longbourn. Mrs. Bennet was of a mind to force Lizzy to marry him even before this disaster occurred. A marriage to him would secure her future, you see. However, now she is more resolute and since he is my heir, it would seem the logical solution."

"If Mr. Collins is the vicar at Hunsford, it would prove you have no care for your daughter's happiness. For *that* Collins is my aunt's vicar. I am acquainted with him and I find him an obsequious fool."

A quick intake of breath from where Charles sat alerted William that he had managed to insult Mr. Bennet's family.

"Pardon me. I should not have disparaged your cousin, no matter how horrid I find him."

Charles dropped his head in his hands, clearly expecting the worse.

"I think him a fool, too, but at least Lizzy would not be subjected to the ridicule of the *ton* if she marries him."

"For a woman of her intelligence, her *joie de vivre*, to be shackled to such a man would be the cruellest fate imaginable. And mark my words: she would suffer ridicule from her peers for having such a husband."

Instantly, Mr. Bennet realised that this man understood Elizabeth, perhaps even deserved her, and his spirits rose. "How do you plan to convince Elizabeth to marry you? She is stubborn and will not have you just because you wish it."

"Let me speak with her."

"I will. But it shall be here in my study and in my presence. I will have no more secret conversations."

"Agreed. And I have a request as well." Mr. Bennet lifted his chin in anticipation. "I would prefer if you did not mention to Miss Elizabeth the things I related about Andrew."

Bennet's eyebrows rose in question. "Why not?"

"I would not want my poor opinion of him to influence her decision."

Thomas Bennet's eyes narrowed. He had rarely met someone so principled. "Very well."

As he went to find a servant to fetch Elizabeth, William exchanged glances with Charles.

"Are you sure of this, Darcy? Even if you love Miss Elizabeth, marrying just to prevent a scandal might not be the wisest choice for you."

"If I marry her, it will be only because I love her."

A short while later

The sunlight now filtering through the windows did little to alleviate the gloom that permeated the entire house since news of Lizzy's lack of discretion reached Longbourn. Mrs. Phillips had appeared at their door whilst they were in the breakfast room, barely recognisable in her solemnity. Usually her visits were punctuated with giddy anticipation as she waited to share the latest gossip, but today, after simply relaying the facts, she had departed as downhearted as when she had arrived.

In one corner of the parlour, Mrs. Bennet and her three youngest children sat at a table in front of a large window. Fanny scarcely focused on the embroidery she had picked up to settle her nerves, instead stealing glances at the door that led to Mr. Bennet's study while straining to hear what was being said.

Barely able to contain her curiosity, she was certain that this meeting meant the difference between ruin and salvation, for she scarcely believed Mr. Collins would still want Lizzy if he learned of the scandal. Having been sick since her sister's visit, relief had washed over her at the news that Mr. Darcy had come. Surely it signified that he would make Lizzy a legitimate offer.

Secretly, she was pleased that Thomas had to face his culpability in the matter, for she had warned him often enough that coddling his favourite daughter was a grave error and now she felt thoroughly vindicated. There was no doubt that Lizzy's belief that she was not like other young women, or subject to their rules, had led to this disaster.

Suddenly, loud voices could be heard coming from the study, causing those in the parlour to go eerily quiet. Realising that she could hear much better outside Mr. Bennet's study—especially if the windows were open to catch a breeze—Mrs. Bennet threw her sewing on the table and hurried from the room.

Everyone in the parlour was left staring at the door through which she fled.

Mr. Bennet's Study

When Elizabeth entered her father's study, she anticipated having to face the man that she had refused the night before, for in response to her pleadings for information, Mrs. Hill told her that a Mr. Darcy was waiting with her father. Then she had patted Elizabeth's back, her way of showing support, before opening the door. A slight smile was all Elizabeth had time to bestow on the servant before her father beckoned.

Refusing to glance at the man who sat on the left, Elizabeth kept her eyes firmly fixed on her father until she stood in front of his desk. This exercise caused her to realise that he seemed to have aged overnight and a pang of guilt pierced her heart. Drowning in regret, she barely heard his words.

"Elizabeth, I believe you know Mr. Darcy."

Only the wave of his arm towards the left, gave her to know that he had spoken. Swallowing hard, she turned and her heart almost stopped. Expecting Andrew, she was mortified to find *the other* Mr. Darcy rising to greet her. The expression on his face was puzzling, for he looked at her with such kindness that she could scarcely believe it. Suddenly lost in a pair of piercing sky-blue eyes, she felt lightheaded and dropped her gaze to the floor.

"Yes. We have met."

William bowed. "I am sorry that we meet again under these circumstances, Miss Bennet. Please allow me to apologise for my cousin's complete disregard for propriety and lack of common sense. I ask for forgiveness for the pain he has caused you and your family."

Relieved that an apology must be his grounds for coming, Elizabeth looked up at him through her lashes. He seemed sincere. Glancing to her father, she noted that he was watching them both keenly.

Her throat seemed as dry as sand as she replied, "I… I accept your apology. But you are too kind, for I am at fault as well. I allowed Mr. Darcy to talk with me privately, knowing we should be chaperoned. I fear that I fancied myself in complete control and was flattered to be noticed by someone of his station. My pride overruled my better sense. Now I, as well as my family, will suffer for my foolishness."

"Your humility serves you well, though it is my contention that my cousin deserves the greater part of the blame."

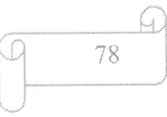

Greatly relieved that the apology was over and expecting that he would leave, an awkward pause ensued. She was stunned when, instead of leaving, Mr. Darcy pulled a chair out and waited patiently for her to sit down. Surprised, she complied and watched as he took the chair opposite her. Then her father spoke.

"Mr. Darcy has proposed a way to minimize the effects of the rumours now entertaining the good citizens of Meryton. I am inclined to agree with his solution, so you will hear him out."

Minutes later, when Mr. Darcy had finished speaking, Elizabeth sat as motionless as a statue. Too overwhelmed to think clearly, she opened her mouth, but no words came. Instead, her mind swirled with thoughts.

What an absurd idea! I could barely envision being married to Andrew Darcy, for he is so far above my circumstances, but marriage to someone of Fitzwilliam Darcy's rank would be utter madness! Never mind that I have no regard for him; what would his family have to say? Would they demand the marriage be annulled? Would Miss Darcy accept someone beneath her for a sister? No! It is impossible! Preposterous! I would rather be a governess!

Mr. Bennet observed her face go through a plethora of emotions, paling a little more with each. Standing, he reached for a decanter and poured three glasses of wine. Handing one to Mr. Darcy, he set one on his desk and handed the other to Elizabeth. She nodded her gratitude. Taking a sip of the fragrant liquid, she closed her eyes and willed herself to relax. She sat in this manner for a time, then cleared her throat and addressed Mr. Darcy.

"Sir, I understand that you feel somewhat responsible, and I appreciate your selflessness in offering to marry me. What I cannot fathom is why you have not considered the reaction of your family to such a marriage. Clearly, you were born into a higher sphere and you are expected to uphold a certain standard. I do not represent that standard. My dowry is little or nothing compared to any debutant the season might field, and I have not the background required."

Mr. Bennet dropped his eyes, uncharacteristically ashamed.

"Miss Elizabeth, I am seven and twenty. My father's death left Pemberley to my management at twenty. My sister, who is almost eighteen, was only eleven when he died. And though I have regard for my family, I have run the estate and taken care of my sister on my own since that day. I answer to no one. As for a dowry, I am wealthy. Lack of a dowry is no obstacle."

"But you need a wife who is schooled in the ways of the *ton*."

"I have to disagree, for I despise the *ton*. Why should I want you to emulate them? Besides, your manners are suitable to me."

Elizabeth was becoming irritated. *Can he not be made to see reason?* "What of your sister? Might not her chances for a good match be lessened by choosing me?"

"I have considered that as well, but Georgiana's dowry is thirty thousand pounds and she is handsome. My choice should have no bearing on her prospects. And, if need be, I can increase her dowry."

Now Elizabeth was exasperated. "While I am deeply appreciative, sir, I simply cannot accept."

Mr. Darcy's expression changed to astonishment. "I would not have thought it possible. You are afraid."

Her face coloured. "My courage always rises with every attempt to intimidate me." [3]

"Your refusal speaks louder than your words."

Mr. Bennet saw what Mr. Darcy was doing and joined in. "I think Mr. Darcy is right, Elizabeth. I have never known you to back down from a challenge. You must be frightened of the prospect of being under the scrutiny of the *ton*."

Elizabeth stood up and paced the room. "Do you not see how foolish this whole notion is? This is ridiculous! Yesterday I would have sworn that you hated me, Mr. Darcy. Now, you want us to marry. How can I trust your judgement? Will you coerce me into this marriage only to regret your action once your family rejects me? And they will."

"Do you mean to make certain of that? Otherwise, I have every confidence in your ability to gain the support of most anyone you choose."

One of Elizabeth's eyebrows rose. "Most?"

"Every family has one member who tries to manipulate the world to their liking."

"You are impossible! A marriage between us would never work. I had rather never marry and become a governess, or… or a companion."

"If these rumours are not squashed quickly, they will fester and grow. As a result, you may never become a governess or companion. After all, who will want a woman with a scandalous reputation teaching their children or accompanying a loved one?" William's voice rose along with his temper. "I will tell you who—only a rake who will look upon you as easy prey!"

Elizabeth's brows furrowed, and her face began to burn with anger.

"I beg you to reconsider. My parents hired several gentlewomen who were reduced to being servants. I would not wish on any woman what they endured before coming to Pemberley. What is more, even if you are willing to take that chance, would you condemn your sisters to such a fate?"

Ignoring his plea, she snapped, "Are you implying that Mr. Bingley will hold this against Jane?"

"Charles is not one to change his mind once it is made up. But please allow me to explain what may happen. I have spent years assimilating him into my circle, as his fondest wish is to be a landowner. He is now involved in many dealings with my friends who regard him, if not as an equal, as someone I highly regard as trustworthy. Regrettably, a marriage to your sister will not elevate him in their eyes, but neither shall it harm him if I support his choice. However, if the rumours presently circulating escalate and spread to Town, Miss Bennet's chances of being accepted by society are practically nil and Charles' influence and income will be severely affected."

By the time he finished, Elizabeth was frowning in comprehension and Mr. Bennet took that opportunity to press a point.

"Lizzy, I believe that this is the best solution; however, you should know that your mother has been insisting that I force you to marry Mr. Collins. In fact, as we speak, he is on his way here from Cambridge for he returns to Kent. Your mother has led him to believe that if he offers for you, you will accept. I do not think him the kind of husband you deserve, but your own foolishness has brought this upon you." He waited until she looked at him. Taking a deep breath, he concluded the speech he had been dreading. "It is your choice. I think you already know that Andrew Darcy is not about to marry anyone, and from what I have just learned, he could not support a wife if he were of a mind to do so. Therefore, either you will accept Mr. Darcy, or I shall insist that you marry Mr. Collins. I will not waver with your sisters' futures at risk. You must decide now."

Elizabeth took a deep breath, her chest rising with the effort. She stood and walked over to the window to stare into the garden of her home. Just days ago, she had wondered if she could ever be happy anywhere else. Tears filled her eyes, and she blinked to keep them from falling.

Blinded to my own foibles, I have subjected my sisters to ruin. And while I dislike Mr. Darcy immensely, he has offered me a way out, though I can only imagine his motive. In the end, it comes down to one thing. I would rather die than be shackled to that horrible vicar!

Without a word, she nodded.

William had stood when she went to the window, watching with barely concealed angst. Her nod was not enough confirmation, so he looked to her father.

"Elizabeth?" Mr. Bennet enquired.

She strangled a fierce tide of feeling that welled up within. "I... I will mar... marry Mr. Darcy."

From somewhere in the garden outside, shrieks of joy could be heard as Mrs. Bennet raced back to the front door.

Chapter 8

On the road to Netherfield

Luckily for William, the first few minutes of the ride back to Netherfield were filled with Charles' nonstop chatter and he was able to escape into his thoughts, for in recalling all that had been said, the realisation that Elizabeth had been vehemently opposed to marrying him was now unmistakable. The impact was jarring. During their meeting, pride had caused him to counter every objection she raised to their union. Upon reflection, he now questioned if he had been blind to Elizabeth's contempt because of his newly acknowledged feelings for her.

Is it possible to find felicity with a woman who thinks so little of me? The voice of reason interrupted. *What did you expect? She was evidently quite fond of Andrew, and for years that cad has blamed you for his state of affairs. She may think you a far worse choice than he.*

Across the carriage, Charles was still carrying on a one-sided conversation, barely stopping to take a breath of air. "... and Caroline cannot object to my marrying Jane if you are married to Miss Elizabeth! No, that will end that argument entirely!"

William absently fiddled with his signet ring. It was a habit that anyone familiar with him would recognise as a sign that he was lost in thought and not listening.

"I cannot thank you enough!" Bingley blurted. Then noting that his friend was staring blindly out the window, he added, "Darcy? Darcy? Are you listening?"

He leaned over to touch William's arm and the action brought his friend back to the present.

"Wha... what is it?"

"I said that I cannot thank you enough for offering to marry Miss Elizabeth! The gossip about Andrew will surely end now that there is an even bigger happening to discuss."

"At least you are pleased by the prospect."

Bingley's brows furrowed. "I have to say, you do not sound the joyful fiancé! Are you having regrets about your decision already?"

"No." William heaved a ragged sigh. "Well, not exactly."

"I do not like the sound of that."

"Do not fear. I am a man of my word, and I shall marry Miss Elizabeth, but, in hindsight, I fear I may have been blinded by my feelings for her and too eager to force her acceptance. While I have tender feelings for her, I now believe that she loathes me."

Bingley interjected, "Surely not."

"The more I dwell on it, the more certain I am. She not only took an extraordinary amount of time to reject Collins, she showed no particular regard for me."

"Obviously, Andrew has told her his usual pack of lies—how you cheated him of his inheritance and reduced him to poverty. Once she learns the truth on that subject, she shall change her mind. Besides, you are something Andrew will never be—a good man. Just allow her to see that side of your character."

"I have no idea what you mean, Charles. I am what I am; there are no sides."

Bingley shook his head. "I disagree. Most people see only the Master of Pemberley—a decisive man, taciturn at times, and one who brooks no foolishness. I have seen the other—a man who quietly sets to right his cousin's crimes. For heaven's sake, you were the only one concerned for his castoffs! You have treated him far better than he deserves. I would have washed my hands of him years ago."

"Father always said, 'To whom much is given, much is required,'" William replied. "Since my own cousin was the reason for the situation, I was duty bound to help them. That is all."

"Precisely my point! The world is full of men who do not do their duty. If Miss Elizabeth learns the full story, not the vitriol Andrew spews, then she cannot help but respect you, and respect will lead to love. Just tell her the truth!"

William sighed. "With regard to Andrew, I fear she will not accept the truth from me."

"I shall be glad to speak to her."

"Hearing it from you would be equivalent to hearing it from me. In her present state, she will assume I cajoled you into taking my side."

"You may be right, though I advise you to tell her anyway. Women are strange creatures. They may pretend not to believe you, but if you create a doubt, they will not stop until they learn the truth."

"Pray tell, how do you know so much about women?"

"My mother and I were very close, and, in the interest of my finding true felicity when I marry, she gave me some valuable insights. I must say, it has helped in dealing with Caroline."

The mention of that name made William groan. "That brings up another subject. Since I am off to London to obtain a special license, I would like to stay in your townhouse so my family will not know I have returned. If Caroline should decide to return to Town as well, it would necessitate changing my plan."

"I understand completely. Of course, you may use my townhouse, and I shall make certain Caroline stays here." Bingley's expression grew more sombre. "So, you are not going to tell your relations of your wedding? Not even Georgiana?"

"If word of the wedding reaches my uncle, he will try to stop me, and I have no doubt that Georgiana would do all in her power, as well."

"I had not fully considered the cost, Darcy. You shall be up against your entire family."

"Not Richard or my mother's youngest brother and his wife, who are presently residing at Pemberley."

"It is good to know that at least a few have your interests at heart." Then Bingley scratched his head. "News of your impending wedding shall travel to London faster than a fire in a hay field. How in the world will you sneak into Town, procure a special license and return by the end of the week without being found out? A special license alone takes several weeks, I am told."

"The worst part will be keeping my presence a secret. As for the license, my godfather is the Bishop of London."

"Something else I never knew about you. That could come in handy if Jane and I were to—"

"Mrs. Bennet was extremely upset to learn that Miss Elizabeth and I shall be married within the week. It took Mr. Bennet's ire to convince her that we had to marry immediately to quell the rumours. I feel certain that she would have liked to drag the engagement out for months, so I doubt seriously that she will allow Jane to marry in the same manner."

Charles tilted his head and raised his shoulders in a gesture of resignation. "You are right." Then he smiled brightly. "I shall simply be content then that we can marry without any scandal hanging over our heads and without having to listen to Caroline's objections."

"At least you shall have the satisfaction of knowing that Miss Bennet will look forward to your wedding. A long engagement is nothing, if the parties are blessed with mutual affection."

Bingley grasped William's shoulder. "You shall be blessed with affection, too, my friend. I am sure of it."

"I pray you are correct. My mother once said that a woman would endure a great many faults as long as she felt cherished. And while I may have had misgivings about marrying Miss Elizabeth in the beginning, it was not for lack of affection."

"There you are! Even your mother agreed with me. Love her, and she will love you in return."

William turned to the window, staring forlornly. "For years I have longed for a wife and children. I do not know if I could bear being married to someone who has no affection for me."

This time Charles could not answer for the lump in his throat. He dared not reveal more of his mother's advice—never marry a woman who was not even-tempered. Jane's lovely face came to mind as he recalled her description of Elizabeth. Though said in a teasing manner, she allowed that her sister was quick to judge and not inclined to admit fault, even when it was evident that she was wrong.

Glancing to William, his heart went out to the one who had risked alienating the *ton* in order to be his friend, and a prayer formed in his heart.

Please let Miss Elizabeth learn Darcy's true character before things are said that cannot be taken back. He deserves this chance for happiness.

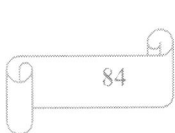

As Caroline descended the grand staircase that evening, she called to her brother, who was heading in the direction of the dining room. "Charles, wait for me."

Quickly catching up to him, she smiled condescendingly. "I wish for you to escort me into the room. Mr. Darcy can examine me longer if you are by my side, and I wish him to see this new gown I had designed with him in mind."

Bingley smiled but said nothing as he led her into the room. Immediately noting that Darcy was not there, she let go of his arm and turned in a circle.

"But I knocked on his bedroom door and there was no reply, so he must be downstairs!" She glanced back at the door. "Perhaps he is in the library or your study."

"He is no longer here, Caroline. He was called upon to help a distant relation."

"But he only arrived yesterday!"

"And he left today. Now, no more about Darcy. Let us enjoy the feast set before us."

"But, but—"

"Enough, Caroline. I will brook no more discussion about Darcy."

Caroline took a deep breath, puffing out her cheeks before expelling the same with great effort. Glancing at Charles, she realised that she had no choice but to obey… for now. She motioned to the servant who began to fill her plate.

Just you wait and see, Charles Bingley. When I am Mrs. Darcy, I shall see that your invitations are always lost in the post.

London
Darcy's Townhouse
The next day

When Colonel Richard Fitzwilliam entered the dining room, he found it abounding with all manner of delicious food. Breathing in the enticing aromas, he marvelled that Darcy's cook would go to such trouble for only one person, for, in his estimation, there was enough fare spread across the table to feed his entire regiment.

Darcy must owe a fortune to the butcher and another to the grocer.

He took the chair at the end of the table normally occupied by his cousin. Taking a bite of the food and a sip of hot coffee, he began to study his surroundings.

I fear your generosity in hosting me so often, Cousin, has been my ruin. I allow that I am spoiled, though that may soon be of no import. For you seem determined to marry, and what woman would suffer seeing my face across the dining table as often as you? No, I shall not be residing here or at Pemberley as often if you carry through with your plans.

Still, I am not against you marrying, for I know how lonely you have been since your parents died. Georgiana has offered you little companionship, preferring first the company of Andrew and then my parents. But you—you were formed for marriage, with lots of little ones at your feet and a doting wife at your side. Unfortunately, that means you must first take a wife.

It is your current choice that worries me. Lady Susan, and those of her ilk, will have you leg-shackled faster than a raw recruit can flee a volley. And you, Cousin, will not survive a marriage of convenience. You are too tender-hearted, whether you know it or not. It would send you to an early grave. So, I shall just have to help you see reason. I shall begin by investigating Susan's behaviour since her marriage and departure from Derbyshire. Perhaps I shall uncover something that will dissuade you from her.

Having formed a plan, Richard relaxed and began to eat in earnest. *After all*, he chuckled, *who knows when I shall eat at this table again, and I would not want to waste a farthing of Darcy's money.*

Longbourn

The unexpected arrival of the Gardiners' coach brought both angst and joy to the Bennet household. Angst for Elizabeth, for she dreaded for her aunt to learn how close she had come to ruining the family, and joy for Mrs. Bennet, for she had gained no satisfaction from her daughter's newly engaged status, as she had no one to tell. Her husband had forbidden members of his household to go into Meryton, sure that if they kept silent, the *new* version of what had happened, as spread by Mrs. Phillips, would overshadow the old.

Fanny's sister had appeared early the day after Darcy's offer and had listened raptly to the news that her niece had not been compromised, but instead had received an offer of marriage from the tall, dark gentleman seen with her in the gazebo. The fact that Fitzwilliam Darcy of Pemberley, a man of ten thousand a year and owning half of Derbyshire, was betrothed to her niece was a far more interesting subject than any elicit kiss, and Mrs. Phillips was eager to spread the fact. After all, the news that a local girl was to be so well situated made their neighbours willing to overlook their former disapproval.

And thus it was that the Gardiners' coach was met with great exhilaration, with all but Mr. Bennet and Elizabeth coming out of the house to greet them.

"Sister, it is so good to see you!" Mrs. Bennet exclaimed, greeting Madeline Gardiner with a hug as she stepped from the coach. Glancing inside the vehicle, she added, "But where are the children?"

"The children are staying with my sister in Lambton for a month."

"I had no idea you were going to be visiting. Did you send me word? I do not remember a letter." As she spoke, she pulled Madeline towards the front door. "Well, that is of no import! You are here now, and your arrival is most fortunate, as I am in great need of your advice."

Mr. Gardiner exited the coach just as his wife disappeared inside Longbourn. Jane, Mary, Kitty and Lydia still waited patiently on the other side. The three youngest looked eager to learn what gifts he might have in his pockets, for he always brought small bags of sweets, as well as buttons and ribbons from his warehouse.

"Come now," he teased as he came around the back, "is no one looking for

any treats?" Instantly palms appeared in mid air. "I thought so."

After receiving their gifts, the three youngest hurried into the house, leaving Mr. Gardiner and Jane alone. She had stayed back to allow the younger girls to go first.

Winking at her, Gardiner said, "Are you too old now for bribery? I still have your favourite blue ribbons, or have you decided for another colour?"

Jane blushed. "I still favour the blue."

He pressed several gifts in her hand. "And here are some pearl buttons and a nice lace handkerchief." Then he glanced about. "Where is Lizzy? I have the same gifts for her, only her ribbons are lavender."

"I... I cannot say for sure. Perhaps she is still in her room."

Noting the sadness that instantly overtook his eldest niece at the mention of her sister, Edward Gardiner placed an arm around Jane's shoulder. As he directed her towards the house, he asked, "Is there something I should know?"

"I believe it best if Aunt Gardiner tells you, and I am certain she will."

He stopped short, inspecting Jane for additional clues as to what was wrong. Then mindful that he should not prod, he said gently, "Very well. But know that I shall do everything within my power to help, if I am allowed."

"You have always cared for us above what is your responsibility, Uncle, and for that I am most grateful."

He kissed her cheek. "Believe me when I say that it pleases me to do so." Then trying to cheer her, he continued. "Let us go find Miss Lizzy, and see if she still favours lavender ribbons, or if she has changed her mind."

Elizabeth's Bedroom

As Madeline Gardiner raised her hand to knock on the door, she hesitated. To say she had been shocked to learn that her favourite niece had acted in a manner more indicative of Lydia would not be true—she had been incredulous. Then after being told the name of the man Lizzy was to marry, she had been speechless. Now, an hour later, she had reined in her emotions, resolved that the best thing she could do was to try to keep the arrangement from ending in disaster. Knowing Lizzy, she was certain that it might.

Fitzwilliam Darcy's reputation was well known to her, as it would be to anyone with ties to Lambton. Though she had never met the man, she had seen him on occasion, and while the circumstances of the engagement were unfortunate, she had every confidence that the union would be the making of Lizzy—if she would allow it. In the last few years, Mrs. Gardiner had worried over this niece's future more than all the other girls, uncertain if any man would see the unique treasure hidden beneath the intrepid exterior.

Surely a man such as Mr. Darcy will see and value Lizzy's intelligence. And if I can convince her not to be so candid... She shook her head. *... Well, that will be a tall order.* Gathering her resolve, she knocked lightly.

"Lizzy, may I come in?"

Elizabeth opened the door and fell into her aunt's arms in an anguish of penetrating remorse, though only her trembling body signified that she was crying. Embracing her niece, Mrs. Gardiner pulled her to the bed where they sat down, and she gently rocked her. Several minutes passed while she prayed for the right words to say.

Elizabeth, however, was first to speak, stuttering out a confession between loud sniffles. "I… I know that I was foolish, but does foolishness warrant being sentenced to spend the rest of my life with a man I loathe?"

"I must confess that I cannot imagine what objections you have to Mr. Darcy. I have known him all his life, howbeit not formally. But he and his family have always been well regarded in Lambton. They are reputed to be kind and generous to servants and tenants alike, in addition to providing for the common good of Derbyshire. They built and furnished the church, a physician's office, a home for widows and another for orphans—"

Elizabeth broke in, "Perhaps the parents were good and kind, but the son does not share the same virtues."

"Lizzy, I visit my relations in Lambton quite often, and they have nothing but good things to say about him. Where have you heard such nonsense?"

"From his own cousin!"

"The one who compromised you? And you believe him?"

She nodded, saying defiantly, "It is because of Fitzwilliam Darcy that Andrew Darcy could not offer for me in the first place," then added less vehemently, "not that I would have accepted him."

Mrs. Gardiner noted the proviso. "It is plain that you had reservations and would not marry him, though you accept as truth his criticism of Fitzwilliam Darcy. Could something else have coloured your perception of the one you are to marry?"

"His conduct left me no reason to doubt the charges Andrew Darcy lay at his feet."

"Then suppose you tell me everything, starting with when you met Fitzwilliam Darcy."

Relating their entire association, ending with the tale Andrew had shared about his degradation at Darcy's hands, Elizabeth waited confidently for her aunt to acknowledge that she was right. When she did not, Elizabeth glanced to find Madeline Gardiner regarding her with an expression akin to disappointment. Her aunt's attitude annoyed her, and she added, "And he was not the only man Fitzwilliam Darcy denied an inheritance. He did not give Mr. Wickham the living bequeathed to him, either."

"George Wickham? The steward's son?"

Hearing the misgivings in her voice, Elizabeth nodded a little less earnestly.

"Rumours have swirled for years regarding Andrew Darcy and George Wickham, but as I had no firsthand knowledge of the facts, I always kept them to myself. However, it is well known that Mr. Darcy had Mr. Wickham escorted from Pemberley shortly after his father's death, and Andrew Darcy was removed to his estate two years past under similar circumstances."

"Does that not prove his disagreeable temper and support his cousin's allegations?"

"It only proves whichever point of view you wish to defend. Until the truth

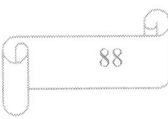

is known, both sides of an argument should be given the benefit of the doubt." She waited, but her niece kept silent. "It is logical to give more credence to the party with the better reputation. Andrew Darcy and George Wickham have been associated with some very appalling behaviour. Andrew Darcy's actions in regard to you only reinforce what has been said."

Elizabeth's head dropped, so her aunt lifted her chin with two fingers. "The only thing that matters now is what you do next. This debacle has been unfortunate in so many ways, but in another sense, Fate has granted you an opportunity few will ever experience. Give Fitzwilliam Darcy the chance to make you happy, I beg of you. Do not throw everything away by being resentful."

Instantly, Elizabeth's brows knit. "I am not resentful!" Then more calmly she asked, "Am I?"

"Though I love you dearly, I must speak the truth for your sake. I have seen such a trait in you since you were a babe. You have always resented being forced to do things, even though you might do it later if left alone. It was an attribute that your father encouraged. He thought it entertaining, though now I have to wonder if he still thinks the same."

"Am I really so dreadful?"

"Not dreadful, my dear, only inflexible in that one area. But you must grasp the truth now, or it will destroy any chance for happiness in your marriage." Trying to lighten the mood, she added, "And you are also most fortunate in another way."

"How so?"

"Fitzwilliam Darcy is not only wealthy, he is very handsome. I dare say that most of the women in England would clamour to take your place."

"I care not if he is handsome. I would give them my place willingly."

"Enough of this, Lizzy," she said firmly. "You are no longer a child, and your father is right. You must marry in order to save yourself and your sisters. If you hate Mr. Darcy so much, why did you not choose Mr. Collins?"

"Mr. Collins looks as though he never bathes. His clothes, his breath and his hair all smell and his teeth need cleaning."

"Then you have told a falsehood." One of Elizabeth's brows rose in question. "You boasted that you care not for physical attributes, but it seems you chose Mr. Darcy over Mr. Collins because he is the more attractive of the two."

Elizabeth rolled her eyes.

"I think you should thank God every night that the man to whom you are engaged is not only handsome but cares about your welfare."

Elizabeth stood and walked to the window, where she pulled back the curtain to peer into the garden. Sighing raggedly, tears filled her eyes. "I swore that I would marry only for the deepest love. Now I shall be bound forever to a man who offered for me simply out of pity. I shall never be good enough for his family or acquaintances. Even he considers me beneath him."

Madeline Gardiner rushed to the window and wrapped her arms around her niece. "Oh, my dear, now I understand why you struggle so against this arrangement. But all of us, Bennets and Gardiners, are beneath his society. Your task, should you be mature enough to accept it, will be to show him that rank does not make the person. Show him your true worth."

"My true worth," Elizabeth repeated woodenly. "I no longer know who I am, much less what I am worth. This entire matter has me so lost. I do not know if I can trust my instincts ever again!"

Mrs. Gardiner pushed her to arm's length, gripping her shoulders. "Well then, pay heed, for I shall tell you exactly who you are! You are Elizabeth Bennet—a lively, beautiful, inquisitive and intelligent young woman who will make an excellent wife and a loving mother. And I have every confidence that once Mr. Darcy sees your true character, he shall consider himself the most fortunate of men."

Elizabeth managed a wan smile. "And if he does not, may I count on you to point out the obvious?"

Relived that her niece was at least trying to be jovial, she smoothed some curls from Elizabeth's face.

"Most certainly! For I am convinced that if you give him a fair chance, I shall never be forced to act."

"I shall try very hard to be a good wife."

"That is all I ask."

Manchester
Winfield Hall

The sound of loud banging on the front door brought Mrs. Lightfoot scurrying to the foyer, drying her hands on her apron. Unbeknownst to her, Mr. Lightfoot was coming from the opposite direction, and they met on the marble floor below the grand staircase. With so few servants, it took everyone performing several duties at Winfield Hall, and the housekeeper was as likely to answer the door as the butler. Despite both hurrying to the front, neither was keen to find out who might be raising such a fuss. With the master away most of the time and guests but a memory, any unforeseen arrivals brought uncertainties.

The knocking grew louder and more insistent.

"Who do you suppose is here at this hour? It is almost dark."

"We are expecting no one. Perhaps I should look through the glass before we open the door, my dear. With Bivens presently at the stables, there is not a footman in the house, and it could be one of those beggars who dared to knock on Glenbrook's door last week."

"I agree. Better to be safe than sorry," her husband said.

Tiptoeing to one of the large windows that flanked the door, the housekeeper eased the curtain aside. Though able to see a tall figure, she could not make out his face. She had just turned to shake her head at her husband when a voice boomed from outside, "Open the door, for God's sake, Lightfoot!"

Recognising their employer, Mrs. Lightfoot instantly threw open the door, only to watch as Andrew Darcy stumbled inside and fell to the floor. It was obvious that he had been in a scuffle, as his coat was torn and blood-spattered, and there were bruises and blood on his face.

"Close the door and bolt it!" he ordered.

Having frozen at the sight of him, the housekeeper quickly moved to follow his orders. While her husband knelt by his side.

"Good heavens, sir, what happened to you? Shall I send Mrs. Lightfoot for help? Mr. Petty is not in town this week, but she can fetch Mr. Carnes. He was once a physician's apprentice and may be able to help with your injuries. Besides, the two of us cannot get you up the stairs without assistance."

As Mrs. Lightfoot hurried towards the back of the house to fetch Carnes from the stables, her husband made several attempts to get Andrew on his feet. Finally successful, he assisted him into the foyer, Mr. Darcy moaning with every step. Easing him into one of the chairs that flanked a large mirror, the elderly servant ventured, "Should I send for the constable? Were you robbed?"

"I... I was attacked when leaving the inn not three miles away, but they did not take anything from my person. Most likely they were tenants from Marsden Park."

"Why would someone from that estate do such a thing?"

"You have not heard of Miss Harrington's death?"

"Yes, sir. But what has that to do with you?"

"Apparently, Effie Harrington has drowned. How it came about, I have no idea since I was not here. But it appears that I am being blamed for her death. I have no idea why. I am a scapegoat, if you will."

Lightfoot's brows furrowed. "I see," was his only reply.

"Veiled threats were made against my life, so I left the inn, hoping that would be the extent of their intimidation, but four or five men must have followed me outside, for as I mounted my horse, I was instantly dragged to the ground. They began to pummel me, and had I not managed to grab my pistol as it fell from my inside pocket, they might have finished me. As it was, when I wielded the weapon, they scattered. My horse ran away when the scuffle began, and I feared they might return, so I walked the rest of the way here through the forest."

Just at that moment, Mr. Bivens and Mr. Carnes rushed into the foyer and helped Andrew to his feet again. As they carried him up the stairs, he shouted orders over his shoulder, "Post guards around the house. I want every available man on guard tonight. Tell the coachman to have my horse ready for departure early tomorrow, for I shall leave this damnable county behind at daylight."

"Where will you go?" Mr Lightfoot asked.

Thinking he might have said too much already, Andrew said, "I have friends in York and Newcastle, so I may decide for there. Remember, tell no one I was here or where I have gone."

Lightfoot only nodded, for by then the men and Andrew had disappeared down a hallway. Not long afterward, his wife met him at bottom of the grand staircase.

"Do you still think him to blame for Miss Harrington's death, Homer?"

Lightfoot looked around before answering. "I certainly believe that he raised her expectations. After all, I once heard him tell Landers that we might all be working with the staff from Marsden Park in the near future. That was right before he left for London as if his life depended on it."

As they began down another hall that led to their quarters, she offered, "His boast about having us work for Marsden Park was strange to say the least."

"Strange and incriminating, if you ask me. If I knew for sure that he caused that poor girl's death, I would consider sending word to Marsden Park."

Mrs. Lightfoot stopped short. "Calm down before you have another one of your spells. You cannot make Mr. Darcy behave like a gentleman, no matter how much you may wish it."

"You are right, Eunice. Still, if there is any justice, whoever is responsible for that young woman's demise will be held accountable."

"They will. You have only to consider what the Bible says: 'Vengeance is mine; I will repay, saith the Lord.'" [4]

"Sometimes one just needs reminding. Thank you, my dear."

Chapter 9

London
Bingley's Townhouse

As Colonel Richard Fitzwilliam alighted from his stallion in the rear of Charles Bingley's house, he was full of anticipation. The note delivered to him at Darcy House early that morning had been very clear. He was not to bring attention to himself by making the trip in any conveyance with the Darcy markings or to be seen entering the front of Bingley's house. This was different from his cousin's normal *modus operandi,* and he was keen to discover the reason for such secrecy.

Examining the tall, red-brick mansion as he gained his footing, he could not help but smile. *Surely Darcy is not hiding right under Caroline Bingley's nose!*

A groom rushing to take Titan's reins interrupted his thoughts, and, nodding at the man, he ordered, "Give him some oats." As Richard watched the animal being led away he added, "And a good rubdown."

The man nodded. "Yes, sir."

Might as well let ol' Bingley take care of Titan in the manner in which he has become accustomed at Darcy's stables.

Chuckling, he walked more spryly than usual to the rear entrance of the mansion and rapped on the door with the back of his knuckles.

Instantly it flew open and a footman stepped aside. "Mr. Darcy is in the library, Colonel Fitzwilliam."

"Thank you," Richard answered, wondering how the man knew his name. He shrugged. *Most likely he knew only to expect a Colonel Fitzwilliam.*

Being familiar with Bingley's residence, he went straight to the front of the house and entered the large library. Once inside, he stopped to look around, a bit irritated that William was nowhere in sight.

"Darcy?"

"Over here."

Making his way around a large, freestanding bookshelf, he spied his cousin atop a ladder that slid on rails across the length of the shelves occupying the wall.

"Hiding something the ladies are not supposed to see?" he teased.

"I believe Charles is the one who was not supposed to see. I have found the books that I lent him when he first considered renting an estate. They contain information regarding animal husbandry, irrigation, crop rotations and the like. However, when I arrived at Netherfield, he could not account for ever having seen them, and since Caroline was the only one here when I brought them, I suspected she had a hand in making them disappear." William held up a book with a puce coloured cover. "Luckily, this volume is an odd colour, so it was easily spotted from the floor."

A loud guffaw escaped the colonel. "Why would Miss Bingley do such a thing?"

"Most likely she thought if she could keep Charles ignorant of how to turn a profit, he would give up the lease and leave Hertfordshire. All her conversation consists of is demeaning the county and the neighbours, and she laments the fact that she is not in London society."

"I cannot fathom why you put up with either of Bingley's sisters or Mr. Hurst. Bingley is amusing, but that unholy trio makes his company intolerable at times."

"It is simple. I am fond of Charles." William dropped a book. "Here, take this one! And do not leave, as there are more."

After having retrieved all of the missing books, William came down the ladder with the last one in his hand. Richard took the book, making a show of opening it. Instantly, he turned the book sideways to examine a drawing depicting animals mating. His eyebrows rose in mock horror.

"I must say, Darcy, these books definitely belong on the top shelf. They are not fit for delicate eyes." William shook his head at Richard's antics as he began stacking the remaining books.

Glancing up when William walked over to place them on a table near the door, Richard declared, "Let us get straight to the point, old man. Why you are staying here instead of Darcy House, and why are you being so secretive?"

"I do not want my relations to know I am here, for I am making arrangements to be married."

The volume Richard was holding slipped from his hands, hitting the carpet with a thud. As he bent down to retrieve it, he searched clumsily with one hand while keeping his eyes trained on William. "You, married? When?"

"In three days' time."

Swallowing with difficulty, Richard added, "Dare I ask to whom?"

"Miss Elizabeth Bennet."

Sighing audibly, Richard made a display of swiping his hand across his forehead. Then remembering that only that morning he had hired a former Bow Street Runner to investigate Lady Susan's past, he weighed whether he should cancel the mission. Upon brief reflection, he decided not to.

"At least it is not Lady Susan! But who in the world is Elizabeth Bennet? Have I met her?"

"She is the woman I met on my first visit to Netherfield—the sister of Bingley's new love. If you recall, you thought her a spectre."

"I remember." Richard's hand found the handle of his sword unconsciously. "And while I am relieved that you are not marrying Lady Susan, this development concerns me. Only days ago, you were adamant that you would never offer for that woman. What has forced your hand?"

"It is a long story."

"I have all the time in the world." Sinking down in a large upholstered chair, he motioned to another. "Suppose you begin."

William did as he was asked, knowing that his cousin would demand the truth before coming to his aid; thus, the next half-hour was spent telling all that had occurred after he reached Meryton the second time. When he was finished, Richard looked sceptical. Then he stood, scratched his head and began to pace.

"Let me see if I understand. In essence, you are marrying Miss Bennet to put right another of Andrew's misdeeds, and she does not appreciate that you are sacrificing your entire future to help her."

"No!" William snapped. Then he took a deep breath and released it resignedly. "Very well, yes… in a manner of speaking."

"What manner, Darcy? Andrew compromised her, and you offered to make the scandal disappear. Still, she refused you. Why in God's name would you insist on marrying her? Why not let her headstrong ways be her undoing?"

"As I was waiting in the carriage while Bingley went in to speak to Mr. Bennet,

I began to evaluate the manor house. You know my penchant for evaluating property I have never seen before." Richard nodded. "As I studied the upper stories, I spied Miss Elizabeth on a balcony, barely visible from where I sat. Unaware that anyone was watching, she began to sob. Then her sister came out to embrace her. They looked so young and vulnerable. Instantly, I thought of what happened to Miss Harrington and knew what I had to do."

"Any caring person would feel dreadful about Miss Harrington's death, Darcy. But that is no reason to sacrifice your life if there is no mutual affection to be had in the bargain. You could aid Miss Bennet and her sisters by finding them employment if she did not want to accept Collins."

"You do not understand. I have had tender feelings for Miss Bennet since leaving Netherfield. And to see her again, not as the woman I remembered, but changed entirely—'shattered' is the word that comes to mind."

"Shattered by her tender feelings for Andrew," Richard reasoned, "otherwise she would not have been in this predicament. Remember, she was seen kissing him in the moonlight."

"She swore to her father that he kissed her against her will and that she is not in love with him."

"And she made it clear that she is not in love with you."

William stood, moving to the window. He offered no rebuttal, though Richard could see his jaw twitch, as it did whenever he was upset.

"I am puzzled as to why, so unexpectedly, you are prepared to settle for an arranged marriage without even the solace of a large dowry or superior connections to sustain you when discontent comes. And in marriages of convenience, discontent shall come."

"All I ask is that you trust me." William turned to him. "Trust that I know what I am about."

Seeing the pleading in his eyes, Richard's stance softened. "Well, I suppose this Miss Bennet cannot be any worse than Lady Susan or most of the ladies of the *ton*, for that matter. At least she is not after your fortune."

William managed a small smile.

"I do have concerns about her eyesight, though."

"Her eyesight?"

"Please, Cousin! You are a handsome fellow! All the ladies throw themselves at your feet whenever you enter a room. Yet she seems totally unaffected by your pretty face. Perhaps she is in need of spectacles."

William relaxed under Richard's teasing. "I would say that she is just not impressed with my fortune or my face."

The colonel's bearing lightened, and he crossed the room to stand next to the man he loved like a brother. For a long time, they watched silently as a goodly portion of the populace of London entered and left Hyde Park, which was visible through the tall windows.

Finally, Richard spoke. "I assume that your godfather is expediting a special license."

"Yes."

"How may I be of service then?"

"I wish you to stand up with me."

"Is that all?" Richard jested. "No mustering the troops to thwart a counter-attack from the Fitzwilliam clan? No fear of General Catherine de Bourgh blocking your gate?"

"This is no laughing matter, Richard. Your father will be livid when he learns that you stood with me." William gripped his shoulder. "Are you sure you want to be involved?"

"If you are prepared to be shackled to a wife, I am prepared to help you."

"Thank you. I could not imagine being wed without you there."

Trying not to look as touched as he felt, Richard asked, "But what of Georgiana? You do realise that she will be livid if you purposefully leave her uninformed."

"I considered taking her with me to Meryton and then revealing the truth. But she would never agree with my decision, nor would she act in a civil manner during the ceremony."

"I agree. It is best if you say nothing to her." Richard looked a little sheepish as he continued. "I apologise if I upset you with my misgivings. In truth, there is a part of me that had begun to believe that Miss Bennet might be the perfect wife for you."

"If you have any encouragement, please do not hold back."

"The first time you described her to me at Pemberley, I noticed something astonishing. Just recalling everything about her brought a light to your eyes, a liveliness to your spirit, which I had not beheld in years. I remember thinking that any woman who could produce such emotion in my staid cousin after so brief an acquaintance had to be someone special."

"Let us hope neither of us is wrong." Reaching into his coat pocket, William brought out a letter. "I would like for you to deliver this. I do not want Bingley's servants comparing notes with mine—you know how servants like to gossip. These are instructions for Mr. and Mrs. Barnes, telling them of the marriage and when to expect us in London."

"I will be happy to do so." Suddenly, Richard began to chuckle aloud.

"What is so amusing?"

"I just pictured my parents, Edgar, Georgiana and Lady Susan in the receiving line of that fancy ball Mother is giving in her honour. You know it is to be held right after your marriage. Would it not be entertaining if you and Miss Elizabeth arrived at the ball as a married couple? I would give half a year's pay to see the expressions on their faces!"

"I am counting on the activity surrounding the ball to mask the fact that we have returned to Town. The only thing preventing me from going directly to Pemberley is the fact that I would not want Miss Elizabeth to spend her wedding night at a post inn. I would like to stay in Town for a day or two before removing to Derbyshire."

"Then you intend to hide her away at Pemberley? What of Georgiana?"

"Georgiana shall be welcome to accompany us back to Pemberley, if she promises to be civil to Elizabeth. Otherwise, she may remain in Town with your parents and reconsider her attitude. Frankly, she has been ill-mannered to me for months, and her inconsiderate behaviour towards our uncle and aunt was the last straw. I find myself wishing she were married, if only for some peace of mind. That is not how I wish it to be between us, but that is what it has come to."

Richard threw an arm over William's shoulder. "You have tried, Cousin. Her attitude is not your fault; I would lay it at Andrew's feet. He was the one who turned her against you, in my opinion."

"I know that she adored Andrew and believed whatever he told her. After I insisted he live at his own estate, she completely ignored me, turning to your parents if she needed advice." William shook his head as though to rid himself of the memory. "As for introducing Elizabeth to the rest of the family, I may consider bringing her to London after six months or so. Hopefully, by then they will have run out of slings and arrows."

"Let us pray then that your wedding proceeds without them finding out, for I fear that slings and arrows shall be the least of your concerns if they do. I look for Father and Aunt Catherine to mount heavy artillery and cannons if they hear about it in advance!"

"You certainly know how to lift my spirits."

"That is my forte, Darcy. And, no, you do not have to thank me."

"I was not planning to."

Pemberley
In a garden

A favourable sky, marbled pearly white, greeted the Fitzwilliams as they settled into the swing that marked the end of the gravel trail that wound through one of Pemberley's most beautiful gardens—the one comprised entirely of wildflowers. Though there were many gardens on the premises, one containing an elaborate maze, another comprised of every imaginable rose and still another featuring manicured lawns and statuary, this was Olivia Fitzwilliam's favourite, for it reminded her of the day her husband had proposed, bearing only a bouquet of buttercups and daisies. Over the years, those memories sustained her as life brought some heavy sorrows.

As she took a deep breath of fragrant air, Joseph began to move the swing with his foot, at the same time bringing a daisy from behind his back. As he held it out to her, she took it and rewarded him with a kiss.

"You certainly know how to make a lady feel special."

"You have always been special, Livy. I do not have to make it so."

"Do you think you may be prejudiced?"

"Of course not!" He kissed her lips softly. "I am the most unbiased man in all of England."

Olivia leaned into him, and his arm went around her, pulling her tightly against his body. "Are you comfortable? I can fetch your shawl if you wish."

She patted his hand. "Just stay right where you are, and I shall be fine."

They were silent for some time, both pleasantly diverted, watching all the activity that accompanied so large an estate. If one paid attention, there was always something taking place. In addition to the grooms and gardeners going about their jobs, just past the stables was a lake where several ducks and their hatchlings cut a swath across the smooth surface. Beyond, on a hillside meadow, a trio of horses raced up a verdant grassy knoll, while in the next pasture scores of black-faced sheep grazed as their young leaped about in play. Nearer, birds bathed in a small fountain fashioned just for them, while a cat and several kittens hovered next to a small pond where fish darted in and out under lily pads. Every so often the mother cat would swipe at a fish sending water flying and the kittens scampering.

"Do you remember the last time we were here? Anne was still alive, and Fitzwilliam was just a boy?" Olivia ventured.

"Yes, it seems like only yesterday."

"While we are here, Joseph, I want you to spend more time with Fitzwilliam, for he has no father to turn to, and you would be a steadying hand. And Richard, poor boy, has no relationship with his father, I just know it. He needs your presence in his life, as well."

"You know that I will continue to do everything in my power to help both my nephews, Livy. But this is not about Fitzwilliam or Richard. What do you wish to say?"

She laughed softly. "You know me too well." Then with a deep inhale to fortify herself, she said, "If I should die first, I want you to remember that you still have family who need you and look to you for wisdom. Never forget that."

A great pang gripped his heart. "Nothing will happen to either of us, darling, for a long, long time. You and I are just experiencing the changes that come with age."

She kissed his cheek. "I know you are right, but I wanted to speak of this while it was on my mind. I do not want you moping around should I precede you in death. I want you to be happy and to enjoy those who love you. And, to be frank, if you found someone you could love, I would wish for you to marry again. You were not formed to be alone."

Joseph stood up, visibly irritated. "Olivia Fitzwilliam, never say such a thing to me again! I have never loved any woman but you, and I never shall. How you can conceive of such a thing is beyond my imagination!"

She grabbed his hand and pulled him back down beside her on the swing. "I apologise if I offended you, but I wish only for your happiness."

He leaned in to kiss her tenderly. Afterward he pulled back to look into her eyes. "Know this, Olivia Angelina Stratford Fitzwilliam, you will be the only wife I will ever have on this earth, and, the Lord willing, you shall be my wife throughout eternity. Oh, I know it is taught that there will be no husbands and wives in heaven, but I could never forget that you are mine."

Tears filled her eyes, and she cupped his face. "Joseph Marshall Howard Fitzwilliam, I am blessed to be your wife, and I shall forever love you."

A longer kiss followed, and then Olivia settled back into his arms, content once more, for she was certain that they would face whatever came as they always had—together. And now that they had reunited with Fitzwilliam and Richard, she knew her Joseph would be in good hands.

Almost a half-hour later, Mrs. Reynolds came down the gravel path carrying a tray. She coughed so as not to interrupt, and Olivia called out, "You did not have to bring us refreshments, Mrs. Reynolds. You have far too much work to do as it is."

The housekeeper smiled as she set the tray on a nearby table. "I wanted to bring the tray. I was tired of being inside." She brought her hand up to shade her eyes as she surveyed the sky. "It is a beautiful day. Just enough clouds to keep it pleasant."

"Yes," Joseph answered, "and Pemberley is one of the most beautiful places on earth. I do not think I could ever get tired of it."

The housekeeper smiled at them. "I have been here the greater part of my life, and I never tire of waking up each morning to the view. If heaven is half as beautiful, I shall be satisfied. I shall leave you to enjoy the garden. I think I shall walk down to the stables to see how the new colt that was born yesterday is faring."

"I may check on him later while Livy takes her nap," Joseph replied.

As she nodded and turned to leave, the long-time servant could hear the rest of their conversation, and it made her smile.

"I may not take a nap. I feel much better than I have in days."

"Still, you do best when you rest for an hour. If you wish, I shall wait until you awaken, and we shall both walk to the stables."

"If you insist on a nap, I would love to go with you afterward."

As she walked further from them, Mrs. Reynolds was thinking of something that had crossed her mind almost every day since the couple had come to Pemberley.

I imagine Mr. Darcy and Lady Anne would have been much like the Fitzwilliams, had they lived. It would do the Master so much good to have them remain here. I pray they decide to stay in England.

Longbourn
The sewing room

Elizabeth was growing weary. For hours she had stood on a stool in the sewing room while Mrs. Hill and her Aunt Gardiner walked around her, pinning and tucking a length of cream-coloured duchesse satin to her frame. Her aunt thought it providential that she happened to have the bolt of luxurious material in a trunk on the coach. Having just visited Lambton, she had brought along six bolts of fabric for a friend's daughter who was getting married. That young woman opted for a white satin, leaving the cream available for Elizabeth.

Regrettably, Mrs. Bennet had not been impressed with Elizabeth's wishes for the dress, protesting that, while the silk was pretty, it would be too plain without adding yards of lace. While not opposed to some lace, Elizabeth was not in favour of covering the entire dress with it, which led to a disagreement. The dispute finally became so loud that Mr. Bennet left his study to learn the reason. Afterward, he forbade his wife from entering the sewing room until after the dress was finished. Though thankful for his intervention, by now her mother's hysterics and the hours spent standing perfectly still had given Elizabeth a pounding headache, and for a moment, she closed her eyes. A sudden touch on her hand caused them to fly open again.

"Well?" The look on Mrs. Gardiner's face meant that she was expecting an answer. "I asked if you had any preferences for the lace. Edward happened to bring home a lovely bolt of Belgium lace, three inches deep, that I have been embroidering with pink roses across the top. Embroidered lace is highly sought after by the *ton*, thus I add flowers to some of the best pieces that come through the warehouse. I believe the piece I am working on now will complement this dress beautifully."

"I care not. I shall leave it for you to decide."

Mrs. Gardiner seemed unhappy with her reply. "Mrs. Hill, would you excuse us, please?" The elderly housekeeper curtseyed and left the room, giving Elizabeth a concerned look as she pulled the door closed.

"Elizabeth Bennet! If you do not care about your appearance, I certainly do. Many wealthy men have portraits done of their wives in their wedding dress, and there are indeed enough at Pemberley to support my claim. Do you want to be ashamed every time you pass your portrait in the great hall?"

"How do you know so much about Pemberley?"

"I grew up in Lambton, if you remember. When I was a child, they allowed the public to tour the house in the summer months, and I went every year."

"Is it really that grand?"

"I think it the most beautiful house in all of England. Even nicer than many of His Majesty's palaces, according to some who know, for it is not ostentatious, and the grounds... the grounds are lovelier than Hyde Park. I venture to say that you will love discovering all the wonders of Pemberley, especially during your walks."

"If I am allowed to walk," Elizabeth sighed. "Mama says that proper ladies

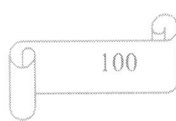

do not traipse all over the country afoot; they ride in carriages or on horseback. And while I do not mind an occasional horseback ride, I dearly love to walk."

"Surely Mr. Darcy will not forbid something that you love so well."

"Oh, I do not know about that. He agreed with Caroline Bingley that he would not want his sister walking to Netherfield, as I did when Jane was ill."

"I imagine that he would not want you walking from Pemberley to Lambton, either, especially if the roads were muddy. But keep in mind that the people of Lambton speak well of him; he cannot be too unpleasant."

Lizzy cocked her head to the side and scowled. "Not ALL the people."

"Elizabeth Rose Bennet, you promised me!"

"I am trying, but surely you do not expect me to change overnight," Elizabeth said sheepishly.

"What if, after you marry Mr. Darcy, he begins to note and resent all your imperfections? After all, you are not without fault."

"You have always made me feel faultless," Elizabeth tried to tease.

"That is because I am your aunt, and aunts are supposed to spoil. But, you know of what I speak."

"Yes." Elizabeth became serious. "I suppose both of us had better look for the silver lining if we are to survive."

"Precisely my point." She took her niece's hands and rocked back on her heels to examine her. "Oh, Lizzy! I think your bridegroom is going to be very impressed when he sees you come down the church aisle."

Turning her niece so that she could see her reflection in the large mirror that stood in one corner, she was pleased when Elizabeth whispered reverently, "It is going to be beautiful. Thank you."

She held out her arms, but Mrs. Gardiner only gave her a peck on the cheek. "I fear it would be too painful to hug you with all the pins."

Mrs. Hill came into the room again, having been summoned to help unpin the gown and then re-pin it on a dress form used for that purpose.

"I must begin the supervision of dinner, but I shall be glad to sew the front to the back once I have the preparations well in hand."

"Thank you, Hill," Madeline Gardiner said. "Your help has been invaluable. Between us, I believe we shall finish this dress in time for the wedding. I will continue working on the lace and, hopefully, once I am done with it, you will have the gown in one piece."

Mrs. Hill beamed, proudly dropping a curtsey before leaving. As she exited the room, Jane came rushing in, untying her bonnet as she walked.

Breathlessly she exclaimed, "I wanted to see you wearing your dress, Lizzy, but it seems I am too late!"

"You shall have a better view of it tomorrow, for I believe Mrs. Hill will have finished the seams by then. Hopefully, the next time I try it on there will be no pins to avoid."

"How was your luncheon with Mr. Bingley's sisters?" Mrs. Gardiner asked Jane.

"Mrs. Hurst was nice enough, I suppose. Though I have to wonder at her inviting me in the first place, for she never listens to anything I say. But it was a bit odd, for Miss Bingley was nowhere in sight. According to her sister, everything she has eaten disagrees with her."

Lizzy and her aunt exchanged glances. Caroline's tantrum in response to Mr. Darcy's impending nuptials was the talk of Hertfordshire.

"Mrs. Hurst tried to blame her sister's behaviour on spells she alleges Miss Bingley has suffered all her life. However, in my opinion, she is simply acting childish over your impending marriage."

"Good for you, Jane!" their aunt declared. "I believe you have assessed the situation adeptly."

Jane smiled at the accolade, blushing a bit because she was not used to being so forthright. "Well, let me change out of these clothes. Then you can tell me all about your dress and what I may do to help you." With that, Jane kissed both ladies before rushing from the room.

"I worried that Jane would try to smooth over Mr. Bingley's sister's outrageous behaviour. Apparently all that has happened has made her bolder."

"Or cynical."

"Not cynical, but perhaps more pragmatic," replied her aunt, "and I, for one, am relieved. Jane was too apt to try to find good in everyone before this happened." Suddenly she began chuckling. "I know I should not laugh, but I find it amusing that Miss Bingley is sick because Mr. Darcy is marrying you."

Lizzy could not repress a smile. "If she only knew that I was sick at the thought of marrying him." The smile on her aunt's face quickly vanished, and Lizzy rushed to add, "I was only making light of the situation."

"Teasing can be another way of showing resentment."

Elizabeth thought about that for a moment. "You are right. Though Papa and I have perfected the art, teasing can be used to do great harm."

Her aunt beamed. "That is why I love you. You are willing to listen and to change if proven wrong."

"Let us pray that Mr. Darcy is willing to change as well, for I fear he has no idea what he is getting into by marrying me."

"I will pray that you both are pleasantly surprised."

Elizabeth sighed. "So will I."

Later

That evening a different kind of weariness washed over the occupants of Longbourn, for as they sat around the parlour after dinner, Mrs. Bennet was back to reasserting her authority and making plans. If she was to be shut out of everything to do with the dress, she would not be overruled when it came to the wedding breakfast; thus, she proclaimed to one and all her ideas on how to impress the gentleman from Derbyshire.

"I shall have Hill fix a nice salmon. Oh, and a joint of beef must be provided—all great men love roasted beef! And of course I shall have Hill round out the fare with mutton, fowl and tongue. Surely, Mr. Darcy will favour one or more of those."

She went on to describe all the vegetables and sauces, droning on for so long that even Lydia and Kitty had quit listening by the time Mrs. Bennet began to describe the desserts. Elizabeth, who was sitting in her favourite upholstered chair with shoes off and feet drawn up under her, wanted nothing more than go to her room in order to have peace and quiet. Moreover, as her eyes met Madeline Gardiner's across the room, there was no doubt that she wished for the same. Nonetheless, both were aware that her mother wished to have an audience and would take offense if they retired. So they remained, though they added nothing to the conversation.

At some point, Elizabeth managed to completely block out her mother's voice while she considered her aunt's counsel. Madeline Gardiner had been like a mother to her for as long as she could remember, always concerned for her wellbeing, and she trusted her completely. In addition, the advice she gave reinforced all that Elizabeth had learned from reading the Bible and listening to sermons every Sunday. At last resigned to her fate, she silently vowed to put forth her very best effort to be a good wife.

After all, the good Lord says we should love our enemies and bless them that curse us.

The absurdity of applying that verse to her upcoming marriage almost made her giggle, and she covered her mouth. Seeing that no one had noticed, Elizabeth assumed a solemn expression while trying to recall a more appropriate one to adopt as her motto.

Turn the other cheek? No, that will never do! I know! Love your neighbour as yourself! Surely I can love Mr. Darcy as much as I love Charlotte.

Suddenly her heart was lighter. *At least God said that He shall not put more on me than I can bear.*

She glanced up to heaven. *I am counting on You to keep that promise.*

Chapter 10

Matlock House

As Georgiana awaited her guest in the spectacular library at Matlock House her expression fell, for she was reminded of how much this room resembled the one at Pemberley. It had the same magnificent, polished wood panelling and wall-to-wall shelves rising all the way to the ceiling, with ladders to access the books on the top shelves. Despite the fact that the carpet was emerald green instead of royal blue, the likeness was remarkable. Closing her eyes, the smell of books, both new and old, transported her back to her childhood home, and she longed for it. Oddly, she also found herself longing for her brother.

After she had decided to punish William for making Andrew move to Winfield Hall, their once close relationship had deteriorated. When first she had stopped speaking to him, it was to be for only a few days. Certain that he would relent quickly, she was surprised when William distanced himself from her because of her petulance. And because he did not beg her forgiveness and she was too proud to admit culpability, she had expanded on her protest. Instead of seeking his advice, as in the past, she began writing her uncle and aunt for their opinions. William was very hurt when she flaunted their counsel, and from that moment on, he had stopped trying to reason with her. Now recalling all that had transpired between them, tears filled her eyes, and she blinked to keep them from falling.

What do I care if you do not fawn over me as in the past? Uncle thinks I am right to ask his opinion. Besides, when I was a child, Andrew was more of a brother than you ever were!

Her mind flew to the day her world had turned upside down—the day Fitzwilliam had left for Eton. All that she had shared with him—horseback rides, swimming, fishing and exploring the grounds—had suddenly come to a halt. Some time afterward, Andrew, George Wickham and Lady Susan, their nearest neighbour, had begun including her in their activities, though it was never the same as being with her brother. For years afterward, even after going to Eton himself, Andrew would make time for her when he returned to Pemberley each summer. In contrast, when William was home from school, his time was spent locked in their father's study. It was not until their father's death that any semblance of closeness had returned.

Only Andrew truly cared to spend time with me when I was a child. The small voice of her conscious whispered a rebuttal. *You remember overhearing your father insist that Andrew watch you while he instructed your brother on estate matters. Besides, when given the opportunity, Fitzwilliam never failed to ask if you wished to join him for some activity. But you refused because Andrew was a livelier companion and, truth be known, because you wanted to punish Fitzwilliam for deserting you.*

Tossing that thought aside as easily as she would an outdated gown, Georgiana lifted her chin. *If Brother truly cared to reconcile with me, he would! I shall think on this matter no longer.*

Just as she made that resolution, the Matlocks' butler appeared in the doorway.

"Lady Susan has arrived."

Stepping aside, a tall young woman who closely favoured Georgiana, only with lighter blond hair and blue eyes, rushed past him. She almost bumped him in her haste. His raised brows showed his disapproval and Mr. Soames sniffed with indignation as he quickly turned to resume his post.

"Georgiana!" Lady Susan kissed the air on either side of her head. "How wonderful to see you. You look lovely!"

Blushing, Georgiana replied, "You say that every time we meet." They both giggled as Georgiana pulled her over to a beautiful brown leather sofa. "Let us sit here while we plan our strategy."

Lady Susan glanced across the room. "Should we not close the door?"

"My aunt would wonder what we were hiding if we did. We shall just talk softly so as not to be overheard."

"As you wish."

"I am optimistic that my brother will be in town the night of your ball. When my aunt told him of the event, she emphasised her desire that he escort you."

"I hope he was listening," Susan replied. "He can be so slow-witted at times! It is as though he does not wish to comprehend."

Georgiana sighed. "I know exactly what you mean, though he is anything but dull. He remembers what he wishes to remember."

"Agreed." Then Lady Susan's face became animated. "Tell me what you have planned for the ball. Your note was so intriguing. How do you plan to spur him into offering for me?"

"It is simple. My uncle has agreed that I may attend, even though I am not out yet. Of course, I cannot dance, but I shall attend in any event. So, right after supper, I thought that I would send a note to William via a footman, saying that I must speak to him and will await him in the gazebo. Only you shall be there, not me. I shall hide until I see him walk towards the garden. Then I will find my aunt and persuade her to accompany me to the garden, saying William is there and I fear he is ill."

"But if you and his aunt are the only witnesses… "

"Oh, there will be others. Before the ball begins, I will solicit several young women of my acquaintance to follow when my aunt and I exit the ballroom, letting them think it is a game of sorts. When we find Brother holding you in his arms—and you MUST manage to fall into his arms—he will have no choice but to marry you. Is that not clever?"

Susan's brow furrowed. "Your brother may rebuff me, should I try to fall into his arms. From what I hear he has avoided being caught in compromising situations many times before."

"You simply have to act the part of a helpless woman. I have found that his stoic facade crumbles the moment I begin to cry. Just fall into his arms crying."

"I shall impress everyone with my theatrics."

"Excellent!" Georgiana declared.

"What is excellent?" Lady Matlock enquired as she entered the room, her expression all anticipation.

For a moment Georgiana faltered. "I... I... "

Susan rose to greet the countess, answering effortlessly, "I was just describing the gown I am wearing to the ball, Lady Matlock. It is the most gorgeous shade of blue. My modiste assures me that it will bring out the colour of my eyes."

The countess took both of Susan's hands. "Oh my dear, I do not think you need anything to make your eyes more beautiful. You will look lovely regardless of what you wear."

"If only your nephew thinks so."

"My nephew needs an heir, and I am certain that, with a little prodding, he will act now that you are available again. After all, you have known each other all your lives, and since Fitzwilliam is reluctant to meet new people, he cannot object to you."

Without awaiting an answer, Lady Matlock turned back to Georgiana. "I have just now received a note from Madam Bouvier asking us to revisit her shop. It seems your measurements have changed substantially, especially your bosom, and she wants to be sure that her assistant did not make an error before she proceeds."

As Georgiana blushed, her aunt glanced at Lady Susan. "I apologise for interrupting your little *tête à tête,* but it could not be helped if Georgiana's gown is to be finished in time. You are welcome to accompany us if you wish, and we shall make a day of it—visiting the millinery, the coffee shop and the confectioners."

"That sounds wonderful!" Lady Susan exclaimed. "I cannot think of anything I would rather do today."

Privately, she was not as enthusiastic. *I cannot believe I have to spend the rest of the day with the two most boring people in Town. After I marry Fitzwilliam, I shall immediately find you a husband, Georgiana. Hopefully, one who lives in Ireland or, at the least, Scotland. And once I am a member of the family, I shall invent excuses for not spending time in your company either, Countess.*

Shortly thereafter, they were all ensconced in the Matlocks' carriage, headed for Madam Bouvier's, with neither of Darcy's relations the wiser regarding the woman who accompanied them.

Longbourn
Late Evening

Watching his eldest daughter and her fiancé stroll through the gardens outside his study window brought a slight smile to Thomas Bennet's face, the first one in days. Mary was not twenty steps behind them, keeping pace, though her attention was fixed on the book in her hands. So focused was she that every so often she would trip over a rock, a stick or a tuft of grass and struggle to catch her balance. It made for a most amusing sight.

At least Jane is well matched. Though undoubtedly she and Mr. Bingley are both so agreeable that they will be cheated assiduously by their servants, and be so generous with the rest, they will always exceed their income. [5] *In any event, I do not worry about their felicity as I do Elizabeth's. What happened to her is my fault, and that makes it all the more painful. I raised Elizabeth to be more like a man in temperament. Had she not been so bold and confident, she would never have met with that blackguard alone.*

Glancing now at the papers in his hand, delivered that morning, Mr. Bennet was reminded of the taciturn fellow who would soon abscond with his favourite child. Though Charles had given his word that *this* Darcy was honourable, it had not allayed his reservations substantially. For while Bingley was near to Jane's age, with little or no experience in running an estate, Lizzy's fiancé was many years older and had been the master of Pemberley since his father's death. No doubt he was used to being obeyed without question, and Elizabeth was used to questioning before obeying.

Turning so that the faint sunlight illuminated the pages, he rubbed his chin appraisingly as he read the settlement once more.

Though his demeanour was unflappable and he did not act the lovelorn suitor, Mr. Darcy must care for Elizabeth, else why would he settle on her so large a sum? Still, he hardly knows her, and I have to wonder if he will continue to care so keenly after he learns her nature.

A knock at the door interrupted his thoughts. Reminding himself that he had no alternative but to follow through with what he had decreed, he called, "Come!"

The door opened much more slowly than usual, revealing that Elizabeth stood just outside. She hesitated a moment before stepping inside, her eyes fixed on the floor the entire time. His heart broke, for only a few weeks before she would have bounded into the room and run to plant a kiss on his cheek.

"Shut the door, Elizabeth." She complied and, when she turned back to face him, he added, "Sit down, please."

As quiet as a mouse, she took her usual seat in front of his desk. Realizing that this might be the last time they would share his study in this manner, a large lump filled Mr. Bennet's throat. Nevertheless, taking a deep breath, he began.

"I do not understand how you came to know *this* Mr. Darcy in the short time you were at Netherfield, but it seems that you made quite the impression." Elizabeth looked up through her lashes, her expression quizzical. "I have never seen nor heard of a more generous settlement in my life."

"You need not tease me, Papa," she answered cynically. "I am resigned to marrying Mr. Darcy."

"I assure you that I am not teasing," He slid the papers across the desk. "I would like for you to read this."

Shrugging with indifference, Elizabeth took the proffered pages and settled back in the chair. The further she read, the more her mouth fell open. "Surely this cannot be correct."

"It is true. Mr. Darcy sent a letter summarizing what he was settling on you and on any children you may have. There is no error."

Elizabeth counted the zeros again. Shaking her head, she murmured, "I cannot fathom anyone needing that large a sum or anyone granting it."

"He is most generous."

Elizabeth laid the papers on the desk, stood and walked over to the window to stare at her sisters and Bingley, who were still circling the garden. Crossing her arms, she ran her hands up and down her forearms.

"Mr. Bingley told Jane that Mr. Darcy's fortune was far more than the 'ten thousand a year and half of Derbyshire' that everyone was so keen to note," she said.

"After seeing this, I would have to agree."

"Still, I am puzzled as to why he would want to marry me. There are many women who would suit him much better, even Caroline Bingley."

"You have only to say the word and I shall reject his settlement and send Mr. Darcy away. When I received the settlement, I also received a letter from my cousin saying he will arrive before dark. If you would rather marry—"

Elizabeth whirled around. "You cannot be serious! Mr. Collins is ridiculous! Moreover, he looks as though he never bathes and he smells of cheap cologne."

"And Mr. Darcy?"

She sighed. "At least he looks clean, though I have not been close enough to notice if he smells."

Mr. Bennet could not suppress a chuckle, causing Elizabeth to break into a smile. Rising from his desk, he moved to where she stood, turning her around so that they both observed the garden as he slipped his arm around her shoulder. While their eyes followed the three people circling the pathway, he offered some counsel.

"Everyone thinks Jane and Mr. Bingley are well matched, and so they are for they are both even-tempered and easily pleased. Jane would not know what to do with someone as, shall we say, *intense* as Mr. Darcy." He glanced to Elizabeth, noting that her brows knit with his words. "But you are not Jane, and I believe your rejection of Collins is for the best. You need someone who is his own man—someone intelligent, strong and authoritative. Should you settle for someone you can rule, you will be miserable."

Elizabeth bristled. "Am I so unbearable?"

"I am not criticising you. In fact, your spirit is one aspect of your nature that I have always encouraged, though I fear that I may have done you a disservice. For not many men desire a headstrong wife."

"I am headstrong in that I do not like men who are easily swayed with every wind. Still, Mr. Darcy seems a bit stern. Do you think a man can be too authoritative?"

"Only if he uses that authority for evil, and Bingley has vouched for

Fitzwilliam Darcy's character, so I do not think him that kind of man."

She nodded, seemingly still not convinced, but past arguing.

"I think that with a little patience, Mr. Darcy will make a good husband. But I caution you to remember that he has been master of a large estate for many years and is used to being obeyed." Elizabeth wrinkled her nose. "A man of seven and twenty is set in his ways. You must give him time to become accustomed to being married and to consider your opinion. Do you think you can do that?"

"Aunt Gardiner said the same thing when we talked, and I told her that I shall give it my best effort."

"That is all one can ask." Then turning her so that they faced one another, he pushed an errant curl behind her ear. "I am sorry that you and your sisters do not have more choices in marriage. I should have provided you with stouter dowries."

"I would not be forced to marry had I not thought myself so very clever in meeting Andrew Darcy alone."

Thomas Bennet's eyes got teary. "I want you to know that I have always wished for you to marry a man who would appreciate your uniqueness. I pray Mr. Darcy is clever enough to be that man."

"Perhaps we shall both be pleasantly surprised."

They stayed at the window, arms about each other, watching the impromptu parade as the sun began to set. Finally, a knock came at the door.

"Dinner is being served, sir."

"Thank you, Hill."

The Bennet Dining Room

The Gardiners were at their sister Phillips' home and would not return until late, so only the Bennets were gathering around the dinner table that evening. They had barely taken their seats when the noise of a carriage in front of the house caught their attention. Mr. Hill hurried to the front door while Mrs. Hill stopped in her tracks for fear that dinner was about to be delayed. As the room grew quiet, Mr. Collins could be heard speaking as he came into the foyer.

"Already eating, you say?" The sound of footsteps coming toward the dining room was quickly followed by the door flying open. "Oh, my dear cousins!" Collins exclaimed. "What a feast! And it seems I am just in time to join you!"

Without waiting for an invitation, he turned to Mrs. Hill. "Where may I wash my hands?" She motioned towards the door to the kitchen, and he strode in that direction, calling over his shoulder, "Do not wait for me! I shall return shortly."

The deep breath that Mr. Bennet took did not bode well. It was obvious to those at the table that he was not happy with his cousin's presence or his directive and was trying not to fly into a rage.

As Hill and her husband began to place the food on the table, he found his voice. "Do not say anything to my cousin regarding Lizzy's engagement. I shall inform him after dinner in my study. Is that understood?"

No one had time to reply because the vicar came back into the room and took the empty chair next to Elizabeth. As he did, he looked at her appraisingly, his inspection ending with a smirk as he placed his napkin under his chin.

"I am delighted to be back amongst my family," he said, thoroughly convinced that Mrs. Bennet had made Elizabeth understand that she must accept his suit.

Lydia and Kitty snickered. Mr. Bennet stopped them with a glare.

"I have written to her ladyship that I shall have good news to share when I return, and she will be most pleased… most pleased!"

During this pronouncement, he gave Elizabeth a large smile, revealing that his teeth still needed a good cleaning.

"Fortuitously, whomever I marry will benefit from my patroness' advice. I have been astonished that she has concerned herself with my humble abode, but she has instructed me on the specifics of adding shelves to closets, the correct shades of paint for each room and even provided a use for old curtains. In addition, she explained how to lay out my garden and provided a cure for ridding the garden and my home of any type of pest."

"*Including a stupid vicar?*" Mr. Bennet mumbled under his breath.

This brought more snickers from Kitty and Lydia, who were close enough to hear, and a shake of the head from Mrs. Bennet.

After another hearty bite of potatoes, Collins replied, "I am sorry, Cousin. I did not hear your last remark."

"I was wondering how someone of her ladyship's station has such a vast knowledge of pests."

Mr. Collins beamed, most eager to explain. "Her ladyship is very intelligent! She often knows what is needed before you are aware that you are in need."

"I see," Mr. Bennet replied dryly.

"By the by, whilst I was visiting the vicar at Tipton, I received a letter from her ladyship enquiring if I had previously encountered her nephew, Mr. Fitzwilliam Darcy, in Meryton. It seems her sources reported that he had been in residence at Netherfield. Is he still in the neighbourhood?"

Mr. Bennet bristled. "She has her nephew spied upon? The Darcy I met is no child and would not appreciate being treated thusly, I imagine."

"Oh, it is not like that at all. Mr. Darcy is her daughter's fiancé and she worries for his safety."

Mr. Bennet looked to Elizabeth, her expression indicating that she was as astonished as he. As calmly as he could, he challenged, "Her daughter's fiancé? Surely you are mistaken. I spoke to the man not a week past, and when he told me of his current situation, he never mentioned being engaged."

Collins looked cautiously about the table. "I do not think my patroness would mind if I told you the particulars of the engagement. After all, she speaks of it quite freely to all who will listen."

"Then why do you not enlighten us."

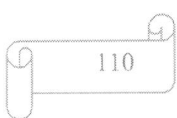

"It is an unusual arrangement. It was agreed upon by their mothers whilst they were yet in their cradles."

Thomas Bennet huffed. "Unusual—I would say unenforceable. An engagement of that sort would not be binding to either party, in my opinion."

"Oh, I assure you that it is! Mr. Darcy is bound by duty and honour to marry his cousin, Miss Anne de Bourgh!"

Forgetting herself completely, Lydia retorted, "La! It seems he takes no care for duty, since he has offered for Lizzy!"

Realising too late what she had done, Lydia clamped her hand over her mouth and slunk down in her chair under her father's stern gaze.

"Engaged to Miss Elizabeth! That is preposterous! Mr. Darcy would never marry someone so beneath his station!" Collins exclaimed, even as he turned to Mrs. Bennet for confirmation. "Did you not say that she was ready to accept my offer?"

"I... " was all that Mrs. Bennet could manage before her husband interrupted.

Incensed at Collins' pronouncement, Mr. Bennet declared, "I assure you that Mr Darcy does intend to marry Elizabeth. I received his settlement just this morning, and it is very generous."

Collins stood abruptly, causing his chair to fall back and hit the floor. "I cannot stay under this roof another minute! My esteemed patroness will be most displeased when she hears this news. Most displeased! And I shall not have her thinking I had any part in it. Please have a servant fetch my bags and drive me into Meryton. I shall take a room at the inn."

Instantly, he was out of the dining room, the door slamming shut behind him as proof. The silence was deafening as all the members of the family held their breath. Then Mr. Bennet spoke.

"Well I, for one, am grateful that we will not be made to suffer through another night of Fordyce's sermons!"

With that pronouncement, he stood and was out the door as hastily as Collins. For a brief moment, no one moved. Then Elizabeth began to giggle, and the others joined in one at a time. Even Mrs. Bennet gave in, finding a new use for her handkerchief as she used it to wipe the tears now streaming down her cheeks, the result of having laughed so heartily.

London
Younge's Boarding House

As Andrew Darcy reined his horse to a stop, he looked at the dilapidated building that comprised Younge's Inn, located just minutes from London Bridge. He had thought to go north when he left Manchester, but soon realised he could hide more readily in Town than in some obscure village where he might stand out; thus, he donned the old clothes he kept for whenever he wished to avoid being recognised and headed straight to the Mint. [6]

According to Wickham, in this area he could get lost in the rabble that occupied the lowest level of society. Mrs. Eunice Younge, a widow and one of Wickham's old paramours, would accommodate anyone who had the funds to pay. Her late brother, one of George's associates, had stolen enough to pay for the inn before his death, leaving her with a way to make a living, howbeit a difficult one, for she dealt with the vilest of men.

Hesitating to dismount, Andrew considered how far he had sunk. No decent man would ride through this area, must less reside here, unless he had good reason. And he had. He must remain hidden until the misfortune of Miss Harrington's death was not as sorely felt, and Lord Warren had calmed enough to think more clearly. Thus, with no alternative, he threw his leg over his mount and dropped to the ground.

Wearily slapping his hat against his breeches in an attempt to remove some of the dust, all he managed to do was create a cloud of dirt. He was taking the steps to the front door when a woman with weary brown eyes and unkempt red hair appeared in the doorway. She was briskly wiping her hands on a stained apron. He noted that she was plain and probably in her late thirties, though the wrinkles on her face made her appear older.

"What can I do for you?" she asked, though her tone was not solicitous.

"George Wickham said that you might have a room for rent."

She studied him carefully. "Wickham, you say? How do you know him?"

"I grew up at Pemberley when his father was the steward. We have been friends since I was eleven."

"You must be the other Darcy—not the heir to Pemberley. Why would a man of your station be dressed like a pauper or wish to stay here?"

"I need to hide from an irate father, and I do not think he will look for me here." Andrew looked about anxiously. "George assured me that you could help, but if not—"

"Do not get distraught, Mr. Darcy. I like to know what I am facing, that is all. I have room six available."

"Very well, but please, refer to me as Mr. Smith, if you do not mind."

"Just so you understand, if an irate father or the law comes looking, I will tell them only that a Mr. Smith is renting room six; however, I will not prevent them from searching the room and it will be your problem to escape by the back door or a window if they find you. I will try to warn you if I have the opportunity, but I cannot guarantee anything."

"Agreed."

As they entered the building, she became a bit friendlier. "When was the last time you saw George? That blackguard owes me a thruppence." [7]

Andrew flashed his best smile, always the charmer. "I saw George about a week ago. He is a lieutenant in the militia now."

"So he joined, did he? He swore he would, but I never believed him. I imagine all the ladies admire him in his red coat. He was always a handsome

"He does cut a fine figure in his uniform." Andrew reached into his coat pocket, bringing out a shilling. "Perhaps you will allow me to pay you what George owes and a little towards my rent?"

Mrs. Younge took the coin, biting it to ascertain it was genuine. Satisfied, she dropped it in her bosom. "Since you are George's friend, the room will cost you a ha-penny a day. Washing and meals are extra."

"Excellent. Just keep the shilling, and when I owe you more, let me know."

"You can rest assured that I will. Now, let me fetch the key."

Chapter 11

Meryton
Longbourn

Longbourn was straining at the seams, but Mrs. Bennet was in her element as hostess of the wedding breakfast for Mr. Darcy and her least favourite child. Moving from one guest to another, suggesting that they try this or that dish, she was certain that Meryton had never seen, nor would ever again see, a more sumptuous banquet. Nor, she thought, would the majority of her neighbours have many opportunities to associate with more august personages than her new son and his cousin, Colonel Fitzwilliam—the son of an earl, no less! Her reputation for hospitality would forever be fixed in the annals of local society.

Pausing from her exultation to take in the scene, she managed a small smile for Elizabeth, who was standing alongside her husband. That gentleman, she thought, looked as though he would rather be elsewhere. However, the line of neighbours waiting to offer felicitations was just now thinning after nearly an hour, so she allowed that her new son's expression could merely be the result of fatigue.

One would think he could force a smile on his wedding day! Oh well, indulging the throng is simply the price one pays for being so wealthy. When the rich deign to marry, the entire county wants to see the spectacle!

Her fear that Mr. Darcy would not return to Hertfordshire had subsided only after his coach stopped in front of the manor last evening— the fluttering in her heart ending as abruptly as her criticisms. Though Mr. Bennet and the Gardiners had expressed confidence in Darcy's constancy, she had uttered an audible sigh of relief when the gentleman from Derbyshire finally repeated the vows that tied him to Elizabeth forever. For her, this union meant that she would always be cared for in a superior fashion, should Mr. Bennet expire. While Jane's beau was well off, Mr. Darcy was rich beyond imagination and, after how he had stepped in to save Lizzy, Mrs. Bennet had no doubt that he would do right by the rest of his new family.

She was about to address the newlyweds and insist that they partake of the breakfast when her sister Phillips pulled her aside to relate the latest news from Meryton. Thus occupied, Mrs. Bennet completely forgot about Elizabeth and Darcy, which was for the best, for Madeline Gardiner had her own plans and, nodding to her husband, they both proceeded towards the vanishing receiving line.

As the last guest shook Mr. Darcy's hand and wished Elizabeth joy, Madeline Gardiner approached. "Elizabeth, may I assist you in changing into your travelling clothes?"

Behind the offer, Elizabeth sensed that her aunt wished to speak privately.

Turning to her new husband, she ventured, "Mr. Darcy—"

"Elizabeth, what did we agree upon last night?"

"I am sorry. I meant to call you Will."

He smiled as warmly as possible. "Thank you. What is it, my dear?"

"I am going to my room with Aunt Gardiner; I shall return shortly."

"I will eagerly await your return," he said sincerely, bringing her hand up to place a kiss on the back of it.

Seriousness lurked in the depths of her dark eyes as she apprised him. *Does he really mean that?* Then she chided herself. *What have you just sworn? To obey, serve, love and honour him in sickness and in health, forsaking all others, so long as we both shall live. At the least you could attempt to trust him.*

She nodded and answered, "I shall hurry then."

In mere seconds, she disappeared from the room, and the crush of humanity almost overwhelmed William. Being tall, he looked over the tops of the guests' heads and located Richard in one corner of the room. He was surrounded by Elizabeth's sisters and a few other young ladies. It seemed that he was occupied with answering a plethora of questions, one right after the other. Sighing, William realised that he could not count on his cousin to rescue him.

"I imagine that you could use a drink right about now."

Turning, he found Mr. Gardiner was holding out a small glass of brandy. Taking the proffered liquid, William finished it in one gulp. "Thank you."

William had been pleasantly surprised to meet Elizabeth's aunt and uncle upon his return to Longbourn. Edward Gardiner acted every inch the gentleman and could carry on an intelligent conversation regarding the pressing issues of the day, be it business or politics, while his wife was everything lovely and genteel.

"You are welcome. I remember that I once needed a brandy whilst I stood in the receiving line at my own wedding," Elizabeth's uncle chuckled, "but no one thought to fetch me one."

"I am glad that you thought of it," William replied. Then he sighed heavily. "I had no idea that our small wedding would attract such a crowd."

Gardiner chuckled anew. "My sister would never let Elizabeth marry so illustrious a person as yourself without the entire county being invited to witness the ceremony. She relishes being known as the most excellent hostess in all of Hertfordshire. With you to put on display, it was everything she could have ever wished for!"

William tried to smile. "I am happy to have pleased one of the Bennets."

With that pronouncement, Edward Gardiner studied his new nephew sombrely. "I believe you pleased Elizabeth's father as well. He had only good things to say about you." Gardiner looked around to see that several people were listening to their every word. "Would you consider accompanying me to the terrace? I did not have opportunity to speak with you in private last evening."

"Certainly."

Though not prepared for another *talk*, William was keen to breathe some fresh air and escape the stares of the Bennets' neighbours.

Elizabeth's Room

As she unbuttoned her dress, Madeline Gardiner studied her petite niece. Having closed her eyes while waiting for the buttons to be unfastened, Elizabeth looked almost childlike in her innocence and considering the circumstances of her marriage, Madeline's heart went out to her. On several occasions, she had tried to have *this* talk, but Fanny Bennet had intruded. Nonetheless, she had no intention of allowing Elizabeth to face her wedding night ignorant of what to expect, so she had taken advantage of this opportunity.

"Lizzy, has your mother talked to you of what to expect on your wedding night?"

Elizabeth's face flushed as her eyes flew open and she nodded mutely.

"Was it enlightening?"

"Mama tried, but her thoughts were disjointed, and neither Jane nor I could make much sense of it."

Making a mental note to speak to Jane too, Mrs. Gardiner asked, "Do you mind telling me what she said?"

Swallowing hard, Elizabeth began. "Wealthy men such as Mr. Darcy and Mr. Bingley usually take mistresses who cater to their baser instincts. So we had only to worry about pleasing them for a short while after we marry."

"Preposterous! Not every great man takes a mistress. What else did she say?"

"On the wedding night, he will come to our bed and most likely remove our gowns. We are to lie still no matter what he chooses to do and not make a sound. Once he is finished, he will quickly remove himself to his own bedroom, but, she cautioned that there are a few men who are not so easily satisfied. Those may stay until completely sated—which could take several attempts."

"Is there more?"

"Mama said that he would visit our bed until we became with child and then leave us until the child is born. If the child is the heir, he would likely trouble us no longer, so it is important to have a son on the first attempt."

Seeing the confusion in Elizabeth's expression, Mrs. Gardiner pulled her niece into her arms, hugging her as she explained. "I fear your mother's advice may be what she heard from her mother. Perhaps in a marriage of convenience those things might happen, but it certainly does not apply where there is mutual affection and caring partners. And I can tell that Mr. Darcy cares for you. It is evident in his eyes whenever he looks at you."

"What if I do not yet care for him as I should?"

She took both of Elizabeth's hands and looked into her eyes. "If you will focus on fulfilling his needs as a wife, you will fall in love with him. I promise."

A faint smile graced her niece's lips. "You make it sound so simple."

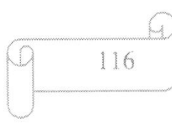

"It is simple, I assure you. Edward and I have mutual affection and the moments we spend as husband and wife are something that we both look forward to and cherish."

Elizabeth looked puzzled. "Then if Mama is wrong, what can I expect?"

"I imagine that you have found the illustrated book hidden on the top shelf of your father's library."

"How did you—" Lizzy sputtered, stopping at her aunt's chuckle.

"I was not certain he had one until now," Mrs. Gardiner admitted. "Almost every gentleman has a copy in his library; at least, that is what Edward said when I found his copy in ours."

"I confess that when I looked at the illustrations, I wondered if the drawings only meant to titillate."

"Edward assures me that the book has often been passed down from father to son in order to instruct the next generation in methods of pleasing a spouse." She lifted Elizabeth's chin so their eyes met. "I can say truthfully that except for a little pain when you are together the first time, there is nothing to fret over, and the pain is quickly forgotten in the pleasure that follows."

"Then I shall trust your advice and try not to worry. Please speak to Jane as well for I am certain she is just as confused. And thank you for relieving my mind. At least I am no longer dreading tonight."

"I am glad." Having worked to get Elizabeth out of her wedding gown and into her travelling clothes the entire time they were conversing, Mrs. Gardiner stood back to admire her handiwork. "I know that I have seen this lovely gown before, but somehow I cannot place it."

"Hill had just changed the colour of the trim from green to blue the week before Mr. Darcy—*Will* offered for me."

"Yes, that is it! I remember the green. It looks almost new now."

"It is passable and, in any event, it and a few others will have to suffice until I can order more clothes. Papa has given me several pounds to do so once we reach London."

"Have your bags all been packed?"

"There is only one," she giggled. "Everything decent to wear in proper society fit into one piece of luggage, which, believe me, is not full."

"How good to hear you teasing, Lizzy! Laughter will see you through so many difficulties. I pray that you never lose your sense of humour. Just remember that you are a pearl in a sea of sand."

Preparing to return to the breakfast, Elizabeth stopped to examine herself in the large standing mirror. "Let us hope my husband sees the pearl."

Satisfied with how their talk had gone, Mrs. Gardiner led her beautiful niece back down the stairs to the celebration, praying that Edward had time to speak to Mr. Darcy.

On the terrace

"I hope you do not think me presumptuous in speaking to you on your wedding day."

"Not at all," William said, though he was unsure what to expect.

"I asked Elizabeth's father if your father was still living, and when I learned that he had died years ago, I thought I should, at the least, do what another man did for me and offer you my counsel." At William's raised brows, he chuckled. "Not that you may want my counsel. However, as a married man of nearly fifteen years and because Elizabeth is like my own daughter, I felt I must offer. I know the value of having someone experienced in marriage to confide in when questions arise. And they will."

William was listening, so he continued.

"You and I have much in common." Gardiner hastened to add, "Oh, not in wealth or station, but my father died when I was but one and twenty, and a year before his death I assumed management of the importing business that he had founded. In fact, I did not marry until I was almost thirty because I would not offer for Madeline until I was certain the business would support a wife and a family.

"Fortunately, when we wed I gained a wonderful father in the bargain. Mr. Gavin was not only a very kind gentleman, but a wise one as well. He treated me as though I were his own son and encouraged me to confide in him when difficulties arose that I could not manage on my own. I believe the success of my marriage is partly attributable to him.

"And in that spirit, since you have not known Lizzy very long, I would like to share a few things about her in hopes of creating a better understanding between the two of you."

William's ears perked up. "I welcome anything you care to tell me."

"Elizabeth has one attribute of which few women can boast. She is without guile. While everyone else may rush to tell you what they believe you wish to hear, you can count on her to be truthful—oft times painfully so."

William smiled. "That was the main thing about Elizabeth that captured my attention when we first met. Most of the women I have known agree with whatever I say. They hold no opinions of their own."

"Oh, you do not have to worry about that with Lizzy. Tribute does not come easily for her, having learned to be analytical at her father's knee. Sadly, trust does not come easily either. To be brutally honest, if one cannot trust one's father to provide adequately for their future, how does one trust a husband?"

"I can see how that might be the case."

"Just have patience with her. Give her time to adapt to your society; that is all I ask, for I know she shall surprise you."

"You have my word that I shall be patient. And I intend to keep every promise I have made to her, before man and God. She shall never have occasion to doubt my constancy."

"I am glad to hear it." He held out his hand and William shook it. "Welcome to the family, Mr. Darcy."

"Fitzwilliam," urged William.

Before Mr. Gardiner could answer, the door flew open and the noise of the congregants inside spilled onto the terrace like a bucket of cold water, along with Mrs. Bennet.

"Oh, Mr. Darcy, there you are!" Mrs. Bennet sputtered, grabbing his arm as she threw a glare in Edward Gardiner's direction. "You simply must come inside. The guests are asking about you! And I cannot allow you to leave until you have sampled the fare that I spent hours planning. Lizzy has already changed into her travelling clothes, but now she is refusing to take a bite of anything. Surely you can convince her to eat something before you leave. How will she ever travel all the way to London on an empty stomach? Why, she shall faint of hunger if… "

With that, the matron of Longbourn pulled Mr. Darcy back into the madness that was now Longbourn, leaving her brother shaking his head sympathetically.

I wish you all the patience in the word, my boy, all the patience in the world.

On the road to London
In Darcy's Coach

William pulled back the curtain at the window to look at his cousin. Richard was returning to London, too, but he was riding alongside on his red stallion, refusing to intrude on the newlyweds by sharing their coach. Since the colonel was a little ahead of the vehicle at present, William let the curtain fall back into place and withdrew his pocket watch. Flipping the case open, he noted that they would be in Town in another hour. Glancing at Elizabeth, he saw that her eyes were still closed and her breathing was shallow and steady. He smiled.

It would have been no bother for Richard to travel inside. He might even have provided some company.

Elizabeth had fought sleep at first, but eventually was lulled into it by the sway of the vehicle. Deeply disappointed that she insisted on sitting on the seat opposite him, in time William came to realise that the choice provided him with the perfect view from which to watch his wife. *His wife.* The thought made his heart glad, and he slid to the middle of the coach in order to see her better.

Rejecting his suggestion that she lie down, she was still sitting upright, though with each rut in the road she slid further down in the cushion. The corners of his lips lifted when her nose twitched—the result of some feathers her mother had insisted on sticking in the top of her bonnet. That monstrosity now sat lopsided atop a few items in her lap—the long thin feathers touching her nose whenever the coach pitched. He considered moving the offending item but feared waking her. After all, Elizabeth had declined his earlier offer to place it on the seat beside him.

Though he did not wish to dwell on it, the question that had troubled him since his conversation with Mr. Gardiner came to mind again. If Elizabeth did not trust easily, then would it not be better to defer consummating their marriage until she trusted him? Surely it would assure a better start to their marriage if she came to his bed of her own volition. A greater part of him wanted simply to ignore the subject. After all, he had waited years to enjoy connubial bliss, so why not assert his rights as a married man? Recalling the teasing that ensued at White's the moment a newly married man entered the door, his face burned. If any of his acquaintances ever suspected that he considered delaying consummating his marriage, he would be laughed out of Town, if not accused of favouring men.

Sighing, he studied Elizabeth even more closely. The shawl she had wrapped around her had begun to slip, exposing the soft ivory skin of her décolletage. It did not help that her travelling gown was cut much lower than her usual gowns, and her pert breasts beckoned him like a siren. Instantly, his body reacted, and his heart began to pound. Blood rushed through his veins so quickly that the thrumming in his ears was deafening. The temperature in the coach became unbearable and, swallowing hard, he forced a finger under the knot of his cravat in hopes of loosening it. He wondered if Elizabeth would be shocked to wake and find he had removed it altogether. Dismissing that notion, he pushed back the curtain and opened the window wider. As he did, Richard noticed and smirked, touching the brim of his hat in a salute. A little perturbed that his cousin had likely guessed why he needed more air, William nodded curtly. Not easily dismissed, the colonel guided his horse closer to the coach.

"What is the matter, Darcy?" he asked, leaning so low that William thought he might fall from the saddle in order to keep the postillions from hearing what he said next. "If things get too hot in there, you can always ride with me!"

Discomfited, William jerked the curtain closed to the sound of his cousin's laughter.

Laugh all you want, Cousin! For when we get to London, I shall have the upper hand. You forget that you reside at Darcy House by my good will.

London
Matlock House

Lady Matlock hurried down the grand staircase as quickly as she dared in order to comply with her husband's wishes, for a countess never ran. Nonetheless, the summons to Edward's study had been as fear-provoking as it was curt. *Come at once!*

In over thirty years of marriage, he had never interrupted her when she was entertaining in her private parlour. Most especially, he should not have today, knowing that her guest was one of the ruling members of the *ton* and someone she was counting on to ease Georgiana's entrance into society— Countess Esterházy. [8] That august lady now waited upstairs while she rushed to obey his directive, and as she did, Lady Matlock's mind flew wildly from one presumed disaster to another. Edgar had been present this morning when they broke their fast, so most likely he was well, but her younger son was another matter entirely. Had something happened to Richard? Given his current assignment for the army and his propensity for accidents, she worried for his safety, for between their sons, Richard had always been the one who required a bandage, if not stitches, every so often.

Suddenly, she was standing outside the room she never entered except by invitation. A footman watched her sombrely, awaiting her command. Lady Matlock took a deep breath and straightened to her full height—all five feet and four inches of it. *I refuse to fall apart while there is company in the house.* Nodding, she watched the servant knock on the door.

A disembodied voice called, "Come!"

The footman opened the door, and she stepped inside. Noting that Edward was red in the face and standing, not sitting, behind his desk, she knew straightaway that he was angry. However, almost immediately a diminutive man in an ill-fitting coat who had been seated began to stand. The smile on his face led her to conclude that he was quite pleased with himself. Convinced that he was of no import, she ignored him and addressed her husband.

"To what do I owe this summons? I am certain that you are aware that I have company awaiting me, even as we speak."

"Blast your company!" the earl bellowed, slamming his hand against the wall and causing a picture to tilt precariously. He rubbed his fist. "And for heaven's sake, sit down, Collins!"

The now-trembling guest sat down, nervously glancing between the two.

The earl's gaze returned to his wife. "This is Mr. Collins, Catherine's new vicar. He has brought grave news... grave news indeed."

The countess' heart stopped to realise that a man of the cloth was bearing bad news. She asked, "Is it Richard?"

"What? Richard?" the earl sputtered. "No, no! It is Darcy!"

She sank down in a nearby chair, stunned. Though they did not always agree, Fitzwilliam was like one of her own children. "He is dead," she said woodenly.

"Dead? What gave you that silly notion? No, it is far worse! Collins came to inform me that my nephew is slated to marry some nobody from Hertfordshire! Despite having no confidence in his account, *The Morning Post*[9] was on the corner of my desk, so I opened it to the society pages to find the announcement was made this very morning— in bold print no less!"

With that declaration, he slid the paper across the desk. Confused, Lady Matlock picked it up and read the offending item. Then she eyed the vicar. "How would you have known of this before the announcement?"

Lord Matlock answered in his stead. "Collins is heir to a small estate in Hertfordshire called Longbourn, where this fortune hunter resides. He tells me that that little chit has no connections and, worst of all, no dowry to speak of!"

When the truth of the matter finally became clear, Lady Matlock became light-headed with relief. Her face brightened as she whispered, "He is not dead, only married."

"My Lord, woman! You act as though it is a good thing! It would be better had he died!"

"You cannot mean that."

"My nephew has not only ruined himself, but our dear Georgiana in the bargain. Her chances for a good match have been lessened considerably, if not destroyed. And we shall all be tainted by the scandal that is sure to follow."

Mr. Collins nodded furiously all while the earl spoke, then suddenly interjected, "I knew that as head of the family you would want to know immediately, and since it would take much longer to reach Kent to advise my noble—"

"SILENCE!" the earl bellowed. Collins' face drained of all colour. "Now, tell my wife what you told me."

The vicar complied, though his voice quivered. When he finished, the silence in the room was deafening. The earl had taken his seat as Collins related the tale once again and was now rubbing his chin with one hand and staring into space. This was a posture Lady Matlock had seen regularly over the years—whenever her husband was about to force his will on others. The countess decided she must be the voice of reason.

"Mr. Collins, I am sorry that you must return to Hunsford immediately."

Comprehending the command hidden in the politeness, Collins stood and picked up a satchel lying on the floor. He bowed quickly towards Lord Matlock and then the countess.

"If you will excuse me, I must take my leave."

Neither Matlock replied as he headed to the door. However, just as he touched the doorknob, the earl declared, "You WILL keep this information to yourself, Mr. Collins."

Collins turned around, stricken with fear. "But... but what of Lady Catherine?"

"I shall inform my sister WHEN I decide."

Collins swallowed hard. "Her ladyship will be livid if she learns that I knew and did not tell her."

"She shall learn of Darcy's folly soon enough; however, I will not have you hastening it along. I cannot deal with my nephew and Catherine at the same time! Your involvement will only become known if you disregard my order."

The earl stood, his eyes narrowing as he leaned across his desk and braced himself on his out-stretched fingers. "And believe me—that would be a very foolish thing for a man of your station to do."

The warning could not have been clearer, and the vicar's knees began to knock. "Of... of course, Lord Matlock. Lady Catherine will not hear a word of it from me."

As swiftly as possible, Mr. Collins quit the room and then practically ran from the house. It was not until the large front door closed solidly behind him that he let go of the breath he had been holding. Drained, he stepped away from the door, leaned against the wall and let his head fall back. How had it all gone so awry? Though he had succeeded in informing Mr. Darcy's uncle of the disaster, he would not be allowed to tell Lady Catherine, and that could cost him his employment. Sighing, he pushed away from the house and rushed down the steps. There was nothing to do but to return to Hunsford straightaway and pretend he knew nothing of Darcy's wedding.

I shall simply tell Lady Catherine that I never returned to Longbourn! Yes, that is it! I was too busy to stop by the Bennets' household on my way back to

London, and I never got the chance to ask if anyone had seen Mr. Darcy.

Relived that he had thought of a plan, he hurried towards the nearest coach stop to board a vehicle to Kent. After all, there was a sermon to prepare for Sunday and likely a list lying on his kitchen table. Lady Catherine believed in keeping track of things that needed doing, just in case he should forget. She was very thoughtful in that way.

※

Meanwhile, in the earl's study, Lord Matlock paced the room without saying a word. His wife knew this was never a good omen; thus, she tried to appeal to her husband's more rational side.

"Edward, we must appear to support Fitzwilliam, otherwise your prediction will come true—whatever gossip is bandied about will turn into a greater scandal if it appears that our family has turned against him."

"Humph!" Edward huffed. "I *should* cut him off from the family."

"May I make a suggestion?" Lady Matlock ventured. The earl nodded. "Since Countess Esterházy is here, I will disclose to her what has happened, being sure to emphasise that Fitzwilliam met this young woman only a few weeks ago. I will add that he confessed to being so besotted that he could not wait to marry her. The *ton* is more forgiving if a marriage appears to be a love match."

The earl whirled around. "A love match, woman? He had to have been entrapped!"

"You are not ignorant of the number of fortune hunters Fitzwilliam has thwarted. Do you see him blithely falling into a country girl's snare? I do not. If he is in love with her, all you will accomplish is to alienate him. We must act wisely."

"It appears Darcy has schemed behind my back, and I have no doubt that Richard knows and supports him wholeheartedly!"

"You should not criticize our son without the facts."

"The fact is that Richard and Darcy defy me as a team, which makes each of them bolder. Nevertheless, I shall bring the full force of the family to bear on both if I feel it necessary. Obviously, the woman's character will speak for itself. But, mark my words; I will not sanction a marriage of unequals."

"Oh, Edward! Must you be so dramatic? If Fitzwilliam is married, I have no doubt that she is proper, even if she is not wealthy."

He sniffed. "No one is truly proper without wealth."

"I shall not belabour that point, as we shall never agree," Lady Matlock sighed. "Now, we must decide who shall tell Georgiana."

"I am of the opinion—"

"Good heavens!" the countess interrupted. "I completely forgot about the ball! This will be devastating for Lady Susan. Fitzwilliam was to be her escort."

"Lady Susan is fully grown, and I have no doubt that she will survive. My fear is what Georgiana will do when she learns of her brother's folly. As I do not cope well with crying young ladies, I will leave the telling to you."

"As you wish. Now, I must return to my guest before she decides I have disappeared entirely. After our talk, I am certain she will leave in order to share the news with others. At that point, I shall seek out our niece and explain what has happened. While I am occupied, try not to do anything without speaking to me first. You know how irrational you become when you are angry."

"I am never irrational, Evelyn. You simply do not understand my motives because the future of the entire family rests on my shoulders and not yours."

"Things are not as they were when your father was earl, my dear. Today many are accepted into our society who are only one generation removed from trade. And peers are marrying whoever they wish, even their mistresses."

"Still, it is not proper."

Lady Matlock shook her head slowly. "I fear for your sanity if you persist in keeping to the old order."

The earl did not reply but proceeded to pour himself a glass of brandy. Lady Matlock could not wait on his concurrence, however, so she left the room, heading in the direction of her parlour. Entering, she found Countess Esterházy gazing at Hyde Park from the window, holding a cup of tepid tea in her hand.

"Forgive me for taking so long. I have called for a fresh pot of tea and a new tray of cakes, as I have some wonderful news that I simply must share or I shall die! It concerns my nephew, Fitzwilliam Darcy."

Her enthusiasm was palpable, and Countess Esterházy hurried to sit back down. Instantly, the tall, dark and handsome Mr. Darcy came to her mind. A twinge of regret crossed the lady's face as she replied, "I remember your nephew fondly."

In truth, she had been infatuated with that gentleman since they met at one of Lady Matlock's balls several years before. As a rule, she had no difficulty seducing vibrant young men, but Mr. Darcy had proved to be the exception. Even now, she recalled drowning in his light blue eyes the night he politely declined her invitation to become her next lover.

"I shall be pleased to hear whatever you wish to share."

"Wonderful! For I am bursting to tell it."

Chapter 12

London
Darcy House

As William's coach rolled through London just after noon, a downpour began in earnest. It pleased him greatly, for the rain meant that there would be fewer people on the streets to notice the crest on the side of the coach. The only unfortunate aspect of the weather was the fact that Richard was getting wet astride his stallion. He considered asking his cousin to join him inside the coach, but dismissed that idea.

Serves him right for teasing me! Besides, he has on his greatcoat, so he will not be too soaked.

In fact, by the time the worst of the storm had begun, the vehicle was nearing the back drive of his townhouse, so he leaned across to wake Elizabeth. At his touch, she sat straight up, her eyes as wide as a young deer he had once found in the woods. He was troubled to see the same fear in them.

"Elizabeth, there is nothing amiss. We have arrived at Darcy House. It is raining, so you may want to don your bonnet though a footman should appear with an umbrella as soon as the steps are lowered."

He accompanied this bit of advice with a wide smile, hoping to reassure her, but she still appeared uncertain. Tugging her shawl so that it once more covered her shoulders, she dismissed the bonnet, tossing it aside. Then she clasped her reticule, a book and a small satchel that she had held possessively the entire trip.

"You may leave the bag," William urged. "The servants will bring everything inside."

"I prefer to keep it with me."

Though his brow knit in question, William nodded. "As you wish."

When the coach halted, William descended the steps first and then turned to hand her out. As soon as Elizabeth's feet were on the ground, however, she walked briskly up the gravel path towards the door with the servant hurrying alongside, trying to shield her from the rain. Unfortunately, at one point there was a place where the downpour had washed away most of the gravel, creating a stream of water not easily crossed by one so petite. Seeing her hesitation, William, who was right behind, instantly swept her into his arms without so much as a warning and carried her over the water and into the house.

Elizabeth had no time to object, and, as a result, clung to him in confusion. Though she would never admit it, she found the experience exhilarating. He had always cut a handsome figure, with his broad shoulders and narrow waist, and, despite her best efforts, she had come to admire his lean frame. But now, with arms akin to steel bands around her and the hard muscles of his chest rippling beneath the hand that rested there, something unexpected transpired—an odd tingling sensation began. Starting at her toes, it raced upward to the pit of her stomach. Desires she had never experienced before, along with thoughts of being in those arms tonight, made her feel faint.

However, her imaginings ended brusquely when William set her on her feet inside the house. As she smoothed her skirts, feigning calmness she did not feel, Elizabeth stole a glance at her husband. Had he experienced the same emotions? She could detect no discomfiture in his manner; thus, she concluded that he had not. As she pondered all this, a cry came from behind, and she turned to see an older couple rushing towards them. A woman she assumed was the housekeeper spoke first.

"Oh, Mr. Darcy, we were expecting you and Mrs. Darcy to come in the front door! All the servants are eager to greet you and it will only take a moment to assemble them."

She offered a restrained smile to Elizabeth, almost as though she was not quite sure whether she approved of her or not. The gentleman was not smiling but instead studied her closely. William made the introductions.

"Mrs. Darcy, allow me to introduce Mr. and Mrs. Barnes. They have served my family as butler and housekeeper for longer than I have been alive." The housekeeper bobbed a curtsey while her husband bowed.

Elizabeth smiled warmly. "I am pleased to meet you. I imagine that you know many tales of my husband's childhood that he would rather forget. Mayhap that information will be useful to me in the future."

Her reply caused both servants to relax. Instantly, William took her arm, intending to escort her to the front of the house. "My wife will meet the other servants later. She is tired and would like to rest. Barnes, will you see to the luggage?"

As the butler passed them on his way to supervise the unloading of the coach, Elizabeth scowled at William. He did not notice.

How would he know if I am tired? He has not asked! I slept most of the way from Longbourn, so I am certainly rested enough to greet the servants.

Biting her lip in a bid not to contradict her new husband, especially in front of the servants, she concentrated on matching his long stride as he walked towards the front of the house. Elizabeth could not help but notice how enormous the house was as they passed one room after another. From what little she could see, it was very elegant and much more richly furnished than even Netherfield. Almost in a trance at the novelty of it all, Elizabeth barely attended to the conversation occurring between her husband and the housekeeper once they reached the stately foyer. For she was turning in a circle, admiring the paintings, tapestries and mirrors that covered the walls two stories high, before her attention was caught by the stained glass skylight in the ceiling. Mesmerised by its beauty, only the mention of her name penetrated her consciousness and brought her back to the present.

"Tell her that will not do! Indeed, Madam Bouvier needs to be here first thing tomorrow, as I have Mr. Curry scheduled directly afterward to make his sketches. Stress that her commission will be substantial, as Mrs. Darcy will need an *entire* wardrobe, something for every season, including slippers to match her gowns and boots for the rugged terrain in Derbyshire, so I expect her to bring the shoemaker, too. It is my wish that a good many clothes be completed right away; the others can be shipped when finished. Assure her that, in the event she needs to hire more seamstresses, I will pay extra to have the items expedited."

"Yes, sir. And, I managed to locate a lady's maid," Mrs. Barnes stated. "She should be here tomorrow."

"Excellent!" William responded. "No doubt my wife will be pleased."

My wife! He talks as if I am not standing two feet away! Her ire rose along with his overbearing attitude and Elizabeth felt her face turn crimson. Unfortunately, William did notice that.

"Are you well, my dear?" Without waiting for an answer, he addressed Mrs. Barnes, "A headache powder for my wife, please. We are off to the mistress' suite. You may bring it there, along with some strong tea. That should make her feel better. Are the baths ready?"

"They shall be shortly, Mr. Darcy. We have the water hot, but were waiting until you arrived to bring it up."

William began leading Elizabeth up the stairs. "Come, I shall show you to your suite." Remembering something else, he called over his shoulder, "Please inform me when the baths are ready. And we shall dine at eight."

As they disappeared out of sight, the housekeeper heard a chuckle and turned to see Richard staring at the top of the stairs. She pressed her lips together to keep from smiling.

"Darcy seems eager to show his bride the bedroom." Seeing Mrs. Barnes blush, he added, "Well, if my cousin should ask, though I imagine he will not, I am off to stay at Bingley's house for a time. He was kind enough to offer his hospitality and I accepted. Tell my cousin he can find me there if he needs me."

"Your room is ready, Colonel Fitzwilliam, and Cook has prepared your favourite roasted lamb for dinner," she offered. "Will you not at least wait until you have eaten to leave? After all, the master assumed you would be staying here."

"You have talked me into staying for dinner, Mrs. Barnes. But only because I am famished and Mrs. Colton's lamb is the best in England." Richard started up the stairs and then stopped to ask, "Is there hot water enough for me?"

"Of course," she replied. "We could never forget about you."

With a big smile, Richard turned and practically ran up the stairs, disappearing as quickly as the Darcys had before him. Mrs. Barnes looked about to find she was all alone. Consequently, as she headed to the kitchen to inform Mrs. Colton when dinner was expected, she could not help but contemplate her new mistress.

Wait until I tell Mrs. Colton! Mrs. Darcy is nothing like we envisioned. Instead of being tall and willowy like Miss Darcy or Lady Susan, she is very shapely and petite. I imagined her hair to be the colour of corn silk and very straight, instead it is dark brown and curly. And it seems she uses none of the powders and rouges that are all the fashion, though her complexion looks flawless. If asked, I would not describe her as beautiful though she is certainly pretty. Perhaps the secret lies in those eyes—dark as coal, though they almost sparkle with fire at times.

She chuckled. *If I am not careful, I shall be as bewitched by the mistress as Mr. Darcy seems to be.* Then she smiled. *At least she does not act pretentious.*

Reaching the kitchen, she was disappointed to find it empty. Suddenly, her husband came down the servant's stairs from the upper floors, busily brushing water from his coat. He stopped when he caught sight of her.

"All of the luggage is inside and unpacked." Then out of the blue, he craned his neck to be sure that the room was clear of other servants and sidled up to her. "I will say this, Mrs. Barnes. The new Mrs. Darcy does not seem to have come from wealth. Everything she brought with her fit into one piece of luggage—other than the small satchel she carried herself. That was the extent of it."

Mrs. Barnes' brow knit. "She does not seem the type to marry a man for his fortune, nor does she seem to be with child. Nevertheless, I cannot form an opinion on why they married so abruptly with so little evidence. All we can do is act as though everything is well and pray that it truly is."

"I agree. We must trust that Mr. Darcy knows what he is about. But I hope that she is good to him, for he has had more than his share of heartaches."

A footman stuck his head in the door at that moment, informing them that the hot water was being carted upstairs. Sighing, Mrs. Barnes said, "I must supervise, or else they will soak all the floors with it."

"And I need to get out of these wet clothes."

Thus, each hurried in different directions, questions still swirling in their heads.

Matlock House
Georgiana's bedroom

The scene that unfolded when Lady Matlock informed her niece of Collins' news was nothing short of astonishing—though not in a good way. The countess was stunned to see her niece fly into a fit of rage and begin to pick up various items and throw them at the hearth. Costly vases and crystal met the same fate as less expensive figurines. Never had she witnessed someone of Georgiana's age act so childish and it was worrisome. For the first time, Lady Matlock wondered if she and Edward had been responsible for spoiling their niece for she knew that Fitzwilliam had not.

Having tried to reason with her to no avail, she was relieved when a maid interrupted the melee to say that Lady Susan had arrived. Georgiana insisted that her friend come upstairs immediately and she rushed into her arms the minute she appeared in the doorway. Without delay, she blurted out all the particulars of William's marriage, never considering how the news might affect her confidant. However, Lady Matlock noted that, oddly enough for someone who wished to be the next Mrs. Darcy, Susan took the news almost too well. And when she pulled Georgiana over to a settee to console her, the countess took the opportunity to leave them alone.

In the hallway outside, she leaned against the door, exhausted. *Edward and I must do something about Georgiana's temper. We must rein her in, or she will be out of control by the time she is twenty!*

She then hurried in the direction of the grand staircase. *I would give my favourite slippers for one of Mrs. Soames' headache powders this very minute!*

Now that her friend was here, Georgiana's anger escalated even more. "I will not have it!" she declared, standing and stomping her foot. "He cannot marry some nobody, ruin my chances for a good match and expect me to be happy for him. I hate him, and I shall hate her as well!"

Lady Susan reached out for her hand. "Oh, dearest, you are handsome, and there will be no dearth of wealthy, refined gentlemen offering for you. After all, you are Lord Matlock's niece."

Georgiana brightened, pulling her handkerchief out of her pocket to blot her eyes. "Do you truly believe that?"

"I do. However, you must be very careful what you say and do at this point. If you insult your new sister and anger your brother, there will be no way for you to assist me. And I shall need your help now more than ever."

"How can I help you now? It is over and done with! Brother is married!"

"Yes, but it does not follow that he shall *always* be married. If I am ever to have him, I will need you to be my eyes and ears—to tell me what goes on between the two of them. And you must keep this a secret."

"Whatever do you mean?"

"Marriages do not always last, Georgiana. There are annulments and divorces—admittedly few and far between—but they do happen. If we can uncover some secret in her past that will make Fitzwilliam angry enough to divorce her—"

Georgiana's face brightened. "I… I had not thought of that!" Then she became serious. "But why would you still want to marry him after he has treated you so cruelly?"

"I had hoped to be married to your brother before revealing my reasons, but I suppose it is best that you know now, especially if you are to help me."

Reaching into her reticule, she brought out a small portrait. Regarding it, she smiled at the image before holding it out to Georgiana.

"I have never seen this likeness of Fitzwilliam before. How did you come by it?"

"That is not your brother."

"But, who—"

"That is my son. His name is William."

Georgiana gasped! "Brother is the father?" Lady Susan nodded. "But… but he would never…" Georgiana's voice trailed off as she studied the child's image.

"Do not judge him harshly, dear. When he and I... well, when our son was conceived, he was not sensible. In fact, Fitzwilliam was very drunk."

"And all these years he has berated Andrew for doing what he has done! He is nothing but a hypocrite!"

"I fear that Andrew's problems were the catalyst for your brother's state that night. You know in your heart that he would never have done such a thing had he been sober."

"What happened?"

"We were both at Lady Montclair's ball in London. I happened upon him in the garden and saw immediately that he was inebriated. I helped him back into the house by a side door, and we ended up in the library. One thing led to another. I recognised the very next day that he did not remember anything that had taken place. A week later he was off to Scotland."

"I remember when he toured Scotland," Georgiana murmured woodenly.

"Two months later I realised that I was pregnant. It would have been futile to try to locate your brother, as he planned to stay only one night at each location during his trip." As Georgiana regarded her sceptically, Susan added, "And, to be truthful, I knew he would not welcome the news. He always swore he would not marry until he was thirty. So, when Lord Hartley offered for me, I accepted."

"Let me tell Brother about his son! I am sure he will leave that woman at once to secure his heir."

"NO!" The force of Lady Susan's answer caused the younger woman to startle. "I mean, please do not. He could take my child away from me entirely. You know how the courts favour men."

"I had not thought of that."

"I shall keep our son hidden until his father is free again. Then I shall reveal the truth."

Georgiana continued to glance at the replica. "Did your husband not see the resemblance?"

"Yes. As William got older it was very noticeable. However, we had a frank talk about the past, and Fletcher told me that he did not hold it against me. That was just before... " Susan faked a small sniffle. "He was lost to me."

"Would you mind telling me how he died? I have always wondered, but I was afraid that it might make you sad to speak of it."

"Since we are friends, I will tell you. Once a year, we would travel to the coast. His family owns a home at Land's End in Cornwall that sits atop a cliff and overlooks the sea. We would stay there while he conducted business with his contacts in nearby villages." She stared into space as if reminiscing. "It is a beautiful place; we spent our honeymoon there."

She gave her friend a wan smile. "Unfortunately, William was ill, and I did not go with Fletcher on his last trip. According to his valet, my husband went for a ride one afternoon and never returned. The valet did recall hearing a gunshot earlier, but thought nothing of it, as Fletcher often shot birds for sport. When evening came, the valet went looking for him and found only his horse standing near the edge of the cliff. There was no sign of Fletcher. The local constable ruled that he was likely shot and then fell into the ocean, since his body was never found."

"How awful!"

"Yes, it was a most difficult time," she said, her voice breaking at just the right point. Then, just as quickly her mood improved. "Nonetheless, that is behind me now and I must make the most of what life has for me in the future."

"I agree. What role shall I play in order to be of service?" Georgiana made a face. "I do not think I can convince Brother, but *she* may be dull enough to believe I like her."

"No. You are correct. If you act overly welcoming, Fitzwilliam will suspect your motives, even if his wife does not. It would be better if you act reserved but accepting of her—as though you have no choice. Then as time goes on, you can pretend to warm to her."

"I shall give a performance worthy of the theatre!"

Lady Susan smiled. "I am sure you will. Just remember that no one can know of this. It is between the two of us."

"I understand completely."

"Good. Now what shall we do about your plans for the ball? Am I still to meet Fitzwilliam in the gazebo now that he is married?"

"Now more than ever!" Georgiana declared. "Only I shall make sure that his new bride, not my aunt, catches you kissing him. That should get their marriage off to a rocky start."

"I never knew you could be so cunning," Susan said teasingly.

"For some time, Fitzwilliam has forced me to rely on my own devices. It is time that he learned what has come of his cruelty."

It was not long afterward that Lady Susan left Georgiana, eager to be by herself. Shocked to hear of William's marriage, it was all she could do not to scream and throw things, just as Georgiana had done earlier. Yet, she could never let anyone see her desperation, least of all Lady Matlock.

I shall make him regret his decision, if he does not already. After all, she mused, *for Darcy to marry so quickly and to a woman of no consequence, it had to be coercion.* She stopped suddenly to study that thought. *Unquestionably, it was a compromise.*

By then she had reached the landing of the grand staircase and Lady Matlock was on her way up. At the sight of her, the countess spoke. "I was just coming to find you. Please forgive me for leaving you to console my niece alone, but I was having no luck with her and I thought your counsel might be just what she needed. I do hope she listened to you."

"No need to apologise, I assure you, my lady. I had a good talk with Georgiana and she agreed that she must accept her new sister for her brother's sake, as well as her own. I told her that no good would come from despising the woman Fitzwilliam chose to wed."

"I can hardly credit such wisdom in one so young!" The countess declared, her voice filled with admiration. "And to think that your heart was broken to hear the news, yet you consoled my niece and convinced her to be forgiving."

"When one has lost a husband, one grows up quickly. I would not recommend it as a way to mature, but Fletcher's death did make me a wiser person."

"Well said, my dear," Lady Matlock replied, reaching out to lay a comforting hand on Susan's arm. "And I am sure that your reintroduction to society will be successful, despite my nephew's newfound status. I shall have Edgar escort you to the ball instead, and I am confident that you shall charm the masses, just as you did in your first season."

"You remember my first season?" Susan asked. "I hardly remember it myself."

"Come, have a cup of tea before you leave, and I shall tell you all about it. Cook is preparing a new pot as we speak. Besides, if you are as weary as I from consoling Georgiana, you can use some strong tea."

Arm-in-arm, they came down the stairs and walked across the foyer to the parlour, chatting animatedly, even laughing occasionally. Meanwhile, the Earl of Matlock had exited his study to find his wife, and when he saw her talking to Lady Susan, he stopped short. He was not anxious to interrupt, lest he be brought into their conversation, so he went in another direction.

That is odd. I assumed Lady Susan would be inconsolable at the news of Darcy's marriage, as she seemed determined to have him this time around. But she seems completely unaffected. I shall never understand women!

With a huff of irritation, he walked towards the billiards room. It always helped to work out his frustrations with a cue stick.

⁂

Longbourn
The same day

Though the breakfast should have ended hours ago, Fanny Bennet was in her element and encouraged everyone to stay a while longer and have another bite to eat. Truth be known, there was an excess of food and drink still to be consumed, for she had spared no expense in an attempt to impress her new son and his cousin, not to mention the Bingleys. As a reward, she had the opportunity to brag to her heart's content about her new son and his wealth, as well as of all the fine things that her second daughter would have at her disposal as Mrs. Darcy. In actuality, she was reluctant for the whole thing to end.

Seeing the Bingleys leaving for Netherfield reminded Aunt Gardiner that she had not seen her oldest niece in quite some time. Concerned that Jane would miss Lizzy the most, she hoped to comfort her if she were distressed. She could not find Jane among the crowd, so, at length, she walked to the bedroom that her two eldest nieces always shared. Arriving at the door, she found it ajar and pushed it open a bit to peer inside. Jane was sitting in the window seat that overlooked the garden, so occupied with her thoughts that she did not hear her aunt enter the room.

Her niece's head swung around at the sound of her name, and Madeline

Gardiner discovered that Jane was weeping. Closing the door securely, she rushed to the window seat, pulling her niece into her arms. "What is the matter?"

Jane began to weep in earnest then and could barely speak for several minutes. Then she stuttered, "I... I cannot say. It is not one thing but many. So much has happened in so short a time."

"There, there," Mrs. Gardiner said, patting her back before reaching into her pocket for a handkerchief. After dabbing Jane's cheeks with it, she pressed it into her hand. "Calm down and begin with the first thing that is wrong."

Taking a ragged breath, Jane said, "I am going to miss Lizzy so much!" Drying her eyes with the handkerchief, she sniffled. "It is hard to think that we shall never share a room again or... or lie in bed talking of our hopes and dreams. Everything has changed forever."

Her aunt smiled knowingly. "Perhaps it will not be the same, but you and she are too close not to correspond regularly or to visit, so you may still share your hopes and dreams. Only now, they will include your husbands and, before long, babies."

"Babies," Jane repeated woodenly. "I still have not reconciled myself to Lizzy being married, so I cannot picture her as a mother. Not yet, anyway. And I hate to speak of it, but I worry for her happiness. That is another reason for my melancholy—she did not wish to marry Mr. Darcy." Her eyes implored her aunt. "Do you truly think she will be content with him?"

"I do." Madeline cupped Jane's face, smiling in a motherly fashion. "Edward is convinced that Mr. Darcy is a good man, and I know that he has an excellent reputation among my family in Lambton—throughout the county, for that matter. In addition, Mr. Bingley speaks well of his character. Do you not have faith in your own suitor's judgement?"

Jane nodded, forcing a wan smile. "Yes, I believe Char—I mean, Mr. Bingley's report."

"You may call him Charles when speaking to me. I know how close you are."

Jane nodded. "What I worry about most is that while Mr. Darcy might not be unkind to Lizzy, he may completely misunderstand her, for she is unique. You and I know that she can be brusque—she takes after Papa—but underneath has a very tender heart."

"I understand. We can only trust that both of them shall give the other the benefit of the doubt. If you will pray for that to happen, I shall, too. You know the Bible says that if 'two or more agree as touching any matter—'"

"It shall be done," Jane finished, smiling genuinely now. "I shall agree with you."

"Then it is sure to happen eventually! Now, while we are on the subject of marriage, have you and Mr. Bingley settled on a date? I know there has been no formal announcement, but it is clear that you and he have an understanding." Jane blushed, but did not refute her words. "Will there be enough time to bring you to London to shop for your trousseau in the proper manner, or will your engagement be as rushed as Lizzy's?"

The question made her niece giggle. "You know Mama will never agree to let me marry quickly, though I think Charles would like to follow his friend's example. She wishes to parade us all over the county and brag of his circumstances for at least six months, I think—perhaps even a year."

"But what of you? What do you want?"

"While I wish to marry him, I am in no rush to get married. All of the theatrics that have occurred since Andrew Darcy compromised Lizzy have put me off anything to do with weddings. I wish to calm down—to breathe again—before undertaking such an important step."

"You are sensible. But, of course, you were always the sensible one."

Jane could not help but smile at the compliment. "Lizzy says I am too nonchalant, that things do not ruffle me when they should."

"Maybe a little, but that is not necessarily a disadvantage. You look before you leap, while others—well, this entire debacle was a result of not thinking before leaping. God bless her, Lizzy has often been too apt to run headfirst into danger. Do you remember the time she decided to remove the hornet's nest from the apple tree in the garden?"

Jane laughed aloud. "Do I? I have never run so fast in my entire life! We could not go out of the house for days, fearing we would be stung."

"I know, for I was here!" Mrs. Gardiner pushed a hair from her niece's forehead. "It is good to see you smile again."

"Thank you for making me smile." Jane grew pensive. "Do you think the wedding has quelled what is being said about Lizzy and Andrew Darcy?"

"If the number who attended the wedding and packed into Longbourn to fete the bride and groom is any indication, it has already been forgotten."

Just then, the door flew open, banging against the wall behind. "Jane! Why are you up here chatting with your aunt when we have guests? Come down this minute and help me. And do not be slow about it."

Instantly, she was gone. Mrs. Gardiner winked at Jane as they stood up.

"Duty calls," Jane sighed.

"Remember. In no time at all you will be married and no longer subject to your mother's whims, if that is any consolation."

"I believe I shall miss even her whims when I am no longer here," Jane said pensively.

Aunt Gardiner patted her hand sympathetically. Then they quit the room and began to descend the stairs arm in arm.

Somewhere in the tumult below, Mrs. Bennet could be heard over the din, saying, "And to think! He has ten thousand a year and half of Derbyshire!"

Chapter 13

Darcy House
That evening

Having finished dressing for dinner, William decided to see if Elizabeth was dressed as well. Since she had no lady's maid as yet, he was not sure if she was alone or if the maid who had helped with her bath was still attending her.

Going to the door that connected his bedroom with the mistress' suite, he opened it cautiously, peering inside the sitting room that they shared. Not seeing Elizabeth there, he gingerly proceeded across to the door that led to her bedroom. Trying that knob, he found it unlocked, so he gave several loud raps upon it. Hearing no answer, once again he opened it cautiously only to find that she was not there either. Consequently, he crossed that room, stopping in the middle to make sure she was not on the balcony. Not seeing her outside, William continued to the door of her dressing room which, unexpectedly, had not been closed all the way.

From that vantage point, he could see Elizabeth standing in front of her dressing table, bent over at the waist, brushing her hair. She was tossing the thick, glossy locks to one side of her head, brushing them vigorously, then flipping them to the other side and repeating the deed. Her endeavours seemed to cause the curls to relax a bit in waves. Suddenly, she stood up straight, letting the ebony mass cascade down her shoulders and back. It was magnificent, reaching more than halfway down her back and shining like crystal. William was awestruck. And in that moment, he longed to feel those tresses soft against his skin more than he wished to breathe.

Elizabeth, totally unaware of his presence, then began to braid her hair. Apparently in too much of a hurry, she dropped one of the strands.

"Drat! I shall never finish," she said, stamping her foot in frustration.

"May I be of service?"

Elizabeth jumped, startled to hear Mr. Darcy's voice. Her hand flew to her heart as she turned to face him, completely forgetting that she was wearing only her chemise and a thin dressing gown. William's heart began to beat faster at the sight of her breasts straining against the diaphanous fabric, the dark centres easily recognisable. For a moment, he stared without thinking. Noting where his eyes were trained, Elizabeth crimsoned, crossing her arms over her chest. Instantly he began to speak, though his voice was unsteady.

"Please excuse me. I did not mean to startle you. I knocked on the door," he tilted his head towards the door he had entered, "but you must not have heard me."

"I… I did not," Elizabeth managed to say. "But it is no matter. It is your house, and you are free to come and go as you please."

"No. I should have made another attempt to alert you. After all, these are your rooms now and I should knock before entering."

She paused, seeming a bit confused. "That is very kind of you." Then she added, "Still, I am uncertain of *how* you might be of service."

"I have some experience in styling hair," he said confidently. As one of Elizabeth's eyebrows rose in question, he added, "With Georgiana's hair."

"Oh, I see, and what do you propose to do with my unruly curls?"

"I am very good at braiding in the French style," he answered triumphantly. "When my sister was very young, my mother was so ill that Georgiana had a French governess who helped with her care. She began to braid her hair in the custom of her country, which was more intricate than any braids I had ever seen. Often, I watched her, mesmerized by how she accomplished it. When she had to return to France, she taught me how to braid Georgiana's hair in the same manner."

"I am surprised that she taught you and not another maid."

"You have to understand the circumstances," he explained. "My sister is tender-headed and at the age of nine would not allow just anyone to brush her hair. She was used to my help, so I was the one she chose to master the technique. Besides, at that age, I was keen to give it a try, just to see if I could do it.

"I see. So now you fancy yourself an expert?"

"Not an expert! In fact, it has been years since I have attempted it, but I am willing to try my hand at it. The lady's maid that I asked Mrs. Barnes to engage will be here tomorrow, so you shall never have to put up with my skills again."

Elizabeth studied herself in the mirror, making a face at the image staring back. "I suppose it cannot look any worse."

William swept an arm towards a chair and she sat down. He took his place behind her, a little giddy at the thought of being able to touch her hair. As he began to gather the long locks in order to braid them, they were just as silky as he had imagined and unknowingly he released a sigh.

"Defeated already? Are you discouraged before you begin?"

Embarrassed that she had heard him, he mumbled, "I… I was just admiring your hair. It is beautiful."

She blushed, her eyes falling. "I need to have it cut, as it is getting too hard to manage without a maid."

"No!" William exclaimed. Seeing her look of surprise, he added less vehemently, "I meant to say that you shall have all the help you need very shortly. And, to be honest, I do not wish for you to cut your hair. I would be very disappointed if you did."

The corners of Elizabeth's mouth lifted slightly. "I shall keep that in mind."

Relieved, William proceeded to braid Elizabeth's hair in an intricate pattern that ended at her shoulders, leaving the rest loose. When he was done, he reached for a small mirror on the dresser and handed it to her. She stood and turned in order to examine his handiwork.

"You are hired to do my hair," she teased, which caused him to beam. "But I think I should fashion what you left undone into a bun. To wear it loose is more the fashion for young girls."

"My wife shall wear her hair as she wishes or as I wish. And, for now, I wish it to be down so that I can admire it."

"Then would you will be so kind as to call a maid to help me dress." She saw the gleam in his eye. "Do not tell me that you have experience as a lady's maid."

"What can I say? My mother was ill so much after Georgiana was born that I often looked after her. It was nothing for me to button or unbutton a gown."

Her eyebrow rose higher as her eyes twinkled. "I would have liked to have seen how you handle stays. But, unfortunately, they have gone out of favour with the new styles."

"Alas, I have no experience with stays. By the time Georgiana was a young woman, she had conceded to having a lady's maid do her hair and help her dress." His sky-blue eyes twinkled even more brightly as he struggled not to smile. "However, I am willing to learn anything that may be useful to you. That is, if you wish it."

Elizabeth's smile vanished. William immediately noticed the change and guessed the reason for her reluctance.

"Elizabeth, there is something that I have wished to say to you since we left Longbourn." She tilted her head questioningly. "I do not want you to feel that you must... that we must... " As he searched for the right words, her wide, dark eyes blinked continuously, and he struggled not to get lost in them.

"I do not want you to think that I do not desire you... as my wife. I do—more than you shall ever know. But I am willing... " He swallowed hard, forcing himself to continue. "I am willing to wait until you decide that you are ready to consummate our marriage... if that will ease your mind."

Instantly, her eyes filled with tears, and she flew into his embrace. She hugged him, barely managing not to cry. Delighting in the feel of her body next to his, his arms instinctively tightened and for a moment he regretted ever making the offer. He began to pray that she might refuse his offer, but it was not to be; for just as quickly as she had embraced him, she pushed away.

"I am so grateful for your understanding, and you are correct—it will ease my mind... very much."

Nearly overcome with desire, he could barely reply. "Then it is settled. I shall wait until you come to me. And until then, I think it best that we maintain separate bedrooms."

That remark was confusing to Elizabeth, for her parents had always kept separate bedrooms and, according to her mother, that was the way of all married couples. So she made a mental note to ask her Aunt Gardiner about it, for she was not about to broach the subject with William—especially since he had been so generous.

"I agree," she whispered. Taking a deep breath, she pasted on a smile. "Now, if you would ring for a maid so that I may finish dressing, I am sure that your cousin is wondering what has become of us. He must be starved."

The mention of Richard lightened the mood. "I imagine my cousin could not care less where I am, and he never starves, I can assure you of that. But you are correct, for most likely he is already at the table. I shall ring for a maid and wait in the hall until you are ready, Elizabeth."

Immediately William was out the door, closing it quietly behind him; however, Elizabeth had seen his smile disappear the moment he turned away from her, his disappointment palpable.

Clearly he wished for me to object. After all, what man would not want to consummate his marriage on his wedding night? She shrugged guiltily. *But I cannot pretend that I am not relieved to have more time to know him better.*

With that confession, she hurried to the bedroom that was now hers, though she did not feel comfortable claiming it. Shaking off her misgivings, Elizabeth entered the closet to find the few gowns that she had brought from Meryton hanging neatly in a row. They looked pitiful in the cavernous space, and she stepped forward to study each critically, convinced that none would do for her first dinner as mistress. Nonetheless, she set aside her reservations.

After all, she mused, *I cannot go downstairs in my chemise.*

That thought made her giggle just as she heard the bedroom door open and close. Assuming a more appropriate expression, she stepped out of the closet to greet the maid. The servant was young and pretty, with hair so light it was almost white. She curtseyed at the sight of Elizabeth.

"I am Maggie, Mrs. Darcy. Mrs. Barnes sent me to assist you."

Elizabeth motioned to the closet. "Thank you, Maggie. If you would be so kind as to help me into my green gown, I shall join my husband for dinner."

The gown in question was of plain white muslin, featuring a light green bodice and sleeves, as well as a matching border at the hem. Other than being serviceable, there was nothing to recommend it. Clearly the maid was surprised that it was not of better quality, for her face fell as she brought it from the closet into the light.

"I shall be happy to," she managed to murmur. Before long Maggie was fastening the buttons, though she kept stealing glances at her new mistress in a large mirror that stood in one corner of the room. "There, all finished," she announced sombrely. "Do you wish me to do anything else?"

"No, thank you. You are free to go."

The young maid bobbed another quick curtsey and left.

Opening the door to the hallway, Maggie found that Mr. Darcy was still leaning against the door directly across from his wife's bedroom, just as he had been when she came up. His head was down, as if deep in thought, and one of his legs was bent, with an expensive boot propped against the doorframe. He looked so very dashing that she could not help but smile as she passed him, though he never looked up. Curious, she hurried to the landing at the top of the grand staircase, turned the corner and then peeked back down the hall to see how he would react when his wife came out. She did not have to wait long, for in a moment the door opened and she appeared. Mr. Darcy was instantly at her side. Though she could not hear what was being said, the look on his face as he gazed at his bride was unmistakable.

Well, it was evidently a love match on his part! I suppose there is no accounting for taste.

Looking around to make sure no one was watching, she ran towards the steps that led to the kitchen, for it would not do to let Mrs. Barnes see her spying on the Darcys. She knew how particular the housekeeper was about servants keeping their mouths and eyes shut when it came to their employer.

Downstairs
The Dining Room

Colonel Fitzwilliam had been in the dining room for some time before William and Elizabeth appeared. Though one could not tell, he had lifted the silver covers from the serving dishes to see what Cook had prepared and, being hungry, pinched a roll, dipped it into the gravy that surrounded a pheasant, and finished it off in a few short bites. Quite pleased with having gotten away with that manoeuvre, he justified his actions because his hosts were late for dinner.

After all, they make me wait while they are upstairs doing... Richard paused to consider what they might be doing. A wide grin followed. *Whatever they do! But I cannot live on love! Hence, I must eat at regular—*

"Have you been waiting long, Cousin?" William asked as he and Elizabeth entered the room and he directed his wife to a chair. Across the table, Richard stared at her with his mouth agape. Though William was proud that her beauty would cause such a reaction, he was equally jealous that it had.

"Have you been waiting long, Cousin?" William asked as he directed his wife to a chair. Across the table, Richard stared at Elizabeth with his mouth agape. Though William was proud that her beauty would cause such a reaction, he was equally jealous that it had.

"Richard, you are staring," he said, taking his place. The tone of his voice carried a warning, bringing the colonel out of his stupor.

"I apologise, Mrs. Darcy, but other than when Georgiana wore her hair in that manner, I do not think I have seen anything as lovely."

Elizabeth blushed, her eyes falling to the tablecloth. "You are too kind."

The talk quickly turned to more mundane things, such as what the cook had prepared for dinner. While the wine was being poured, a loud commotion in the foyer drew everyone's attention, and dinner was quickly forgotten. Recognising his father's voice, Richard stood immediately and left the room without bothering to excuse himself.

William rose to follow, leaning over to say to his wife, "Please finish your dinner, Elizabeth. This may take a while, and I would not want your food to grow cold. I shall return as soon as possible."

Without awaiting a reply, he flew out the door. The sounds of Richard confronting his father could easily have been heard in Hertfordshire, and it killed Elizabeth's appetite. She sat still for a moment, wondering what she should do, but soon she decided she must hear what was being said, for, in truth, she realized she was the topic.

By the time she gained the dining room door, the quarrel had moved into the large front parlour. Cautiously peeking into the hallway, she found no servants loitering about, as they were prone to do at Longbourn. Realising that the few candles that lit the hallway left shadowy places in which she could go undetected, Elizabeth slipped out of the dining room and edged her way towards the voices. Nearing a large palm tree in a pot by the entry to the parlour, she was pleased to see that no one had thought to close the door, thus, she had a view of who was speaking as she peeked through the opening.

"I will not be taken to task like a schoolboy," her husband said to an older man who favoured the colonel. William's face was crimson, and he fairly shook with anger as his hands formed and reformed fists. Elizabeth had never seen his celebrated self-control so near to crumbling, and it was a little frightening. "I am my own man, and I have chosen the woman *I* wished to marry. It is settled!"

"You have chosen to defy me. That is what you have chosen! First you refuse to marry Anne and now this!"

A lovely older woman in an expensive gown of blue damask came forward, urging each to be calm and suggesting they lower their voices, though neither seemed to heed her counsel.

"Darcy is right, Father!" Richard declared, though he was not visible until he walked over to stand beside William. "He is not a Fitzwilliam; he does not have to obey you!"

"Of course, you would take his side!" the earl exclaimed, casting a disgusted look at his son. "You would defend him if he married a courtesan! In fact, I would not be surprised if she was his mistress."

"My wife is a gentlewoman and everything that is good and decent. You have no right to criticise someone you have never met and know absolutely nothing about!"

"And why do I know nothing about her? If she were someone of import, I would know her. Produce her so that I can see for myself that she is not some little tart that is heavy with child!"

"My wife will not be subjected to your vitriol on her wedding day! In fact, I do not intend to subject her to you in the future, either."

"What is the matter? Are you afraid she could not pass inspection?"

As William took a step towards his uncle, Richard grabbed his arm. William nodded at his cousin and said, "You have made your feelings perfectly clear, Uncle. Now, let me be clear. You are no longer welcome—"

"Fitzwilliam?"

At the sound of Elizabeth's soft voice, every head in the room turned. To his credit, after meeting her eye, the earl looked away, for he had been excessively cruel in his remarks.

William came to his senses and rushed to shield her from his family. "Sweetheart, please go back to the dining room and wait for me there."

"Are you not going to introduce me? After all, this is your family, is it not?"

"You will meet them at another time."

Suddenly, the elegant woman stood beside them, extending her hand. "I am your husband's aunt. I apologise for what you may have overheard, my dear. Things are often said in anger that we do not mean."

Elizabeth took the hand graciously. "I have found that to be true."

"Lady Matlock," William felt impelled to say, "and Aunt Eleanor, may I present my wife, Elizabeth Bennet Darcy."

"I am pleased to meet the woman who has captured my nephew's heart," Lady Matlock said as Elizabeth curtseyed. Then, putting her arm around Elizabeth's shoulder, she ushered her around William and towards her husband. The look she directed at Lord Matlock meant that she would brook no further incivility on his part.

"May I introduce my husband, the Earl of Matlock?"

William's uncle had been examining Elizabeth closely from the moment she spoke. It was quickly evident that she was gently bred and certainly not with child. For the first time in years, his face flushed with embarrassment as she stood before him now.

"I am pleased to meet you," Elizabeth said softly, dropping another curtsey.

Though the earl barely nodded, he managed to murmur, "Forgive me for my harsh words. I was angry with my nephew for not doing his duty towards our family, but I should not have directed my anger towards you."

Elizabeth barely had time to react before Richard began pulling his father aside to speak privately. The countess, who still stood beside her, said in a lower voice, "I apologise for upsetting you on your wedding day. Please allow me to make amends. Say you will attend my ball the day after tomorrow so I may introduce you to society as my new niece. If my husband and I show our acceptance of your marriage, it shall help to gain the approval of the *ton*. That, of course, can only be an advantage for Fitzwilliam's sister, Georgiana, when she comes out."

Elizabeth could think of no polite way to refuse. "I should like to attend."

William, who had moved closer in order to intervene if needed, spoke up. "None of my wife's *new* gowns will be ready by then, Aunt. It would be best to postpone Mrs. Darcy's introduction to society to a later date."

Elizabeth's brows knit. *Is he so ashamed of my clothes that he would rather wait until I have better?*

"I am sure that any gown Mrs. Darcy wears will be lovely, Fitzwilliam. Moreover, it is essential that the family present a united front now in order to thwart what the scandal sheets may print."

She turned back to Elizabeth, oblivious to William's scowl. "The gossips love a spur-of-the-moment wedding, my dear, but if we act quickly, they will have less reason to criticise. Please say that you will come."

"If my husband will escort me, I shall."

Lady Matlock smiled. "If he will not, send me a note, and I shall have my eldest son, Edgar, come for you."

Unsure of what to reply to that, Elizabeth said nothing, but she was certain that William was not pleased with his aunt's offer. The glower on his face made that plain.

"I shall escort my wife whenever she needs an escort!" William declared.

"Good! Then I shall expect both of you at Matlock House at seven. The ball begins at eight, and I want you to have plenty of time to meet with Georgiana beforehand."

Before William could object, Lady Matlock quickly joined her husband as he and Richard walked towards the foyer. That gave opportunity for him to address Elizabeth.

"My dear, you have no idea of the level of cruelty among the women of the *ton*, especially if they perceive that you are not of their sphere. Do you really want to reap their attention by attending a ball in one of the gowns you brought from Hertfordshire? Why not wait until after your new gowns are finished before subjecting yourself to their inspection?"

"Were you embarrassed by my wedding dress? For that is what I thought to wear."

"Certainly not! But as lovely as it is, it might appear plain next to the current fashions. I would not want you to lay yourself open to their insults—that is all."

Recalling her promise to her aunt, Elizabeth swallowed the retort on the tip of her tongue. "If you will excuse me, I am tired and wish to retire. Good night, Mr. Darcy."

With those words Elizabeth quit the room, leaving William bewildered. *Mr. Darcy? What happened to calling me Will?*

He had pictured them inhabiting the library after dinner, where he intended to read some newly published poetry aloud while they shared the vintage champagne he had saved for his wedding day. Afterwards, he planned to present her with the wedding gift he had commissioned when he was in London last—a perfect strand of pearls, painstakingly chosen to match. Alas, that was not to be, for by the time William fully understood that Elizabeth was actually retiring for the night, he moved to the door only to watch her walk away. As she vanished up the stairs at the rear of the hall, his dreams sank along with his heart.

He considered going after her to clear the air, but decided against it, fearing that if he suddenly appeared at her door, she might think he was reneging on his pledge not to consummate their union until she was ready. In any case, he could not get over the feeling that he had just been dismissed.

While lost in thought, William had not noticed that the house had gone eerily silent. Hearing footsteps, he glanced to see Richard striding towards him.

"Thank God they are gone!" Richard said, walking past him to stick his head in the parlour and look around the room. "Where is Mrs. Darcy? I wish to apologise for Father's insults."

"Elizabeth is exhausted and decided to retire. However, I am certain that she does not hold you personally responsible for what your father says or does. You owe no one an apology."

"Still, I want to apologise to her and to you. My parents had no right coming here today, of all days. And my father should never have said the things he did, especially in your home and within earshot of your wife. It was unconscionable."

"Your mother is not so much unkind as she is a hostage to the dictates of the *ton*."

"But Father can be intentionally unkind! And he went too far today."

"I will admit that he pushed me near to my breaking point. It is one thing to insult my intelligence, but quite another to insult Elizabeth's character."

"Quite right," Richard stated, releasing a heavy sigh. "At any rate, I think I shall follow your wife's example and retire to Bingley's residence now. I have no appetite after all that has happened."

"You are not staying here tonight?"

"No, and I have already informed Mrs. Barnes. I am not so thick that I do not know that newlyweds need their privacy, so I am encamping at Charles' home for a while."

"Bingley lent you his house?"

"Yes. He thinks, as do I, that a newly married couple does not need a houseguest, so he offered to let me stay there before we left for London. I do not mind, as it will be nice having the house to myself and you may reach me there at any time."

"Very well, but let me have Cook pack you a basket in case you wish to eat later. After all, she prepared a lot of food, and someone has to eat it."

Richard offered a tired smile. "You have talked me into it."

As they headed to the kitchen, the colonel suddenly stopped as though he had remembered something important. "What of Richmond? Do you still plan to visit the children and their mothers while in Town?"

"Yes, I am obligated to see that the children are raised in a decent home. So, I must check on the progress on the estate before returning to Pemberley. I hoped you would accompany me."

"I intend to, but what of your wife? Are you not going to tell her?"

"There is no point in Elizabeth knowing anything about the situation at this point. She will find out soon enough and will be deeply disappointed, I am sure."

"Any decent woman would grieve to hear of illegitimate children," Richard offered soberly.

By then they had reached the kitchen. After entering the heavy door, it slammed shut behind them, effectively cutting off their conversation to anyone outside that room.

"And since Elizabeth was very fond of Andrew, I know it would come as quite a shock to learn of his debauchery. I am not willing for her to be upset again so soon by a member of my family."

"You are a too kind-hearted, Cousin! I hope it does not come back to haunt you. I, for one, would expose that cad in a second!"

"He will be exposed soon enough, I believe. He is running out of options and places to hide. I cannot help but wonder what happened when he got to Manchester. If he had been shot by Harrington, I think I would have heard by now."

"That blackguard is too slippery to be caught so easily." Richard replied sarcastically. "I imagine he is hiding in some gutter, even as we speak."

"You are probably right."

"I know his kind well. I pursue them all over England in service to His Majesty— deserters, rebels, conspirators, ne'er-do-wells and the like. They come to a bad end."

Just then Mrs. Colvin came through the door from to servants' quarters. Seeing the master and his cousin awaiting her, she smiled and bobbed a curtsey.

"How may I be of service, sir?"

In a dark corner of the foyer, Elizabeth stood as still as a statue, stricken to her soul by what she had just heard and wishing she had not come back downstairs.

Once in her bedroom, she had realised that she needed to speak to her Aunt Gardiner about her frustrations before being swept off to Pemberley, and since the Gardiners were to return to Town after the wedding, they were most likely home already. Thus, she had gone in search of William in order to tell him that she intended to visit them first thing in the morning by herself, assuring him of her intent to return before the moddiste arrived at nine. Regrettably, as she neared the foyer, she overheard snippets of a conversation between her husband and his cousin that pierced her heart.

... visit the children and their mothers while you are in Town...

... obligated at least to see that the children are raised in a decent home...

... but what of your wife? Are you going to tell her...

... There is no point in Elizabeth knowing anything about the situation... She will find out soon enough and will be deeply disappointed...

... Any decent woman would grieve to hear of illegitimate children...

Visualizing the faces of the illegitimate children that William was *obligated* to support made her stomach begin to churn. Looking about and seeing no one, Elizabeth quickly made her way back to the safety of her bedroom. Once ensconced there, she turned the key in the lock and leaned back against the door with her eyes closed. Silently she commanded, *Breathe!*

Suddenly, her eyes flew open. Noting the other doors—one that led to a joint sitting room and the other to her dressing room—she ran to lock them. At last done, she lay down across the huge bed that now belonged to her. Tears refused to obey and gathered in her eyes, though Elizabeth fought to keep them from falling.

You WILL not cry! You will make the best of the situation because you have no other choice! One thought kept running through her mind, though: *What else do I not know about Mr. Darcy?*

William and Richard exited the front door and paused on the portico. Below, a carriage was waiting to take his cousin to Bingley's residence, and William nodded to a footman who instantly leapt down to open the door.

"So you will allow me to impose upon you again, then? Since your mother

invited Elizabeth to the ball for Lady Susan, I feel I have no choice but to go, and I could use your help."

"You do realise that attending the ball can only create more trouble."

"Why do you think I want you there? Though I imagine your mother means only to quell the gossips, our presence may be a bigger disaster than anything the gossips could invoke. I cannot see any good coming from introducing Elizabeth to Lady Susan at this time."

"Or Georgiana, either. She cannot be happy about your marriage, and I fear what she may say or do."

"As do I, so you see my dilemma. I need your help to shield Elizabeth from those who would like nothing better than to tear her to shreds, even those members of my own family who have not had their chance as yet."

"Like Edgar, for instance, or, God forbid, Lady Catherine."

"Exactly. At least our aunt is not likely aware of the marriage yet, or if Collins has managed to get back to Kent, she will not be able to travel to London in time for the ball."

"It was not my aim to attend. I could not fancy myself being a part of anything honouring Lady Susan, but I shall attend for Mrs. Darcy's sake."

"Thank you, Richard."

"Do you remember what I said when we were in Town last—about how entertaining it would be if you showed up during Mother's ball for Lady Susan with a wife?"

"Now that you mention it, I do."

"Forget I ever said such a foolish thing! After tonight, I could do without any more drama."

"I feel the same. I shall not sleep a wink until this whole ordeal is over and we leave for Pemberley."

Chapter 14

Darcy House
Darcy's dressing room
The next morning

If Mr. Martin thought it odd that Mr. Darcy spent his wedding night in his own bed, he tried not to let it show as he laid out his employer's clothes. He had not been entirely taken aback, for last evening he had heard two maids nattering about the new Mrs. Darcy retiring early—by herself. It seemed that one of the tattlers was supposed to help the mistress undress, but she found all the mistress' doors locked and could not rally her to open them. Upon spying him, however, both women had hurried away. He knew that it was his duty, so he intended to inform Mrs. Barnes of the gossip today.

In the meantime, while it was yet dark Martin had entered the master's dressing room, as was his usual custom, only to find the subsequent door to Mr. Darcy's bedroom standing wide open. In addition, a light was emanating from within, and it drew him to the door to see if candles may have been left burning. A strong stench of liquor assaulted him immediately, causing his nose to crinkle. Still, assuming that the room was empty, he was surprised to find William asleep in the bed. Moreover, the bedclothes were dishevelled, as though he might have fought a legion of ~~████~~ during the night. Pillows were scattered over every inch of carpet and the sheets no longer covered the mattress or the man. There was nothing to be done but to close the door quietly, so he did and went about his duties.

Recalling it now as he brushed his master's coat a little too zealously, Martin let out a ragged sigh. *This is not a good omen.*

Having been George Darcy's valet since before Fitzwilliam was born, Mr. Martin was very familiar with the son, whom he had come to admire even more than the father. So familiar, in fact, that he was acutely aware of how isolated his charge had been for much of his life, especially since his father's death and the estrangement with his sister. Their rift was something of which the entire house was aware, though the wise never mentioned it—well, other than when he discussed it with Mr. and Mrs. Barnes. The three of them, employed the longest, knew all of the family secrets and always closed ranks to protect the master from tittle-tattle being spread amongst the other servants.

If you ask me, young Miss Darcy could use a good scolding for turning her back on her brother in allegiance to that rogue, Andrew. I suspect that no one more unworthy of the Darcy name will ever appear in the annals of the British Empire!

Suddenly William appeared in the doorframe, rubbing his eyes, and Mr. Martin came to attention. "Good morning, sir," he said crisply.

William's response was so muffled that Martin could not make it out, and the odour of brandy became even stronger as William approached the bowl where he always washed his face. It took all of the valet's strength not to reach out to steady him as he passed; however, he was keenly aware that Mr. Darcy did not like to appear helpless.

After splashing his face and drying it with a towel that Martin produced, William stood and stretched, groaning a bit as he reached towards the ceiling. "I did not realise it was so late. Do you know if Mrs. Darcy has gone downstairs to break her fast?"

"I have not so much as heard, sir. However, I have been up for about an hour and have heard no voices or footsteps in the hall to indicate that Mrs. Darcy is awake."

Just at that moment there was a knock at the door and William and the valet exchanged curious glances. It was not customary for anyone to bother Mr. Darcy in the mornings before he got dressed.

"Come," he called.

The door opened, revealing that it was Mr. Barnes who had knocked. Strangely, after entering the room the butler stood stock still and silent, his eyes focused on the floor. The best evidence that something was amiss, however, lay in the fact that he kept wringing his hands. In his entire life, William had never known Barnes to act in such a manner and he was especially concerned when he would not look him directly in the eye. Thus, his imagination began to run wild.

Something has happened to Elizabeth!

"Good Lord, Barnes! Out with it, man, what has happened?"

Gracechurch Street
The Gardiner's residence

"Lizzy!" Madeline Gardiner exclaimed, looking past her niece to the imposing Darcy carriage parked on the street below. She glanced down the pavement in either direction. "What in the world are you doing here at this hour? Has something happened?"

"It has," was all that Elizabeth managed to say before falling into her aunt's arms.

Mrs. Gardiner held her until she composed herself and drew back, wiping her eyes with the backs of her hands. Then she pulled Elizabeth into the house, closing the door and instructing her housekeeper, "Please bring some tea and scones to Mr. Gardiner's study."

Once inside her husband's study, Madeline shut the door soundly. Then she led Elizabeth to a small sofa in front of the hearth, where they sat down beside one another.

"Edward has already left, so, other than the children, we are alone in the house. You may talk freely."

"I am so sorry to be a nuisance so soon after my wedding, but I simply could not leave for Derbyshire until I had your advice."

"You could never be a nuisance. Besides, it was my intent to be available to you should you need me. What is troubling you?"

"It is a conversation that I overheard last night."

Madeline Gardiner's brow rose in surprise. "Your wedding night?"

Elizabeth shrugged. "It might as well have been any other night, as we spent it apart."

Her aunt's countenance fell further. "You slept in separate rooms?"

Elizabeth nodded. "And before you chastise me, it was Mr. Darcy's idea. Since I was so set against marrying him, he thought it best if… " She hesitated then hurriedly finished. "He is letting me decide when I am ready to… to come to him."

"I am surprised that any man would be so generous."

"And he said that until I do, we should keep separate bedrooms. I find that thoroughly confusing, for Mama said all married couples have separate bedrooms. She and Papa do."

"Again, your mother is wrong. Edward and I have never maintained separate bedrooms. In any event, I must say your husband's offer proves he has a kind heart."

"He is thoughtful in some ways, but not in others. For instance, he treats me as though I am either a child or invisible much of the time. He talks about me as though I am not in the room and makes decisions concerning me without bothering to ask what I want."

"And this is your entire complaint? For you and I have already spoken of how you must give him time to—"

Elizabeth broke in, growing flustered. "I am fully aware that I agreed to be patient with his officiousness, but I did not know the extent of his controlling character until after we married. Nonetheless, that is not the reason I am here at this hour. I overheard a conversation between him and Colonel Fitzwilliam that has pierced my heart."

Mrs. Gardiner cupped her face sympathetically. "Oh, my dear girl. What could be so painful to hear?"

"My… my husband has… " Elizabeth sniffled. "He has fathered more than one illegitimate child. Apparently, he purchased an estate in Richmond to house them, along with their mothers. His only concern seems to be that he is obligated to support them."

"Oh, Lizzy, I am not sure that I believe—"

"It is true!" Elizabeth interjected fervently. "They even spoke of keeping it a secret from me."

"Repeat exactly what you heard."

Elizabeth did so, growing more emotional with the telling than she ever imagined she would. She was crying by the time she finished, and her aunt pulled her into another embrace, patting her on the back.

"Oh, my dear. I can understand why you are upset, but if you think about it, your husband did not say that they were *his* children. And from what I know about the Darcys—"

Elizabeth jerked away. "They are saints! I should have known that is what you would say, as you champion them at every opportunity." Suddenly ashamed, she sank back into her aunt's arms, cradling her head in her hands.

"Forgive me. That was disrespectful. You have always been my anchor, and I know that you have my best interests at heart at all times. But I am so afraid that, though you may have known his parents, you do not know the true Fitzwilliam Darcy."

"And you do?"

"No. I realise I do not know him at all." She stood then and moved to sombrely gaze out the window. "I fear it will destroy my marriage if this secret proves true. For it will crush any regard I may have begun to have for him. Love grows from respect and if I cannot respect—"

"Listen to yourself, Lizzy! You are leaping to conclusions and *that* will destroy your marriage. Of that I am certain. You must speak to Mr. Darcy about what you heard."

"You are right. I must confront him, if only for my own peace of mind."

"Confront is such a harsh word, Lizzy. Talk with your husband, calmly and without making accusations. I think you will find that there is more to what you overhead than you can even imagine."

"I pray you are right. Though I am not in love with him, I committed my heart and soul to making my marriage work because I believed Fitzwilliam Darcy an honourable man."

"Let me hear from you after you speak to him of this matter, for I will worry until you do."

"I shall." Elizabeth pasted on a wan smile. "I must return now, as he has arranged activities for the entire day."

In no more than a few minutes, Elizabeth was in the carriage on the way back to Darcy House, planning what she would do.

I shall wait until after the ball to speak to him. For if what I heard proves true, I shall never be able to feign any degree of cheerfulness at the ball.

The Library
An hour later

It was nearing nine o'clock when Mr. Barnes peeked inside the library to find his employer still pacing the floor, hands clasped firmly behind his back. Except for not bearing a weapon, Mr. Darcy put him in mind of the guards at St. James' palace, so steady was his stride. The master had been livid since realising that Mrs. Darcy had left at dawn for the Gardiners' house, and he had not been notified until after awakening. Never mind that the new mistress had expressly forbidden Barnes from waking Mr. Darcy to tell him. He would not be placated.

Barnes understood, truly he did, for he had tried to dissuade his mistress from going, but to no avail. Moreover, her husband had reason to be concerned for her safety, for accompanied only by a driver and two postillions, she had gone to an area of London usually shunned by those who lived in the finer districts. Cheapside—even the name conjured up seamy images.

At least, he thought, *I sent an extra man to see to her safety; if only Mr. Darcy had allowed me to explain.* For now, the only thing the elderly butler had to be thankful for was that Mrs. Barnes had not been a party to the debacle—for she was still asleep when Mrs. Darcy left.

Barnes sighed. *It seems that pleasing the new mistress AND the master is not going to be an easy task.* He shook his head despondently and returned to his duties, praying as he had all morning that the mistress had known what she was about. *After all, she assured me that her aunt and uncle lived in Cheapside and that she had visited them every summer, without incident, since she was a child.*

Inside the library, the sounds of a carriage rumbling down the street penetrated the trancelike state that had swept over William, and he rushed to the tall windows facing Hyde Park. From there, he had an excellent view of the street and his front steps. This particular vehicle was not his, so he went back to pacing. Each time the scenario was repeated, he resumed his exercise with renewed vigour. Truth be known, it took all his strength not to rush to Gracechurch Street and escort his wife safely home; thus, wearing the carpet down to bare threads was his way of coping.

The sound of another carriage brought him back to the window, and the Darcy crest on the door made him go fairly limp with relief. As Elizabeth stepped from the carriage, for a moment, he feared that he might burst into tears. Since that would never do, he crossed the room to one of the large mirrors on the wall to see if his appearance might betray him. Other than bloodshot eyes and his hair being chaotic from constantly running his hands thought it, he felt that he looked presentable. Using his fingers, he managed to smooth it somewhat and, satisfied, he straightened his cravat and waistcoat, buttoned his coat and assumed his normal mask as he hurried to meet Elizabeth. As he gained the foyer, he noted that she was handing Mr. Barnes a plain, muslin pelisse that looked like it had seen better days.

"Mrs. Darcy, will you join me in the library, please?"

Elizabeth stopped and slowly turned to face him, though she did not reply. Her refusal to greet Mr. Darcy caused Barnes to freeze in mid-step.

Elizabeth hesitated for only a moment before a simultaneous tilt of her head and lift of her shoulders demonstrated that she felt she had no choice. As she passed her husband, however, she would not look at him. Glancing past her, William locked eyes with Mr. Barnes, who instantly lowered his head and hurried in another direction. William then followed his wife.

Once inside the library, he closed the door soundly. Elizabeth was already at the windows, standing in the exact spot he had stood only moments before. Instead of joining her, he took a calming breath. Then he walked over to prop his elbow on the huge mantle that spanned the hearth—one expensive boot coming to rest on a bronze box that held strips of wood for starting fires.

"Sit down, please."

Elizabeth did as he asked, her manner submissive. She looked so very young and vulnerable at that moment that any anger William might have felt quickly dissipated. Her demeanour brought to mind the many times he had had to correct Georgiana in this very room, and he did not wish to deal with

his wife as he had his sister. Yes, he had been angry that she had left without a word, and he was frantic with worry for her safety, but he was not angry that she had visited her relations. He needed her to understand that.

"Elizabeth."

Her name hung in the air for a moment before she looked up at him through her long lashes. Her expression was indecipherable, and it pained him that he knew so little of her thoughts by observation.

"Why did you go to the Gardiners' home at such an ungodly hour? And, more importantly, why did you wish to go without telling me?"

Her chest rose and fell heavily before she answered. "I... I missed my aunt terribly and... and I felt that I simply must see her before we left London."

"I would never forbid you from seeing the Gardiners. Surely, you know that. And I would gladly have accompanied you... had you asked."

"You had made so many plans for today that I felt sure you would tell me to put off visiting, perhaps even until tomorrow or... or later."

"And it was crucial that you go today." With those words Elizabeth squirmed under his gaze but did not reply. "Regardless of your reasons, I am certain that you will agree that there are parts of Cheapside where a woman should not go unescorted." He waited but she did not reply. "Mr. Barnes also explained that you had expressly forbidden him from waking me to let me know."

Suddenly, she took a good look at William. In contrast to his normal appearance, his eyes were red-rimmed, his hair dishevelled and his clothes needed a good pressing. Clearly, he had not slept well last night, if at all.

"I apologise if I worried you. I am very impulsive at times, and I felt a sudden urge to see my aunt; that is all. In fact, my uncle had already left for his warehouse, as he does each morning, so he does not even know that I was there." He waited as though expecting more. She sighed heavily. "In truth, I did not desire your escort. I wished to go alone."

"Evidently," William said solemnly. Then he crossed to the windows and stared into the distance, clasping his hands behind his back in his usual manner. "Still, all actions have consequences. Mr. Barnes has been reprimanded and the under-coachman, Mr. Saulder, will be shortly."

"Oh, no! It is entirely my fault! You should not—"

A raised hand halted her plea. "Your safety is my responsibility, Elizabeth. It does not fall to Mr. Barnes or Mr. Saulder." He looked in her direction, though he did not move. "Wealth can be a curse as well as a blessing. As my wife, you are a valuable commodity to any blackguard who might seize you. Just last year, Lady Carrollton was kidnapped and savagely ..." William dropped his head, unable to continue.

"I did not think—"

"I would never forgive myself if you were subjected to what that poor woman endured," William broke in.

"But Mr. Barnes instructed Mr. Saulder to send another postillion."

"While I am grateful for his diligence, that is immaterial to this discussion. I decide how best to protect my wife, not my servants. It is my duty to know

where you are at all times, not theirs." He softened his voice and expression. "Can you understand why I am upset?"

"I... I can. And I apologise for creating problems for your servants, as well as for upsetting you." She lifted her chin decisively. "It will never happen again. You have my word."

Before William could answer, there was a knock on the door. With fatigue evident in his voice, he responded, "Come."

Mrs. Barnes opened the door and stepped inside. Noting the friction in the air, she did not attempt to be cheerful. "Begging your pardon, sir. Madam Bouvier has arrived."

"Show her to Mrs. Darcy's sitting room and explain that we are running a bit late. Have Cook send up a tray of tea and sweet rolls. Perhaps that will entertain her until my wife and I are prepared to join her."

"Certainly."

The housekeeper left and he addressed Elizabeth again. "Have you eaten? If not, the fittings can wait until you have had an opportunity to do so."

"No. I was offered food at my aunt's home, but I was not the least bit hungry. I still am not."

He considered her for a long moment. "Very well. Then you are ready to begin?"

As ready as I shall ever be! Elizabeth thought, but said aloud, "I am."

Later
Elizabeth's sitting room

It was nearing eleven o'clock when Elizabeth swooned, falling from the stool on which she had stood for the last few hours as different materials had been wrapped, draped, or, on occasion, pinned about her while her husband and Madam Bouvier argued the merits of each design and fabric as though she were not there. Despite being surrounded by the moooiste, three associates and Mr. Darcy, not a one of them had realised that she was literally on her last legs until she collapsed.

Fortuitously, William had seen her begin to fall and had swooped in, took her in his arms and carried her into the bedroom, laying her on the bed. At the same time, he shouted for one of the seamstresses to fetch Mrs. Barnes. He was busily massaging Elizabeth's arms and entreating her to wake when the housekeeper rushed in.

"Have you sent for the physician?" he asked anxiously.

"No. I have not had time. I was in a nearby guest room when I was summoned, and I sent a maid after my bag of medicine. I suspect that Mrs. Darcy could just be weak from not having eaten. After all, not a one of you finished dinner after the visitors arrived last night, and Mrs. Darcy did not break her fast this morning, to my knowledge. And being that yesterday was her wedding day, I venture to say that she might not have eaten much before or after the ceremony."

William was nodding his agreement. "Her mother mentioned that she had not eaten. How could I have been so imperceptive? I should have insisted that

she eat this morning."

"You are not used to having a wife, Mr. Darcy. You will learn in time."

"I do not deserve understanding, for I insisted that we order all her clothes this morning, even her footwear. She must have been famished, but she never said a word."

At that moment, a young maid deposited the housekeeper's black bag beside her on the bed, and Mrs. Barnes retrieved a bottle of smelling salts from inside it. Waving it under Elizabeth's nose, it caused her eyes to blink open.

"There you are!" Mrs. Barnes smiled warmly at her. "How do you feel, Mrs. Darcy?"

"Wha... what happened?"

"You fainted," William answered.

Sending the maid for a cup of tea and a sweet roll from the tray in the sitting room, Mrs. Barnes sat down next to Elizabeth. "Help me raise her, sir, so that she may take some tea. It should be lukewarm by this time and will do nicely."

William did as asked, propping some pillows behind Elizabeth's back after he got her settled. She eagerly drank the entire cup of tea.

"Very good. Now, Cook fixed these rolls just this morning and they are fresh. Try to eat a few bites."

"I do not think—"

"You must eat, Elizabeth," William said gently but firmly, "or I shall be forced to send for the physician, and he will no doubt concoct some horrible-tasting potion for you to drink, so please listen to Mrs. Barnes. At least try to eat part of the roll."

Turning her eyes to the housekeeper, Elizabeth nodded and began eating the roll one small piece at a time, with more sips of tea in between.

After it was done, the housekeeper ventured, "Would you allow me to bring you a cup of Mrs. Colton's vegetable soup? She has just prepared it, and I feel certain you will do much better with something more nourishing in your stomach." Elizabeth conceded. "Wonderful," the older woman said. "Rest for now, and I shall bring it up shortly."

After she exited the room, Elizabeth grew uncomfortable under William's watchful gaze. Not wishing to argue with him, she closed her eyes, hoping he would leave. He did not. Instead, he took her hand and brought it to his lips, kissing the back of it as tenderly as one would a child's.

"Forgive me. It was wrong of me to insist that you order everything you will need as Mrs. Darcy in this one session. It is just that there are no first-rate modistes in Lambton, and I would not have you lack for anything. I expect my neighbours to invite us to many soirées once we settle at Pemberley. They will be keen to make your acquaintance, thus the reason for the sheer number of gowns and slippers. Additionally, the weather in Derbyshire is more severe than in Hertfordshire. We have colder winters with much more snow and ice. Your cloth pelisses and cloaks, not to mention unlined boots, will be insufficient, to say the least. You really must have fur-lined boots and cloaks."

Elizabeth only nodded. It would not do for him to know how furious she had become over the course of the morning, for he had decided every pattern, fabric and colour of her new gowns—even the trims—without consulting her. And the modiste was no better, for once when she expressed reservations about how revealing the décolleté would be on a certain pattern, Madam Bouvier had stopped in mid-sentence to gawk at her. Then she returned to her conversation with Mr. Darcy without replying. It was unsettling not to be taken seriously, and thereafter she had remained mute in protest. She winced at the memory. *I had to faint in order to gain their attention!*

Her expression instantly gained William's attention. "Elizabeth, I think it best that we send our regrets to my aunt and forego the ball. You are clearly exhausted."

"No, please. Your aunt expects us, and I have done enough harm to my own sisters' prospects; I do not wish to add Georgiana to the toll. Besides, I wish to attend."

William looked dismayed. "If that is your wish, then we shall, but only if you eat well for the rest of the day and are clearly in better health tomorrow."

"All will be well. You shall see."

"Do you feel like having Mr. Curry do his sketches today, or shall I send him away? He is to be here in less than an hour."

"I have forgotten. Who is Mr. Curry?"

"He is an artist who has done our family portraits since I was small. I have asked him to do your wedding portrait. His method is to do a few quick sketches of the subject here in London. Then in his studio he will expand upon the sketches, creating different poses and backgrounds. When he comes to Pemberley to complete the portrait, you will be able to visualise how each pose will look and choose the one that suits."

"I have never heard of such a thing," Elizabeth said listlessly. "Of course, I have never had a portrait done."

William smiled as he pushed a curl behind her ear. "While I am sure that he would rather have you pose in your wedding gown, I may be able to talk him into sketching the gown itself, and then do a few brief sketches of you. Or, I can put him off if you would rather—"

"Just let me have a few minutes to lie here and rest. When he arrives, I shall be fully able to pose."

"If you are sure."

"I am."

"Then I shall leave you. I have business that needs attending, and I shall be in my study if you need me."

With those words, William quit the room, and Elizabeth breathed a sigh of relief to be alone at last. She had wanted to think over her aunt's advice of that morning, but had not had a minute to herself. Taking a deep breath, she let it out slowly, recalling everything that was said.

In less than an hour, Mrs. Barnes came to inform her that Mr. Curry and her husband were awaiting her in the study. Having fallen asleep briefly after her meal, she was well rested and ready to begin again.

Inside Madam Bouvier's Carriage

Having served the women of London for the last fifteen years, Elena Bouvier was now at the pinnacle of her career. The foremost modiste in Town, if not in the entirety of England, none of the leading ladies of society dared appear in public wearing a gown by anyone else. A fiery redhead of Sicilian ancestry, handsome and well-figured, having never borne children, she was the best at her craft, and all who mattered knew that.

Her shop now flourished next to Humphrey's Print Shop [10] near Boodles on St. James' Street and just up the lane from White's. She had not always been in such august company, however. As a young woman, she had arrived in England with her first husband, a Frenchman, whom she supported with her seamstress skills while he entertained other women. He returned to France shortly after with his lover, and that became the turning point in Madam Bouvier's life. She vowed then and there never again to support anyone but herself. That did not mean, however, that she did not occasionally enjoy a man's company, so she took some lovers, all wealthy and more than glad to contribute to her success by steering their wives to her shop.

Engaged in a woman's province, she was privy to a good deal of gossip, for she was very discreet, and the women she dressed trusted her explicitly. Thus, it was not unusual for her customers to discuss the most desirable men in their circles. Over the years, one name came up more frequently than others—Fitzwilliam Darcy. Every season, he seemed the target of most of the newly arrived debutants, all the younger widows, as well as a goodly number of married women.

Madam Bouvier understood the attraction well. Having fallen under his spell the first time he walked into her shop to enquire about gowns for his sister, she was still speechless whenever he appeared unexpectedly. For not only was exceptionally handsome, but there was an air of inaccessibility about him that begged to be conquered, and she had tried, dropping numerous hints over the years that she would welcome his *company*. The fact that he had completely ignored her and was still unmarried had finally persuaded her that, most likely, he did not favour women. That had changed today!

Departing Darcy House as swiftly as her well-equipped carriage would move, she had people to call on. Rumours had been swirling concerning the woman who had stolen Mr. Darcy's heart and, fortuitously, she had been chosen to dress her. Now that the appointment had concluded, she was eager to pass along her impressions of Mrs. Darcy to her confidants. Many were not only willing to pay for silks and satins, but even more generously if the gown came with a bit of gossip. And today she had gossip in abundance.

It had truly been an enlightening experience. Who would have thought Mr. Darcy was as red-blooded as the next man, totally besotted with the dark-haired pixie that was now his wife? Not only had he commissioned enough garments to insure that she had the finest wardrobe in all of England, but when his young wife had swooned, he had been reduced from the idol of the *ton* to a mere mortal, frantically begging her to open her eyes and speak to him.

Enthralled by such a display of affection from so detached an icon as Fitzwilliam Darcy, she had been unable to move a muscle until the tender scene had played out.

Wait until I tell them that he is besotted! That shall astound the lot of them.

Unaware of the thoughts running through her employer's head, her assistant, Loreli, asked, "Do you think we shall be able to finish the gowns that Mr. Darcy wishes to take with them when they leave for Derbyshire? Frankly, I do not know how it can be accomplished."

Pulled from her reverie, Madam Bouvier shrugged. "Working day and night, we may be able to finish several before they leave. I shall summon all our extra seamstresses back to work and postpone all other orders until we get Mrs. Darcy's wardrobe done. That will be a small price to pay for the privilege of dressing her. She shall be the object of everyone's attention for years to come. Even if he hides her away in the north for a time, she will have to come back to London at some point. And when she does, what she is wearing will be the talk of the *ton*. It can only enhance my reputation."

Loreli leaned over to whisper to her employer, unwilling that the two seamstresses riding across from them hear. "I have to say that I do not see the attraction. She is pretty but not as handsome as some who have pursued him. Mrs. Darcy is certainly not the type of woman I thought Mr. Darcy would choose to marry—not that I thought he ever would. He seemed much too fastidious."

"Oh? Did you picture him marrying someone like Lady Susan, perhaps? To be truthful, so did I, but I was wrong, and it seems I have been entirely wrong about his proclivities. What was evident to me today is that he is truly in love with that young woman, and I have to say that I am pleased for her, as well as him."

"Pleased? I thought that you fancied him yourself."

"I have long since abandoned that goal," she laughed. "However, I am a romantic at heart. And to see a man that I thought so unfeeling act the schoolboy," she shook her head in awe, "well, let me just say that my belief in true love has been restored, and that is no little feat for one as jaded as I."

Loreli sighed. "I cannot deny that I had a tear in my eye when he was begging her to awaken. Would that some man would act as besotted over me!"

"Or even half as besotted." Madam Bouvier sighed wistfully. Then she chuckled. "However, I doubt that shall ever happen. And there is no sense dwelling on it, as we have much to accomplish in a short period of time."

The rest of the trip was spent discussing the amount of fabrics, lace, trim and such needed to make Mrs. Darcy's wardrobe, as well as the names of all the women they would need to contact to help with the endeavour.

Chapter 15

Pemberley

Mrs. Reynolds hurried towards the gardens, eager to find the Fitzwilliams and deliver the letter that had arrived for them not ten minutes before. Clearly, it was from Mr. Darcy as it was on the same paper as he had used for her own letter and was in his script. She felt certain that their missive shared the same information—he was married!

As she progressed, the housekeeper recalled her shock when opening the letter addressed to her. The news contained therein had almost caused her heart to stop, and she had sunk into one of the chairs in the foyer, almost in a trance. Only Mr. Walker's immediate intervention had brought her around, for seeing the shock on her face, he had called her name and patted her hand until she recovered her senses. Afterward, enquiring as to what had alarmed her so seriously, she had shared the letter with him. Mr. Walker had been with the Darcys almost as long as she and was like a member of the family as well. The news had left him equally as bewildered.

"What do you suppose happened?" Mr. Walker asked. "Do you think our dear boy has been ensnared by a fortune hunter?"

"It is never a good thing when a man of Mr. Darcy's stature marries on the spur of the moment, without a formal engagement and accompanied by all the public and private celebrations that someone of his sphere merits. To just announce that he is married, especially to a woman we have never met nor heard of—well, that is just not done!"

"I agree entirely."

"I am certain that this letter to the Fitzwilliams informs them of the same. Perhaps they can shed some light on the situation. Maybe they know the lady, or at the least have heard of her. I cannot enquire, of course, but they may say something to ease my mind."

"If not, I would be tempted to ask," the butler interjected.

"I shall be sure to let you know if they divulge anything significant in my presence."

<hr />

In the garden

Joseph and Olivia Fitzwilliam sat on a thick woollen blanket that lay on the ground under a large oak tree. Though Joseph rested his back against the tree trunk, his wife sat nearer the edge of the blanket. She had been trying for days to entice the kittens that frequented that part of the garden to join her. Today, they had warmed up to the idea and crept onto the blanket where she petted first one and then another. The more frightened mother cat had even moved to within a few feet, which was unusual, as she had never gotten that close to anyone at Pemberley, according to Mrs. Reynolds.

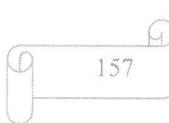

"You mentioned keeping one for a pet, Livy. Which one do you favour?"

"The white one is curious, the orange striped wants only to play, but the gray loves to be held. Oh, I cannot pick just one!" Olivia Fitzwilliam lamented. Then she laughed as the black and white kitten licked the ends of her fingers. "I fear that this one has found the residue from the sweet roll I just finished."

Joseph left his spot to lie down alongside Olivia, rolling over to prop on one elbow as he watched his wife work her magic on the shy kittens. As always, he was amazed at her ability to befriend the most timorous of creatures—be it animal or human.

Out of the blue, the mother cat suddenly edged forward. His wife held out her hand to the calico and the animal gave it a sniff before nudging it. Olivia stroked the cat's head, continuing until its eyes began to close. It was not long until the animal was lying beside her while some of her kittens nursed and the others fell fast asleep.

"God certainly gifted you with a special ability to communicate with all living creatures, Livy. I would never have thought the calico would have given in so easily."

"Often the one most in need of a gentle touch offers the greatest resistance. Some creatures feel hurt more deeply and if their spirits are wounded when they are young, they are not as likely to open their hearts again."

"Why do I think you are no longer speaking of cats?"

"Because you are right. For some reason, I have had Fitzwilliam on my mind a good bit lately. He has even frequented my dreams, though I see him as he was when last we visited, at about six or seven years of age. I have not said anything about it, but when greeting him upon our arrival, I instantly felt a deep sadness emanating from him. It was almost palpable."

"I am not surprised. His lot in life has not been easy, what with Anne's many miscarriages, stillbirths and her early death. And George was dead by the time he was twenty. It would be overwhelming to take over the reins of an estate the size of Pemberley at any age, but Fitzwilliam was full young and still had to act as guardian for Georgiana. I am amazed at how well he has managed it all."

"I am not sure he has coped well at all, for he has shunned courtship and marriage to raise Georgiana, and now he is all alone. I am certain that the love of a good woman would help to heal his wounded spirit, if only he would open his heart to one."

"Wounded spirit," Joseph repeated. "What a sad phrase!"

"But appropriate, I believe. I still remember how close he was to Anne the summer we were here. He was so solicitous, bringing her flowers and whatever other treasures he found in the yard. I can only imagine his heartache when she died. After all, he was still just a young…"

Olivia voice trailed off as she noticed Mrs. Reynolds rounding the gate that led to the fish pond and their hideaway. She waved.

The housekeeper waved in answer, the bucolic scene just ahead causing her to stop for a moment in her tracks. What would Mr. Darcy's marriage mean for the Fitzwilliams?

My hope is that they would stay here instead of returning to Ireland, but everything will likely change now that there is a new mistress. I can only pray it changes for the best.

Darcy House
The next day

As Elizabeth came downstairs to break her fast, she found Colonel Fitzwilliam in the foyer, talking with Mr. Barnes. He instantly turned to greet her.

"Mrs. Darcy, it is good to see you again. I hope that you are well."

"I am, thank you," was all she had time to reply before her husband walked out of the dining room.

William looked very handsome in his dark brown suede riding breeches, matching coat and black boots with brown tops that came to the knee. Her breath caught and she looked away, unwilling to expose her discomposure.

"Elizabeth!" he called jovially, crossing to where she stood next to Richard. "I was coming to find you. My cousin and I have some very important business we must attend to in Richmond this morning. I will not be back until late this afternoon."

And no doubt that business involves illegitimate children, Elizabeth thought as her mood instantly darkened. "It would only take a short while for me to dress and accompany you," she said, testing his resolve not to tell her.

"I do not think that reasonable. Only yesterday you were unwell, and the ball is tonight, so I think it best if you rest. Besides, Richard and I are travelling by horseback and it would not be comfortable for you to come with us."

"I see."

William instantly addressed his cousin. "Have you eaten?"

"Yes, Bingley's cook has been most attentive. In fact, I may have a hard time choosing whether to stay at his house or yours in the future, for the fare at both is excellent!"

"I, for one, am glad to hear it, though I fear that Charles will not be able to keep up with your appetite, especially for expensive brandy!" William teased.

"Thank you for the reminder of where his hospitality falls short. You will be glad to know that I have settled on your house over his, after all."

"Perhaps I was too hasty in disparaging Bingley's liquor cabinet," William said wryly. "Are you prepared to leave, then?"

"When you are!"

Both men turned to Elizabeth, who had been watching their banter and was growing more irritable with each joke. *I cannot believe they can be so jovial when they know what awaits them in Richmond!*

Seeing her expression, William instantly became concerned. "Are you well, Elizabeth? You look as you did when you fainted. Perhaps I should cancel my plans."

"I am perfectly fine!" Elizabeth exclaimed almost defiantly, her hands coming to rest on her hips. "Go and do whatever it is you must. I have many things to occupy my time, so I doubt I shall even notice your absence."

With those words she turned and disappeared into the dining room. That left the cousins to share puzzled looks.

"Is she ill, or angry, or both?" Richard whispered.

"I hardly know," William replied. Then he heaved a loud sigh, holding up his hands in frustration. "I am afraid that I do not understand women. Sometimes it is as though they have a language all their own."

"I suggest that you learn the language soon, my friend, or you shall be more miserable than when you were a bachelor."

"Please do not remind me."

Elizabeth's sitting room
Several hours later

With William gone, Elizabeth curled up in the window seat of her sitting room, pleased for the opportunity to record her deepest thoughts in her diary. Since leaving Longbourn, she had kept her treasure hidden in the small satchel that she carried in her lap in the coach. Now it resided in the farthest corner of her cavernous closet underneath her empty luggage. Having written her thoughts until she was satisfied, Elizabeth was not upset when a knock came at the door. Hiding the book under a pillow, she called, "Come."

Mrs. Barnes entered, dropped a small curtsey and was followed by another woman who did the same. The unfamiliar lady was of average height and weight, about five and forty, with brown hair and eyes. Elizabeth was instantly reminded of her sister Jane, for her eyes were just as kind.

"Mrs. Darcy, this is Mrs. O'Reilly. She is to be your lady's maid."

Elizabeth nodded. "Mrs. O'Reilly."

"It is a pleasure to meet you, Mrs. Darcy," the maid said, her gaze meeting Elizabeth's.

"Has Mrs. Barnes gotten you settled in, then?"

"Yes, ma'am. I am well situated, thank you. As I told Mrs. Barnes, I am prepared to help you straightaway with anything you may need. I understand that you are to attend a ball tonight and I shall be glad to assist. In fact, if I might see what you plan to wear, I can decide how to style your hair."

Mrs. Barnes broke in, "I shall leave you to your work, Mrs. O'Reilly, and if I may be of service please do not hesitate to ring, Mrs. Darcy."

"Thank you, I will," Elizabeth answered. Waiting until the housekeeper left the room, she then addressed her new maid. "I have something dreadful to confess. I am afraid that I am not used to having a lady's maid, at least not one to myself. I have four sisters and we shared one maid."

Mrs. O'Reilly smiled. "Then we shall each get used to the other."

"If you will follow me, I will show you my closet. I fear you will find it quite bare, as I brought few things with me. In fact, I shall wear my wedding gown to the ball tonight, for it is the nicest thing I own. Nevertheless, rest assured that I shall have a full closet before long. My husband has just ordered enough gowns to dress half the ladies in London."

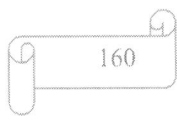

The maid chuckled. "He must love you very much."

Elizabeth's lips formed a tight line, which she turned into a smile. She did not reply, however, instead she led the way to her bedroom closet. It did not take long for O'Reilly to go through her few gowns, making remarks about what she could do to update each one. When she was through, she laid the wedding dress on the bed and studied it.

"This is a very beautiful gown. It is not gaudy, as is the fashion with the *ton* at present." The maid now eyed Elizabeth's hair. "And I know the perfect hair pins to go with it. They have faux pearls attached, fine enough that they appear authentic, and they will highlight your lovely dark hair. They were a present from my last employer, though Lord knows I have no occasion to wear them."

Elizabeth blushed. "I am sure I will be pleased with whatever you decide."

"If I may be so bold, whoever braided your hair did an excellent job. Seldom have I seen so intricate a pattern, though I have been schooled in braiding myself."

"My husband will be pleased to hear it, for he was the culprit," Elizabeth said. "As you are aware, I have been without a lady's maid since arriving in London. I had washed my hair and it was so unruly that he offered his help."

"Now I understand. In any case, I would say that Mr. Darcy is very talented."

Elizabeth and O'Reilly were still talking when Mrs. Barnes returned to announce that Miss Georgiana Darcy was downstairs in the drawing room. Elizabeth froze, unable to speak for an embarrassingly long time.

Then, with more equanimity than she felt, she said, "Please inform my sister that I shall be down shortly." As the housekeeper turned to leave, she added, "And have refreshments sent to the drawing room."

As Mrs. Barnes rushed to do as she asked, Mrs. O'Reilly said, "Begging your pardon, Mrs. Darcy, but are you well? You look as though you have seen a ghost."

"I... I am perfectly well," Elizabeth responded, assuming a smile she did not feel. "You may return to your room for now. I shall not need your services until another hour or so. That should give me plenty of time to dress and have you style my hair before the ball."

"Yes, ma'am."

O'Reilly was out the door in a flash, leaving Elizabeth to ponder why in the world Mr. Darcy's sister had come today. After all, his aunt had said that they would meet before the ball at Matlock House.

I suppose there is nothing left to do but find out.

The drawing room

Elizabeth paused at one of the large mirrors hanging in the hallway on her way to the drawing room. Frowning at her likeness, she smoothed the skirts of her blue muslin gown in a bid to erase the wrinkles produced by sitting with her feet drawn under her in the window seat. That did not help. Then she smoothed her hair, trying to tame the few curls that had escaped from the braids. A deep breath, followed by the puffing of her cheeks and a noisy sigh heralded her defeat.

This will have to do!

Shrugging, she continued on her way. Once at the door, she spied a tall, blond woman standing at the windows, her back to the door. For a brief second, she studied William's sister silently. Georgiana must have felt her presence, for she turned, and Elizabeth was obliged to greet her. She walked towards his sister with more serenity than she felt, hand outstretched.

"I am Elizabeth Darcy. I am most pleased to meet you, Miss Darcy."

As Georgiana met her halfway across the room, it was evident that she was not as old as she appeared from behind. Elizabeth thought her very pretty, though she certainly did not favour her brother with her dark blond hair and green eyes. Even her complexion was paler, as demonstrated by the freckles across her nose and cheeks.

"Finally, we meet," Georgiana replied a bit sarcastically, though she took the proffered hand. She looked Elizabeth over from head to toe before releasing it. "Please call me Georgiana. I apologise for coming here today, especially since Mr. Barnes informed me that my brother is out. However, I realised that the jewels I wished to wear to the ball tonight are here… in the safe in my room."

"There is no reason to apologise. This is your home. You could have retrieved them without informing me."

She curled her lip with a defiant scorn. "Now that Brother is married, you are the mistress of this house. I would not dare come and go as I please."

"I assure you that—"

"Georgiana!"

The sound of William's deep baritone startled Elizabeth, and she turned to watch him walk into the room. His tone of voice was cautious, rather than welcoming, and a look of trepidation marred his features. He crossed the room to stand next to Elizabeth, slipping his arm protectively around her waist. The gesture brought her a new and unexpected feeling—gratitude.

Elizabeth began to explain. "Georgiana was just—"

"I apologised to your wife for coming here today," her new sister interrupted. "I would never have come, had I known you were out. I only wish to retrieve my jewellery case from the safe in my bedroom, as I plan to wear the necklace Mother gave me at the ball tonight. In the future, I shall leave the case in my room at Matlock House where it will not be in the way."

Elizabeth glanced up at her husband, noting how he struggled to appear unaffected. Unmistakeable, though, was the fact that he was not happy with his sister's attitude.

"Your room is ready whenever you wish to reside in it and you are welcome to leave your jewellery here if you like. It is certainly no bother."

Georgiana tilted her head and raised her shoulders simultaneously, as though dismissing his statement. "In any event, I am pleased to finally meet your wife."

She faced Elizabeth. "I fear that Brother failed to inform any of his family that he was courting you, much less that you were to marry. Since we are strangers, would you consider telling me something about yourself?"

"Now is not the—" William said, only to be cut short by Elizabeth's protestation.

"It is normal, I think, for her to be curious." She felt William's arm tighten as she began to explain. "I am the former Elizabeth Bennet of Longbourn, located just outside Meryton, a small village in Hertfordshire. My father is Thomas Bennet and his family has owned the estate for well over eight hundred years."

"Bennet? I do not believe I have ever heard the name. Is the estate very large?"

"Not very—only some eight hundred acres."

"I see. And are you an only child, Miss Bennet?"

William started to correct Georgiana, but Elizabeth swiftly answered.

"I have four sisters. Jane is the oldest, I am second, Mary is in the middle, and the two youngest are Catherine and Lydia, who is but fifteen." She tried to lighten the atmosphere. "We are all only a year or so apart, so we are devoted to one another."

"*No* brothers?"

Aware of the implications, Elizabeth simply shook her head.

"To be honest, you look barely older than I am."

"I am one and twenty."

Now the arm around her waist felt like a vice, and Elizabeth shifted to make William loosen his grip. After the next question, however, he gave an audible sigh, as though he had had enough of his sister's enquiry.

"And your mother? Would I be familiar with her family?"

"I do not imagine you would. My mother is also from Hertfordshire, the former Frances Gardiner. Her father was the local solicitor before his death, her sister is married to his former clerk, who is now a solicitor, and her brother owns a warehouse."

"A warehouse? In Hertfordshire?"

"No, in London." Elizabeth answered. "Near Cheapside."

Georgiana's nose crinkled. "Cheapside? I am afraid to shop in that area."

At that point William put an end to the inquisition. "Elizabeth, if we are to be on time for the ball, we must begin preparations now. If you will please excuse us, Georgiana."

Georgiana looked triumphant. "Of course, you are correct. Neither of us would want to be late to our dear friend's ball." She looked directly at Elizabeth again. "Brother has told you about Lady Susan, has he not? My aunt is honouring her with the ball."

Elizabeth's brows knit. "Lady Susan? No. I cannot say I have ever heard the name."

"She is Brother's lifelong friend... I should say of our entire family. Since her family's estate is situated next to Pemberley, she practically grew up with us. She recently returned to Derbyshire after being widowed, and we have since grown as close as ever. In fact, she is helping me prepare for my presentation next year. A lovelier person you will never meet."

"I am sure I will find her delightful."

William took his sister's arm, directing her towards the door. "This will have to wait until later. If you would, please inform our aunt that we shall not come early, since you and Elizabeth have already met."

Georgiana seemed amused. "I shall be glad to." She looked over her shoulder at Elizabeth. "As I said before, I am pleased to finally meet you."

Elizabeth forced a smile. "The pleasure is mine."

As William continued to walk her to the door, Georgiana shook off his grip. "I am perfectly able to see myself out."

Then she swept out of the room, her sateen skirts rustling as they swept the floors. William stood in the doorway and listened as the butler addressed her in the foyer, followed by the opening and closing of the front door. His entire demeanour relaxed as he came back into the room.

"Forgive me! I should never have left you here alone. I gave no thought to my sister coming here while I was out."

"Coming to her own home?" Elizabeth chided. "She has more right to be here than I do."

"No, she does not. You are my wife—the mistress of my homes, Elizabeth. Georgiana has refused my advice and my company of late. That is why she is residing at Matlock House. It follows that she might not treat you with respect, either."

"Was I the cause of the breach in your relationship?"

"You? Heavens, no! It started years before I met you." Then his expression softened as he tried to lighten the mood. "I do not have the time or inclination to discuss my difficulties with my sister now. We really must begin preparations if we are to attend the ball. I am assuming you still wish to go."

"I do."

"Then, come! I shall escort you to your dressing room. I understand that your new lady's maid is to arrive today, but in the event she has not, I am prepared to help with your hair."

"She arrived just before Georgiana."

"I am sure you are pleased, if only because you will not have to suffer my help any longer."

"I cannot disparage your help. You did very well."

They were ascending the stairway when Elizabeth remembered where he had been and her spirits fell. "Did... did you complete your business today?"

"Yes, I did. All is well in Richmond."

Would that all was well in my heart.

Elizabeth's dressing room

Dressed and ready to leave, William paced the hall outside of his wife's rooms. Pulling his pocket watch from its place inside his coat for what seemed the hundredth time, he flipped it open and read the dial. Quickly closing it, he knocked on the door.

"Come," Elizabeth called.

Entering the room, he found her sitting in the chair in front of her dressing table as Mrs. O'Reilly placed the last few pins in her hair. When finished, she nodded, dropped a curtsey and practically ran from the room.

Elizabeth was amused. "I think you frightened Mrs. O'Reilly."

"Who?"

"My new maid."

"Oh." William looked at the door through which she had disappeared. "I fear I took no notice of her."

As he looked quite dashing in his black coat, breeches, gold waistcoat and stark white shirt, Elizabeth could not suppress her admiration. Nonetheless, as her gaze moved from his boots to his face, she noticed that he wore a strange expression.

At once, her smile disappeared and a worrying hand flew to one cheek. "Have you spied a smudge on my complexion?"

"I apologise if I was gaping. It is just... you look so very beautiful."

Elizabeth flushed, uncomfortable with his compliment. She suffered no illusions about her looks, for her mother had often lamented her lack of beauty. Besides, Mr. Darcy had never professed to admire anything about her, save her humility.

"You owe me no compliments, sir. I am well acquainted with my defects."

"I can assure you that I have found none." At that moment, William seemed to remember something and began to fumble in a pocket of his coat. "I meant to give you this on our wedding day, but—" He tilted his head in a shrug. "I hope you like it."

He held out a long black velvet case. Elizabeth hesitated only a moment before taking his present and setting it on the dresser in front of her. Lifting the top, a small gasp escaped her involuntarily. It was a pearl necklace, each barely pink pearl perfectly matched to the next. As she looked up through her lashes, she could see William watching her in the mirror, a hesitant look on his face.

"It is beautiful," she whispered.

Reaching over, William picked up each end of the necklace and fastened it around her neck. Elizabeth's hand instinctively came up to glide over the silky beads.

"I have never seen anything quite so lovely. I... I did not expect you to give me a wedding gift. I have nothing for you."

"You are my gift, Elizabeth. Besides, I enjoy giving gifts, and now that I have a wife, well, you will just have to indulge me."

At that moment, Mrs. Barnes appeared in the open door. "Sir, you wanted me to inform you when the carriage was out front."

"Thank you, Mrs. Barnes. We are ready, it seems."

With that, William began to escort Elizabeth from the room before noticing something was amiss. "Would you fetch Mrs. Darcy's shawl, please?"

"Certainly," the housekeeper replied.

In no time at all, they were settled in one of William's finest carriages as it

rumbled over the cobblestones of Grosvenor Square on the way to Matlock House.

Chapter 16

Matlock House
The ball

Attending the ball at Matlock House was more exhilarating and frightening than Elizabeth could have imagined. As their carriage made its way forward in the steady procession of expensive vehicles depositing their occupants in front of the manor, she found her stomach filling with butterflies. From her vantage point, Elizabeth could see the members of London society, each more finely clothed and coiffed than the last, ascending the double row of steps to the imposing front entrance, which was flanked on both sides by several footmen in extravagant gold and blue uniforms, holding Union Jacks and banners with the Matlock crest.

The portico, gravel walks and lawns literally overflowed with huge pots and baskets of colourful flowers resplendent with greenery, while the steps sported coloured lanterns down each side. The lanterns, along with the torches spread throughout the grounds, lit the scene so spectacularly that it reminded Elizabeth of Vauxhall Gardens. Glancing up to the pinnacle of the manor house, she was stunned to realise that, like Darcy House, it was only three stories high, since from further down the street it had appeared much taller.

Glancing timidly at William, Elizabeth found that he was not paying any attention to the scene playing out in front of Matlock House. Instead, he stared glumly out the other window. There was an expression of dread on his face, and Elizabeth began to wonder if she should be as anxious about this soirée as he. Then concluding that it was too late to fret, she steeled herself to face whatever might occur as the carriage lurched forward again.

While it may have seemed to Elizabeth that William was not paying attention, this was far from the truth, for since leaving Darcy House, he had done naught but consider how to shield his wife from the cruelty of his peers. He despised balls in general, and this one in particular, certain that insults would be aimed at Elizabeth not only by Edgar and his friends, but likely by Lady Susan Hartley and her supporters. It would be no hardship for him to refrain from dancing in order to stay by her side, but, knowing Elizabeth, she would accept an invitation to dance and that would spoil his best means of protecting her. His thoughts instantly flew to how she had taken his breath away when he had first seen her dressed for the ball. *If only she were not so very beautiful.*

Barely recognisable was the gown she had worn on their wedding day, for candlelight seemed to give the fabric an ethereal quality. Her new maid had piled her ebony locks atop her head, leaving a few long curls to hang over one shoulder. Pearl pins interspersed throughout her hair emphasised its rich darkness, in addition to matching the necklace he gave her. Smiling, he recalled the look on her face as she opened the case.

"Do you think I look presentable?"

Her hesitant question returned his thoughts to the present, and, unable to resist, he slid the tips of his fingers gently across her cheek.

"You are everything that is lovely tonight, Elizabeth."

A small smile lifted the corners of her lips, and suddenly his heart was full. Wishing to say more, the opportunity was ruined when the door to the carriage abruptly jerked open and a footman began lowering the steps. Disappointed, William exited the carriage, straightened his coat, and reached in to hand Elizabeth out.

"We are late. Do you think your aunt will be cross?"

"She knows I never arrive until the receiving line is finished. I do not relish the stares of those brainless spectators standing about."

That being said, they began up the steps. The few guests still lingering there and on the portico turned to take their measure of Mr. Darcy and his new wife. And, if the increase in the hum of conversation was any indication, they found plenty to like—or dislike. Nonetheless, William noted that Elizabeth stood her ground with the most perfect dignity, and his chest swelled with pride.

Perhaps I underestimated her ability to take on the ton!

The Darcys had barely entered one of the large double doors that led into the ballroom when the music began for the first set. Despite the crush of people who circled the perimeter of the room observing those dancing, Lady Matlock spied them and came in their direction.

"There you are! I am so relieved you are here. I was about to send Edgar to find you."

William looked about the room, his anxiety rising when he realised that his favourite cousin was nowhere in sight. "Where is Richard? I would have thought he would be the first to greet us."

"That horrible General Lassiter has detained him in Highbury. I got a note earlier saying that he would come as soon as he could get away." Then the countess lowered her voice so that only they could hear. "Georgiana told me what she did. Please believe me when I say that I did not know she had left the house. I was not at home at the time."

"No apology is necessary. I know how hard it is to monitor my sister."

"Thank you for being so understanding." She brushed an imaginary piece of lint from William's shoulder. "You look handsome, as always, Fitzwilliam." Then taking both of Elizabeth's hands, Lady Matlock stepped back to examine her. "Your husband should not have worried, my dear, for your gown is quite lovely, as are you."

Then her expression became absolutely serious. "Now, I really must introduce you to as many of my friends as possible. Your uncle is dancing already, so he will be of no help." Her voice lowered again as she learned in closer, "Besides, he is still cross with you both."

She directed Elizabeth towards the location where she always held court—a corner that featured two small settees, bordered on either side by palm plants in huge pots. Though there were several more such havens on either side of the room, Lady Matlock preferred this one, as it was closest to the doors to the terrace. If there was a breeze to be had, it would be enjoyed from that advantageous place.

Already several members of Almack's occupied the area and, as they approached, the countess immediately began one introduction after another. That was how the next half-hour or more passed. If those meeting the new Mrs. Darcy had any reservations as to her suitability, most hid them behind masks of civility for the countess' sake, for Lady Matlock was a formidable foe if crossed. The very few that offered less enthusiastic greetings were far outweighed by the ones eager to move in the countess' circle.

Nevertheless, at some time during the exercise, Elizabeth began to wonder at the futility of it all, for by the time the countess stopped to catch her breath, sending a footman to fetch a glass of punch, Elizabeth could not put one name with any of the faces. She sighed unknowingly.

William noticed and took her hand, leading her to the other side of one of the large palms. "Are you well, Elizabeth?"

"I fear I have met so many people that I do not remember any of their names."

He chuckled and his eyes held kindness as he lifted her chin so that she looked directly at him. Unexpectedly, her heart began to beat faster.

"I can readily understand. It would overwhelm anyone to meet this many of my aunt's friends in such a short span, but you have done exceptionally well. I am proud of you and I think you deserve to escape for a time."

"Escape?" She could not suppress a grin. "How, sir?"

"We could always dance the next set."

"Dance? I thought, from what you told Mr. Bingley, that you despised dancing."

"In the past, I often used that excuse to avoid ..." he coughed a little self-consciously, "certain women."

"Yet you married a woman of no consequence."

Instantly, the playfulness left his eyes. Remembering how Aunt Madeline had said that teasing could be used to harm, she instantly regretted her words. "Forgive me. I meant only to—"

"Darcy, old man!"

William groaned, for he knew that voice only too well, and it was obvious that the man it belonged to was intoxicated.

Suddenly, Edgar slapped him on the back. "What are you doing behind this planter? Hiding from Mother?"

Edgar guffawed and simultaneously a group of men standing nearby laughed raucously. William narrowed his eyes in their direction, causing those with good sense to look away. He recognized the usual pack of wolves that tagged after his cousin, laughing at his every word and deed and making him feel superior. Angrily, he took Elizabeth's hand, intending to lead her to the dance floor, but Edgar stepped in front of them, blocking their retreat.

"Frankly, when Father told me you had married, I found it impossible to believe. It was one thing to defy him over sickly Cousin Anne, but quite another to marry someone… " His voice trailed off as he got a good look at Elizabeth. "However, seeing this exquisite creature, I cannot say that I blame you. Are you not going to introduce us?"

William stiffened. "May I present my wife, the former Elizabeth Bennet. Elizabeth, this is my cousin, Edgar Fitzwilliam."

"Viscount Leighton," Edgar corrected tersely as he took Elizabeth's hand and bowed over it. "Having no title himself, Darcy apparently cannot remember mine." Kissing her knuckles, he added, "Elizabeth. What a lovely name!"

Elizabeth's eyes went wide, though she said nothing in reply. Empowered at her discomposure, Edgar smirked. "Would you do me the honour of dancing the next set? I would love to hear what arts and allurements you used to persuade my dull cousin to marry. I am quite sure the details will far exceed anything I could have imagined."

A roar of laughter from Edgar's cohorts saw the end of William's patience. His face was set like stone as he leaned in to whisper, "If it is your wish to face me at dawn, keep to your present course, and I shall gladly oblige."

Edgar's visage paled instantly, and he swallowed hard. Darcy's expertise with sword and pistol were well known, and though he enjoyed pushing the limits of decorum, Edgar was a coward. Glancing to his associates, he tried to appear unaffected though his next words were more prudent.

"One would think you took me seriously, the way you glower, Darcy!" He bowed again to Elizabeth, saying loudly enough for all to hear, "It was a pleasure meeting you, Mrs. Darcy. Perhaps we shall dance another time."

As Edgar rejoined his friends, more ribald laughter ensued, causing William's colour to rise. As he took a step in their direction, Elizabeth grabbed his hand and squeezed it. That gentle act redirected his attention, for when he felt her hand slide into his, he stilled to look at her. Seeing the smile offered just for him, the corners of his mouth lifted.

"I would have known that he and Richard were brothers for they certainly favour one another, though the colonel is a good bit taller," she whispered.

"Fortuitously, any resemblance to Richard is limited to appearances only. Richard has all the character while Edgar has naught but the title."

"The viscount did impress me as a man who thinks highly of himself."

"You have assessed his character skilfully."

Suddenly, there was a crush of people as the first set ended. Elizabeth turned to find that Lord Matlock was coming in their direction. One of the most beautiful women she had ever seen was hanging on his arm. Tall and blond, she immediately reminded Elizabeth of Georgiana, though her hair was a good deal lighter than her sister's. She was not aware of just who the lady was until the stranger fixed her eyes on William and smiled beguilingly.

"Darcy!" Lady Susan exclaimed, letting go of the earl's arm to rush to where William stood. Sliding her hand up the front of William's coat familiarly, she quickly removed it as though she had forgotten herself. "I told Georgiana earlier that if you were not here, it would simply ruin my entire evening, but I just knew that you could not be so cruel as to ignore my ball."

William stood as stiff as a statue and remained speechless. Her arm still threaded through his, Elizabeth managed to nudge him with her elbow, causing him to speak. "Lady Susan, may I introduce my wife, Elizabeth Darcy."

"Charmed, I am sure," Susan said frostily, brashly taking Elizabeth's measure from head to toe.

"Elizabeth, Lady Susan is the widow of one of my oldest friends, Fletcher, the late Lord Hartley."

William's impervious manner only served to embolden Susan, who fumed behind the facade of a smile. "You forget, Darcy, that you and I were close friends long before you ever met Fletcher."

Suddenly the band began to play, reviving the woman's previously lively manner. She smiled deviously at Elizabeth. "You may be newly married, but since your husband and I are such dear, dear friends, I know that you shall not mind if I steal him for a dance."

Lady Susan wrapped her arm around William's free arm, intent on forcing him to let go of Elizabeth and escort her to the dance floor. He did not budge, however, so Susan became insistent, which served to gain the attention of those nearby. Then, Georgiana appeared from out of nowhere.

"Surely, you would not refuse to dance with Lady Susan, Brother. After all, the ball is in her honour." Then she implored Elizabeth. "Please tell him you do not mind, else he may think you are jealous and refuse."

As every eye locked on her, Elizabeth tried to smile unaffectedly. "Fitzwilliam does not need my permission. He is a grown man, after all."

There was scattered laughter among the onlookers. Left with no choice, since Elizabeth offered no objection, William escorted Susan to the floor.

Curiously, as she watched him walk away, a feeling Elizabeth had never experienced washed over her—jealousy. It completely bewildered her.

"So, we meet again, Miss Bennet."

At the sound of *that* voice, Elizabeth whirled about to face the one man she hoped never to see again. Georgiana was still there, and she looked enquiringly between the two of them.

"Elizabeth, do you know my cousin?"

Andrew Darcy jumped in to answer, a wry smile on his lips. "I met Miss Bennet in Meryton several weeks ago. Though I was only there a short time, we became quite good friends."

"I am Mrs. Darcy now."

"So I have been told."

Andrew noted the uncertainty on Elizabeth's face and was elated, for that followed perfectly Lady Susan's plans. "Since my cousin is dancing with his dear friend, Lady Susan, I thought I might have this dance with you."

"I... I was not going to—"

"I would love to reminisce about the events in Meryton during my stay there. Surely you would not deny me that, and what better way to discuss it than while dancing?"

Comprehending his meaning, she acquiesced. Placing her hand on his arm, they went towards the other dancing couples while Georgiana observed curiously. Elizabeth was relieved to see that her husband and Lady Susan were on the opposite end of a long line.

As they walked, she whispered, "Pray, say whatever it is you wish to say as quickly and quietly as possible. I do not plan to dance the whole set."

"I shall get straight to the point then. How is it that as soon as I left Meryton you married my cousin? From what you told me, he was poorly thought of by all of Meryton, including yourself. In fact, you despised him enough to encourage me to expose his true character to Bingley."

"I found that Mr. Darcy improves upon acquaintance," Elizabeth replied as they took their places in the line.

"Or perhaps his wealth improves upon acquaintance."

Elizabeth stiffened. "I would never marry for money."

"Then why did you marry him?"

She came forward to take Andrew's hand and exchange places. "To save my sisters from the scandal created by your actions; someone saw us in the garden."

"I would have returned to marry you, had I only known."

"You said that you could not afford to marry. Your cousin reiterated that during his offer."

They both completed loops around another couple and then Andrew answered.

"And why could I not afford to marry? Make no mistake about it, I would have married you regardless of my circumstances, had I only known, but it is Darcy who reduced me to poverty. No doubt, as soon as he learned that I had feelings for you, he made an offer. Do you not see? Your marriage was strictly another way to punish me."

"I do not think my husband would marry in order to punish anyone."

The dance came to a point where they waited for other couples to circle the entire group, which gave Andrew leave to speak freely.

"Clearly, you do not know him. Only days before your marriage, London was abuzz with his interest in Lady Susan Hartley. Why do you think his aunt gave this ball in her honour? Do you really believe that, at some point, he will not regret his haste in marrying you?" He was heartened to see uncertainty flash across Elizabeth's face.

"My husband has made his choice," she answered with more bravado than she felt.

"You will learn the truth soon enough. Fitzwilliam has always been a selfish man, used to getting his way and punishing those who do not follow his dictates."

The first part of the set was coming to an end, and it was plain that Elizabeth had heard enough.

"I think you have made yourself perfectly clear, sir. Now if you will excuse me."

She walked away, leaving him staring after her. Hesitating only a moment, Andrew went in the opposite direction. Pleased at how well their meeting had gone, he was well aware of his need to escape before William found him.

Well, Susan, you were very fortunate to find me at Mrs. Younge's inn this morning. Let us see if your plan works and my talk with Elizabeth helps or hinders. It is up to you now!

⁓∞⁓

Relieved to have returned to London so soon, Colonel Richard Fitzwilliam strolled into the ballroom with his usual flair. A favourite among the ladies for his good humour and superior dance skills, he was aware that his regimentals gave him an advantage over the dull clothes worn by most men. Even though a second son, he was in high spirits, for his objective had always been to choose a wife from among the prettier debutantes—one with a large dowry. And though that would not occur anytime in the near future, he felt it his duty to inspect the latest offerings. Dutifully scanning the room, absorbed in deciding which young lady to charm that night, Richard's eyes fell on Elizabeth. She was preoccupied and passed him without notice.

"Mrs. Darcy?"

Elizabeth halted, a look of confusion quickly changed to a wan smile. "Colonel, you have come at last."

"Yes, I only just arrived. I hope Darcy is not too angry with me for being late." Richard looked past her uneasily. "And just where is my stoic cousin? Surely he has not left you alone in this throng?"

"He left me with Georgiana, who has completely disappeared, it seems. As for my husband, he is dancing with Lady Susan."

"Lady Susan?" Instantly, he began searching the dance floor. Spying the couple, he growled, "I am not surprised, not surprised in the least. That woman has always tried to manipulate Darcy to her will."

"Whatever do you mean?"

"Let me explain it this way. She was but ten years of age the first time she told me she intended to marry him. And she has never changed her mind on that subject."

"Not even when she married another?"

"In my opinion, not even then."

Richard spied his mother across the room. "Mother is motioning for us to join her. If you will allow me, I shall escort you in the direction of the lions' den."

Elizabeth could not help but smile at his jest. "I fear I have no choice."

Just as they joined Lord and Lady Matlock, his mother pulled Richard aside so that Elizabeth could not hear. "Richard, did you see Fitzwilliam's horrid cousin, Andrew Darcy? He was dancing with Elizabeth only a moment ago."

A scowl crossed Richard's face, and his eyes narrowed as he examined the room. "Then apparently that rascal accomplished what he set out to do and left before my cousin or I could confront him."

"I can only imagine that Edgar invited him, for I certainly did not!"

"I think likely it was Lady Susan who invited him. After all, they have always been such *good* friends."

"I thought their friendship only a childish fixation. If she still maintains the relationship, I have to wonder at her intelligence."

"Wonder no more, Mother, for she is immature and infantile in her choices."

"Are you not being too harsh?"

"No. I have seen her side with Andrew against Darcy far too often over the years."

"I am horrified to hear it, for I thought so well of her." The countess glanced to Elizabeth, who was standing elegantly alongside Lord Matlock. "Perhaps my nephew has chosen well after all."

"I can assure you that he has."

"I really must redouble my efforts to champion her, then."

Leaving Richard, the countess moved to stand next to her new niece. "I lost track of you, my dear. When I asked Georgiana if she had seen you, she pointed out that you were dancing with Andrew Darcy. I have to admit I was taken aback, as my nephew does not think well of that man."

"While I did not care to dance with him since my husband does not hold him in high esteem, I agreed so as not to draw attention. That is all."

The countess looked as though she might say more, but suddenly the music ended, along with the set. Once more a throng moved to and from the dance floor. This included William and Lady Susan, who still clung to his arm like a leech. Fortuitously, Lord Selfton stepped out of the crowd to ask her for the next set, and fixing a false smile on her face, she had to agree. Thus liberated, William hurried towards his family. His eyes located Elizabeth in the group and then Richard.

As his aunt moved to converse with Elizabeth, William took her place next to Richard, saying, "Could you not have gotten here earlier?"

"I could, had I wished to be court-marshalled. General Lassiter is not used to being told no when he asks me to accompany him. I apologise for not being here as we agreed, but I arrived as quickly as possible, given the circumstances."

"Not soon enough to thwart Andrew, it seems. Whilst I was forced to dance with Lady Susan, he managed to partner my wife. I was just about to quit our dance and confront him when Elizabeth stalked away. Afterward, I saw him quit the room entirely, so he could be as far as Cheapside by now."

"No doubt. What amazes me is how he avoided Mr. Harrington's and Lord Warren's wrath to end up here tonight."

"I share your amazement and intend to find out how that happened before I leave London."

Elizabeth strained to hear the exchange taking place between her husband and Richard, however, Lady Matlock was holding court next to her, and her voice drowned out everything else. Nonetheless, as the countess took to the dance floor again, William was suddenly by her side.

"Did you enjoy your dance with my cousin?" he asked testily.

Rising to her full height, Elizabeth proclaimed, "I was asked to dance, and I felt that I could not refuse."

Unable to control his jealousy, William's arm circled her waist. "Could not or *would* not?"

Elizabeth was not sure if she should be angry at his temper or pleased that he was jealous. Yet she had no time to decide, for Countess Esterházy and her escort, Lord Tottenham, rudely interrupted.

"Mr. Darcy, your aunt and I have been busy planning your sister's coming out. Perhaps it is time that you *and I* schedule a meeting of our own." The invitation was issued in a sultry voice and accompanied by a slow scan of every inch of William's body. Afterward, she boldly locked eyes with Elizabeth saying, "Merely to discuss what we have planned thus far, you understand."

Tottenham, a member of White's board and one whom William despised for his adulterous ways, clearly thought the whole thing very amusing and could barely contain his mirth. William cast him a sinister look before responding, "That is impractical, my lady, for I plan to return to Pemberley straightaway. I fear that I shall be occupied with more important matters before I leave. Besides, anything my aunt proposes will suit, of that I am certain."

Taking another cursory inspection of Elizabeth, the countess replied, "That is a shame, for I dearly wanted your participation." Fortuitously, the music began and she exclaimed, "Come, Totty! Let us show London how a waltz is supposed to be done."

As they walked away, William relaxed. Elizabeth could not, for she was certain that her face was bright red. The countess' proposition, delivered in front of family and strangers alike, had been calculated to humiliate—and it had. Even though William had rejected the *offer*, the countess had considered her an easy target. It stung to know that most of those here tonight probably thought the same.

Completely oblivious to Elizabeth's dismay, William noticed that Richard was now the focus of a lovely red-haired woman with green eyes who smiled shyly at him from behind a painted fan. Feeling guilty for complaining so soundly to his cousin only moments before, he tried to make amends.

"Since I can see to Elizabeth's safety, as I do not plan to dance again, why do you not enjoy yourself by dancing the next set with your young lady?"

"Who?"

"The one who has been making eyes at you for the last few minutes."

"Oh, that one," Richard replied, amused that Darcy had noticed. "I think I shall do just that."

As Richard sauntered over to greet Lord Shaw and his daughter, William turned around to speak to his wife. Unfortunately, she had struck up a conversation with one of his aunt's friends, Lady Clarkson. That conversation continued, to his dismay, until the bell rang for supper.

The meal had concluded and almost everyone had reassembled in the ballroom. The music had resumed and William had asked Elizabeth if she wished to dance.

"I would rather watch," had been her curt reply.

Though he was unsure what Elizabeth was perturbed about, her refusal to dance could not have pleased him more. He truly despised dancing in public, though he thought he would enjoy dancing with his wife if they were alone. As it was, Richard stood nearby, entertaining yet another young debutant with his wit, while his aunt and uncle danced with each other.

To the entire family's relief, Edgar had joined the men in the card room, leaving Georgiana the only family member unaccounted for, and William felt sure that she was still in the dining room with Lady Susan. It seemed the honouree had had a little too much punch and continued to hold court at the head table long after most of the guests had quit the room.

Very pleased that the evening had passed without further ado and was now coming to an end, he was content to stand with his beautiful wife while all the men who had not done so before, came closer to steal a look. His mind now forming lists of what he needed to accomplish upon his return to Pemberley, William did not notice a footman approaching from the side. As the servant held out a silver salver with a note lying upon it, he took the paper and unfolded it to read.

Come to the gazebo. G.

Refolding the missive, he shoved it into his pocket, saying to Elizabeth. "Georgiana needs me."

"Then by all means go to her. I shall be quite safe until you return."

"Are you sure?"

"Richard is nearby."

William's eyes flicked to his cousin and back to her. He nodded. As Elizabeth watched her handsome husband walk in the direction of the terrace and then exit the ballroom, woman after woman turned to follow his progress and a new awareness settled in her heart—she cared more deeply for her husband than she wished to admit. That realisation caused her to shiver.

"Where is my brother?"

Elizabeth's brows knit in confusion as she turned to see Georgiana approach from the opposite direction. "I… I think he is looking for you."

"Would you accompany me to find him then? I am ready to retire, and I wished to say goodnight."

"Certainly."

In the garden

William reached the gazebo only to find it empty. Turning in a circle, he could see no evidence of his sister anywhere in the garden. Confused, he went up the steps and sat on one of the benches, hoping she would soon appear. No sooner had he taken his place under the vine-covered edifice than Susan entered the structure from the other side—the one barely visible due to large shrubs on that end. Instantly, the hair on the back of his neck stood up.

"Lady Susan! I was expecting Georgiana. She asked me to meet her here."

"That is my doing. I wished to speak to you privately." From the way she slurred her words, it was evident that she had had too much to drink.

"This is highly improper. I must leave before someone sees us."

As he stood to go, Susan lunged in front of him. "I WILL have a moment of your time, or I shall follow you inside and have this conversation in front of your little wife." He hesitated, unsure of what to do. "For weeks you led me to believe that you were going to make me an offer. Then, out of the blue, you return to Town married to this... this nobody!"

"That is not fair. I never gave you any reason to think—"

"Yes, you did! Even your sister and your aunt believed we would marry! At the least, you owe me an apology."

"Very well." William hesitated. He did not want to say anything to cause her to react more irrationally. "I am sorry. Things transpired... things that I did not have a hand in, but that needed to be rectified. Thus, Elizabeth and I married. Believe me when I say it was never my intention to hurt you."

Seeing that he meant to leave, Susan threw her arms around his neck, rising on her toes to kiss him full on the lips. Stunned, for a moment William did not react. Once he recovered his senses, however, he removed her arms none too gently.

"Please, Lady Susan. You embarrass yourself!"

"Lady Susan? I would have been Mrs. Darcy if you had been gentleman enough to offer for me. I practically threw myself at you the summer you graduated from Cambridge, but you ignored me. So I had to marry Fletcher! Even now, I would be your mistress, if you asked."

"Madam, it is evident that you are not yourself. I shall leave you and send a servant to assist you."

"Do not bother," she whined. Seemingly overtaken by the liquor, she sat down on a bench. "You are the only one who can comfort me."

William hurried away from her as fast as he could walk, praying that Susan would not follow and that no one had seen them alone together. As he neared the house, he wondered if he looked as flustered as he felt. Straightening his clothes, he stepped into the ballroom again, praying under his breath for good fortune.

A few minutes earlier

"Perhaps my brother thought I was in the garden," Georgiana said innocently as she led the way down the stone steps of the terrace and onto the gravel path that formed a circle through the yard.

"A footman handed him a note and then he said that you needed him."

"How singular," Georgiana said convincingly. "I cannot imagine why he thought it was from me, for it certainly was not."

She could barely contain her excitement as they neared the gazebo, for her brother's voice carried easily over the night air and it was evident that he was talking with a woman. Still, they could not quite make out what was being said without getting closer.

"That is Brother!" Georgiana said, her voice a combination of curiosity and a bit of panic. "Hurry!"

"It could be him," Elizabeth agreed, her voice betraying the apprehension she was beginning to feel. As they arrived at the gazebo, his words suddenly became perfectly clear.

"I am sorry. Things transpired... things that I did not have a hand in, but that needed to be rectified. Thus, Elizabeth and I married. Believe me when I say it was never my intention to hurt you."

They came around the corner just as Susan flung her arms around William, kissing him soundly on the mouth. Georgiana was pleased to see a wounded expression cross Elizabeth's face, and, taking her arm sympathetically, she began to pull her in the direction from which they had come.

"Oh, Elizabeth, I am sorry you witnessed that. Please try not to be upset. You have to realise that he and Lady Susan have been more than friends all their lives and—"

"Stop!" Elizabeth halted in mid step, her voice as cold as ice. "You need never defend him to me again. Now, if you will excuse me."

She hurried toward the terrace, leaving Georgiana behind with a huge smile on her face. Hearing footsteps, Georgiana hid and watched as her brother followed the same path his wife had just taken.

Chapter 17

Matlock House
The ball concludes

An unexpected grief washed over Elizabeth as she hurried back to the house, for William's betrayal was not only a cruel blow to her pride, but it also proved that he had no respect for his wedding vows. In spite of never professing to love him, the sight of him kissing Lady Susan had an involuntary effect—it produced a deep, searing pain in her chest. She found it hard to breathe and slowed her pace, her hand flying to her heart. Beating as though it might leap from her body, Elizabeth took several deep breaths to quiet it. Now blinded by threatening tears, she resumed the path to the house, chastising herself with every step for accepting William's soft words and gentle touch as proof that they could have felicity in their union.

Elizabeth fought the desire to blame her aunt for defending him. For after receiving his wedding present, she had been persuaded to agree with Madeline Gardiner's view on the illegitimate children. After all, his kind-heartedness was contradictory to the cruelty she had ascribed to him.

Regardless, everything was perfectly clear now. A liar thought nothing of feigning kindness to further his goals. Thus, the small reservoir of regard that had begun in Elizabeth's heart disappeared along with her trust, leaving only a desire to strike out at him for making her care. Unfortunately, the voice of reason refused to grant her that luxury.

What did you expect? Yours was never a love match. Did your mother not warn you that wealthy men all have mistresses? Why are you shocked to find him in the arms of another woman? Toss away your romantic notions and accept your marriage for what it is, else you will be disappointed time and again for the rest of your life.

Upon reaching the terrace, she was convinced that every person inside knew that her marriage was nothing but a farce. Fearing she might become ill if she were required to smile and make normal conversation, Elizabeth longed to vanish into thin air so she began to contemplate slipping out of the house and walking home. After all, Darcy House was only a few streets away. As all of these thoughts swirled in her mind, a couple came towards the terrace doors, and she timidly lowered her head and entered the ballroom as they came out.

Richard had just danced a set with yet another debutant and had begun to walk in the direction of a group of his fellow officers when he spied Elizabeth moving hurriedly through the crowd. Thinking it odd that Darcy was not beside her, he followed as she went into the hallway. By the time he reached the foyer, he could hear her conversing with one of the footmen.

"Mrs. Darcy? May I be of service?"

Elizabeth looked anxiously over her shoulder and then turned to face him. Her eyes flicked to the floor. "I... I was just explaining that I need to leave. I feel a bit poorly, and a breath of fresh air will be the perfect solution."

"Leave?" Richard looked behind to see if his cousin was perhaps slow in coming. "I did not see Darcy. Let me—"

"No!" She exclaimed, then smiled calmly. "I meant to say that I do not wish him to leave because of me. He seems to be enjoying himself. Besides, I am perfectly able to walk back to Darcy House. It is not nearly as far as I often walk in Meryton."

Richard's brows furrowed, and he motioned to a more secluded section of the foyer. "Perhaps we should step over here so we may talk privately."

Glancing back to the hallway that led to the ballroom, Elizabeth's unease seemed to grow and, for a moment, Richard thought she might bolt for the street. Instead, she conceded and they stepped away from the footmen. As soon as they were out of his hearing, he began to speak.

"Please understand that I cannot allow you to strike out on foot. London is not Meryton, and no woman is safe walking at this hour of the night, even in Grosvenor Square."

Elizabeth looked to the front door, as though pondering the validity of his claim.

"Could you have our carriage brought round then? I can always send it back for Mr. Dar—for my husband, once I am home."

Richard did not have time to answer, for at that very moment, William entered the foyer from the ballroom.

"Elizabeth! I have been searching everywhere for you."

Richard knew from Darcy's expression that he was upset and that they could best solve their problems without his interference. "If you both will excuse me, Mother is probably searching high and low for me."

William waited until his cousin was out of sight before taking the measure of his wife. "Elizabeth, what were you and Richard discussing so seriously?"

"If you must know, a short while ago I felt unwell. I was speaking to your cousin about returning to Darcy House."

"Should I send for a physician?"

Her lips formed a tight line. "There is no longer a need, for whatever ailed me has passed."

William look puzzled. "So, you were going to return to Darcy House by yourself?" She nodded. "Why in heaven's name would you not just tell me?"

"I did not wish for you to have to leave as well."

"Nonsense! If you are ill, I want to know and to escort you home. There should be no ambiguity on that subject."

William signalled for one of the footmen, who instantly responded and was just as quickly sent to make sure their carriage was brought to the door.

Though they had not spoken since entering the carriage, William could tell that Elizabeth was in a dark mood. She had taken the seat across from him, and whenever the street lamps shined through the window, her cheeks looked as though they were wet. It caused his heart to go out to her.

"Forgive me if I have done anything to offend you." She did not reply, so he continued. "I was not pleased with having to attend and I may not have acted as a gentleman should."

Still she said nothing.

"Elizabeth, will you please tell me why you are upset? I am not very good at reading minds."

"I am only tired. That is all."

By then the carriage was coming to a stop in front of Darcy House and footmen began to swarm around it like ants, opening the door and lowering the steps. At the portico, the front door swung open. Mr. Barnes stood waiting. Elizabeth hurried up the steps the moment her feet hit the ground.

After Elizabeth was dressed in her nightgown and Mrs. O'Reilly had returned to her own quarters, there was a knock on her bedroom door. Hesitating for a moment, she went to the door, turned the key and opened it partially. William stood without in his dressing gown.

"I just wanted to remind you that we are leaving very early tomorrow for Pemberley."

"I realise that."

Still, William waited awkwardly. Finally, he heaved a sigh. "Again, I apologise if I did anything to upset you tonight. It was not my intent."

Elizabeth said sharply, "I have already said that I am just tired. What more can I say? Now, if you will excuse me, I need to rest in order to rise early."

"Yes... yes, of course. Goodnight, Elizabeth."

The door shut soundly in his face without a similar sentiment from his wife. Dejected, William turned and entered his bedroom.

The next morning

The sun was full in the sky by the time Elizabeth realised that she had not risen early as was expected. According to her husband, they were to have left for Pemberley just after daylight. As she sat up in bed, she noticed that even the curtains had not been opened, which was the maids' customary way of letting her know it was time to rise. Sliding from the bed, she ran to the door to her dressing room and opened it, only to find that the trunks that had been placed there the day before were still there.

Suddenly the door to the sitting room opened, and Mrs. O'Reilly came in. "Oh, Mrs. Darcy. You are awake."

"Yes, I am, but I fear I have overslept. My husband must be livid. Is everyone waiting for me?"

"No ma'am. In fact, Mr. Darcy left instructions this morning that you were not to be disturbed. According to Mrs. Barnes, there was a matter of great urgency, and he left for Richmond very early this morning."

A frown crossed Elizabeth's face. "Richmond?"

"Yes, and as I understand it, we shall not be travelling to Pemberley until he returns."

Just at that moment two maids appeared in the open door, one carrying a tray with tea and scones and the other with her arms full of linens.

"I hope you do not mind, but I had Cook send up tea. I know that you do not usually eat too heartily in the morning. The dining room has already been cleared in anticipation of a light luncheon if the master and Colonel Fitzwilliam should return by then."

"What time did you say my husband left for Richmond?"

"It was still dark, Mrs. Barnes said."

With all the possibilities of what might have happened in Richmond spinning in her head, Elizabeth sat down to eat, though later she had no recollection of what she had consumed.

An hour later, she was dressed, and Mrs. O'Reilly had styled her hair. No longer needing her services, Elizabeth dismissed the maid. Her heart was set on reading in the conservatory, since it was raining, so she opened her sitting room door and peered into the hallway. Hoping to avoid all of the tumult that would ensue if the servants found out that *Mrs. Darcy* had left her rooms, she entered the hall and tiptoed to the stairs at the rear of the hall. This route was her best chance of getting downstairs without having to answer a thousand questions.

She made her way to the conservatory before realising that she had left her book upstairs. Undaunted, she reasoned that the library was only three doors away, and she could select another book to read. She had no more than disappeared behind the last row of bookshelves when she heard her husband and his cousin talking as they entered the room. Since she had no desire to speak to William, she looked about and spied a small opening at the end of the shelves where the sliding ladder rested when not in use. Squeezing into it, she held her breath, hoping they would not search for a book and find her.

As she listened to their banter, she realised that one of them seemed to be walking with great difficulty, perhaps using a crutch or a cane, for it scraped the floor with every step. Though full of curiosity, she dared not look.

"Sit here, Darcy." There was the sound of a chair being moved.

"Thank you. I fear I cannot manoeuvre the staircase and we can speak privately here until Barnes returns."

"You should have waited in the coach until they could take you directly to your bedroom."

"Can you just imagine the scandal? Fitzwilliam Darcy being carried into his house in the middle of the day? No, better for me to walk into the house on my own two feet, such as they are."

"You are right. The *ton* would have you coming home roaring drunk, the way they distort everything." Then Richard's voice became grave. "I thought you were going to die when the wall fell. I called out a warning, but you were not listening."

"I was thinking of only one thing."

"I understand." Richard replied sombrely. Then his voice grew angry. "I cannot believe that that blackguard accidentally started a fire and then ran

away instead of sounding the alarm! Bloody bastard needs to hang when they find him!"

"There was only one witness who claimed that is how it happened, and I do not know the man."

"Yes, but why would Hobson run if it were not true?"

"I cannot dwell on that now. All I can remember is that poor boy hiding under the bed, thinking he would be safe." Elizabeth heard him take a deep, ragged breath. His voice sounded as though it cracked as he continued, "And his mother perishing as she tried to save him."

"It is not your fault. You thought the man was reliable. After all, he had good references as a steward."

"I cannot help but feel responsible. Mr. Hobson was supposed to see to their welfare, to keep them safe."

"You did the best you could, Darcy. No one can blame you. In fact, you went far beyond what most men would have done. You must believe that."

"I will always wonder if I did enough."

"That is because you are goodhearted. Now, I must return to Bingley's to wash this soot off and get some clean clothes. Then I shall notify the young woman's family and arrange for the burials. That, at least, will be one thing that you will not have to handle."

"Her parents will want her and the child buried in Lambton, of that I am certain, for our tenants have always made use of the cemetery next to the church. Do whatever is necessary and send the bills to Pemberley."

"Of course." Elizabeth heard footsteps going towards the door.

"Richard, I do not know what I would have done without your support throughout this entire ordeal. You not only helped me to keep this entire scandal quiet, but you have kept my spirits up. At times, the children and their mothers seemed only another burden on my shoulders. You have made it less so."

"You know that I was only too glad to be of service." He hesitated. "I hate to bring this up, but do you think you will be able to attend the services?"

"I suppose I shall have to leave that to Mr. Graham."

"Yes, Barnes has sent for him. I expect he will be here at any time."

Just then Elizabeth heard the voice of Mr. Barnes telling William that the footmen were ready. There was a lot of scuffling of feet, a few groans she attributed to the injury they mentioned and then the room went silent.

After waiting for what seemed an eternity, she chanced a peek out of her hiding place. Satisfied at seeing no one, she slipped to the end of the bookshelf. The library was empty, so she rushed to the door and peered down the hallway. It was vacant as well; thus she headed back to her room the same way she had come. Reaching the second floor, Elizabeth was just in time to see the backs of several men carrying someone into William's dressing room. As that door slammed shut, she ran for her own door and quickly disappeared inside.

Leaning back against the door, she considered all that she had just heard and began to cry, her heart broken for those who had perished in the fire.

And to think he considered his own child merely a burden!

Later that Day

Elizabeth kept to her room the rest of the day, having a light lunch served on her balcony. She did not even bother enquiring if her husband had returned from Richmond. As upset as she was with William after the ball, she considered herself fortunate to be able to hide in her rooms, for she had worried what she would say the next time they met. However, her luck in keeping out of sight was coming to an end.

It was nearing time to come inside, for the sun was waning, when she looked up to find Mrs. Barnes standing at the door to the balcony where she still sat reading. It was obvious that the housekeeper was studying her with an entirely different expression than the friendly, welcoming one of yesterday. Her mien was formal and detached, which did not surprise Elizabeth. After all, she reasoned, the servants were loyal to her husband, not her, and it was plain that they had noticed her insensitivity with regard to his injury. Especially in light of his being carried to his room, something she would have seen or heard, or, at the least, learned from Mrs. O'Reilly.

The fact was that her lady's maid had informed her; however, Elizabeth had shocked her by declaring that it could not have been too serious an injury if no one had bothered to notify her. That had disappointed Mrs. O'Reilly, it seems, for she had silently returned to her rooms.

"Excuse me, Mrs. Darcy, but Mr. Darcy asked that you come to his bedroom."

Elizabeth decided to play ignorant. "Why did he send you to summon me? Could he not simply come here and talk as we normally do?"

"Are you not aware that he was injured in Richmond this morning?"

"Yes, but I assumed it was minor. Else, I would have been consulted."

"Mr. Darcy did not wish to upset you, but he is unable to leave his bed until Mr. Graham gives him permission, so he asked that you come to him."

"Mr. Graham is…?"

"He has been the Darcys' physician for many years," Mrs. Barnes said curtly.

"I see. So tell me, how serious is the injury?"

"If you will forgive me, it is his place to say, not mine."

Elizabeth stood up. "Of course."

She followed the elderly housekeeper across the hall to her husband's dressing room. After Mrs. Barnes opened the door, she stepped aside to let Elizabeth enter first. The smell of sandalwood immediately assaulted her senses. That fragrance was the main ingredient in the cologne William preferred and his coats always smelled of it. She would never admit it, but she had loved the scent ever since the first time she had been close enough to him to notice it.

As she passed through the room, Elizabeth found its dark furniture very masculine and the blue and cream wallpaper striking. Entering his bedroom she found it even more impressive, for it was decorated in the same manner, but also had a recessed ceiling featuring a fresco of an Italian villa. Her eye was drawn upward, and she was still looking up when William spoke.

"Please come closer, Elizabeth."

The housekeeper immediately left them alone and Elizabeth edged closer to the right side of the bed. He was lying with his right foot out of the covers, propped on a pillow and both ankle and foot were wrapped in bandages. Determined not to look at or enquire about his injury, Elizabeth tried to focus on his face. Instead, her eyes keep returning to the musculature of his naked chest which was covered by fine black hair. That aspect of his body was noticeable now that he wore no cravat and his shirt was open. The sight made her heart beat so fast that it thrummed in her ears, and she was silently cursing her vulnerability when he began to speak.

"As you know by now, we will not be going to Pemberley as I planned."

"Oh? I am deeply disappointed. The Gardiners are to return to Lambton next week to retrieve their children and I assured them that I would see them there."

"I am sorry to thwart your plans. Something occurred to prevent my being able to travel."

"What happened?" she asked, her voice sounding oddly unsympathetic.

"You have heard me speak of Richmond."

"Yes."

"I have an estate there, and on the property are two houses. Last night one of them caught fire and burned to the ground."

Her courage rose. This was her opportunity to let him know she was not ignorant of his children and she did not appreciate his cavalier attitude towards them.

"Was anyone hurt?"

"Yes." His eyes dropped. "A woman and child lost their lives in the fire." He nodded towards his injury. "That was how I was injured, trying to recover their bodies. I intend to make sure they are given a decent burial in Lambton."

"How noble of you," Elizabeth replied, forgetting all of Aunt Gardiner's counsel. "You are in control, even in death."

William's brow knit in bewilderment. "I do not have the pleasure of understanding you."

"No, I imagine you do not, for you have no idea that you are selfish. However, from the very beginning, you took charge of my life, convincing my father that I *must* marry you to thwart a scandal. And you did not stop there. No, you had to control the smallest details of my life, as well. You decided when I was tired, or hungry. You would not even allow me the privilege of selecting the colour, pattern or materials for a single gown ordered from Mrs. Bouvier! They were all made by your design!"

As William looked at her with his mouth agape, she felt invigorated. It gave her reason to continue.

"More important of all, you have been most selfish in regard to those who died at Richmond. I cannot imagine losing a child," she retorted, "but I know I would have more love for my child, even if he were illegitimate, than to ever refer to him as a burden."

"*Excuse me?*"

"I was in the library, searching for a book, when I overheard you tell Colonel Fitzwilliam that you thought of your own children as burdens on your shoulders. You cannot deny it."

Instantly, William's eyes narrowed, and he tilted his head as though to hear her clearly. "Did you say *my children*?"

"Do not act innocent, for I know about them. The night the Matlocks came here to confront you, I went back downstairs to tell you that I was going to the Gardiners' the next day; however, once downstairs, I heard you and your cousin discussing your illegitimate children in Richmond and the fact that you did not want me to know about them."

Suddenly William began struggling to sit up, a small groan signifying his efforts. The medicine that Mr. Graham had administered earlier for his pain had not taken effect.

Biting her lip at the rebuke sure to come, Elizabeth stood her ground; for, after all, she was in the right.

William's breath was laboured by the time he was sitting upright, and he replied through gritted teeth. "And this is your opinion of me! This is the estimation in which you hold me! I thank you for explaining it so fully. My faults, according to your calculation, are heavy indeed!"

"I have every reason in the world to think ill of you. I saw you kissing Lady Susan in the garden during the ball and any trust I had in you was lost. And no motive could excuse the unjust and ungenerous part you acted in the misery of the poor women and their children at Richmond. You dare not, you cannot deny that you have been the principal reason those poor souls were brought into the world fatherless."

Suddenly it was though a curtain fell between them. William's entire countenance changed, and his voice sounded dull and lifeless with his answer.

"You have said quite enough, madam. I perfectly comprehend your feelings. Forgive me for taking up so much of your time. I am sure you have more important things to do."

Elizabeth was stunned that he made no attempt to defend himself. She had planned a rebuttal to every argument he might possibly put forth. Now, it seemed, she would not have the opportunity to use them. When it became clear that he was not going to refute her charges, she rushed from the room, slamming the door behind her.

Insufferable man!

The next day
Elizabeth's bedroom

Mrs. O'Reilly came into her bedroom while it was still dark, waking Elizabeth from a deep sleep. As she rubbed her eyes, she could not believe that her maid was up so early.

"Wha… What time is it?"

"I am not quite sure. Just before dawn, I should think. You and I are off to

Pemberley today."

"Only the two of us?"

"I heard Mrs. Barnes tell her husband that Colonel Fitzwilliam has to go to York, and he will be escorting our coach."

"And my husband?"

"Oh, Mr. Darcy cannot travel until his ankle is much improved."

The realisation that her husband was sending her to Pemberley but was not going himself, made Elizabeth feel peculiar. What would the servants here think, and more importantly, what would those at Pemberley think, since they had never met her? In the end, she knew that there was nothing she could do to change William's mind, so she climbed out of bed and began getting ready.

Truth be known, if Mr. Darcy wanted to send me to , he could do so without any questions asked. And he may very well wish to after yesterday.

William's bedroom

As Richard entered shortly after daylight, Mr. Graham was already in William's bedroom, attending to his injury. William was very pale, likely due to the physician's manipulation of his ankle. When the fallen beam landed, it had cut through his boot and burned a large portion of skin before the others could lift it off. The sight of it made Richard's nose crinkle, for he well remembered the putrid smell associated with these type of injuries during campaigns in His Majesty's service. Silently, he moved closer.

"I was just about to treat the burns and rewrap it, Colonel," the physician stated, retrieving a jar from the black bag that was beside him on the bed. "I would have liked to have gotten a look at this ankle before it swelled. As it is, I am not certain if any bones are broken, though I think not. Otherwise, I believe there would be even greater pain. Would you like to examine the wound before I finish up? I know that you have experience with such things, what with your occupation."

"I have had more than my share." Richard conceded, leaning in for a better look. "I would never have thought a charred beam could inflict so much damage."

"If the boot had not split, we would only be dealing with the damage to the ankle. Burns add complications of their own, as you well know."

"Discounting the swelling, I will say that the burns are not as red today." What was left unsaid was that Richard had seen many men lose their limbs with less serious damage.

"I agree," the physician replied, his eyes locking with Richard's in a silent acknowledgement of the true severity of the injury. "Nonetheless, we must pray that infection does not set in." Mr. Graham held up the jar. "This may prevent that from happening, though it is not a pleasant remedy to endure." He met William's eyes. "It will sting, sir."

William nodded. Bracing as the man dabbed the potion on his ankle, he closed his eyes and grasped the covers. Afterward, the physician reapplied the bandages. Satisfied, he prepared to leave, putting everything back into his bag.

"I have given Mrs. Barnes a draught you must take three times a day. It is bitter, but it is essential to your recovery."

Resignedly William nodded.

"I shall come every morning to change the bandages and check your progress. I do not want you on your feet; however, if you have men enough to carry you, you may occupy other rooms to alleviate boredom. Just be sure to keep your foot elevated."

Richard answered in William's stead. "Thank you for your service, Mr. Graham. Be assured that my cousin will follow your orders, or his staff will report to me." He grinned at William. "And he does not want me administering the draughts and supervising his care, I assure you."

William rolled his eyes while the physician laughed. "On that note, I shall bid you good day then, Mr. Darcy. Colonel."

Instantly the physician was out the door, leaving Richard and William alone. Richard wasted no time getting directly to the point.

"I got your note this morning. Let me see if I understand. You are sending your wife to Pemberley whilst you recuperate here, and since I must go to York at General Lassiter's behest, you wish me to escort her. Is that correct?"

"Yes."

"I cannot believe this. It goes totally against your character to send your wife on to your home alone. Why not keep her here with you until you are well enough to travel?"

"Elizabeth planned to meet her relations, the Gardiners, in Lambton next week. I see no reason to prevent that just because I am incapacitated."

"How absurd. She could always see them in Town after they return. Try again, Darcy."

William groaned. "Must you be so inquisitive?"

"Yes, I must. I enquired of Barnes how Mrs. Darcy was handling the fact that you were injured and was informed that she had showed no concern whatsoever. If you expect me to escort her to Pemberley, I insist on an explanation for her behaviour since the ball; for to be truthful, at present I am not predisposed to like her any better than Lady Susan."

With no other option, William told Richard all that Elizabeth had said when they argued the evening before. By the time he was finished, Richard was angrily pacing across the floor.

"I cannot believe you did not refute the rubbish she spouted—*your* illegitimate children indeed! And anyone who knows how you feel about fidelity in marriage would know that you did not instigate the kiss with that viper!"

"I suppose that after the fire and my injury, I was too despondent to bother explaining. I blame myself for those deaths and to hear her blame me... In a way, she is right."

"Good Lord, Darcy, listen to yourself! You are not to blame for anyone's death. And, you should tell her everything so that she will see your true character."

"She has already sketched my character to her satisfaction," William said woodenly. "Already she believed me capable of imposing myself on innocent women and fathering illegitimate children, so it was not difficult for her to believe that I am a philanderer after she saw Lady Susan kiss me. And though those are her gravest charges, she allows that there is still more to despise about me."

"More faults. Such as?"

"She hates me because I am selfish and opinionated. In short, even if I were exonerated of Andrew's transgressions, I am still an overbearing arse."

On any other day Richard would have teased him about those aspects of his personality, but not today.

"First, you have been a bachelor for a long time; second, you were forced to take charge of Pemberley and raise your sister at a young age. Blast it all! If you are domineering, you acquired it honestly. Besides, any good woman could tease a decent man out of those trifling habits. I would be glad to apprise her of your integrity."

"I wanted to win her love, not have her care because someone convinced her of my honour." William was silent for a long moment. "You were right. I should not have forced her to marry me. In her mind, I will always be the one to blame for Andrew's actions because I left him impoverished. It follows that he could not marry any of the women he ruined because of me."

"That blackguard took advantage of those women, never intending to marry them. And he left his children for you to raise simply because he is a degenerate!"

"God help me, I do not care what Elizabeth believes at this point. I need you to escort her and her maid to Pemberley. You are the only one I trust to see to their safety."

"Are you sure this will not make matters worse between the two of you?"

"Can they be any worse?" Richard shrugged in acknowledgment.

"Please help me, Cousin," William pleaded with no pretence of cheeriness. "I need time alone to prepare for the kind of a marriage I never wished to suffer." He forced a smile, though his eyes did not share in it. "Whilst my ankle recovers, hopefully I will recoup my common sense and return to my former outlook regarding the great institution of marriage. Then I shall be able to go on with my life. I imagine that my wife will welcome a reprieve from me, as well."

"If that is your wish," Richard agreed, sounding as despondent as his cousin. "Thaggart is travelling with me, and we shall ride alongside the coach. Knowing Mrs. Darcy's mindset, I dare not ride inside, for if she utters any more of that rubbish, I cannot promise to keep silent."

"However you wish to ride is up to you. Since her lady's maid is accompanying her, there will be no problem if you decide to share the coach."

"Thank you, but no. By the way, I told the general that if you were worse, I would stay in London, and he was very understanding. He even offered me time away, if need be. So you have only to send for me if I am needed. I can take a few months' leave, if necessary."

"I appreciate your concern."

"So, I suppose I am ready to leave then; however, I do require something from you in return." William looked puzzled. "I expect you to follow Mr. Graham's instructions whilst I am gone. I do not wish to return and find that you are no better or, God forbid, worse."

"You have my word."

"Excellent." Richard leaned over to shake his cousin's hand. "If only your wife knew the man that I know."

William smiled wanly. "She would think him daft for presuming she could ever have loved him."

Richard just shook his head before hurriedly exiting the room.

I fear you are right, Cousin.

Chapter 18

Darcy House
Later that Morning

Within an hour of rising, Elizabeth had broken her fast and was dressed and ready to leave. The large trunks that had been piled in the foyer, due to the number of new clothes Mrs. Bouvier had completed, were now missing, and she presumed they were aboard the coach. The only thing left was for her and Mrs. O'Reilly to board. Fully expecting William to send for her before they departed, she was stunned when Colonel Fitzwilliam came down the grand staircase and made an announcement.

"Time to leave!" he declared, stopping in front of Mrs. Barnes. "You will keep me informed about Mr. Darcy's progress. Rest assured that I shall return at the slightest sign of a problem, so an express would be appreciated in that event."

"You can rely on me, Colonel," the housekeeper answered. Then she cut her eyes towards Elizabeth. "We all think so very highly of Mr. Darcy. We will be on tenterhooks until he shows true signs of recovery."

"As will I," he said worriedly. He looked at Elizabeth, who appeared to be paying no attention to their discussion. "Mrs. Darcy?" When she glanced at him, he motioned to the front door. "It is four days to Pemberley and we have no time to lose, so let us take our leave. It will likely rain again this afternoon, and the roads are already impassable in some places. I fear that any more bad weather will impede our progress markedly."

Elizabeth glanced warily to the top of the grand staircase. "Does my husband not wish to speak to me before we leave?"

"I just left him, and he did not mention it," Richard said brusquely. "Would you like me to ask?"

Her face crimsoned. "No... no, I just thought... "

Ignoring her, Richard said loudly, "Mr. Barnes, I believe we are ready to board. Where did Thaggart go?"

"He was having a sweet roll in the kitchen when last I saw him," the butler offered, noting the tension between the master's cousin and wife. "I shall fetch him for you."

Richard made no attempt to escort Elizabeth; instead, he strode to the front door and stood observing the scene on the street below. If Elizabeth thought anything of his slight, she did not show it as she walked past the colonel, out the door and down the steps, followed by her maid. At the bottom, a footman held the door open as they entered the imposing Darcy coach.

Summarily, Thaggart was located, and he and Richard came down the front steps, each mounting an imposing stallion being held by a groomsman. As the coach got underway, they took a place on either side of the vehicle.

On the road to Pemberley
Stag and Boar Inn

The first two days on the road were spent in the same manner—the ladies rode in the coach, the men alongside. Even in the afternoons when showers came from out of nowhere, the colonel and his batman stoically rode in the rain, despite attempts by Elizabeth to get them to ride inside. Upon reaching the post inns where they changed horses, William's cousin stayed with the coach, while Thaggart escorted Elizabeth and Mrs. O'Reilly inside the building. There they would occupy a table and enjoy a cup of tea and often a biscuit until the coach was ready to resume. At that point, Thaggart would come back inside to fetch them. Everything was accomplished with as little conversation between the Colonel and Elizabeth as possible, something not lost on her. She assumed that her husband had told his cousin of their argument and accepted that it had resulted in being shown the cold shoulder.

Just as during the day, when they reached their destination in the evening, they spoke very little. Since a servant had been sent ahead to arrange rooms and horses, all Richard had to do was sign the register. Then he would retire to his room, not to be seen until the next day, while Thaggart supervised the luggage and the horses. Mr. Darcy was well known along the route from Pemberley to London, so each proprietor wished to please the new Mrs. Darcy and, by extension, her husband; thus, they offered every courtesy to their party, including hot water for baths and meals in their rooms. This aspect of being married to a man as powerful as Fitzwilliam was something that Elizabeth had never anticipated, and the luxury of invoking his name to obtain good service brought feelings of guilt and shame. After all, why should she benefit from his name when it suited, and spurn the connection otherwise?

As a result of the tension, Elizabeth had reached her breaking point by the third day of travel. Dawn broke with an enormous thunderstorm and, tired of pretending that she was not wounded that Richard treated her as the culpable party, her frustration gave rise to righteous anger. When the chance to confront him materialized, she decided to act, knowing that it would also prove that she was the better person.

How dare he act as though I am the one at fault? Indeed, he is almost as wicked as Mr. Darcy, for he helped keep the children a secret. A sensible man would at least admit that my husband is no saint and not be like my Aunt Gardiner—blind to his every defect because of his rank in society. Today, I shall brook no opposition. Colonel Fitzwilliam and the sergeant shall ride inside the coach, whether they speak to me or not. My concern for his wellbeing will at least prove that I am not without concern for the welfare of others, as is the wont of some.

As she marched out of her room, Elizabeth met a maid coming towards her with a pail of water.

"I need to speak with Colonel Fitzwilliam, who is a member of my party. Could you tell me which room he was assigned?"

The young girl stopped, dropped a curtsey and replied, "Yes, ma'am, he is in number seven, at the end of the hall, but I believe I saw him downstairs already."

Elizabeth thanked the girl and, giving a quick glance in the direction of his room, decided to trust the maid's recollection. In a few seconds, she was standing in the common area, dotted with small tables already packed with customers. In this room, anyone with the means could purchase food and drink, and a good many waiting out the rain had done so. She noted that Thaggart was at a corner table, playing cards with three men. Immediately upon seeing Elizabeth, he rose and made his way to her.

"Sergeant, could you tell me where I might find Colonel Fitzwilliam?"

"The colonel went outside several minutes ago, ma'am. I assume he was going to the stables to talk with the liveryman. He told me earlier that he was not sure if the roads would be passable due to all the rain." As though a testament to the truth of that statement, a huge clap of thunder rattled the windows at that very moment. "He said that I was not to worry about anything until further notice."

"I see," Elizabeth replied, looking anxiously at the storm raging outside the structure. The wind was as fierce as she had ever seen, whipping the rain sideways, whilst bending small trees almost to the ground.

"I shall be glad to locate him for you."

"That will not be necessary, Sergeant. You may return to your table." Thaggart nodded and hurried to rejoin the card game.

Pushing the door open against the force of the wind, Elizabeth held fast to her bonnet as she walked onto the narrow porch. Though covered by a slanted roof, the structure was not well protected from the elements and she realised immediately that she should have worn a cloak, for her dress was quickly soaked. Deciding she had no choice but to go back inside, a movement caught her eye as she turned. Richard was standing on the opposite end of the porch, barely visible in the billowing mist. Wearing his cocked hat and his greatcoat with its collar turned up against the rain, he looked in the direction of the stables, oblivious to her presence, so she called his name.

Turning, Richard said angrily, "Mrs. Darcy! What in the blazes are you doing out in this downpour?" All the while he spoke, he was removing his coat and then proceeded to place it around Elizabeth's shoulders. "Where in the world is Thaggart? He was supposed to keep an eye out for when you came downstairs."

"I spoke to the sergeant, and he offered to find you. Please do not fault him, for he did not see me go out the door." She squirmed under his continued censure. "Sir, I know that you would rather not speak to me; you have made that perfectly clear. However, in light of the severity of the weather, I feel we must address your determination to ride outside the coach, along with the sergeant. In a downpour of this magnitude, both of you will surely catch your death, not to mention the danger from lightning."

As if to prove her point, lighting struck a tree on the other side of the road, causing a huge limb to hang precariously. Elizabeth ducked at the sound of it, but Richard never flinched.

"Please, I beg you, ride inside the coach today."

"How very noble of you!"

The irony of repeating the exact words she had said to Fitzwilliam was not lost on Elizabeth. Regardless, she was determined to be the better person.

"I see no reason why we cannot put our differences aside, if only while the weather is so fierce."

"That is not the issue."

"I do not understand."

"The issue, Miss Bennet—*oh excuse me, Mrs. Darcy*—is whether I wish to ride with someone who disparaged my cousin so meanly after he rescued her, nay her entire family, from certain ruin. And, I might add, against my advice. I am not sure I can keep silent from here to Pemberley in the face of such ungratefulness."

"Ungratefulness!" Elizabeth's colour rose as she lost her resolve to be civil. She sputtered, "I should be grateful to be married to a man who has fathered illegitimate children? Children you helped him to hide!"

"Only someone wholly unacquainted with him could believe Darcy capable of ruining innocent women and fathering bastards."

"I *know* him capable because I heard it from his own mouth... and yours."

"And what exactly did you hear, pray tell? Did you hear me or my cousin actually say the children were his?"

A puzzled expression crossed Elizabeth's face. Try as she might, she could not recall the exact conversation. Seeing her hesitation, Richard expounded on the truth.

"You did not hear that, Mrs. Darcy, because the children are not your husband's; they belong to your favourite—Andrew. His dissolute ways brought those poor children into the world and ruined their mothers' lives. Out of the goodness of his heart, my cousin rescued them, set them up in a decent home and began a fund to provide them with an education. Not unlike how he rescued you because of his generous heart."

"I... I did not—" Elizabeth mumbled, her mind too muddled to think.

"Did not what?" Richard's probed unsympathetically. "Did not consider why he should give a care if you or your sisters were ruined? Did not recognise that he is a good man? Did not give my cousin the benefit of the doubt? Not even once?"

Finally pride stepped in, and Elizabeth's hands formed fists. "Why should I trust you to tell me the truth? Or him, either? I found him kissing Lady Susan at the ball. Any man who would forsake his marriage vows would—"

"For someone I once thought so clever, I am amazed at your inability to see what is right before your eyes. For reasons known only to God, he is utterly in love with you. Even my father, who is usually unobservant, said that Darcy looked like a lamb to the slaughter as he led Lady Susan to the dance floor. And she boasted that she had your blessing, I am told. I warned you that she desires him, always has. It was *she* who tricked him into coming to the gazebo, and *she* who instigated the kiss—not the other way around."

Stunned, Elizabeth was left speechless.

"Excuse me," Richard said wearily as he passed her, meaning to leave. "The weather is too poor to chance the roads. We shall spend another night here. Hopefully, the weather will improve, for, to be truthful, I much prefer Titan's company. At least he is clever enough to feel gratitude when he ought."

Continuing down the narrow porch, when he got to the door, Richard glanced back to where Elizabeth stood in shocked silence. "I suggest you come in out of the rain, Mrs. Darcy. That is what any *sensible* person would do."

With his jaw firmly set in a scowl, he entered the inn and went straight to his room to rest.

Pemberley

As Mrs. Reynolds stood in the hallway outside the library reading the express just delivered, her expression turned to one of bewilderment. Mrs. Fitzwilliam happened to be walking to the library at that particular moment and, seeing the housekeeper absorbed in the missive, stopped to enquire if all was well. Flustered to be caught unawares, the grey-haired servant uncharacteristically sputtered her answer.

"I do not… that is to say, I am sure… it is just that… "

"That?" Olivia said kindly.

"Mrs. Fitzwilliam, would you mind very much if I asked you… well, the circumstances surrounding the master's marriage have taken an unexpected turn and… "

Olivia reached out to pat the long-time servant's hand. "I know that you are not one to gossip, Mrs. Reynolds. If you have concerns, they are fuelled by your wishes for my nephew's wellbeing. If I can answer your question without betraying a trust, I will be happy to do so."

"I have just received this express saying that Mrs. Darcy is to arrive tomorrow."

"How wonderful!" she declared. "We are at last to meet the young lady who has captured Fitzwilliam's heart. I am just as ignorant of her as you, and I am excited to see the one he found irresistible."

"Yes, but this express raises even more concerns. Mrs. Darcy is coming alone, escorted by Colonel Fitzwilliam. It appears that Mr. Darcy sustained an injury to his ankle after a fire at his estate in Richmond and cannot travel."

"Good lord! Was Fitzwilliam badly hurt?"

"He says not, but it would be like him not to tell me the full extent of any injury to keep me from worrying. Once Colonel Fitzwilliam arrives, I shall have the truth of it."

"Hmmm. So I imagine that you are wondering why Mrs. Darcy would not stay with her husband in London while he recuperates."

"Exactly. It just does not seem… normal. Added to the fact that he married someone entirely unknown to us and without an engagement… "

"The tendency is to think the worst, is it not?"

Mrs. Reynolds nodded silently, her eyes searching William's aunt for assurance.

"Well, we who love the boy will just have to trust that he knows what he is about. I cannot imagine anyone as particular as my nephew marrying a lady who is improper or sending her to Pemberley alone without good reason. There has to be a worthy explanation."

The older woman smiled faintly. "I forget sometimes that the Master is no longer a boy to be watched over. Since he took over the estate, he has always done the right thing for Pemberley and for Miss Darcy. I am thoroughly ashamed that I have not trusted his judgement regarding his wife."

"Do not be ashamed. Mothers always wonder if their children's spouses will be good enough for them, and you have been like a mother to Fitzwilliam. I remember when my Arthur was sweet on a local girl and I feared that she was not the right one for him. After he died, I regretted ever feeling that way, for her suffering was as great as Joseph's and mine. For years afterward, she would visit, and we would reminisce about Arthur. Four years passed before she married, though she sought my blessing before accepting his offer." Olivia sighed raggedly. "She would have made the perfect wife and the perfect daughter."

"I did not mean to revive sad memories. I well remember when we received word of your son's death and, though your daughter died years ago, it is etched in my memory how hard Lady Anne took the news in both instances. Your children and hers were so close in age that it was especially poignant. Both deaths saddened everyone at Pemberley, Darcys and servants alike."

Olivia smiled through tear-filled eyes. "Thank you for saying as much. It is a peculiar thing, but reminiscing about my children makes me both happy and sad; however, the alternative, never to speak of Arthur or Jenny again, is far worse. For then it is as though they never existed."

"I agree completely. I dearly miss Mr. Darcy and Lady Anne, but the thought of never mentioning their names just because it makes me so sad, well, it is insupportable."

Mrs. Fitzwilliam took the housekeeper's hand and gave it a squeeze. "Then we agree on that point. Now, what shall we do about Mrs. Darcy? What say you to doing our best to make her feel welcome when she arrives? We can decorate the door and the foyer and, of course, have all the servants form a line to greet her. Afterwards, we can serve punch and cake for everyone. That should mark the occasion as memorable."

"I think that a brilliant idea! I only wish I had thought of it first."

"I am certain that you would have after the surprise of this express wore off. Now, let us go to your office and plan what we will need to carry this out."

Mrs. Reynolds and Mrs. Fitzwilliam walked arm-in-arm towards the front of the house, chatting and laughing as they made their plans.

⚭

Meryton
The parlour

Surreptitiously looking over the top of the newspaper he was reading,

Thomas Bennet tried not to smile. Mr. Bingley was pretending to be absorbed in yesterday's news when, in fact, he was only mooning over Jane, who sat on the settee with her mother. Unable to resist, Mr. Bennet laid down his copy and reached out to turn the paper Charles was holding right-side-up. Embarrassed to be found out, Bingley turned as bright red as his hair.

Pretending to take a better look, he opined, "No wonder I was having difficulty making sense of it."

"Yes. Holding the paper in the correct direction often helps one read," Mr. Bennet said dryly. "What is most puzzling is that you did not notice the drawings were upside down."

This caused a new round of laughter from his youngest girls, and he pursed his lips in order not to join them. Bingley only smiled drolly and shrugged.

Feeling sorry for her fiancé, Jane enquired, "Have you heard from Mr. Darcy? I have yet to get a letter from Lizzy, and I am beginning to become cross with her. She has never been away so long without at least one letter."

"La! Your sister is a newly married woman," Mrs. Bennet said authoritatively, as she continued knitting a pair of gloves. "You cannot expect her to write as often as she once did. I imagine Mr. Darcy requires most of her attention at present. Of course, his interest in her will lessen as time goes on, and things will return to normal. You shall see."

Mr. Bennet huffed, pulling his paper up to cover a scowl. He was unwilling to dwell on what activities his favourite daughter might be engaged in with Mr. Darcy.

"I have not gotten a letter from Darcy, though I did hear from Colonel Fitzwilliam. I thought it odd that he did not mention his cousin or Mrs. Darcy, but his missive was short, and he may have been pressed for time. In any event, he informed me that he was off to York, so he will no longer be staying at my townhouse."

Mrs. Bennet beamed. "I imagine Mr. Darcy will not rush to Pemberley, but stay in Town a while longer so that he can introduce Lizzy to all of his friends."

"I do not know about that. Darcy is not one for the social scene, and most of his friends are his neighbours in Derbyshire," Charles allowed. "Other than the opera and theatre, he rarely attends events when in Town."

"Well, I imagine that all changed when he married!" Mrs. Bennet crowed. "What man would not want to show off his new bride?" She sighed. "I cannot wait until they host a dinner for us, Mr. Bennet."

The newspaper crumpled to the tabletop. "What earthly reason do you have for thinking he shall host a dinner for us?"

"Because that is the proper thing to do—throw a dinner party and introduce your wife's family to your own family, as well as to your friends. I, for one, cannot wait."

Sighing heavily, Mr. Bennet retreated once more behind newsprint, murmuring sardonically, "Do not hold your breath, my dear."

Shrugging off his advice, Mrs. Bennet focused on Charles. "Do ask Mr.

Darcy if he has given any thought to a family dinner party the next time you correspond with him."

Bingley nodded cheerfully. "I shall."

All of a sudden, a grand idea seemed to come to Mrs. Bennet. "I do not know why I did not think of it until now, but if the colonel is not staying in your townhouse, that means it is available for Jane and me to occupy when we visit Town to select her trousseau."

A smile brightened Bingley's face. "That sounds splendid! Of course, all of you would be welcome should you wish to come, and I could accompany you and stay at my brother's townhouse, for the Hursts are not in Town, and Caroline is travelling with them."

While Lydia and Kitty danced in a circle, exclaiming their joy at going to London, Mr. Bennet let his sentiments be known. "I have no wish to go to Town. I shall be perfectly happy to remain here by myself."

"It shall only be Jane and me," Mrs. Bennet declared, causing her youngest daughters to whine and her husband to frown. "For Madeline, Jane and I must have time to concentrate on finding the finest materials and locating the best seamstresses, not supervising the lot of you."

Her pronouncement sent the two youngest Bennets into a tizzy of crying and whining even more loudly. Mr. Bennet stopped reading to warn them to cease complaining or to go to their rooms. Lydia bounded up the stairs, hoping her mother would call her back, and Kitty followed, as she always did; however, Mrs. Bennet appeared to be dreaming of staying in Bingley's fine home and did not seem to care that her favourite child was disappointed.

She laid down her handiwork and walked over to a table where she withdrew pen and paper from a drawer before sitting down. At once, she began a list of all the things she needed to accomplish while they were in London, including listing all the materials she would peruse at the various warehouses, including the Gardiners'. As she wrote, she named each item aloud, and the enormity of the expense of Jane's wedding began to make Mr. Bennet feel ill. Citing a need for peace and quiet, he left the room in favour of his study.

London

As the Gardiners sat at a small table in the confectioner's shop enjoying tea and sweets, they were entertained by watching the inhabitants of London going in and out of similar shops nearby. In her condition, Madeline craved the chocolate biscuits, strawberry scones and vanilla fudge unique to the establishment. Never being one to deny his wife anything, much less when she was with child, when she mentioned Colette's Confectionary that morning, Edward decided to surprise her by coming home early and escorting her there.

Enjoying refreshment at Colette's had become a habit of Madeline's, as it was a true respite from supervising the children, for though they might be in the care of their nurse, they were never truly out of her mind when she was at home. Normally, she and Edward stayed no more than an hour, but with her relations in Lambton presently keeping all the children, they were free to stay as long as they wished. And desirous of purchasing a few new items for the coming child, with Edward along to give his opinion, she could not have been more pleased.

Edward, who was also enjoying the break from work, had fixed his gaze on a gentleman coming out of a boot shop across the way and began to rise from his seat. He intended to cross the street and bid the man to join them, as he was positive that it was Lizzy's husband. Then the gentleman turned to face them, and he quickly sat back down, for it was obvious at that point that he was not Fitzwilliam Darcy. Seeing his perplexing behaviour, Madeline's brows rose in question.

"I know you think my actions curious, my dear, but I could have sworn that that was Lizzy's husband across the street."

"Which gentleman?" Madeline asked, narrowing her eyes to scan the crowd across from them. "Oh, I see the one you mean. My goodness, he does favour Mr. Darcy, does he not? Except with better scrutiny, he is not nearly as handsome."

"No, he is not. But from behind, I could have sworn it was he."

"In any event, that reminds me. I am worried about Lizzy," Madeline Gardiner said.

"So soon? Has something happened I should know about?"

"She came to see me early one morning after you had left for work. It concerned something she had overheard Mr. Darcy and his cousin, the colonel, discussing. I, of course, told her she should not jump to conclusions. I advised her to tell him what she thought she had heard and give Mr. Darcy the opportunity to explain. I did not mention it to you because I thought it would be resolved quickly."

"And did she speak to him?"

"That is why I am worried. I told her I would be uneasy until I heard from her. She promised to let me know, but I have not heard a word."

"Mayhap she has not found time to talk with him as yet. I think our Lizzy would not purposely keep you uninformed and certainly not in your condition."

"I agree, but I cannot help but think the worse."

Edward patted her hand. "You know that anxiety is not good for the baby or you," he said lovingly. "I shall call on Mr. Darcy tomorrow if he and Lizzy are still in town. I wanted to inform him that I received a shipment of the cigars he mentioned preferring, and that shall be as good an excuse as any. While there, I shall determine if there are any problems. Perhaps then your nerves will settle."

"My nerves," she laughed. "You make me sound as awful as Fanny!"

Edward chuckled. "I did not mean to imply that you are anything like my sister, dear, but when you are with child, you are more excitable."

"I suppose I am," Madeline said thoughtfully, "but it is something completely beyond my control."

"I know, dear. That is why I offered to ease your mind. Now, I think it is time we left. I must return to the warehouse."

As they rose to leave, Edward Gardiner noted that the man who favoured Darcy was just entering the shop owned by the tailor, Mr. Poindexter. Pondering the probability of two men looking so similar without being related, he pushed the thought from his mind when his wife reached out for his arm.

On the road to Pemberley
Stag and Boar Inn

Rain of biblical proportions was still falling outside the inn as Colonel Fitzwilliam observed it all through the large front windows. He was beginning to wonder if the structure was high enough to avoid the flood sure to follow, as water was spilling over the banks of a nearby stream. If the rain continued to fall at the same pace, he was certain that water would come under the front door in less than an hour. Uneasy, he went in search of the innkeeper to enquire if he had sacks of sand with which to reinforce the thresholds. After all, most establishments located near water were used to flooding during the rainy season and kept them on hand for just such events.

While Richard was seeking to prevent a disaster, Elizabeth was praying about how to repair a catastrophe of her own. Grateful that Mrs. O'Reilly had been in her room and not a witness to her set down, she had spent the hours since her quarrel with Colonel Fitzwilliam staring numbly out the window of her bedroom. Immediately upon hearing his blistering defence of William, a voice deep inside affirmed that he was telling the truth, and since then she had been oppressed by a deep melancholy.

Perhaps, she reflected, *it was your voice, Lord, finally penetrating my stubborn heart.*

Now all she could do was ask Him for wisdom, for she was certain that only He could repair what she had destroyed. Still, no matter how hard she prayed, she had no peace and no viable solution came to mind.

Perhaps you are angry with me, too. And who could blame you, Lord, for I was quick to condemn the husband you sent—the one I vowed to love, honour and obey only a week past. Tears welled in her eyes and began to slide slowly down her cheek. *Just because he was domineering, I was eager to believe the worst about him.* Angrily, she wiped the tears away with the back of her hand. *Why cry, Lizzy? After all, you were not the one disparaged.*

Once more the truth overwhelmed her. William had never been guilty. Before this morning she thought him completely lacking in compassion and principles. Now it was plain that it was she who lacked these attributes. And just as when her beloved Grandmother Bennet had passed away, she found herself mourning a loss. Only this time, she had lost something intangible and irreplaceable—her husband's esteem.

A knock at the door penetrated her thoughts, and numbly she answered it. Colonel Fitzwilliam stood without and, for a moment she considered closing it, though only because she felt she had suffered as much pain as she could handle in one day. Nevertheless, she opened it wide before silently resuming her place at the window.

The colonel walked in the room hesitantly and said nothing. This caused

Elizabeth to glance sideways at him, noting that he did not seem as angry as earlier.

"Mrs. Darcy," he finally began, clearing his throat self-consciously. "I wish to apologise."

Elizabeth's brows furrowed as she turned to him but did not reply.

"Not for telling you the truth, but for the manner in which I spoke to you. Fitzwilliam is a true gentleman and would never sanction any man speaking to a lady in that manner, especially not his wife. For that, I am sincerely ashamed. Forgive me. I shall apologise to him, as well, when I see him next. I suppose if I must blame my actions on any one thing, it is that I have always held a deep regard for my cousin. While I consider myself a gentleman, his commitment to doing what is decent and proper far exceeds my own and, to be truthful, any man of my acquaintance. He abhors deceit of any kind, and to hear him accused of the unkindest deceit, that of ruining women and fathering… " Richard paused to gain control. "By the one person he cares the most—"

Elizabeth broke in, her voice almost too low to be heard. "I understand completely. It is I who should apologise to you and to my husband, Colonel. In fact, allow me to apologise now for thinking you would support Fitzwilliam had he compromised those women, or that you would ever have conspired to hide the facts."

Richard eyed her warily, uncertain that she could have been so easily swayed by his argument of that morning. "Your apology is accepted, though I never felt like the offended party."

"You are too kind. Please believe that I realise to whom I owe the sincerest of apologies, even if he no longer wishes to hear it."

"I know it is not my place to say, but I do wish my cousin to have felicity in his marriage, for he has had far too little happiness throughout his life. So, if I may be so blunt, you would do well to ask questions instead of believing everything you hear. For if you had bothered to ask, you would know that my cousin is likely the most honourable man in the whole of England, and you are fortunate that he chose you to be his wife."

"I believe you," she said sombrely. "Colonel, I realise that you have no reason to think well of me. I do not think well of myself just now, however, I shall be eternally grateful that you were truthful with me. All that is left is to pray that Fitzwilliam will let me make amends and that I can be the wife that he deserves."

With a curt nod, he departed, and an unsteady truce settled between them.

Chapter 19

London
Matlock House
The next day

Georgiana's maid, Florence, had been positioned from birth to be a valuable source of the latest gossip in London. Her aunt, being a sought-after lady's maid, was a confidant of every lady's maid of any significance in Town. So, as a matter of course, because Florence was family, she was taken into the confidence of her aunt's friends, which meant that she, too, was well-positioned to find out anything one wished to know. Thus, when she overheard her mistress and Lady Susan speculating about the current state of Mr. Darcy's marriage, Florence was eager to be of service. Her motivation? Her mistress was very generous when she was in a good mood, buying new gowns and passing still-lovely gowns to her. The result was that she was one of the best-clothed servants in Town.

Having gone to the baker's shop early that morning to learn what she could, as Florence approached Matlock House with a small box of biscuits as a decoy, she looked about to be sure no one had followed. Lady Matlock frowned on the practice of any servant passing along gossip, sure that such a servant would divulge the secrets of her own household just as easily. And she was correct. Florence was not above passing along what she overheard as a sign of good faith. In the event she needed a favour—such as today—she had merely to mention parts of the Matlocks' private conversations, especially those about the viscount's dissipation, in order to attain her goal.

As she slipped into the house and up the back stairs to Georgiana's sitting room, Florence let out a sigh of relief at not having been seen. Once inside the room, she set the biscuits on a table and hurried to the bedroom door, knocking and praying that her mistress answered. When there was no response, she quietly turned the knob and peeked inside to find Miss Darcy missing. A glance to the balcony was equally disappointing. Suddenly, however, the sitting room door opened, and Georgiana entered into the room, followed by one of the Matlocks' maids.

"Florence! I wondered where you were! No one seemed to know," Miss Darcy said, obviously annoyed. "I asked my aunt to borrow a maid, as I needed someone to style my hair. You know that I cannot brush it out myself."

This was true, for Georgiana's hair was thick, and only a good brushing every morning could keep it manageable. Nonetheless, Florence felt certain that her absence would be forgiven once her mistress knew the circumstances.

"I hoped to return before you awakened. I went to the baker's shop to purchase some of those biscuits you favour, as you had eaten the last of them."

At Georgiana's puzzled look, she tilted her head meaningfully in the direction of the other maid. Instantly, Miss Darcy knew what she wanted and dismissed the Matlocks' servant. Only after the woman closed the door soundly, did Florence continue.

"I overheard you tell Lady Susan that you wished to know the present status of your brother's marriage. If there is gossip to share or you wish to enquire about *certain* situations, the lady's maids patronize the bakery the first thing in the morning. That is where I was."

Georgiana's face lit up, recalling what Florence had shared previously about the camaraderie of the women in her occupation. Pulling her towards the window seat, they both sat down.

"Tell me. Have you any news regarding my brother? I fear not, for his servants are trained not to gossip."

"Well, Mr. Darcy's regular servants are well-known for being tight-lipped."

Georgiana nodded her agreement. "However, there is a new upstairs maid at Darcy House who likes to talk, and she shares everything with a maid who works for Lady Appleton. That maid is sister to Lady Thornton's lady's maid, who happens to be a good friend of mine."

"So, what have you learned?"

"Your brother was injured the day after the ball, which postponed his return to his country estate."

Georgiana's eye went wide. "Injured? I was not notified, nor was my aunt or uncle, so surely it was not serious."

"He is rumoured to have a severely swollen ankle. Apparently it did not require a surgeon, but he must spend several weeks off his feet. However, what happened the next day caused a new round of gossip."

"Pray tell!"

"Well, the very next day, Mrs. Darcy, accompanied only by her personal maid, boarded a coach for Derbyshire. Rumour is that it was escorted by your cousin, Colonel Fitzwilliam, who was on his way to York in service to General Lassiter."

"Brother sent his wife to Pemberley but stayed behind?"

"If the rumours are true, he did. Is that not very unusual? Especially for a newly married man?"

For a long moment Georgiana seemed deep in thought, and then she began to smile like a Cheshire cat.

"You are pleased with the information?"

Georgiana wiped the smile from her face. "I am satisfied that you were able to learn things that my brother would never share with me. He does not want anyone worrying over him so, of course, he would not send word of his injury. As a result of your information, I shall make it a point to go to Darcy House today and see how he is faring." Rising, she walked towards her bedroom door. "Come. Let us look through my closet and choose which gown I will wear and perhaps find a few that you might like. After all, I have five new gowns that should arrive next week, and I barely have space as it is."

Now it was time for Florence to smile, and she did as she followed her mistress to the closet.

Darcy House
William's study
Later that morning

Sitting behind his desk, howbeit sideways with his foot propped on a stool, William tried to ignore the pain that radiated from his ankle and focus on the stack of correspondence sitting before him. He had sprained his ankle before, but it had not prepared him for his present agony—for the burns he suffered along with the swelling caused his leg to ache constantly. Yet, stoically he refused to be medicated, handling the results of his injuries with his usual tenacity by turning his attention to a property dispute between two of Pemberley's tenants, as explained in a letter from his steward, Mr. Sturgis.

Most of his tenants were decent, hard-working men, and he seldom had to preside over contentious misunderstandings. But this problem presented a special conundrum, for both men seemed to be in the right, according to the maps each offered as evidence of their claim. Well aware that some of the tenants' ancestors had farmed Pemberley's acreage for centuries, William was equally aware that many of the original parcels' boundaries overlapped a bit on the maps. Both men were profitable farmers, and Pemberley benefited from their diligent handling of the land. Because he did not wish either to suffer a hardship, he decided to give each of the men half the disputed land, adding a section from one of his adjoining pastures to each farmer's plot to make up for what each must forfeit. Writing his instructions on the bottom of the letter from Sturgis, he folded the paper and added it to a pile that he had already resolved and picked up another letter.

Just then there came a knock at the door. Irritated at being interrupted when he had expressly told Mr. Barnes he did not want to be disturbed, he called out testily, "Come!"

Instead of Barnes entering, however, his sister walked into the room. At once William steeled himself. Nothing good had come of their talks lately.

Georgiana saw the distrust in William's eyes, but pretended not to notice. "I heard that you were injured and just had to see your condition for myself."

"I suppose I should be amazed my business has spread through London so quickly," William replied, throwing the paper in his hand on his desk. "But I am not. Gossip travels faster than the plague these days."

"If not for gossip, I would never have known you were hurt. I do not think even Aunt and Uncle know, for they have said nothing to me."

"I am well enough, as you can see. I saw no need to alarm you or them."

Georgiana walked over to take a good look at William's ankle. Though it was covered in bandages, bruises and swelling far exceeded the covered part, which spoke of the seriousness of the injury.

Making a face, she asked, "What happened?"

"You have heard me mention the estate I purchased in Richmond."

"I do remember that you purchased one."

Since Georgiana did not know about the women and children who resided there as a result of Andrew's debauchery, William was vague. "There was a fire at the estate, and a building was destroyed. I was going through the rubble when a charred wall fell and a beam landed on my ankle."

"It looks ghastly, but I am sure that Mr. Graham was summoned, so you must be receiving the best available care."

"I am."

"Then I shall not worry dreadfully over you, which is fortuitous, for I must return to Matlock House before Aunt Evelyn finds that I am missing. She acts as though I am a small child whenever she learns I have gone out with only my maid." She hesitated. "Nonetheless, I should greet my new sister before I go. Would you send for her, please?"

William was not fooled. "If you have heard about my injury, I am sure you know that Elizabeth is not here."

"Truthfully, I did hear that she had left for Pemberley with Richard, but I was no more certain of the truth of that rumour than I was of your injury."

"Richard had to travel to York, and he graciously agreed to escort Elizabeth to Pemberley. Her relations are to be in Lambton next week—her Aunt Gardiner being from there—and she wanted to host them at Pemberley. I felt there was no reason to delay her plans just because I could not travel. As soon as I am able, I shall join her."

Seemingly unconvinced by his explanation, Georgiana said dryly, "I would have thought she would insist on staying to see to your health."

"I insisted that she go."

Her expression resembled a cat that had just cornered a mouse. "I see."

"Now, I have a question for you." The satisfied look left Georgiana's face. "Why did you send me a note during the ball asking me to meet you in the gazebo? As it turned out, Lady Susan was waiting when I arrived, not you."

"I felt ill after dinner and took the night air in hopes of recovering. When that did not suffice, I sent the note to you via a footman and waited at the gazebo, as I wished to say goodnight before I retired. However, you were so long in coming that I finally went to look for you. I was not aware that Lady Susan was even in the garden."

William was not swayed. "From what she said, the note was to lure me there."

"I have no knowledge of that, though she could have overheard my exchange with the footman. When I left her in the dining room, she had drunk too much wine, likely a result of her unhappiness with your marriage. So I do not think she was herself after dinner, nor would she remember anything correctly."

William looked as though he thought she was lying. Colouring, Georgiana quickly added, "Susan still cares for you, and I am certain that when she learns you are injured, she will rush right over to see you."

"She will not be welcomed or admitted."

"You cannot mean that! She is our friend."

"After what she did at the ball, I no longer consider her a friend." Georgiana opened her mouth to speak, but was cut off. "And if you continue to pretend not to know anything about it, you will lose all integrity with me." With that, William groaned as he moved his leg in an attempt to get some small relief. "Keep to your present course, Georgiana, and I assure you that you will regret it. Now, if you will excuse me, I have estate work to finish."

Although she was angry at his dismissal, Georgiana was determined to do as Lady Susan asked, so she pasted on a smile and ignored his warning. "Always the dutiful master," she said facetiously.

Intent on leaving, she hesitated at the door. "Even if we do not always agree, I do care about your welfare. So I shall come by every day or so to assess your progress, and I instructed Barnes to keep me informed. When you are well enough to return to Pemberley, I have decided to go with you so that I may get better acquainted with my new sister."

Flashing a false smile, she went out the door, leaving it wide open.

William rubbed his eyes wearily. Weighed down by the myriad of estate issues regarding Pemberley, he had managed to forget his disastrous marriage for a short while. However, Georgiana's visit had served to plunge him back into the maelstrom and, as his thoughts flew to what had transpired between him and Elizabeth, his father's voice spoke as clear as day.

You cannot wallow in pity, Son, when so many lives depend on you! You are a Darcy, and Darcys do not buckle!

William sighed. *I know, Father, and I shall get through this. Just give me a few days. Presently, I have neither the desire nor the stamina to consider my crumbling marriage.*

Another headache was beginning, and his eyes felt as though they were full of sand. He considered requesting one of Mrs. Barnes' powders, but they made him sleepy, and when he slept he dreamt of the awful things Elizabeth accused him of doing. It was one thing to recall her words while he was awake, but quite another to relive them in his sleep, for then he would awaken in a cold sweat with his heart pounding. Thus, he had decided to forego all medication for the pain. Bringing his other foot up to rest on the stool alongside the swollen one, he lay his head back against the padded cushion of the leather chair and closed his eyes. *Only for a moment,* he pledged.

Still, the second his eyes closed, despair took hold. Entirely beaten for once in his life, William was weary of duty, of honour and of doing the right thing regardless of the consequences. Even more, he was sick of being disappointed with life's twists and turns. He had failed to win the love of the one woman who possessed what he desperately needed—*joie de vivre*—a quality he initially noticed the second evening in her company at Netherfield.

It was after Charles asked about Jane's health that Elizabeth's entire demeanour had transformed. She fairly radiated joy as she explained that her sister felt much better and would likely go home the next day. And as she and Bingley continued to converse, he was drawn like a moth to a flame, moving to a chair closer to her. It was then that the idea of her smiles being directed at him had materialized.

Tenting his fingers over his bowed head, William silently berated himself for presuming he could ever make her smile. He was totally unaware that Mr. Barnes had returned and was watching him with a worried expression before he knocked on the door.

Immediately, William opened his eyes. "Yes?"

"I wished to apologise, sir. Miss Darcy entered the house through the back entrance. When I encountered her in the hallway, she would not allow me to announce her."

William's smile was more of a grimace. "It is no matter, Barnes. I know that my sister does as she wishes. Still, I do not want the knocker on the front door."

"Yes, sir. Begging your pardon, but you do not look as though you feel well. Do you wish to return to your bedroom?"

William shook his head. "It is too awkward to get up and down the stairs. I wish to work at least another two hours. Just let me close my eyes for a time and I will be fine."

"Very good," Barnes said glumly. "If you would like, I can have Cook prepare a pot of coffee. I know you enjoy it when you are trying to sort out estate matters."

"Thank you for suggesting it. Coffee does seem to clear my mind. I shall look forward to having a cup."

"I shall get right to it, sir."

As the butler disappeared and William's eyes closed again, his greatest fear refused to be silent any longer.

What kind of marriage can you expect if she hates you? She may even refuse to bear you an heir.

The likelihood hung like a verdict in the air.

Stag and Boar Inn
The next morning

The lightest of blue skies with not a cloud in sight greeted the guests, some of whom had been deathly afraid when water had covered the porch and lapped at the doors the previous evening. Pools of water, pieces of limbs, foliage and debris were now scattered everywhere, evidence of the destructive nature of the flood. In addition, a thick mud covered every inch of ground and formed deep ruts in the road.

Colonel Fitzwilliam was at the stable, assessing the situation with Darcy's driver and the inn's stable manager. Travelling before the mud dried sufficiently meant the horses might falter in the muck and break a leg, or the coach could lose a wheel to a rut. Still, after their talk, he ordered the coach readied and cautioned the driver to take his time on the road. He felt he had no choice, for the general expected him in York on a certain date and he could not leave his cousin's wife unescorted.

Making his way back to the inn, Richard noticed Thaggart standing at the end of the porch.

"Are we leaving today, Colonel?" Richard nodded. "Shall I supervise the horses?"

"Yes."

Instantly, the batman was off the porch, heading towards the stables. Richard's answers had been clipped because his mind was elsewhere—specifically, what he planned to say to his cousin's wife. They may have reached a truce yesterday but he still felt it best if he and Thaggart rode their stallions, for the more weight on the coach, the more it would sink in the mud. Since one last conversation with Mrs. Darcy would be necessary before they got underway, he went back inside the inn to find her.

Elizabeth was at that moment descending the stairs, followed by Mrs. O'Reilly. At the sight of the colonel, she halted.

"Mrs. Darcy, will you join me on the porch?"

"Of course."

Following Richard, they walked to the far end to speak privately. Once there, he wasted no time getting to the point.

"As I said yesterday, my hope is that you and Darcy may still reach an understanding and have an agreeable marriage. To that end, I know that it would embarrass him immensely if those residing at Pemberley were to learn of your disagreement. I know that he would rather they believe that he made a prudent match."

Elizabeth's eyes dropped as she said softly, "As would I."

"Precisely. I propose that you and I act as though there is nothing amiss. If anyone at Pemberley should learn about what transpired in London, it shall be because you or my cousin told them."

"That is kind of you."

"Would you like to hear another of my suggestions?" She numbly nodded again. "With my cousin still in London, you have the perfect opportunity to begin anew at Pemberley. Prove to Darcy—nay, to all those who think or hope that you will fail—that you are worthy to be the mistress of his estates."

"I would rather prove that I am worthy of being Mrs. Darcy," Elizabeth said quietly. Then she added, "I hope it pleases you to know that I came to the same conclusion last night. I intend to perform the duties of mistress with all my heart, even if my efforts never atone for my blunders."

Richard offered encouragement. "It certainly cannot make things any worse. And while Darcy may nurse his wounds for far too long, he has always been a forgiving soul. Otherwise, he would never have put up with Andrew all these years. Besides, given time, he will come to the conclusion that he is not without fault either."

Mention of Andrew brought to mind something Elizabeth wished to ask of Richard. Reaching into a pocket of her gown, she pulled out the brooch that Andrew had given her that night in the Phillips' garden.

"Andrew Darcy gave this to me when last I saw him in Meryton. He said it would prove his good intentions, as he was unable to marry me at present. I refused, saying I would not be secretly engaged, but he would not have it back." When Richard did not speak, she continued. "I... I would have thrown it away; but since it was his mother's, I thought perhaps that would be unkind. Would you see that it is returned to him?"

Richard took the brooch and, without a word, tossed it into the high weeds and bushes across the road. Elizabeth's eyes were wide as saucers when he turned back to her.

"That is not his mother's brooch. And, though it may appear expensive, believe me when I say that it is not. Andrew has used these trinkets for years to soften the hearts of his targets. If I were you, I would never mention it to anyone."

The realisation that she once thought Andrew a better man than William caused Elizabeth to wince. "I am glad to know the truth of it."

"Now, if you are ready, we really should get started. Even if we must go slowly, on account of the roads, we can make Pemberley by sundown if we do not suffer any unforeseeable difficulties."

Not long afterward, the Darcy coach pulled away from the inn on the last leg of the journey to Pemberley.

London
Darcy House
That evening

As Barnes looked in on his employer for seemingly the hundredth time, he was relieved to find him asleep. Having been moved back to his bed after hours downstairs, William's foot was now held aloft by a blanket suspended from the ceiling by a rope and pulley. The contraption was fashioned by their coachman after one used to steady horses in need of sutures. His ingenuity had quickly gained the respect of Mr. Barnes. Though sceptical when it was first suggested, once it was installed, the butler found that the device made keeping the injured appendage at the right height much easier. No longer did the foot slip off the pillows, causing Mr. Darcy to wake in agony.

Assured that his charge was resting peacefully, Barnes left to resume his duties downstairs. Descending the grand staircase, the butler heard someone knock at the door. Frowning, for any sensible person knew that no knocker on the door meant that company was not welcome, he rushed to peer through the curtain at the intruder. As the man walked down the steps, he followed him with his eyes; however, when the visitor stopped at the bottom to look back at the door, he did not recognise him.

"Humph!" Barnes said, turning to go in the direction of his wife's office. "That man should learn some manners."

All of a sudden, the footman who always stood at the front door called out and he turned to find him holding a card that must have been slipped through the slot in the door.

"He left this calling card, sir."

Barnes stopped, took the card and read: *Mr. Edward Gardiner.*

Having never heard the name, he laid the card on the silver salver that held the mail. There it would stay until William awakened.

Gracechurch Street
The Gardiners' residence

As the maid came to clear the soup bowls and serve the entree, the Gardiners became silent. After they were alone again, Mrs. Gardiner spoke.

"Are you certain that no one was at home?"

"Well, the knocker was not on the door and no one answered, so I am almost certain the Darcys are not in residence." Then he chuckled. "Though it is not unheard of for a newly married couple to disdain company for as long as possible."

Madeline smiled. "How well I remember! Besides, it would be odd if Lizzy left London without telling me the outcome of their discussion. It is not like her to worry me."

"I agree, dear. And perhaps she is still trying to fit everything into her schedule as Mr. Darcy's wife. I am certain that you will hear from her as soon as she settles in." He hesitated for a moment. "Perhaps I am entirely wrong, but I have been thinking about the man we saw—the one who favours Mr. Darcy."

"Yes, the similarity was uncanny."

"I am convinced that he has to be the cousin who caused the scandal in Meryton. What was his name?"

"Andrew Darcy, if I remember correctly."

"Yes! That is it! It must be him, and I have to wonder if Fitzwilliam has any idea that he is in London."

"I imagine that he cannot keep up with his cousin's comings and goings, what with all of his responsibilities. It is not a good situation to be sure. Being cousins and looking so much alike will not serve when one is definitely not a gentleman."

"No, it will not. I think I shall, at the least, send Mr. Darcy a letter mentioning that I saw someone who could be his cousin here in London."

"A fine idea, my dear. One cannot be too careful when dealing with someone who would do what he did to our Lizzy and then disappear."

"Exactly."

Pemberley
That Evening

It was getting late, and almost everyone at Pemberley was drained. Having been on high alert all day for the arrival of Mrs. Darcy, all of the servants were dressed in their finest uniforms. They tried valiantly not to soil them as they went about their daily tasks. Even Joseph and Olivia Fitzwilliam had donned more formal attire than usual in anticipation of greeting their new niece and had occupied the primary drawing room most of the day in hopes of being close by when the coach arrived. Now, however, Olivia showed signs of fatigue, for she had also helped Mrs. Reynolds supervise the decoration of the house the day before.

Their efforts had not been in vain, for Pemberley looked splendid. A huge wreath filled with colourful flowers was hung on the front door to welcome the new mistress. Inside the foyer, garlands of greenery were wound around the bottom of the grand staircase and the entire house sported crystal vases filled with exotic flowers from the conservatory. This was a special touch that Mrs. Reynolds remembered Lady Anne employing when she hosted dinner parties and balls. In the drawing room, a round table had been placed in the centre, complete with a lace tablecloth. It awaited the myriad of small cakes and pastries that Mrs. Lantrip had created especially for the occasion. They were scheduled to magically appear, along with a bowl of punch, the moment word came from their lookouts that the coach was in sight. All that was left was to wait patiently.

"My dear, why do you not let me help you upstairs where you may lie down? Rest assured that I shall wake you the moment there is any news, so you will have enough warning to be presentable." He chuckled. "Though I think you are always lovely."

"How you do go on!" Olivia Fitzwilliam said as she leaned her head back against the soft cushions of a large, upholstered sofa. "But I shall not be gainsaid on this. If they have weathered the recent thunderstorms, they may be only seconds away."

Joseph accepted defeat. "Yes, dear."

Just then a footman appeared at the door. "Excuse me, but Mrs. Reynolds wanted me to inform you that a sentry has arrived on horseback to notify her that the coach has entered the grounds."

"Thank you."

The footman nodded and hurried back to his post as William's uncle turned to his wife. She was beginning to stand, but her legs were a little weak from having been seated so long.

"Wait, Livy, let me help you."

"I am well enough to stand on my own," she protested, though clearly she was not. "I get light-headed when I stand too quickly, that is all. Just let me get my bearings, and I shall be as good as new."

Not long afterwards Mrs. Reynolds rushed into the room, her face animated as she proclaimed, "She is almost here! Oh, I do hope the new mistress will be pleased with our preparations."

Recovered sufficiently, Olivia reached to take the housekeeper's shaking hands. "She shall be delighted; you shall see. Do not worry, Mrs. Reynolds, you have never failed to make any person feel welcome at Pemberley."

"But this is not just anyone."

"No, but you must remember, our dear boy would never marry someone who would not fit into the family creditably. I am sure Mrs. Darcy is kind-hearted."

The housekeeper nodded even before she finished speaking. "You are absolutely correct." Then she glanced to the tall windows overlooking the drive that led to the front of the house. "Look! There is the second sentry. That means they are only a few minutes away. Let us hurry to the portico. Everyone should be on the steps before the coach stops."

Mrs. Reynolds rushed on ahead, while William's aunt and uncle followed at a slower pace. By the time the Fitzwilliams entered the foyer, the housekeeper was taking to task some servants who had forgotten their places in line, something she had gone over the day before. As they watched with no little amusement, she put them in proper order. The footmen outside were already lined up on the right side of the steps to the portico, while the inside footmen hurried to take their places alongside them. Next, Mrs. Reynolds, Mr. Walker and Mrs. Lantrip led a line of maids down the opposite side—a line that reached all the way back to the grand staircase. Still, this left plenty of lesser staff for Mrs. Darcy to meet later, for Mrs. Reynolds reasoned that the mistress could not be expected to greet every last member of the staff upon her arrival.

As the Fitzwilliams took their places on the portico, it seemed an interminable wait until the coach came into sight at the end of the long drive. Suddenly, Richard and Thaggart left the coach to gallop on ahead, and the Fitzwilliams started down the steps. In no time at all, two footmen stepped forward to take their horses as Mr. Darcy's cousin and his batman reached the house. Dismounting, Richard removed his gloves as he walked over to his aunt and leaned down to kiss her on the forehead.

"I must say that you look lovelier each time I see you, Aunt Olivia."

She chuckled, patting his cheek lovingly. "Then perhaps you should leave and return several more times."

He laughed and shook his uncle's hand. "Uncle Joseph, it is good to see you again."

"Likewise, my boy!" Joseph said, slapping him on the back. Glancing behind him, he added, "And who is this fine credit to His Majesty's service?"

"May I present Sergeant Louis Thaggart, my batman and one of the finest men I have been privileged to serve alongside." Richard smiled to see Thaggart turn red with his compliment. "Sergeant, allow me to introduce my favourite Fitzwilliam relations, my uncle, Captain Fitzwilliam, and my Aunt Olivia."

Thaggart saluted Joseph and bowed to Olivia. "It is my pleasure, Captain. Mrs. Fitzwilliam. Colonel Fitzwilliam speaks so admirably of you both that I am delighted to meet you at last, however, I do not recall him mentioning that you were a captain, sir."

"Retired from the navy," Joseph explained. "To Richard, I am just Uncle Joseph." Thaggart nodded.

By that time, Richard was looking for Mrs. Reynolds, and, seeing her at the top of the portico, he hurried there. "Thaggart will be occupying the room next to mine, Mrs. Reynolds," he said, quietly enough that none overheard.

"Of course, Colonel. We shall be honoured to have him."

At that moment, the sound of the huge Darcy coach entering the freshly laid gravel of the circular drive caught everyone's attention and, in what seemed like seconds, it halted at the bottom of the steps. Everyone held their breath as Richard ran back down the steps, and the footman jumped off the back of the vehicle to open the door. As the servant turned the handle and pulled the door open, William's cousin leaned in to hand Elizabeth out.

As soon as her feet hit the ground and her head came up, her heart sank.
What have I gotten into? This is so much grander than I ever imagined.

As though in a daze, Elizabeth barely remembered being introduced to William's aunt, uncle, butler, housekeeper, cook, and more maids and footmen than she could ever remember. She hoped that her smile looked sincere, for she earnestly wanted them to like her; however, Elizabeth's knees were knocking so hard that she feared everyone could hear.

After all the introductions were accomplished, she was escorted into the drawing room for a small party that included refreshments for everyone. The room and its furnishings were so opulent that at first Elizabeth had a hard time focusing on the members of the household, but everyone was so kind that soon the knot in her stomach relaxed and she began to enjoy herself.

Within a short time, Olivia, a woman with whom she had felt an immediate kinship, leaned over to whisper, "Mrs. Darcy—"

"Please, call me Elizabeth."

"If you will call me Aunt Olivia." Elizabeth nodded, smiling warmly as her new aunt. "I know you must be exhausted."

"I confess that I am a little tired."

Olivia patted her hand. "What do you say to resting a bit so that you do not fall asleep at the dinner table?" She chuckled. "To be honest, I fear we shall want to keep you up all night getting acquainted."

Elizabeth smiled. "A short nap would be most welcome."

Satisfied, Olivia addressed the room. "Mrs. Darcy has had a long trip, and I believe we have engaged her long enough with our little celebration. Be assured that the festivities shall continue, though Mrs. Darcy is retiring to her room for a rest." There were nods of approval as Olivia turned to the housekeeper. "Mrs. Reynolds, you have worked tirelessly to be certain that everything is in order. Thank you. Now, if you will be so kind as to show Mrs. Darcy to her rooms."

Excitedly, Mrs. Reynolds set aside the tea service. "I shall be delighted." She swept a hand towards the drawing room door. "Shall we, Mrs. Darcy?"

Elizabeth followed the kindly servant, and the room went silent as everyone watched her leave. Just as soon as she and the housekeeper cleared the door, however, the level of conversation returned.

A little embarrassed, the housekeeper said, "Please forgive us if we seem in awe of you, Mrs. Darcy. A good many of the servants have never served under a mistress, so this will be a new experience for them."

As they began up the stairs, Elizabeth asked innocently, "What of Miss Darcy? Did she not act as mistress when she became of age?"

Mrs. Reynolds seemed to consider her answer. "Miss Darcy has lived a very sheltered life and, in many respects, is still very childlike. She was never comfortable assuming the obligations Lady Anne fulfilled. Other than being the hostess at a few dinner parties, Miss Darcy has assumed no other duties."

Wondering if she had misspoken, Elizabeth said no more as they continued their trek up the long staircase. She found herself mesmerised by the opulence of the rest of the house. It was absolutely breathtaking, and the farther she went, the more she felt as though she were an intruder—one soon to be found out and quickly expelled. Nevertheless, she did her best to mask her distress and carry herself with all the dignity she could muster.

Chapter 20

Pemberley
The Mistress' Bedroom

Finally, Elizabeth and Mrs. Reynolds stood before one of a number of ornate doors in an upstairs hall. The housekeeper began sorting through a large ring of keys that she had pulled from a pocket in her skirt, each of which looked exactly like the last. She settled on one and proceeded to try the door. To Elizabeth's amazement, the door opened, and at once the servant stepped aside to let her enter first.

The room was huge—at least three times the size of her bedroom at Longbourn, with equally large furniture, all in gleaming mahogany. She took several steps and halted inside the cavernous space as her gaze was drawn to the deep red and gold patterned wallpaper. Though the appearance was regal and the room large enough to handle the vibrant colours, she thought it much too bold for her taste.

What caught her attention next was a huge, canopied bed which dominated the space. It was covered with a dark-gold counterpane, while sheer scarf-like curtains in royal colours of blue, red, green, gold and purple decorated the canopy overhead. As she studied the bed itself, she pictured all of her sisters occupying it at once, and a giggle escaped. Quickly she covered her mouth, though it was too late, for Mrs. Reynolds stopped reciting all of the features of the room and turned to her.

"Forgive me," Elizabeth said sheepishly. "I was just contemplating such a large bed for someone of my size. I cannot fathom how I shall be able to climb into it."

The housekeeper smiled knowingly. "I understand completely. Lady Anne was tall, as are all the Fitzwilliams, so the bed was no problem for her. But I can imagine it looks quite high to one so petite. Let me show you what the furniture maker added to aid those who might wish some assistance."

As she talked, Mrs. Reynolds moved towards the bed and pulled back the counterpane near the floor. She exposed a lever that, when engaged, let down two small steps.

"When the master was a small boy, Lady Anne would leave these steps down so that he might come into her bed whenever he was afraid." Her hand flew to her mouth. "Oh my! I should not have mentioned that. I am not sure that Mr. Darcy remembers it, and he might be embarrassed for anyone to know."

"Rest assured that I will never repeat it, but might I say something?" When the housekeeper nodded, she continued. "Though I am not as familiar with him as you, Mr. Darcy does not impress me as the type of person to ever be frightened—even as a child."

"There may be an air of invincibility about him now, but when he was very young, perhaps four or five, he did have night terrors for a long while. They began after one of his siblings was born a month early and his father was away on an unavoidable business trip. The local physician was summoned but did not reach Pemberley in time to assist with the birth. I had to aid Mrs. Darcy and, having my hands full, I did not realise that the master had slipped into this room and was watching. He hid in the corner, behind that chair."

The housekeeper's face took on a painful mien as she looked towards a high-back chair in the corner. Silent for a time, it was as though she were reliving the event. Then abruptly she began again to explain more fully.

"Evidently, he witnessed his brother take his last breath not more than twenty minutes after he was born. It was only much later, when I passed through the sitting room, that I heard crying and found him hiding behind the curtains, inconsolable. As I questioned what upset him, it became clear that the poor boy thought that his mother had died along with his brother. Blessedly, Lady Anne fainted after the baby died, so when her wails ended, he believed she had died as well. My dear master has had his share of heartaches; that is certain."

"If I may ask, did his parents lose any other children?"

"Other than the boy I spoke of, there were two stillbirths, both girls, and, if I recall correctly, four miscarriages. We were all astounded when Miss Georgiana was born with little trouble. It brought everyone great happiness, including her brother."

"I can only imagine. Thank you for sharing this with me, and be assured that I shall never mention it."

"Thank you. Now, as I was saying before I began on that subject, this suite has not been refurbished since Lady Anne died. When Mr. Darcy sent word that he was to be married, he instructed me to obtain samples of the latest wallpapers, paints and fabrics from London. He intends for you to decorate the rooms to your liking, even ordering new furniture if you wish."

Elizabeth sighed. *More evidence of his thoughtfulness.*

Not aware of Elizabeth's dismay, the housekeeper continued to explain. "I have placed all of the samples on the desk in your private study, so you may undertake the changes whenever you have time. Should you decide to replace the furniture, I have also ordered brochures from the finest furniture makers, though they have not arrived as yet."

Elizabeth managed to stammer, "I... I have a private study?"

"Yes, ma'am. It is located on this floor at the end of the first hall to the right. It has a balcony which overlooks the rose garden. Lady Anne loved to work there—even out on the balcony when it was a pretty day. From her perch, she could supervise the placement of new selections." Mrs. Reynolds chuckled softly. "She often laughed about how, from that vantage point, she could find so much more that needed doing. And she was fond of telling the gardeners that God loved beautiful gardens; after all, He created Eden."

Elizabeth laughed aloud, which seemed to delight the housekeeper and caused her to continue. "Lady Anne once told me that she overheard a young apprentice, who did not realise that she was listening from above, say, "I do hope God is not as persnickety as Mrs. Darcy!"

"What a lovely sense of humour!" Elizabeth exclaimed. "She must have been a wonderful person. I am sure you miss her terribly."

"Words cannot say," Mrs. Reynolds replied wistfully. Then taking a deep breath, she assumed her usual demeanour. "However, we are all of us delighted to have a new Mrs. Darcy at Pemberley. If I am allowed to say, I was beginning to doubt we ever would."

"Why would you say that?"

"Most men of his station are already married by his age. I believe he waited because Pemberley is too dear to him to entrust to just anyone."

Elizabeth's heart sank. "I... I do not know what to say."

"You need not say anything. Your presence attests to the fact that my master trusts you with those things that are nearest to his heart."

Remembering all the charges she had thrown at William, Elizabeth was mortified and could not form an answer. Her silence gave the housekeeper the opportunity to take her leave.

"Mrs. O'Reilly has been assigned several rooms below stairs, next to my own. I understand that she is already settled in and resting. When it is near time for dinner, I shall direct her here so that she may learn which rooms are yours. She will be here in time to help you dress, if that is agreeable to you."

"It is, thank you."

Mrs. Reynolds smiled widely. "If you would like to undress before your nap, I began as a lady's maid and have not forgotten my craft. I shall be pleased to help you or, should you desire, I can send for Mrs. O'Reilly now."

"I do wish to be freed of this corset, but there is no need to disturb Mrs. O'Reilly. If you will undo the buttons and untie me, I can handle the rest. After all, I shared one maid with four sisters, so I can do a great deal for myself."

Looking somewhat confused by Elizabeth's confession, Mrs. Reynolds said nothing as she helped her new mistress undress. Once she was finished, she curtseyed and left the room.

Unburdened of her tight corset, Elizabeth took a deep breath of air—something she could not do when dressed as a proper lady. Then after taking another turn about the handsome room, examining exquisite items perched on every surface, she returned to inspect the beautiful bed. Pulling back the counterpane, champagne-coloured silk sheets beckoned and, after running her hands along the cool, smooth fabric, she proceeded to step onto the stool and crawl to the middle of the bed. Like a child, she fell back into the pile of plump pillows and slid her hands and feet up and down as she did when creating snow angels, while giggling in sheer delight.

Only seconds later, the enormity of her present circumstances came rushing back, bringing all frivolity to a standstill. Elizabeth's heart filled with dread as she considered what she had ruined... perhaps forever.

Never lose sight of the fact that your childish behaviour is what got you in this predicament! You have made a shambles of your marriage, and if you have a chance of redemption, you must attempt to be the best mistress Pemberley has ever known. Even that may not be enough to repair the damage done.

The burden of regret brought even more fatigue and, when she closed her eyes, she instantly fell into a restless sleep.

London
Younge's Boarding House
The next day

Andrew Darcy was not unaware that he would be looked upon as an easy target by most of his fellow boarders at Mrs. Younge's establishment, for normally he wore the clothes of a gentleman, and that alone caused him to stand out among those who frequented the place. Thus, to avoid being noticed, he rose early and departed the premises, not returning until late in the evening, just before dark. In addition, he wore an older, shabbier overcoat whenever he went out. This caution kept him on an entirely different schedule than those who drank until dawn, slept all day and rose at dark to steal from the unsuspecting, afterward using the pickings to gamble.

Nonetheless, in spite of his watchfulness, as Andrew returned to the inn this day, the proprietress waved at him before he could take the stairs. Though he fervently wished to disappear from sight, he had no alternative other than to find out what she wanted. As Eunice Younge approached, she gave him a look that he assumed was supposed to be enticing, one he pretended not to notice.

"*Mr. Smith,*" she said with a wink. "I have not seen you in days."

"I have business."

"I just imagine you have, for ole Brumeloe is waiting to speak to you."

With the name she gave a nod of her head towards a table in the corner where a lone, rough-looking man sat watching them. Swallowing hard, Andrew tried to appear not to know to whom she referred, though he guessed half of London knew that the man had a reputation for doing whatever needed to be done—for a price. That was why he had hired him.

"I am sure I do not know the man, but I shall see what he wants." To distract the innkeeper, he dug several coins out of his pocket and handed them to her. "Here is a bit more on my account."

"Indeed!" Mrs. Younge said, her eyes lighting up as she added the coins. "You are a far cry from most of my customers who slink out in the dark without paying. You are welcome to stay here as long as you wish."

"Your hospitality is appreciated," Andrew said, as he began towards Mr. Brumeloe. "Now I shall see what this fellow wants with me."

Once he had reached the table, Andrew looked back to see that Mrs. Younge had returned to the kitchen. He leaned over the table. "I thought I told you not to come here!"

"Excuse me, gov'ner, but I needed a pint, and this was as good a spot as any ter 'ave one while I waited for ya."

"Fine!" Andrew declared, visibly irritated. "Follow me to my room before

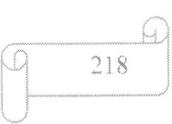

someone sees us together."

Both men went up the stairs. It was not until the door closed soundly, however, that their discussion began.

"That Miss Bunting—that one wot 'ad yer boy—she would not agree ter sail ter tha Americas, even wif promises of passage and coins. She told me that yer cousin was takin' care of 'er and tha lad proper, and she 'ad nah intention of messin' wif ya again."

"What of Miss Carden?"

"Precisely why I am 'ere. I did not 'ave a bloody chance ter talk ter her, for I was found out straightaway."

"What do you mean found out?"

"Yer cousin 'ired a steward called Mr. 'obson. Tha old fool over'eard me talkin' ter Miss Bunting in tha kitchen and threw a proper fit. Said 'e was gonna 'old me for Mr. Darcy, 'e did. When 'e tried ter shout for 'elp, we got in a struggle. I don't mind sayin' 'e was powerful strong for 'is age and almost got tha bloody better of me. It took an iron pan ter get 'im off me. That would 'ave settled it, I suppose, but suddenly tha 'ole room was in flames."

"A fire? You started a fire at Fitz's estate?" Andrew groaned, sinking down on the rock hard bed. "Oh, my Lord!"

"'Tweren't me. It was tha old man! While we was fightin', 'e knocked a can of kerosene over, one wot was too near the 'earf. Once the oil hit the 'earf, there was no goin' back."

By now Andrew was on his feet again, pacing. "Then what happened?"

"As I regained my feet, tha woman ran through tha door ter tha parlour, I suppose after tha lad. Tha old man tried ter folla, but tha fire spread too fast. As I went out tha back, 'obson passed me 'eadin' ter tha front. It weren't nah use, for tha building was ablaze by then. Seein' that it was 'opeless, 'e gave chase after me. That old man must 'ave followed me through tha bleedin' woods for 'alf a mile before I lost 'im. I 'eard later that tha woman and boy was killed in tha fire."

Andrew covered his face with his hands. "Fitz will kill me," he mumbled. Then taking his ire out on Brumeloe, he hissed, "My cousin will not only hunt you down, but he will see that you hang and me along with you."

Brumeloe's eyes narrowed. "Won't be tha bloody first time I've been 'unted. That is why I came fer me bread and 'oney. I'm off ter Scotland ter let me 'eels cool for a while."

"I said I would pay you if you got those women to leave England. I never told you to kill anyone," Andrew spit out.

"Tha results tha same, if ya ask me. That one and 'er brat won't be costin' ya another farthin'." Brumeloe pulled a long knife from his boot and began running his finger over the edge of the blade. "Tha way I sees it, I almost got killed, and I 'ad ter walk miles through tha woods, leaving a good 'orse behind. I deserve me wages."

Knowing that he would likely extract the money if he did not give it willingly, Andrew reluctantly handed over the twenty pounds he had promised.

"Get out of here! I never want to see you again."

"Fine by me, Darcy!"

Even as he watched the miscreant leave, Andrew Darcy began making plans, for when William had the fire at Richmond investigated, and he had no doubts that his cousin would do just that, the trail could lead to Brumeloe and then to him.

I shall forget about trying to convince old Poindexter to let me have my supplies and head north. Perhaps I can find sanctuary with some of Wickham's cohorts in Derbyshire. What was the name of the man he claimed to have robbed coaches with before he joined the militia? The one who lives just north of Lambton? Denham? Denny? Yes, that is the name! Perhaps Denny will provide me with shelter for a while.

Darcy House
William's study

As Mr. Barnes showed him through the elegant residence, Mr. Gardiner was just as astonished as his niece had been upon her first glimpse of Darcy House. The furnishings were of the finest quality and tastefully done, which was not always the case with the homes of the *ton*.

Edward Gardiner would know. By virtue of his import business, he was acquainted with many gentlemen and had been invited to several of their houses through the years. He had come to expect flamboyant furnishings that screamed of wealth more than common sense. Pleased to discover this was not the case with Lizzy's new husband, he was still pondering that fact when he was shown into William's study.

"Mr. Edward Gardiner," Barnes announced.

"Thank you, Barnes. Mr. Gardiner!" Fitzwilliam Darcy exclaimed from where he sat behind a huge, wooden desk. "Please forgive me for not rising to greet you."

"No apology needed! When I received your note this morning relating your injury and asking me to call again, I rushed over to see how you were faring."

"To be truthful, I have eschewed most company. However, you are always welcome, and I have instructed my servants of that. I had no idea that you called until I saw your card last night."

"Yes, well, I came to tell you that I believe I saw your cousin in Town."

William's eyes narrowed. "Andrew?"

"From a distance, the man I saw could have been you—same looks and height. It was only when he turned to face me that I discerned the difference. Still, he looks enough like you that there is no mistaking your kinship."

"I had the *pleasure* of seeing Andrew at the ball, though he did not stay long enough for me to confront him. Where did you see him?"

"Across the street from Colette's Confectionary. He was entering Poindexter's shop."

"The tailor?"

"Yes, that is the one."

"Andrew always dressed far better than he could afford. Thank you for telling me. I shall consult Poindexter to make sure he is not charging items to my account as he has done at other shops in the past."

Mr. Gardiner came around the desk to get a closer look at the injury. "My, my! You have done as fine a job as I have ever seen of rendering yourself unable to walk. What in the world happened?"

William gave him the explanation he had given Georgiana regarding Richmond, and the same justification for Elizabeth's absence. Afterwards, he presented his new uncle with what he thought was a sincere smile. His performance must have fallen flat, however, for instead of being reassured, Mr. Gardiner stared at him with a look of total unbelief. Still standing, his eyes narrowed as he clasped his hands behind his back.

"Forgive my straightforwardness, but I know no other way. I detect that there is something amiss between you and my niece." William started to object, but Mr. Gardiner held up both hands. "Please spare me the awkwardness of arguing that I am wrong. I am certain that no newly married man would willingly part company with his wife so soon after the wedding, especially if he had no idea when they would be reunited. I can only conclude that separation from my niece was preferable to being under the same roof."

William's fabricated smile vanished as Mr. Gardiner continued. "As I said on your wedding day, if you wish my advice on any situation, I promise not to judge. I know the extra strains upon your marriage due to the circumstances, and I am very aware of how stubborn my niece can be when she thinks she is right."

While he spoke, William's hands came up to cover his face and, for the briefest moment, Mr. Gardiner thought he might break down. After what seemed a long while, William dropped his hands and shook his head in despair. Edward's heart ached for the young man, so he leaned across the desk, bracing on his fingertips.

"Please. Allow me to help."

"I… I thought that if Elizabeth knew… if she understood how deeply I care for her, I could change her heart as well as her name. I no longer believe that will be the case."

He dropped his hands to stare intently at a portrait of his father on the wall. To Mr. Gardiner, it seemed as though what William said next was meant as an apology to that man.

"My father raised me with the expectation that I would have sense enough to use good judgement. With Elizabeth, I let my heart overrule my head. I knew she was opposed to the marriage; however, I had no inkling how much she truly hated me, not just the idea of being forced to marry. That is, until now. In hindsight, in every circumstance before and since our union, she has chosen to believe the worst of me."

"What could possibly have caused you to come to this conclusion?"

Completely devoid of the strength necessary to keep up the charade, William told Elizabeth's uncle everything. When he was done, Mr. Gardiner was dumbfounded by what he had heard and completely unable to speak.

For a long time he gathered his thoughts. Finally, he managed to say, "I completely understand your feelings despite the fact that I can see things from my niece's point of view too. Having said that, I have always known Lizzy to be headstrong, but I imagined she would be more discerning when it came to charges against her own husband. Am I being presumptuous to enquire if you have lost all desire for a reconciliation?"

William's voice was barely a whisper. "Even if I were to tell her the truth regarding Andrew's children, and Lady Susan's schemes, I have no expectations that she would believe me. After all, in her eyes I am a liar. Besides, it seems there are still many aspects of my character that she found abhorrent from our first meeting. Things I never thought to question before."

"Do you mind telling me what they are?"

"No. I am sure she will enlighten you in any case. Apparently, I do not know the difference between settling an issue and being dictatorial. In Elizabeth's eyes, I am a selfish, officious tyrant who thinks only of himself. Regrettably, I never before considered it unkind to take charge when circumstances dictated action."

"Not an uncommon complaint among women, I think," Gardiner said, trying to garner a smile with his tease. "Even my wife has charged me with that on many occasions."

William's silence made the hair on the back of his head stand up. *Are the wounds still too fresh, or have Lizzy's criticisms cut too deep?*

"Fitzwilliam, if you will allow, I will share everything you have told me with my wife. I am certain she will wish to counsel Lizzy when we get to Derbyshire, as will I."

William sighed. "You may share the details with Mrs. Gardiner, but please do not try to convince my wife that I am worthy of… " His voice trailed off, the sentence left incomplete.

Mr. Gardiner walked around behind the desk and clasped William's shoulder. "Nephew, please try to remember that things always seem insurmountable when you are in pain. And it is a cruel trick of fate that my niece's accusations came at the same time as your injury. But, in spite of what you may think, Lizzy is not insensitive, and when she realises how badly she has erred, she will be distraught. Then she will try valiantly to make amends; that is her nature. The question is, can you forgive each other and move forward?"

"The Lord commands us to forgive if we are to be forgiven, so I must. I just do not know if I will be able to forget. My greatest fear is that all that has occurred has created a wall that will forever divide us."

"That is understandable," Mr. Gardiner said, his heart heavy with concern. "Now, I shall take my leave. You have only to send word, though, and I shall be here in a shake of a lamb's tail. Unless I hear from you, however, I shall not call again before we leave for Lambton." All he received in answer was a nod, so he added, "Try to keep your spirits up. Give it time. Things will get better."

"That was my father's favourite admonition," William said, without

emotion. "Though, as I recall, it rarely worked out that way."

Mr. Gardiner went to leave, but paused at the door to glance at Lizzy's husband. William was gazing listlessly at his father's portrait.

Oh, Lizzy! Knowing how headstrong you are, I pray that you are ready to listen when next we meet.

Not long after Mr. Gardiner departed, Barnes came back into the room. "Sir, a Mr. Harahan and a Mr. Coleridge are here to see you. And, perhaps I should not say, but I found it a little odd that they came by way of the back alley?"

"All is well, Barnes. They are retired from the Bow Street Runners, and I asked them to come via the back entrance so that those who are familiar with their work will not suspect that they are working for me. Please show them in."

Presently a very tall, muscular, ginger-haired man entered the room. Patrick Harahan was six-foot three. He was followed by an equally brawny, bald-headed fellow who was nearly as tall, Dale Coleridge. William noted that they both had the scraggly features of men who had been in plenty of scraps, similar to those who made a living as pugilists.

"Gentlemen, as you can see, I am unable to rise." William greeted them, nodding to his foot. Both men glanced at his ankle. "So, if you will, please be seated and we shall begin."

When the men left an hour later, they were both employed by William. Richard had wished him to hire them as protection against Andrew's schemes, but he felt that he had more pressing needs. Since he was unable to walk and Richard was busy with his career, he had to have men he could trust to investigate the things that weighed on his mind. As a result, Harahan was sent to Eastbrooke Manor to investigate the fire and to try to locate Mr. Hobson, and Coleridge was charged with finding out where Andrew was staying and what happened between him and Mr. Harrington at Marsden Park.

With these two mysteries in good hands, William was beginning to relax when his shattered marriage came rushing back to mind. Immediately, his spirits fell as Richard's warnings taunted him anew.

"Any caring person would feel dreadful about Miss Harrington's death, Darcy. But that is no reason to sacrifice your life if there is no mutual affection to be had in the bargain. You could aid Miss Bennet and her sisters by finding them employment if she does not want to accept Collins."

"You do not understand. I have had tender feelings for Miss Bennet since leaving Netherfield. And to see her again, not as the woman I remembered, but changed entirely—'shattered' is the word that comes to mind."

"Shattered by her tender feelings for Andrew," Richard reasoned, *"otherwise she would not have been in this predicament. Remember, she was seen kissing him in the moonlight."*

Unable to bear any more reminiscing, William slammed his fist down on his desk, sending papers flying in every direction. He reached for a bell that Mrs. Barnes had provided him and rang it steadily. He kept at it far longer than was necessary, intent on drowning out the recollections that mocked him. In the end, the effort proved futile, as he was still ringing the bell when his housekeeper rushed into the room.

Pemberley
The next morning

If anyone thought that Elizabeth would take her time assuming the duties of mistress, they would be mistaken, for she was on a mission of redemption. Thus, early the next morning when the Fitzwilliams encountered the housekeeper as they came downstairs to break their fast, they learned that the new Mrs. Darcy already had plans.

"Is Mrs. Darcy awake?" Olivia enquired of Mrs. Reynolds.

"Oh my, yes. According to Mrs. O'Reilly, she arose at dawn, though she did not come downstairs until she was certain the rest of us were awake. At present, she is in the dining room with Colonel Fitzwilliam and Sergeant Thaggart."

"I assumed that she would sleep late. After all, she had been on the road for days, and we kept her up last night getting to know her better."

"I must say that I am impressed," Mrs. Reynolds continued. "Already Mrs. Darcy requested a meeting with me when she is finished eating. She wants to go over all the ledgers, and she mentioned getting to know the tenants as soon as possible."

"That bodes well," Olivia stated. Then she looked to Joseph. "Let us hurry then, before Elizabeth finishes eating. Otherwise, we may not get to speak to her today."

As they walked into the small dining room, everyone seemed focused on their plates of food and not on conversation. Noticing their arrival, however, Richard broke the silence.

"I am so pleased that you have deigned to join us!" A wry smile accompanied his tease. "Thaggart and I are to leave right after we are done eating, and I wished to see you before we do."

"Do you have to leave so soon?" Joseph Fitzwilliam ventured. "Livy and I were hoping to visit with you again. We see you so infrequently."

"I would love to stay longer. In fact, I have several months' leave accrued and had intended to return straightaway, since Darcy always insists I take my leave at Pemberley." He chuckled. "Who am I to refuse his entreaty?"

"Who, indeed!" Joseph joked.

"At any rate, I cannot do as I please, for I have been ordered to take Colonel Franklin's position while he is on leave. As a result, I now serve as aide to General Lassiter until Franklin resumes his post. Then I shall have my leave. So, if you stay a good while longer, we may visit."

Suddenly he remembered that things had changed with his cousin's marriage. "Excuse me, Mrs. Darcy, if I sound presumptuous. Though Darcy has always asked me to stay here when on leave, I should not assume the invitation still stands, now that he is a married man. I would not want to interfere with your felicity, and I can always stay at my parents' estate,

Matlock, which is a little over ten miles from here."

"Colonel, nothing at Pemberley shall change. Those who were welcome to stay here before our marriage will be welcome now. Actually, I look forward to getting to know my new family when they visit."

Richard studied her a moment and, satisfied that she was sincere, said, "We look forward to knowing you better as well." Then he addressed his batman. "Are you ready, Thaggart?"

"I was ready, Colonel. Now, I think I have eaten too much and need a nap or, at the least, another strong cup of coffee before we leave." Everyone chuckled.

"I tell you what I shall do, Sergeant. I will have one more cup of coffee with you. This will allow my aunt, uncle and Mrs. Darcy to finish eating and to walk out with us. How does that suit?"

"Most kind of you, Colonel, most kind."

Several minutes later everyone was on the portico, waiting for the horses to be brought around to the front of the house. A footman hurriedly placed their bags at the base of the steps, just as Olivia stood on tiptoes to kiss her nephew's cheek.

"Please stay safe, Richard. Joseph and I worry so much about you. The roads can be dangerous, what with highwaymen and all."

Before he could answer, Thaggart did. "No need to worry about the colonel, ma'am! I keep a good watch on him."

Richard nodded at the younger man. "Thaggart does make my job a lot easier. He is always there to offer his support. And two on the road are safer than one."

Olivia smiled at the sergeant. "Then I thank you for doing a fine job of protecting him."

"You are welcome, ma'am."

While Joseph shook both their hands, Mrs. Reynolds spoke up. "Mr. Darcy would want me to insist that you come back to visit us whenever you can, Colonel Fitzwilliam."

"That is enough coddling, Mrs. Reynolds! Now Thaggart shall pester me to come in this direction every time I leave London," Richard declared, chuckling.

Then he met Elizabeth's eyes. "Mrs. Darcy, I pray that my cousin heals quickly and joins you soon. I know that you will be glad for that as well."

"Yes, I will. Thank you for all you have done, and please—now that we are family, call me Elizabeth." Something profound seemed to pass between the two as they studied each other.

"If you will call me Richard."

A small smile turned up the corners of her mouth. "Done."

Then Richard grabbed a small bag and mounted his horse, calling over his shoulder, "If you want to keep your rank, Thaggart, you had best get moving."

Quick as lightning, the sergeant was on his horse, kicking it into a trot. Richard pursed his lips to keep from smiling as he followed his batman. About fifty yards out, as he turned to wave one last time to his family still on the portico, his eye caught Elizabeth's.

I hope you succeed, for your sake as well as Darcy's. Then he kicked Titan into a gallop, never looking back.

⁂

After everyone had gone back inside the house, Elizabeth excused herself, saying she had to meet with Mrs. Reynolds. As she followed the housekeeper to her office, the Fitzwilliams were left to themselves.

Watching them walk away, Joseph leaned in to his wife. "I can see the wheels turning in your head, Livy. Something is bothering you."

Olivia cut her eyes to her husband. "You know me well." Then she gave a quick tilt of her head in acknowledgement. "Let us walk in the park where we may speak without being overheard."

With that, she took the arm he extended, and they went down the hall and out the back entrance of the manor. Once in the gardens, they selected one of many gravel paths and began to walk down it. When they had gone several hundred feet without conversation, Joseph could be silent no longer.

"It was evident last night that you were taken aback that Elizabeth never mentioned Fitzwilliam—well, not until you asked about him."

"To begin, let me say that I like Elizabeth, I truly do. I sense that she is a decent and kind person; however, she has something very heavy weighing on her heart. I was already apprehensive because she came ahead while my nephew lay injured in London. Nonetheless, I hoped that when she arrived all my doubts would be dispelled."

"She did not oppose discussing Fitzwilliam, I think, as much as she did not know what to say," Joseph Fitzwilliam added. "Not a one of my questions regarding his injury, what treatment was being rendered or when he might be expected to join her, was in her power to answer. And I know if we were in a similar situation, you would have had all the answers."

Olivia stopped walking to face her husband. "My thoughts exactly. I have tried to assuage Mrs. Reynolds' fears, even as my own have overwhelmed me at times. Nevertheless, I must and I will support Elizabeth, for she is Fitzwilliam's choice. I just pray that things are not as grave as they appear at present."

"Did you get the impression that she and Richard reached a truce of some sort just before he left, or was I the only one who sensed that?"

"On the steps?" Olivia asked. At her husband's nod, she continued. "Yes, I saw that as well."

"Since Richard always defends Fitzwilliam in every situation, if he has made peace with Mrs. Darcy, then things may not be as serious as they seem."

"I pray that is so. For now, I must be sure not to let the servants sense my reservations," Olivia stated. "I believe I shall have my hands full with Mrs. Reynolds, though. She is not easily fooled."

"I have faith in your ability, my dear," Joseph Fitzwilliam said as he brought one of her hands up for a kiss. "After all, you convinced our children that my family cared for them, though most had no concern for them at all."

"That was effortless, for I loved Jenny and Arthur. And I would not have them think that anyone wished them ill, even if it meant attributing kindness to those who had none."

She leaned into his chest as his arms went around her waist. Then he kissed the top of her head, whispering into her hair, "Thank you for loving me despite my family."

"I had no choice. I could not stop myself."

Joseph leaned down to capture her lips and this kiss lasted far too long for propriety's sake. He cared not if every servant at Pemberley saw them.

Let them look, if they are obliged, for they shall be able to boast that once in their lives they witnessed a perfect love.

Chapter 21

Pemberley
The stables
One week later

Elizabeth knew the stables would be alive with activity even at the break of dawn. After all, from the time she could walk, she had accompanied her father to their stables almost every morning—perhaps because they were the only two members of the family awake at that hour. Watching the various animals exiting the huge barn the first thing each day had been very exciting for a child, for it reminded her of the story of Noah's ark she had heard in church. To this day, Elizabeth could not suppress a smile whenever she remembered pretending to be Noah as she sat safely atop the paddock fence where her father had placed her. So, making her way in the foggy mist of this new morning, a childlike eagerness filled her heart.

As she neared the buildings, however, it became readily apparent that Longbourn's stables paled in comparison to Pemberley's. Viewing them through the trees from the balcony of her bedroom had not prepared her for seeing them up close. Not only were there separate buildings for the different livestock, many hidden from view one behind the other, but also there were literally scores of men scurrying from building to building. None of them seemed to notice her in the shadows, for she had eschewed bringing a lantern. After all, she had reasoned, she would not need one in another half-hour. Nonetheless, the closer she got, the more nervous Elizabeth became. What would the servants think of her traipsing about at this hour in the dark?

Suddenly a booming voice came from out of the darkness. "What are you doing here?"

Startled, Elizabeth turned to see a bear of a man walking towards her with his hands on his hips. The shawl she had draped over her head fell to her shoulders, and immediately the man recognised her.

"Mrs. Darcy! Please forgive me. I… I did not know it was you, ma'am. I thought—never mind what I thought. I am Travis Miller, the coachman." He performed a quick, unpractised bow.

"Mr. Miller, I apologise for coming here unannounced. I awoke early and suddenly decided that I needed to choose a horse for my personal use this morning. Mr. Sturgis, my husband's steward, has been kind enough to drive me around to the tenants' homes in a carriage, but he informed me that the last few families can only be reached via horseback."

"It is true that there are a few in the farthest sections where a carriage is not practical because of the terrain. Usually the only vehicles seen in that area are sturdy wagons." Then his brow furrowed as he looked back to the manor. "Are you going out alone?"

"Mr. Sturgis is too busy today to accompany me, so I must."

"I will send for a footman to go with you then. I am sure Mr. Darcy would—"

"That is not necessary. I have ridden by myself for years."

"But Pemberley is a vast estate and you are not familiar with—"

"I have a good memory and I remember the way to the tenant houses. I can assure you that all will be well."

"If you say so, ma'am," the coachman said in the end, though his voice and expression were both doubtful.

"I much prefer walking, but that is not practical for my purpose. If possible, I would like a jumper, if you have one, as I have been known to take fences if it means not having to ride miles out of the way. And I prefer a mare."

Mr. Miller nodded, still unconvinced. Then, taking a deep breath, he ventured, "If you will follow me, I shall try to find one to suit."

In the semi-darkness, the man kept glancing over his shoulder as they walked towards the buildings, as though he expected her to disappear. This tickled Elizabeth, though she managed to suppress a smile. When they reached the horse barn, two grooms were just opening the huge, double doors.

Mr. Miller stopped to shout, "Hold off releasing the mares until I have time to look them over." The grooms nodded before going on inside. "Wait here, please, Mrs. Darcy. When the horses are released from their stalls, they tend to head to the pastures like they have been locked up for years. One could easily get trampled, especially by a stallion."

Elizabeth wanted to tell the man that she was aware of the danger, but she did not. "Thank you for the reminder."

It was several minutes before Miller returned, leading a dappled-grey horse. It was now getting light enough to see well, and Elizabeth smiled, for the animal was very handsome.

"This one we got in trade from Lord Dutton last month. Mr. Darcy wanted a stallion, and this mare was part of the bargain. According to his lordship, his daughter rode the horse until her marriage, after which she moved to Scotland. The mare is very gentle. I know, for several of the young grooms have ridden her."

Elizabeth ran her hands over the horse's head, pushing the mane from her dark brown eyes. "You are a lovely girl." Then she addressed Mr. Miller. "What is her name?"

"I don't rightly remember hearing anyone say. I suppose that you may call her whatever you please."

"Then I shall call her Phoebe," she said, rubbing the horse's neck. "Do you have a saddle?"

"I do. Miss Darcy has used several saddles over the years and I can think of one that may be a good fit for you."

In no time at all, Mr. Miller returned with a saddle and a blanket. After all the cinches were tightened on the saddle, he led the mare to a very old set of steps leaning against the paddock fence.

When he turned to see that she had not followed, he declared, "Begging your pardon, Mrs. Darcy, but this is how Miss Darcy used to mount a horse before she grew so tall."

Elizabeth pursed her lips, amused at his unease, and walked to the steps. After she had mounted the horse, Mr. Miller handed her the reins, and she kicked Phoebe into a trot. She made several effortless rings around the paddock before taking the lane that led to the pasture. Having noted that if she followed the fence line, she would eventually find the tenants they had missed previously,

Elizabeth was determined to do just that.

Watching her leave, Mr. Miller was pleased to see that she sat the horse well; in fact, it was as though she and the grey had been partnered for years. Thus, it was with a small sigh of relief that he returned to his job. Knowing Mr. Darcy as he did, it was a given that the master would not be happy that he had helped his wife pick a horse and would tell him so in no uncertain terms. And he would like it even less when he learned that she had ridden out alone. Regardless, the look in Mrs. Darcy's eye when he had questioned her made it plain that it was futile to argue. As he paused one last time to look in the direction she had ridden before entering the barn, Mr. Miller came to a conclusion which brought a smile to his face: *I have the feeling that Mrs. Darcy will have her way when it comes to a lot of things around here.*

It was late in the afternoon by the time Elizabeth visited the last of the tenants' houses she could manage in one day. She was tired, but pleased that she had thought to bring along bread, cheese and an apple, allowing her to keep to her plan without having to worry about eating. For at the last house she visited, she had discovered a family in great need of baby clothes, towels and bed sheets before their family increased.

Mrs. Becker was a very friendly woman, though a bit pale and drained from her circumstances. She told Elizabeth that she was four and twenty and was expecting her second child in about a month, though from all appearances, the baby could come at any moment. There was a child in the house already, a girl of five named Mazie, who was quite the talker. Elizabeth found her inquisitiveness delightful, and that had been one reason she had stayed longer than planned. Mr. Becker was nowhere to be seen, but his wife had said that was not unusual because he worked from sunrise to sunset.

Now heading back to Pemberley with visions of how to help this couple swirling in her mind, Elizabeth kicked Phoebe into a canter. The sun was beginning to wane, and it seemed the faster she rode, the faster the sun set. Thus, by the time she turned down the road leading to the stables it was almost dark, and Elizabeth could barely make out a group of men up ahead. They were saddling horses as she entered the paddock, and each turned to watch her in total silence. At once, it became painfully obvious that they had been preparing to begin a search for her.

Saying a quick prayer that her cheeks were not as red as they felt, Elizabeth held her head high as Mr. Miller stepped forward to take Phoebe's reins, his scowl showing his displeasure. As she slid off the horse she meant to apologise but Joseph Fitzwilliam suddenly appeared at her side.

"Elizabeth, we were all worried sick about you." He took her arm and began to lead her towards the manor. "What in the world kept you out to this hour?"

"Nothing out of the ordinary, I assure you," she said as confidently as possible. However, she sounded a little breathless as she continued, for it was hard to keep up with her uncle's long strides. "The time simply slipped away before I knew it."

Joseph Fitzwilliam stopped to look at her as though she had grown two heads. And when next he spoke, he reminded her of Fitzwilliam during their last conversation.

"Did it never occur to you that this entire estate hinges on your welfare? You are their mistress, and the staff—from the lowest gardener to Mrs. Reynolds— has been frantic, thinking you may have come to harm. Not to mention that Olivia is beside herself, imagining all sorts of things. I need not remind you that my wife is ill and does not deserve to be excessively worried when it is easily avoided."

"I... I did not—" Lizzy sputtered.

Joseph was not finished, and he interrupted as he walked her towards the house. "My nephew is not here to protect you, but he would assume that I had sense enough to do so in his absence. I beg you. Never again leave the premises without leaving word where you are going and taking a footman, a groom or the steward along. Even I am willing to escort you, if need be."

Elizabeth said defensively, "Mrs. Reynolds was aware that I was going to call on tenants this week."

"Yes, but she thought you were riding out with Mr. Sturgis again today. When she encountered him this afternoon, she was shocked to realise that he was here but you were not. It was only after checking with the liveryman that she learned you had ridden out alone."

"I have called on the tenants of Longbourn by myself for years now."

"How large is Longbourn? Can it compare in any measure to Pemberley?" Before Elizabeth could answer, he added, "Where you grew up it may be perfectly safe for a woman to ride out alone and be gone all day without a word, but that is not the case here. On this vast estate, packs of wild dogs, capable of taking down a horse, occasionally pass through. And if that does not frighten you, from time to time vagrants have been found living in the shepherd's shacks, hay barns and other structures dotted throughout the fields, forests and pastures. They live off whatever they can forage or steal, if not from my nephew, then from the tenants. While the guards who circle the perimeter rout them whenever they encounter them, Pemberley is so large that it is a constant struggle."

"But if the tenants are safe in the far reaches of Pemberley, other than missing a few items—"

"The tenants are not valuable to use as ransom. Mrs. Darcy is!"

Suddenly they neared the manor where torches were spread out evenly across the grounds, while the house itself looked as though there were candles lit in every room. Mortified that she had caused such a disturbance, Elizabeth's audacity fled and she fought back tears.

"I apologise. It was inconsiderate of me to cause such upheaval." She looked to her new uncle. "I promise that it shall never happen again."

Then Joseph Fitzwilliam did something totally unexpected. He pulled her into an embrace, hugging her very tightly before remembering himself and pushing her to arm's length.

"Now it is I who must apologise for being so outspoken. It is just that... " He took a ragged breath, and his voice broke as his expression became pained. "You are only a bit older than my Jenny would have been, had she lived. When I thought something might have happened... " His voice trailed off and his tear-filled eyes dropped to the ground.

Elizabeth laid a hand on his arm. "I understand completely. Thank you for caring for me." Then she looked to the terrace where Olivia had just walked out to get a better look. "We should go in before Aunt Olivia takes a chill."

Joseph nodded and together they hurried on to the house. When she gained the terrace, Elizabeth fell into Olivia's open arms. It was obvious that her aunt was crying, for her shoulders shook, but she did not utter a word of reprimand.

Elizabeth was grateful as she whispered, "I am sorry."

Over Olivia's shoulder, Mrs. Reynolds stood wringing her hands, and as soon as she had kissed her aunt and slipped from her embrace, Elizabeth went to the housekeeper, giving her a hug as well. Again, there was no lecture, not that the housekeeper would have said whatever she thought in any case, but Elizabeth apologised profusely for the worry she had caused.

"I am just so relieved that you are home. You must be starved," the elderly servant said softly. "I shall send a tray up to your room, for you must eat before you retire."

Harmony was restored at Pemberley once again as all the candles were snuffed and a myriad of servants went to bed, for they had to rise early. In her own bedroom at last, Elizabeth was too tired to converse with Mrs. O'Reilly who, fortunately, was uncharacteristically quiet as she helped her undress. After she was left alone, Elizabeth stared at the ceiling in the darkness and considered how drastically her life had changed.

Gone were the carefree days of wandering alone wherever she desired. From now on, her every move would be watched and chronicled, whether she wished it or not. Suddenly the enormity of the situation brought her to tears. She was married to a man she barely knew and, in her unhappiness, had judged poorly, accusing him of despicable acts he had not committed. It remained to be seen if he could ever forgive her. If that were not bad enough, she had upset the entire house today because she had chosen to do things her way.

Congratulations, Lizzy! You have managed to make everyone at Pemberley think you are a foolish child during your very first week as mistress.

A knock on the door announced that the supper tray had arrived, so she let the maid in. The events of the day had taken a toll on her appetite, but to show her gratitude for Mrs. Reynolds' care, she consumed a goodly portion of the fare as well as a welcome cup of tea. Afterward, she crawled into the big bed and plopped wearily back onto the pillows.

It was a long time before she fell asleep, however. Besides her conduct this day, Joseph Fitzwilliam's words kept running through her head—not his reprimand, but his mention of Jenny. Now Elizabeth comprehended the source of the sadness that was ever present in her aunt and uncle, and it was painful to think she had added to that sorrow, even unintentionally.

London
Darcy House
The study

Now that William was back on his feet, howbeit not all day long, he was more satisfied. Of course, standing caused his ankle to swell again, but if he propped it up every hour or so for a quarter-hour, it was tolerable. Already, his local bootmaker, Hoby, was designing a special, wider boot which would both accommodate the injured foot and would match his regular footwear, should he need to appear in public. Nonetheless, William hoped that he might be able to wear his regular boots by the time he left for Derbyshire. That remained to be seen, however, as Mr. Graham was not in the least bit happy that he insisted on being afoot so soon. Nor was he happy that William was using brandy to dull his pain.

Nevertheless, William was in his study one afternoon when Mr. Harahan was announced. Noting that the man looked as though he had just returned to Town and had not taken the time to bathe before meeting with him, William tried not to stare. Harahan's clothes were covered in dust, as was his face.

William stood to extend a hand. "I did not expect you so soon, Mr. Harahan."

Harahan wiped his hand on his pants before shaking hands, "And I did not expect to find you on your feet."

They both chuckled as William sat down, and Harahan followed suit, taking the chair directly in front of the desk.

William was hopeful. "You must have some news, else you would still be in Richmond."

"I do. In investigating the fire, I found out that there was a visitor that day—a man who apparently left his horse behind. One of the grooms saw him ride up to the house that later burned, but he did not see what happened afterward, for he was attending to some work. After the fire, the horse was found tied to a tree and was stabled. I examined the animal and discovered it had a brand on its flank."

William's brows rose. "Will that help us to find the one who rode it?"

"Perhaps. It was a number like the army uses to identify its horses. I intend to trace the number to the outpost that sold the animal—all older horses are sold after a certain time, you see. Perhaps the buyer's name is recorded. Of course, it could have been sold, traded or even stolen afterward, so we cannot be sure. But it is something to go on. Besides that, there was a receipt in a pouch on the saddle. It is from a warehouse in Cheapside."

William scratched his chin. "That could prove helpful." Then he remembered his other concern. "No news of Hobson then?"

Harahan's mien became sombre. "I hate to inform you that while I was there, Mr. Hobson's body was found by some men hunting in nearby woods. The body was about a half-mile from Eastbrooke Manor, and I was summoned to have a look. The skull was crushed, but there is no doubt it was Hobson, for there were papers in his coat. Whoever killed him was in a great hurry to leave, as they took nothing from him—even his pocket watch was still there. I think that clears him of any suspicions, for if he had set the fire, he could have taken any number of horses and ridden off. I surmise that he may have been chasing the perpetrator who left the horse behind."

William silently studied his desk for a moment, and then he looked up. "Has Hobson been buried in a pauper's grave?"

"Yes, sir. It was necessary to bury the body immediately."

"I will pay for Mr. Hobson's remains to be reinterred wherever his family may wish. Can you find out if he had any next of kin?"

"I will see what I can learn."

"Thank you." Then William sighed heavily. "You have helped me tremendously. There are extra rooms in the servants' quarters or you may choose to rent a room elsewhere, your choice. I will order a hot bath for you if you decide to stay here. In any case, please take a few days to rest before you continue your work. You have only to ask for whatever you may need—supplies or funds."

"I had just as soon stay here and I should really like a bath. I imagine I am beginning to smell ripe," Harahan joked. "I just felt that I should report to you first."

"That is appreciated."

William rang the bell on his desk, as it was still too painful to stand and use the bell-pull. In an instant, Mr. Barnes came to the door, and Mr. Harahan was shown to his rooms.

Left to contemplate what it all meant, William wondered if Mr. Coleridge was having as much success in his quest to find out about Andrew's circumstances. Thinking about his cousin, however, brought Elizabeth back to mind. William had not written to her since she left, not from a wish to be hateful, but because he knew not what to say. He had received letters from Mrs. Reynolds and his aunt and uncle, congratulating him on his marriage and promising to take care of his wife until he could join them at Pemberley. The prospect of joining her, however, gave William pause. He was not sure if he could act as though nothing was amiss when they met again. All eyes would be on them, and he would be obligated to portray a happily married man. He wondered if he was that skilful an actor.

Frustration mounted and he pushed everything from his mind, save work. Grabbing the pile of letters that lay unanswered on his desk, he began to read the next one in a bid to forget. Between the letter and another glass of brandy,

William was able to focus on the problems of irrigating some of Pemberley's fields—at least for a short while.

Later that day

Weary from working steadily without a proper break, William had already rung for Barnes by the time Charles Bingley appeared at Darcy House. This meant that the butler was not at the front door to greet him, for he was looking for Mr. Martin in order to dispatch him to their employer's bedroom to help the master undress, remove the bandages and reapply new ones before dinner. Therefore, Bingley was met at the front door by a long-time footman who recognised Mr. Darcy's friend and let him in.

Never one to bother with formalities, instead of waiting for Barnes to return in order to announce him, Charles headed down the hall towards the study where William could normally be found at this hour. When he reached the open door, however, Bingley stuck his head inside instead of entering. Seeing that William had lost weight and looked dishevelled, immediately his suspicions were raised.

"Darcy?"

William looked up, his frown taking a minute to transition into a wan smile.

"Bingley? What are you doing here?"

"That is a fine how-do-you-do!" Charles said as he walked on into the room. "One would think you did not want me here."

"No, not at all. I was just… just surprised to see you, that is all."

"We are friends, and shortly we will be brothers. Why would you be surprised that I stopped by?" Reaching the desk, he had a good view of William's ankle. "My lord, Darcy! If you are an example of what marriage does to a man, I am not sure I want to have a go at it."

When William did not smile, Bingley realised he had hit a nerve. Quickly taking a seat, he leaned forward, propping his elbows on the desk. "Is something the matter?" A loud sigh was evidence it would not to be a simple explanation.

"You can count on my loyalty, friend. I shall not breathe a word of anything you say."

Not wishing to add to Bingley's worries, William decided not to expose his marital problems. After all, Charles had to be loyal to Jane, and she would, of course, be loyal to her sister. So William quickly stated the fact that Elizabeth was not there and changed the subject.

Charles was somewhat familiar with the women and children Andrew had ruined, so William recounted all the circumstances of the fire at Eastbrooke Manor, including how he came to be injured. There was a long period afterward when neither man spoke while they contemplated the tragedy.

"I am so sorry to learn of this," Bingley said at last. "You must know that you did all you could to help the poor souls while they lived." Then he added, "May I have a look at your ankle? Just to satisfy myself that you are doing as well as you claim?"

William said wryly, "Are you saying that I would lie?"

"I know you well enough to know that you will lessen the importance of any injury. You always do."

"Fine. I was just about to return to my rooms. If you want to join me, you will see that I have been truthful, for Mr. Martin will work his magic on my ankle. By the way, if you have not made plans, I would love to have you stay and dine with me. Cook has promised a roasted pheasant and a caramel flan this evening."

There was a strange loneliness in William's eyes, so Charles accepted. "That sounds wonderful. I am on my own today. Jane and Mrs. Bennet are with Mrs. Gardiner, examining fabrics and such. The Gardiners leave for Lambton tomorrow, so this is the last day she will be able to direct them to the best warehouses. As my expertise was not needed, I told them I would stop by to see if you and Mrs. Darcy were still in Town."

Suddenly Charles' expression changed to puzzlement. "Tell me again why your wife is at Pemberley and you are here. I know Mrs. Bennet will be displeased when she finds out, and she will interrogate me thoroughly. I wish to be ready with an answer."

William was already limping around the desk when the question made him stop and snap at his friend. "Please listen this time, Charles, for I do not feel well enough to keep repeating it. Elizabeth wished to be at Pemberley when the Gardiners arrive in Lambton to retrieve their children. Since Richard had to be in York, he agreed to escort her there, as he was travelling in that direction. It is as simple as that."

William walked past Charles towards the door, the pain in every step apparent. For a moment, Bingley pondered why the mention of his wife would irritate Darcy so. Shrugging his shoulders, he pushed those misgivings from his mind as he walked to catch up with his host.

Maybe you are making too much of it. After all, surely his irritation is a result of the horror at Eastbrooke Manor and his present pain. That is all.

⁓⁂⁓

Bingley's townhouse

Charles had promised Mrs. Bennet word on her daughter and new son, and he knew that if he waited to bring the report, she would never forgive him. Having no choice, as he approached his own residence he began to dread what the woman would say when she heard the news he carried. Nonetheless, taking a deep breath, he forced himself to knock on the door and smiled at his own butler when it swung open.

"Mr. Bingley, sir! Do come in!" Snipes greeted, stepping aside and taking Charles' hat and gloves. "Mrs. Bennet and Miss Bennet are in the drawing room at present."

"Thank you, Snipes. I shall join them." He began in that direction, then stopped and turned. "Would you bring me a large glass of brandy? I think the decanter in the drawing room is empty. And if the ladies do not already have refreshments, have Cook bring a pot of tea and a tray of cakes."

"Right away, sir."

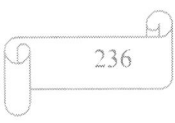

As he watched the rotund man walk away, he could not suppress a smile, for with his black coat and white shirt, Snipes always reminded him of a penguin. Shaking his head to clear that impression from his mind, Charles hurried towards the room where his angel waited.

Immediately upon entering the drawing room, Mrs. Bennet exclaimed, "Oh, Mr. Bingley, there you are! You will never guess what we were able to find in the warehouse district today. Never! Never! Never!"

"Then I suppose it shall be fruitless to venture a supposition," Charles declared, all the while smiling at Jane, who was seated on a settee with an unopened magazine in her lap. When she returned his smile, his heart leapt.

"Oh, but you must guess!" Jane's mother replied. "I shall give you a hint. It is white and very delicate."

"Hmmm. Lace?"

"You are absolutely correct! And the most beautiful lace there ever was. It is from—" She turned to Jane. "Where was it from, dear?"

"Belgium," Jane dutifully answered.

"That is it! Belgium! And it is lovelier than any I have seen in my life. Jane will be the most beautiful bride in all of England."

Bingley beamed. "She already is, without any lace."

Jane flushed the same shade of rose as her gown and could not reply. Alas, Mrs. Bennet was not as affected. "Now, tell me. Did you call on Darcy House? Are they in London or not?"

Charles said timidly, "One of them is?"

"Whatever do you mean? One of them?"

Bingley told her of Darcy's injury and repeated exactly what he had said about Elizabeth going on to Pemberley; however, this did not satisfy Mrs. Bennet.

"Lizzy left Mr. Darcy in London and went to Pemberley by herself? I have never heard of such a thing. A bride leaving her husband in this manner is beyond comprehension." Standing, she began to pace and rant. "That means there will be no dinner party for us! What could she be thinking to leave him, especially with him so near death?"

Charles tried to interject, "He is not near death," but was drowned out by Mrs. Bennet's steadily increasing volume.

"She must have made him angry, and he sent her away." She moved to stand in front of Jane. "You are my witness that I warned Lizzy to keep her opinions to herself." Then she turned to accost Charles. "Did Mr. Darcy seem very displeased with her?"

"I assure you, Mrs. Bennet, that that is not the case at all. It is simply Darcy being considerate. That is all."

"Humph!" Mrs. Bennet declared. "No newly-married man would permit his bride to go off without him—not if he was satisfied with her. I imagine we shall learn the results of this ere long. He may send Miss *I-know-better-than-you* back to Longbourn before the ink dries on the marriage license."

Just then a maid entered with a glass of brandy, a pot of tea and some cakes. As Mrs. Bennet rushed over to take a bit of cake and stuff it in her mouth, Bingley tried once again to pacify her.

"I am sorry if I gave you the wrong impression, but I can assure you that nothing is wrong with my friend's marriage. You shall see as time goes on."

By now Mrs. Bennet was busily pouring herself a cup of tea and choosing another cake to satisfy her sweet tooth, so she was not as keen to keep arguing her point.

"I hope you are right, but I fear that I have the truth of it," was all she managed to say as she took another bite of a chocolate éclair and dabbed a napkin on her lips.

At least Mrs. Bennet's preoccupation with food gave Charles a chance to sit down beside Jane. He glanced back at her mother and, seeing her occupied, leaned over to whisper, "I missed you ever so much today."

"I missed you just as truly," Jane replied, which brought a wide smile to her fiancé's face. Then she whispered, low enough that her mother could not hear, "Do you really think all is well with Lizzy's marriage? After all, it does seem strange that she would leave Mr. Darcy while he is injured. I know I could never have left you."

At that declaration, Charles reached to take her hand and squeezed it tightly.

He considered his answer for a brief time before replying.

"I do. Darcy is not one to make decisions lightly. He loves your sister, of that I am certain, and he has never been a good patient. He becomes irritable and short-tempered when he is not well. Most likely, he thought it best that Richard escort Lizzy on to Pemberley; that way she would not be subject to his complaints and bad humour."

Jane watched Charles intently as he spoke, and hearing his explanation, she relaxed. "I shall trust your instincts then. Thank you for calming my nerves." A giggle escaped and she covered her mouth. "I am beginning to sound like my mother."

"Do not say that again, my love. You could never be like your mother."

They both snickered, which drew Mrs. Bennet's attention. "What are you two laughing about? I must have my part in the conversation."

"Oh, Mama, we are just happy that we shall be married before long."

Mrs. Bennet smiled. "Well, it shall not happen until after an appropriate betrothal. I will not be deprived of a proper wedding with all the trimmings this time!"

Then she went off on a long discourse of what constituted a proper engagement and wedding in her opinion. Jane and Charles heard not a word of it, as they held hands and stared into each other's eyes.

Chapter 22

Pemberley
A drawing room

The magnitude of their niece's new circumstances rendered Madeline Gardiner almost speechless as she and her husband trailed Mrs. Reynolds through the elegant halls of Pemberley, for even though Mrs. Gardiner had toured the home often as a girl, the enormity of the residence became clear only when one entered the private quarters. In addition, seeing the manor again after so long a time made it apparent that her remembrances were a poor substitute for seeing it first-hand.

Having reached her childhood home only a scant few hours earlier, Mrs. Gardiner was very weary. Nonetheless, after a footman had appeared with an invitation for tea at Pemberley, she had immediately accepted. She felt that she had no choice—not with what she knew of the current state of her niece's marriage. Thus, she and Edward now found themselves following a servant through a maze that would lead them to Elizabeth. Finally, an open door appeared just ahead, and upon reaching it, the housekeeper immediately stepped inside.

"Mr. and Mrs. Gardiner," they heard her announce.

Madeline entered the well-appointed room apprehensively, with her husband close on her heels. Just as she noticed that some unfamiliar faces were examining her, Elizabeth sprang from a chair and rushed to greet them.

"Aunt! Uncle!" Elizabeth cried, hugging their necks enthusiastically, one after the other. "Forgive me for sending an invitation so soon. Knowing that you were to arrive this afternoon, I simply could not wait to see you, though I know you must be exhausted from your trip."

"No apologies are necessary, Lizzy," Madeline Gardiner replied with a restrained smile. "It was only a few more miles, and we are always pleased to see you. We just cannot stay long."

"Then perhaps you will come again once you have a chance to visit with your family. We could have a picnic and include my cousins."

"We shall see."

Elizabeth noticed that her aunt's gaze was fixed over her shoulder at the Fitzwilliams, who stood when they entered the room. Remembering her manners, she turned to address William's relations.

"Uncle Joseph, Aunt Olivia, please allow me to introduce my uncle and aunt, Mr. Edward Gardiner and Mrs. Madeline Gardiner of London."

The Fitzwilliams smiled pleasantly at them as Elizabeth continued the introductions, "May I present Captain Joseph Fitzwilliam and his wife, Olivia Fitzwilliam, my husband's aunt and uncle? They are visiting from Ireland."

The couples exchanged pleasantries, and when Elizabeth mentioned that her Aunt Gardiner had been born in Lambton, Olivia Fitzwilliam's eyes lit up.

"I lived in Lambton for a time when I was a child," she said excitedly. "I was a Stratford before my marriage."

A big smile split Mrs. Gardiner's face. "I knew your family well, for my best friend when I was young was Mary Stratford. My maiden name is Gavin."

Olivia laughed. "Mary Stratford is my cousin! And the Gavins were our neighbours when we first moved to Lambton. I do remember your name, though there were so many Gavin siblings that I was better acquainted with the older girls."

"I understand completely, for I have five sisters and three brothers. Mary and I were the youngest in our families so we became quite close. She moved to Edinburgh, did she not?"

"Yes. Her husband's ancestral home is there," Olivia replied. "It is unfortunate that she moved so far away after she married. For years now, we have only corresponded in letters; however, I shall write to her and tell her about our meeting."

"If you would give her my regards and pass along my address, I should love to hear from her again."

"I will, and I know she would love to hear from you as well."

Before long, they were on a first name basis. While Edward, Joseph and Lizzy consumed refreshments and listened, Olivia and Madeline talked animatedly of their childhoods. Lambton was so small when they were children that they learned they had many friends in common, despite the fact that there was more than ten years difference in their ages.

A half-hour later, Olivia stood and addressed her husband, teasing, "We should leave Elizabeth to visit with her family, my dear. Otherwise, I fear I shall continue to dominate the conversation."

"Perhaps you can persuade them to come again," Elizabeth ventured. "You could resume your reminiscing at that time."

"That is a splendid idea, Elizabeth. Madeline, please come again before you return to London," Olivia pleaded.

"We shall try our best," Mrs. Gardiner responded. And with that, the Fitzwilliams said their goodbyes and quit the room.

The door had no more than closed when Mrs. Gardiner's expression changed to one of deep concern as she addressed her niece. "Lizzy, I must be frank. Though I am fatigued, I accepted your invitation to come today because I thought it imperative that we talk as soon as possible. Your uncle had occasion to meet with Mr. Darcy before we left London. We were both stunned to learn that your marriage is in turmoil. Did you heed none of our advice?"

Mortified that her favourite relations were aware of the mess she had made of her marriage, Elizabeth reacted badly. "So my husband felt it necessary to inform my relations of our problems. I suppose he ran to tell Jane and Mr. Bingley, as well."

Mr. Gardiner stepped forward, a scowl deepening as his hands formed fists and rested on either side of his waist. "Must I remind you, young lady, that *your husband* cannot *run* anywhere? He is injured, as you well know."

Elizabeth flinched at his declaration. Trying to add that her husband had given her no choice but to leave London, she began, "But he—"

"Furthermore, had I not stopped by Mr. Darcy's house to see why you had not contacted Madeline, we would still be ignorant of it all. To be truthful, Mr. Darcy tried to excuse your absence as nothing out of the ordinary. It was I who detected something was amiss and would not be satisfied with his explanation. He only told me what happened after I demanded that he be honest with me."

Elizabeth's bravado collapsed entirely and when she spoke again, her voice was rough with emotion. "Forgive me, Uncle. I had no right to take offense." Then she addressed her aunt. "As to your original question, I had taken all your advice to heart. I intended to challenge Fitzwilliam about the conversation I heard between him and his cousin, but the house in Richmond burned in the meantime. A child and his mother died... " She took a ragged breath, adding, "I lost all reason when I heard him speaking of that tragedy as though he had no part in the blame."

"Which was entirely true," Mr. Gardiner interjected.

"Which was true," Elizabeth repeated faintly. "I was so confident that I was in the right that it took Colonel Fitzwilliam telling me the truth during our journey here to convince me otherwise. He informed me that Andrew Darcy was the man who ruined the women and fathered those poor children living in Richmond. It was only after his reprimand that I comprehended my utterly baseless indictment of Fitzwilliam in regards to that matter. And, my hurtful behaviour towards him from the very start of our marriage proves that I have no business sketching anyone's character."

"What is done is done," Aunt Gardiner said sympathetically. "What matters now is that you are truly sorry and that you will try to make amends."

"I do not know if I shall be given the opportunity. My husband cannot stand the sight of me or else he would not have sent me away. And, it follows that soon all our family will know why."

She sank down into a chair, her hands covering her face. The Gardiners exchanged worried looks when she mumbled, "I fear that when Fitzwilliam returns to Pemberley, he may send me away from here as well. What will Mama do if he sends me back to Longbourn?"

"Lizzy, I do not believe for a moment that Mr. Darcy wishes his family or anyone else to know of your... *difficulties*," Mr. Gardiner offered. "After all, I practically had to draw the story out of him. I just happened to catch him at a very vulnerable time, what with his injury, for it was obvious that he was in great pain and despondent. If I remember correctly, his words were 'my greatest fear is that this will always stand between us.'"

Silently, Elizabeth rose and walked over to a large bank of windows. Folding her arms, she pictured William's face the day she had confronted him in his bedroom. He looked so weary and in pain, but she had ignored his wellbeing in favour of pressing her case. The memory brought tears to her eyes, and she began to run her hands up and down her arms. It was a habit—something she always did when she was upset.

With a tilt of his head in his niece's direction and a doleful look, Mr. Gardiner indicated that perhaps they were being too severe; thus, Madeline crossed the room to stand next to her, slipping an arm around her niece's waist.

Elizabeth seemed focused on the lawn where a calico cat with kittens trailing behind her was pursuing a bird as it flitted from one place to another. Each attempt to catch the bird resulted in its flying higher—first on top of the fountain, then on a lower limb of a tree and finally to the very top of the tree.

"Do you see how the bird evades the cat?" Mrs. Gardiner asked. Elizabeth nodded. "When your husband returns, he will likely be just like that bird."

Elizabeth's expression became puzzled. "I do not understand."

"From what Edward told me, you must have hurt Mr. Darcy tremendously by having no faith in his character. Most likely he will deal with the pain by avoiding you. However, you must be as tenacious as that cat. As much as possible, be near him, even if it is just to sit and read while he works."

"I cannot impose myself on him."

"You can and you will!" her aunt insisted. "That is, if you wish to save your marriage. Mr. Darcy must understand that your opinion of him has changed and that is impossible if you are never in each other's company."

"I... I would be embarrassed to—"

"Pride has always been your Achilles heel, Lizzy, and it has served you ill. You have wounded your husband very deeply, and there is no easy way out. Trust between a husband and wife is a fragile thing. Once it is destroyed, it is very difficult to restore—sometimes it is impossible."

"I have ruined everything," Elizabeth said softly.

"Do not say that again!" Madeline Gardiner declared, turning Elizabeth so that they faced each other. "If you have given up, then everything is lost already. I do not know Mr. Darcy well enough to make predictions, but in light of his reputation, I know him to be a fair man and not vindictive. That speaks well of his character and leaves hope for the future."

"He has every right to be despondent over our marriage. For had he readily believed such evil of me from the beginning, I do not think I could ever have forgiven him, or forgotten."

"That is because it has always been your nature to hold grudges," Madeline Gardiner said more light-heartedly. "I hate to say that, but it is true."

Elizabeth could only nod for Jane had often said the same thing.

"On the other hand, you have many fine qualities—one of which is to put your whole heart and soul into whatever you find worth doing. I have faith that you can still find felicity in your marriage, but the burden shall be upon your shoulders. Since he is in physical pain, he is likely to keep to himself as men are prone to do in those circumstances."

"I have already resolved to do everything in my power to be a good mistress," Elizabeth said. "Since my arrival at Pemberley, I have gone over the ledgers with Mrs. Reynolds and memorised the procedures for recording expenditures, and I helped with planning the dinner menus. In addition, I recently finished calling on all the tenants and making a list of their needs. I have put into motion plans for addressing them, including providing baby clothes, towels and sheets to a prospective new mother."

Madeline hugged Elizabeth. "This is the Lizzy we know and love. Taking your duties seriously will convince Mr. Darcy of your sincerity. He will see that you wish to be a good mistress."

Elizabeth blinked away tears as she whispered, "I would give everything to convince him that I also wish to be a good wife. In fact, I wish that more than anything."

"All in good time, dear. The opportunity will come, wait and see."

"I hope so," Elizabeth sniffled, unable to keep a few of her tears from escaping. "I truly, truly hope so."

Not too long afterwards, the Gardiners took their leave, returning to their family in Lambton. Elizabeth stayed in the drawing room for a while longer, emerging with red, swollen eyes and quickly seeking the sanctuary of her rooms. Fortunately, she managed to evade most of the servants, as well as the Fitzwilliams, who had decided to visit the gardens after leaving the drawing room.

London
Matlock House
Georgiana's sitting room

When she walked into Georgiana's sitting room, Lady Matlock was shocked to find her niece sharing tea with Lady Susan. She had grown increasingly wary of that woman's motives for being Georgiana's friend, especially following the episode at the ball. Tactfully, she had suggested that the widow was too old to be Georgiana's particular friend and expressed hope that she would make friends closer to her own age. It was obvious, though, that Lady Matlock's ploy had not worked yet, for here she sat. Still, there was nothing to be done but to act pleasantly.

"Lady Susan, I am surprised to find you here!" Surreptitiously, she threw a displeased look at Georgiana, who instantly looked away. "My niece did not mention that you were coming today."

"I... I forgot she was to visit," Georgiana sputtered.

"We talked of it the night of the ball, so I am sure it merely slipped her mind," Susan lied.

Mention of the ball caused the countess' brows to rise, which said much more than mere words. She had been livid at the rumours flying about Lady Susan and her nephew since that evening. However, as she did not wish a confrontation, nor did she have the time, she addressed Georgiana instead.

"Whatever the case may be, I need to speak to you privately, Georgiana. Would you join me in your bedroom for a moment?" She offered an artificial smile to Susan. "I am sure that Lady Susan will not mind."

With that, the countess and Georgiana left the room. No sooner had the door closed to Georgiana's bedroom than Susan ran over to place her ear against it. She was able to hear all that was said easily, for the countess talked very loudly when she was upset.

"Your uncle and I must go to Darcy House this very minute. We received a letter from your Aunt Catherine saying that she would be in London today. She intends to confront your brother about his marriage."

"I... I do not wish to go with you."

"That is just as well, for we thought it best to leave you here. I simply wanted you to be aware that Lady Catherine is in town. If she were to come here, you have my permission to send your maid down with your regrets. Just say that you are unwell. I shall make sure that Soames knows."

"Thank you, Aunt."

"Now, let me be off, or Edward shall leave without me."

Having said that, Lady Matlock walked back into the sitting room and nodded at Susan, who had barely regained her seat. Hastening into the hallway, the countess disappeared with no further ado.

"My goodness! Is there some emergency?" Susan asked, standing up just as Georgiana walked solemnly back into the room.

"You could say that. She and my uncle are off to Darcy House. It seems my aunt, Lady Catherine, is in town to see my brother."

"And you are not going?"

"No. When I was much younger, Lady Catherine tried to persuade Fitzwilliam that it was in my best interest to live with her at Rosings. She said that I needed my cousin's influence, but Brother would have none of it. He knew that I was fearful of my aunt's temper and that Anne and I had little in common. She got very irritable with him... and me. To this day, I try never to be in her company."

"She must be here because she is unhappy about Fitzwilliam's marriage. I heard Lady Matlock say often enough that Lady Catherine wished him to marry Anne."

"Yes. For years she insisted he must marry my sickly cousin, but my uncle put an end to that. I do not know why she must berate my brother about it again today."

"I think her visit today will be about berating Elizabeth Bennet. After all, her dowry and connections prior to her marriage render Mrs. Darcy's status to hardly more than a servant."

When Georgiana looked down without replying, Lady Susan became suspicious. "I thought that you wanted your family to realise he has made a horrible mistake."

"I did... I do. But with Brother's injury... " She sighed. "There will be plenty of time for that after he is well again."

"Which brings up another subject—I want to visit Darcy. I must express my concern for his injury and wish him a speedy recovery. But, as you well know, he is still angry with me over that little kiss. Could you not take me with you the next time you visit?"

"Fitzwilliam has forbidden me to bring you, and I will not defy him on that point. He could easily restrict me from the house if I did."

"He would never go that far."

"You have no idea. He has changed since Eliz—his wife left for Pemberley."

Lady Susan could not suppress a smile. "At least we achieved that! She is gone, and he remains in Town. What does that say for the state of his marriage?"

Georgiana looked contemplative. "It is one small accomplishment, I suppose. But it has definitely made his temper worse."

"Of course, it has! You realise that, if there was any other solution, Fitzwilliam would never have encouraged gossip by sending her to Pemberley while he stayed in London. Can you imagine what a shrew he has married, if the only way he could get any peace was to send her away?"

"That is exactly what I have been saying. He is entirely different."

Lady Susan reached to pat her hand. "Do not fret, my dear. For when I am his wife, it will be as it was when we were young."

A small smile lifted the corners of Georgiana's mouth. "We were all so happy then."

"And we shall be again. It will not be long until Eliza Bennet will be history, and we shall be sisters."

"But she would have to die for Brother to marry again, as divorce would take years and still might not be permitted. I know that much from listening to my uncle rant about the unsuitability of his match when they married."

"Oh, but if she disappeared—say, by leaving on a ship under another name—she could be declared dead after several years and I can make certain that happens. Once society realises that my son is Fitzwilliam's child, they will accept that we have been in love since we were children, and that I am the rightful Mrs. Darcy. Ours will be a genuine love story, the kind that poets love to immortalise."

"I suppose you are right."

"I am!" Susan quickly kissed the air on both sides of Georgiana's head. "Now, I must go, for I have many things to accomplish." She started towards the door then stopped to peer over her shoulder. "Do you still wish me to come again tomorrow?"

"Perhaps it would be better if I called on you. My aunt is worried that I spend too much time gossiping and not enough time on my lessons."

"If you wish, but I simply must know what Lady Catherine has to say, so please come as soon as possible."

"I promise to come, but I do not know if Aunt Evelyn will tell me what is said."

"Of course, she will," Lady Susan declared cheerfully. "Now, have faith, for we shall see that hoyden out of Darcy's life before too long. I just know it!"

In seconds, Susan was gone, and for a long time, Georgiana stared at the door. Then she walked over to close it and went straight to the window seat. Gazing listlessly into the Matlocks' gardens, she considered what the scheming she and Lady Susan had done would actually accomplish.

Once Elizabeth is gone and Susan marries Brother, things will return to the way it was when I was a child. It must or I shall…

The voice of reason spoke. *You shall what? What is it that you really want to accomplish? Do you wish to command everyone else about? Is it your ambition to be like Lady Catherine?*

She huffed to herself. *I am nothing like her!*

Her conscience disagreed. *You want to control your brother's life, which makes you no different than she.*

Having had enough introspection, Georgiana stood and irately reached for the bell pull. *I shall concentrate on my painting.*

Before long, Florence appeared and helped her change gowns. After all, one never wore good quality gowns when painting, for the least bit of paint could ruin delicate fabrics and lace. Later, as she hurried to the conservatory where her easel was set up in one corner, her conscience managed to have the last word.

How peculiar! You realise that a small amount of paint can ruin a gown, but cannot see that infantile behaviour, left unchecked, will ruin your character.

Had Florence not been beside her, Georgiana might have shouted for her conscience to be silent. As it was, all she could do was grit her teeth and walk faster.

⁖

Darcy House
William's study

The light rain that had begun that morning turned into a deluge during the day. It made the study dark, rendering it necessary for Mrs. Barnes to light even more candles in order for William to see properly. After she had left the room, lightning began such an impressive display outside the window that he rose wearily and hobbled over to watch. Trees were bending with the wind and a steady stream of water was busily washing leaves and trash down the sides of the street. Strangely, William was pleased, for the weather now more closely mirrored the turmoil inside his heart. Sunshine and blue skies were a mockery when one's life was in tatters.

A sigh escaped his chest. He had no choice but to go home immediately, as there were problems with some tenants that only he could resolve. Furthermore, his injury was no longer a valid excuse. It had improved to the point that the journey could be undertaken with little worry about riding in a coach for hours at a time. At least that was his estimation, though he doubted that Mr. Graham would agree. However, he would not fault the man for worrying excessively about his patients.

In any event, he did not relish the idea of seeing Elizabeth again so soon, though he knew that his duty to Pemberley must take precedence over his personal problems. Mr. Sturgis, his steward, required his help. That gentleman had been meeting with two tenants regarding repairs to a bridge that stood between their properties. Now it seemed they were both agreeable to having a new bridge built instead of trying to repair the old, but they disagreed on where the bridge should be situated. Each tenant favoured a different plot of land, while Sturgis favoured yet another. Only a look at the boundaries of the properties could render a proper judgment, and he was duty-bound to return to Pemberley to make the final decision.

With this occupying his thoughts, William returned to his desk resignedly, determined to get to the bottom of a stack of correspondence before he left for Derbyshire.

A knock on the front door brought Noonan, a footman, scurrying to answer it, for Mr. Darcy had allowed the knocker to be replaced on the door that very morning. On the portico, he found a woman wholly unrecognisable by virtue of a parasol that obscured her face. Two formidable-looking postillions stood on either side of her. Accepting the calling card offered, Noonan requested that she wait in the foyer while he located Mr. Barnes. Then he hurried to search for the butler, for he was the only one who could disturb the master when his door was closed.

Not one to follow orders, as soon as the footman was out of sight Lady Catherine motioned for the men to follow and immediately crossed the foyer. She had been in Darcy House often enough to know where her nephew's study was located and that he was likely there at this time of day. Mr. Barnes was coming down the hall outside William's study when Noonan spied him and handed him the card. Quickly scanning it, Barnes turned immediately to knock on the door.

"Come," William called.

Opening the door, Barnes stepped just inside. "Sir, the Countess of Matlock is here to see you."

William was about to request that he show her in, when a scuffle broke out behind Barnes. The butler turned to find Noonan struggling to keep two men from barging into the master's study, followed closely by Lady Catherine. Noonan's shouts for assistance were answered by enough servants to cause the men to step back. Nonetheless, the altercation distracted Barnes, letting Lady Catherine slip through and enter the room.

Immediately the butler sputtered, "But... but the card is Lady Matlock's!"

"What of it!" Catherine de Bourgh declared. "I used my sister's card, for I assumed I would not be welcome." Her eyes narrowed as she focused on William. He had stood with her entrance—not from respect, but because he was furious. "You can be at no loss, Nephew, to understand the reason for my coming. Your own heart, your own conscience, must tell you why I am here."

William knew her mission, but chose to annoy her by playing naive. "Indeed, you are mistaken, madam. I cannot account for having you here. Most especially when I expressly forbade you from entering this house ever again."

Lady Catherine ignored his retort. "I am almost the nearest relation you have in the world, and I had to learn that you married some country nobody from this!" She threw a copy of the paper announcing his wedding on the desk. "I have come to demand that you have this ridiculous marriage annulled."

His eyes narrowed. "That will never happen."

"Where is she? Have her summoned, so I can see this Jezebel for myself!"

William's spirits rose. *At the least she does not know of our separation.* "I shall not subject my wife to your vitriol."

"Honour, decorum and prudence—nay, interest, requires that you cast her aside. For you wilfully acted against the inclinations of your family when you refused to marry Anne and you mock my daughter by choosing someone so far beneath her as to be laughable. This Bennet woman is without status, wealth or connections. She will be censured, slighted and despised by everyone connected to you. Your alliance will be a disgrace; your name will never again be mentioned by anyone of worth."

Knowing full well Elizabeth's true feelings for him, still William could not resist taunting his aunt. "Those are heavy misfortunes indeed. However, as my wife will have extraordinary sources of happiness necessarily attached to her situation, I believe that, upon the whole, she will have no cause to repine. And, I will never regret our marriage."

"Headstrong, obstinate man! I am ashamed of you! Is this your gratitude for my guidance all of your days? Is nothing due to me on that score?"

William walked around his desk to stand toe-to-toe with his aunt, being sure not to limp or grimace as he did so. "I have never sought your advice, nor have I ever followed it!" he roared. "I do not understand why you think I would begin now."

Lady Catherine slammed her cane on the floor. "Tell me, once and for all, will you annul this marriage?"

"I WILL NOT."

"I am shocked and astonished that you are not more reasonable, but do not deceive yourself into believing that I will ever give up. I shall never stop until you have done your duty to Anne."

"Are you so obtuse as to assume that by throwing aside Elizabeth it will make marriage with Anne more probable? The arguments with which you have supported this extraordinary lie have been frivolous, as well as ill-judged. You have widely mistaken my character if you think I can be worked on by such persuasions as these."

He turned as if to sit down again, for his ankle was beginning to ache.

"Not so hasty, for I am by no means finished. I am no stranger to the particulars of Miss Bennet's humiliation in Meryton, which involved your own cousin, of all people! It was a patched-up affair, at your expense. Heaven and earth, what were you thinking? Are the shades of Pemberley to be thus polluted?"

William hissed through clenched teeth, "I warn you, say no more. Leave now or I shall not be responsible for my actions!"

"Stay this course and I will not be responsible for mine, either. For if I do not get satisfaction, I shall visit our joint solicitor and demand that he surrender my part of the family trust in cash. That will insure that there is nothing left in the account to fund spring planting for Pemberley or for Matlock, for that matter, until all the investments mature and are sold. Simply said, I shall receive the cash reserves for my holdings, while your portions will be tied up in stocks and bonds."

Suddenly, the still partially-open door flew back against the wall with a thud as Lord Matlock marched into the room, his wife right on his heels. "Catherine, I order you to cease your threats and leave these premises immediately!"

The lady whirled around. "You cannot order me about as though I am one of your servants!"

"I can and I do!" the earl declared. "I am the head of this family, and your threats hold no alarm for me."

"They should! As I told Fitzwilliam, I will withdraw all my funds from the family trust, so that you will no longer have anything to hold over my head. I shall handle all of my affairs and Anne's from hence forth!"

A look of arrogance crossed Lord Matlock's face. "If you think Lewis left anything in your control, you are sadly mistaken. He did not trust you with his legacy or with Anne's inheritance. That is why he left me solely in charge. You have no authority to withdraw from the family trust without my approval and, pray tell, what do you think my answer will be should you ask?"

Lady Catherine's face paled, but she hesitated for only a moment before trying another line of attack. "Do you have no regard, then, for the honour and credit of our nephew? Do you not care that marriage to that hoyden has disgraced my daughter, as well as him, in the eyes of everyone we hold dear and by association, you and me?"

"Catherine, my sentiments have not changed since you first tried to force Fitzwilliam to marry Anne. Like it or not, Darcy is a grown man, and he must face the consequences of his actions, good or bad. Regardless if I agree or disagree with his choice, I will not interfere now that it is done."

Her head whipped back to William. "You are resolved to have her then?"

"I am only resolved to act in a manner which will, in my own opinion, constitute my happiness."

She huffed. "Very well! I shall know how to act. Do not imagine that Miss Bennet's ambition will ever be gratified by me, nor by any of my friends. I shall never accept her. NEVER!" Then she marched to the door where she stopped to add, "I take no leave of you, Nephew. You deserve no such attention. I am most seriously displeased."

With a nod to her brother, Lady Catherine went out the door. She could be heard barking orders to the men who had accompanied her, and a few seconds later the slamming of the front door announced her departure. Immediately, William slumped as if completely drained and closed his eyes. Then he grimaced as he limped back to his chair.

Lady Matlock exchanged worried looks with her husband as she said in a motherly tone, "Fitzwilliam, we have tried to abide by your wishes and have not hovered over you since Georgiana informed us that you were injured. She has kept us apprised of your recovery, but if your current state is any indication, you do not seem to be doing well at all."

Still wincing as he tried to find a comfortable sitting position, William replied, "I am better, I assure you. My ankle is healing, but it is painful to stand for any length of time, as it causes the foot to swell again. Unfortunately, I have been on my feet since dawn."

Instead of leaving, Lord Matlock guided his wife to a seat in front of William's desk and took the chair next to hers. He looked uncomfortable as he began to speak. "I wish to apologise for Catherine's behaviour. Apparently, she still believes she is God."

Normally that would coax a smile, but William could not be teased today. "I am used to her ways. And let me say that while I appreciate your concern, I do not understand why you thought it necessary to come here to protect me."

"Now, now, Nephew. I have accepted that you are well able to defend yourself. However, I was concerned that she would strike at a moment of weakness—what with your injury. Furthermore, I felt it necessary to remind my sister once more that I am the head of this family. Nevertheless, I apologise for appearing in your house uninvited and unannounced."

William accepted his apology with a slight nod.

The countess nudged her husband's foot, and he cast a glance her way before adding uncertainly, "Might I enquire about Mrs. Darcy's absence?"

Frustrated, William exclaimed, "Does everyone in the whole of England know that Elizabeth travelled to Pemberley without me?"

William's aunt could restrain herself no longer. "Why would that surprise you? Your marriage was already THE topic of conversation before the ball and afterward, what with all the rumours of a dalliance in the garden between you and Lady Susan." She sighed loudly. "We have tried to take your part in this, but how are we to proceed if we do not know the particulars?"

William's temper flared. "I have never had a dalliance, or anything else, with Lady Susan. She, most likely with Georgiana's help, tricked me into going to the gazebo the night of the ball. Lady Susan flung herself into my arms and kissed me. I rebuked her and left immediately. That is all there is to that." He took a deep breath and let it go noisily as he addressed the other point. "As for sending my wife on to Pemberley, her relations were to be in Lambton this week, and she wished to show them her new home. In light of how ill-tempered I am when I do not feel well, I saw no sense in subjecting her to my bad humour while I recuperated. Thus, I sent her on to Pemberley with Richard as he returned north."

"I remember Anne saying you were never an easy child when you were sick or hurt," Lady Matlock ventured, trying to sooth his temper.

"And I have only gotten worse with age," William confessed. "If it suits, you may announce to one and all that I am leaving for Pemberley tomorrow, as my ankle is greatly improved. Perhaps that will assuage the gossips."

The earl interjected, "If all that limping and grimacing just now is evidence that you are greatly improved, I am pleased I did not see you sooner."

"Precisely why I sent my wife away."

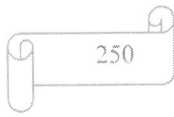

"How kind of you to think of her," Lady Matlock offered weakly.

In truth, she wondered if kindness had anything to do with sending Elizabeth on to Pemberley. Newly-married couples, those who were compatible, would never have parted so effortlessly. In any event, seeing no need to press that subject, she went on to another.

"A while back, Georgiana said that she intended to return to Pemberley when you did. Are you willing to take her now, or do you wish more time alone with Elizabeth before she returns?"

"If she wants to go now, she can. However, she must sleep here tonight for I shall leave very early tomorrow."

The earl and countess stood to go. "Then we shall take our leave, Fitzwilliam," the earl said. "If Georgiana still holds to the notion of going with you, I will have her escorted here this evening. Otherwise, we are bound for Matlock later this month, and she can travel to Derbyshire with us."

"Then she has only to decide."

Later that evening after his bath, instead of going straight to bed as was his practice, William dismissed Mr. Martin and eased his aching body into the large leather chair in the corner of his bedroom. Propping his feet on the matching stool, he glanced at the supper tray on a nearby table, noting that Mrs. Barnes had placed one of her sleeping powders thereon. Rejecting the idea of taking it, he moved the candle on the table closer and reached for the book he had selected from the library. Staring at its cover blankly for some time, he eventually tossed it aside. Tomorrow he would face his ▓▓▓▓ and force all his desires and hopes regarding his marriage into the furthest chamber of his heart. But tonight… tonight was meant for exploring the tattered remains of his love for Elizabeth. His eyes fixed on a miniature portrait of his mother atop the chest of drawers.

It is fitting, William thought, *that my grief over Elizabeth will reside alongside my grief for you, Mother.*

Pushing up from the chair, William hobbled to his dresser, opened the top drawer and moved the clothes to one side. Withdrawing a small black box secreted within, he stared at it for a time before lifting the lid. Inside, wrapped in a soft cloth, was a gold wedding band. Wishing for Elizabeth to have a ring that was hers alone, he had commissioned this band when he travelled to London for the special license. It had not been finished until after the wedding, so he had hidden it in this drawer, awaiting the right time to give it to her. Though the sentiments engraved thereon represented his heartfelt pledge of love and faithfulness, it was obvious that Elizabeth would never be interested in hearing it now. Nonetheless, holding the ring near the candle, he read four ornately engraved words, each punctuated with a diamond in between. *First. Last. Only. Always.*

Returning to the table, he picked up a half-full crystal decanter and poured another glass of brandy. Sighing heavily, he set the glass down and proceeded to his luggage which lay open on a large stool. Hidden on one side was a special drawer that already contained pieces of their mother's jewellery that

Georgiana had left in London. When not in use, the Darcy jewels were always kept in the walk-in safe at Pemberley. He dropped the ring inside there and locked it. Once he was finished, a thought came to mind.

Perhaps I can have it melted down and made into something less sentimental for Georgiana's birthday.

Crossing the floor to the leather chair, he dropped tiredly back into the comfortable piece of furniture, letting his head fall back and closing his eyes. Instantly, memories of Elizabeth flooded his mind, beginning with the first time he had seen her at Netherfield and concluding with the day she had rushed angrily from this very room. Now he was left with only one question: How had the desire for a marriage of mutual love and affection gone so awry?

The voice of his conscious was quick to taunt. *It went awry because you let your dreams override common sense.*

Angrily William's head flew up, and he took a swallow of brandy. *I tried to resist! I left Netherfield when I realised I was attracted to her.*

The voice would not be hushed. *You left, but you let the notion of true love get a foothold in your heart. You had already fallen in love.*

William huffed. *How could I have fallen in love then? The first time I saw her she was covered in mud, and her hair was loose and wild. Even Caroline Bingley said she looked positively medieval with her hem six inches deep in mud.*

His lips betrayed him, involuntarily curling at the memory of how beautiful she had been at that moment. His head fell back again. In truth, it mattered not when he fell in love with Elizabeth. What mattered was that she had not fallen in love with him.

Why did I not listen to Richard? At least he saw my marriage for what it was—a desperate attempt to fill the emptiness in my life.

The brandy had eased his pain somewhat, and he reflected that, at the worst, he and Elizabeth could live separate lives. He hoped she might agree to have a child, for he desperately wished for an heir. If she was not agreeable to that, he was not sure what his next step would be.

Then tossing down the last of the brandy in his glass, William stood and limped over to the bed. Divesting himself of his robe, he crawled onto the huge mattress and adjusted the hanging contraption that elevated his leg. Then he grabbed a pillow and positioned it under his neck. Suddenly he remembered Georgiana's intention to return to Pemberley. With his present problems, he did not think he could deal with her pettiness and Elizabeth's revulsion at the same time.

Moaning an oath, he pulled another pillow over his head, refusing to even consider that possibility tonight.

Chapter 23

The Pig Whistle Inn
North of Lambton

The small post inn was a stop for people travelling between the village of Lambton and the town of Sheffield, though it was located nearer the smaller village. Dark and dirty, the majority of its clientele were equally as unkempt and unwashed. In fact, except when necessary to change horses, respectable folk never stopped at the Pig Whistle Inn. And in the few instances where bad weather gave them no choice, many chose to sit at the tables in the common room rather than take advantage of the tiny rooms with dirty beds that the proprietor had to offer. The conditions had grown progressively worse over the years until the patrons now consisted of ne'er-do-wells, highwaymen and others wanted by the law—or soon to be. Such were the two men who currently occupied one of the four tables in the common room.

Nate Burton, the proprietor, was no stranger to their kind. Short but stocky, with a full head of brown hair and a beard to match, he had an eye for trouble. He had met enough men like these while serving a sentence in Newgate [11] as a boy. Never mind that his crime was stealing food to feed his younger siblings, most of his patrons felt a kinship with him because of his familiarity with the inside of the prison. That kinship gave Burton the opportunity to hear things of interest to the constables and Bow Street Runners who pursued men with prices on their heads. Feeling no loyalty to those who frequented his inn, if a lawman had questions and it meant more coins in his pocket, Nate was happy to provide answers.

Moving closer to the men in question, he made a mental note of their attributes, as was his practice, observing that the one called Denny was fair with green eyes and red hair, tall and well-proportioned. The other man, one he had never seen before, had the same muscular frame, though he had dark brown hair and eyes. Getting closer, Nate strained to hear what was being said. Unfortunately, they chose just that moment to go upstairs to a room.

"Bring a pitcher of ale up to my room, Nate!" Denny called as the owner swept up trash below a nearby table. Nate nodded in acknowledgement while Denny proceeded up the stairs to the first room on the right, followed closely by Wickham. Once alone in the room, Denny motioned for his friend to have a seat at a small table near the window. He was truly glad to see Wickham again, for since their stint in the militia together, he trusted him like no other.

"I am pleased that you joined me today, George. When I saw you in Lambton, there was no time to explain. I was forced to stop because my horse threw a shoe on the way to our safe house. Pate's farm is where we divide up the spoils, and then he and Duke stay hidden there until our next job."

"I wondered why you were so curt. You mentioned that you had another job planned, insisted that we meet here today and were off before I realised what had happened!"

"I apologise. It is necessary to stay out of sight just after a job. You should have contacted me months ago, in any case," Robert Denny declared. "I was under the impression that you did not like the militia any more than I."

"Had I not been chasing a bit-of-muslin with a large dowry, I would have. That did not work out as planned, and afterward I had to wait for the right chance to desert."

"I see."

"So, tell me more about the plans mentioned in your letter. How do you decide who to target? And, most importantly, how have you managed to evade the law?"

"When you are willing to pay for information, word gets to the right people," Denny explained. "I now have several *associates* who regularly bring me information about the travels of the rich pricks of the *ton*. Their sources are, for the most part, servants with a bone to pick. The servants tell my contacts who, in turn, pass it along to me. As long as we are careful not to kill anyone during the robberies, we may be able to keep at it a good while because George Lyon [12] is drawing most of the Crown's attention."

"What do the snitches get for their trouble?"

"I pay my associates for every clue that results in a profit. As far as the servants go, some seek only revenge, while others expect a reward. The latter get a few shillings, depending on the value of the information. Some servants have even begun to glean information from their counterparts at other estates and pass that along. We only rob a coach every few weeks or so—alternating routes. I tell you, George, I have accumulated more money in the last six months than in the last six years. I save most of it, for I intend to sail to the Americas when I get a stake large enough."

"That sounds like a good plan."

"Better than slaving in the blasted militia."

"The only problem is that you can hang for being a highwayman," Wickham replied, a little too loudly.

"Shhh!" Denny cautioned, glancing around. "These walls are thin."

Wickham looked sheepish as he continued in a somewhat softer voice. "But should it get around Derbyshire who is paying for the information—"

"I do not intend to hang," Denny interrupted. "I have taken care to raise no suspicions. Once a month, I come to this inn to settle debts and gather new information. None of my men are involved with this aspect, so their identities are kept secret. Likewise, after today, you and I will never be seen together at this place."

"I suppose the risks involved are no worse than some of the things the militia forced on us, like putting down factory riots," George replied.

"Precisely the point."

"You mentioned needing another man."

"Including you, there are four of us, but we could use five."

"I have an old friend who is in need of funds, and he is an ace shot. He is actually a gentleman who is down on his luck."

"I do not care if he is a duke, as long as you trust him."

"I do. So I shall send a letter to a friend in London and see if I can locate him."

Denny walked over to the bed, bent down and pulled a satchel out from under it. Reaching into it, he brought out two bags and threw them on the table. Opening the first sack, he poured many coins on the table, mostly half-crowns, crowns and sovereigns. Wickham's eyes went wide.

Smirking, Denny said, "This is a part of what I have made thus far in my new profession. If you are smart, you will save some of what you earn as well."

Then Denny laid a cloth on the table and emptied the other sack. It contained seven rings, six necklaces, six bracelets, several pairs of earrings, a silver flask and a gold watch.

"All of this is yours too?"

"No. Only a portion. It falls to me to sell these items because one cannot approach just *any* jeweller and ask him to buy stolen goods. I happen to be acquainted with a man in Sheffield who has no problem with the fact that the pieces are stolen. I have him list each one and what he paid for them. Then I give Pate and Buck their share afterward."

"That seems a lot of jewellery to take in one robbery."

"Our sources reported that the mark was to stay in London for several months and the lady of the house always took numerous family pieces when she went to Town. We were fortunate to find her jewellery case hidden under the seat of the coach; else the pickings would have been slim." Grasping an emerald necklace, he held it up to the window for a better look. "What do you think? My guess is that we will get close to two thousand pounds for the whole lot!"

George Wickham huffed, picking up another piece. "This watch alone is worth seven hundred pounds, the pearl necklace a thousand and the diamond necklace three thousand at the least! Five thousand for the whole lot would be a joke."

"Yes, but they are stolen!" Denny countered. "And old Castleman takes a risk whenever he sells one. What if someone were to recognise the pieces? He may be able to reset the jewels and reuse the gold, but he cannot do anything about the watch, the flask or the pearls, for the most part. And unfortunately, the watch and flask are inscribed, so while he may be able to buff out the inscriptions, it will be noticeable. I cannot see him paying more when he faces so great a peril!"

"*He* faces peril!" Wickham exclaimed. "You could have been shot!"

"True, but he could easily hang for his part."

"Then perhaps you should find another jeweller who is willing to pay more. I know one in London who would be happy to get his hands on items this grand."

Denny sighed. "Selling stolen goods in London is difficult because most of those we rob spend at least part of the year there. They are likely to buy replacements, at least for their wives' jewellery, and they may notice the stolen items in their favourite shops."

"I see your point."

"Good. Now, I plan to leave this area today. I am not like Pate or Duke, for I require a lively place to rest between jobs."

"But in Lambton you mentioned another job—a wealthy earl you had in your sights."

"As it turns out, Lord Cochran was not a good target. I learned that he has lost his family's fortune and his wife's jewellery betting on the horses. Every necklace, ring and earring she wears is paste, though she has no idea. In fact, next month he will no longer be travelling in his luxurious coach, as it will be sold to pay his creditors."

"I see why you do so much research," Wickham replied. "I would not want to put my life on the line for nothing."

"Which is why I thoroughly investigate everyone first," Denny replied as he stood. "I am off to Sheffield to sell the jewellery, and I have plans to visit the brothel there while I do. There is a certain redhead I have my eye on. Are you going with me?"

"I thought you did not want us to be seen in each other's company."

"Only here. Outside of this region, it is unlikely to gain notice."

"Then yes, I might as well join you."

"Good!" Denny replied. "After I leave, take your horse to the stable, and have the blacksmith check for loose shoes. That should take enough time to quell any suspicions. I will leave straightaway and wait for you on the road ahead."

Immediately after they entered the room, Nate slipped into the one next to it. He managed to hear enough of the conversation through the walls to know it could prove useful, for highwaymen gained more notoriety than the usual thief. They preyed upon those most likely to have the Prince Regent's ear—the wealthy. That meant that eventually a special prosecutor would likely be commissioned to bring them to justice and a nice reward offered as an inducement for information. Even so, as he heard the door open and the sound of their boots on the stairs, his main concern was for the monies due him now.

Hurrying from his hiding place to confront Denny before he cleared the inn entirely, he called out, "Are you leaving, Mr. Denny?"

"Yes, my business has concluded," Denny replied. Then realising the reason for the question, he reached into his pocket. As he tossed several coins to Nate, he added, "I almost forgot to settle with you. Thank you for reminding me."

"Glad to be of service," Nate answered, smiling insincerely. "Will you be back next month?"

"I have no plans to at present," Denny responded, "but you can never tell."

Nate watched as Denny went out the door, mounted his horse and took the north road towards Sheffield. He was still standing on the front porch a few minutes later when Wickham came out of the stables, mounted his horse and went in the same direction.

There you are, Nate said to himself. *I figured you would be following Mr. Denny.* He scratched his beard, adding, *It shall not be long until someone comes looking for the likes of you, and I shall be here when they do.*

༺ঔৣ༻

London
Darcy House

On a beautiful May morning, the elegant Darcy coach stood ready and waiting for the master of the house to emerge from the rear entrance. As Mr. Coleridge threaded his way through the servants milling about the back garden, he stepped up his stride when he realised that Mr. Darcy must be leaving at any minute. Though his mission had taken some time, he was pleased with what he had discovered and was eager to present it to his employer. Gaining the back door, he reached for the handle, only to have the door fly open in his face. A footman quickly stepped outside and held the door for the man he had come to see.

Nodding with a curt bow, Coleridge declared, "Mr. Darcy, it seems I have been fortunate enough to catch you before you left. I have information regarding what we discussed when I was here last. I hoped to present it to you today."

Knowing exactly what he meant, William nodded. "Then let us go back to my study and review it before I leave."

Abruptly, William turned and began hobbling down the hall. Coleridge noticed that his employer was trying to shift his weight to one foot, and the novelty of it caused him to watch until William was halfway down the hall before he remembered to follow. Running a bit to catch up, he slowed as they neared the study. Once at the door, William opened it with a key and motioned for him to go in first. As soon as his employer entered, the door was closed solidly behind them.

William walked past him gingerly, making his way around his desk and easing his body into the large chair behind it. Swiftly, Coleridge took the chair in front of the desk and opened the satchel he carried. Pulling several rolls of paper from within, he laid them on the edge of the desk. William's brows furrowed as he studied the papers.

"I traced Andrew Darcy to a boarding house belonging to a widow, Eunice Younge. The establishment, if you can call it that, is located in the Mint."

"It is fitting that Andrew is staying among the thieves and beggars. To think, he is not ten minutes from here."

"Yes. It seems he lodged there the entire time he *was* in London."

"Are you saying he has gone?"

"From all indications, yes. However, I learned something very interesting about your cousin. He was also renting a room from Mr. Poindexter and has for some time."

"The tailor?"

"The same. Poindexter said that he rented an upstairs room for the last year or more. Only a few days past, however, they had a disagreement about how much rent was owed. Poindexter refused him entry to the room, saying he would keep all the supplies therein and sell them to recover some of his losses."

"What kind of supplies?"

"Art supplies—paints, canvases, brushes. It seems Andrew Darcy is quite the painter, or portraitist, if you will."

"I had no idea he could even draw."

"From the funds you advanced, I paid Mr. Poindexter the rent due in order to acquire the contents. I thought there might be clues in what he left behind." William nodded his head. "And I was quite shocked at what I discovered in a locked closet. I would say ole Poindexter would have been shocked as well, had he forced the lock as I did."

"Such as?"

"Numerous drawings of nude women—very important women, if my memory serves. For I have seen some of their likenesses on the pages of the society section of the news, not to mention on the arms of their husbands and fathers in Hyde park on Sundays. These were not scullery maids and shop girls."

"I cannot believe Andrew had access to such women, or that they would pose nude for him if he did."

"Here are several." Coleridge laid three rolled up drawings on William's desk. "There are more in two locked trunks I left at the stables with your livery manager. I was not sure where else to put the supplies or the pictures."

William reached to take the first and unroll it. His face registered disdain as he went from one drawing to the next. Shaking his head when he was done, he rolled all them up together.

"I do not, for one minute, think any of these women posed for my cousin."

"Truthfully, neither do I," the former Bow Street runner said, "for I also found these."

Reaching into the satchel, he brought out two more drawings—each a nude completely finished except for the face. "I would say that he draws the body and adds the face afterward, so they resemble any woman the buyer wishes to humiliate. After finding these, I enquired around Town, and my sources say that there is a market among the *ton* for this kind of thing, especially at White's. Some have even commissioned coloured portraits in lieu of charcoal drawings."

"And Andrew is the source?"

"At least one source, if not the only one."

William stood up. "Disgusting! One could have what is purported to be a nude portrait of my wife or my sister in their study or even their bedroom!"

"Exactly!"

Reaching to pour himself a brandy, William downed it in a few gulps. "Andrew will pay dearly when he is found out. Most men would call him out if they knew their loved one had been debased in this manner. I would not hesitate to do so."

"Yes. I marvel at his audacity—thinking he will never be found out."

"Andrew has never lacked audacity." Then William added, "What have you learned regarding what occurred at Marsden Park?"

"I am sad to say that Mr. Harrington expired only days after his daughter."

William whirled around. "Expired? No wonder I did not hear from him. How did he die?"

"A heart ailment, they suspect. I imagine that is the only reason your cousin escaped his wrath, for I was told that he was determined to exact revenge for his daughter's death."

"And Lord Warren? What news of him?"

"Lord Warren was charged with arranging Mr. Harrington's funeral and with trying to locate the next of kin who inherited Marsden Park. I understand it is a distant cousin who lives in Wales. At least that is the rumour. I do know that Lord Warren has not been in London since Harrington's death."

"I would hate to be in Andrew's shoes when Lord Warren finishes his obligations and goes after him."

"Yes. I can imagine he will exact revenge on your cousin himself."

William took a deep breath of air, puffing up his cheeks and blowing it out noisily. "Well, I refuse to worry about what happens to Andrew because of his dissolute ways. I have enough problems of my own." Slamming his glass down on the desk, he declared, "Keep after Andrew. I want to know where he is at all times. You may contact me at Pemberley."

"I am off to Manchester tomorrow, and I shall report to you when I know more."

"Take two days of rest if you wish. I know you have not been slack in your pursuit. The day after tomorrow will be soon enough to head to Manchester."

"Thank you, sir. I believe I shall."

With that, William headed out the door. After he and Coleridge were again in the hall, William locked the door and walked towards the rear entrance. Coleridge watched him until he left the house and then went in the direction of his room.

Pemberley
Elizabeth's Study

Mrs. Reynolds watched Olivia Fitzwilliam glide down the hall as quietly as a mouse, her silk damask skirts barely rustling as she walked. She could not wipe the smile from her face, for William's aunt reminded her of Lady Anne. Having grown to care for her since she came to stay at Pemberley, the housekeeper was delighted that someone of her calibre was around to advise the new mistress.

Only minutes before, Olivia had stopped to enquire where the new Mrs. Darcy could be found, and she had gladly directed her to the mistress' study, where Elizabeth was busy making baby clothes for the tenants. Though she had suggested to her mistress that another venue was available as a sewing room, Elizabeth insisted that she had plenty of room for a table in her study, and its presence would remind her of what she needed to finish. Thus, footmen had transported an unused table from the attic to her study, moving a sofa and two chairs closer to her desk to accommodate it. The last time Mrs. Reynolds had looked, the table was covered in bolts of cloth, patterns and a collection of completed baby items. Pleased with how well her new mistress had taken to her role, the long-time servant sighed contentedly and went back to her duties.

"Elizabeth!" Olivia Fitzwilliam declared as she walked into the study. "What in the world have you started?"

Elizabeth looked up from her sewing and smiled. "I am making baby clothes. Jane and I sewed all the clothes for the tenants' children at Longbourn, so I am well versed in making gowns for newborns. I have these patterns that I use to cut out the pieces," She held several up. "When I get enough cut out, I stitch them together. I find that I can finish them faster in this fashion."

Her new aunt held up one tiny gown and winked. "Are you trying to tell us something?"

Elizabeth's heart sank at the realisation that she might never have William's child. Still, she quickly resumed her smile, for she had no wish for his aunt to suspect her heartache.

"No. They are for Mrs. Becker, a tenant who is due to give birth at any time. She has not been well and has had little time to make baby clothes."

Olivia did not seem to notice when the smile left her new niece's face. "I must say that you sew very well. These stitches are small and perfectly straight." Then she became sombre. "Elizabeth. I hope you will take this advice in the spirit that it is given, for I do not wish to interfere in your private affairs. But as a newlywed, I wish to tell you what my mother told me."

Elizabeth could only nod, her eyes growing wider. *Does my aunt suspect what a muddle I have made of my marriage?*

"Do not fret if you do not get pregnant straightaway." Olivia walked over to pat Elizabeth's shoulder. "A child will come in its own good time."

Elizabeth breathed a sigh of relief. "Thank you. I shall remember that."

Olivia changed the subject, which suited her niece perfectly. "Do you knit?"

"I do, but not very skilfully." She reached into a bag to bring out a small pair of yellow socks. "This is all I have accomplished thus far," Elizabeth declared with a chuckle. "If you look closely, you will notice that I missed some stitches along the ankle, but at least they will keep the baby's feet warm."

Olivia took the socks and studied them. "You did well, Elizabeth. If you would like some advice, I am sure I can help you do better. I would love to join your cause by knitting some socks, sweaters and blankets for the expected child. I do not mean to brag, but my husband says no one can knit as well or as fast as I."

"Oh, I would be so grateful for your instructions and your help. If you

could make socks and sweaters, I will make gowns and blankets. We should have a sufficient number ready before the baby is born, and we can always take more later."

"Then let us get to work!" William's aunt exclaimed. "I shall return to my room to fetch my needles. I cannot do well with any others, for I have used the same needles all my life. Besides, I have an abundance of threads in every colour in my luggage."

Aunt and niece soon formed a bond as they worked. In addition, it gave Olivia a chance to learn more about Elizabeth—her upbringing in Meryton and her family—though, noticeably, she never mentioned Fitzwilliam. Being a wise woman, Mrs. Fitzwilliam decided to bide her time, praying that as they became closer, Elizabeth might share what lay heavily on her heart.

London
Lady Susan's Townhouse
The next day

Though situated in a less exclusive area than the Darcy or the Matlock townhouses, Hanover Square was still a fashionable area of Town, since it was part of Mayfair. And today it was the destination of a carriage carrying Georgiana through the streets of London. The farther she travelled, the more her stomach filled with butterflies, just as it had this morning when she received the message from Lady Susan: Come as soon as possible!

Unable to imagine what would require her presence right away, she was obliged to fool her aunt and uncle in order to comply. As it was, the earl and countess believed she was on her way to visit Lady Amelia Callaway, whom her aunt thought the perfect friend because she was of the same age and background. Georgiana suspected that her aunt's disapproval of Lady Susan was the result of her helping the widow lure Fitzwilliam into the garden the night of the ball, for ever since that night, her aunt had done everything in her power to discourage the friendship.

Sighing heavily, Georgiana complained furiously to herself. *Now I shall have to persuade Amelia to lie if my aunt asks about our visit. And what if she decides not to help me? She is so submissive that she probably never lies. What will my aunt and uncle do if they find out? Fitzwilliam is angry with me, and if I make them angry, too, I will have no allies.*

It was truly ironic that just when she vowed to be less involved with her brother's affairs, Susan insisted that she must have her help.

I do not appreciate Susan pushing me to take an active part any longer, and I mean to tell her so today. This does not mean I like Elizabeth! It only means I no longer want to be instrumental in separating her from Fitzwilliam. After all, a union so unequal is bound to falter on its own. All I need do is wait for the inevitable.

The carriage had barely pulled to a stop in front of Lady Susan's townhouse when it began to rain very hard. Thus, when the front door swung open and a footman came hurrying down the steps with an umbrella, Georgiana was grateful. Once inside the house, Lady Susan rushed from the parlour just as the butler was taking her shawl.

"Georgiana, I am so pleased you managed to come today!" She began to pull Georgiana towards the parlour. "My cousin is here, and I so wanted you to meet him before he has to leave for Liverpool."

A man suddenly appeared in the parlour door, and as their eyes met, Georgiana's heart stopped, for rarely had she seen anyone as handsome. He appeared to be about four and twenty, of average stature, with sandy blond curls and bright green eyes. He looked at her as no man had done before, and it caused her to feel quite giddy. As she and Lady Susan reached him, he quickly stepped back.

"Cousin, I wish to introduce my best friend, Miss Georgiana Darcy of Derbyshire."

"Charmed," the gentleman declared as he took Georgiana's hand and placed a chaste kiss on her glove.

"Georgiana, may I present my cousin, Lord Attaway, of Gracehill Park in Liverpool."

"I... I am pleased to meet you," Georgiana stuttered, blushing profusely.

"Had I known my cousin's friend was so lovely, I would never have promised to return to Liverpool so soon," he said smoothly. "In fact, I think I shall send a letter stating that I plan to delay my trip by another day."

This caused a new round of blushes, though Georgiana was too shy to reply to his flirtations. Susan, however, never seemed happier.

"If you are no longer planning to leave, Matthew, I shall call for a pot of tea, and you two may get better acquainted. I should love for you to become good friends."

Once the three of them entered the room, they did not depart until it was time for Georgiana to return to Matlock House, for they found much in common to discuss. Afterward, when they said their farewells and Georgiana descended the steps to her carriage, Lady Susan and Lord Attaway stood on the portico, waving until she was gone.

"So? Did I play the part of the love-struck fool well enough?" Lord Attaway leaned in to whisper as the carriage rolled out of sight.

Susan whirled around, entering the house and looking about to see if any servants were listening. "Never discuss such things until we are behind closed doors."

Shrugging his shoulders, Matthew followed as she led the way back to the drawing room. When the door was shut soundly, she turned with a triumphant smile. "You were absolutely perfect! I am sure that she is already in love with you."

"When do I get the five thousand pounds?"

"I promised five thousand pounds *if* you help me for as long as needed to accomplish the deed. That means coming with me to Derbyshire and staying as long as necessary. If I pay you now, I shall not see you again until you are destitute."

His hand flew to his heart in mock horror. "You wound me with your sarcasm and distrust, my dear."

"I know you too well to trust you again."

Lord Attaway quit any pretence of civility. "Fine!" he growled. "Then at least advance me a thousand pounds so I can pay something on my gambling debts. Else you will be looking for another lackey to woo your friend. The man who holds my markers has no patience, and he promised to break both my legs if he is not paid a thousand pounds by tomorrow."

"How have you come to this? You received thirty thousand pounds as well as your mother's jewellery when your father died last year. Besides, Gracehill Park must do well, not to mention that it would bring a fortune on the market!

"It is not as you think. Father left Gracehill deep in debt. Nevertheless, I could never sell it, for what is a gentleman without an estate? And mother's jewellery was not as valuable as he led me to believe. Besides, it is not my fault that gambling has always been my weakness. I inherited it from him."

"Spare me the pitiful details," Susan interrupted as she stood and walked to the door. "I shall have the funds for you in the morning. But take this warning to heart: If you disappear this time without carrying out your end of the bargain, I shall never help you again. Even if you are tossed into prison, I shall not pay your debts."

"You need not worry. After meeting Miss Darcy, I am half-persuaded to charm her into marriage. I have heard that her dowry is thirty thousand pounds, and that would pay my debts and more. Besides, she is handsome, if naive."

"You had best keep in mind that her brother is no fool. He can spot an exploiter instantly. He will investigate your circumstances soundly before he agrees to let his sister marry you."

Lord Attaway shrugged. "I am not worried about Fitzwilliam Darcy. After all, he did not spot the woman who compromised him, did he? Moreover, if I charm Georgiana into caring for me, it will be her problem to convince her brother to let her marry."

"At any rate, I do not want you offering for Georgiana until I am completely satisfied with my quest. Is that understood?"

He performed a sloppy salute. "Understood, General Hartley!"

"You jest, but you had best remember that I am in charge. And keep this in mind. If I get what I want—Fitzwilliam Darcy—then I will help you win Georgiana."

"I like how you think," he replied. "So, shall I just stay here for now?"

"Yes. In three days, I plan to strike out for Derbyshire. Georgiana talked of accompanying the Matlocks to their country estate next week, so that will give us a few days at Monthaven Manor before she returns to Pemberley. Once we are there, my plans can begin in earnest."

"As you wish, Cousin. I look forward to fleecing the Darcys as a team."

"You may only desire to swindle Georgiana, but I truly want to rescue Fitzwilliam from the chit he married."

Lord Attaway did not respond, for he could not say what he thought. Susan had been selfish all her life, and she saw everything through greedy eyes. Thus, as he nodded and began up the grand staircase to his rooms, he pursed

his lips to keep from chuckling.
But who shall rescue Mr. Darcy from you, my dear?

Chapter 24

Pemberley
Three days later

It was late afternoon by the time the elegant Darcy coach entered the ornate, wrought-iron gate at the entrance to the mile-long drive leading to Pemberley. This sent a sentry from the guardhouse scurrying via horseback to alert the occupants of the manor of the master's return. The journey had taken the usual number of days from London, for William had insisted on keeping to his regular schedule, despite his physician's instructions to add additional time to the trip in order to stop more often and stretch his legs. There was no denying that by refusing this advice William had paid a price, for the swelling that had subsided to manageable levels in Town had returned with a vengeance. So much so, that shortly after William entered the coach that morning, he abandoned the extra-wide boot crafted to accommodate his right foot and rode in only his stocking.

As a result, when the coach came to a stop in front of Pemberley, William struggled to get the boot back on. In light of his infirmity, Mr. Martin, the valet who normally resided in London, had accompanied him, and it took both of them to accomplish the task. Thus, his exit from the coach took an inordinate amount of time, causing anxiety to rise among those waiting to greet him. When William finally emerged, it was with a forced smile, meant to convey that all was well; however, a noticeable limp sent an entirely different message, and though the servants pretended nothing was amiss, that was not the case with his aunt.

"Fitzwilliam!" Olivia cried. "Your letter said that you were better, but you can barely walk."

"I am better, I assure you. My ankle is merely stiff from sitting in one position for so long." He stepped forward and placed a kiss on her forehead, rewarding her with a rarely-seen dimpled smile—a gesture that had never failed to reassure his late mother. "The journey aggravated the injury, but it should heal quickly now that I am home."

As he spoke, he glanced to his uncle, eyes pleading.

"The boy is right, Olivia. All the jostling can only have made things worse. He should heal rapidly now that he is home." William smiled gratefully as Joseph stepped over to slip an arm around his shoulder, adding quietly, "You and I will discuss this later."

Nodding in acknowledgement, William looked to the portico where he expected to find Elizabeth. Realising that she was not there, his forced smile was quickly replaced by a puzzled expression. Noting the change, Olivia hastened to explain.

"Oh, I was distracted and forgot! I meant to tell you that your lovely wife is waiting for you inside—at my insistence, I might add. Only minutes ago she felt faint, and I was afraid that she might actually tumble down the steps if she stayed out in this unbearable heat. Mrs. Reynolds is with her."

William nodded absently, for two factions were warring within him. The first wished to rush inside to make certain she was well, while another cautioned that Elizabeth's light-headedness was simply the result of having to be in his company again. Distracted, he did not reply.

Olivia patted his arm sympathetically as they started up the steps. "It is likely just her nerves, for she has been anxiously awaiting your homecoming."

A frosty retort flew to William's mind. *I just imagine she has!*

Entering the house, he found Elizabeth sitting in one of the chairs that flanked the ornate table and mirror in the foyer while Mrs. Reynolds diligently fanned her. When she saw him, Elizabeth stood, though she did not move to greet him.

She was even more beautiful than he had remembered and, for a split second, he mourned what might have been. Even so, as their eyes met, the uncertainty in hers served as a grim reminder of their last conversation, and instantly all thoughts of that nature vanished.

Taking a deep breath, he smiled as he walked towards her. Those in attendance were expecting to witness the reunion of a happily-married couple, and William meant to oblige. Her eyes were firmly fixed on her shoes by the time he took her clasped hands, which he was surprised to find were trembling. Wishing the public display to be over as quickly as possible, he leaned in to place a chaste kiss on her forehead.

His voice was composed as he said, "Mrs. Darcy, you look well." Then his brow furrowed in suitable concern. "However, my aunt shared that you were faint only minutes ago."

"It... it was only the heat," Elizabeth managed to say without actually meeting his gaze. "I am well."

It was as though all present heaved a collective sigh of relief, for the silence in the foyer was soon replaced with the sounds of maids scurrying about, footmen bringing the luggage inside and his aunt and uncle conversing with the butler and housekeeper, respectively.

Suddenly, Elizabeth whispered so that only he could hear, "I... I am sorry for your injury... that it has not healed."

Her confession caused William to regard her warily before he answered, "I thank you for your concern." Then immediately, he addressed his aunt. "I wish to wash off the dust of the road and elevate my foot for a bit. And I am sure that Mrs. Darcy has much to share. So if you will excuse us, we shall join you again at dinner."

"Of course, dear, go and rest," his aunt said warmly.

William turned and held out his arm. Tentatively, Elizabeth placed hers atop it, and they began to make their way up the grand staircase. It quickly became obvious that William was struggling not to grimace with each step, and by the time they entered the sitting room connecting his bedroom suite with hers, his false smile disappeared completely. Wordlessly, he removed her arm and hobbled in the direction of his bedroom door. He turned the knob before halting and looking over his shoulder.

"It is best if everyone assumes we are happily married. That is why I suggested that you join me; however, you are free to do as you wish. Although, if you feel you must return downstairs, you might wait at least an hour in order to give the impression that we actually had a conversation." He paused. "As for me, I intend to soak my ankle and rest before dinner. Good day, Mrs. Darcy." With that, William disappeared into the room, closing the door softly.

Elizabeth's heart sank. Since learning that she was mistaken regarding his character, she had prayed continually that God would prompt William to forgive her, but obviously her prayers had had no effect. Knowing that her distrust had singlehandedly built the wall that was between them, she was unable to hold back the tears that had threatened since she first saw him. Thus, hurrying into her bedroom, she locked the door and fell on the bed, sobbing until there were no tears left.

At Dinner

Had there been guests for dinner, they might never have noticed the detached manner between William and Elizabeth, for outwardly everything seemed normal as the newlyweds entered the dining room sporting smiles and conversing with practiced politeness. Nevertheless, due to the odd beginning of the Darcys' marriage, the Fitzwilliams were conscious of even the smallest of aberrations. And since they were on a mission to quell all their doubts, throughout dinner they asked many questions.

"We have never heard how the two of you met, Fitzwilliam," Aunt Olivia stated after the entree was served. "Do share the story with us."

William appeared more reticent than usual, blotting his mouth slowly before answering in a cautious manner. "It was in Meryton. I was staying at Netherfield Hall as a guest of Charles Bingley. I am certain I have mentioned him to you before." His aunt nodded. "Elizabeth was also a guest at Netherfield during that time. That is how we met."

Olivia waited, but when he said no more, her eyes flicked from her nephew to Elizabeth. One might expect a newly-married couple to, at the least, exchange shy smiles in recollection of their first meeting, but such was not the case. Olivia found that very strange.

"And did you fall in love with Elizabeth at first sight?"

When he did not immediately answer, she looked to Elizabeth, as if posing the question to her instead. However, instead of answering, her niece's eyes fell to her plate, while William replied woodenly, "No. It was not like that."

The brevity of his reply made it clear that he was not enjoying her enquiries so she became silent. Joseph, however, stepped in to fill the void.

"So tell me, Fitzwilliam, what did Mr. Graham recommend to get your ankle back in shape?"

"I have a list of exercises—manipulations, if you will—that are supposed to strengthen the muscles," William said straightaway, apparently eager to change subjects. "They involve flexing the foot in various positions." He smiled wanly. "I tried to do them on the trip here, and they proved quite painful; however, there is nothing I can do about that. In addition, he insists I walk every day as far as possible, stopping to rest if the pain becomes unbearable."

"How long does he think it will take until you are fit again?"

"He is unsure, but estimates that I will be much better in two weeks if I exercise faithfully."

"I am sure that Elizabeth will be a great asset to you then, since she is so fond of walking. No doubt we shall now see the two of you walking around the lake very soon."

William glanced to his wife, who quickly busied herself by pushing food about her plate. "Unfortunately, Elizabeth prefers to walk at dawn, while I prefer late in the evening," he said charily. A confused expression crossed Elizabeth's face, though she said nothing. "Besides, I would only hinder her exercise, as I have to walk at a snail's pace."

Olivia raised another issue. "Tell me about the burns you suffered. Have they healed? Elizabeth was unable to allay our fears regarding their severity because she had not seen them."

Perturbed at the reminder of his wife's indifference, William answered matter-of-factly, "Thanks to Mrs. Barnes, all but the largest two have completely healed. In fact, Mr. Graham claims that her salve is far superior to any he has seen, and he offered to pay her for the formula."

"I imagine that Mrs. Barnes was more concerned with helping you than making a profit," Joseph interjected. "She and her husband have been devoted servants of the Darcys as long as I can remember."

"Yes, they are most devoted," William repeated. "And Mrs. Barnes offered the formula for free, saying she was glad to provide relief to any who may suffer."

Olivia addressed Elizabeth. "I can only imagine how pleased you will be when Fitzwilliam has completely regained his health. Had this happened to Joseph on our honeymoon, I would have been beside myself with worry."

If possible, Elizabeth looked even more ill at ease. "Of course," she said, but not before stealing a furtive glance at her husband. "What wife would not wish for her husband to be well?" At her assertion, it was William's turn to stare awkwardly at his plate.

Now thoroughly convinced that their marriage was in trouble, and upset that her worries had proven true, Olivia sought her husband's reassurance. But just at that moment, William announced that he was tired from his journey and was retiring for the night. Elizabeth stood up immediately, saying she was retiring early, too. Consequently, after the young couple exited the dining room, Joseph walked over to shut the door behind them.

"Well, my dear, I have to admit that your suspicions were well-founded. It seems that something is definitely wrong in paradise."

"Paradise is not a word I would use to describe their marriage," she said sadly. "After the aloofness and formality I witnessed tonight, I would not be surprised if ere long they were complete strangers passing in the halls."

Joseph walked over to help his wife from her chair. "Perhaps we are being too cynical. After all, Fitzwilliam is not well. Perchance once he is rested and his ankle heals, their relationship will improve. After all, I imagine that they have not shared a bed since he was injured. That alone would be frustrating for a newly married couple."

"Let us hope that is the case." She grasped his hand. "For if not, I do not foresee any felicity in their union, and I did so want Fitzwilliam to find someone who would love him as he deserves." Standing, she added, "We might as well retire as well. I promised to visit a tenant with Elizabeth in the morning."

"You did not mention that earlier."

"I completely forgot."

"As long as you do not wear yourself out, I have no objection to your going." They got as far as the door of the dining room when he stopped and faced her. "We are blessed that nothing serious ever came between us."

"We were blessed to fall in love. When a couple does not have that kind of love in the beginning, there is so much room for misunderstanding."

"So you believe their marriage was not a love match?"

"I have not witnessed any true affection, and my heart aches to see how uncomfortable they are in each other's company. So I would say no."

He tilted his head, offering a slight smile. "And, naturally, you feel obligated to put right all that is wrong."

"Do not tease me, Joseph. You know that I cannot just sit by and watch these young people destroy their lives. I must try to help."

"I know, Livy. Please, just remember that Fitzwilliam is eight and twenty. He is not a child that we can lecture and expect to mind. And, while Elizabeth is young, she, too, is an adult. As much as is possible, we must let them sort out their marriage without interference. You do remember how we hated my family's meddling."

"And I will remind you that we are trying to unite them, not separate them, which was the goal of your family."

"You are quite right, my dear."

"I shall simply let Elizabeth know that I am willing to listen if she wishes to talk. Hopefully, by doing that, she will realise that their struggle has been noticed."

"Well, you cannot save the world tonight, sweetheart, so let us be off to bed."

Olivia laughed. "I suppose I shall have to begin tomorrow then!"

Slowly, they made their way back to their bedroom, holding hands. And, as with every night since their marriage, they forgot the cares of the world by falling asleep in each other's arms.

Sheffield
A pub

After several days of searching for Wickham, Andrew Darcy was greatly relieved when his friend walked into the pub he was occupying in Sheffield. The farther north he had gone, the more Andrew had begun to doubt the rumours that George had travelled north from Lambton, but there he was, as plain as day and looking every inch the gentleman. Walking in the direction of where George now sat at a corner table, he hesitated when he noticed that he was seated beside another man; however, his cohort spied him across the room and waved him over, and the decision was taken from his hands.

"Andrew! Sit down. It is good to see you, my friend."

"And you, Wickham," Andrew said, shaking his hand and taking a seat.

"Let me introduce to you another friend of mine, Robert Denny," Wickham exclaimed, sweeping his arm towards his companion. "Denny, this is the man you have heard me speak so often about—Darcy's cousin, Andrew Darcy."

Both men nodded in acknowledgement of the other, but before either could speak, Wickham hurried on, "What on earth brings you to Sheffield? Last I heard, you were still in London."

Andrew looked about and lowered his voice. "It got a little uncomfortable in Town."

"Oh?" Wickham said, lowering his voice proportionately. "Were you forced to leave?"

Andrew did not answer. Instead, he glanced at Denny.

"You can trust him," Wickham said bluntly.

After studying Denny for a long moment, Andrew continued. "Yes. I heard from a friend that my fool cousin had men on my trail, not to mention that it was rumoured that Lord Warren was returning to Town."

"Does all of this pertain to the woman who drowned herself?"

"It is not known if she drowned herself or it was an accident. In any case, Lord Warren blames me for her death. I am certain that he has men searching for me, even as we speak."

"I would never have guessed you to be afraid of Lord Warren. After all, he is old enough to be your grandfather," Wickham teased, causing Denny to chuckle. This raised Andrew's ire.

"I am glad that you find it funny, for I do not. Warren may be old, but he has never lost a duel, and the last one was only six months ago."

"Calm yourself. I was only teasing. So how was it that you came here?"

"I was looking for you. I cannot return to Winfield Hall, for Warren's men are in Manchester, and Fitz will never again let me stay at Pemberley. I learned that you had left the militia and returned to Lambton. In Lambton, it was rumoured that you headed north. I hoped that we might be able to do some business together. You have always had good ideas, Wickham."

"What about your allowance?"

"Fitz has cut off my allowance entirely until I agree to meet with him. I am almost destitute."

Wickham jerked his head towards the stairs that led to the rooms for rent. "Let us go to my room. We can talk privately there."

Once they were situated around the small table in the room, Wickham began to explain. "Denny and I, plus two others, have found a way of *acquiring funds*. I had already thought of you as a possible fifth member of our group. However, you must swear to keep your mouth shut about what you hear, or face certain death. If you join us or decide not to, none of us would hesitate to do away with a snitch."

"You can trust me."

George began to explain how he, Denny, Pate and Buck made a living robbing coaches. When he was finished, he was a bit annoyed to find Andrew regarding him with scepticism. "You look as though you do not believe me."

"I admit that I find it hard to believe that so many servants would actually betray their employers."

"We have found it to be so. Apparently almost every estate has one disgruntled servant who feels they have been mistreated, abused or paid far too little."

"Do they not realise they will hang if they are caught?"

"I suppose the draw of getting revenge and possibly making a few pounds outweigh the risks."

"Why let me in on something that is obviously working well?"

Denny replied, "During the last robbery, a footman managed to pull a pistol. He dropped the weapon when we threatened to kill his master, but we would rather not use violence. With an additional man, we could better watch all sides of the coach."

"Well, are you in or out?" Wickham asked.

"I have been reduced to poverty, George. What choice do I have? I am in."

"Good!" Wickham exclaimed. "Hungry men make good partners."

Andrew looked around the threadbare room. "Is this where you live when you are not *working*?"

"No," Wickham answered. "We are only in Sheffield to pawn the jewellery from the last robbery and to visit the ladies at the brothel. Pate's father owned a large farm seven miles west of Lambton. His mother still owns the old house, though most of the land around it was sold. Since she moved in with his sister, Pate lives there and pays the taxes, which keeps a roof over his head. We stay there between robberies."

Denny stood up, pulled a pocket watch from inside his coat and flipped open the top. "It is merely minutes until Lily's opens. Will you be joining us or staying here?"

"I am practically penniless, George, and I do not think the ladies will extend me credit on my looks."

"You will not have to worry about that ere long," Wickham chuckled, pulling a few pounds from his pocket. "Here! There is no need to repay me."

Andrew took the money and stood. "I was never foolish enough to pass up a good time, especially at someone else's expense."

With that, all three men left the inn to enjoy the favours of the ladies at Lily's Pleasure Garden.

Longbourn

Though Thomas Bennet walked as fast he could, it was not fast enough to escape into his study before Mrs. Bennet caught up to him. Presently, she was on his heels as he navigated the hallway between the parlour and the study, spouting the same nonsense she had uttered ever since her arrival from Town. Never doubting that Jane and Charles had to listen to her opinions all the way from London, he considered himself very fortunate to have stayed home.

"I tell you, Mr. Bennet, there is something terribly wrong with Lizzy's marriage. You must go to London and find out what has happened. Perhaps you can convince Mr. Darcy not to divorce her." She waved her handkerchief like a flag. "I cannot imagine what I will say to the neighbours if he sends her back to us."

Now sufficiently cross, Mr. Bennet turned to confront her just as he reached the study door. "Mrs. Bennet, I heard the same report from Mr. Bingley as you. Mr. Darcy never mentioned divorce! On the contrary, he made it clear that he was only thinking of Elizabeth when he sent her on to Pemberley. Why can you not just accept his explanation?"

"Because no man who is pleased with his wife would send her on to his estate while he stayed behind. Especially if he was injured! It is Lizzy's place to see to her husband's health, not to go off to Pemberley alone."

"For the last time, do not ask me again to interfere, for I will not! And I admonish you to quit reading more into the situation than is there."

With that, he stepped inside the study and slammed the door, letting his body fall back against it. Listening to her mutterings as she went in the direction of the parlour, once it faded completely away, Mr. Bennet let go of the breath he was holding. Then he hurried to his desk and settled into his favourite chair to consider all he had just learned. Though he had argued with Fanny that there was nothing wrong with his favourite daughter's marriage, she had managed to create some doubts in his mind. Secretly, he found the whole thing as peculiar as she, and he wished to know the truth. Reaching into his desk, he pulled out pen and paper and began to write to his brother Gardiner.

At least he is sensible enough to relate the facts without embellishment.

Once finished with the note, he sealed it and slipped it inside his coat pocket, for he knew that if Fanny caught sight of it, she would pester him to know what it contained. Returning the pen and paper to the drawer, he briefly considered his part in forcing Lizzy to marry.

I pray that I did not make a mistake, Lizzy.

Laying his head back against the chair, he closed his eyes. It was too late to go into Meryton today and post the letter. That would have to wait until tomorrow. And until he knew for certain that something was amiss, he was determined not to worry.

After all, he mused, *if I am not careful, I could end up with Fanny's nerves.*

Pemberley

The next morning proved a great disappointment to Elizabeth. For though she had Mrs. O'Reilly come at first light to help her dress and style her hair, when she entered the dining room at daybreak, William was not there. In fact, according to Mrs. Reynolds, his ankle was so improved that he had left the house with his steward while it was still dark, and was not expected back until after dinner. Though Elizabeth accepted the news with a stoic smile, she was hurt. She had no doubt that this prolonged absence was designed to avoid seeing her. Nonetheless, her new aunt and uncle chose just that moment to enter the dining room, which left her no time to dwell on that fact.

After they had greeted one another and sat down to eat, Joseph Fitzwilliam asked, "Would you ladies like me to escort you today? I have no plans that are pressing."

"It is not necessary, dear. A footman can accompany us," Olivia replied. Then she addressed Elizabeth. "You mentioned taking a gig."

"Normally, I visit this tenant on horseback because they live where a carriage is not very practical. But, since you are joining me and we have several baskets of clothes, a gig will suffice." Elizabeth smiled at her uncle. "And you need not worry, Uncle Joseph. I have driven a gig too many times to count."

Joseph Fitzwilliam's brows furrowed. "But you tire so easily, Livy. I would worry less if I went with you. That way, if necessary, I can bring you home and return for Elizabeth later. Besides, I would like to see the location of the new bridge that Fitzwilliam told me about. I understand it is near where you are visiting."

Acutely aware that her husband did not speak to her of such things, Elizabeth shared all that she knew. "Mrs. Becker told me that it lies between their property and the next. And just so that you need not worry, I always tie my horse to the back of the vehicle in case she is needed. One never knows when one might be stranded by a broken wheel. Should the need arise to return Aunt Olivia to Pemberley, I can always ride Phoebe home."

"That would defeat the purpose of being your escort, my dear," Joseph said, dabbing his lips with a serviette. Then he smiled. "I intend to escort you both there and back. Since that is settled, I can be ready to leave shortly."

"Well, I am not ready," Elizabeth teased. "For I fear I must have another sweet roll and another cup of tea."

Olivia laughed. "I do not know how you stay so slim, Elizabeth. You have such a healthy appetite."

"My father says that I am completely hollow. But it is only that I take after his side of the family, for they are all slim. Even to this day, Papa can wear the suit he wore when he and my mother married."

"Oh, for a constitution like that!" Joseph declared, as he stood and patted his stomach. "I find the older I get, the harder it is to maintain a decent weight."

"You look just as handsome as the day we met," Olivia said.

Leaning down to kiss the top of her head, Joseph replied, "You would say that, even if it were not true."

"But I have no reason to lie."

"As long as you think so, my love. Now," he said purposefully, "I just remembered why I do not like to wear these boots. They are too narrow, and they pinch my feet. So I shall go change them." With that, he walked towards the door.

As Olivia followed his retreating figure, Elizabeth whispered, "You are so blessed to have such a marriage."

She turned back to her, noting her wistful expression. "I agree. And I pray that you find as much felicity with Fitzwilliam as I have had with Joseph."

Tears filled Elizabeth's eyes. "I pray for that, too." Then as quickly as turning a page in a book, her expression changed to forced cheeriness. "Please excuse me. I think I shall check to be sure that all the baskets have been packed."

As Elizabeth hurried from the room, it appeared to Olivia that she might have begun to cry, so it was with a heavy heart that she went in search of her husband.

Chapter 25

Pemberley
The same day

Annie Becker was so grateful for the generosity of Elizabeth and Olivia that she could not hold back tears. The ladies had made enough baby clothes that she would not have to wash them every day, as well as a new supply of towels and sheets that were sorely needed. Moreover, a large basket was filled with jars of pickles and jams, while breads, cakes and sweets packed another. Seeing her mother cry, however, provoked Mazie to cry, and in an effort to cheer the little girl, Elizabeth reached into a bag containing a surprise just for her. It was a small doll, fashioned from scraps of plain, white muslin and dressed in a colourful print dress, white petticoat and cloth shoes. While Elizabeth had created the doll, even embroidering eyes, a nose and a mouth, Olivia had knitted and attached plenty of blond hair, which made it very similar to Mazie herself.

"For me?" Mazie cried in delight as she reached for the doll.

"Just for you," Elizabeth confirmed. "Mrs. Fitzwilliam and I thought you might want a new baby to care for too."

The little girl was still sniffling as she wiped her cheeks with the backs of her hands. "I have never had so pretty a doll."

Her mother smiled as Mazie examined her treasure. "What do you say to the ladies, Mazie?"

"Thank you, Mrs. Darcy and Mrs. Fizz… Fizzwilluuu… "

"Fitzwilliam," her mother finished.

"Yes, that!" Mazie said, her face beaming.

"You are welcome," Olivia and Elizabeth replied in chorus.

"Mazie, did you let Star out of her stall so she can go into the paddock?"

The girl's hand flew to her mouth. "I forgot."

"She cannot reach the water unless you do. So put the doll down and let her out, please."

"Yes, Mama."

As she raced from the house, Annie explained, "Star is Mazie's pony."

"But Mazie is so small," Elizabeth observed. "Are you not afraid for her to ride?"

"No, ma'am. She has been riding with her father since she could sit up. And after her third birthday, she began to beg for a pony of her own. She mentioned wanting one to Mr. Darcy, and he brought Star back from Wales just for her. The pony is barely three feet tall and as gentle as a lamb. Mazie adores her, and when Tom is home, he watches while she rides."

"So Mr. Darcy provided the pony?" Elizabeth asked.

"Yes, she was a gift. The Master has always been very fond of Mazie—

well, all the children. He also helped Tom find a good draft horse for the wagon for a reasonable price."

"I see," Elizabeth said numbly, her mind recording this new evidence of her husband's goodness.

"Mr. Darcy has always been so very kind, and you have provided all these wonderful things." She motioned to the baskets Elizabeth had brought. Her eyes dropped to the wooden floor. "I feel guilty asking for anything else."

"Good tenants are an asset to Pemberley, and we want to help you whenever we can. Please do not be afraid to ask for what you need."

"It is just that… " She took a shuddering breath as she studied her feet. "Two years ago, I lost a child at birth—a son. The midwife said that he died because he was not healthy enough to survive, but he looked just as healthy as Mazie when she was born. There was no difference."

Olivia sat closest to Annie, so she grasped her hand and gave it a squeeze. This gave her the courage to continue.

"There was no one here to send for the midwife when my time came. I was in labour all day before Tom came home that evening and I… " She met Elizabeth's gaze. "I wonder if the child might have lived, had the midwife gotten here sooner."

"Oh, my dear!" Elizabeth said, reaching to pat her arm.

"I just pray that someone is here when my time comes, for I cannot send Mazie to fetch her father and I have no family near to stay with me."

"If you agree, I can have a maid stay with you until the baby is born," Elizabeth said. "She can help with your work, as well as fetch your husband when the need arises. Would that ease your mind?"

Annie smiled now. "Oh yes, ma'am, very much."

"Good, then—"

The door flew open and Mazie rushed breathlessly to her mother. "Mama, Star is gone! I forgot to lock the paddock, and when she came out of the barn, she nudged the gate and it opened! I tried to catch her, but she ran away!"

"If only Joseph had not driven over to meet Fitzwilliam," Olivia lamented. "If he were here, he could bring her back."

Instantly Elizabeth was on her feet. "It should not be that hard to retrieve so small an animal. I shall take Phoebe and fetch her." Then she bent down to speak to Mazie. "Could you show me in which direction she went?" The child nodded earnestly.

"You will need to give Mrs. Darcy the rope to lead her, Mazie," Annie Becker said. Then to Elizabeth she added, "Star is wearing a bridle, so all you need do is run the rope through the ring on the bottom."

Elizabeth nodded. "I should get started." When she and Mazie reached the door, she called over her shoulder. "Do not fret if it takes me a little while to find her."

With those words, Elizabeth was out the door. After untying Phoebe from a tree, she followed Mazie to the paddock, where the child pointed to a rope hanging on one of the fence posts. As Elizabeth took it, Mazie was already looking at something across a vast field.

"Can you see her? Star is underneath that tree."

A small golden pony was barely visible on the horizon, grazing as though she belonged there.

"Yes, I see her. Now go to your mother, and I shall bring your pony home."

As Mazie ran back to the house, Elizabeth pulled Phoebe to the paddock fence and stepped on the bottom board. Mounting the horse, she kicked the mare into a trot. Almost immediately, what had seemed an easy task quickly became an ordeal, for at the sight of Elizabeth coming towards her, the pony decided she had best escape. The scene repeated itself over and over, until Elizabeth found herself in unfamiliar territory. Stopping to get her bearings, she looked back but could no longer see the Beckers' chimney.

A dense stand of trees lay straight ahead, while a clearing lay to the left. She concluded that Star must have taken the open path, so she headed to the left. Just as soon as she rounded the copse, however, she immediately pulled Phoebe to a halt. Just ahead was a meadow, and in the middle of it stood a small brick house. It looked well-maintained, for it had a manicured lawn with beds of flowers along the front and each side of the dwelling. A neat gravel path led from the front steps to a small shed on the left, as well as to a gazebo on the right. Since Star was nowhere in sight, there was a chance that the animal had gone behind the house, so she kicked Phoebe into a trot, intending to find out.

Circling the structure, Elizabeth found Star eating the flowers in the beds along the back entrance to the house. It was quickly obvious how the animal got her name, for the golden pony had a perfect white star on her forehead, as well as four white stockings.

Elizabeth chuckled. "So you enjoy eating flowers, do you?"

Star was too busy chomping the flowers to care that she had been found; thus, Elizabeth managed to dismount and slip the rope though the pony's bridle without scaring her away. Then tying Star to one of the porch posts where she could continue to eat, she looked about. A large well, sheltered by a roof, stood in back of the shed, so she grabbed Phoebe's reins and pulled her in that direction, hoping to get a drink of water. It took a good bit of effort, but by turning the handle, she eventually wound the bucket to the surface. Then grabbing a gourd dipper that hung from a leather strap, she drank her fill of the cool liquid.

Afterward, Elizabeth poured the balance of the bucket into a nearby trough. While Phoebe drank, Elizabeth turned her attention to the house. It looked as though no one was there, and, being very curious, she tied her horse to the well-housing and slipped over to peek in a window.

The Beckers' House

When Tom Becker returned home, he was accompanied by two of the gentlemen who had been at the site where it was decided that the new bridge would be constructed—Mr. Darcy and Mr. Fitzwilliam. Mr. Sturgis, Darcy's steward, had been sent straight to Pemberley, for he was clearly exhausted.

Being weary himself, Becker was hoping that those who accompanied him would collect their wives and leave promptly, for all he wished was to eat and go straight to bed, though he had no way of knowing that was not to be. For as soon as he opened the front door, he was surrounded by three anxious females, all asking if he had seen Mrs. Darcy. Assuring them that he had not, his wife began to explain.

"Mazie's pony escaped and Mrs. Darcy went in search of her. We expected her back before now. She has been gone for a long while."

"Star is missing?" He looked to Mazie. "How did your pony get out of the paddock?"

"It was my fault, Papa," she said meekly. "I forgot to lock the gate."

He reached down and picked the child up, planting a kiss on her forehead. "I know you did not mean to forget, but you are going to be a big sister soon, and you must try to remember what we tell you."

"I will. I promise."

"Good. Now, tell me what happened."

William and Joseph reached the door just as Mazie was explaining all that had transpired and each edged further into the cramped room in order to hear what was being said. Upon learning that Elizabeth was missing, Joseph glanced to his nephew to see what effect the news had on him. Except for the furrowing of his brows, William was expressionless, though he did ask the first question.

"You say she has been gone for an hour?"

"Yes, maybe more," Annie replied, wringing her hands. "Oh, I do hope she has not met with some misfortune."

"Most likely she has just lost track of time," William stated calmly. "I shall go after her."

"But surely your ankle must be bothering you," Joseph interjected. "Let me go instead."

"As a matter of fact, I have hardly noticed my ankle today. I suspect the exercises I have been doing are the reason for such improvement." He glanced to Olivia, noting her fatigue. "You had best take Aunt Olivia home, for it will be dark soon."

"I... we can wait here until you return." Olivia offered.

"Fitzwilliam is right, my dear," Joseph quickly overruled. "I shall take you back to Pemberley, and afterward I will be able to help him look for Elizabeth if she is still missing."

"I can accompany you now, sir," Tom Becker volunteered. "Just let me saddle my horse."

"The child could come early, so I would rather you stay here," William countered. "If more help is needed, I have men at Pemberley who can be of assistance."

"I know the way Mrs. Darcy went," Mazie volunteered.

William smiled at the girl. "I would like it very much if you could show me." Mazie nodded, proud to be of service.

Then he addressed the others. "I am confident that Mrs. Darcy is well.

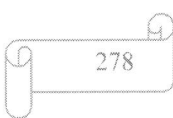

However, if it gets dark before I locate her, I will return to Pemberley and organise a search party. For now, let us not panic." He donned a slight smile for his aunt and uncle. "I hope to see you at dinner, along with my wife."

William went out the door and walked towards the barn, with Mazie running ahead of him. The child was sitting on the fence when he arrived, and after he mounted Zeus, she pointed in the direction that Elizabeth had taken. In mere minutes, man and beast were out of sight, and Mazie went back to the house.

At the cottage

The heavy curtains on the back windows permitted no view of what was inside the house. Nonetheless, Elizabeth's curiosity had been aroused by this mysterious dwelling, and, against her better judgement, she decided to see if, by chance, one curtain may have been left open. Alas, she found none. Suddenly remembering the narrow windows on either side of the front door, she hurried there. The windows were etched with bucolic scenes to provide privacy, but still she hoped to spy something amid the trees, flowers and birds. Cupping her hands around her eyes and squinting, she was frustrated to learn it was impossible; thus, she decided to knock on the door. There was no answer.

Well versed in good manners, Elizabeth knew better than to invade another's privacy, but she simply could not resist trying the doorknob. It opened effortlessly. Turning in a circle to find no one about, she took a deep breath and entered. Stepping hastily over the threshold, two things became immediately clear. First, the house was definitely fashioned after a woman's taste, and, second, her husband's cologne still lingered in the air. That realization gave her pause. Not once had she considered that William might have another woman.

What if he had a mistress before we married and this was their rendezvous? Is it possible that he sought comfort in her arms again after I disparaged him? At once, she thought of how often he had been unavailable since his return. Swallowing against the lump that had risen in her throat, she shook her head decisively. *No! You will not jump to conclusions again, Elizabeth Darcy! Fitzwilliam is not that kind of man.*

Forcing all those thoughts from her mind, she began an examination of the house. The structure was comprised of four rooms with a narrow hall down the middle. As she walked further inside, she found a parlour and a bedroom on one side and a dining room and kitchen on the other. Beginning her examination with the parlour, she entered it and pulled back a curtain to let in more light. Two beautifully upholstered, jade-green chairs immediately caught her eye. A small table, holding a candelabrum, sat between them. A mahogany bookcase, filled with books, stood against the far wall, while a settee, upholstered in jade and rose, sat across from the chairs. Two landscapes on the walls and an oriental rug completed the decor.

A book was lying open on the top of the bookcase, and, curious to learn about the resident, Elizabeth picked it up. It was a copy of her favourite poetry by Thomas Moore, and the notion that they might share the same taste in literature proved somewhat unsettling. It was even more disconcerting to find William's name written inside the front cover in his elegant script. She ran a finger over it reverently before placing it where she had found it. Downcast, she was about to quit the room when she noticed something white tucked under a pillow on the settee. Uncovering it, she discovered a delicate shawl. Holding it aloft to admire the intricately knitted pattern, without thinking she flipped it over her head in one smooth motion. It came to rest on her shoulders, leaving a familiar scent in the air. Elizabeth recognised it straightaway—lavender.

Leaving the parlour, she glanced to her left. The dining room consisted of a round table and two chairs, with a small chandelier hanging overhead. Each chair was upholstered with dark blue fabric and embroidered with colourful flowers. The same fabric had been employed for the tablecloth, and the colours were repeated in an oriental rug beneath. The walls sported two plaster sconces holding vases of dried flowers and candles. Deciding there was nothing extraordinary about this area Elizabeth went to inspect the bedroom.

Elegantly carved woodwork defined that room, which was painted white from floor to ceiling. Even the furniture was white, howbeit with a striking gold trim. The curtains and counterpane were of gold damask, while a gold and red print fabric covered the pillows on the bed. Though the room was stunning, Elizabeth's curiosity about the resident of the house outweighed everything. So when she spied several items on a tray on the bedside table, she rushed to sit on the edge of the bed to better examine them.

A wooden tray carved in an oriental design held a bottle of perfume, a mirror with an oak handle, a brush and a comb. Taking the bottle, she removed the stopper and brought it to her nose. Lavender! *I was right.*

Putting the bottle aside, the brush caught her eye. Picking it up to investigate more closely, she found several dark hairs still in the bristles. Numbly, Elizabeth placed it on the tray and opened the table drawer. Inside was a leather-covered box. She withdrew it, setting it in her lap and lifting the lid. She discovered a bracelet fashioned out of small beads, strung on a string and tied clumsily. Clearly something created by a child, she absently slipped it over her wrist to find that it fit perfectly. Hurriedly, she returned it to the box and put the box back in the drawer.

Noting that the mantle over the hearth held several small portraits, she walked in that direction and her foot collided with something sticking out from under the chair. Leaning down, a new pain pricked Elizabeth's heart, for, there was a pair of boots that perfectly matched those William wore every day. Refusing to dwell on the implications, she went on to the hearth.

Noting that all of the portraits were encased in ornate, silver frames, she began her study with the first in a line. It was the image of a boy of perhaps four years of age with dark hair, piercing blue eyes and a decided frown. She almost chuckled, for the subject of the portrait was obvious. Still, her forehead knit with concern when she realised that this portrait suggested William had been sad, even as a child. Unsettled, she placed it on the mantel and picked up the next.

A little girl with golden curls, clutching a doll, smiled back at her. Georgiana looked about three years of age, but she was centuries removed from the cynical sister Elizabeth had met in London. Wondering what could have caused so drastic a change in her, Elizabeth set that portrait back as well.

Her breath caught when she spied the next portrait. For it was of a beautiful woman, perhaps four and twenty years of age, with dark blue eyes and black hair. *Is the hair in the brush hers?*

Taking the portrait to a window, she drew back the curtain until light illuminated the features. And as a prayer rose to heaven, Elizabeth searched for any resemblance to William.

A voice abruptly ended her deliberations. "How did you get in here?"

Startled, Elizabeth whirled around to find William in the doorway. Knowing how appalling her trespass must appear, her mind went blank.

Clearly annoyed, he continued, "That door is always locked. So I ask again, how did you get in?"

"It... it was not locked today."

"Then I shall have to have a stern talk with the sentry for this area. He keeps check on the house and apparently forgot to lock it."

William stared at her as though expecting something more. Suddenly remembering the shawl and the portrait in her hand, Elizabeth became mortified. Hurriedly, she returned to the mantel to replace the portrait and whipped off the shawl.

"Please forgive me," she said as she held the shawl toward William. "I should not have intruded."

"This house is kept private." William replied, as he took the shawl and folded it reverently. Then his eyes roamed over the bedroom, as though taking in every inch of it. "For now, I do not want to discuss why."

"As you wish."

William stepped back into the hall and motioned for her to go ahead of him. As she entered the hall, he began to follow her to the front entrance and address another matter.

"Finding a pony on so vast an estate as Pemberley is best left to the men I pay to do such things. You could get lost in certain areas, not to mention encountering poachers and such. In taking matters into your hands, you have worried a number of people unnecessarily."

"I only meant to be of help," she said dejectedly.

"Sometimes being helpful means letting the servants do their jobs," he said flatly, as they exited the front door. Then turning to lock it, he added, "We must hurry. It will be dark soon."

"What of the pony? Should we not take her back to the Beckers?"

"We shall take her with us to Pemberley. A groom will deliver her to them in the morning. For now, I do not want my aunt worrying about your safety a moment longer."

"I apologise if my actions caused Aunt Olivia or anyone else to worry for me. It was not consciously done."

Still out of sorts, William stalked off to fetch Phoebe and Star. Bringing them to the front of the house, he helped Elizabeth into the saddle and then mounted Zeus, leaving Star to trail behind them. The sun had already set, and it was dark when they reached the circular drive of Pemberley and footmen rushed out to take their horses. Nonetheless, because the Fitzwilliams had insisted on delaying dinner, William and Elizabeth were able to dine with them.

Immediately after dinner, Joseph Fitzwilliam declared that the events of the day had been exhausting and he wished to retire early. Olivia knew that he claimed as much just to spare her, for, in truth, her health was the reason he wanted to retire. In any case, they said goodnight to the young couple and exited the dining room.

After they did, Elizabeth's eyes flickered to William. He had closed his eyes, she assumed from weariness, as he sipped the last of a glass of wine. That gave her the rare opportunity of studying his features without his notice. Even though he was tired, he was so very handsome that her heart ached.

With nothing to lose, she spoke with hurried eagerness. "The library here is spectacular. I have never seen so many books in one place; however, I have been so busy with other things that I have neglected exploring it fully."

William's eyes opened. "There is no reason you cannot spend the rest of the evening in the library. I dare say that you will not be disturbed."

"But, I... I thought to share the evening with you."

"Elizabeth, I have had a trying day. I seek only a hot bath to relieve my ankle and some sleep."

"But you were walking so well today that I thought perhaps your ankle—"

"It still pains me," he interrupted. "I try not to complain, lest others worry unnecessarily. Now, if you will excuse me, Adams has a hot bath waiting, and I imagine he would like to retire at a reasonable hour." He stood up, dropping his serviette on the table. "I hope you enjoy the library."

Her hopes fell as she watched him walk away.

The next morning

As Mrs. Reynolds crossed the foyer toward the dining room, she was surprised to find William's aunt coming down the grand staircase. Having a weak constitution, Mrs. Fitzwilliam was not usually awake at dawn and the fact that she was not accompanied by her husband left the servant wondering if something was wrong. Regardless, she greeted her cheerily, hoping that was not the case.

"Good morning, Mrs. Fitzwilliam. Are you ready to break your fast?"

"Good morning," Olivia parroted. "I am not hungry just yet. Actually, I hoped to speak to Mrs. Darcy before she left for the day. Have I been successful?"

"Mrs. Darcy just finished eating and went upstairs to her study. She said that she wanted to fetch a basket she had left there."

"Then I need to hurry." With that, Mrs. Fitzwilliam went back up the stairs to find Elizabeth.

When she reached the door to Elizabeth's study, Olivia was surprised to find it open. Her niece stood at the windows, holding a letter in her hand and staring at the lawn below as though in a trance. Olivia watched her for a while before calling her name.

Elizabeth's head swung around, and, seeing who it was, she pushed the letter deep into her pocket and smiled wanly. "Aunt Olivia, you startled me."

"I am sorry. I hope I am not intruding."

"No, not at all."

Olivia pulled the door shut behind her. "I hoped to catch you before you left the house. I feel that I must address something that has been worrying me."

One of Elizabeth's brows rose in question. "Oh?"

"Yes. I am beginning to fear for your health, my dear. Since my nephew returned, I have not seen you stroll around the lake even once. And while I commend your diligence to your duties as mistress of this house, I fear that you are trying to match Fitzwilliam's long hours." Elizabeth's expression fell at the mention of William. "You will soon exhaust yourself at this pace."

"I like to keep long hours. It takes my mind off the fact that my husband is gone from sunrise to sunset."

"And why do you think that is?"

"I... I suppose that a surfeit of estate problems cropped up in his absence."

"Perhaps they have, but consider this. Fitzwilliam pays his steward a good salary to oversee Pemberley. Other than something he might have to witness in person in order to make an informed decision, he gives orders and Mr. Sturgis carries them out. That is how a man of his station conducts business. For the most part, Pemberley's affairs can be handled from Fitzwilliam's study or via post when he is out of town."

Meeting her aunt's eyes, Elizabeth looked like a child caught in a lie. "Then I have no idea why he is gone all day."

Olivia walked over to Elizabeth, reaching out to gently cup her face. "I think you know very well, but you are afraid to admit it to me or anyone else. I promise not to judge you, if you want to tell me what is wrong. I dearly want to help, but I cannot, for I do not know what has made you and my nephew so very unhappy."

Her tender gesture caused Elizabeth to break down and sob. Olivia pulled her into an embrace, holding her until she stopped crying and began to wipe her eyes. Then they sat down, and Olivia heard the entire story of how her nephew and niece met and all that had transpired until the present. For a few seconds after Elizabeth had finished, Olivia was speechless, and then, taking both her niece's hands, she smiled at her lovingly.

"Mistakes were made, but it is not the end of the world. I happen to know that my nephew would never have married a woman for whom he felt no attraction. And no matter how hard he tries to feign indifference, I have seen the longing in Fitzwilliam's eyes when he thinks no one is watching."

"Longing? For me?" Elizabeth said, her voice breaking with emotion.

"Yes, my dear, for you." She squeezed Elizabeth's hands. "As long as a man still desires a woman, there is hope."

"The letter I was holding when you came into the room is from Aunt Madeline. She asks if I have spent time in William's company, and it pains me to confess to her that I have not been successful."

"How I wish Madeline had returned to Pemberley before leaving for London. Perhaps then, you or she might have confided in me."

"Their sudden return to London was unavoidable, as my uncle had a crisis with one of his suppliers."

"I completely understand. Still, I cannot help thinking that I would have known all of this sooner." She sighed. "In any event, now that I know, the question is what shall we do about it?"

"I fear there is nothing anyone can do. Last night, after you retired, I hinted that I wanted William to spend time with me in the library, but he refused. I cannot say that he was not tired, for that was evident. Even so, each day that goes by takes him one step farther away from me."

"Oh, Elizabeth, try not to think in that vein. The Lord helps those who have faith. We shall both continue to pray and believe."

"I try, but each day brings new doubts. Something I stumbled upon yesterday made me wonder if I am being foolish to think I can still win his love."

"What did you find?"

"While looking for the pony, I discovered a small, brick house on the far side of Pemberley. Plainly, it has been kept up and it was fashioned for a woman. It is just—well, Fitzwilliam's cologne was in the air, and boots like those he wears daily were in the bedroom. And a book, with his name in the front, lay open. And while I firmly believe that he is not the type to take a mistress, when Fitzwilliam found me there, he acted as though I had intruded into a private sanctuary. He made it clear that he would not explain anything about the house, and I was not to question him about it."

"Hmmm. Perhaps Joseph can learn something from my nephew about the house. I am certain it is not what you fear."

"Oh, please do not jeopardise your relationship for my sake! William made it clear the house was not to be discussed. Besides, he would know that I was the one who told you. So do not mention it, I beg you."

"As you wish, though Joseph talks to the gardeners, sentries and such, so he may be able to learn something without Fitzwilliam's knowledge."

"Uncle Joseph must be discreet with his enquires, for it would further damage my husband's opinion of me if he thought I was using you to find out about the house."

"I concur. Now, will you allow me to share what you have told me with Joseph? He will be your ally, I promise. He is just as anxious to see your marriage flourish as I am."

"I suppose it makes no difference now."

"Good. Once Joseph knows everything, he can best determine how to talk with Fitzwilliam. Perhaps he can help him to see that felicity in marriage is always salvageable where there is love—and I am certain that he loves you."

"Would that I believed that," Elizabeth whispered. Then she forced a small smile as she stood to her feet. "There is much to do, and I must get started."

"Oh, I forgot." Olivia pulled a small knitted cap from her pocket. It was white with a blue ribbon threaded around the edges. "I finally finished this to go with the sweater I made for Mrs. Becker's baby. If you are visiting her, will you take it?"

"I shall stop by to see how she fares and will be happy to give it to her. My intention today is to visit two tenants who were poorly when I last called on them—Mrs. Brown, who suffers with persistent headaches, and Mrs. Walters, who strained her back and can barely walk. She is fortunate that she has such a large family to help her, allowing for rest.

"As you probably know, Mrs. Reynolds has recipes for every imaginable ailment, so I have packed plenty of her salves, tinctures and powders for them, as well as cakes and biscuits for the children. While I am there, I shall list all the children's measurements. That is something I wish I had thought of the last time I called on all the tenants."

"What are you planning?"

"I am compiling a list for Christmas. I want to give all the children a new pair of shoes from the cobbler's shop in Lambton, as well as a new coat. I sewed coats for little girls when I lived at home, and Mrs. O'Reilly said that she has made coats for her nephews. She is excited about helping me. Even Mrs. Reynolds and Mrs. Lantrip said that they would like to help. I think I shall need them all, if I am to get everything finished in time."

"You can rely on me, you know that. And Mrs. Kelly, who acts as my lady's maid, may no longer be young, but she can stitch a seam straighter than most. I think she would be delighted if she were asked to help."

Elizabeth hugged her aunt. "I depend on you so much. You are too kind."

"No one can be too kind to another person. I have lived long enough to know that kindness always comes back to bless the one who gives it freely."

"Oh, and I forgot. Mrs. Samson, who runs the foundlings' home in Lambton, sent a letter asking me to visit. So I shall call on her. It seems my husband built the home, and every year he makes certain that the children are not forgotten at Christmas. She has made a list of their needs and wanted to give it to me in person." Elizabeth shook her head dolefully. "What does that say about my judgement? I was so foolish that I deliberately chose to think ill of a man who is practically a saint!"

Olivia chuckled. "I assure you that I know him better than you, and while he is kind-hearted, Fitzwilliam is no saint! Have you not experienced enough of his temper to realise that?"

"Well, compared to most men, he is everything good and generous." Then taking hold of the basket, she added, "If I do not leave now, everyone will worry about where I am. I have been chastised for causing worry, so I shall take my leave."

"Be careful and try not to tire yourself." Olivia kissed Elizabeth's forehead. "Trust in the Lord. He shall hear our prayers and sustain your marriage."

Elizabeth smiled sincerely. "It gives me hope to consider everything in that light. Thank you."

With another quick hug, Elizabeth went out the door, and Olivia followed to watch her walk down the hallway.

She is young, Lord. Help her to stand strong until Fitzwilliam remembers that he must forgive in order to be forgiven.

Olivia made her way back to the dining room, knowing full well that Joseph would be waiting there, and that he would not eat until she joined him.

Chapter 26

Pemberley
Several days later

Having just locked her office, Mrs. Reynolds turned and was surprised to find Mr. Walker waiting for her.

"Mrs. Reynolds, do you recall speaking to me about the footman—the one you caught several times talking clandestinely with the new maid?"

"Are you speaking of Mr. Barrows and Molly?"

"Yes, those two. Well, as I was coming up the stairs from the servants' quarters this morning, I saw them again. They were halfway down the west hall, as though it were natural for them to be in that area of the house at that hour, however, the moment they saw me, they separated and quickly vanished."

"Did it seem to you that there was any impropriety involved? That they might be infatuated with one another?

"I cannot say that it did. They were just talking."

"I see. Well, since last we discussed this, I learned that Molly told another maid that Mr. Barrows comes from the same small village south of Birmingham where she was born. It seems that they were neighbours as children, though both grew up and left the village to find work. Apparently, it was only a coincidence that they both ended up at Pemberley and were hired within days of each other."

"They have been here almost a year, if I remember correctly."

"Your memory serves you well."

"Do you still want me to let you know if I see them together in the future?"

"Most certainly. It is my business to know what is going on under this roof."

"No one is more conscientious than you, Agnes Reynolds."

Mrs. Reynolds pursed her lips to keep from smiling. Surreptitiously, she looked about to make sure no one had overheard. "Now, what kind of example are you setting for the other servants by using my given name, Mr. Walker?"

"I apologise, Mrs. Reynolds," John Walker said with a smile that assured her that he was not sorry in the least. Then he hurried back to the front of the house.

Mrs. Reynolds chuckled and turned to go in the opposite direction. She had gone no more than half the length of the hall when the master suddenly came out of the smoking room. She stopped and waited for him to speak.

"When my wife comes downstairs to break her fast, please inform her that we are to attend a ball the day after tomorrow at Creighton Hall, Mrs. Reynolds. It is likely that our paths will not cross, as I have many things to attend to today."

Mrs. Reynolds sputtered and spoke without thinking, "Attend a ball with two days notice?"

"Yes, I completely forgot to mention to Mrs. Darcy that the Creightons wished to hold a ball in honour of our marriage. I tried to put them off, using my ankle as an excuse, but Lord Creighton would not hear of it. I am aware that this is short notice, but there is nothing to be done about it now."

The housekeeper stuttered, "I am sorry, sir. After you mentioned the ball, I completely forgot that Mrs. Darcy is not here."

"Not here?"

"It has been her practice to rise early and begin her day shortly afterward. Would you like me to find where she is today? She leaves a calendar on her desk in case I need to locate her."

"No. I imagine she is merely exploring another area of Pemberley that I have asked her to avoid." Then he said, "Forgive me, I should not have given voice to my thoughts." Mrs. Reynolds could not think of how to reply, so she did not.

He began to walk away, but when he was only several feet down the hall, he stopped to add, "If you need me, I will be in my study for the next two hours. Afterward, I will travel to Lord Concord's estate to bring home Georgiana. This afternoon I will meet with Sturgis again."

"Miss Darcy has returned?"

"She accompanied Lord and Lady Matlock back to Derbyshire. My uncle had to meet with Lord Concord on business, so he brought her as far as Monthaven Manor."

Recalling the carriage accident that injured that gentleman last year, Mrs. Reynolds ventured, "May I ask how Lord Concord is faring?"

"Apparently, he is doing as well as can be expected for a man of his age. Lady Susan told Georgiana that her father will never be able to ride again, but he can walk unassisted with a cane for short periods."

"I remember that when your mother passed away and Lady Concord died shortly thereafter, he and your father spent a great deal of time together playing cards and billiards or riding."

"Yes, he and Father were great friends, but never more so than when they were united in grief." Looking a little melancholy, William abruptly dropped the subject. "I should get something accomplished before I leave. I will be in my study."

Completely lost in her own thoughts, Mrs. Reynolds watched until he was completely out of sight.

It is sad that Lord Concord's daughter ruined the relationship between the families. I never liked Lady Susan. She was manipulative, even as a child. And since she has been widowed, she has used Georgiana to try to get close to the master again. I can only imagine how she must disparage Mrs. Darcy.

Suddenly, her conscience spoke. *No more so than Mr. Darcy at times.*

Faced with that truth, the old servant sighed. *If only the boy could see how industrious Mrs. Darcy is and how she is admired by one and all. Yet, it seems that he is determined not to see.*

A loud commotion in the foyer disrupted her thoughts, and she hurried in that direction. She found that a young maid had dropped an entire tray of dirty dishes on the marble floor. Frustration rose in her chest, though she spoke calmly to the crying young lady.

"No need to cry over spilt milk, Violet. Just pick up the pieces and put them on the tray. I shall have Cassie come mop the floor."

However, as Mrs. Reynolds walked in the direction of the servants' quarters, her thoughts were not as charitable.

The young people of today have no earthly idea how to accomplish the smallest tasks. One would think that their parents had never given them any chores!

Her complaints continued until after she located Cassie and sent her on her way. By then it was nearing time for a meeting with the cook, so she headed towards the kitchen.

Monthaven Manor
Later that day

As the Darcy carriage entered the long drive leading to Monthaven Manor, all of the hours William had spent there suddenly came to mind. He could not help smiling as he thought of the races between Pemberley and here that he, Richard, Andrew, George Wickham and Susan had participated in almost weekly—races he or Richard usually won.

When his parents were young, they were close friends with Lady Susan's family, who happened to be their nearest neighbours. So they could as easily be found here in the summer as at home. And the same could be said of Lord and Lady Concord, along with their daughter Susan, who spent copious amounts of time at Pemberley. It was only natural that the children would become friends, but while the parents' friendship lasted until their deaths, the children were not as fortunate.

As they grew older, their relationships were beset by jealousies and mean-spiritedness, primarily caused by the inclusion of George Wickham, the steward's son. Always envious that he was not born a gentleman, from the day that Andrew came to live at Pemberley, Wickham encouraged him to resent William. By continually pointing out that Andrew's father was the firstborn and that Pemberley should rightfully have been his to inherit, he managed to sever all civility between Andrew and William by the time George Darcy died.

In addition, Lady Susan had set her cap for William by the age of ten, so it was a wonder the friendship survived as long as it had. Susan was never above using both Wickham and Andrew to try to make William jealous, though her tactics proved futile. For William, the most troubling part of the dissolution of the friendship was that the others had managed to influence Georgiana to turn against him.

As thoughts of his sister filled his head, the carriage entered the circle in front of the manor, and he found himself staring at Georgiana on a balcony overhead. She was not alone, for precisely the moment William spied her, a man leaned close to whisper something in her ear, and she laughed. Anger instantly rose, but William tried to conceal it as the carriage came to a halt at the front steps. Quickly exiting the vehicle, William took the steps to the portico two at a time. Once on the portico, the front door swung open, and the Concords' butler stood ready to take his hat and gloves. As he obliged, he realised that Lady Susan was watching him from halfway up the grand staircase.

"Fitzwilliam! I am so delighted to see you again and even more so to see that you are healed. You will never know how many sleepless nights I spent worrying about your health. When I was in London, I had no luck convincing Georgiana to let me accompany her to Darcy House to see for myself that you were in no danger of dying."

"Georgiana was only following my orders, Lady Susan. And, although I appreciate your concern, it was totally unnecessary. I have wonderful servants and an excellent physician," William said stiffly. Then he glanced up the stairs. "Would you be so kind as to show me to my sister? I spied her on one of the balconies as we neared the house."

"Oh!" Lady Susan exclaimed, "When I saw your carriage approach, I came straight here to greet you and left our dear Georgiana with my cousin, Matthew."

"Your cousin?" William said, as he went up the stairs past her, not waiting for her guidance.

Susan hurried to catch up. "Matthew is Lord Attaway. I am certain that you must have met him. He attended most of mother's dinner parties when we were children."

William did remember. He had never liked the conceited boy.

"You may remember that he inherited Gracehill Park after my uncle died. He is one of the most eligible men in England, if I say so myself. And when he stopped by to see me in London, we had such a grand time reminiscing that I invited him to come to Monthaven. He has agreed to spend the rest of the summer with us."

"It was thoughtless of you to leave him alone with Georgiana," William said brusquely.

"Surely you cannot object to her being in his company for a few seconds. My cousin is a fine gentleman, not a cad to be avoided."

"A gentleman would know better than to be alone in the company of an unmarried young woman. Georgiana is not a child, and her reputation is as easily tarnished as the next young woman's."

By the time he reached the landing, he looked to the right, trying to decide which room to enter. Susan stepped in front of him.

"Come! Let me show you the way."

When Darcy reached the balcony, Attaway was propped against a wall, one knee bent and his boot flat against the bricks. Upon seeing William, he pushed away and stood up straight. He eyed William haughtily as Lady Susan made the introductions.

"Fitzwilliam, this is my cousin, Lord Attaway of Gracehill Park in Liverpool. Cousin, may I present Fitzwilliam Darcy of Pemberley, Georgiana's brother. I told him that you may remember each other from mother's dinner parties."

"I do not recall meeting you," William said coolly.

"That is of no import," the young man retorted with a smirk, "for I do not remember meeting you, either."

Annoyed, William walked over to kiss his sister's forehead. "I am pleased that you have returned, Georgiana. You look very well."

"Thank you, Brother. I am pleased to find you so much improved. I was telling Matt—Lord Attaway of your accident before you got here."

The familiarity with which she spoke of the young man irked William, but before he could say a thing, Attaway interrupted.

"I am surprised to even see you on your feet, old man! From what Georgiana told me of your injury, I would have expected you to be using a cane."

"My recovery was merely a matter of pushing ahead in spite of the pain," William answered matter-of-factly.

Lord Attaway laughed. "I have to say that I am not one to intentionally cause myself pain if it can be avoided."

William took the gentleman's measure, all the time praying that his sister was not infatuated with this immature man. "Then at some point in your life, I fear you will let something defeat you that could have been conquered with a little determination."

Before Attaway could respond, William addressed Georgiana. "Unfortunately, I am needed immediately at Pemberley, so we must be on our way."

"Our uncle is talking with Lord Concord at present. Surely you mean to speak to him before you leave. I shall just wait here for you and enjoy another of Lord Attaway's stories of Liverpool. They are so diverting." Georgiana blushed when Attaway gave her a wink.

"Diverting or not, we must be on our way. I think it best if you come with me now."

Taking his sister's hand, William began to lead her from the balcony while she, Lord Attaway and Lady Susan protested. It was to no avail, however, for William never slowed his pace.

As Attaway watched them walk out of sight, he huffed, "Darcy acts as though he has saved her from a fate worse than death."

"If you had not tried to be so clever, perhaps he might have let her stay with you while he talks to Father. As it is, you antagonised him. What in the world were you thinking?"

"I think that I do not care to bow and scrape to a man who feels he is my superior. Georgiana is in love with me, I am certain, and I intend to pursue her. It is obvious that she is headstrong, and once I convince her that I want to marry her, nothing will stop us. Her dear brother will have a whirlwind on his hands, should he try to separate us then."

"You are a fool if you think Fitzwilliam Darcy is someone to challenge. It would have been smarter to try to make him like you. As it is, you have only made both our tasks more difficult! Now stay here and do not move."

Lady Susan rushed to prevent William from leaving without seeing her father. For months she had inundated Lord Concord with pleas to seek William's help with their fall plantings, reminding him that he could no longer ride. And with his steward newly retired, who else would know exactly which fields should be ploughed under and which to leave fallow, save someone like William. If only he would agree to help, that would assure his presence at Monthaven for at least a week. And she meant to spend every minute of it with William, even if she was on horseback the entire time.

Catching up to them just outside the study, she found William talking to a footman, and she intervened. "Jimmerson, you are dismissed."

The footman nodded and walked away, while Susan smiled predatorily at William. "I am sure that Father will insist on seeing you," she said as she knocked on the door. "He has talked of nothing else in his letters."

"Come," a voice rang out. She opened the door and stuck her head inside.

"Father, Fitzwilliam is here. I know that you wished to speak to him before he left."

"Yes, I do. Come in, my boy."

Shortly thereafter, the Darcys were in their carriage on their way back to Pemberley. Never especially thrilled to see his uncle, William had cut the visit as short as possible without insult. Both men had asked about Elizabeth, and though he assured them that she was well, that was all he had said on the subject. Neither man noticed his reticence to elaborate on the state of his marriage, for they were used to his wont for privacy.

Lord Concord had quickly brought up the subject of the Creighton's ball, something of which Lord Matlock and Georgiana had no knowledge. Lord Matlock claimed that the countess must have forgotten to tell him, but he was certain they would attend. While Georgiana declared that her invitation had likely gone astray during her travels, she intended to attend as well.

After a bit more conversation, William pleaded that he had work to do and excused himself and Georgiana, but not before Lord Concord seized the opportunity to ask William to help with his winter planting. Having no excuse to decline graciously, he acquiesced.

The carriage ride to Pemberley gave William time to think, and his mind spun with ways to avoid being in Lady Susan's company. He had no doubt that she was behind her father's request and would be waiting like a spider when he returned. Suddenly, an idea came to him, causing a rare smile. It was the perfect solution—he would send his steward, Mr. Sturgis.

A remark from Georgiana drew his attention. "You said little about Elizabeth when our uncle and Lord Concord enquired about her and even less now. Is something wrong?"

He sighed. "What is your point, Georgiana?"

"Obviously, Elizabeth is not of our sphere. I can only imagine that being

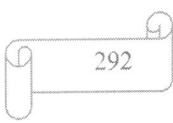

mistress of an estate the size of Pemberley must seem a daunting task to someone so unprepared for such responsibility."

William stiffened. "Upon my return to Pemberley, Mrs. Reynolds informed me that Mrs. Darcy had already mastered the household books and had begun to plan the menus. In addition, she has already called on all the tenants; therefore, to imply that she is ill-equipped is erroneous, to say the least."

"We shall see," Georgiana answered petulantly. "Calling on tenants does not a mistress make. How she handles the problems that occur—that is the measure of the mistress of a great house."

William sighed. "Given that I am not worried about her ability, neither should you be. Moreover, Elizabeth is my wife, and I expect you to treat her with respect."

"I have an excellent knowledge of decorum, thank you." Georgiana said coldly, turning to look out the window.

"Then tell me, if you are such a model of decorum, how is it that I found you alone with Attaway?"

Her head swung around. "It is not as if we were in public. Besides, we were alone for only a few minutes."

"Have you considered that Lady Susan may be promoting a match between her cousin and you in order to gain access to me?"

"Everything is not about you, Brother! Perhaps Lord Attaway simply finds me attractive. I hope so, for I think him very charming."

"You do not know him well enough to form an opinion," William argued.

"And you do? Have you already decided against him, just as you decided against George and Andrew without a word to me?"

"I have sound reasons for my actions toward George and Andrew. You will just have to trust me."

"That is always your answer—trust me! Never a word of explanation! So tell me, what is it you dislike about Lord Attaway?"

"I find him very arrogant for one so young, and someone of his self-importance has likely made many foolish mistakes already. I have only to learn what they are."

"I am sure that, if you try, you can find something not to like about anyone. But be forewarned, Brother. I like Lord Attaway, and I do not intend to dislike him simply because you do."

By then the carriage had slowed in front of Pemberley. Just as it came to a stop, Georgiana opened the door. She was poised to step out unassisted, and when the footman lowered the steps, she did just that. As William watched, she ran up the steps to the portico, disappearing into the house through the front door that was now open. William sighed deeply.

I do not know if I shall survive both you and Elizabeth under one roof.

Wearily, William stepped out of the carriage and followed Georgiana inside.

Pemberley
After Dinner

With Georgiana's return, dinner was even more excruciatingly awkward for the Fitzwilliams than it had been before she left for London. Not only did she continue to act as though she was unhappy with their presence at Pemberley, but throughout the meal, she seemed determined to find something to criticise about Elizabeth's taste. Everything from the menu to the new tablecloth and napkins displeased her; however, it was a question about a tenant that served as a catalyst for another row with her brother.

"Elizabeth, did you have opportunity to visit Mrs. Becker?" Olivia Fitzwilliam asked innocently. "I could not help but wonder how she is faring, poor girl. She could barely walk when I visited."

Elizabeth smiled warmly at her aunt. "I did, and I gave her the bonnet you made for the baby. She said to tell you that it is lovely and to thank you for being so kind. As to her health, she is the same. She had nothing but praise, though, for the maid I sent to help her. She allows that Jessie has taken over the cooking and the wash, in addition to helping with Mazie, which was far more than she had expected."

"A maid? You loaned one of our maids to a tenant?" Georgiana said in disbelief. She sought the faces of the others at the table as she added, "Can Pemberley afford such generosity?"

"I... " Elizabeth bit her lip and glanced to William. He did not look up, though his head swung slowly side to side.

Elizabeth swallowed hard. "It will not cost Pemberley a farthing. I explained to Mrs. Reynolds that I mean to pay her wages while she assists the Beckers."

Previously, William had been feigning interest in his pheasant, hoping not to get in another argument with Georgiana, but now he realised that that was not to be.

"Elizabeth, why do you think you should pay the maid out of your account? Pemberley will pay her wages. After all, the Beckers are our tenants."

"It was my idea to loan them the maid, so I felt that I should pay for it."

"That is hardly the point!" Georgiana interjected. "Brother, do you not see the madness in a precedent of this nature? Now every tenant will expect similar treatment if they are incapacitated. Every broken bone or aching back will require that we send a servant to cook and clean."

Slowly William lay down his cutlery—a symbol of the gravity of what he was about to say. Then he focused entirely on his sister.

"If Mrs. Darcy wishes to lend a servant to one of our tenants, that is her prerogative. I am quite certain that every gesture of benevolence will be predicated by circumstance. If a tenant is fortunate enough to have family who can help them, then that is another matter."

Elizabeth spoke quietly. "Fitzwilliam is right, Georgiana. I only sought to help Mrs. Becker because she has no family nearby and no one to send for help when the baby comes."

Georgiana shrugged. "As far as I know, Mother never thought something of that nature was necessary." Standing, she dropped her serviette on the table. "If you will excuse me, I am weary from my trip. I am retiring." With that, she left the room.

A collective sigh of relief went up, though it went unacknowledged. For a time the room was silent as William stared solemnly at his plate, then he looked up and forced a smile.

"Well, for once I am not ready for bed. Uncle, if you are finished eating, would you care to join me for a cigar?"

Joseph Fitzwilliam was holding his wife's hand under the tablecloth. He squeezed it in silent recognition of a chance to speak to his nephew alone.

"Certainly." As he stood he added, "Perhaps my wife will consent to exhibit on the pianoforte when we rejoin the ladies. In my opinion, no one can hold a candle to her talent on the instrument."

Every eye looked to Olivia, who smiled shyly. "I shall play if Elizabeth will agree to sing."

As William looked at her with a puzzled expression, Elizabeth crimsoned. "I sing a few Scottish tunes my grandmother taught me and only for pleasure. I dare say I am not proficient enough to entertain."

"Oh, but I beg to disagree. Do you remember when we were at the Beckers' and I came outside to see if you wanted a cup of tea? You were sitting on the back steps singing 'Barbara Allen' [13] to Mazie. I never let on that I heard you, but I thought you sang beautifully."

Elizabeth chuckled. "Mazie asked if I knew a certain song and, unfortunately, I did not. So, I sang that song, as I remembered the words to it."

"Will you sing it for us tonight?" Uncle Joseph asked.

Elizabeth looked ill at ease. "I shall, but only if you will not insist that I do another."

"Then we have a bargain!" Joseph said. He slipped an arm around William's shoulder and changed the subject as they went toward the door. "Richard said that you import cigars from the Americas. Is that correct?"

When they could no longer be seen or heard, Olivia addressed Elizabeth. "Shall we hurry to the music room and practice?"

"It seems you have left me no choice," Elizabeth teased, though she looked unsettled. "I fear that Fitzwilliam will be greatly disappointed, since I have never sung in public."

"He will enjoy your singing, of that I am sure. And I shall not apologise for requesting that you sing. Fitzwilliam should know that you have talent. Men are proud of their wives' performances, and I shall tell you a secret. According to my husband, they like to feel that you exhibit solely for them."

"But what if others are watching?" Elizabeth asked as they both stood.

"The key is to act as though there are only the two of you. Look up while you are singing and meet his eyes lovingly. I promise that his regard will rise dramatically."

Elizabeth reached to squeeze her hands. "I shall take your advice."

The smoking room

At the liquor cabinet, William poured first one glass, then another, of his finest imported brandy. When done, he held one out to his uncle. A small smirk lifted the corners of his mouth.

"This is the only reason I see Richard as often as I do. He declares it the best in the country, and he should know."

Sipping the amber liquid, Joseph Fitzwilliam stopped to laugh. "I can see why. After tasting this, I have to agree that the French certainly have the upper hand in the brandy market."

"And my source knows the very best that France has to offer and how to smuggle it out of the country. Lord Matlock has hounded me for years to divulge the information, but I struck a bargain, and I will not break my word."

"Then I can only imagine that it must drive him mad. My brother has always believed he could intimidate anyone into doing his will. In fact, in that aspect, he is exactly like Father."

By then William was standing before a table holding a large, wooden humidor. However, as he began to lift the lid, Joseph made a confession.

"To be truthful, I would not care for a cigar. Livy has a cough much of the time now, especially when she lies down. Smoke seems only to make it worse. Even the smell of smoke on my clothes can trigger an episode."

William hurriedly closed the lid. "I had no idea. I shall not smoke, either."

"Please, do not abstain on my account or Livy's. Any smoke on your clothes should not be a problem as long as she does not get too close."

"To be honest, I prefer brandy to cigars. I keep a supply on hand for my guests and join them in a smoke occasionally, for it is expected."

Joseph tossed the rest of his brandy down this throat. "A world of misery lies in that phrase."

William looked puzzled. "That phrase?"

"*It is expected*," his uncle repeated flatly. "When I was a boy, I never questioned my lot in life. I was an earl's son, and I was expected to act in a certain way. And I did. By the time I left for university, I was sick of the hypocrisy of it all, especially in regards to marriage. Marriages of convenience, like that of my parents, more often than not made both parties miserable, as well as their offspring. We all knew of father's succession of mistresses. Even mother knew, though I doubt she cared, for she lived her life apart from him—apart from us all, actually."

"I never—Mother never mentioned that."

"No. She would not have. Your mother was too kind-hearted and made excuses for both our parents." Joseph stood and walked over to the liquor cabinet. "Do you mind?"

"Of course not. Help yourself."

Joseph poured another glass of brandy and took a sip. "I was expected to follow Father's order to marry a debutante he had handpicked for me. If I remember correctly, her dowry was a hundred-thousand pounds. It was exceedingly large, I suppose, in order to compensate for her, shall we say, equally large size. The poor woman weighed more than my horse."

William could not help but chuckle, though he covered his mouth. Undeterred, his uncle kept talking.

"I was expected to redeem Father's bad investments by sacrificing my life. But I had already fallen in love with Livy and could never have abandoned her. By then she was my life."

"You suffered greatly for your refusal to obey Grandfather," William stated. "Mother often lamented the fact that you were ostracised by most of the family."

Joseph shrugged. "Looking back, it was the most intelligent decision I have ever made. I am grateful that God gave me the courage to choose my darling wife. She has made me very happy all these years."

"Even now, you have no regrets?"

"My only regret is that I do not have another lifetime to love Olivia. This one has been much too short."

Deep in reflection, William silently replenished his own brandy. Then he stared absently at the liquor as he swirled it in the glass.

"Fitzwilliam, clearly something is wrong between you and Elizabeth. You act like strangers, hardly spending any time together. Everyone has noticed. I dare say that you have not even fooled the servants."

William's eyes closed and he grimaced. "I appreciate your concern, but I do not care to discuss my personal business, Uncle. Suffice it to say that we are not as compatible as I had hoped."

Joseph could not let William know that he knew everything; thus, he replied, "A broken heart is hard to hide, son."

"My heart is just fine, thank you," William declared harshly, then immediately apologised.

He began to pace the floor, as was his wont when he was upset. "I realise that you are only concerned for my well-being, but the problem with my marriage lies in the fact that I have no one to blame but myself for the outcome. I was too proud to listen to Richard's advice or my own conscience when I decided to marry. Andrew had compromised Elizabeth by kissing her in public, and I thought the only solution was for us to marry. In hindsight, there were other ways I could have helped her that would have resolved the matter better—for her and for me."

"So you no longer fancy being married?"

"I do not fancy being married to a woman who loathes me! I spent my adult life eschewing fortune hunters, for I desired a marriage of mutual affection. Look where it has gotten me."

"Why do you believe Elizabeth loathes you? I have seen no evidence of that. To the contrary, she seems eager to please you."

"I believe she loathes me because she has said as much. Before she left London, she made it perfectly clear that in her opinion I was the lowest form of rake. Why she is pleasant to me now I cannot imagine, unless being at Pemberley has opened her eyes to the privileges that come with being my wife. She may have decided that being tremendously wealthy and perchance having children will balance her distaste for my company. However, she certainly does not care for me."

"I disagree."

William stopped pacing as his head swung around. "How could you know better than I what is in her heart?"

"I am a good judge of character, and I see it in her eyes. Elizabeth looks at you the same way Olivia looks at me."

William laughed mirthlessly. "No. I will never believe any woman's affections can change that quickly."

"You are too cynical," his uncle declared. "Any decent human being, shown the error of their ways, will begin to see the person they misjudged in a new light."

"A light coloured by money perhaps."

Undaunted, Joseph Fitzwilliam continued. "If she should apologise for her mistrust, would you forgive her that? Or would you continue to punish her because she was not in love with you from the start?"

William looked shocked. "I... I have never thought in terms of punishing her. I was focused entirely on my failure. That is all."

"It is understandable that you may have acted unconsciously, but think on this. Forgiveness is essential to happiness—yours and hers. Search your heart. If you still bear any resentment against Elizabeth, forgive her. No matter her motivation for being here and even if she is not in love with you, forgive her. If you do, I know it will lift that burden that weighs so heavily on your shoulders. And you can never tell. You may just succeed in gaining the kind of marriage you always wanted."

William sighed heavily. "I shall think on what you have said. That is all I can promise."

Joseph put his hand on William's shoulder. "That is all I ask. Now, shall we join the ladies and listen to some beautiful music?"

Later that night

As William lay in bed that night, his uncle's advice ran through his head. He had never considered that he was punishing Elizabeth, for since she had revealed her true feelings about him, he had been drowning in a river of regret—a river so deep that he could think of nothing beyond keeping his head above water.

Suddenly he pictured Elizabeth as she had looked that evening. She wore a lovely rose-coloured gown and the same shade of roses in her hair. While his aunt had played the pianoforte, she had sung "Barbara Allen" with a Scottish burr.

Amazed to learn that she had a beautiful voice, William had been equally amazed when Elizabeth sought his eyes as she sang. Now, however, he dismissed that as purely coincidental. After all, his uncle sat next to him on the sofa, so she was likely just looking in that direction.

Turning on his side, William clutched a pillow to his chest, trying to get comfortable. A few minutes later, he pulled another pillow over his head, for Elizabeth's song kept running through his mind. It did not help, however, and it was only after several hours of tossing and turning that he finally fell into a fitful sleep.

Chapter 27

Lambton
Three days later

As William came to the end of the main thoroughfare of Lambton and turned Zeus towards the foundlings' home a hundred yards away, he spied the elderly vicar of Kympton and his wife, Mrs. Moody, standing in front of it, conversing with the children milling about. The vicar was nearing five and sixty, and William smiled to see him bend down, pick up a ball and toss it back to the children with the energy of a much younger man. A few years ago, several parishioners had hinted that the vicar was past his prime and needed to be replaced, but William had not agreed. Moody had been the vicar at Kympton for nearly thirty years, having been appointed by George Darcy, and had baptised him. So, to him, Mr. Moody was practically part of the Darcy family.

Currently, in addition to his work at the church, Mr. Moody was ably handling much of the responsibility for the orphanage. In fact, the construction of the building three years past seemed to have reinvigorated the vicar and his wife, and they spent as much time there as possible. Both maintained that the children deserved to have elders who were quick with a hug and always ready to listen, even if they were related by concern and not blood.

As these thoughts went through William's head, Mrs. Moody spotted him and began to wave. That caused her husband to look up, and when he waved, the children followed suit. It brought a much-needed smile to William's face, and he kicked Zeus into a trot, arriving at the front gate in only seconds. Several boys ran to the picket fence, hoping to be the one selected to take his horse. There were two boys roughly eight to ten years old and another who looked to be about twelve. William nodded to the older, red-haired, freckle-faced boy.

"Colin, will you see that Zeus gets a rub-down and some water?"

"Yes, Mr. Darcy," Colin exclaimed proudly as he pushed through the gate and stepped up to take Zeus' reins. Then noting the sad expressions of the two who had not been chosen, he added, "Would you mind if Jack and Rudy rode Zeus while I take him to the barn, sir?"

William had no objections, but he did have words of warning. "I do not mind, as long as you take Zeus straight to the barn." To the younger boys he said, "Do you promise to sit perfectly still and let Colin help you down?"

The boys nodded enthusiastically, so William picked up first one and then the other, placing them on Zeus' back. He watched until they had gone several feet before turning his attention to the Moodys.

"I am sorry that I am late," he said, nodding to the couple as Mr. Moody bowed and Mrs. Moody dropped a curtsey. "My steward stopped me with some questions just as I started out the door."

"Oh, there is no need to apologise. We have enjoyed talking with the children while we waited," the vicar said. "But I imagine that you have much work still to do, so if you are ready, we can begin."

The Moodys turned to go inside the large, two-story building and William followed. They walked down a long hall with a myriad of children's voices filling the air from all the open classroom doors. When they passed one particular door, something caught William's eye, and he backed up to make certain what he had seen.

Across the room sat a lady who very much resembled Elizabeth. She was at a table with her back to the door, and several girls stood on either side of her, each diligently focused on whatever she held in her hands. From the bolts of cloth, pincushions and scissors on the table, he assumed that they were sewing. He observed for a few seconds before deciding that the idea of his wife being there was absurd. Subsequently, he shook his head and walked on, eventually catching up with the Moodys, who had stopped to wait at the end of the hall. They wore quizzical expressions.

"Mr. Darcy, you seem perplexed," Mrs. Moody said. "Is something the matter?"

"Oh, it is nothing. For a brief moment, I thought I saw Mrs. Darcy in a classroom."

"That *is* Mrs. Darcy. After meeting with the headmistress, Mrs. Samson, she volunteered to help the girls learn to sew. We assumed that you knew."

William did not want to appear ignorant. "She may have mentioned it, but I do not recall. Things have been hectic since I returned from London. Mrs. Darcy and I have often been separated by our duties."

Mrs. Moody smiled and nodded. "I understand. In any case, though this is her first class, all of the girls have admired her from her first visit. They all wished to take lessons, so we limited the classes to the older girls first. After all, they will be the first to marry."

"Now, Lovey," Mr. Moody broke in, addressing his wife with the endearment he always used instead of her given name, "Mr. Darcy is here to talk about the new building and not about sewing lessons." Then he addressed William. "If you will allow me, I can show you the drawing I spoke to you about."

William nodded, and with that, the vicar disappeared into the room on his left, quickly followed by his wife and his patron. Lying on a huge table was a hand-drawn diagram of the layout of the current building with the proposed addition.

"If we build the addition right beside this wall," Moody said, pointing to the plans, "we can remove the windows and insert doors in their places. The top floor of the addition will be living quarters, doubling the number of beds, and allowing us to better segregate the girls from the boys. The bottom will contain a larger kitchen and dining area. We need a bigger kitchen if we are to use it as a classroom to teach our children how to cook. The old kitchen and dining room in this building can then be converted into classrooms."

"It seems that you have planned capably," William replied. "If I may, I shall take this drawing and present it to my builder. If he has no objections, we can have the building plans drawn up. If the weather cooperates, we should be able to begin construction in the spring."

The vicar shook William's hand. "You have been so supportive of the home, and I thank you on behalf of all the children."

"It is the least I can do when you and Mrs. Moody give so much of yourself to make this endeavour a success. By the way, is Mrs. Samson available? I wish to get the monthly report while I am here—that is, if she is finished with it."

"Lovey, will you be so kind to ask Mrs. Samson if she has time to meet with Mr. Darcy?"

Instantly, Mrs. Moody headed toward the door; however, once she reached the hallway she stopped to ask, "Do you wish me to inform Mrs. Darcy that you are here?"

"No!" William said with more zeal than he meant to convey. Then he said more sedately, "I meant to say that I do not want to interrupt her lessons. I would rather you not mention my presence."

The older woman's expression was one of confusion. "As you wish, Mr. Darcy." Then she forced a smile. "If you wait here, I will return in a shake of a lamb's tail."

Being near the door, Mr. Moody moved to peek into the hallway, following his wife's progress. Sincerely he said, "I am blessed to have Lovey as my helpmate." Then he looked back at William. "And you are blessed to have Mrs. Darcy. She is not like most women of her station, but I am sure that you are aware of that. Other than your sainted mother, few women of wealth have such compassion for the poor. It is a tribute to your character that you chose her to marry. I am certain that your parents would have approved."

William flushed, not sure what to say, so he settled on a wan smile. If the vicar noticed his reluctance to praise Elizabeth, he did not mention it. Besides, all was quickly overshadowed by the return of Mrs. Moody with the news that Mrs. Samson would be delighted to meet with him immediately. Thus, with Mrs. Moody's company for propriety's sake, William went up the stairs to meet with the bookkeeper.

Finished with business an hour later, William left the building without seeking out Elizabeth. Rather than accompany her back to Pemberley, he wished to reflect on the fact that he knew nothing of her activities at the orphanage. His uncle's advice played repeatedly in his mind. To his credit, he had tried to interact more with Elizabeth after their talk, but he had not been successful. For now it seemed that she was in the habit of avoiding him as keenly as he had once avoided her.

And now that he thought about it, she had become especially reclusive since Georgiana had reappeared, even refusing the last two nights to join the others after dinner. As he pondered the implications of that, he made a new resolution.

I shall speak to Elizabeth the moment she returns from Lambton by one means or another!

London
Gracechurch Street
The Gardiners' residence

The front door had barely closed before Mrs. Gardiner enquired of her housekeeper, Mrs. Olds, if there were any letters. The servant replied that there was one and handed it to her. Noticing the handwriting, the lady of the house hurriedly opened it and began reading. Then she rushed to her husband's study, for Edward had remained home that afternoon to work on the household finances. He was startled when his door flew open and Madeline came in, speaking as excitedly as his sister Fanny.

"Oh, Edward! Jane is threatening to go to Pemberley! She is not at all satisfied that Lizzy is well and tells me that she has spoken to Mr. Bingley about escorting her and Fanny to Derbyshire. Now that would be a disaster!"

Edward Gardiner removed his spectacles, rubbing his nose tiredly. "I thought that my reply to my Brother Bennet's letter would have eased everyone's suspicions, but I should have known Thomas would not share it with the rest of the family. He was probably afraid that Fanny would ask to read all of it. In hindsight, I should have thought to have you write Jane."

"In the last letter from Lizzy, she appeared content, but I could read the unhappiness between the lines. She was not in high spirits, so I can only surmise that they have not worked out their problems—at least not to her satisfaction. I pray continually that Mr. Darcy will forgive her and that they shall reconcile, at least as much as possible."

"I do as well, but Mr. Darcy seems a good man, and I think him more hurt than revengeful. And, given time, I believe he will forgive and forget. But should Fanny, Thomas or Jane call on Lizzy now, especially with her sisters in tow, all sensibility could be lost in the melee."

"I agree."

"So, you must write to Jane and tell her that you have been in touch with Lizzy and know for a fact that all is well. Advise her not to visit Pemberley until she is invited or else she will be interfering with a couple very occupied with the business of being newlyweds. Perhaps that will embarrass her enough to put off the notion."

"Perhaps." His wife sighed. "But Jane will not be held off for long, if Lizzy does not convince her that all is well. For now, however, a postponement is the best we can hope for.

"I fear you are right."

Pemberley
That afternoon

By chance, as William travelled the road from Lambton to Pemberley, he encountered the very man who had built the original orphanage. Mr. Arrington just happened to be in Lambton visiting his mother and, saying that it was no imposition, he accompanied William back to Pemberley to look over the crude drawing for the new addition. Finding the idea feasible, Mr. Arrington and

William concluded their meeting, and William was seeing him to the door just as Elizabeth came down the grand staircase. While he had been sequestered in his study with Arrington, she had returned from Lambton, had tea with Olivia and was preparing to leave again. Elizabeth stopped abruptly at the sight of her husband and the stranger, waiting as William came over to take her hand and lead her forward.

"Elizabeth, this is Mr. Arrington, the man who built the orphanage in Lambton. He will also be building the new addition in the spring." Addressing Arrington, he added, "Mr. Arrington, my wife, Elizabeth Darcy."

Arrington bowed as Elizabeth curtseyed.

"You did an excellent job with the foundlings' home," Elizabeth said. "I have never seen a finer institute for children. Some elements look more like a home than an orphanage— the large activity room, for example, with all the windows and window seats and the cushioned benches in the kitchen."

"While I cannot take credit for the cushions, we tried to make it comfortable as well as functional."

"And you succeeded admirably."

"Thank you, Mrs. Darcy." Then Arrington shook William's hand. "I shall leave you now. I return to London in the morning, and I wish to spend the rest of this day with Mother. I will contact you the first part of February, after I have finished the specifications."

"Excellent."

Placing his hat on his head and giving it a pat, Arrington nodded and went out the door. William and Elizabeth moved to the front entrance to watch him mount his horse, raise a hand in farewell and gallop down the front drive. For a long time neither moved nor spoke.

Finally, Elizabeth said with forced cheeriness, "I am afraid that I must be going, too, if I am to check on Mrs. Becker and be home before dark."

"May I ride with you? I need to inspect the new bridge, and with my escort, you will not need a footman."

Elizabeth was surprised that he had offered. "If that is your wish."

William gave orders to retrieve his stallion and her mare, and as they waited for the horses, the silence between them grew awkward. Elizabeth felt his eyes upon her, so she boldly glanced in his direction. His blue eyes were piercing as he gazed steadily at her. Unable to endure his inspection, Elizabeth closed her eyes and swayed a bit.

His hand clasped her elbow, making her shiver. "Elizabeth, are you well? Perhaps you should postpone your visit today. Surely tomorrow will be soon enough to check on Mrs. Becker."

"I am well, I assure you." She wiped a faint bead of perspiration from her brow. "It is just that this outfit is unbearably hot, that is all."

William's eyes were drawn to the riding habit, travelling slowly down her body and back again. The habit was dark burgundy with a fanciful, forest-green, leather trim around the collar, the neck and the bottom of the sleeves. Unlike most of her gowns, it fit like a glove from her generous breasts to her tiny waist, with the skirt hugging her hips without flaring until it reached her thighs. She wore a pair of green-leather boots and a jaunty, three-cornered hat, also in green, topped with two pheasant feathers. William slipped a finger under his cravat to loosen it. It was getting warm!

Just at that point, a groom rode around the house, leading Zeus and Phoebe. William stepped in front of a footman who was preparing to help Elizabeth onto her mare. Placing his hands on either side of her waist, William effortlessly lifted her into the side-saddle. Not meeting her eye, he positioned her leg around the top of the saddle and straightened out her skirts. Once he was satisfied, he handed her the reins.

"There, you are set."

He put one foot in a stirrup and swung a long leg over Zeus. "Tell Mrs. Reynolds that we are off to visit a tenant," William said to the nearest footman.

"Yes, sir, Mr. Darcy!" a nervous, young footman replied. "Right away."

William almost chuckled as the young man tripped over his feet in a rush to go up the steps. Then he addressed Elizabeth, "Shall we be off, then?"

At her nod, he kicked Zeus into a trot, and she followed suit with Phoebe; however, as they reached the end of the road and began to cross a field, both horses broke into a gallop. As it was too hard to talk, the entire trip to the Beckers was spent in silence. Once at the tenants' house, William dismounted and then helped Elizabeth to the ground just as the door opened, and Mrs. Becker slowly walked onto the small porch.

William greeted her, doffing his hat and bowing slightly, "Mrs. Becker, I hope you are well."

The woman smiled tiredly. "Thank you for enquiring, sir. I am as well as can be at this point."

Seeing that no one else appeared, Elizabeth asked, "Are you alone? I expected Mazie to rush out." Her expression darkened. "And where is the maid?"

"Tom is at the bridge, and Mazie is picking gooseberries with the maid."

Elizabeth seemed miffed. "I sent her to see after you, not pick berries."

"Please do not be angry, Mrs. Darcy. Mazie has begged for a gooseberry pie for weeks, so I asked Jessie to help her pick the berries." She pointed to a rise on the left. "They are just over that ridge."

William interrupted their talk as he replaced his hat. "I am afraid that I must go on to the bridge, Elizabeth. After I am done there, I shall come back to escort you home." He touched the rim of his hat. "Mrs. Becker."

The tenant watched raptly as William swung into the saddle effortlessly, reined Zeus to the right and galloped off.

"My Tom always says that no one sits a horse like Mr. Darcy. It is a pure pleasure to watch him ride. He makes it seem effortless."

"Yes. I dare say that my husband is a talented horseman," Elizabeth answered, as she, too, watched him leave. Then she took Annie Becker's arm. "Come! Let us go inside. You must long to sit down."

At the bridge site, William found Mr. Sturgis, Tom Becker and the other tenant who relied on the bridge, Mr. Hanson. They were all gathered on a bank underneath the partially framed structure. As he dismounted and walked under it to join them, William was surprised to hear of his steward's displeasure with the project.

"No, no. This will never do! Those boards are bending under the weight! That is not what I ordered," he said, pointing to a certain section. "They must be thicker. And we must have more nails in these supporting timbers."

Tom Becker volunteered, "I can ride into Lambton for more nails, and while I am there, inform the sawmill that the support boards were not thick enough and must be re-cut."

Everyone looked to William to make the decision. "That would be helpful, if you think you can ride to Lambton and back by dark. At the least, that will insure that the boards are on order. I fear it will take several weeks to make enough to replace those that are insufficient."

"I am certain that I can be back before nightfall, sir," Becker answered. Then he scurried up the bank to find his horse.

"Mr. Darcy, would you and Mr. Sturgis consider looking over a field on the far side of my land before you leave? It has begun to stand water, and my attempts to reroute it with ditches have not succeeded."

Knowing that his steward had been up since dawn, William looked to him. "Are you too weary, Mr. Sturgis, or would you rather wait until tomorrow?"

"I am not too tired to give an opinion," Sturgis answered.

"Then show us the field, Mr. Hanson."

As Tom Becker rode toward Lambton, he planned to stop by his house, for it was in the same direction. And, with the baby due at any time, he wanted Annie to know where he would be.

At the Beckers' house, the maid and Mazie were returning with a pan full of gooseberries. Hearing a noise, Elizabeth told Annie Becker to sit still and got up to see who was outside. As she went out the door, Mazie ran to give her a hug and then hurried past her to show her mother the bounty. Jessie lingered behind, for upon seeing Mrs. Darcy, she had a request.

"Since you are here now, would it be possible for me to return to Pemberley early, Mrs. Darcy? I wish to give Mrs. Reynolds a list of things we really need here—things such as meal and flour. That is, if you do not mind."

"Of course not. How did you get here? A carriage or a horse?"

"A horse, ma'am. Mr. Miller, the coachman, lent me one so that I do not have to wait for someone to drive me. I ride very well, so it was the best choice for me."

"Then you had better be off!" Elizabeth declared with a smile. Jessie nodded and turned to hurry to the barn. Elizabeth called after her, "Oh, and ask Mrs. Reynolds to send more breads and sweets if Mrs. Lantrip baked today."

"Yes, ma'am, I will!" Jessie called over her shoulder. "Please tell Mazie and Mrs. Becker I will be back tomorrow."

Elizabeth entered the house to find that Mazie had poured the pan of gooseberries on the kitchen table where they had immediately rolled off. They were now covering the floor, and Mrs. Becker was on her knees trying to gather them.

"Oh, Mrs. Becker! Please do not worry about those. I shall sweep them up." She glanced anxiously at Mazie, who stood with her mouth open in shock. "Mazie, fetch me the broom."

As Mazie ran off, her mother moaned loudly and water spread in a circle around her. Elizabeth knew what that meant! Annie's water had broken, and the baby was coming. Before she had time to react though, Tom Becker came through the door. Assessing the scene, he ran to help his wife to her feet. A hard labour pain caused Annie to cry and bend over, holding her belly. Mazie began to cry.

"Mr. Becker, it is up to you to fetch the midwife. Please take Mazie with you, and I shall make your wife comfortable until you return."

He hesitated until his wife cried, "Do as she says, Tom!" Instantly, he was out the door with Mazie in his arms, screaming for her mother.

"It is best if Mazie is with him, for you need to concentrate on yourself," Elizabeth said as she put an arm around the expectant mother. "Come, I want to get you out of these wet clothes and into bed."

By the time William and Mr. Sturgis had finished inspecting Mr. Hanson's property and suggestions had been made for the standing water, it was late. Tom Becker had not yet returned, so William dismissed Sturgis, who headed straight back to Pemberley, while he went toward the Beckers' house to retrieve Elizabeth. Once there, a strange feeling came over him as he tied Zeus to a post near the front door. No one had come out to greet him, and it was eerily silent. Then a scream filled the hush. One word flew from his lips.

"Elizabeth!"

Hastening inside the cabin, William instantly realised that it was Mrs. Becker's cry he had heard. The door of the Becker's bedroom was partly open, and he could hear Elizabeth speaking calmly but firmly to her. He dared not look in the door, for fear of invading the woman's privacy.

"Remember, breathe deeply and slowly! That is it! Now, let your breath out very slowly," Elizabeth was saying. "You are doing well." He heard the shuffling of feet. "Let me see who has arrived. I shall be right back."

Suddenly, she was before him. "William, thank God! Mr. Becker and Mazie have gone for the midwife, but I need help now."

Elizabeth rushed to a nearby basket and picked up something white. As she held it up, he noted that it looked like what she had on—an apron that covered her chest, arms and lap. Holding it out, she ordered, "Put this on."

Without hesitation, William slipped it over his head, and as she rushed behind him to tie the strings, she almost chuckled. "It is too small, but it shall have to do." Then she began to give more instructions. "Draw some water and put it on the stove, then take several towels from that basket." She pointed to one on the floor. "Make several towels into a soft bed on the table; you will be washing the baby after he is born."

William froze. "But... but the midwife—"

"The midwife will not arrive in time. The baby is coming now!"

As quickly as Elizabeth had appeared, she vanished. Still in disbelief, William grabbed the bucket and headed to the well. As he pumped the water, he considered how scared he was and, consequently, how frightened Elizabeth must be. After all, he was simply heating water; she was delivering a baby.

Once in the kitchen again, he poured the water into a large kettle and set it on the stove. He stoked the waning fire beneath it, and upon seeing how little wood was left to burn, added more. Amid cries of pain so severe that they caused him to cringe, William placed several towels on the table, creating a bed. It seemed forever before the water was warm, but just as Mrs. Becker's cries intensified, coming closer together, he was able to fill a bowl and set it on the table next to the towels. Pleased to have accomplished his tasks, a piercing cry filled the house causing William to hold his breath. It was followed by an eerie silence before Elizabeth rushed into the room with a bundle in her arms. As she opened the blanket he could see the child was not moving and his skin was gray.

"He is not breathing!" Elizabeth said as loudly as she dared in a panicked voice. She lay him down on the towels and ran a finger in his mouth to clear anything that might be obstructing his throat.

"My hands are too slippery!" she protested, her voice breaking. "Pick him up by his heels, but be careful not to drop him when I strike him on the back."

Without questioning, William did as she asked. The moment Elizabeth struck the baby between the shoulder blades, he began to wail. Smiling as tears streamed down her face, she looked at William. Unsurprised at the relief in his face, she took a deep breath and resumed the business at hand.

"I must attend to Mrs. Becker."

"How is she faring?"

"She is doing well, but I must inform her that the baby is perfectly fine—all ten toes and fingers," Elizabeth was smiling now. "It is up to you to wash him whilst I finish up. Keep one hand on him at all times, do not let him roll off the table."

William could not stop smiling as the boy howled. "Hush," he said, soothing the child. "You are part of the world now, young man. No need to keep protesting the abrupt removal from your sanctuary. Besides, the worst of it is over." The baby began to calm a little as he listened to William's deep baritone. "You should know that I have been enlisted to give you a bath. And, while I am no expert at washing babies, the warm water should make you feel a lot better." As William began the washing, the baby's eyes went wide, and his cries became whimpers. "I told you that you would like it."

Just at that second the front door flew open, banging against the wall. It scared the baby, and he began to cry louder than before. Tom Becker was the first to rush inside, followed by the midwife and then Mazie. Tom froze at the sight of his son, but seeing that the baby was well, the midwife rushed past him into the bedroom.

"My wife?" he asked William.

"Mrs. Darcy says that she is doing well."

Mazie, not as reticent as her father, ran to push a chair to the table and climbed onto it. By the time her father joined her at the table, William was wrapping the crying boy in a clean towel.

When at last he handed the child to his father, Mazie challenged him, "Did you hurt him?" she said protectively. "It is not nice to hurt babies."

"Do not be rude, Mazie," her father admonished. "Mr. Darcy did nothing to your brother. He cries because he is hungry." Then he smiled at William. "Thank you does not begin to convey all that I feel, Mr. Darcy. I do not know what we would have done—"

William sought no praise, so he held up a hand to stop him. "I did very little. If you want to praise anyone, then it should be Mrs. Darcy. She delivered your son. I merely bathed him."

Becker looked at the child in his arms. "You picked a fine woman to wed, if I am allowed to say so, sir. Mrs. Darcy has been a blessing to so many." Then he went toward the bedroom. "Come, Mazie. Let us take the baby to your mother. I just imagine she would like to see how he looks all cleaned up. And your brother is hungry."

"Can he have a biscuit? I saved him one of mine," Mazie said as they entered the room.

Her question made William smile and shake his head. Then noting the mess left in the kitchen, including the gooseberries still covering the floor, he began to straighten up. He had just finished and was rolling down his cuffs, when Elizabeth reappeared. Untying her soiled apron, she noticed that William still wore his.

Pursing her lips to keep from smiling, she said, "Here, let me help you out of that." William turned his back and she untied the apron, then he pulled it over his head. Taking it, Elizabeth threw it on top of a basket of dirty clothes. "Jessie will wash everything tomorrow, I am sure."

"Jessie?"

"The maid I lent to Mrs. Becker," Elizabeth said matter-of-factly.

"I see," William said, looking about teasingly. "And where exactly is she?"

"Unfortunately, I sent her back to the manor before the baby decided to be born. She wished to speak to Mrs. Reynolds about a few things that the Beckers needed."

"May I ask you another question?

"Certainly."

"How did you learn to be a midwife?"

Elizabeth laughed self-consciously. "I am no midwife. Until today, I had never brought a baby into the world. Well, not alone."

"Then, how—"

"In this case, I had no choice, but I confess that when I was a great deal younger, I helped Mrs. Harris deliver a tenant's child. Mrs. Harris was the closest thing that Meryton had to an apothecary until I was almost fifteen. She lived alone in the woods near Longbourn, and she had a cure for anything that ailed you. In addition, she delivered all the babies for miles around. She never asked a farthing for her services, so she was especially popular among the poor. I was fascinated with her abilities and, against my mother's warnings, by the age of ten, I spent my mornings following her about. My parents thought that I was merely taking walks."

"But to deliver a baby? It is unheard of for an unmarried woman to watch such a thing, much less a mere girl."

"So it is. But you must realise that my first experience was unplanned. Mrs. Harris and I were at a tenant's cottage when a woman's baby decided to be born during a thunderstorm. With no way to leave, I was stuck for the duration. And with no one else to help her, Miss Harris enlisted my services."

"Were you not afraid?"

"I was, but Mrs. Harris never got ruffled, and she taught me to stay calm." Elizabeth looked off, as though recalling the incident. "I suppose that I did not want to disappoint her, so I pretended bravery that I certainly did not feel. Eventually, with practice, I became less fearful. Before she died, she said that I should consider taking her place." Chuckling, she added, "Can you imagine me as Meryton's apothecary?"

"After tonight, I can imagine just that."

Elizabeth laughed. "Given time, you will learn the folly of your words."

"I suppose we could debate that forever, but we have a more pressing problem."

"Oh?"

"If you do not fancy sleeping in the barn, we must leave now. The sun is near to setting, and the wind has picked up. If it rains, darkness will come earlier."

"I had not thought of that. There is barely enough room for the family, and the midwife in here. Just let me see if everything is still well, and if so, we can leave."

"I shall go to the barn to retrieve our horses."

Elizabeth watched until William was out the door, then she joined the Beckers and the midwife to see how Annie was faring and to admire the baby once more.

When Elizabeth finally exited the house, William was holding a hand over his brow, shielding his eyes from the sun as he scanned the sky in the direction of Pemberley. Elizabeth followed his gaze to a group of ominous black clouds over their home. The contrast between the sunlight where they were and the storm brewing was astounding. Suddenly, a large bolt of lightning flew out of one huge black cloud, striking the earth below.

William began counting. "One... two... three... four... fi—" Before he finished the last word, a thunderous rumble filled the air. "The storm is less than a mile away. We cannot ride all the way to Pemberley, but I think we can take shelter in the cottage." Without waiting for agreement, he untied Phoebe and helped Elizabeth into the saddle. Then he mounted Zeus.

"Are you fearless enough to keep up with me?" He said with a smirk.

Elizabeth nodded. "Then hold on for dear life!"

William was off in a flash, with Phoebe instinctively following the stallion without any prompting from Elizabeth. It took all her strength to hang on to the reins as the little mare galloped for all she was worth, trying to catch Zeus. Rain began coming down in sheets, whipped by the wind, just as the brick house came into view. Finally gaining the yard, William headed straight for the shed that served as a barn. Jumping off Zeus, it took all his effort to open the door against the wind. But once that was accomplished, he motioned for Elizabeth to go in before pulling Zeus in behind her.

They were soaked to the bone, and as William pulled the saddles from their mounts and led them to a stall, Elizabeth began to shiver. Once he was done with the horses, William closed the front door and pulled Elizabeth toward the door on the side next to the house.

"You did not lock the door."

"No. There is nothing here but hay and horses. And I do not think anyone would be foolish enough to steal Pemberley's horses—not unless they wish to hang." William had taken off his hat and slapped it on his leg. "We are both soaked to the skin. Come, let us get inside the house and dry off."

He started to move, but Elizabeth grabbed his arm. "Wait! What about the person who—" William's brow furrowed in confusion. "Someone could be… we could be intruding," Elizabeth stammered earnestly.

"I do not take your meaning. Other than the few occasions when I have stayed here, this house has been unoccupied since Mother died."

Elizabeth rocked back on her heels. "But, you—I thought." Suddenly, she went silent.

"Look! The rain has let up a bit. We should get inside while we can."

The cottage

The downpour intensified just before William and Elizabeth reached the porch and the storm began blowing the rain crosswise. Lightning struck a tree nearby, causing a limb to fall. Since the roof of the porch was not large enough to protect them, William endeavoured to shield Elizabeth by pressing her closer to the door and covering her with his body while he tried the key. It seemed to take forever to unlock the door.

"I have it!" he shouted above another blast of thunder.

Suddenly the door flew open and Elizabeth nearly fell into the house. Fortunately William grabbed her arm in time to steady her. Unable to see well in the darkness, the only thing she could recognise was the outline of a large table in the middle of the room.

"Stand here until I light a candle," William instructed.

Elizabeth's eyes followed William's dark figure as he moved toward a piece of furniture standing against the wall. She heard a drawer open and the sounds of searching inside it. Directly, a tinderbox was placed on the table, and sparks began to fly as a piece of steel was struck with a flint. Almost immediately a flame began and two chamber candlesticks [14] were instantly pulled from a shelf overhead and lit. Then the fire in the tinderbox was smothered with the damper before being placed back in the drawer. Placing one candlestick in the middle of the table, William took the other and headed toward the hall.

"Come. You must get out of those wet clothes."

Elizabeth followed him into the bedroom, very conscious of the fact that she had nothing to wear once her clothes were removed. William set the candle on top of the fireplace mantle and walked over to a panelled wall. Pushing on a particular spot caused two doors to pop open, exposing a long, narrow closet. Inside it, at one end, stood a tall, slim chest with six drawers.

"Although I leave clothes here on occasion, I fear there are none here at present. However, there should be a blanket or perhaps a sheet or two in this chest if my memory serves. In the winter, there are usually quilts as well."

From the bottom drawer, William withdrew a thin blanket, bringing it up to his nose for a sniff. "It still smells clean, though it was likely placed in this chest after last hunting season." He held it out to her. "I fear it will have to do."

Elizabeth took the offering. "Thank you."

Then he made a twirling motion with his finger. "Turn around and I shall undo your buttons for you."

She did as he asked, wondering all the while he worked if he was as affected by her nearness as she was with his. Shaking like a leaf by the time he

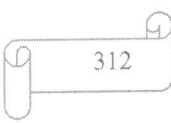

was done, Elizabeth was surprised to turn around and find him gone.

Then from the kitchen he called, "Remind me to tell Mrs. Reynolds to replenish the blankets and sheets and to send two quilts. If someone is stranded here in the future, they would be useful."

He said nothing more as she undressed, so when she was down to her chemise, which was barely damp, she laid her clothes on the only chair in the room, wrapped the blanket around herself and sat down on the end of the bed.

Truth be told, Elizabeth's mind was awhirl with one goal. She felt that God, in His wisdom, had provided the storm to bring them together and it was up to her to make the most of it.

Suddenly, William stepped back in the room carrying a box of wood, which he set near the hearth. Instantly, he crouched in order to add it to the fire. He had divested himself of his coat, waistcoat and cravat and rolled up his sleeves. A perfect specimen of manly beauty, the dark hair on his chiselled chest was visible at the top of his partially unbuttoned shirt. Elizabeth wondered if he had undone the buttons with the aim of taking the shirt off, but had gotten distracted. Whatever the reason, she was grateful for the tantalising view. All at once, a picture of him with shirt open, as he had been in London, came to mind, and a tingling sensation began deep inside her. The sensation was so unsettling that she took two deep breaths to calm herself. It did not help.

"You should be in bed." His voice brought her back to the present.

"My hair is damp. Before I go to bed, I need to let it down and dry it. Else I am apt to come down with a sore throat."

Still squatting, William twisted on his heels to look at her. Then he stood and went to the chest again. "There may be a towel left in here." He opened a drawer. "Yes, here are two." Pulling them both out, he walked to where she sat. "With hair as thick as yours, you may need both."

Elizabeth tried to remove the pins from her hair with one hand while holding the blanket securely with the other. Seeing her struggle, William stayed her hand.

"Stop, Elizabeth. You are only tangling your hair. Let me remove the pins."

Suddenly, he was close—so close she could smell sandalwood and soap. And while his fingertips made soft impressions in her hair, Elizabeth closed her eyes at the sheer pleasure of his touch. Unbidden, a deep sigh slipped from her throat. If William heard, he did not react, and soon afterward all the pins were on the bed. Then grabbing the nearest towel, he began to squeeze sections of her hair with it.

"One of Georgiana's governesses said that hair should be blotted dry, never rubbed. She contended that rubbing the hair breaks the strands."

"So I could have avoided all these curls simply by drying it differently?" Elizabeth teased.

"You mistake my meaning. Your hair is very curly. No amount of blotting will cause it to be less so. This will just keep it from breaking."

"Then I suppose I am to be burdened with this wild hair forever."

William stopped what he was doing, his mien sombre. "Your hair is lovely just as it is. Never change it." Handing her the towel, he walked out of the room.

Not sure if she had angered him, Elizabeth continued to dry her hair the way he had instructed. Presently he returned with one of the dining room chairs, which he set in front of the fire.

"Since your clothes are occupying that chair, I thought that you might want to sit in this one to dry your hair."

Elizabeth did as he proposed and William disappeared. For a time, the sounds of pots and pans being moved about in the kitchen made her wonder what he was up to. But just when she had decided to go look, William appeared with a single cup of tea.

"There was a small amount of tea left in the cupboard and I made this for you. I fear there are no biscuits, other than a few that have seen better days."

"I am not that hungry, truly. I took a biscuit at the Beckers before we left. In hindsight, perhaps I should have taken more." Seeing that there was only one cup of tea, she added, "Is there only enough for one?"

"Yes, but I found half a bottle of brandy, so I drank a glass of that."

"Still, the tea would warm you. Can we not share?"

"I assure you that the brandy has warmed me enough. Please drink your tea before it gets cold."

Resigned, Elizabeth took a sip of the hot liquid. "This is so comforting," she said. "Thank you." Closing her eyes with the next sip, she was surprised upon opening them to find that he had not moved and was watching her.

Upon being discovered, William quickly busied himself by seeing to the fire. Then stepping back to survey the room, his gaze fell on Elizabeth's bare feet. Kneeling before her on the rug, he took one of her feet in his hands.

"My Lord, Elizabeth, your feet are freezing."

As he massaged one foot and then the other, her breath hitched with each stroke of his talented hands. Totally unaware of her predicament, William finished his ministrations and walked over to the bed. There he pulled the counterpane and sheet back before fluffing the pillows and placing them against the headboard.

"The room should stay warm enough now. You should get into bed."

Not wishing to argue, Elizabeth walked to where he stood, regarded the bed, and then looked innocently up at William as she dropped the blanket. That her deed had the desired effect was evidenced by his loud intake of breath.

"Please, Elizabeth! Do not make this any harder than it is." He went past her toward the door.

She went after him, clad only in her thin chemise. "Do you intend to punish me forever for my foolishness?"

Already at the door, he stopped dead still, gripping both sides of the doorframe. "Is that what you think this is all about?"

"How can I think any differently?"

He turned to face her then, his eyes sadder than she had ever seen them. "It has never been about punishing you. Though I confess that I think true punishment is to be forced to pretend feelings for someone you loathe. I appreciate that you are willing to do your duty, even if your heart is untouched, but I would rather wait in the hope that, with time, you might come to care for me just a little. Otherwise, it would mean no more to me than a tryst with a complete stranger."

"You are so mistaken, William. I am not trying to do my duty." Her voice broke as she continued, "I truly want to be your wife, but only because I love you."

"Only days ago, you said that you loathed the very sight of me. In truth, from the very beginning of our marriage, you made it clear that you despised my company though I refused to see it. I find it inconceivable that upon coming to Pemberley you suddenly realised that I was not a degenerate and fell madly in love with me."

She dropped her head. "I deserve that, for God knows that you have no idea why I acted as I did. You may not even believe me if I tell you. I can hardly believe it myself."

"Suppose you let me be the judge of that."

She met his questioning eyes, swallowing hard. "The truth is that I never hated you. I had convinced myself that I did, but after Colonel Fitzwilliam pulled the veil from my eyes regarding Andrew, the truth stared me in the face."

"And what truth is that?" he ventured guardedly.

"The truth that I fell under your spell from almost the minute we met." She strangled a fierce tide of feeling that welled up within her to continue. "Is it so hard to believe that I fell in love with you? Is it so inconceivable that I found you handsome and desired your good opinion from the start?"

"Hmmm." That he did not believe her was obvious.

"But you stayed true to your upbringing and soon dashed my hopes. You even stopped joining my conversations with Mr. Bingley and debating your point of view, though you sat close enough to listen to my every word. I assumed you were afraid that you might have raised my expectations. You were not the first man of your sphere to slight me. And your slight was no worse than the others, except that, with you, I had allowed myself a ray of hope." She forced a smile. "In order to nurse my wounded pride, I began finding fault with you and listening to Andrew's lies. It was easy enough to imagine that you were the villain."

"I confess that I intended to regard you as any other woman not of my circle— someone to avoid." Unwittingly, William took a step forward. "Except that from the beginning, I felt a bond with you that I had never felt with any woman before—a pull on my heart, if you will. You were so lively and intelligent, as well as beautiful, that I was drawn like the proverbial moth to a flame. It was after I realised that I might be falling in love with you that I began to refrain from engaging you in conversation."

"No doubt by then Miss Bingley had regaled you with descriptions of my family and the fact that I had no connections and no dowry."

William's expression became contrite as he moved even closer. "Unfortunately, you are correct. To be honest, it was only after I returned to Netherfield that I concluded that your character was far more significant than your family, your connections or your dowry."

"Lack of a dowry, you mean," Elizabeth murmured.

"Your dowry is your character, Elizabeth," he said solemnly. "And that is worth more than gold." He reached out to take her hands. "But if you want the complete truth, what kept me from offering for you was my fear that marriage to me would ruin your life. You seemed so very joyful just as you were, and given the burden of my responsibilities, my family's wishes and the expectations of society, I looked upon an offer from me as a fate worse than death for someone like you. It was only after Andrew's compromise that I felt that might not be the case."

As tears rolled down her face, Elizabeth brought their hands to her heart. "How odd that you should say that, for in these past few weeks, I have learned that not being your wife is what I consider a fate worse than death."

All restraint crumbled. William stepped forward and tenderly cradled the face of the woman who was the embodiment of all that he had ever desired.

"Oh, my beautiful Elizabeth, what a muddle we both have made by trying to guess what the other was thinking!"

"Then let there be no more guessing. Let us open our hearts to each other."

His mouth captured hers in a fierce kiss as strong arms crushed her to his body. A low groan escaped him as his hands moved down her back to clasp her hips and press them close against the evidence of his desire.

William began teasing Elizabeth's lips to part with his tongue and they did. With each kiss that followed, he plunged her deeper under his spell. In a daze, she barely noticed as his hand slid down her body until it reached the edge of her thin chemise near her thighs. Grasping it, he brought it up and over her head in one smooth motion, breaking their kiss to accomplish the task.

Then breathing heavily, he stepped back to admire her, his eyes ablaze with desire and need. Under his examination, Elizabeth felt vulnerable but refused to shy away, for she wished to fulfil his every fantasy. Suddenly, William was kissing her hungrily once more and, picking her up effortlessly, he carried her to the bed. He broke their kiss to stare into her eyes, then kissed her tenderly and laid her on the mattress. Next, he sat on the edge of the bed and began to undress.

He was so powerfully built, so firm and muscular, that Elizabeth could not look away until he began removing his breeches. With a flick of the sheets, he was in bed with her, pulling her closer and, in one smooth movement, he positioned himself above her. The feel of his hard body pressed into hers was incredibly arousing and the passion inside that had burned so many days unrequited turned into a blaze.

William's lips brushed softly from her mouth to the sensitive spot just below her ear before continuing down her neck. Reaching her shoulder, he nuzzled the soft skin there before placing kisses along her collarbone to her bosom. Elizabeth's breath was becoming as laboured as his, and she moaned aloud when one hand cradled a generous breast, palming it gently before capturing it with his mouth. The centre hardened and he gently nipped it. Writhing with desire, Elizabeth ran her hands into his hair to pull him closer.

"Love me, Will," she said breathlessly.

"Are you ready to be mine for all eternity?"

"Truly, I am. I love you so much."

Within minutes they were joined, the two becoming one flesh in a dance as old as time. The slight flinch of pain that Elizabeth experienced was swiftly forgotten in the bliss of being one with the man she loved with all her heart. Encouraged by her words of love, William kept up a steady cadence and soon the first waves of ecstasy began to wash over her. They had waited for this moment for so long that it took little effort to reach the pinnacle of satisfaction and, as she cried out his name, William was unable to hold back a second longer and joined her in paradise.

Lying in her arms as his breath returned to normal, William lifted his head to look into her eyes. Stunned to find tears rolling down her cheeks, he began apologising. "Forgive me. I never meant to hurt you."

She cupped his face. "No, Will! You did not hurt me." Lifting her head from the pillow to kiss him softly, she then lay back down. "It is just that I have never experienced such joy before."

His concern quickly dissipated, and he smiled crookedly. "I have never been this happy before, Elizabeth. But are you certain that I did not hurt you? Can I fetch you a bit of brandy? You have only to ask."

"I am very certain. I need nothing except for you to recover so we may do that again." She smiled cheekily. "After all, how shall we become proficient without ample practice?"

Now giddy with joy, William tried not to chuckle as he looked at her adoringly. "What makes you think that I need time to recover?"

"I was told that once a man is spent, once he… you know. Then he will most likely return to his room in order to recover. And I heard that most men do not visit their wife more than once a night, some even less frequently."

"I believe, my love, that you have been misinformed—at least in regards to me. For one thing, I intend to share your bed and, more often than not, I will want you more than once a night… *every* night. Of that you may be certain."

"You will hear no objections from me, Will Darcy. I have wanted you far too long to ever turn you away from my bed." She brought his mouth to hers in a fierce kiss.

William's passion was reawakened and his voice was hoarse as he pulled back to say, "Should you ever desire me, Elizabeth, you have only to say so."

"I desire you," she murmured.

She did not have to say it twice. And this time as they made love, they took their time for, having discovered the pleasures of being married, they wished to savour the benefits for as long as possible.

The next morning

A loud thumping on the front door brought William out of a deep slumber. Abruptly sitting up, where he was and what had transpired the night before came rushing to mind and he grinned ridiculously. Elizabeth, too, was starting to rouse, but he kissed her and slipped out of the bed and into his breeches, fastening the buttons as he stumbled toward the bedroom door. Before opening it, he looked back at her. She was now sitting up, rubbing her eyes, and oblivious to the fact that she was naked. He pursed his lips to keep from smiling.

Suddenly aware, Elizabeth blushed as she pulled the sheet up to cover herself. "What is happening?" she asked sleepily.

"Someone is at the door. Stay in bed and keep warm. I shall see who it is and then put more wood on the fire." She nodded and lay back down as he closed the door.

Upon reaching the entrance, he looked through one of the side panels to see his uncle pacing on the portico and his groundskeeper, Mr. Farrow, still astride a horse behind him.

I should have known they would look for us this morning.

Looking thoroughly dishevelled, he turned the key, unlocking the door, and swung it wide open.

"Here you are," Joseph Fitzwilliam said, smiling to himself at his nephew's appearance. "Livy said you might be here."

"How would—"

"Elizabeth told her about this place." William nodded absently. "Are you going to leave me standing out here?"

Stepping aside, William watched as his uncle picked up two baskets at his feet and walked past him. At the closed bedroom door, Joseph smiled before turning to go into the kitchen. There, he placed the baskets on the table.

"Mrs. Reynolds sent food and wine for fear that you had not eaten. The other basket contains clean clothes, lest you were soaked in the storm."

"That woman is a saint," William said sombrely. Then his face became quizzical. "What on earth possessed you to come out so early? It is barely light."

"I wanted to thwart Georgiana, for it was her intention to see if this is where you spent the night."

"Why would she do that?"

"Let us just say that she was livid when you did not return last night. She tried to blame Elizabeth—said that she was the reason you were caught in the storm and that she had only brought you bad luck since your marriage—that kind of balderdash."

"That is preposterous!"

"Of course, it is. When no one agreed with her, Georgiana tried to organise a group to search for you. Mrs. Reynolds did not want to send anyone out in a storm of that magnitude. She was of the opinion that you would not appreciate her doing so, and that you were clever enough to find shelter somewhere on your own estate.

"When I sided with Mrs. Reynolds, Georgiana became angrier. Seeing that she was out-numbered, she agreed to wait until morning. When we assembled at dawn, Olivia mentioned this cottage as a possible safe-haven, saying that Elizabeth had spoken of it. That caused a new round of Georgiana's railings, saying that this was her mother's cottage and Elizabeth had no right to be here."

William sighed heavily. "I shall speak to her. I will not have her talking about Elizabeth in that manner."

"I did not think you would appreciate her attack on your wife. That is why I would not allow her to ride with us. Two footmen went to check with the Beckers, to see if you were still there, and Mr. Farrow and I came here. I had a strange feeling that we would find you here, and I did not want anyone invading your privacy." Joseph chuckled. "Or I should say anyone but me."

William smiled as he glanced to the bedroom door. "You are not invading *our* privacy."

"Then Elizabeth *is* here as well. Thank God! Olivia and I prayed that it would be so."

William could not stop smiling as he recounted what had happened. "We were trapped here by the storm. Being thrown together forced us to confront all of the misunderstandings that have plagued our marriage. We were honest and forthright about our feelings and have reconciled."

"Have you considered that the storm was sent by God's design?"

William considered the possibility. "It could very well have been His hand at work. Mother always believed that coincidences were merely miracles in disguise."

"Your mother was right, Fitzwilliam." Joseph stood. "It is time that I leave you two alone." Then he winked at William. "I shall let everyone know that you and Elizabeth are alive and well and have no need of company."

William smiled unabashedly and stood up. When he did, Joseph glanced down at his nephew's well-worn breeches. "I suggest that you wake your wife and enjoy the repast Mrs. Reynolds has provided as well as the rest of the morning. For you will need to return to Pemberley by early afternoon in order to prepare."

"Prepare for what?"

"Have you been so *preoccupied* that you have forgotten the Creighton's ball?"

William groaned, "Good Lord, I have! Not only do I despise balls, but I would have liked nothing more than to spend tonight with my wife—alone."

"Well, you shall just have to endure it, my boy, for half of Derbyshire will be there to see the new Mrs. Darcy. You would not want to cancel and have them think you are ashamed of her, now would you?"

"Of course not!"

His uncle placed a hand on his shoulder, giving it a fatherly squeeze. "I suggest that you return to Pemberley in plenty of time for Elizabeth to dress. You will learn that women need a good deal more time than we men do."

William smiled. "Thank you for the advice, Uncle, but I learned that lesson a long while ago with Georgiana."

After seeing his uncle to the door, adding extra wood on the fire in the kitchen and putting a tall pot of water on to boil, William picked up more wood and went to the bedroom. Easing the door open, he was a little surprised to find Elizabeth watching him, her eyes almost black in the faint light.

"Sweetheart, I thought you might have gone back to sleep." Instantly he noted that she was holding the bedclothes tightly around her, so he began placing the wood on the fire. "You must be chilled to the bone, but do not worry. I shall have the room warmed shortly and then you may wash up if you like, for there is water boiling in the kitchen."

From behind him Elizabeth's voice was low and enticing. "I do not think I shall ever be able to sleep again without being in your arms."

Desire shot through him like a bullet, and he tossed the rest of the wood on the fire and hurried back to the bed, divesting himself of his breeches on the way. Naked, he crawled back under the sheets and snuggled close to Elizabeth.

"Your feet are cold!" she squealed, playfully hitting him on the shoulder.

"But the rest of me is hot," he growled, kissing her passionately.

The next half-hour was spent in fevered lovemaking. Finally completely spent, Elizabeth collapsed upon William's chest, his arms circling her waist. They lay like that as their breathing returned to normal.

"Will?"

"Hmmm?"

"Have you ever... " She hesitated. "What I mean to say is... " She stopped speaking.

"Whatever you want to know, sweetheart, you have only to ask. We said that there would be no secrets between us ever again."

Propping on his muscular chest she ran a finger over the fine, dark hair there. "Have you ever had another woman?"

He groaned. "I know I said there would be no secrets, but do you really want to speak of this?"

"Yes." She took a ragged breath. "I would rather know."

"Very well, dearest. But I tell you this only to ease your mind. Please remember that it was years ago and not something that I am proud of."

Her face fell. "Then you have."

"I am sorry to say that I have. It was the first Christmas I was at Cambridge. Everyone had gone home for the holidays; however, Father had just died a few months before and Georgiana was spending Christmas with the Matlocks. I could not face being alone at Pemberley, and I did not relish being with the family, so I stayed at school. Several of my classmates who also had unhappy situations at home were there and they begged me to go into town with them. After a while, I acquiesced merely to gain some peace. But once we were at the local pub, they began buying me drinks and, in a bid to forget my sorrows, I let them.

"The next morning, I awoke to find myself at Madam Kate's, a nearby

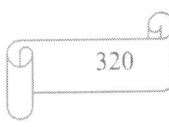

gentlemen's club. According to my colleagues, I drank far more than anyone else before ending up there. Perhaps that is why I have no recollection of what actually transpired at Madam Kate's."

"And you have never had any other woman? Not one of the *ton*?"

"No, no others. As the heir of Pemberley, I was taught to keep myself under good regulation and I managed except for that one instance. Besides, seeing firsthand the ruin caused by being promiscuous, I was resolute that my children's mother would be my wife, not a maid, shop girl or tenant's daughter."

As Elizabeth looked into the face she adored, her eyes brimmed with tears. "Oh, Will. Then in truth, you do not remember any woman but me."

"None but you."

She sniffled as a tear escaped. "Then I am satisfied, for you have no memories with which to compare me."

William's expression grew completely serious. Then he rolled over, capturing Elizabeth beneath him, his face mere inches from hers as he stared into the depths of her ebony eyes.

"My darling wife, I can assure you that what I experienced in your arms these few hours has erased all else from my memory save you."

"Oh, Will," was all she managed to say before he kissed her deeply and the cycle began anew.

Needless to say, it was mid-morning before Mrs. Reynolds' basket was opened and enjoyed, for the newly-reconciled couple had been starving for a lot more than bread and wine.

Chapter 29

Pemberley
Elizabeth's Dressing Room

Having noticed some deep wrinkles on Elizabeth's ball gown, Mrs. O'Reilly had taken it downstairs to steam them from the garment and was presently going back upstairs. Re-entering her mistress' bedroom through the hallway, she crossed at once to the open dressing room door, where she had left Mrs. Darcy in her bath less than a half-hour before. When she walked into the room, she was stunned to find Mr. Darcy holding his naked wife in a passionate embrace. Instantly, she halted and backed out of the dressing room.

Once inside the bedroom, she quietly closed the door and let go of the breath she had unconsciously been holding. The sight of the Darcys sharing kisses and embraces in Mrs. Darcy's suite of rooms was not uncommon since their return, but she had thought that Mr. Darcy was getting dressed and had not expected to catch them in the middle of another, especially with her mistress nude. Taking several deep breaths for composure, the maid gave herself a little talk.

Now, Kathleen O'Reilly, you were married, so you are not ignorant of the passions of a man and a woman. Do not act as though you have never seen such a thing and just be pleased that they have evidently settled their differences. Now, go to the door, knock and announce that you have her dress ready. That should give them time to recover and compose themselves.

After several minutes, she felt ready to try again. So she went to the door, took a deep breath and knocked lightly. Then she called in a calm tone of voice, "Mrs. Darcy, your gown is ready. Shall I bring it in?"

Inside the dressing room, Mrs. O'Reilly's enquiry caused Elizabeth to break their kiss and whisper as firmly as possible, "Will, we simply must stop. I have to dress and so do you. Otherwise, we will miss the ball entirely."

At Elizabeth's protest, William trailed kisses down her neck and across her shoulders. Catching his wife nude had been too much of a temptation as her silky skin beckoned to his baser instincts. He was not about to give up yet, even under threat of interruption.

"Will, please." Elizabeth's heart pounded in her throat as she now murmured more weakly, "Mrs. O'Reilly is waiting for an answer."

"Let her wait," William declared, moving to her breasts and eliciting a small moan from Elizabeth, just as he desired.

"I cannot fight you, Will. I want you as much as you want me. But remember, it is you who will have to explain to everyone, including the earl and countess, why we did not attend."

Slowly her words sunk in, and William ceased his assault with a groan.

Even so, his eyes burned for her as he pulled back to look into her face. "You force me to concede, sweetheart. If not for embarrassing you, I would send our regrets and love you for the rest of the night."

"And while I would love to do just that, we must make the sacrifice and attend. After all, the Matlocks are expecting us as much as the Creightons. But we will have the rest of the night to ourselves once we are home."

A flash of brilliantly white teeth cut across his tanned face. "Yes, we will."

Softly he traced the outline of her jaw before slipping his hand into her thick hair and cupping the back of her head. Pulling her close for a last tender kiss, he whispered, "I shall leave you—for now."

As he stepped away, he looked down at his soaked breeches, unbuttoned shirt and naked feet. A smirk played at the corners of his mouth. "At least I was not wearing all my clothes. Adams will be upset enough that I have ruined my breeches and this shirt. I have no regrets, though." He winked. "It was worth it."

Another quick peck on the tip of her nose and he walked away. Though Elizabeth immediately ached for his return, she forced herself to stand firm by reaching for a towel and wrapping it about her body.

At the bedroom door, William turned to give her a wry smile. Then he opened the door to reveal Mrs. O'Reilly. He stepped aside, sweeping an arm to indicate that she should go inside. "Come in, Mrs. O'Reilly."

Suppressing a laugh at the shock on her face, he disappeared into Elizabeth's bedroom on the way to his own. Very slowly, Mrs. O'Reilly's head swung back around. Elizabeth tried not to giggle at the expression on her face, for she had seen O'Reilly enter the room earlier and rush right back out. And now that William had walked past her in such disarray, she feared that the woman was scandalised.

Pretending that nothing was amiss, Elizabeth declared, "Oh, there you are, and you have my gown."

"Yes, ma'am," Mrs. O'Reilly stepped closer, holding the gown out for her approval. "I steamed the wrinkles from the skirt."

"That looks wonderful. Thank you."

"Now, if we can get you dried off, I may have enough time to fashion your hair in a different style. Since the sleeves are off the shoulder, I thought to leave several long curls hanging over your shoulders and back."

"My husband has often said that he loves my hair down, so I am certain that he will approve."

The maid's eyes twinkled. "I think Mr. Darcy would be pleased no matter how you wore it. He is like a different man today." Catching her breath, Mrs. O'Reilly stammered, "Forgive me, ma'am."

Elizabeth touched her hand. "I know that my previous *situation* was not hidden from you, and my melancholy affected you just as it did me. But that is all in the past now. Mr. Darcy and I are reconciled."

"I have prayed for it to be so."

"Thank you for your prayers." Then Elizabeth smiled. "Now, let us see if you can work a miracle with this hair. The steam from the water has brought out all the curl and it looks a fright."

"Do not worry. I can use the curls to our advantage."

While Mrs. O'Reilly began to work her magic, Elizabeth reached for the one red rose that William had laid on her dressing table when he had entered the room to find her bathing. Bringing it to her nose, she inhaled the scent, remembering his words as he knelt by the tub to kiss her.

A secret sweeter than the soul can whisper, I shall love you forever.

Creighton Hall
The ball

The enormous ballroom was exquisitely decorated from top to bottom, as only those with vast wealth and no concerns could afford. In Creighton Hall this night, there were enough candles, flowers, crystal, silver and linens to outfit three manor homes, for on this evening, one of the most enigmatic men in Derbyshire had not only agreed to appear at the Creighton's ball, but he would also be bringing his new bride.

It was Mrs. Darcy's first formal appearance in the neighbourhood and a feather in Lady Creighton's cap, for she had been the only hostess to secure the Darcys' company since their return to Derbyshire. That their presence was the result of Lord Creighton using his friendship with George Darcy to twist his son's arm was of no consequence to Lady Creighton. This ball was meant to secure her reputation as the premiere hostess in Derbyshire, and if bribery was necessary, then she had no quarrel with that.

As the long line of arriving guests began to dwindle, Lady Creighton leaned out of the receiving line to peer at the Darcys, who were on the other side of her daughter and new son, Lord Bertram. Mr. Darcy had protested being part of the receiving line, but she had been adamant that he and his wife participate. After all, having secured their company, she wished to make the most of it. Nevertheless, Mr. Darcy had won one concession—he would oblige her only if he and his wife were positioned at the end of the line.

Still miffed at that demand, Lady Creighton examined the couple anew, wondering for the hundredth time what had possessed Mr. Darcy to marry someone like his bride when he could have had her Margaret.

Apparently, Margaret was thinking the same thing, for she leaned close to her mother. "What in the world does he see in her? She is certainly no beauty and from the way she smiles mindlessly at everyone, she is merely a country bumpkin."

"Keep your voice down," Lady Creighton said, looking about. "We cannot afford to alienate the Darcys." Seeing that no one was listening, she added quietly, "But I heartily agree. She cannot hold a candle to you, my dear. If Darcy had been sensible, he would have offered for you last season. Then your father would not have settled you on that freckle-faced—"

"Hush, Mother," her daughter said. "Bertram will hear you." She glanced at her portly new husband who was conversing with the Darcys, oblivious of anything they said.

"I cannot help it. Every time I think of how ugly my grandchildren will be—what with his protruding teeth and—"

"Believe me when I say it pains me more than you. I cannot believe Father thought him suitable for me, even if he is a distant cousin of the Prince Regent." Margaret glanced longingly at William, who looked extremely attractive in his black suit. "It would have been so much more enjoyable being bedded by Mr. Darcy." Then she sighed heavily. "He is still the handsomest man of my acquaintance."

As they both studied the man in question, he chose that moment to silently mouth *I love you* to Elizabeth.

Lady Creighton sighed. "That he is, Margaret, and who would have thought him a romantic, too. Just gazing at his masculine figure is a welcome respite from all the unappealing men of the *ton*."

Lady Margaret cut her eyes at her mother. "He is young enough to be your son."

"I am not dead, my dear. You will learn that, while a woman may age, inside she is still a young girl, and she can still appreciate the strapping figure of a virile young man."

"Mother!"

Georgiana Darcy was not dancing. She would have liked to, but the man she most wanted to dance with, Lord Attaway, had been delayed. So after dancing with her uncle and her brother, she rushed to join her good friend, Lady Susan, who was standing with a number of ladies along the periphery of the ballroom. The group she joined were all straining to see every move the newly married Mr. Darcy made, and he was a sight to behold as he took to the floor to waltz with his new bride. If he adjusted his pace to accommodate his sore ankle, it was not evident.

Lady Susan's eyes narrowed as they fixed on the one she desired. "Look at Fitzwilliam!" she hissed to Georgiana in a loud whisper. "I have never seen him so happy to be dancing—and to a waltz at that! One would think he would shun so scandalous a dance. What is more, in the receiving line, he claimed that he might not dance at all, for his ankle still pained him."

"It is odd to see my brother so content dancing. I had to beg him to practice with me after learning to waltz at a friend's house in London. Afterward, he said he thought it only suitable for married couples. I suppose that is why he seems unconcerned tonight—after all, they are married."

Lady Susan's countenance darkened, her gaze never leaving William. "Only days ago you assured me that they acted like strangers. They look well acquainted tonight."

"All I know is that there was a definite coldness between them when I returned, and now there is not."

"And you say that they stayed in Lady Anne's cottage last night because of the storm?"

"Yes. If I did not know better, I would have thought that they married yesterday by the way they acted when they returned. Upon their homecoming, the entire atmosphere at Pemberley changed. From the lowliest maid to Mrs.

Reynolds, everyone was suddenly in good spirits. It is simply nauseating. Not to mention that the Fitzwilliams, who already think Elizabeth is God's gift to our family, are even more giddy than is their usual wont."

"Then why are the Fitzwilliams not here to support them?"

"They allowed that they did not wish to cause discord on a night meant to honour my brother and Elizabeth. Since the Earl and Countess Matlock were scheduled to attend, they decided it was best not to come."

"I imagine you were relieved."

"Enormously. At least they are not here to embarrass me, too."

"In any case, you and I cannot become disheartened. This change in your brother's situation only means that we have more work ahead of us. Given time, we will think of a way to discredit Elizabeth. Then your brother will toss her aside, and I shall be there to take her place."

Feeling uncomfortable for not telling her friend earlier what had happened that day, Georgiana never took her eyes from William as she confessed.

"I am afraid that all is lost in that regard, for nothing can dissuade Brother now."

Lady Susan's head swung around. "Why would you say such a thing?"

"Because when he returned to Pemberley today, he made it plain that he would brook no more criticism of Elizabeth. No doubt, Uncle Joseph passed along what I had to say when they did not return last night. I was very vocal in blaming her for their dilemma."

"What is wrong with that, as long as it is true?"

"Apparently everything! Fitzwilliam said that if I continue to disparage his wife, I will find myself living with the Matlocks permanently. In fact, I had to grovel in order to accompany them here tonight."

"How odd that he would toss his own sister from the house to please some little chit!"

"Actually, I do not think she had a part in it. Brother is… well, I have never seen him so besotted with a woman."

"Oh, I can dissuade him of that notion. And I will. I must!" The latter was added for emphasis before Susan leaned in to whisper. "I have our son's future to consider."

Georgiana looked properly chastised at the mention of the boy, and Susan was pleased that she had hit the mark. "As long as I have your help, Elizabeth Bennet will be on the road back to Hertfordshire before she knows what has happened."

Just at that moment, Lord Attaway came towards them with an enormous smile on his face. "Ladies, I apologise for being late. It was unavoidable." He winked at Georgiana. "I hope that you have not missed me too terribly."

"We hardly noticed you were not here," Lady Susan reproved. It was clear that Georgiana did not feel the same, for she blushed under his examination.

"Miss Darcy, you look so lovely tonight that you simply take my breath away. May I enquire if your next set is open?"

"It is, sir."

"Then may I have the honour?" She nodded. "Excellent. Now, if you will

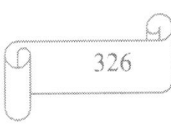

excuse me for a moment, I see an old friend that I must greet before the next set begins."

With that Attaway walked away, and Georgiana turned to watch him leave. Instantly, he joined a group that included several women, all of whom circled him, speaking animatedly. Soon they were giggling at whatever he was saying. Seeing Georgiana's smile fade to a scowl, Susan made a mental note to chastise her cousin for flirting in front of her.

"Do not be overly concerned, dear. Those are merely neighbours of my cousin who live near Liverpool—the Pierpoint sisters, I believe."

"I was merely curious, that is all," Georgiana lied as her head swung back around. "I care not with whom Lord Attaway converses. After all, he is an unmarried man and can entertain whomever he wishes."

"This is true," Lady Susan said, adding cleverly, "though from what he has told me, he may not be single for long."

Georgiana was suddenly in better humour. "What did he say?"

"Oh, I could not betray a confidence, my dear." Lady Susan smiled knowingly. "I will only say that what he plans to do pleases me immensely."

That must have satisfied Georgiana, for she quit keeping an eye on Attaway as he made his way around the ballroom, flirting with one woman after another. And, truth be known, he had great success with his flirtations, for more than one young lady in attendance that evening believed wholeheartedly that his plans for the future included her.

On the dance floor, the main objects of Derbyshire's curiosity were twirling around in time to a German waltz, [15] hardly aware of anything save one another. William, dressed in black except for a dark gold waistcoat and white shirt, was the epitome of what an elegant gentleman should be, while Elizabeth was beguiling in one of the gowns he had commissioned from Madam Bouvier. It was an empire-style gown of pale-pink silk with rose-coloured, embroidered flowers across the bodice and the hem and several flounces of Belgium lace on the skirt and sleeves. The centre of each flower was accented with sequins, and she wore a rose-coloured silk flower adorned with the same sequins in her hair.

Bewitched by his wife, William pulled her closer, murmuring, "Have I told you how beautiful you are, sweetheart?"

Elizabeth smiled lovingly up at her handsome husband. "Yes, but evidently my *beauty* has blinded you to a more pressing problem."

"And what might that be?"

"Each time we circle the floor, you hold me a little closer, Will. If you continue in this fashion, by the time the waltz ends, we shall have scandalised your relations and most of Derbyshire."

William chuckled, whispering mischievously, "I care not if we do. Besides, if you keep calling me Will, you will find yourself involved in a much bigger scandal than that."

One eyebrow rose, a mannerism of hers that had always enchanted him. "Oh? I do not take your meaning, *Mr. Darcy?*"

"Well, *Mrs. Darcy*. Do you recall what activity we were engaged in when you resumed calling me Will?"

She turned crimson. "I do."

"Then can you fault me if using that appellation reminds me of that very activity?"

She whispered as loudly as she dared, glancing about, "Someone may hear you."

"Let them," he declared. "No doubt everyone here has already decided that I am a besotted fool."

She smiled. "Or merely just a fool for choosing me."

They were just then nearing the open French doors that led outside and, without missing a beat, William twirled her though the doors and onto the terrace. As he did, several couples standing near the doors gasped and moved closer to follow them with their eyes.

"Let no one doubt after tonight that I am completely and irreversibly mad for you."

With that, William clasped her to himself in a torrid kiss, then slipped an arm around her waist as he began to lead her down the steps, taking the gravel path lit with lanterns.

"Where are we going?"

"Surely there is a bench or a gazebo in this garden and I mean to find it."

"Oh, Will, you are the guest of honour. You cannot just disappear."

"*We* are the guests of honour, and yes, we can—at least for a short while." He stopped to face her. "It is either steal a few minutes alone with you now or depart for home." He brushed her lips with his. "For I am overwhelmed by the need to be alone with you; moreover, I can always say that I wished to rest my ankle."

"You dance so well that I completely forgot about your ankle. Does it still hurt terribly?"

"It is sore, but not so much that I cannot enjoy a dance with my wife."

It was several minutes until the honourees returned to the ballroom. When they did, Elizabeth's lips were crimson, her face flushed—a silent testament to their activities. Nonetheless, neither she nor William appeared embarrassed as they made their way back into the ballroom, past the stares and whispers of the *ton*, just as a set was ending.

While the Darcys may have invited scandal, the gossips were delighted at their impudence, for their disappearance had provided even more tittle-tattle to pass along to their fellow gossipmongers. And seeing Mr. Darcy so love-struck was truly a unique experience to be able to boast about.

Reaching the spot where his aunt and uncle were standing, William was amused by the uncomfortable expressions on their faces. That and the fact that Lady Matlock was fanning herself frantically were sure indications that they were not in good humour.

The countess recognized that they were the centre of attention, so she managed a smile as she whispered, "You are taxing my nerves tonight, Fitzwilliam."

As the music started again, she addressed Elizabeth politely, "My husband mentioned that he would like to have the next set with you, my dear."

Instantly, the earl stepped forward to offer her his arm. Elizabeth laid her hand upon it and looked wide-eyed back at William as Lord Matlock led her toward the dance floor. William looked entirely lost as she was led away and could offer only a meagre smile to fortify her before she disappeared into the crowd.

With Elizabeth occupied, Lady Matlock turned her attention to her nephew. "Now, if you would be so kind, I should like to dance with you."

William knew that a lecture was forthcoming; still, he had no choice but to comply. "Certainly."

He held out his arm, and the lady laid her hand upon it. As the music began and they walked towards the dance floor, she said quietly, "I expected better behaviour from you."

William rolled his eyes. The rest of the night would no doubt be endless.

In a corner of the ballroom, Lord Attaway stood with his cousin, Lady Susan.

"Just to satisfy my curiosity, why were you late tonight?"

"You do remember that your father had me deliver a stallion to Sheffield yesterday."

"Yes, but you had plenty of time to return and still be here on time."

"Yes, well I would have been, if I had not run into an old friend of ours at an inn just outside Lambton. We had an interesting visit."

"Friend of ours?" Lady Susan's eyebrows rose. "Pray tell, who do we both consider a friend?"

"Darcy's cousin, Andrew. He is still as amiable as ever—nothing like his austere cousin who pretends not to remember me."

She huffed. "I hardly think of Andrew as a friend anymore. He never comes to see me unless he wants something."

"Perhaps that is Darcy's fault. Andrew said that he is no longer welcome to stay at Pemberley, and lately his allowance has been discontinued. Needless to say, he is not pleased with his cousin."

"He has not been welcome at Pemberley for years. That is nothing new. However, the rumours in London are that he and Fitzwilliam are at odds over a woman from Manchester. I assume that is why he is keeping out of sight."

"He did not mention anything about it, but it sounds promising. What happened? Did Fitzwilliam favour her, too?"

"Do not be ridiculous; it was nothing like that. Apparently Andrew raised the woman's expectations and then dropped her unceremoniously. She drowned—whether or not by her own hand is not certain."

"Yes, I can see Darcy punishing him for something like that. He was always a stickler for propriety."

"Except when it comes to his own respectability it would seem," Susan said sarcastically. Searching the dance floor until her eyes lit upon Elizabeth, she tilted her head in that direction, "Just look at the chit he chose to marry.

She is dancing with Lord Matlock."

Attaway saw much to like in Darcy's dark-haired wife, but he knew better than to say as much. "Jealousy does not flatter you, Cousin."

"I am not jealous!" Susan declared. "I am honest. She is beneath him. I should say beneath us all! And she has no real beauty."

"Calm down and lower your voice," Attaway cautioned. "People are staring."

Lady Susan raised her chin and turned to smile at those standing nearby. The observers quickly resumed their own conversations. "So, what else did Andrew have to say?"

"He said that he is staying with a friend outside of Lambton and that he has a new business venture that is producing a good living. I hinted for him to tell me more, but he was quite tight-lipped about what it entailed. I suppose he wants to keep all the profits for himself, and I can hardly blame him."

"I should think it only one of his schemes, for he is not fond of hard work." She sighed. "In any event, should you see him again, tell him to drop by Monthaven Manor. I think I will need his help in disposing of Mrs. Darcy."

"How so?"

"Rumour is that Mrs. Darcy was *very* fond of Andrew before she moved on to Fitzwilliam."

"A woman after my own heart," Attaway chuckled.

"I pay your heart to prey on Georgiana, not Mrs. Darcy."

Attaway's eyes flew to Georgiana as she danced with Lord Bertram. "She is a pretty little thing, though I find her quite dull."

"Dull? Georgiana is well educated," Susan countered, trying to encourage her cousin.

"Education does not make a woman interesting. She is so gullible that she believes everything I say. Where is the thrill in that? Deceiving her will be too easy."

"I did not hire you to enjoy your work. You are to seduce her in order to keep her on my side and against Eliza Bennet. In fact, I think that your marrying Georgiana would be absurd. It would only make matters more difficult."

"Still, I have begun to relish the idea of wedding Georgiana just to raise Darcy's hackles—well, that and her thirty thousand pounds. He has always looked down his nose at me."

"Do not let your temper make you foolish. If you ruin this for me, you shall regret it."

Lord Attaway sighed. "Do not worry. I shall keep my cards hidden until after you have Mr. Darcy secured."

"See that you do." The set was ending, and as Georgiana was being escorted from the floor, Lady Susan added, "I want you to dance the next set with Georgiana. Invite her to Monthaven for tea. I shall manage to have something to take care of when she comes and leave the two of you alone."

"And what exactly do you want me to achieve at this assignation?"

"The objective is to seduce her, stopping short of taking her virginity, of course. If you went that far, Fitzwilliam would kill you, marriage or no marriage."

"I am not afraid of—"

He was quickly interrupted. "Spare me the bravado! I do not care to hear it. Make her think you love her. Then we can manipulate her to do as we ask."

"That will be no problem." Lord Attaway's eyes began to follow a tall red-haired woman who smiled at him beguilingly as she walked past.

"And another thing! Stop showing interest in other women when Georgiana is nearby, or her brother, for that matter. They need to think you are besotted with her and not just a common rake."

Attaway took a deep breath and let it out noisily. "You drive a hard bargain."

"That is because I am paying well for this bargain."

Pemberley

Absorbed in the scent and murmur of the night, Olivia and Joseph stood on the balcony outside their bedroom, just as they had done every evening, weather permitting, since coming to Pemberley. Watching as a midnight-blue, velvet expanse of sky turned into a blanket of twinkling stars, Joseph stood behind his wife, his arms around her waist. Her head was tilted back against his chest as she gazed upward. Smiling, he leaned down to kiss the top of her head, and she closed her eyes, allowing a deep sigh to escape.

"What is this? A sigh?" Joseph ventured. "Do you regret missing the ball, my love?"

"My only regret is in not seeing Fitzwilliam and Elizabeth being honoured by their neighbours." She turned to face him. "But in truth, I had rather be here in your arms than anywhere in the world."

He smiled. "You have always made me feel that I am the most important man in the world, Livy. I love you for that."

"That is because you *are* the most important man in the world to me, Joseph."

He kissed her tenderly before embracing her more tightly. "Then if the sigh is not from regret, what is the source?"

"It is a sigh of contentment."

"Ah, yes. Our boy is in high spirits, so all is right with the world," he teased.

"He is not *our* boy, but being around him of late, I have come to love him like a son, and since her arrival, Elizabeth is like my own daughter. When they hurt, I hurt." She lifted her head to look into his eyes. "And do not deny that you feel the same, for I know better."

"I shall not deny it; you are right. I almost feel like their father."

"I know what you mean. I often find myself saying things to them that I would have said to Arthur or Jenny." She chuckled, "And with little prompting on their parts."

"I have seen the way Fitzwilliam reacts to you, Livy. He may be a man, but inside he is still a boy who craves a mother's touch. And Elizabeth, it seems, is much the same. Though our niece has a mother and father, from what Fitzwilliam has said, the Bennets look after their own interests first and foremost."

"Elizabeth has told me a few things that make me believe that as well."

They were both lost in thought until suddenly Olivia's face brightened. "Is it not touching to see how the coldness between Fitzwilliam and Elizabeth has completely vanished? It is so moving to see them hold hands and whisper to one another. In fact, I caught them in a kiss when I went unannounced into Elizabeth's sitting room earlier today."

Her husband chuckled. "Yes. The time alone at the cottage must have done the trick. And with their newly found felicity, I can imagine that we shall interrupt many a kiss in the future. Do you remember how frequently we embarrassed our housekeeper the first few months of our marriage?"

Olivia laughed. "I do. Mrs. Stanley was afraid to walk down a hall without announcing her presence." She shook her head as if in wonder. "Even the atmosphere in the house has changed since they returned today. I thought Mrs. Reynolds was going to walk on air when she announced tea, she was so delighted."

"I suppose Georgiana is the only one not pleased that they are happy," Joseph added, "although I cannot understand why. If her new sister and her brother have a satisfying relationship, it can only work to her good."

"One would think she would wish them joy. Truly, I have no idea why our niece is so set against Elizabeth, for she has never treated Georgiana with anything but kindness, despite her many barbs."

"As we have learned, sometimes people are cruel without any provocation. It is a fact of life." He kissed her forehead softly. "I am so proud that you never held a grudge, or allowed me to hold one, either. You have been my compass, Livy, always guiding me to do the right thing. Without you, I would have been a bitter man."

"And you have been my anchor," she whispered.

They kissed then as they had when they were young and newly married. And it was not long until stars and galaxies were forgotten for more important pursuits.

Chapter 30

Pemberley
The next morning

Olivia and Joseph Fitzwilliam had just finished breaking their fast and were leaving the dining room when they saw Mrs. Reynolds coming toward them from the direction of her office. In her hand was the familiar folder that she nearly always carried, which contained lists of household chores, servants assigned to them and other pertinent information needed for the running of the house. Consequently, her head was down and her eyes were locked on the paper she was reading as she walked.

The housekeeper stopped abruptly when her name was called, her concentration broken. Embarrassed to be caught unawares, she sputtered, "Good morning, Mr. Fitzwilliam, Mrs. Fitzwilliam. I hope you found what Cook prepared this morning to your liking."

Both Fitzwilliams smiled warmly, as Olivia replied, "Good morning, Mrs. Reynolds. The food was marvellous, as always. Mrs. Lantrip is to be congratulated for consistently providing delicious meals."

"I shall pass your compliments along to her. I am certain she will appreciate hearing it."

"You are very kind," Olivia stated. "Have my niece and nephew come downstairs yet?"

"No, ma'am, they have not; however, Mr. Darcy left word last night that he wanted breakfast trays sent to their sitting room this morning, though not before ten o'clock."

Olivia cut her eyes to Joseph, smiling knowingly. "Well, after being up so late for the ball, I can imagine that they must be exhausted."

"And they did not return until long after midnight," Mrs. Reynolds declared knowingly. "Did you wish to speak to them?"

"No, no. It can wait. I can always talk to Elizabeth later. Please do not disturb their privacy."

With that, she and Joseph walked past the housekeeper, taking the hall on the other side of the grand staircase that led to the back entrance. When they were out of hearing range, Joseph leaned close to whisper his observation.

"I shall wager that we will see very little of them for days! If you ask me, they shall be pleasantly occupied for quite some time."

Olivia restrained a chuckle. "Joseph Fitzwilliam, how you do love a good ribbing! I can only imagine what you will say to our nephew when you see him next."

"Now, Livy, what is this you accuse me of? I only meant to suggest that they will be so tired after attending the ball that they will *sleep* for days."

"That is not what you meant and you know it."

He chuckled. "If I am correct, they will be making up for all the time wasted being upset with one another."

"And I hope they take all the time they want. They deserve to be happy."

"Everyone should be as happy as we are, my love." Joseph turned and embraced her, kissing her tenderly. Then he pulled back to smile at her. "Do you still feel like strolling about the gardens?"

"Happiness gives me strength. I feel as though I could walk the entire estate."

"Then let us begin, for I think *that* shall take a long time."

He held out his arm, and they went out the door and took the gravel path to the rose garden.

⁕

When the Fitzwilliams stopped to talk at the back door, their lively conversation was overheard by the two maids working in the nearby billiards room with the door open. Though Clara and Polly could not make out all that was said, they still stopped to smile at one another when the sounds of laughter reached their ears.

"Have you ever seen a more amiable couple than the Fitzwilliams?" Clara asked as quietly as possible. "I swear it makes a body feel good just watching them make eyes at one another."

"When they are not kissing, you mean," the younger maid added cheerily. "I am sure I have caught them in a kiss at least once a day since they came to Pemberley. Not that I mind. It warms my heart to see such felicity in a married couple. In my last position, the master and mistress hated one another, and the master was always making vulgar remarks to me and the other maids."

"That happened to me a lot when I was younger. Fortunately, you will never have to worry about that kind of behaviour here. Mr. Darcy is a gentleman and expects gentlemanly conduct from everyone else," Clara replied.

"That is the reason I sought work here." Then Polly suddenly stopped dusting. "May I tell you something? And, if I do, will you promise not to tell?"

"I cannot promise if I have no idea what you are talking about."

"It involves Florence, the maid who just returned from London with Miss Darcy. I overheard her tell the master's sister something that raised a question in my mind."

"You know the rules about gossiping," Clara chided. "You can be fired for passing along things, even if they may be true."

"But I am not passing anything along. I just want your opinion. I thought maybe I should tell Mrs. Reynolds what I overheard."

"Tell me what you heard, and I will give you my opinion as to whether you should tell her. And I promise not to tell anyone, unless I feel it will harm the Darcys."

"That was my concern." Polly heaved a sigh and then began. "I was clearing the dishes from Miss Darcy's sitting room this morning when I heard Florence talking. She was in Miss Darcy's bedroom, and the door was ajar. I was not trying to hear, mind you, but she was not speaking softly."

Clara nodded, motioning with her hand for her to continue.

"I heard Florence say that she knew for certain that the master and mistress are sharing Mrs. Darcy's bed, and she thought Miss Darcy would want to know."

"What an odd thing to say. How would she know where the master and mistress sleep, and why would she think it important enough to tell her mistress?"

"My thoughts exactly."

"What did Miss Darcy reply?"

"Her precise words were, 'I was afraid of that! Until the storm, they were sleeping in separate bedrooms. Thank you for telling me.' Then a cup accidentally fell from the tray I was carrying and they went silent."

Completely forgetting her admonition against gossip, Clara retorted, "Humph! Miss Darcy has had a bee in her bonnet since the master tossed their cousin, Andrew, from Pemberley several years ago. Andrew was her favourite, and she has no qualms telling anyone who will listen that her brother is simply cruel."

"But why would she be unkind to the new mistress? Mrs. Darcy seems so nice."

"I imagine it is to pay her brother back for the perceived *cruelty*. Miss Darcy was raging about Mrs. Darcy bringing bad luck the night she and the master were caught in the rain, so I am not surprised at her. However, I am most troubled at Florence's claim."

"That is my point. After all, *how* would Florence know that the Darcys are sharing a bed? For the present, Mrs. O'Reilly and Mr. Adams are off duty, only going upstairs when summoned, and no one else is allowed in the Darcys' suite save Mrs. Reynolds. We both know that she will not breathe a word about them."

"This is true."

"So, do you think I should I inform her?"

"You could, but Florence would deny she said it, and Miss Darcy would likely back her up, especially if she does not want her brother to learn of it."

"I had not thought of that."

"However, I believe you and I should look for more evidence."

"You are going to help me?"

"I am. You and I can keep an eye on Florence. If we can catch her lurking in the servants' hallway outside Mrs. Darcy's bedroom, then we will have stronger proof."

"So you think she is spying on them from the hallway?"

"How else would she know if they shared the bedroom? And she has no business being in that hall, not with Miss Darcy's rooms clear on the other side of the house. Likely, she sneaks around early in the morning or late at night."

"My room is across from Florence's and the hall floor squeaks whenever anyone passes. I shall have to pay more attention to the squeaks and see who it is," Polly stated.

Clara laughed. "Well, I have a better situation than you. My bedroom adjoins hers and there is a door between us. The door itself is a little crooked, leaving a gap on one side. If I am awake, I can see when there is a light in her room. If she were to light a candle at night, I will know."

"If she is spying on the Darcys, let us hope we discover her soon. It will be hard to work and keep watch over her."

"No doubt. But we must do what it takes to protect the Darcys' privacy."

Polly sighed. "Yes, we must."

Elizabeth's bedroom

An itchy nose awoke Elizabeth. She did not bother to open her eyes but instinctively brushed her hand back and forth across it and, satisfied, she tried to go back to sleep. The mysterious sensation began again and this time Elizabeth opened her eyes to find a long feather being held just over her eyes. Recalling that she was now sharing her bed with William, she giggled and rolled over to face him. Tossing the feather, he used his hand for a more important task—snaking it around her waist and pulling her bare body against his.

"Will!" Elizabeth exclaimed gleefully as she was rapidly swept across the silk sheet. "You are incorrigible! Last night you promised to let me sleep as late as I wished today."

"I shall let you go back to sleep then," he proclaimed, his mien dejected, "if that is your wish."

As the arm that held her tightly was slowly removed, she grabbed hold of it, staying its progress. Instantly, his frown turned into a smirk and she playfully pushed at his chest.

"You knew that I was teasing."

Admiring the dark shadow of a beard that now covered his chiselled chin, her eyes travelled to his well-shaped mouth that called out to be kissed, so she obliged. Soon, what began as a tender kiss became a raging fire as his tongue began to work its magic. She moaned when he suddenly rolled over, trapping her beneath him. Still, he continued the kiss as her arms snaked around his waist and her nails sunk into his back. Soon they were joined once more and lost in the enchantment of making love. The feelings inside Elizabeth built until she felt herself falling off a cliff into a deep abyss, while wave after wave of bliss washed over her.

Still lost in desire, William kept going until he reached the same pinnacle. Then with a loud groan, he collapsed atop her, breathing as though he had run a race. Lying perfectly still until his breath slowed, he rose up on his elbows to study his wife.

"I love you, my darling Elizabeth."

"I love you, too, my darling Will."

He rolled over, taking her with him so that she lay on his stomach. As he ran his fingers lazily up and down the supple skin of her back, he asked, "What do you wish to do today, love?"

She lifted her head and crossed her arms to prop herself on his chest. As she studied him, she said, "What I wish for is to stay here with you."

William tried not to smile too widely. "If we wish to occupy this room for the next month, it is our prerogative."

Elizabeth chuckled. "I can just see the faces of our servants, scandalised because the master and mistress have not left their bedroom for weeks—not to mention your aunt and uncle."

"I do not imagine my aunt and uncle would be at all surprised. The way they act toward one another, I am certain that they still have a healthy physical relationship."

Elizabeth gasped. "Will! What a thing to say!"

"Relations between a man and his wife are a normal part of life, Elizabeth. It is only natural to speak of it. Of course, I would never speak about it to anyone but you; however, to be truthful, I admire that aspect of their marriage. I pray that we shall follow their example, for I intend to occupy your bed until the day I die."

Elizabeth's smile vanished. "Please do not speak of dying, Will. I cannot bear the thought of living without you. Promise me that you will never leave me."

"I cannot promise that I will be here for the rest of your life, Elizabeth, but I can promise that I will love you for the rest of mine."

"Oh, Will," was all she managed to say before their lips met.

William ended the kiss, whispering, "I need to retrieve something from my bedroom. Do not move."

"I do not think I shall be going anywhere, the way I am dressed," Elizabeth teased, holding the sheet back.

By then William was donning his robe and glanced to her display. Sucking in his breath, he said, "If you keep that up, I shall never leave this room again."

Despite what he said, he did hurry from the room and in only seconds returned with a mysterious smile on his face and a hand hidden behind his back.

Elizabeth smiled mischievously. "Just what are you hiding, Mr. Darcy?"

"Close your eyes and you will learn soon enough." She did as asked and felt the bed settle as he sat back down on it. "Now you may open them."

Elizabeth sat speechless, blinking steadily at an exquisite, gold wedding band. It was wide enough that words had been engraved on it and a diamond had been sunk into the space between each word.

He chuckled. "Have you nothing to say?"

"I... it is so beautiful that words fail me."

"Read the inscription." As she took the ring from the box, a small paper fell to the bed. "That is just my order for the ring," William assured her as he scooped up the paper and laid it on the bedside table.

As she read the words aloud, her eyes filled with tears and her voice choked. "First... Last... Only... Always."

"I wanted my feelings toward you inscribed on your ring for the entire world to see. You are my one and only love, now and forever."

"As you are mine," she said raggedly, leaning towards him until their mouths met again in a tender kiss.

"It also has our wedding date inscribed inside. I hope you do not mind trading my mother's band for this one, for I wanted to give you a wedding ring that was truly yours alone."

"It is the most beautiful ring I have ever seen and the sentiments simply melt my heart. I shall cherish it forever, Will. And, if you do not object, I shall wear your mother's ring on my other hand, since it was my first ring from you."

"I think Mother would have liked that very much."

"I cannot imagine when you ordered it, though. I was so unkind to you once we arrived in London that I wonder at your having any feelings left for me," she looked down at the inscription, teary eyed. "Much less ones that are so dear."

"Hush, my darling. No dwelling on the past. As for this ring, I ordered it when I went to London for the special license, but it was not finished until a week later."

She hugged him fiercely, murmuring hoarsely in his ear. "No one else will ever know the strength of my love for you, Will Darcy. For you alone have seen my heart from the inside, for you reside there."

"My precious Elizabeth," he whispered, pushing her back on the bed and kissing her soundly.

Only a knock on the door an hour later and a voice announcing that their meals were waiting in the sitting room, could have lured them from their pleasant endeavours.

Meryton
Longbourn
Two Days later

At another soirée given by Mrs. Phillips in honour of their engagement, Charles Bingley and Jane Bennet were presented, yet again, as living trophies to Mrs. Bennet's cleverness in finding husbands for her daughters. Agnes Phillips had already held a small party in honour of Jane's engagement, but Fanny Bennet insisted that she have a larger, more formal dinner party; thus, to keep peace with her sister, she had acquiesced. So here the lucky couple stood once again greeting their friends and neighbours and receiving their wishes of joy.

As the crush of people began to thin, Jane leaned close so only Bingley could hear and whispered, "I apologise again for Mama's officiousness. I had no idea that she would make Aunt Phillips host another party for us."

Ever the conciliator, Bingley whispered in return, "Do not fret, love. It is nothing to me if we attend a hundred dinner parties. As long as you are with me, I shall be glad to attend them all."

Jane blushed as she examined her handsome fiancé. His blue suit looked so smart with his ginger hair and blue eyes, and when he smiled at her, her heart soared with happiness. "Oh, Charles, you are so good to me!"

"I intend to do everything within my power to please you, now and after we are married."

"Speaking of pleasing me, you no longer need to travel to Pemberley. I received an express post from Lizzy just before we left Longbourn for here."

"An express? What news was so important that it necessitated an express? From your smile, I can only assume that all is well."

"All is more than well. It is wonderful! And as for the express, Lizzy must have taken my last letter quite seriously."

"Whatever do you mean?"

"I threatened to come to Pemberley to see her. Unlike the few letters I have received since her marriage, this one convinced me that she is truly happy." For a moment, Jane seemed lost in thought as a contented smile settled across her face.

"I am glad for that. I would not have you worry needlessly."

"Have you gotten a reply to your letter to Mr. Darcy?"

"Not as yet. I should hear from him any day, though." Charles looked around until he located his future mother across the room, too far away to hear. "Do not expect to glean too much information from any letter from Darcy, though. He is notoriously tight-lipped about his personal life."

"I understand. But if he is as happy as my sister, perhaps he cannot resist telling you. As Lizzy wished, I shared the letter I got with Papa and Mama."

"Is your mother content then?"

"Of course not," Jane replied with a sigh. "She insists that Lizzy would never tell us if Mr. Darcy was unhappy with her. That is why I am curious as to what he may say. Perhaps he will write something that might persuade Mama that all is well."

Bingley smiled sheepishly. "I do not think Darcy would care if I told you what he wrote; after all, we are engaged, but if you shared his thoughts with your mother, he might feel that I betrayed his trust."

"Oh dear, I did not think of that."

"I do believe your mother took Lizzy's trip to Pemberley alone the wrong way," Bingley said, patting her hand consolingly. "I know Darcy well enough to say without hesitation that he is besotted with your sister. And he is simply not the kind to toss her aside. After all, he waited years to meet someone that he wished to marry."

"Still, I must agree with Mama on one thing—there was something amiss between them. My sister has never been able to fool me, even in a letter, and until I got the one today, I was convinced of her unhappiness."

"And now that you think otherwise, a trip is unnecessary."

Jane smiled lovingly, taking his hand to give it a squeeze. "Yes, for now I am satisfied. So, unless you wish to see your friend, you do not have to travel there for my sake."

"Excellent! To be truthful, I had rather stay here. I think Darcy will be too occupied with your sister to relish a visit from me."

Just at that moment, Mrs. Long came over to them. "Oh, Mr. Bingley, I was thinking that we have not seen your sisters in Meryton in such a long while."

"Yes, they have been at the Hurst family estate. They are having so fine a time that they do not plan to return to Netherfield until after the first of the year, or perhaps later. In any case, Miss Bingley is keen to return to London, not Meryton."

"Why, that is unfortunate. I was looking forward to attending another ball at your home. But with no hostess to assist you, I am sure that a ball would be out of the question."

"Yes, it would," Bingley said without further debate, making his intention of not bringing Caroline back to Meryton to act as his hostess clear.

Thwarted in her attempt to promote another ball, Mrs. Long took her leave. As she did, Jane turned to him. "I thought that Caroline has written twice asking to return to Netherfield."

"She has. But I do not relish seeing her, especially after she defied my instructions in regard to Darcy, so my answer was no. She is unstable where he is concerned, and, frankly, she cannot be trusted in regards to our plans to marry, either."

"Surely you do not think she would interfere now that Mr. Darcy is married to Lizzie and we are engaged?"

"I cannot promise that she would not try. In fact, I told Louisa that if Caroline does not reside with them in the future, I shall find a place for her with one of our maiden aunts. I do not intend to have her live with us once we marry."

Jane tried not to smile too widely for, to tell the truth, she was relieved to hear Charles say as much. Just at that point, her mother came toward them talking animatedly and pulling an older woman along with her. Pasting on a smile, Jane steeled herself for yet another conversation.

Lambton
The local inn

The small inn at Lambton also served as a post office, so it was often quite crowded. No more so than today, when heavy rains thwarted many of the patrons' plans to travel further north. Reports of the banks of the river overflowing on the county line had caused several coaches to stop for the night, and their inhabitants now occupied all the rooms upstairs, as well as the common area. Wishing to avoid being seen by his cousin or any who worked for William, Andrew Darcy was pleased by the throng, for it was his wish to retrieve any posts forwarded by Mrs. Lightfoot and hurry back to Pate's farm without being seen. He kept up a correspondence with his housekeeper, for he did not want her or her husband to abandon Winfield Hall like the rest of his staff had done. Today, however, he was not happy with what Mrs. Lightfoot included with her post.

Inside her letter was an unopened letter from Fitzwilliam Darcy addressed to him at Winfield Hall. Fearful of the content, Andrew ripped it open to read it whilst still standing at the counter.

May 26, 1812
Andrew,

I have not heard from you since you left Meryton for Manchester. Other than your conversation with my wife at the ball in London, you have kept yourself well hidden; thus, I have sent this letter in hopes that you will get it in due course.

You have, for the most part, abandoned Winfield Hall. As far as I can see, you have done nothing to raise the estate's income and have, in fact, left even your servants' salaries for me to pay. It was inevitable that your situation has come to this due to your lack of concern.

I feel that I have no choice but to put Winfield Hall on the market, as per the stipulations in my father's will. I shall continue to pay the few servants who still reside until a new owner is secured. If you wish to discuss my decision, I suggest that you make haste, for I am consulting with a solicitor to advertise the property in the London papers this very week.

Fitzwilliam Darcy

Furious, Andrew mumbled to himself as he replaced his hat and stalked out of the inn, the door crashing against the wall as he pushed it open.

Humph! Abandoned Winfield Hall! Not paying my servants! In a few weeks, I will have three hundred pounds, and if he had not withheld my allowance—

"Andrew, old boy! We meet again!"

The cheerful greeting caused Andrew to stop dead in his tracks. Had he been found out? Searching the faces of those coming up the steps to the inn, he spotted the source of the greeting and breathed a sigh of relief.

"Attaway! I am surprised you are still in Derbyshire. I would have thought you would be at Gracehill Park by now."

Lord Attaway motioned for Andrew to follow him to the end of the porch where they could talk in private. Once there, he replied, "Oh no. I thought I made it clear that I am a guest at Monthaven until the end of the summer, at the very least. By the way, I told my cousin that I talked with you on the road. She asked me, if we met again, to tell you to come by and see her."

Andrew's expression darkened. "Did she say what it entailed? I am sure she does not want me to come for old times' sake."

Attaway laughed. "I see you know her well. I suppose then that it will come as no surprise that she wants your help."

"For what?"

"She said to separate your cousin from his wife."

"She told you of her plans?"

"You know Susan. When she is obsessed with something, she cannot keep it to herself. She has even solicited me to help keep Georgiana on her side."

"I fear that this time her plans will not succeed," Andrew huffed. "From what little I saw in London, Fitz is love-struck. And that is saying a lot for that killjoy."

"I agree with you. I saw him and his wife at Lord Creighton's ball, and they looked smitten with one another. But you know Susan. Whatever she wants—"

"She gets." Andrew finished. "But this time she will concede defeat. Besides, I have problems of my own to worry about. That skinflint Fitz is threatening to sell Winfield Hall right out from under me!"

"You cannot be serious! What will you do without an estate to provide an income or legitimacy? What is a gentleman without an estate?"

"I am sure Fitz does not care how it will affect me."

"From what I remember about Fitzwilliam, he likes to be thought of as an authority and to be begged for assistance. You need only grovel."

"I fear that he and I have crossed that bridge already. Fitz is serious about selling Winfield, and I have to figure out another strategy to make him reconsider."

"Then come to Monthaven Manor tomorrow. Susan has always known how to bend men around her little finger. Perhaps she can devise a plan. In any case, you would do well to keep her on your side. She could be useful, especially if you become homeless."

"I see your point." Andrew shrugged. "Tell her I shall visit tomorrow, but I want no one to know I am coming. I fear that if Fitz found out I am this close to Pemberley, he would confront me. I shall see him when I have a plan and not before."

"I will pass that along," Attaway said, tipping his hat. "Until tomorrow then."

Andrew tipped his hat as well. "Tomorrow."

Sheffield

In a shadowy corner of an inn just outside Sheffield sat two retired Bow Street runners, both now employed by Fitzwilliam Darcy—Mr. Coleridge and Mr. Harahan, respectively. They had inadvertently crossed paths as they went about their assigned tasks and decided to have a pint of ale and compare notes.

"So you say that this man, Brumeloe, owned the horse that was left at Eastbrooke Manor in Richmond after the fire?" Coleridge asked.

"Yes. Not only that, but he left a receipt in a pouch that I traced to a warehouse in Cheapside. The receipt proved most helpful."

"How so?"

Harahan smiled wryly. "It was for a used saddle and the proprietor actually remembered the man who bought it—Andrew Darcy."

"He was certain?"

Harahan took another swig of his ale and wiped his mouth before saying dryly, "According to him, it was easy to recall. His family has done business with the Darcys for years, though he had not so much as heard of Andrew Darcy until the day he bought the saddle. That and the fact that Andrew favoured Mr. Darcy made the sale stand out in his mind."

Coleridge let go with a low whistle. "I fear Mr. Darcy will not be happy to hear that."

"I agree. I tracked Brumeloe as far as the Scottish border and lost him near Gretna Green. I understand he has family in Scotland, so it could take years to find him if they help him hide. And Mr. Darcy may not wish to go to more expense tracking him across Scotland when there are no guarantees. No doubt we will never see his ugly face in England again."

"He is probably still running as fast as his legs will carry him."

"What about you? Have you had any luck?"

"I have been one step behind Andrew Darcy for weeks. He pulls up stakes a lot for someone not already on a wanted poster. I know for certain that he did not return to his estate in Manchester after leaving London—I imagine because Lord Warren has men watching it. So I played a hunch that he would return to Lambton and that led me here."

"But you have not seen him?"

"No. I have it on good authority that he was in Sheffield only days ago. Some say that he returned to Lambton."

"Do you think he is aware that he is being followed by you?"

"Truthfully, I believe that he keeps moving because he fears Lord Warren will find him. Bloody blazes! If he did return to Lambton, I might have passed him on the road without knowing it."

"Do not be so hard on yourself! We cannot commandeer and search all the coaches along the road. Unless we run into our suspects at an inn or post stop, we are limited."

"Yes, but Mr. Darcy is not one for excuses, and I owe him another report. I wanted more information than I have presently."

"He is reasonable. Why not accompany me back to Pemberley, and we shall both report our findings."

Coleridge laughed. "Safety in numbers."

"Precisely."

Chapter 31

Pemberley
Elizabeth's Bedroom
A week after the ball

Occupying the chair in front of her dressing mirror, Elizabeth felt quite alone in spite of the fact that Mrs. O'Reilly had returned to help with her bath and was now styling her hair. Though equally as reluctant as she to end their impromptu honeymoon, William had gone downstairs to meet with Mr. Sturgis regarding some business that the steward felt could not wait. An unexpected loneliness had swept over her with his departure, so much so that Elizabeth now pondered how her disposition could have changed so swiftly. Only a month or so previously, she had relished traipsing all alone through the woods for hours on end, and now her heart was literally aching for her husband's return. Shaking her head at the reality of being so smitten, Elizabeth forced herself to try to concentrate on what Mrs. O'Reilly was saying.

"... and I think that it would look lovely in your hair. Not to mention, it is the latest fashion." Mrs. O'Reilly then smiled at her image in the mirror, evidently awaiting an answer.

"I... I think it would too," Elizabeth replied, embarrassed for O'Reilly to know that she had not heard most of what she said. "How do you propose to accomplish it?" she asked, praying that the answer would give her a clue as to the subject.

"Oh, I shall look for a wide lace at that little shop in Lambton. The loveliest bandeauxs are fashioned from lace, in my opinion, and there is a simple pattern in the magazine that Miss Darcy brought back from London."

Letting go a sigh of relief, Elizabeth replied, "I look forward to seeing what you have in mind." Reminded of Georgiana, who had not been very civil to her when she and William returned to Pemberley after the storm, she asked, "Did Miss Darcy lend you the magazine?"

"No, ma'am. Florence, her maid, said that there was nothing in it that interested her or her mistress and tossed it on the table in the servants' quarters. I asked if I might take a look at it, and she told me I could have it."

Elizabeth nodded absently, wondering if William's sister would ever warm to her. Then pushing those concerns aside, she began to make a mental list of what she needed to accomplish whilst William was busy. First and foremost was returning to the foundlings' home to resume the sewing lessons.

Mrs. O'Reilly proclaimed that her hair was complete, and Elizabeth looked up to study her refection in the mirror. Pleased with what she saw, she smiled. "Thank you, Mrs. O'Reilly."

"You are welcome. Now, do you wish me to return tonight to help you undress or wait until I am summoned?"

"I had rather you wait. I have no idea what Mr. Darcy will have in mind." Afterward, Elizabeth blushed at the implication. "I did not mean that quite the way it sounded."

Mrs. O'Reilly smiled knowingly. "I shall be ready if and when you need me." With those words, the maid curtseyed and left the room.

Once the maid was gone, Elizabeth entered her bedroom in search of the book wherein she recorded her sewing lessons. Glancing about, she noted something sitting on the table by the bed. A big smile crossed her face when she realised it was the box that had contained her wedding ring. Without thinking, she held her hand out to admire the evidence of William's devotion and her eyes began to fill with fresh tears. Refusing to indulge in another cry, she took a deep breath and went to retrieve the box. As she did, a piece of paper fell to the floor and she stooped to pick it up.

Blanchard's Jewellery – Gold wedding band, 18ct, engraved on outside of band with "First. Last. Only. Always." Four 1ct diamonds bezel set between each word. Inscribe inside of band with April 28, 1812. One thousand pounds.

Amazed at how much William had paid for her ring, Elizabeth simply shook her head in awe as she folded the paper and put it back in the small velvet box. Closing the top, she placed everything inside a mahogany chest on her dresser. The chest was one of the few nice possessions she had brought with her from Longbourn, a present from the Gardiners on her eighteenth birthday. As she turned to continue her search, the red spine of her sewing book caught her eye. It peeked out from its hiding place beside the cushion of the upholstered chair near the window. Recovering it, she went out of the room.

Astonished to have arrived at her study without having encountered a single servant, Elizabeth was equally amazed to find the door open. Stepping just inside, she immediately spied Olivia on the right side of the room, sitting at the large table dedicated to sewing. Her aunt's head was down, and so focused was she on her needlework, that she did not hear Elizabeth come in.

"Aunt?"

Olivia looked up and smiled. "Oh my! I assume this means you have escaped my nephew. Should I hide you under the table?"

Elizabeth laughed. "I suppose everyone thinks we have deserted them."

"Do not mind me, child. I could not resist teasing you a bit."

"I do not mind… not really, for I am so very content that nothing could spoil my joy."

By then her aunt had put down her sewing and was coming toward her. Hugging Elizabeth, Olivia pulled back to look into her eyes. "That is how marriage should be."

"I knew that you would understand, for it was your marriage that inspired me to find the same felicity in my own."

"I am so pleased to hear that," her aunt said, squeezing her hands. Then she tilted her head toward the sewing table. "I hope that you do not mind. Mrs. Reynolds let me in so that I could work on the coats." She chuckled. "I promised her I would not bother a thing."

"I do not mind at all. My only regret is that I have neglected my part of the bargain."

"Nonsense! You needed to spend this time alone with Fitzwilliam in order to strengthen your marriage and, as for the coats, Mrs. Kelly, Mrs. O'Reilly and several of Pemberley's maids are helping with the sewing. Along with what little I have contributed and Mrs. Reynolds' efforts when she finds the time, we have finished six coats and have two more almost complete." She motioned to a stack of several items lying in an unoccupied chair. "At this rate, we will be done long before they are needed."

"I am so grateful to everyone for their help." Then as Olivia moved to sit back down at the table, Elizabeth added, "I do not mean to be rude, but I must hurry if I am to go to Lambton this morning."

"To Lambton?"

"Yes. While my husband is busy with his steward today, I thought that I would teach a sewing lesson. I came in here to find a cross-stitch pattern I wish to use."

As Elizabeth searched her desk for the pattern, Aunt Olivia teased, "Are you sure that Fitzwilliam will not go after you the minute he is done with his steward? I can just imagine him riding into Lambton and bringing you home on horseback."

Elizabeth laughed. "I had not considered that, but I believe he will be busy for quite some time. After all, he has not met with his steward in over a week." Then she held up a paper. "I found it."

The words had no more than left her mouth than William appeared in the doorway, his face anxious. Just as Elizabeth came around the corner of the desk, with her attention focused on her aunt, he rushed inside. She was both surprised and speechless as he pulled her into his embrace and kissed her hungrily. Logic screamed for her to point out that his aunt was present, but all logic was lost in the sweetness of that kiss. And instead of protesting, she leaned into him.

Finally, he quit the kiss to declare breathlessly, "I thought Sturgis would never finish. I have missed you so much, sweetheart. Have you missed me?" Without awaiting her answer, he captured her mouth again.

"Good morning, Nephew!"

Without letting go of Elizabeth, William's head swung around. "I... I am sorry, Aunt. I had no idea you were here."

"That is obvious." Olivia teased. "But no apology is necessary... except perhaps from me." She stood and began gathering her things. "You had no reason to think I was here. Obviously, your attention was elsewhere."

"Please stay. As I said, I have to leave shortly," Elizabeth protested.

Olivia walked past them, halting at the door. "I really must go. I promised your uncle that I would not be gone all morning." She winked. "You see, just like the two of you, *he* still misses me whenever we are apart."

William and Elizabeth watched her go with smiling faces before facing each other. "You mentioned that you were leaving," he said cautiously.

"Will, you do realise that I have completely neglected the sewing lessons for the girls at the home. What will they think?"

William patiently took the book and pattern from her hand and laid them back on her desk. "Mrs. Moody and Mrs. Samson volunteered to help with the lessons until such time as you can resume them. So there is no reason for you to worry."

The golden facets of her eyes sparkled with many emotions— all of which were enchanting. "And why have you not told me this before now?"

"It is simple. Since our stay at the cottage, I have selfishly desired all of your attention; thus, I was of a mind not to bring up the subject unless you mentioned it."

She beamed, running both hands over the hard muscles of his chest and then around his neck. Entwining her fingers with the long curls at his collar, Elizabeth whispered, "You, sir, are a hopeless romantic."

William's expression grew serious, his eyes darkening with desire. "I am guilty as charged, and I throw myself upon your tender mercy." Another fierce kiss ensued before he tilted his head back to ask, "Do you have any objections to disappearing with me for the rest of the day?"

Her eyes twinkled with naughtiness, and impulsively William swept his wife off her feet, setting off a round of giggles. Then he carried her through the door and started down the hall toward their suite.

"Will! The servants!" Elizabeth exclaimed, kicking her feet weakly as if to protest. "What will they think?"

"They will think I am passionately in love with my wife and they would be correct."

As fate would have it, at the sound of them in the hall, Polly and Clara scrambled to keep out of sight in the room they were about to exit. Immediately after the Darcys passed their door, both maids stuck their heads into the hall to follow their progress. Fascinated, they watched as the man they had always thought of as very proper acted like a besotted schoolboy.

As the Darcys got further away, Clara whispered, "I would not have believed it had I not seen it with my own eyes."

"Nor I," Polly agreed. Then she giggled. "I suppose Florence was right about one thing."

"What is that?"

"If they were not sharing a bed before, they are now."

Just after the Darcys went out of sight around the corner, Mrs. Reynolds started down the hall from the opposite direction. Quickly grabbing their cleaning items, the maids exited the room with stoic faces. Nodding as they passed the housekeeper, Clara and Polly made it halfway down the hall before they could hold back no longer and broke into giggles. Mrs. Reynolds stopped and studied the two, her brows furrowing. Then noticing that the mistress' study door was open, she looked inside and, seeing no one, closed and locked it before going on her way.

Monthaven Manor

As Mrs. Holden made her way up the stairs to the small library on the second floor while carrying a tray of fresh tea and refreshments, she reflected on how much her life had changed since Lord Hartley was no longer there. She had worked for the Hartleys all her life, first for the parents and afterward for their son. Then after he was lost, Mrs. Holden had stayed on with his widow, despite the fact that she had no admiration for the woman, because she felt that she was too old to begin again elsewhere.

Her mistress thought her position entitled her to respect, although she did nothing to warrant it. Not only was her eye critical and her tongue sharp, but none of the servants thought her a good mother to Lord Hartley's heir, for she left him in the care of nannies at the Hartley estate while she wandered all over England. And from what Mrs. Holden had overheard since accompanying her mistress to London, and afterward here, her employer was a manipulator. This was especially true of today's guest, Miss Darcy, whom the maid thought entirely too malleable. She had known the girl's brother, Fitzwilliam, since he and Lord Hartley had attended university together, and she thought well of him.

At least he had sense enough not to fall for Lady Susan Patton's wiles. That was more than I can say for poor Lord Hartley.

By now Mrs. Holden was outside the library and could hear the conversation inside that room through the open door. Looking about and seeing no other servants, she stepped to the side of the door to see what she might learn.

"Andrew, I fear it will not help if I confront Fitzwilliam about selling your estate," Georgiana said, her voice rising with frustration. "In fact, it would do the opposite and strengthen his resolve. Only this week I was told that my opinions are not valid and that I should keep them to myself."

"It is just as I said," Lady Susan interjected. "Your best course of action is to present your cousin with a substantial amount of money toward Winfield's debts. That will prove that you have not been shirking your duty but have been working to keep the estate solvent. With any luck, Fitzwilliam will cancel the sale."

"But you do not understand!" Andrew declared. "Though my new project should prove lucrative, I have just now begun to make a profit. I have only three hundred pounds saved, and that will not be enough to impress Fitz."

"How much do you need, then?" Lord Attaway asked.

Andrew grasped his chin, rubbing one finger back and forth over his lips as he considered his answer. "Most likely an additional five hundred pounds, if I am to convince him that I am serious about saving Winfield Hall."

Sighing heavily, Lady Susan stood and walked over to a window where she stared into the distance for a time. Everyone in the room waited with bated breath until she turned to address Andrew.

"I shall lend you five hundred pounds. With your three, that should be sufficient inducement for Fitzwilliam to give you more time to turn a profit and save the estate."

"That is very kind of you, Susan. Rest assured that I shall pay you back within the next two to three months."

"If I may ask, what is your new occupation, Andrew?" Georgiana asked innocently.

"He will not tell us, Miss Darcy," Attaway broke in with a chuckle. "I imagine he wants to keep all the profits to himself."

Andrew laughed along with him. "If everyone knew about it, there would be too many investors and not as much profit. I abhor people who are self-seeking, but with Fitz on my back, I truly need this enterprise to keep Winfield Hall afloat."

Lady Susan pressed him. "So when will you talk to Fitzwilliam?"

"First I have some business to conduct, but in several days, I should have time to schedule a meeting with him."

Georgiana set a delicate teacup on the table next to her and rose from the sofa. "I hate to leave good company, but I simply must. Brother thinks I am riding at Pemberley. He would be furious if he found out I came here without his permission."

Susan rushed to her. "Thank you for coming. I am so glad that you not only joined us for tea but had the opportunity to see your cousin again."

Georgiana smiled at Attaway. "I am glad that I got to see everyone." Then she turned her smile on Andrew. "You especially, Cousin. You will never know how dull Pemberley is now that you are gone and Fitzwilliam is married."

"So it is not as it was when you and I used to entertain one another with our jokes?"

"Not at all! Now Fitzwilliam spends an inordinate amount of time in his rooms with Elizabeth. So much so, that the house seems more a mausoleum than a home."

Susan broke in. "That will change soon, dear. Mark my words."

Apparently unconvinced, Georgiana tilted her head and shrugged her shoulders. At that exact moment, Mrs. Holden knocked on the door and walked into the room with the tea and biscuits.

"Will you not stay and have a fresh cup of tea before you go?" Susan asked Georgiana.

"No, thank you. I must leave."

As Georgiana walked toward the door, Susan hurriedly caught up with her, putting her arm through her friend's as she looked back over her shoulder and addressed the maid.

"Please pour for our guests, Mrs. Holden. I shall return as soon as I have seen Miss Darcy to the door."

As the two ladies quit the room, Andrew and Attaway went over to the table where the maid began filling cups with tea.

After Georgiana's departure

When Lady Susan re-entered the library, she began speaking immediately.

"I apologise, Andrew. I know that you asked that your presence here be kept a secret, but Matthew had asked Georgiana to come for tea and she decided, out of the blue, to come *today*. We had no notice."

"No need for apology. Georgiana has always been a close ally. I know she will not give me away."

Noticing that the maid was standing off to the side, Lady Susan said, "You may go, Mrs. Holden. I shall ring if I need you."

"Yes, my lady," the maid replied, curtseying and exiting the room. Once more she waited just outside the door to eavesdrop.

"Now, let us discuss things best kept secret from Georgiana at present. What can you do to help me discredit that woman Fitzwilliam married? Rumours are that you and she were once *close*, so tell me something I can use against her."

Andrew shrugged. "I admit that on first acquaintance thoughts of offering for her did cross my mind; after all, she is a pretty little thing with fine eyes and a lot of spirit. But by the time my cousin arrived in Meryton, I had decided that her lack of a fortune made an offer impossible. Still, I had plans to parlay her sympathy of my position to my advantage. Of course, Fitz ruined that."

"Then you have no evidence to prove she was a harlot?"

"If they consummated the marriage, then Fitz knows very well that she was a virgin when they married. How can I refute that?"

"Well, she could have committed indiscretions without going that far."

"I am sure that he would not take my word over his wife's, if that is what you are implying. Especially if he is as smitten as Georgiana says."

"Then I shall have to reconsider my offer to help you. Why should I lend you five hundred pounds if you cannot help rid Pemberley of her?"

Andrew grew anxious. "I... I can think of only one thing that might convince Fitz that she is not the woman he believed her to be when they wed."

"Pray tell me what it is then," Susan said sarcastically.

Attaway laughed aloud, catching himself when Andrew gave him a formidable scowl.

"I can draw unflattering portraits of her and arrange for them to fall into Fitz's hands. Of course, he must never know that I was the artist."

Lord Attaway snickered now, causing Lady Susan to sneer at him before confronting Andrew. "You draw pictures? How ridiculous is that!"

"I can draw; I have all my life! In fact, I paid my way with that talent while I was in London, but I kept it quiet for my protection."

Susan sneered, "Why would you need protection? And how would *unflattering* pictures turn Fitzwilliam against that chit?"

"In one word—nudes. I have been creating nude portraits in charcoal of any woman that a man may desire."

"Even another man's wife?" Susan asked.

"Mostly other men's wives. And you can understand that if a relation of one of my subjects saw the portrait, there would be hell to pay; thus, the reason for the secrecy."

Attaway chimed in. "How could a man bring such a drawing home?"

"The gentlemen who commission my drawings claim that they hang them where their wives are never allowed—like a study, an office or a bedroom."

"So any man can possess a nude that bears a resemblance to another man's wife, daughter or sweetheart for his private enjoyment?" Attaway asked in awe.

"Exactly," Andrew said.

"How ingenious!" Attaway exclaimed. "I have someone in mind already."

"I pay you well, so keep your mind on the task at hand," Susan declared hotly. Then she questioned Andrew. "But if they order from you, do they not think you are the artist?"

"I have convinced them that I am the go-between for a friend—a portraitist. I tell them that I get a portion of the sale and it helps keep the artist from starving between commissioned portraits. Still, I would be suspect if word got out."

"I see," Lady Susan said circumspectly. Then a small smile appeared on her face. "It might work. Fitzwilliam is such a prude that he would die if he thought his wife had posed nude for any man."

"There is only the slight chance that it might work," Andrew said. "Clearly Miss Ben—Mrs. Darcy is not that kind of woman. Besides, if Fitz is in love—"

"Save the sentimentality! What choice do I have at this point? How soon can I have the drawing?"

"As I said, I have business to handle and then I shall return and talk to Fitz."

"Good! Have the drawing when you return, and we have a bargain."

"As you wish."

Pemberley
That same day

As Colonel Fitzwilliam's stallion galloped the final hundred yards toward Pemberley, his rider was filled with a mixture of exhaustion and apprehension. The exhaustion resulted from Thaggart's absence and a head cold that had lingered interminably. His batman had come down with a stomach ailment just as they were to leave and Richard had no doubt that it was due to the large amount of stew and wine he had consumed the night before. But in spite of Thaggart's infirmity, General Lassiter expected Richard in London by week's end, so he had no choice but to leave without his aide. In hindsight, he was surprised at how having Thaggart along to handle the horses made the journey less wearisome; thus, he vowed to draft someone to serve in his place the next time something of this nature happened.

His apprehension was the result of not having heard from Darcy lately. His cousin's last letter contained nothing that would lead Richard to believe that he and Elizabeth had reconciled their differences; in fact, Darcy's misery had been evident on each page. It tugged at his heart, for Richard had great hopes for his cousin's marriage when he departed Pemberley for the north, certain that Elizabeth had seen the error of her ways. Presently, however, he was beginning to think he may have been far too optimistic. Nonetheless, he had little time to dwell on that, for a footman was already running down the front steps of Pemberley to take his horse.

"Colonel Fitzwilliam, sir, it is good to see you again."

Richard squinted against the sun's glare to see if he could identify the man. "Thank you. Wainwright, is it not?"

"Yes, sir, it is!"

At that moment, the front door opened, and Mr. Walker and Mrs. Reynolds walked onto the portico, smiling a greeting in their usual manner. They waited until Richard had dismounted and began to climb the stairs before they welcomed him almost in unison.

"Colonel Fitzwilliam. So happy to see you again!"

"It is always a pleasure to have you at Pemberley."

Mrs. Reynolds looked over his shoulder and her brow furrowed. "Where is your shadow?"

"Thaggart became ill in his stomach just before we were to leave. I think he is just weary of travelling and decided to play sick."

"Oh, I did not think him the kind to miss a stay at Pemberley," the housekeeper chided with a smile.

Richard guffawed. "When you put it that way, I have to agree."

As they all entered the foyer, the colonel was a little surprised that William was not there to greet him, so he ventured, "Where is everyone?"

Mrs. Reynolds glanced at Mr. Walker nervously before answering. "Your aunt and uncle are visiting Mrs. Fitzwilliam's aunt in Lambton. A cousin who is travelling through here on his way to London will be there today. Georgiana is exercising her horse, but she should return at any time."

Richard's eyebrows shot up. "And my cousin and his lovely bride?"

"Mr. and Mrs. Darcy are... " she lifted her chin a bit protectively, "in their rooms."

A wry smile crossed Richard's face as he tried not to laugh aloud. "They are still upstairs?"

Mrs. Reynolds nodded in answer.

"And have they been in their rooms all day?"

"Mr. Darcy met with his steward this morning," Mr. Walker ventured, trying to be helpful.

A big smile split Richard's face as he pulled a pocket watch from inside his coat and flipped the case open to see the time. "I see! And do you expect them to come downstairs for tea?"

"I—we had not planned on it, what with the Fitzwilliams in Lambton. Besides, the master and mistress have taken tea in their rooms lately."

Satisfied that something good must have happened since he was away, Richard declared, "Please do not disturb them on my behalf. If they are not down for dinner, then I shall have you inform Darcy of my arrival, but not before." Then he leaned close to Mrs. Reynolds, saying mischievously, "What are the chances of getting a basin of hot water to wash the dust off?"

"It would be no trouble at all. However, we can provide a hot bath in less than an hour. That is, if you would rather bathe."

"A bath would be like heaven! And I would be most appreciative."

The housekeeper smiled. "A bath it is, then." She addressed Mr. Walker. "If you will have the men bring in more water, I will have the maids heat it and let you know when to fill the tub."

Walker nodded and walked away, so Mrs. Reynolds turned back to Richard. "Mrs. Lantrip is preparing cakes and finger sandwiches for tea. I can fetch something for you now, if you are hungry."

"Let me see," Richard said, bringing one hand up playfully to cup his chin. "If the Darcys do not come down for tea, then send the tray upstairs. If they do decide to grace everyone with their presence, send word and I shall come downstairs."

"Of course, Colonel. Your room is ready and waiting, as usual." Then she added. "You *do* realise that I shall have to tell Mr. Darcy that you are here sometime before dinner."

"I suppose you must," Richard chuckled, "but if he does not come out of his rooms for tea, let us leave off telling him until nearer the dinner hour. After all, we would not want to *interrupt* anything." With those words, he went up the grand staircase, laughing to himself.

Mrs. Reynolds could not help but smile as she watched him ascend the stairs. Then remembering the bath water, she hurried towards the kitchen.

Chapter 32

Pemberley
The next morning

Dawn found Richard making his way as quietly down the grand staircase as his boots would possibly allow, sporting a smile that he could not expunge. Last night William and Elizabeth had joined him, Georgiana and the Fitzwilliams for dinner, and the couple's newly acquired felicity had been unmistakable. Not only were they amiable to one another, but they acted very much in love, and the transformation had lifted everyone's spirits, including his. Well, everyone except Georgiana's, that is.

He had managed a private word with her as they removed to the music room after dinner, but Georgiana had been her usual aloof and haughty self. Recalling it now, Richard wondered at the futility of trying to get through to her and questioned how long Darcy would tolerate her attitude. His mind thus occupied, he was unaware of William's presence until he heard his name called. Stopping on the last step, Richard turned to gaze up toward the landing and found his cousin hurrying towards him down the stairs, pulling his coat on as he came. William's hair was unkempt and he was unshaven. He wore no cravat, and his shirt was open. It was so unlike his staid cousin to be in such a state of disarray that Richard broke into a wry smile.

"Darcy, I hope I did not *disturb* anything important."

"*Richard*," William said, dragging the word out in warning.

"What?" Richard declared innocently. "Do not begrudge me the opportunity to tease you, Cousin. I have watched you carry on without the love of a good woman for far too many years. Now that you have found Elizabeth, the least you can do is allow me a bit of fun whilst your marriage is still new."

William's smile returned and he shrugged. "I suppose you are right."

"I am always right."

Shaking his head at Richard's bravado, William added quietly, "To be truthful, I would not have left Elizabeth except that she is fast asleep, and I must discuss a few things with you before you leave." By then he was standing on the same step as Richard. "I shall instruct Mrs. Reynolds to send food and drink to my study so that we may break our fast whilst we talk in private—that is, if you have no objection."

Being in such close proximity, it was hard not to notice some incriminating red marks along William's neck. Consequently, it took all the colonel's strength not to smirk with his reply.

"That suits me. And I imagine you would rather have this discussion done with and return to more pleasant pursuits."

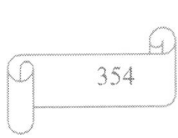

A good while later, empty plates were set aside and coffee cups were refilled as the conversation became more serious.

"So, you are saying that the Bow Street Runners had no luck?" Richard ventured, somewhat perturbed as he leaned back to prop his boots on the edge of William's desk. "I felt sure that by now they would have tracked down whoever was responsible for the fire."

"I did not say they had *no* luck. Harahan learned the identity of the man who left the horse at Eastbrooke Manor. He is called Brumeloe. Most likely it was he who killed Mr. Hobson and set the house on fire. Harahan tracked him as far as Gretna Green before losing him."

"That is reasonable. Most of the miscreants I track head straight to Scotland. It is easy to get lost there, as very few Scots will help an Englishman looking for someone on the run, but I suppose if I were a Scot, I would not either."

"I agree. And there is more. The receipt found in the saddle led Harahan to a warehouse in London. The proprietor remembered the sale—a used saddle—and to whom he sold it. You see, the family name was familiar to the man because he had done business with that particular family for years."

"What name is that?"

"Darcy."

Richard's feet came off the desk as he stood. "Andrew?"

"It had to be, for the shopkeeper told Harahan that he resembled me. Though I shall never be able to prove it unless someone confesses, I will always believe that Andrew sent the man to Eastbrooke Manor. Perhaps he believed he could scare the women into leaving England, but things got out of hand. If the women and children were no longer around, it would have relieved him of future obligations, like the children's education." William stood up now, angrily tossing his serviette down on the desk. "I would give anything if I had never told him about the estate. I hoped that he would take an interest in his children—perhaps even decide to see them now and again."

"You are not God, Darcy. And you could not have known this would happen," Richard declared, gripping William's shoulder in a brotherly gesture. "As usual, you were only trying to help."

William dropped his head. "Still—"

"I will hear no more talk of that!" Richard interrupted, taking his seat again. "However, I agree with you, for why else would Andrew have provided the man a saddle. Have you located him yet?"

"Coleridge says he is on the run. In the last letter I received, he was heading to Sheffield to see if Andrew was there. I do expect to hear from both detectives this week, however."

"If you do, send me word in London with the details. You have the address."

"I will, if you have not returned." William sat back down, taking another sip of the hot coffee. "When are you going to come for a real visit?"

"I am not sure at this point," Richard smirked. "But do you ask because you miss me or because you are worried that my visit would disrupt your honeymoon?"

"My honeymoon, as you call it, will never end if I have any say about it!"

There was a loud guffaw. "Oh? And how do you propose to get any work done if you stay in bed all day!"

"Tease me all you wish," William said, suddenly smiling like a fool. "I am too happy to get upset."

Richard considered him fondly. "You cannot know how much it pleases me to see you happy—nay, deliriously happy. I have spent many years worrying about your penchant for melancholy, especially after Georgiana tossed aside your good opinion in favour of Andrew's useless approbation."

William's face fell, and he began to toy with the Darcy crest ring that never left his little finger. "Ah, yes, my sister. I had hoped—" He stopped to control his emotions. Then shaking his head in resignation, he continued. "It appears that she has no intentions of behaving kindly towards Elizabeth, and if that continues, I feel I have no choice but to send her to live with your parents. At any rate, she is now more akin to your father in temperament than to me."

"I did not want to bring it up, but I spoke to Georgiana last night, and I am of the same opinion. She is unwavering in her bias against Elizabeth."

"That comes as no surprise." William shrugged, then chose to change the subject. "To tell the truth, I was hoping you might return from London quickly and stay for the rest of the summer."

Richard looked puzzled. "And why is that?"

William saddened. "Unfortunately, I have business in Chesterfield next week—business I was going to have you handle if you were here."

"Chesterfield? Laughlin Manor?"

"Yes, in regards to the horses Pemberley provides so that Lord Laughlin can meet his obligations to the army."

"Perhaps Uncle George got along well with that man, but you and Laughlin are so dissimilar that I marvel that you can agree on anything."

"We have always been in opposition, but he has changed for the worse since Lady Laughlin's death. He is certainly not the sort of man I would seek out for company. Still, his contract with the army brings in considerable income for Pemberley. He never has enough stallions, and with my help, he fulfils their demands."

"Do you feel your ankle is well enough to ride that distance?"

"It still gets stiff if I ride for long periods, but it is not unbearable."

"I see. Well, since you and Elizabeth are inseparable, have you thought of taking her along?"

"That will never happen! Since Lady Laughlin died and the viscount is still unmarried, there is nothing respectable about Laughlin Manor. One might think they were at White's or Boodles for the surfeit of gambling taking place there, not to mention the number of questionable ladies who magically appear after dark."

The corners of Richard's mouth lifted. "It sounds more like my kind of gathering than yours?"

"Precisely."

"And the talk is that Viscount Barrett inherited his father's reputation as a rake."

William's eyes darkened. "Another reason I have no intention of subjecting Elizabeth to their company. I had planned to send Sturgis to negotiate a price, but Laughlin would not hear of it. He keeps to the old ways and is unwilling to meet with a mere steward, but *you* could take my place with no argument."

"That is because he and father are old friends."

"And because you are an earl's son and one who can hold your own in an argument. Lord Laughlin loves to negotiate." William stood and began to pace. "That is a practice I find abhorrent when we both know how to arrive at a fair price."

Richard smirked. "I see your point; you have always detested arguing." Then his expression softened. "Sorry, Cousin. I would gladly go in your stead, but I have no idea when I shall be able to return to Pemberley. General Lassiter may keep me in London for a week, maybe more, before sending me this way again."

"I understand."

"So what will you do if I do not return in time?"

"There will be no getting around it. I shall have to go; however, I am determined to go via horseback if I must. By taking Mason's Pass, it is a day's ride there and another back. With one day to work out an agreement, I should return in three days." Walking over to a window, he pulled back the curtain and stared into the distance. "Three days apart from Elizabeth will seem forever."

Richard almost laughed at the absurdity of his statement, but caught himself when William looked back to him. There was definitely nothing humorous about the anguish in his eyes. So he stood and walked over to William, gripping his shoulder with one hand.

"How would this suit you? When I get to London I shall ask the general what his plans are, and if I can make it back in time to go to Chesterfield, I will send word."

A smile crossed William's face. "I knew I could count on you to make an effort."

Richard was somewhat uncomfortable being praised. "Just as I have always relied on you."

At that moment, there was a knock on the door. "Come," William called. The door opened slightly and Mr. Walker appeared.

"Begging your pardon, sir, but the colonel asked me to inform him when his horse was ready."

"Thank you, Walker. I shall be right there," Richard replied, then addressed William as the butler retreated. "I must be on my way. As always, I appreciate your hospitality, Darcy, but I cannot express strongly enough how pleased I am to find you and Elizabeth so content."

"And it is, in no little part, thanks to you." William said with a grin. "Elizabeth told me that you spoke to her—against my express orders, I might add—when you escorted her to Pemberley."

"You are well aware of my propensity for stating my opinions, especially when I think someone is wrong. So if I spoke out of turn, it is clearly your fault for asking me to escort her."

William slid his arm around his cousin's shoulder as they walked toward the door. "Regardless, I am glad that you completely ignored me in this case."

"If it makes you feel any better, I almost always ignore you."

They chuckled as they walked into the hallway, the sound of their laughter causing several maids and footmen to stop, listen and smile before continuing their duties. Moving into the foyer, though, they were surprised to find their aunt and uncle waiting patiently at the bottom of the stairs.

Richard was the first to speak. "I thought I made it clear that you were not to rise at this ungodly hour to see me off."

Olivia Fitzwilliam's expression grew serious as she placed her hands on her hips. "Richard Fitzwilliam, you are never too old for me to discipline!" As everyone quietly laughed, her face softened. "I would not have you leave without saying a proper goodbye. In my lifetime, I have learned a hard lesson—no one is promised tomorrow. Thus, I say what I wish to say whenever the opportunity arises."

Richard looked properly chastised. "You are right."

"Of course I am," she teased, stepping forward to place a kiss on Richard's cheek and cup his face in a motherly fashion. "Joseph and I just wanted you to know that we love you very much, and we shall pray for a safe journey to London."

Touched at the display of affection, Richard could only nod. Next, Joseph stretched a hand out for his nephew to shake and with the other gripped his shoulder. "Be watchful, Richard. Without your batman, you are more vulnerable to those up to no good. Keep an eye out for highwaymen, and let Fitzwilliam know when you arrive, so we will not worry."

"I shall."

"Good. Then Olivia and I shall leave you and Fitzwilliam to say your goodbyes while we break our fast."

As they walked away, Richard turned to find a concerned look on William's face. "I had not thought about it, but would you object if I send a footman along with you?"

Richard chuckled. "I have travelled many years without an aide. I think I can manage to get to London all by myself."

"It would certainly be no problem. He could attach himself to Darcy House once you arrive in London."

As Richard walked toward the front door, he teased, "You do know that marriage has changed you?"

"In what way?"

"It may just be the novelty of having your lovely wife dependent on you now, but you are beginning to sound just like our aunt. And I am not sure I can cope with another aunt."

As they went out the door, loud guffaws could be heard coming from the portico.

That afternoon

Zeus appeared totally unaffected to be carrying both William and Elizabeth up one of Pemberley's many hillsides towards a stand of trees, whilst a pack horse, tethered to a rope, trailed behind. Standing eighteen-hands high and weighing 1300 pounds, he was the largest stallion in Pemberley's stable and well able to shoulder the load. The smaller of the two horses had been enlisted solely for the purpose of carrying the two large baskets filled with items that Mrs. Reynolds deemed necessary for a picnic. Though Elizabeth feared riding so large an animal alone, from her perch sitting sideways in front of William, she felt secure. So secure, in fact, that instead of focusing on keeping her seat, she was enjoying a view of Pemberley that she had not seen previously. And as her head swung from one side to the other, William could not have been more pleased.

"Will, I was just thinking… the idea for this picnic was so unexpected. Only yesterday you said that you did not want to leave our rooms for the rest of the week." Her voice was even more subdued when she added, "Has the teasing from your cousin made you uncomfortable about spending so much time alone with me?"

Suddenly Zeus was reined to a halt and two strong hands framed her face, turning her so that they were eye-to-eye. William willed her to see inside his heart.

"I shall never be embarrassed by my feelings for you, Elizabeth. In his usual manner, Richard did tease me this morning about keeping you locked away and it made me consider if I was being selfish. I know how much you enjoy being out of doors, and I thought this picnic might provide a welcome respite while still providing us with complete privacy."

A crooked smile crossed her face, and Elizabeth turned back around, leaning languidly into his chest. "Thank you for being so thoughtful, but I can assure you that I do not regret any of the hours we spent in our rooms." Then she became curious again. "There is one other thing though—why did you insist I ride with you when Phoebe was available?"

His lips pursed as he tried not to smile at his cleverness. "Zeus is well able to carry us both."

"Still, it seems unfair for him to bear the weight of the two of us."

"It is obvious that he is not struggling, sweetheart. Besides, I love having you close to me, and I thought it simpler if you rode with me so I could do this." He took a handkerchief from his pocket and tied it around her head, covering her eyes. "I have a surprise for you."

Elizabeth giggled. "Another surprise? Will, you are going to spoil me."

He kicked Zeus into a trot. "There is no such thing, my darling."

After only a short while, the horse came to a stop again and William dismounted. Then Elizabeth felt his hands around her waist as he pulled her from Zeus, placing her firmly on the ground.

"Now you may look."

She reached up to remove the blindfold and gasped. In front of her lay a fairytale setting—a large pond with a waterfall fed by a stream, surrounded by a carpet of multi-coloured wildflowers.

"Oh, Will, it is beautiful!"

Reverently she advanced toward the pond, her face growing more animated with each step as William's chest filled with pride.

"This is where my parents brought Georgiana and me whenever they wished to enjoy life as a family—just the four of us, with no servants." William came up behind her, slipping his arms around her waist. "Do you see the large boulder that juts into the water near the falls?" Elizabeth nodded. "That is where I learned to swim."

"It looks idyllic," she answered. Suddenly she looked down to see something dart across the sunny, pebbled bottom of the pond. "Will, I see fish!"

"The pond is full of fish, though only this area is shallow enough for anyone to see them. That is why my parents let us play here unsupervised. The section just under the waterfall is deep; that is where we swam. By the way, can you swim?"

"I can. Father taught me almost as soon as I could walk and against my mother's wishes, I might add. Who taught you?"

"Father tried to teach me the summer I was three, but I was too young to grasp the idea. The next year Richard showed me again, and I took to it straightaway. When she was old enough, I taught Georgiana.

"Just under that end of the waterfall," he pointed to a narrower stream of water on the right, "is a good-sized cave. Richard and I discovered it the summer I was eight. Once, when we did something we should not have, we decided to hide in the cave. It never occurred to us—until it began to get dark—that we would have to face our parents eventually." He shook his head. "Nevertheless, by the time we walked back to Pemberley, our mothers were so relieved to see us that our punishment was not quite as severe as it should have been. Of course, we never told a soul about our hideout."

"Until now," Elizabeth said, tilting her head up so that he caught the twinkle in her eyes.

"Until now," he breathed, pressing a kiss to her upturned face. As she looked back to the pond, she nestled deeper into his arms.

"And what horrible crime did you and Richard commit?"

"We entered a pasture to ride a young bull; however, we did not close the gate securely, and while we were concentrating on our goal, all the other livestock in that pasture escaped."

"Why on earth would you want to ride a bull?"

"Richard's older brother, the viscount, dared us. Silly motive, I know, but when you are young, a dare can be a challenge to your manhood. We were lucky to escape with our lives, and it took the staff several hours to round up the animals that had escaped. Needless to say, our fathers were furious. It was left to our mothers to save our hides."

Elizabeth giggled. "So I should remember never to challenge your

manhood, or you might do something foolish?"

William nuzzled her neck then kissed it. "I hope I am no longer as cheeky as I was at eight, but I shall meet any challenges you care to issue regarding my manhood, Mrs. Darcy."

"Oh, but I would never need to issue such a challenge," she replied impishly, "for now that we are lovers, I have no doubts about your manhood."

Instantly, she was being turned around and kissed passionately, his lips melding with hers, while his fingers caressed her back. When she moaned in response, William broke the kiss, though he was breathing heavily.

He tilted his head towards a stand of trees. "There is a place just inside there." His voice was rough with desire as he continued. "It is hidden from the world. When the responsibilities of Pemberley threatened to overwhelm me after Father died, it became my sanctuary. Would you like to see it?"

"I would love to."

Sweeping her into his arms, he walked in that direction. Not far after entering the trees, they came upon a small clearing. Elizabeth's thoughts flew to a book she had once read about a secret garden. The place was a perfect oval, filled with wildflowers and a thick carpet of grass. On the left was a small replica of the white gazebo that stood near the lake, though this structure's intricately designed walls were hidden by flowering vines. In the centre of it stood a small table with two chairs of wrought-iron and a matching footstool to one side. Opposite the gazebo, hanging from a tall tree was a wooden swing, also painted white. Completely captivated, Elizabeth looked skyward to see glimpses of blue sky and rays of sunlight filtering through the canopy of trees.

"This place is very secure... very private," William said. "No one can see in here just in passing. Do you think we might—would you possibly consider... " His voice trailed off and he hesitated.

Turning to face him, she slid her fingers slowly up his chest, hearing his sharp intake of breath when at last they entwined the long hair at his collar.

"Will, I think this would be the perfect place to conceive a baby. What do you think?"

Immediately, she found herself engulfed in his embrace and being twirled in a circle. Then, inexplicably, he stopped and stepped back. "The blanket!" he exclaimed. "It is in one of the baskets. Wait right here, sweetheart!"

Instantly he vanished, leaving Elizabeth to giggle as he rushed away. Having no choice but to wait, she walked into the gazebo. In the middle of the table was something she had not noticed at first: a wooden box. Flipping open the lid, she found several books, including a Bible. Picking it up, she opened the cover to find stamped in gold *Fitzwilliam George Darcy*.

"That is one of my Bibles."

William's voice startled her and she turned. "I was just curious to whom it belonged."

His white teeth flashed as he smiled. "I keep the Bible here because it is my habit to consult it whenever I have important decisions to make. I find the solitude of this place helps me to think more clearly."

After she replaced the Bible in the box, Elizabeth took a handkerchief she had embroidered with her initials from the pocket of her gown. She placed it in the box and shut the lid. At William's puzzled look, she explained, "I like the idea that something of mine is here with something that belongs to you. The handkerchief will have to do until I can replace it with a book of my own."

William could not restrain himself from sweeping her off her feet and kissing her soundly. "I love how you think, Mrs. Darcy. Now, before I went to fetch the blanket, you were saying something about this being a good place to conceive our child."

"I believe I was."

The animals of the forest were witness to the passion shared by William and Elizabeth on the blanket in the grass. And though there had been a marked increase in tittering among the squirrels and birds, the lovers were too occupied to notice. Later, when both were satiated and the forest was silent again, William lay on his back with his coat rolled up for a pillow, while Elizabeth lay in his arms. She faced him on her side, her head resting in the crook of his neck and one arm splayed across his chest.

"Is there anything I can get for you, my love? Some wine, perhaps, or something to eat?" William asked, pulling the blanket closer around her.

She smiled languorously. "I am not hungry. Just let me lie here for a little while longer. I want to remember this day forever."

Warmth infused William from head to toe. "I will hold you as long as you wish." Softly brushing his lips over hers, he then studied her with a wistful expression. "I have heard that love grows stronger with time, but I do not think I could possibly love you more than I do at this moment, my darling."

Joyful beyond measure, he laid his head back and closed his eyes, and they promptly fell asleep. An hour had passed before the chatter of two red squirrels that had come down from the tree to get a closer look at the intruders woke the lovers.

Now they *were* hungry and ready to sample the fare that Mrs. Reynolds had sent. Overwhelmed by the array—fresh bread, cheese, ham, homemade pickles, fig preserves, grapes and apples, cakes and biscuits, and a bottle of wine—Elizabeth expressed amusement, saying the picnics at Longbourn were much more modest. In his usual meticulous way, William explained that Mrs. Reynolds always included a large variety in order to provide them a selection, and they were not expected to eat everything.

For his trouble, a grape hit him in the forehead, falling into his lap as Elizabeth giggled mischievously. "Will, we are from such different backgrounds that I am amazed that we are so well-suited."

Chuckling at her sauciness, he fed her the grape. "We may have differed in our stations, but we are alike in our integrity, our goals and our desires."

"Well said." Elizabeth replied. Then her thoughts flew to another subject. "May we wade in the water as soon as we finish eating? I love the feel of pebbles under my toes. We have a stream at Longbourn, and I used to wade there all the time."

"Whatever you desire, we shall do."

Later, except for a quick detour to pick some wildflowers which he fashioned into a crown for her head, they went directly to the shallow end of the pond. Vowing not to get her dress wet, Elizabeth removed her shoes and stockings, gathered her skirts and held them aloft. Even so, she complained that it was unfair that she had to go to such trouble while William's tall boots kept him dry.

William winked. "That is just the way it is, sweetheart. I am a man; I stay dry because I wear the boots in the family."

Seeing how pleased he was with himself, Elizabeth plotted her revenge. Waiting until his back was turned, she began soaking him with water. When he ran after her, splashing her in retaliation, she got so tickled that she slipped off one of the rocks that served as a bridge across the water and wet the bottom of her gown. Running also played great havoc with her hair, causing it to escape its pins. The results were ringlets of dark curls framing her face while the rest cascaded down her back.

She had no way of knowing, but the sight of her fine legs and unruly hair caused a noticeable reaction in William. Not wishing to interrupt her amusement, he had turned away; however, after she splashed him with water, all resolve vanished and he chased her back to the secret garden. Once more, the blanket—abandoned only a short while before—proved the most useful item Mrs. Reynolds had packed for the trip.

With the sun waning, Elizabeth found herself sitting in front of William again as Zeus slowly made his way back down the hillside. Weary from their activities, she had unbuttoned her husband's coat, wrapped her arms around his waist and hid her face in his chest. Glancing at her now, William smiled at the crown of flowers she had placed in her hair again. Utterly happy, he placed a soft kiss atop her head as he tightened his grip. Then recalling all the times he had asked God for a wife, he smiled contentedly.

You are everything I have ever wanted, my darling Elizabeth. I could not have chosen anyone more perfect.

If the servants were surprised to see the master and mistress dismount in front of the manor house with their clothes and hair in disarray and soaked with water, they were trained not to show it. William found it hard not to smile as Elizabeth walked past the footmen with a crown of wildflowers in her hair, and Mrs. Reynolds greeted her as though she looked perfectly normal. He coughed to cover a laugh.

"Mrs. Darcy," the housekeeper said with a practiced smile, "I was beginning to wonder if you and Mr. Darcy were going to be home before dark."

Elizabeth looked back to William with a mischievous grin. "If it were up to my husband, we might have spent the night under the stars."

Unable to resist, William took her hand and led her toward the stairs. As he did, he addressed the housekeeper.

"Mrs. Reynolds, my wife and I are in need of a nap. Please advise everyone that dinner will be served an hour later."

"I shall be happy to, sir."

Watching until they were completely out of sight, the long-time servant then broke into a wide smile.

This is how it should have been all along.

Pate's farm near Lambton
Two days later

The old house was sturdy, if not fancy, and that proved especially advantageous today, for while it was pouring rain outside, the house was warm and dry. Nevertheless, the men encamped at Pate's old farmhouse were not in the mood to count their blessings, given that their last robbery had been a complete fiasco.

"I thought you said that Lord Cottingham would be travelling with a fortune!" George Wickham complained, throwing an empty satchel to the floor. He picked up some rings on the table and eyed them once again. "There was nothing in his entire coach worth going to Sheffield to sell, not even these paste emeralds!"

"I cannot guarantee that every tip I get is sound!" Denny protested angrily. We win some and lose some. If you do not like the odds, then perhaps you should go back to whatever you were doing and leave us alone!"

Wickham shrugged. Denny was right. "I am sorry. I know it is not your fault old Cottingham was travelling with little cash and fake jewels. What bothers me is that we shot a footman over this... this rubbish. Now that someone has died, we shall attract more attention from the law."

Pate spoke up. "I had to shoot him. He pulled a pistol from his coat, and there was nothing left to do."

"Pate is right," Andrew proclaimed. "He could have killed one of us."

"This is a ridiculous discussion!" Denny cried. "We all knew from the start that there was the possibility we would have to kill someone. We were just lucky it did not happen before now."

"That is how I see it," the man called Buck volunteered. "We have to keep ourselves alive first and foremost."

"Aye," Pate agreed, "but we had best be more careful, for George is right. We will be known throughout the region now."

Denny walked over to the hearth, propping one dirty boot against it. "The more I think of it, the more I believe we had better stay where we are, maybe for as long as several months. Make them think we have quit before we strike again."

"But... but," Andrew protested. "I need money now in order to redeem my estate."

"That is your problem, not ours," Denny said matter-of-factly.

Andrew's expression grew angry, but a hand on his shoulder caused him to look up at Wickham, who shook his head. Then George walked to the front door and opened it, revealing the deluge still raging outside.

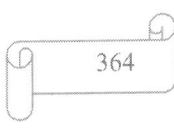

"Care to help me tend the horses, Andrew?"

Having abandoned the horses in the barn in a rush to look through the plunder, it was past time to unsaddle and feed them. And since the only servant was an elderly woman who cooked and kept house, it fell to them to care for the animals.

Realising that Wickham wished to talk in private, Andrew agreed, and they both went out the door. Once inside the dilapidated barn, they set about unsaddling the horses while they talked.

"There is no need to say anything more to Denny," Wickham said as he pulled a saddle off a chestnut stallion and set it on the wall of a stall. "He is right, you know. We have to put a halt to the robberies."

"How am I to make any money?" Andrew retorted as he unsaddled his own bay.

"It seems to me that you should do what Susan said. Take what you have and what she will lend you and make an offer to Darcy. Who knows, he may agree and let you have more time."

"I have the feeling that Fitz has given up on me."

"Well, in any case, that is the only option. We can always do something drastic if your overture fails."

"Such as?"

"I have said all along that you should kill that tyrant, Fitzwilliam. You can still wrap Georgiana around your little finger, and no doubt she would be nicer to you with her brother out of the way."

Andrew threw down the bridle he was holding. "Are you insane? Richard would see me hang, and you, too, if he thought you were involved."

Wickham shrugged. "Not if he could not prove it. In any case, it is just a suggestion. For now, use Lady Susan's plan and see what happens."

"I have no choice. I shall visit Monthaven tomorrow."

"I think I shall join you this time. After all, I have not seen my old friend for far too long."

"As long as you behave, you may accompany me."

Wickham put his hand on his heart. "You wound me."

"I *shall* wound you if you ruin my arrangement with Susan. Just remember that."

Wickham did not reply, for too many thoughts were running through his mind. There was money to be had in fleecing Pemberley, and now that his only avenue to riches was closed, he wanted to be a part of it. If Andrew was too frightened to kill his cousin, he was not. And Wickham was convinced that once Fitzwilliam Darcy was dead, the path to Georgiana's fortune would open like a music box for Andrew—and for him.

Perhaps, he mused, *the path to the new Mrs. Darcy's riches will open, too.*

"What are you day-dreaming about?" Andrew barked. "I have asked three times if you are ready to go back inside."

George smiled. "I was considering all the money we will have once we resume the robberies. And to answer your question, yes, I am ready to go inside."

"Do not count your chickens before they hatch." A loud clap of thunder signalled another downpour. "No need for us to wait! This rain is not going to let up!"

With that, Andrew rushed out into the rain. Shrugging, Wickham pulled his collar up and followed.

Chapter 33

Monthaven Manor
The next day

After Lord Attaway returned from running an errand for Lady Susan's father, he walked into the main library at Monthaven expecting to find Andrew Darcy conversing with his cousin. After all, Susan had received a note saying Andrew was coming today. Instead, standing next to her by the windows was George Wickham, a man he had never liked. He and Lady Susan were talking very secretively and promptly became silent upon his entry. Still, as both turned to face him, he pasted on a smile.

"Wickham! It has been ages since I last saw you. When was it? At my cousin's ball in London three years past?"

"I believe that is correct," Wickham replied blandly.

Attaway nodded and then addressed Susan. "Where is Andrew? I thought he was to be here today."

Susan, who had been drinking almost steadily for the last hour, finished the brandy left in her glass before answering him. "Had you returned on time, you might have seen him. Andrew stayed only long enough to get what he wanted—my money— and then headed straight to Pemberley."

Attaway was surprised that Susan would discuss her arrangement with Andrew in front of Wickham. Seeing his perplexed expression, she declared, "Do not be alarmed. George, Andrew and I have been confidants all of our lives. What one knows, the others know."

"I see," Attaway said, still a bit hesitant. "Then you will not mind if I ask if Andrew brought the portrait of Mrs. Darcy. I was hoping to see it."

Lady Susan laughed mirthlessly. "I should have known that you would. George and I think it a good likeness of Miss Bennet's face, though God only knows the breasts had to be exaggerated."

Wickham guffawed. "I would not agree with you on that."

"Enough rubbish, George!" Susan said jealously. "I am sure that Andrew enhanced them, for that is just like a man." She walked over to a table and picked up a paper that was rolled up, holding it out to him. "Tell me what you think."

As Attaway unrolled the drawing, his eyes grew in direct proportion to another part of his anatomy. Mesmerised by the erotic image before him, he was lost in thought until his cousin's voice broke through his musings.

"Stop gaping, Matthew! She has nothing that any other woman does not have."

"Except in greater measure," Wickham mocked.

Susan stalked over to the liquor cabinet, where she promptly poured herself another brandy. Throwing it down her throat in an unladylike display, she retorted, "Is no man impervious to her charms?"

It was obvious that she was becoming inebriated, so neither man replied. After a short pause, Attaway brought up another subject.

"Well, I, for one, wish Andrew luck with his mission! Perhaps he will be successful in changing Darcy's mind."

"He will need more than luck," Wickham said. "Fitzwilliam Darcy is the most tight-fisted man I have ever known. He would gladly sell Winfield Hall so as not to be under any obligation to help Andrew."

"Well, I know little of the circumstances, but should Andrew not be paying his own obligations?"

"You are right!" George Wickham retorted. "You know very little of the situation, or you would keep your nose out of it!"

Attaway flinched, but Wickham's words caused Lady Susan to glower. "You will not speak to my cousin in that manner. Especially not in my home, do you hear?"

Instantly Wickham stood down. "Please excuse my outburst, Attaway. I fear my anger stems from my own experiences with Fitzwilliam. Just the mention of his name makes my blood start to boil."

Attaway simply nodded. Lady Susan, however, was not pacified.

"Be that as it may, George, I intend to marry the man just as soon as I run that hussy back to Hertfordshire. And once I am Mrs. Fitzwilliam Darcy, you shall have to mind your manners if you expect to be invited to Pemberley."

Wickham laughed. "That will never happen. Darcy hates me."

Lady Susan huffed. "You have no idea of the power a good woman has over a man. I shall change him completely after we marry. Just you wait and see."

As she poured herself another glass of liquor, Attaway and Wickham's eyes met. Without exchanging a word, both knew that neither believed Susan's plans had the smallest chance of success.

"Am I the only one who wants a drink?" she exclaimed, her words now slurred as she held up the liquor decanter.

Acutely aware that putting up with her drivel was easier with a stiff drink in hand, both men headed in her direction.

Pemberley
That same day

Having gone to his study to meet with Mr. Sturgis regarding the list of horses available to sell to Lord Laughlin, William was surprised when Mr. Walker rushed into the room without waiting for his permission to enter, to say that Andrew Darcy had arrived by horseback and was now out on the drive. Having been instructed never to allow him entrance to Pemberley again, Walker winced when William dismissed his steward and instructed him to show Andrew into his study, but he followed the master's order by immediately going to meet Andrew at the front door.

While William waited in his study, he walked over to the portrait of his father that hung on the wall and pondered what he might say about his decision regarding Andrew. He was still studying the portrait when Andrew walked into the room. Their eyes locked, and the cousins stared at one another for a long time in silence. Then Andrew broke the stalemate.

"Well, from the looks of it, Fitz, I would say that marriage agrees with you."

William stiffened. He had hoped that Andrew would not bring Elizabeth into their conversation. "It does."

When he said nothing further, Andrew ventured, "Am I to receive no welcome? After all, it has been a year or more since I last darkened the door of Pemberley."

Not long enough, William thought. "Let us not pretend that we separated under normal circumstances. To get straight to the point, what brings you here?"

Andrew barked a laugh, shaking his head in disbelief. "You pretend not to know. I think that highly improbable, given the letter you wrote regarding the sale of *my* estate. "

"I was not sure you had received the letter. After all, I sent it to Winfield Hall, but it seems you no longer reside there."

"How would you know that unless you have someone watching? Did he talk to my staff? Will you stop at nothing to humiliate me?"

"Humiliate you?" William's voice rose despite his best intentions. "You are the one who has disgraced the name of Darcy—fathering children with women you had no intentions of marrying and raising the hopes of a well-brought-up young woman who ended up dead under mysterious circumstances."

"Oh, that is compassionate. Bring up mistakes I made years ago and things over which I had no control! Can you not give me the benefit of the doubt? I have not been at my estate because I have been trying to accumulate enough to pay my expenses. Look here!" Andrew reached into the satchel he had set in a chair and brought out a small bag. With great ceremony, he dumped the entire contents of the bag on William's desk.

"Eight hundred pounds to pay on my debts—I wanted to prove that I am serious about my obligations."

Barely glancing at the contents, William could not hold back a laugh full of contempt.

"Are you shocked that I was able to accumulate so much?"

"I only fear that I would be shocked to know how you came by that sum, but that is for another day. The point is, Andrew, that it is too little, too late. The estate is still on the market, and it will be sold."

At this pronouncement, Andrew lost his temper. "What do you mean too late? You have the only say in this matter. You have no one to ask, nothing to consult but your own conscience. That is, if you still have a conscience."

"My conscience told me long ago that I should let you stand on your own two feet, but I did not listen. I have given you chance after chance to take responsibility for yourself, yet you have not. As soon as I have a valid offer for Winfield Hall, I shall take it. Then I will repay Pemberley for what was spent on your obligations and put the rest of the proceeds into an account. All interest on that account will be paid to you for a living."

"What do I owe Pemberley?"

"You know as well as I that you have not fully repaid Pemberley for the land and the houses sheltering your children—I should say *child*, as there is only one now."

"I did not authorise you to furnish them such *fine* accommodations. Why should I pay for them?"

"Because I decided that you would. And just so you know, the man that you hired to intimidate the women at Eastbrooke Manor, the one who triggered the fire, was almost apprehended by one of my men."

Andrew's eyes grew large. "I... I have no idea what you are talking about."

William knew that arguing was fruitless. "You and I both know what happened at Richmond, even if I cannot prove it."

"So your suspicious nature has motivated you to leave me homeless, as well as penniless?"

"You will have the interest on your funds. If you cannot live on that, you will simply have to find useful employment or convince one of your wealthy widows to take you on."

"You cannot do this, Fitz!"

"Actually, I can."

"You always said that I could live on what little the estate made. Why are you selling it now?

"Because you are not paying your staff out of what little it makes. I am."

"But, but... " Andrew looked like a cornered deer as he crumpled the brim of the hat in his hand completely out of shape. "If you continue with this madness, you will sentence me to poverty."

"You have sentenced yourself, Andrew. Whether or not you live in poverty is up to you." William motioned to the money on the table. "This proves you have some ability to acquire money, so I suggest you continue."

"You shall rue this day, Fitz!" Andrew shouted as he began gathering the money and stuffing it back into the bag. "This shall come back to haunt you, mark my words."

Having said that, Andrew picked up the satchel and marched out of William's study.

Entering the back entrance of Pemberley, it quickly became clear to Joseph Fitzwilliam that there was an argument in progress somewhere in the house. Relieved that Olivia and Elizabeth had waited in the gardens whilst he went inside to see what was keeping his nephew, he walked in the direction of the raised voices. Had he not heard the quarrel, he would have known something was amiss merely by the presence of three burly footmen and the butler outside William's study. So focused were they that his arrival went unnoticed until he stood beside them. It was at that very moment that the door flew open, slamming back against the wall, and Andrew Darcy stalked out. It all happened so swiftly that there was no time to react, and by the time the butler followed him to the front door, William's cousin was kicking his horse into a gallop.

Worried about his nephew, Joseph stuck his head inside the open study door. William looked upset as he ran his hands through his hair and paced the floor. Concerned, Joseph walked into the room and shut the door behind him.

"You may tell me it is none of my business, but is there anything I can do?"

William stopped pacing at the sound of his uncle's voice. Meeting his eye, he shook his head wearily and sat down. "You know that I have struggled since Father died with my cousin's irresponsibility."

"From what little you have told me, your burden has been great."

"Recently I informed Andrew that I am going to sell Winfield Hall. I am washing my hands of paying his staff as well as my own. He has no intention of making it profitable, and now he will be forced to stand on his own."

"You do not seem too at ease with your decision."

William sighed. "It gives me no pleasure to see him struggle. My father coddled him since the day he came to live with us, and I have let him have far too many chances, so some of it was our fault. Nonetheless, now that I have Elizabeth and my own family to look forward to, I decided he cannot be my responsibility any longer."

"I agree. He is a grown man, after all." Then Joseph smiled. "From the way you and Elizabeth have been hidden away, I should think an announcement regarding a child should be forthcoming very soon."

William's countenance improved greatly. "Both of us want children as soon as God wills it."

"Then let us hope that you do not have to wait long. Now, your wife sent me to find out why you had not joined us, so I shall return and report that you are on your way."

"I would like to keep Andrew's visit a secret from Elizabeth. She has suffered enough over her history with that cad. Now that we have found happiness, I do not want to bring the subject up again."

"I am not in the habit of keeping anything from Livy, so I shall tell my wife and explain why you do not want Elizabeth to know. Will that suffice?"

"Of course. Now, let me speak to Mrs. Reynolds about instructing the servants not to mention his visit."

"Do not take too long, or Elizabeth may begin to wonder."

"I will hurry."

Pemberley
Two Days Later

The night had seemed interminably long, and Elizabeth was still awake. This was the day William would leave for Chesterfield, and the sense of dread that had filled her upon first hearing of the trip had only gotten worse. From the way William had tossed and turned through the night, she knew that he had not rested soundly, either; however, for the last hour his breathing had settled into a steady rhythm, and Elizabeth prayed that he was finally asleep. Glancing in his direction, she could barely make out his form in the darkness and was greatly disappointed. She loved to watch him sleep for, unfortunately, that was the only time that his forehead did not furrow with the cares of his duties, and he appeared much younger.

Truth be told, Elizabeth had slept little since William had informed her two days past of his plans to travel to Laughlin Manor, a trip he fully intended to make without her. At first, she had tried to convince him to take her, but after hearing the valid reasons why he did not think it a good idea, she had reluctantly agreed. Still, the thought of being separated from him for three whole days had caused such unease that, for the first time in her life, Elizabeth was unable to sustain her usual good humour. Thus, when a lone tear rolled down her face and a sniffle escaped, she scolded herself once more with an admonition that sounded strangely like her mother.

Do not make him rue the day he married you, Lizzy. Stop acting like a child!

Suddenly William rolled over. Lying perfectly still, she prayed she had not awakened him, but soon gentle hands began to touch her.

"I know that you are awake, sweetheart. What is the matter?"

Against her resolve, she burst into tears. Immediately, William's arms encircled her, and he whispered soothing words of love. His reassurances only made her feel guiltier.

"Do... do not pay any attention to me," she stammered at last. "I... I am just being foolish."

"Shhh," William whispered. "Do not say such a thing. To be truthful, as I lay here this morning, I was attempting to think of a good excuse not to go to Chesterfield. So you see, I am just as reluctant to go as you are to have me leave."

"Oh, Will!" Elizabeth said, framing his face in the darkness so she could bring his mouth to hers. "I do not know what is happening. I have never been this easily upset in my life."

"Nor have I," he reassured her with another kiss. "But, then, neither of us has been in love before."

Another sniffle followed. "That is true, but how shall we ever be able to overcome it?"

"I do not think two people who love one another as we do will ever overcome it, nor should they. I believe that when the Bible says a man shall leave his father and his mother and shall cleave unto his wife and shall be one flesh, it pertains not only to the act of love but to their relationship. They are one, and when they are separated, they should feel as if the other half is missing."

"I love being one with you, Will," she murmured passionately.

Her heartfelt declaration was all the encouragement needed for William to make love to her again, and by the time they were finished and breathless, sunlight was filtering through the curtains, and sounds emanating from the hallway made it evident that most of Pemberley was awake; thus, when Mrs.

O'Reilly knocked on Elizabeth's bedroom door, there was no denying it was time to rise.

"One moment," William called loudly as he slid from the bed, donned his robe and tied the belt around his waist. Just as he finished, Elizabeth's arms encircled him from behind and she hugged him. Closing his eyes briefly at the sensation, he turned and clasped her to his chest, rocking her back and forth.

"I shall dress and then we shall eat before I leave," he murmured, kissing her hair.

Elizabeth nodded, her heart too full to speak. She then watched until he went out and Mrs. O'Reilly entered just as quickly. The maid greeted her in her usual, cheerful manner.

"Good morning, Mrs. Darcy. It looks as though it will be a beautiful day. At least Mr. Darcy will have nice weather for his trip."

Elizabeth lifted her chin and tried to smile. "Yes. At least that will be a blessing."

Later that day

As Elizabeth emerged from the library carrying several books that she hoped would induce sleep that night, she almost collided with Georgiana. Her sister, who looked beautiful dressed in a blue riding habit, exhaled an exaggerated sigh and stepped aside, allowing Elizabeth to pass.

"I am sorry, Georgiana," Elizabeth stopped to say, her smile apologetic. "I fear I was thinking of Fitzwilliam and not paying any attention to where I was going."

Georgiana shrugged. "There was no harm done." She studied the books. "You must be completely at loose ends with my brother away. Since the storm, you have hardly been out of each other's company." She tossed her hair, adding irritably, "So, of course, he ignores me whenever I do see him."

"I am sure he does not intentionally ignore you. It is just that Will is so busy, what with the completion of the bridge for the tenants and the new addition to the foundlings' home and—"

"Catering to your every need," Georgiana said under her breath.

Not sure if she had heard correctly, Elizabeth said, "Excuse me?"

"Never mind! I shall be late if I do not leave now." With that, Georgiana headed toward the foyer.

"Late?" Elizabeth said, following her. "I had no idea that you had an engagement today. Will did not mention it, and you have said nothing to me about it."

Georgiana bit her lip. "I only meant that I need to leave if I wish to return from my ride before dark."

Having walked on during their conversation, Georgiana vanished out the front door before Elizabeth could question her further; thus, when Olivia Fitzwilliam caught up with Elizabeth, she was standing on the portico, her hand shading her eyes, and watching Georgiana gallop towards Pemberley's open fields on her bay stallion.

"Elizabeth?" She turned, her expression puzzled. "Would you like to walk around the lake with Joseph and me? I know how you love to walk, and with Fitzwilliam gone, I thought perhaps you would like some company."

Seeing the hopefulness in her aunt's eyes, Elizabeth conceded. "Thank you. I would love to join you. Just let me take these books up to my room, and I shall meet you at the back entrance."

As they walked back inside the house, Olivia watched until Elizabeth disappeared at the top of the stairs; she then went in search of Joseph.

Standing just inside the garden, upon seeing his wife coming towards him, Joseph ventured, "Well?"

"She has agreed. Now, remember. Do not mention Fitzwilliam. I want to get her mind off him and on to other things."

"Small chance of that! Our nephew is all she talks about. I have never seen two people as much in love." He reached out to brush the tips of his fingers across her cheek. "Except us."

"And that is precisely why I must ask one more thing of you."

"Which is?"

"Try not to show me too much affection when she is in our company. She will feel Fitzwilliam's absence keenly enough as it is."

"I had no idea how much his being away would affect us," he teased. "I am afraid that I shall be as down in the mouth as Elizabeth by the time he returns."

Olivia chuckled. "Do not be so dramatic, darling. We must refrain from showing affection only in front of our niece. When we are alone, we can be ourselves."

"I suppose I have no choice. I shall sacrifice for the benefit of our niece."

Olivia patted his cheek mischievously. "My poor beleaguered husband."

Soon Elizabeth came out the door and was walking towards them. Hooking her arm through Joseph's, Olivia held out a hand to her niece.

"Let us be off! If we are to circle the entire lake before tea is served, we had best get going."

Somewhere between Monthaven and Pemberley

By the time Georgiana arrived at the spot where she and Lord Attaway had planned to meet, the sun was colouring the horizon in shades of orange, red and purple. The landmark, the tallest tree on the border between Monthaven and Pemberley, proved more remote than she had remembered. That had caused her to be late; however, it also made the perfect rendezvous point where no one would likely see them. Still, Georgiana chided herself for not leaving sooner and only brightened when she saw that Matthew was there. He had dismounted, tied his stallion to the fence and was leaning against the tree truck. As she went through the fence gate and reined her horse to a halt, Attaway stepped forward to take the reins.

"I thought you had changed your mind," Matthew said, helping her to dismount.

"I forgot the way here. But now that I have found it again, I shall have no problem returning."

Tying the animal beside his own, he added, "Well, we will barely have any time at all before you have to leave."

"I am not worried about being late," Georgiana retorted. "Brother is not at home, and I care not what Elizabeth will say."

"What of your aunt and uncle?"

"Their opinion means nothing, either. Besides, I am almost eighteen, and once I am presented at court next year, I shall be in the marriage market. So the days of being told what to do are quickly dwindling."

"So you are thinking of marriage already. May I ask who the lucky fellow is?"

Georgiana blushed. "No, you may not."

"Well, what do you suppose your future husband would do if he were to learn that you met me in the woods all alone?"

She studied Lord Attaway. "I... I thought you were a gentleman. A gentleman would never tell."

Attaway laughed. *If only this foolish girl knew how close she was to being compromised. If I did not fear her brother and my cousin, I would show her that she is not as smart as she thinks.* "You are lucky that I am a gentleman and can be trusted. But we are in the middle of nowhere, and if we should be seen, it would mean marriage."

"I do not think that would be a punishment," she said coyly.

"I am glad you feel that way, for after you are presented at court, I intend to ask Fitzwilliam for permission to court you. What do you say about that?"

Georgiana smiled. "I should like that very much."

Attaway drew her into his arms. "Then you would not object if I kissed you?"

She shook her head, and immediately he captured her mouth. At first the kiss was gentle, but gradually it grew more fervent. His hands were drifting into dangerous territory when he suddenly broke the kiss and pushed her to arms length.

"What is wrong?" Georgiana sputtered, swaying under his persuasion. "Why did you stop?"

"It is getting late, and I do not want you riding after dark. We can meet here again in a day or two, if you will promise to be on time."

"I will. I promise."

"Then I shall send you a note via a trusted servant. Be on the lookout for it."

"I shall."

Attaway helped Georgiana onto her horse and mounted his own. Pulling up beside her, he leaned over to kiss her lightly on the lips.

"Until we meet again," he declared. "Now, ride on! I shall not leave until you are completely out of sight."

He waited until she had disappeared. Then he kicked his horse in the direction of Monthaven Manor.

Stupid, stupid girl.

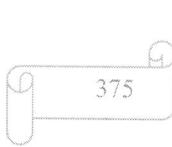

Georgiana galloped as fast as the horse could carry her back to Pemberley. It was pitch black when she reached the front steps of the manor to find her uncle and several grooms mounting a search party.

"Where have you been?" Joseph Fitzwilliam asked irritably as he took charge of her horse.

"I... I was riding in the woods. I took a trail that Brother and I used to ride, but came upon a tree that was down across it. I had to take another path, and I got lost. By the time I found familiar territory, it was getting dark. So, I hurried home as fast as possible."

It was evident from their faces that none of the men believed her, not even her uncle, who just stared at her without comment. Not caring, Georgiana walked past him into the house where Elizabeth and Olivia began peppering her with questions.

"I have already told my uncle what happened, and I do not feel I should have to explain it all over again. I am tired and am going to my room." Then she addressed Mrs. Reynolds. "Please send a tray to my sitting room. I do not wish to come down for dinner."

Mrs. Reynolds nodded and Georgiana swiftly went up the stairs, leaving everyone to stare at her back. Those left standing in the foyer only had time to share exasperated looks before Mr. Walker announced that dinner was ready to be served; thus, Elizabeth, Olivia and Joseph enjoyed a much more pleasant dinner than they might have, had Georgiana not returned.

Chapter 34

Pate's farm near Lambton
The next day

Since his trip to Pemberley, Wickham had found Andrew Darcy more distant and irritable than ever and drinking more than usual. The only information that Andrew had shared was that Fitzwilliam had not been swayed by the money offered as proof of his change of heart.

However, contrary to what he told Andrew, Wickham could not have been more thrilled that his friend's ploy had not worked because, after all, this humiliation played right into his plans. Subsequently, that morning when Andrew walked out of the house, George quickly followed him in order to speak privately. He found him sitting on the rail that circled the old wooden porch, drinking from a flask of brandy he kept in his coat and staring forlornly into the distance.

"Andrew, you may not wish to discuss your situation, but I feel I must point out something—something you may not have considered." As Andrew rolled his eyes, he hurriedly explained. "Have you taken into account that your cousin's unreasonableness may be a blessing in disguise?"

Andrew Darcy huffed. "And how did you come to that conclusion?"

"I have been after you for years to do the sensible thing."

"Oh, so once again you are going to tell me that I should murder Fitz?"

"He has had you under his boot all your life. If he were dead, you could easily sway Georgiana to your wishes and… " he paused for emphasis, "the Widow Darcy would be ripe for the picking, too. Did you not say that she favoured you in Meryton, or at least until your cousin's arrival?" He could tell that Andrew's mind was swirling with the possibilities. "Think of it! If your father had not been stupid, you would have been the Master of Pemberley. And you may have another chance, if you play your cards right."

"I do not know, George. Mrs. Darcy was not as, shall we say, impressed with me the last time we talked. I fear that Fitz has filled her head with all of my failings."

"Oh, come now! You can charm any woman into your bed, and you know how vulnerable a new widow can be. All it takes is a little sympathy and a well-chosen compromise, and you are man and wife!"

"You make it sound so simple. Besides, it would be impossible to get anywhere near my cousin without plenty of servants milling about. To be seen would be a sure death sentence."

"A confidant told me he has gone to Chesterfield by himself. You are aware that every year he and Lord Laughlin meet to haggle over horses. And I am betting that he will stay for only one night, for Laughlin is not his type of company. All we need do is lie in wait at Mason's Pass. It is an excellent place for an ambush."

"That pass through the mountain is only accessible via horseback, and it is perilous due to falling rock. Why would you think he would take that way when he can return safely via the main route?"

"Because it cuts hours from the trip, and, if all the talk of the Darcys' felicity is true, he will be eager to return to his wife."

"I do not like it. It is too near Pemberley. If gunshots were heard—"

"It is on the far side of Pemberley, and there is nothing for miles but woods. Unless someone was travelling it as well, gunshots would go unnoticed. And how often have you seen anyone on that road? Have you been through it?"

"Only once, and I vowed never again."

"My point exactly. That is what makes it the perfect spot."

"Colonel Fitzwilliam would suspect me straight off, especially after our recent argument."

"I have thought of that. Write a note today and send it to your cousin, apologise for getting angry and tell him that he has every right not to trust you. Tell him you are returning to Sheffield to find more work. Send a letter to Lady Susan telling her of your departure for Sheffield as well."

"That will be insufficient to convince Richard."

"Let me finish!" Wickham snapped. "You shall kill Darcy, and then we will head straight to Sheffield. If there is any investigation, my friends at Lily's Pleasure Garden will swear that we have been there since you left Pemberley. For a few pounds and promises of more when you get control of Darcy's wealth, they would gladly say anything."

"What of Denny, Pate and Buck?"

"If they suspect anything, they will keep their mouths shut. They can't afford to draw attention to themselves. Besides, we can always promise them a little something to keep quiet."

"If we did, we would have to pay them for their silence for the rest of our lives."

"Or for the rest of theirs, which would be shortened."

"I never have had the stomach for murder, George."

"Then it is time you developed one. We must move if we expect to be in place before he comes back home. Come! Let us tell the others we will be visiting an old friend in Manchester for a day or so. That will pacify them."

Andrew sighed. "I suppose you are right." He stood up, downing the last of the liquor in the flask. "It is time I stood up to Fitz."

Monthaven Manor

It was a beautiful, sunny afternoon, so Lady Susan and her cousin were taking tea on the terrace. More irritable than usual after Andrew Darcy had not come by when he left Pemberley, Susan was unusually quiet. Trying not to rile her any further, Matthew did not wish to raise that subject so, instead, he recounted his meeting with Georgiana.

"It was so infuriating! After all, it was she who chose the place we were to

meet. Why could she not at least have met me at the time she settled on? And when she finally arrived, she had the gall to claim that she had gotten lost. I waited two full hours, and the sun was going down when she rode up. We had only enough time for a brief conversation before she had to return to Pemberley. Spoiled little chit!"

"Watch your language!" Lady Susan commanded, looking about nervously. "You have no idea how the maids at one estate will gossip with the maids of another. It would never do for anyone to know your true thoughts about Georgiana."

"I shall keep that in mind," Attaway said, lowering his voice. "It is just that her attitude makes me livid. She acts as though I am at her disposal."

"Until I get what I want, you are at her disposal. Try to remember that." Still visibly angry, Attaway let go a sigh which Susan did not notice, for her mind was elsewhere. "I have to think that Fitzwilliam turned Andrew down and that is why he did not return yesterday. Now that I think on it, I should have made it clear that he could not keep the loan if Fitzwilliam would not agree."

"I cannot imagine him thinking that he could."

"That is because you do not know him as well as I do."

At that precise moment, Mrs. Horton hurried out onto the terrace to announce Miss Darcy, who was right on her heels. Georgiana flounced right past the maid and into their company without waiting, so the maid curtseyed and returned to the house.

Surprised, Lady Susan rose to greet her, barely kissing each of her cheeks. "Georgiana, my dear, what in the world are you doing here? I did not expect to see you again so soon."

Oblivious to the unease her presence had caused, Georgiana began to explain. "With Brother out of town, there was no one sensible to talk with at Pemberley, so I decided to come here." Her eyes flicked to Attaway. "I hope I am welcome."

"Of course you are, my dear," Susan lied. "Is she not, Matthew?"

"Any time you can join us, we are grateful."

Georgiana beamed. "While Fitzwilliam is no longer any company for me, when he is home, he keeps Elizabeth out of my way. She must think she is my keeper when he is away, for she had been following me about, trying to make conversation. And she asks where I am going whenever I mount my horse."

"That must be irritating," Matthew offered. "Especially for one as independent as you."

Georgiana seemed pleased with his observation. "It is."

"May I enquire..." Susan ventured, "Did Fitzwilliam mention anything to you about Andrew before he left?"

"Not a word. Has Andrew already met with Brother about his estate?"

"Yes, and I fear it did not end well because your cousin did not come back here afterward. I feel sure he would have let me know if the decision had gone his way."

Georgiana bristled. "Fitzwilliam simply has no goodwill towards Andrew.

I have no idea why, as he can sympathise with tenants, but not his own flesh and blood. I wish my opinion mattered, but it does not."

"There is no reason for you to feel regret, Georgiana," Susan ventured. "Your brother is his own master. You could do nothing to change his mind if he did not wish it."

"How well I know!" Georgiana stood to leave. "Thinking of my poor cousin being homeless has dampened the day, I fear. My company will only distress you, so I shall return to Pemberley."

"Please do not go, dearest," Lady Susan said. "We are all downhearted, so it matters not if you are, too."

"She is right," Lord Attaway chimed in. "We are all melancholy, so we should keep each other company and talk of more pleasant things. Later, I shall ride back with you as far as the oak tree."

Georgiana tilted her head and shrugged. "If you both insist, I shall." Then she smiled at Attaway. "I should enjoy the ride back much better with your company."

"Fine. Now that that is settled, what say you to looking at the latest sheet music from London?" Lady Susan stood. "The package came this morning, and it is in the music room. I told Matthew when it arrived that you could do the new music justice, whereas I can barely pick out the melody."

Amidst Georgiana's protestations that Lady Susan could play as well as she, they all walked back into the house and made their way to the music room. It was several hours later when Georgiana prepared to leave for home.

Pemberley
Elizabeth's sitting room

With William gone, Olivia Fitzwilliam had worked tirelessly to keep up her niece's spirits, for it seemed that all Elizabeth wished to do was hide in her sitting room under the pretence of reading. In truth, every time Olivia had entered the room, she found Elizabeth on the balcony, staring into the distance. Today proved no different, so she quickly went to the French doors and called to her.

Startled, her niece turned and, seeing Olivia, pasted on a wan smile. "Aunt, I thought you and Uncle had gone into Lambton."

"Joseph has been in conference with the coachman all morning. It seems the horse he normally rides has a slight limp, and they are trying to determine if it is serious. So I decided to work on the children's coats today. That is, if you do not mind letting me in your study."

"No, not at all." Elizabeth passed her aunt, entering the sitting room and going directly to her bedroom with Olivia following. "The key is inside the chest atop my dresser." Once at the dresser, she opened a highly-polished, mahogany box. "Here it is," she said, handing the key to her aunt.

By then Olivia's attention was focused on two large books stacked on the end of the dresser. It appeared that the stem of a flower was sticking out from between them.

"What, pray tell, is that?"

Elizabeth looked to where her aunt's gaze was concentrated. "Oh, those are flowers that I am saving." She removed the heavy book on top to reveal two yellow flowers sandwiched between two sheets of fine paper. "I have always pressed flowers in this manner, and when Fitzwilliam made these into a crown for my hair during our picnic, I knew I would want a few in my memory box."

"Memory box?"

"This is my memory box," Elizabeth chuckled, tapping the mahogany box. "It is where I keep my treasures—all things that remind me of significant times." She opened a secret drawer on the bottom of the box, exposing several more pressed flowers, including a white rose with a white ribbon. "This was in my wedding bouquet."

"What a marvellous idea. I have a jewellery box, but nothing large enough to keep all my treasures. I shall have to ask Joseph to get me one for our anniversary."

"The Gardiners gave me this box for my birthday. My uncle keeps many in his warehouse of all sizes and types of wood."

"I shall write to Madeline, then and ask her to recommend one. By the way, have you heard from her lately?"

"Yes. In fact, I got three letters the afternoon William departed—one from my aunt and one from Jane. She also included a note from Papa."

"How is your family, if I may ask?"

For the first time since William's departure, Elizabeth's expression settled into an easy smile. "There is nothing much to say regarding Jane and Bingley. They are truly as happy as two people so alike can be. Jane did ask me to come home for a visit, for she wants me to see her wedding dress and decide on a material for my gown. I am to stand up with her, just as Fitzwilliam is to stand with Mr. Bingley."

"That is understandable. After all, you and she are very close, and it only follows that she would want you to be a part of her wedding plans. As for Mr. Bingley, Fitzwilliam has had nothing but good things to say of him since they were both in university. So it is not surprising that he is Bingley's choice."

At Elizabeth's nod, she continued, "I take it all your family is well, or Jane would have mentioned it, but I have to wonder how your father is taking your absence."

"My family is well. As for Papa, he is an observer of people and a man of few words, but he admits to missing me terribly, which touches my heart. He would normally never say anything of that nature." She looked thoughtful. "He allows that he has no one sensible with whom to discuss literature now that I am married. I believe that to be true, not because I am so clever, but because, other than Jane, my sisters are not interested in improving their minds. And, of course, now Jane is too busy with wedding plans."

"It is a shame your younger sisters do not wish to learn, for I believe that a woman needs to know all she can about the world she lives in, and a wide variety of interests is healthy."

"If only they felt the same but, alas, they do not. Lastly, there is the letter from my aunt. She writes that she is doing well, but increasing so fast that all her dresses have had to be let out. And she allows that she finds it difficult to get in and out of the carriage." She giggled. "I believe she is exaggerating."

"She looked so slender when she was here that I forget that she is expecting. And I do not recall when she said the child is due."

"The middle of November."

"Yes, now I remember thinking it will arrive before Christmas. Speaking of babies, you should be expecting soon, if you are not already."

A flame of scarlet crept across Elizabeth's cheeks. "There is something that I wanted to share with you, but I was afraid that you would think I was jumping to conclusions. And I would never confide in Fitzwilliam, not until I was absolutely sure, but—"

Olivia gently squeezed her hand, "Whatever you say is between us, and nothing is too small to mention."

Elizabeth shoulders relaxed. "My courses are a week late. Of course, that has happened before—whenever I come under great stress. And, heaven knows, my relationship with Georgiana has been strained. I did not think she could be more unsociable, but she is worse since William and I have reconciled our differences."

"Do not fret over Georgiana. Believe me when I say that you are not the cause of her behaviour. It started long before her brother met you. Now," she smiled conspiratorially, "you are correct in that a week is not long enough to say for certain that you are with child."

Elizabeth's smile waned as she looked down. Olivia lifted her chin so their eyes met.

"I know how you feel, dear. You want so badly to share your hopes with someone who is not your husband, for you fear raising his expectations and then having to say that you were wrong."

"It is as though you can read my mind."

"Remember, I was once a young bride, too. And with you and Fitzwilliam as my children by choice, I am still a mother. So feel free to confide in me anything you wish—hopes, dreams and concerns. I welcome the chance to be useful."

Elizabeth threw herself into her arms. "Oh, Aunt Olivia, you are so much more than useful; you are loved! Thank you for being like a mother to me."

As they held one another, swaying side to side, Olivia could not hold back a few stray tears. Then, after a while, Elizabeth stepped back. She was grinning. "If you still want to work on those coats, I should like to join you."

"I was hoping you would. A task is made so much lighter when it is shared."

Chesterfield
Laughlin Manor

The first full day at Laughlin Manor, William assumed that the men who filled every available guest room were there to participate in the three-day bird shoot the viscount had organised, for no wives were present and the sport occupied all but him and his host. He and Lord Laughlin, of course, were busy looking over horses, making plans and agreeing on prices. Nonetheless, the earl made it clear that after dinner he expected William to join him and his other guests at the card tables. Never one to gamble, William still felt obligated to be sociable, so he agreed to play a few rounds, then he intended to excuse himself and retire. Truthfully, his only aspiration was to go to bed early in order to rise equally early and return to Elizabeth.

However, immediately following dinner and whilst seated at a card table, a curious and inexplicable uneasiness washed over him when he noticed that the room was full of ladies—that is, if one referred to everything in a skirt as a *lady*. By the time his first game had concluded, a strange phenomenon had occurred. Laughlin Manor had transformed from manor house into something akin to a fancy brothel. Suggestively dressed women were everywhere—sitting in laps, leaning over the shoulders of those playing cards and latching themselves onto arms as they strolled up the twin staircases to the bedrooms above. It was obvious, too, that this state of affairs suited most of those present, though not William.

Unfortunately, he was clearly the handsomest man there and the chief target of the majority of the women. Watching his growing discomfort seemed just the thing to keep his hosts amused. For both Lord Laughlin and his son eagerly anticipated seeing the staid Mr. Darcy prove human by succumbing to temptation. Even so, as each woman dared to approach him, they provoked the same reaction. First, they would try to make conversation, whilst he all but ignored them and his face fell abruptly into stern lines. Then they would surreptitiously drape themselves over his shoulders, feigning interest in his cards. This would precipitate his coming to his feet and tactfully suggesting they find someone else to admire. It proved extremely entertaining, and the audience grew until, unable to keep his mind on the game, William slid his chair back, mumbled something about getting a drink and walked toward the decanters that Lord Laughlin had set up against one wall. He had barely taken the first sip of his glass of brandy, when a hand gripped his arm. This caused him to flinch and turn to the interloper with fire in his eyes.

"Calm down, Darcy," the earl smirked. "It is only me."

Several men standing nearby, including the viscount, laughed aloud. This irritated William, and, instead of replying, he took another swallow.

"My son and I noticed that you do not seem to appreciate all the *forbidden fruit* right under your nose. Some of the ladies, ripe for the picking I might add, came all the way from London just for these three days. I would have thought that a man such as you would jump at the chance to sample a *bit of muslin*. After all, Mrs. Darcy is not here, and she will never know."

William stiffened, which caused Laughlin to remove his arm and step back. "Then it appears that you do not know me well at all. Besides, though she is absent, I would never break my vows to my wife."

By then the viscount had walked over, followed by his friends. Hearing what William said, he drunkenly replied, "Who would have thought that the great Darcy enjoyed being under a woman's foot. I considered you a real man until now."

"A real man keeps his word to his business associates, his friends and foremost, to his wife. Any man who will break his vows to his wife will break his word to you. Now, if you *gentlemen*," the inflection he gave the word made it obvious that he did not think they were, "will excuse me, I am going to bed. I leave at dawn, and I wish to be well-rested."

The viscount guffawed, too inebriated to realise that he had been insulted. "If rest is what you seek, then you have come to the wrong place. I imagine the celebrating will keep you up all night."

"Perhaps it may, but not because I am a part of it. Goodnight."

With that, William set his glass down and walked towards one of the twin staircases. As he did, one of the more handsome ladies silently followed him. Seeing her trailing his reluctant guest, the earl winked at his son.

"Maybe Darcy will be up all night, after all." Then he looked around the room. "Come! Let us find wenches to keep us company."

Reaching the door of the room he was assigned, William began to relax as he turned the knob and entered. However, before he could shut and lock the door, a woman slipped in through the slight opening. Instantly he reacted, grabbing her wrist before she could go further. As he took note of her auburn hair, green eyes and lush figure, she gave him a brilliant smile. Yet her smile did not seem to have the desired effect on her prey.

"I know who you are, Mr. Darcy," she whispered lustily, trying to move closer to him. His iron grip prevented her ploy. "My name is Flo, and I used to see you in London all the time. Once Viscount Leighton escorted me to the theatre and the two of you spoke in your box whilst I waited behind him. You looked straight at me that night, and I fancied that you liked what you saw, for I had wet the bosom of my gown, and nothing was left to the imagination."

"Frankly, that would have revolted me, madam. Now, I suggest you return downstairs where your cleverness is more likely to be admired."

She was not deterred and smiled even more sweetly. "Hear me out. I have desired you ever since that night, and I vowed to have you if the opportunity ever came my way. Your cousin says that I am the best whore he has ever bedded, and I will not ask for a farthing in payment. I just want us to enjoy ourselves."

This time William's grip tightened enough that her wrist began to hurt. "Hear me, and hear me well. I am married to the kindest, most beautiful woman in England, if not the entire world. I love her dearly, and you could never, *ever*, tempt me to betray her."

As the truth sank in with finality, Flo did something totally unexpected. She began to laugh.

"When we were told what men would be here tonight, all of us talked of how we would be the one to seduce you. Now I learn that not a one of us could have succeeded. I have never known any man to turn down my favours, Mr. Darcy. You are the first! Will you tell your wife something for me?" At William's raised brow she added, "Tell her that she is a very lucky woman."

With that, she tried to kiss his cheek, but he would not allow it. Chuckling, she walked into the hallway. There she issued a final warning as he closed the door.

"May I suggest that you put a chair under your doorknob?" She pulled a ring of keys from her pocket. "Lord Laughlin has given all the ladies a set of keys that will unlock any room, even yours. Good night, Mr. Darcy."

With those words of caution, she left. Immediately, William shut the door and locked it. Then thinking of what she had said, he moved a nearby chest until it blocked the door. No one would be able to move it without waking him. Satisfied, he quickly undressed and crawled into bed. He was dreaming of Elizabeth almost as soon as his head hit the pillow.

Chapter 35

Pemberley

The day dawned sunny and bright at Pemberley, with summer clouds floating feathery overhead. On such days Mrs. Reynolds was normally in an excellent mood, and she should have been this day, since she planned to visit a friend in Lambton. The rain of yesterday had ceased, which meant she could travel there swiftly and be back at Pemberley in plenty of time to greet the master when he returned. Most of the household, including Mrs. Darcy, assumed that Mr. Darcy would not arrive until nearly dark, but after inadvertently catching him and his wife in a passionate embrace before he left, Mrs. Reynolds had a feeling that he would return much earlier than expected.

Despite the beautiful weather, however, the housekeeper's mood was gloomy, for she was not so focused on Mr. Darcy's return as she was on what she must relate to him when he returned. Two of the maids, Clara and Polly, had been in her office about a week past with a tale regarding Miss Darcy's maid, Florence. Mrs. Reynolds had no reason not to believe them, and she had listened intently as they related the results of their surveillance of the lady's maid. Both claimed to have observed Florence in the servants' hall outside Mrs. Darcy's bedroom with her ear to the wall. This was highly irregular, as she had no business in that hall. She had assured the maids that she would investigate and charged them not to tell anyone else. That night, the one before Mr. Darcy left for Chesterfield, she had discovered Florence there herself. Several loud footsteps had sent the maid scurrying back to her own quarters.

Not one to speak before thinking it through, the old housekeeper had not confronted Florence nor brought up the matter with the master before he left. She preferred to wait until his return, for Miss Darcy was very fond of her maid and would no doubt stand up for her. Mrs. Reynolds worried that this might be the final conflict that would sever the bond between the Darcy siblings—a tenuous one that Andrew Darcy had left mostly in tatters before he was thrown out of Pemberley.

As all of these things went through her head, Mrs. Reynolds hurried down the hall that led to the back entrance. Mrs. Darcy and the Fitzwilliams were in the gardens, and she wanted to let the mistress know that she was ready to leave. As she stepped out the back door, the scene playing out before her made her laugh aloud. For at that exact moment, Elizabeth had jumped up from the swing where she was sitting to chase one of the master's hound puppies. It had the ribbon of her bonnet in its mouth and was running towards the fish pond as fast as its small legs could carry it. Mrs. Darcy's aunt and uncle, who were sitting on a nearby stone bench, were laughing just as heartily.

"I wonder if my nephew is teaching his hunting dogs to dislike bonnets as much as he does," Joseph Fitzwilliam declared, winking at his wife.

"He might do just that," Olivia Fitzwilliam concurred between great gasps of air, having laughed so hard that she was out of breath.

At length, their niece overtook the puppy, but not before the bonnet was soaked from being dragged across the pond. As Elizabeth pulled it from the dog's mouth, she held it up in triumph, flashing one of her crooked grins. Just at that moment, the brim of the hat buckled and a stream of water poured out. This caused the others to laugh even more.

As she came towards them, Elizabeth quipped, "I hate bonnets almost as much as Will, for I cannot see as I wish because of the brim."

"Why do you bother taking a bonnet with you everywhere?" Olivia asked.

Elizabeth declared cheekily, "Because, should I run into someone of import, I can always put it on."

"So, Livy and I are not important enough to warrant seeing you in a bonnet?" her uncle teased.

"I am afraid not!" Another giggle escaped. "And, Aunt, it could just as well have been *your* bonnet in the pond."

"I loathe for Livy to wear those silly bonnets, for I had rather see her beautiful face," Joseph punctuated this statement by gently feathering fingers across his wife's cheek. "If need be, a parasol will do splendidly against the sun. Frankly, I find it ridiculous that society decrees that a proper lady does not appear in public without a bonnet. That is just nonsense."

"I agree," Elizabeth and Olivia happened to say in unison. This set off a new round of laughter.

At this point, Mrs. Reynolds approached and performed a quick curtsey. "Mrs. Darcy, I am ready to leave now. Rest assured that everything is in order and that I shall return before noon."

"There is no need to hurry," Elizabeth answered. "Enjoy your visit with Mrs. Shelnut. Please tell her that I shall continue to pray for her health to improve. You did prepare another basket of food, did you not?"

"I did. Last visit, she told me that the food is a real blessing, since she has not been able to cook as much as in the past and that the prayers sustain her."

"Ask the vicar to send word as to how she is faring after he calls on her. And, if you think we should send someone to help with the cooking, please let me know."

"I will pass your request along to Mr. Moody and evaluate her needs while I am there."

"Then we shall see you later today."

Just as quickly as she had appeared, the long-time servant disappeared into the house. Elizabeth said sombrely, "I do not know what we would do without Mrs. Reynolds. She is priceless."

"My thoughts exactly," Olivia said. "Fitzwilliam has no idea how fortunate he is to have had her all these years."

"Very few servants are as devoted," Joseph echoed thoughtfully.

Suddenly the sound of the mother hound's howl caused every eye to glance toward the stables. As the white and rust-coloured dog crossed the paddock, every few steps she would stop and call her missing pup—the one that had stolen Elizabeth's bonnet. Her other offspring, all seven of them, stayed close by her heels, apparently too afraid to wander off.

Upon hearing his mother's call, the adventurous little pup's head popped up from among some wildflowers, and he began to bounce across the lawn. All floppy ears and tail, tripping and falling over his own feet, he flew as fast he could toward his mother. The spectacle brought a smile to all their faces.

"I think I shall visit the new hounds," Joseph Fitzwilliam said. "Your husband promised me the pick of the litter, Elizabeth, and I think I have already found him. Are you coming with me, Livy?"

"No. If you do not mind, I shall sit here in the shade with Elizabeth and wait for your return. Besides, we might have some confidences to share."

Her husband gave her a ▓▓▓▓ smile and a wink. "My ears shall burn if you talk about me, but I still hope you do."

As he strolled leisurely towards the stables, Olivia could not bring herself to look away. His frame was as lithe and muscular as the day she had met him in Lambton, and he looked every bit as handsome. Suddenly overwhelmed, her hand came to her throat and her eyes filled with tears.

"You love him very much," Elizabeth whispered reverently.

Olivia nodded, and though her gaze did not veer from her husband, she stretched a hand toward Elizabeth. When their hands touched, their fingers clasped.

"Yes," Olivia murmured. "If I was not allowed another day with my Joseph, I could never utter a complaint, for God has allowed me more than my share of love." Then she smiled at Elizabeth. "Never forget how blessed you are to have a good man's love."

"I promise. I will never take Will's love for granted."

◈

Laughlin Manor
Daybreak that same day

William waited on the front portico for a footman to find a groom to bring Zeus around to the front steps. A haunting and heavy oppression seemed to brood upon the air, whilst a thick mist covered the ground. Involuntarily William shivered from the dampness. Having awakened well before dawn, he had thrown his clothes back into the small satchel he carried via horseback and tiptoed down the halls of the manor, hoping to avoid waking anyone, especially any of the *ladies*.

The viscount had been correct. He had gotten little sleep. Drunken revellers had carried the downstairs merrymaking to the floors above, with a few of the celebrants waking him from a restless slumber in the early morning hours by trying to gain entrance to his room. Rowdy, slurred voices had stopped outside his door, discussing loudly whether to drag him out of bed while they jiggled the doorknob. And though they gave up and moved along, he did not rest again. Consequently, all William wanted was to put this place and these people as far behind him as possible. He thought he had accomplished that feat when the groom came walking around the corner of the house leading Zeus, however, a voice from behind, calling his name, proved him wrong.

William's shoulders slumped. Then taking a deep breath, he turned to face Lord Laughlin, who was now standing at the front door. His hair was unkempt and his face blood-red. He was half-dressed and still pulling on his coat when he finally stepped onto the portico. William was reminded of the drunkards who begged for handouts on the steps of White's in London.

"Why are you leaving so early? You have not even broken your fast," the earl said groggily. "There will be plenty of food in an hour or so."

With an air of affected civility, William replied, "I am not hungry. Besides, I have business to handle as soon as I get home, and I wish to get an early start."

"Business?" Laughlin laughed wickedly. "Is that what you call taking care of your new wife? Elizabeth? Is that her name?"

William's expression hardened. Elizabeth was too precious to be mentioned by the likes of Lord Laughlin and, at that point, he flung diffidence to the winds.

"Lord Laughlin, while I appreciate that my father had a long relationship with you in regards to the contract with the army, unless I can deal with you without being subjected to what occurred last night, our partnership is finished. I came here strictly on business, expecting to spend the night in your home. I might as well have booked a room in a gambling den with a brothel thrown in for good measure. Rumours have abounded concerning the deterioration of Laughlin Manor, but the rumours were nothing compared to the reality."

"What are you saying? I only meant to provide amusement for those here for the hunt. Certainly you do not intend to end a profitable partnership over the presence of a few card tables and some beautiful ladies? Are you mad?"

"First, those are not *ladies* by any stretch of the imagination. Second, it has been my experience that gambling usually leads to lost fortunes, hot tempers and challenges that often leave foolish men dead. And, thirdly, I am not mad, you are. For if you keep to this behaviour, you, sir, will lose everything your ancestors took centuries to build. You have already lost your good name, for the most part, and so has your son."

Laughlin looked stunned but said nothing.

"I dare say that you have no idea how much money you lost last night." When the earl did not reply, William added, "I thought as much." He turned, intending to leave. However, memories of his father prompted him to try one last argument.

"I remember accompanying Father to Laughlin Manor as a boy and hearing him speak eloquently all the way home about how it was one of the finest estates in all of England, and what a fine job you had done managing it. But after Lady Laughlin died, you seemed not to care. If you do not worry for you own reputation, you should at least be concerned for your son's. If he keeps to the current path, I cannot imagine any respectable lady accepting him, and with no heir, what will become of your estate?" He hesitated, letting that thought sink in. "It gives me no pleasure to say this, but unless you stop this downward spiral, Laughlin Manor is doomed."

By then Zeus was waiting below, so William touched the brim of his hat, nodded and went down the steps. After he had mounted the stallion, he glanced back at his host, who stood frozen in place. Kicking Zeus into a trot, he was out of sight in mere moments.

Looking about as though waking from a stupor, Laughlin noticed several footmen staring uneasily at him. Lifting his chin defiantly, he marched back into the house.

Arrogant man! Who is he to criticise me? If Darcy does not want to associate with Laughlin Manor, many others would be only too happy to take his place.

Nevertheless, a niggling thought had taken root and would not be silenced. For deep inside, the earl knew that everything William had said was the truth.

Mason's Pass

The trail through Mason's Pass had always been treacherous because it was bordered on both sides by rocky cliffs, thus making it vulnerable to falling stone. William realised that recent rains must have caused a new rock slide, for several large boulders now sat in the middle of the path, boulders that had not been there when he travelled to Chesterfield. Still, he considered himself most fortunate not to have been caught in the middle of the slide, as had happened to him when he travelled with Richard years before. It had been a close call, but being young and foolish, it did not deter them from taking the same route to Chesterfield, even after his father expressly forbade it. The pass cut a good twenty miles off the trip, and time was all that mattered to young men eager to join friends in manly pursuits. William smiled. *Or a man eager to return to his beautiful wife!*

That memory was busy in his heart and mind whilst he guided Zeus around the obstacles, and he was totally unmindful of what lay ahead; thus, when he came around the bend that signalled the last stretch of rocky terrain before the beginning of the backwoods of Pemberley, he was astonished to find someone waiting several yards ahead. Reining Zeus in, it took a few seconds to comprehend that it was Andrew atop the horse, and he was holding a pistol that was pointed directly at him.

"Andrew? What in the are you doing here?"

"This is not Pemberley, dear cousin. I have every right to be on this road."

William noted that his words were slurred and that he swayed a bit. He was drunk. Still, the pistol Andrew waved so carelessly was reason for concern.

Suddenly Andrew shouted, "Pull that pistol you carry in your coat out slowly, and drop it on the ground. Then raise your hands."

Having no recourse, William did as he was told. Aghast at his own helplessness, his heart drummed as he tried to recall if he had put the small derringer back in his boot this morning or left it in his bag. He had a knife, but that would do little good against a gun.

"I... I have to stop you, Fitz. You left me no choice."

Andrew seemed reluctant to carry through with whatever he had planned, and William took it as a good sign. *If I can keep him talking, perhaps I can convince him to stop.*

"Put the gun down, Cousin. Let us talk sensibly."

"No!" Andrew shouted in a fiery exclamation. Instantly, his arm straightened and he took aim. "I cannot allow you to sell Winfield Hall."

"Maybe I acted too hastily. If you ride back to Pemberley with me, we can discuss it."

It looked as though Andrew was considering his words, for his arm lowered slightly and the pistol with it. William had just released the breath he was holding when a gunshot rang out. Zeus reared. Since his hands were in the air, William did not have time to grab hold of the horse's mane. He fell backward and a stomach-churning groan pierced the air when his left shoulder hit the rocky surface first. Instantly his head snapped back, striking a large flat rock with a sickening thud.

Andrew sat stunned and speechless. Quickly sobering with the magnitude of what had happened, it dawned on him that he had never fired his weapon. As if on cue, Wickham came charging up on his horse.

"Did I get him? Is he dead?"

A ghastly whiteness had overspread Andrew's face. "You... you shot Fitz!" He murmured incredulously.

"I knew all along that you would not have the nerve to do it! What difference does it make who shot him, as long as he is dead?" Grabbing Andrew's weapon from his hand, he declared, "Give me your pistol! I need to make sure that he is finished!"

Dismounting, Wickham took a few steps in William's direction before the sound of someone shouting stopped him in his tracks. "Damnation!" he cried as he rushed to remount his horse. "We have to get out of here."

Still cursing the fact that his plans had been interrupted, Wickham jerked his horse to go in the opposite direction. To his surprise, Andrew still sat motionless, staring at Darcy. Grabbing the reins to Andrew's bay, Wickham kicked his own animal into a gallop, pulling his friend along with him. They had just cleared the rocky pass and entered the road that meandered through the forest when Wickham cut off from the road. Plunging through the woods via a secret path that only someone who grew up at Pemberley would be able to find, they were safely hidden in the woods within minutes.

Earlier that day, Sergeant Thaggart had convinced his superior officer to take the shortcut through Mason's Pass on their way to Lambton. Their final destination was London, where Thaggart would re-join Colonel Fitzwilliam as his batman. Though he assured Colonel North that, contrary to local lore, the trail was safe and passable and that it would cut miles off their journey, saving time had not been his primary motive. In truth, he wished to steer their little band toward Pemberley, for he felt certain that Mrs. Reynolds would offer to feed them. And after eating army rations for the last five days, all he could think about was the fine fare at the Darcys' table.

Additionally, he and the colonel, as well as Sergeant Whitaker and the six new recruits, were bone tired from having travelled for the past two weeks, and a night spent in the hay of Pemberley's stables was preferable to spending another night in a tent on the hard ground. Having taken a great deal of ridicule for his suggestion to use Mason's Pass after they encountered the rock slide, Thaggart was feeling quite down by the time he heard the shot ring out.

One of the new recruits shouted, "That was gunfire!" Another added, "I think it came from just ahead!"

By the time that every man had drawn his weapon, a large black horse was hurling down the trail towards them. Having nowhere to run, Zeus halted, reared on his hind legs and whinnied as only a frightened horse would.

"That's Mr. Darcy's horse!" Thaggart exclaimed. "I would know him anywhere."

"Darcy? Colonel Fitzwilliam's cousin?"

"Yes. Pemberley's backwoods start at the end of this pass."

By then Thaggart was already on the ground, attempting to calm the frightened animal. "There, there, Zeus. You remember me. Calm down, boy. All is well."

Ultimately, he was able to grab his reins, and Thaggart ran a hand down the animal's shoulder. "There's the Pemberley name on the saddle." Then stroking the horse's nose, he noticed a trickle of blood running down Zeus' ear. "If I had to guess, I would say that his ear has been nicked by a bullet."

"That does not bode well," Colonel North declared. Then he ordered, "Be on alert men, and move out!"

It was only seconds before they happened upon Fitzwilliam Darcy lying in the middle of the trail. The colonel was the first to reach him. Having been in the medical corps when he was young, North had a physician's skills and heart. Kneeling beside William, he placed two fingers on his neck.

"He is alive!"

Suddenly, Thaggart was on the ground beside him. "That is him. That is Mr. Darcy."

"I believe his neck is not broken, or he would have died instantly, however, he is gravely injured. Ride to Pemberley straightaway. Have them bring a wagon to transport him there. He needs to lie flat on his back. Moving him may make things worse, but he cannot stay here. A stretcher would be perfect, if they have one."

"I will tell them all you have said, sir!"

Thaggart was already on his horse when Colonel North shouted, "Have them send for the local physician, too! And hurry, Thaggart! Hurry!"

Pemberley
Library

A curious and inexplicable uneasiness had followed Mrs. Reynolds all day. Though most of the inhabitants of Pemberley were oblivious to it, Olivia

Fitzwilliam had become conscious of it the instant the housekeeper joined her and Elizabeth in the library. Making a mental note to ask the servant—out of Elizabeth's presence—if there was anything amiss, her attention was instantly drawn back to the task at hand when Elizabeth asked a question.

"Mrs. Reynolds, do you remember if this fabric came from Lambton or with the samples sent from London?" Elizabeth enquired, holding up a length of material in a forest green with thin burgundy and gold stripes around the hem.

"I… I am no longer certain, Mrs. Darcy. I wrote down where the samples came from when they arrived, but—"

"I lost the paper!" Elizabeth smiled sheepishly. "It is my fault. I do not blame you. I just hoped that you might recall this particular pattern. I must choose between this one and the blue." At that point, she picked up another length of material which featured a dark-gold paisley pattern scattered on a deep-blue background. "I cannot decide which I like best, so I wished to hear your opinion, as well as my aunt's."

At once she stood up with the two swatches of cloth. "Perhaps it will be easier if you see them next to the windows. Come over here, please!"

Olivia was already at the window inspecting the choices when Mrs. Reynolds reached them. Always watchful of the front drive, out of the corner of her eye the housekeeper caught sight of a man on horseback galloping down it. The rider wore a red coat, though his uniform was not as grand as the master's cousin's. The fear that had dogged her all day suddenly washed over Mrs. Reynolds like a river.

"Excuse me, Mrs. Darcy," she managed to say while keeping her voice steady. "I just remembered something I forgot to tell Mr. Walker."

The tone of her voice caught Olivia's attention, and she looked in her direction. Finding Reynolds' face full of trepidation, she started to say, "Is there—"

The old servant shook her head, stopping the enquiry. Elizabeth was too absorbed in her mission to notice, but Olivia's gaze followed her as she left the room. Entering the foyer, Reynolds nearly ran into Joseph Fitzwilliam, who was coming to join his wife. Seeing the worry written on her face, he stopped short.

"Mrs. Reynolds, what in the world has happened?"

"I… I am not certain," she said sombrely, "but I may need your help. There is a messenger at the front door, and I feel in my heart that something dreadful has happened."

Joseph glanced toward the library's door. "Let us say nothing to the ladies. No need to raise an alarm until we know for certain."

He followed the housekeeper to the front entrance, where they found a footman at the open door. Behind him was a soldier they both recognised.

"Sergeant Thaggart!" Joseph said, taking in the man's serious expression as he reached to shake his hand. "You look frightened. What has happened?"

"It is Mr. Darcy, sir! He has been hurt and lies in the road near Mason's Pass!"

Mrs. Reynolds gasped, but Joseph said in a calm voice, "Tell us everything."

He listened intently as the sergeant quickly told all that had occurred and ended with his colonel's requests. Seeing Mr. Walker hurrying forward, Joseph addressed him.

"Send a footman to fetch Mr. Camryn. If he is not at his office, have him go to his home. Then tell Mr. Miller to ready Pemberley's best wagon and collect several grooms to help. Have a footman retrieve a mattress from one of the unoccupied servant's rooms and place it in the bottom of the wagon along with several quilts."

Without questioning, the butler rushed to comply. Joseph turned next to Mrs. Reynolds. "I do not recollect seeing a stretcher here, but we could knock the legs off one of those cots kept downstairs—the one used for visiting servants when the beds have run out."

"That would work!" Thaggart exclaimed.

"Come with me," Mrs. Reynolds said to him. "I shall show you where the cots are kept. It will take a man to saw the legs off." She rushed in the direction of the kitchen.

"Mrs. Reynolds!" Joseph shouted, bringing her to a halt. "As soon as the wagon is ready, fetch me. I mean to go with them." The housekeeper nodded and hurried away.

With that, Joseph Fitzwilliam was left alone. The thought of in what condition he would find his nephew, someone he loved like a son, caused his heart to ache. Closing his eyes, he dropped his head.

Not Fitzwilliam, Lord. Not now. Suddenly, he heard his father lecturing him on duty. *This is no time to crumble. You must act like a man. Be strong!*

His father had been right about that. He had to be strong for Olivia, but most especially for Elizabeth. Taking a deep breath, Joseph schooled his features to look more serene than he felt and headed toward the library.

⁂

"Oh, Uncle, you are here! Come and give me your opinion of—"

Elizabeth's words hung in the air, for when the expression on her uncle's face penetrated her senses, she was stricken mute.

Olivia turned to see what had silenced Elizabeth. Her husband's face was gravely authoritative—an expression she had seen only twice. Trembling, she rose to go to her niece. She slid an arm around Elizabeth's waist, and for a long moment, they stared at her husband.

Finally, he found his voice. "Elizabeth, would you join me on the sofa."

Elizabeth's eyes dilated with fear as she shook her head slowly left to right.

Then she whirled around, covered her face and began to cry. Olivia pulled her into her arms, whispering words of comfort.

At length, she managed to stop crying. Wiping her face with her hands, she faced her uncle. Joseph grasped her forearms gently, hoping he might be able to catch her if she fainted. "My dear, there has been an accident involving Fitzwilliam."

Elizabeth's face crumbled and she squeezed her eyes tight, trying not to cry again. It was fruitless. Tears seeped through her lashes and rolled down her face.

"Sergeant Thaggart's troop found him lying in the road. He is alive, but unconscious."

Elizabeth seemed befuddled, stammering, "He... he is alive?"

Her uncle nodded. "Yes, he is alive. Thaggart's fellow soldiers are with him, awaiting the wagon from Pemberley. I am going with them to bring him home."

"I must go to him!" She tried to move, but Joseph held her in place.

"Elizabeth," he said as calmly as possible, "the house must be readied to receive Fitzwilliam. You are needed here."

Olivia broke in. "He is right, my dear. We must have everything at hand—bandages and towels, boiling water, Mrs. Reynolds' bag of remedies."

"Stay here with Olivia, Elizabeth. I shall take good care of your husband for you."

Grasping the lapels of his coat, she pleaded, "Promise me."

"Anything in my power."

"Tell Will that I love him. Even if... even if you think he cannot hear." Her voice broke. "Tell him that I love him."

It took all his strength not to cry along with Elizabeth as he wrapped his niece in his arms. Joseph held her tight for a moment, reassuring, "I promise." Then drawing back, he kissed her forehead. "I shall bring him home to you."

She nodded and he turned to go to Olivia. Embracing her, he whispered in her ear, "Be as strong as you can for Elizabeth. I love you."

Just then, at the door, Thaggart cleared his throat. "Excuse me, sir, but the wagon is ready."

"Let us be off then, Sergeant."

In the foyer, Mr. Walker joined Mrs. Reynolds as they followed Olivia and Elizabeth onto the portico. All four stood in silent vigil until the wagon and the men were completely out of sight.

The night was eerily quiet as they remained in front of the house. Then in a voice filled with determination, Elizabeth said, "We have lots to get done before Will comes home, so we had better get started."

As she disappeared back inside the house, Mr. Walker, Mrs. Reynolds and Olivia Fitzwilliam exchanged worried glances. Acknowledging each other's fears without saying a word, they hurried after Elizabeth.

Pemberley

After Joseph Fitzwilliam left to bring William home, Elizabeth went straightaway from frightened to resolute. Heading directly to the suite of rooms that she and William shared, she began to study the configuration of William's bedroom and the door entering it from the hall. Abruptly, she ordered a maid to fetch four footmen and then headed to the sitting room.

When Olivia enquired about the need for footmen, Elizabeth explained, "Mrs. Reynolds mentioned that a stretcher was made from one of the cots in the servants' quarters. Short of moving William's huge bed and wardrobe, it will never fit through the hall door. All that is left is to manoeuvre through the sitting room, and if we go through there, it will be easier if several pieces of furniture are removed."

Though still concerned by her niece's sudden change of character, Olivia was impressed that she was able to think at all under the circumstances. Nonetheless, scarcely had she time to consider anything her niece had said before the footmen rushed into the room, and Elizabeth began pointing to the pieces she wanted removed. Then she gave orders to remove the door between the sitting room and bedroom from its hinges. Next, she sent a maid to fetch bandages of various sizes from their supply. Another maid was asked to bring extra towels and to make sure that Mrs. Lantrip had been instructed to heat water.

Disturbed by the racket, Georgiana stomped from her bedroom and, seeing Mrs. Reynolds, demanded to know the cause of the upheaval in the family quarters. Mrs. Reynolds patiently explained all that had happened. Flushed with a suffusion that crimsoned her whole countenance, Georgiana would not let an opportunity pass to undermine her brother's wife. Entering the sitting room where Elizabeth and Olivia were busy working, she made her views known.

"I do not see why it was necessary to disrupt the entire house by moving furniture at a time like this. After all, Pemberley has ample guest rooms with beds much smaller than Brother's. Any of those rooms could easily accommodate a stretcher."

Half choked by rising anger, Elizabeth turned to face her, the calm mask of moments before replaced by an expression of inflexible authority. It caused all those witness to the scene to exchange nervous glances.

"When *my husband* wakes from this terrible ordeal, he is going to be lying in his *own* bed, in his *own* bedroom. I do not have the time or inclination to argue with you today of all days, Georgiana, so please stay out of the way or, better still, go back to your room. I will have someone notify you when Will is brought home."

Having said that, Elizabeth walked into William's bedroom with an armload of towels a maid had just brought up. Georgiana looked about the room, and finding no sympathy in the faces of her aunt, Mrs. Reynolds or any of the servants, she marched out. Going down the hall, she shouted, "Send for me the minute my brother is home."

Everyone was now on pins and needles, watching Elizabeth cope by keeping up a tumult of activity—none more so than Olivia. Thus, when a maid whispered to her that Mr. Camryn, the local physician, was downstairs, Olivia quietly hurried to meet him. He was already on the first steps of the grand staircase when she arrived at the top of the landing. Going swiftly down the stairs, she met him halfway.

"Mr. Camryn, thank you for coming so swiftly."

"I could do no less for Mr. Darcy, Mrs. Fitzwilliam. He is not only a patient of mine, but a good friend. I am heartsick to hear of his misfortune."

"We all are. He has not been returned to the house as of yet but should be here at any moment. I hoped to speak to you before you talk to my niece."

Olivia proceeded to quickly tell him of her worries about Elizabeth's frame of mind. After she was done, he began to reassure her. "In my profession, I have witnessed many a woman in these same circumstances. To all appearances, they seem strong, but inwardly, they are falling to pieces. If I feel it is warranted, I shall not hesitate to prepare something for Mrs. Darcy's nerves."

"There is something else you should know." Olivia looked around surreptitiously, continuing in a low voice, "I swore I would tell no one, so please keep this in strictest confidence. Even my nephew is not aware of what I am going to say."

"I understand completely."

"Only days ago, Elizabeth confided in me that she may be with child. It is only the first signs, mind you, nothing definite. Still—"

"I am pleased that you told me," Camryn interrupted. "Though I would usually prescribe a few drops of laudanum in these circumstances that is out of the question if she may be with child. Perhaps a strong chamomile tea and a headache powder would have the desired effect."

All of a sudden, Mr. Walker appeared at the foot of the stairs. "The wagon has returned." Then he rushed toward the front door.

"Please ask Mrs. Reynolds to prepare the tea, just in case. I must see to Mr. Darcy."

Camryn hurried after the butler, while Olivia hastily returned upstairs. The very second she told her niece that William was downstairs, Elizabeth's self-possessed facade crumbled. Dashing from the room, she ran down the hall, slowing down only when she went down the stairs. Then she crossed the foyer at her former furious pace.

By the time Olivia and Mrs. Reynolds caught up with her on the portico, Elizabeth was frozen in place, stricken to the soul. Both hands covered her mouth, while her eyes, wide as saucers, locked on the bed of the wagon and Mr. Camryn, who was bent over her husband's unresponsive body.

Olivia whispered Mr. Camryn's orders to the housekeeper. As the long-time servant left to instruct Mrs. Lantrip to make the drink, Olivia went to her niece.

"Elizabeth, dear, why do you not come inside?" she said, sliding an arm around her waist. "Let them get Fitzwilliam into the house."

Elizabeth did not budge, and only when the men began sliding the stretcher toward the end of the wagon did she speak. "Please, be careful!"

By then Joseph had joined his wife and niece. Receiving a pointed look from his wife, he said, "Perhaps we should all step back into the house."

The men were already beginning up the steps with William, and Elizabeth declared, "I must show them the way." Stepping in front of the stretcher, she added, "Please, follow me."

She led the way, leaving the Fitzwilliams to watch apprehensively. When the groom slapped the reins, urging the horses back to the stables, they both startled. And, after the wagon had rumbled around the corner of the house, they were left in an eerie silence.

"How is he truly, Joseph? Do not spare me the truth."

Shaking his head forlornly, he took a deep breath to steady his nerves. "It does not look good, Livy. Apparently Fitzwilliam fell from his horse, taking a hard blow to the back of the head. There is a knot the size of a large egg at the base of his skull. I have been at his side the entire time, and he has shown no signs of regaining consciousness."

Olivia sobbed and he pulled her into his embrace, patting her back. After a spell of crying, she sniffled, pulled a handkerchief from her pocket and dried her eyes. "I cannot let Elizabeth see me like this." Once she was satisfied that she could continue, she said, "Do you think it an accident?"

"No. The soldiers clearly heard a gunshot, but Fitzwilliam's pistol was never fired. It was found on the ground several feet away. Also, the tip of his stallion's ear was bleeding, and I agree with Thaggart that he was likely nicked by a bullet meant for our nephew. Someone suggested that a hunter's shot might have gone astray, but the distance from the woods to where Fitzwilliam was found is too great a distance. No bullet would carry that far, let alone penetrate the rock on either side."

"What do you think happened?"

"Colonel North believes that whoever shot at Fitzwilliam did not have good aim, thus he hit Zeus. The stallion reared, throwing him to the ground, and that is when he hit his head. I concur with his opinion. Most likely, the blackguard would have finished him off if the troops had not come through the pass so close behind our nephew."

"Thank God that Colonel North was there."

"The Lord was certainly gracious in that regard."

"I cannot imagine anyone wanting to hurt Fitzwilliam. And knowing it was deliberate will devastate Elizabeth even more."

"It is hard to comprehend such evil. And I have to wonder if we should wait to tell Elizabeth it was no accident until she is better able to deal with the news. In any case, locating the culprit is secondary to seeing after

Fitzwilliam's wellbeing at this point."

"Of course it is."

"There is one other thing. While I think Mr. Camryn an excellent physician, I want to suggest that we ask Fitzwilliam's physician in London, to attend him, too. I believe he said his name is Graham."

"That is an excellent idea. I think Elizabeth will feel better knowing that more than one doctor is attending him. I am sure Mrs. Reynolds knows the man and we should ask Elizabeth if she wants you to notify him, for she has more than enough concerns at present."

"That is not unexpected under the circumstances. Come, love, we need to go inside, as I wish to hear everything Mr. Camryn has to say."

Upstairs, Elizabeth guided the men to the sitting room as if in a daze. Seeing William lying flat on his back in the wagon with his clothes dishevelled and his boots removed had driven home to her the truth of what had happened. Her once vibrant husband looked so vulnerable, and it had taken all her strength not to collapse then and there.

Suddenly, Mr. Camryn's raised voice coming from inside the bedroom forced her thoughts back to the present. "Hold steady, men! Good, now slide him onto the bed gently... gently."

After the men with the stretcher reverently filed past her, Elizabeth walked into the bedroom, followed shortly by her aunt and uncle, Mrs. Reynolds, Mr. Adams, Darcy's valet, and Georgiana, who had been summoned when the wagon arrived. Mr. Camryn seemed oblivious to the growing number, as he was totally focused on his patient, but once he stopped to take in the scene, his worried gaze settled on Elizabeth.

"I would like Mrs. Reynolds to stay, for I may need to borrow a few items from her bag. Mr. Adams, I could use your help in cutting Mr. Darcy's clothes from his body. If everyone else will be good enough to wait in the sitting room, I will come in and give you my opinion of Mr. Darcy's condition once I have finished my examination."

"I will not." Every eye turned to Elizabeth. Though it was obvious that she was trembling, her expression was unyielding.

"I assure you it will only take a short while, Mrs. Darcy."

"This is my husband, Mr. Camryn. I will stay."

The physician's chest deflated wearily as a loud sigh escaped. "Very well."

Though the Fitzwilliams started to leave, Georgiana did not move. Instead her expression stiffened into obstinacy. "He is my brother. I have as much right to stay as Elizabeth!"

At the end of his patience, Joseph Fitzwilliam took his niece by the elbow. "You will wait with us, Georgiana." None too gently, he ushered her from the room.

After they were gone, the physician addressed the housekeeper, "Mrs. Reynolds, do you have two pairs of sharp scissors?"

"I have only one in my bag," Mrs. Reynolds said, extracting a pair from it without delay.

"I keep a pair in Mr. Darcy's dressing room," Mr. Adams said. Instantly he disappeared into the adjoining room and, just as quickly, reappeared holding up another pair of scissors.

"Good! We dare not risk bending his arms or legs until we know for certain if bones are broken. So, let us get started. We shall remove his coat, waistcoat and shirt first. I shall begin on this side, if you will do the other."

Physician and valet worked swiftly, and soon William was naked from the waist up. Camryn began the examination by feeling along the length of both arms and legs. Seemingly satisfied, he manipulated William's neck before running his fingers over every inch of his head, front and back.

"There is a lump, but, thank God, his neck is not broken. Help me turn him slightly, Mr. Adams. Lift him just enough so that I can accomplish what I must." The valet rolled William toward himself. "That is good. Hold him steady."

The physician peered under William's back, looking for wounds whilst running his fingers over the area. Then he manipulated his shoulder blade and the ribcage before saying, "Now, the other side."

Repeating his actions on the left side, Camryn was soon finished. Rubbing his chin in reflection, he said, "Mrs. Reynolds, I assume you have smelling salts. May I borrow them, please? I left mine at a patient's cottage yesterday and have not had time to retrieve them or prepare more."

The housekeeper immediately handed a brown bottle to the physician. A pungent smell filled the room when he removed the stopper. Holding it under William's nose, he waved it slowly back and forth several times, but there was no response. New tears rushed to Elizabeth's eyes and they were shining when he turned to face her.

"The good news is that I see no open wounds, Mrs. Darcy. Two, possibly three, ribs are cracked on the left, which would likely mean he hit the ground on that side. He will no doubt have bruises there, as well as along his left shoulder and arm. In fact, they are forming already. I could detect no other fractures, but small fractures are impossible to detect by manipulation. If Mr. Darcy was awake, he could direct us to any breaks simply because of the pain."

"Do you—When might he wake?" Elizabeth stammered.

The physician glanced at Mrs. Reynolds, who moved to stand beside her.

"Unfortunately, we have no way of knowing when your husband will regain consciousness. I am certain that he has suffered a concussion because he is unconscious, but concussions and their symptoms vary widely according to severity. At this point, I can say only that the injury to his head is my paramount concern."

A ghastly whiteness overspread Elizabeth's cheek. "I... I see."

"Take heart," Mrs. Reynolds said quietly. "Mr. Darcy is strong, and I am certain that, given time, he will make a full recovery."

Overhearing the advice, Mr. Camryn added, "Mrs. Darcy, your husband is young and strong. It is much too early to despair. Even so, there is not much I

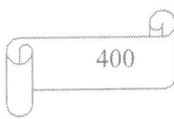

can do to help him until he wakes."

"What about his ribs? I have often seen broken ribs wrapped," Mr. Adams said.

"I will do that tomorrow. Hopefully, by then Mr. Darcy will be awake and can tell me if he is in pain." He smiled benevolently at Elizabeth. "I intend to stay at Pemberley until your husband improves, Mrs. Darcy. Do you have a room I might use?"

"Certainly," she said, as though in a daze. "And if you wish, a tray with hot tea and a light meal can easily be provided."

"That is kind of you. I have not eaten since this morning."

"Mrs. Reynolds, will you see to Mr. Camryn?"

The physician interrupted, "First, let me inform the others of what we have discussed."

As he and the housekeeper moved toward the sitting room, Elizabeth added, "Mr. Camryn, as a girl I helped the local apothecary in Meryton. Consequently, she left me her book of remedies. One recipe in particular is for a wonderful salve for aches and pains. I have a jar in my room."

Seeing hope in the young wife's eyes, the physician smiled kindly. "It certainly could do no harm. Rub Mr. Darcy's arms and shoulders, being careful not to do so too vigorously. At least, not until we are certain what is or is not broken."

Elizabeth nodded, blinking back tears. As soon as he left, she sent Mr. Adams to fetch the salve. Then she rushed to the bed and carefully sat beside William. Tenderly, she brushed a lock of hair from his forehead and placed a soft kiss there. "I am here, my darling."

Through silent tears she addressed the valet when he returned to hand her the salve. "Mr. Adams, please bring a bowl of warm water. I wish to clean my husband's face."

Once the water and a cloth had been brought, she addressed William again, saying, "Your face is so dusty, sweetheart. I cannot bear to see you this way."

Olivia had slipped back into the room knowing her husband would tell her later all that Camryn had said; for now, she was more worried about her niece. Having witnessed the tender display, she could not hold back her tears and when Joseph re-entered the room, she turned into his embrace, hiding her face in his chest. The poignancy of the scene was broken almost immediately, for Georgiana came back into the room spewing nonsense.

"I will send an express to the earl tomorrow morning. He will know the best course of action to take. In any event, I mean to see to it that Fitzwilliam is not left alone, not for a single minute."

"Georgiana, you are not in charge," Joseph stated firmly.

Her eyes narrowed as she glared at him. "Am I the only one concerned about what is best for my brother?"

"We all are," Olivia retorted.

Then Joseph addressed his other niece. "With your permission, Elizabeth, I will send an express to my brother tomorrow and one to Richard. And I would like to ask Mr. Graham to accompany Richard to Pemberley."

Elizabeth, who had ignored Georgiana's outburst, stilled from gently cleaning William's face. "I should appreciate your help in notifying everyone, Uncle. And I would feel better knowing Will's physicians are consulting with one another."

"Of course, Mr. Graham should be consulted," Georgiana retorted, her voice rising indignantly, "but I imagine that the earl will insist on transporting Fitzwilliam to London. Why should you have Mr. Graham set out for Pemberley when Brother will be taken to Town?"

"What in the world makes you think that would benefit Fitzwilliam?" Joseph snapped.

"Because all the best doctors are in London."

Though she never stopped caring for William, Elizabeth said flatly, "My husband will not be jostled about in a coach in his condition. Not as long as I live. Any specialist he may need will come to Pemberley, no matter the cost."

Georgiana huffed, "We shall see," and stalked out of the room.

Olivia returned to a subject still on her mind. "Elizabeth, Fitzwilliam will need you when he awakens, and you will need to be well-rested. Joseph and I will sit with him tonight and call you if there are any signs of change."

Respect forbade downright contradiction, so as Elizabeth dripped the cloth in the water and wrung it out again, she replied, "That is kind of you, but I shall not sleep anyway. It is the two of you who should get some rest; you both must be exhausted." She glanced at Adams. "And you should as well, Mr. Adams. I am sure my husband will need your services when he awakens."

"Elizabeth is right, Livy, you do need to rest."

As all three walked out of the bedroom, Mrs. Reynolds was coming back into the sitting room. Seeing them, she stopped abruptly.

"Miss Darcy is in her bedroom. Forgive me for saying this, but I would give anything if she were still in London."

"Do not apologise. Those are our thoughts exactly," Joseph said.

"We were just coming to find you," Olivia added. "I told Elizabeth that Joseph and I would sit with Fitzwilliam tonight, but she refused, and she dismissed Mr. Adams, as well."

"I am not surprised. Go and rest. I shall sit with her the first half of the night, and Mr. Adams, if you will replace me after midnight?"

William's valet nodded and went to leave. Then he stopped and, with a heart-rending expression on his face, ventured, "Will you send for me if there is any change? I doubt I shall sleep much."

"I will."

As Adams left, Mrs. Reynolds addressed the Fitzwilliams. "Rest assured that I shall keep good watch over Mr. Darcy, as will Mr. Adams."

"We will retire then, hopefully to be of service tomorrow. Please wake us if anything changes, no matter the hour."

"You may depend on me."

The housekeeper waited until they were completely out of sight. Then taking a moment to control her growing fears, she walked into the bedroom.

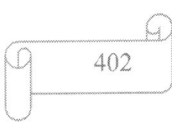

Elizabeth was still absently running a warm cloth over William's neck and shoulders, all the while talking to him as though he could hear.

When opportunity arose, she said, "Mrs. Darcy, I hope you will let me sit with you tonight."

Elizabeth slowed her attentions, though her eyes never left William's face. "I do appreciate your concern, truly I do, but I wish to be alone with my husband tonight."

"Then please allow me to occupy the sitting room. That way, if help should be needed, you have only to call out, and I will fetch Mr. Camryn."

"I... I suppose that is sensible. I do not mean to be unfeeling. I know how much you love Will, but I really need this time alone."

"I understand, ma'am. If there is anything I can do, please call on me. I shall not sleep tonight."

"Thank you, Mrs. Reynolds."

Wearily, the housekeeper proceeded to one of the two chairs left in the sitting room. She removed her shoes and sat down in one, propping her feet on the other. Both chairs were upholstered with thick cushions, and she settled gratefully into the softness. Her body was drained, her heart broken, yet she could not give in to despair, for she had duties to perform. Tonight that entailed listening for Elizabeth's summons and whilst executing that responsibility she intended to pray harder than she had ever prayed in her life.

Finally alone with William, Elizabeth gently applied the salve to the dark purple bruises beginning to manifest on his left arm and shoulder. Now that everyone had left, she felt free to cry, and she did—silently. On occasion, a pitiful sob would escape, and she would turn her head and cover her mouth. Mrs. Harris, Meryton's one-time apothecary, had theorised that people in William's condition could hear what was happening, even if they could not communicate. That realisation came from a patient who told of hearing her family plan her funeral while she was unresponsive; thus, Elizabeth strived to keep her conversation encouraging.

"Darling, this salve helped me tremendously when I twisted my ankle, and I pray it brings relief to you. It contains lavender and may make you smell like me." She tried to laugh, but did not succeed. "Somehow I do not think you will mind. You always said that you love the scent of my hair."

Her cheerfulness ebbed with her next words. "Do you remember what you said to me when you gave me my wedding ring? You told me that these words spoke of your undying love." She repeated them slowly, "First. Last. Only. Always. And you vowed to love me forever."

Elizabeth swallowed, though a large lump in her throat made it difficult. "Surely you know by now, my darling Will, that I love you exactly the same. There shall *never* be any man in my life but you. So, you see, you simply must—" Her voice cracked; still she had to finish. "You simply must get well, because I need you." She leaned over, softly kissing his lips. Then peering at his face for any sign of recognition, she concluded, "And, most importantly, our child needs you."

Gently, she laid her ear against his chest. Listening to the steady drumbeat of his heart gave her hope, and she prayed silently.

Come back to me, Will. Please come back to me.

It was near midnight when Olivia Fitzwilliam stepped into the sitting room to find Mrs. Reynolds with her head down in prayer. Turning to leave, the housekeeper spoke before she could.

"There is no need to go, Mrs. Fitzwilliam."

William's aunt turned back to the faithful servant who was now attempting to stand. "Please do not get up on my account. I did not wish to disturb you, it is just that I could not sleep, so I decided to check..." Olivia glanced toward the bedroom.

"You are not disturbing me. I am glad for the company," Mrs. Reynolds said. "Besides, I have been sitting in one position too long." Looking toward the hall door, she teased half-heartedly, "I am surprised, though, that your husband is not with you."

"Poor Joseph must be exhausted, for he did not wake. Normally, he sleeps with one eye open."

"If he is that tired, then he should rest. But you should be resting, too."

Olivia smiled. "And who are you to lecture on rest?"

Mrs. Reynolds shrugged sheepishly. "Mr. Adams will be here shortly. Then I shall take my turn."

"How is my nephew? Has anything changed?"

"I looked in on Mr. Darcy less than an hour ago, and he is the same."

"And Elizabeth?"

"Mrs. Darcy has talked to him the better part of the night. Only recently she quietened, so I slipped to the door to find out why. I found her lying beside him, holding his hand. She may not be asleep, but her eyes were closed."

The last few words were accompanied by a small sob, so Olivia pulled the housekeeper into her arms. "There, there. We must have faith." She patted Mrs. Reynolds on the back. "You and I must be strong. Elizabeth needs us now more than ever."

"I feel awful breaking down like this."

"It shows how deeply you love my nephew and Elizabeth. Let us, you and I, resolve to cry on each other's shoulders throughout this ordeal. Then we shall be able to bear it and stay strong in front of the others."

Mrs. Reynolds was nodding her agreement when Mr. Adams appeared at the door. Stepping out of Olivia's embrace, the housekeeper greeted him.

"Mr. Adams, are you ready?"

"I am."

"Mrs. Darcy wishes to be alone with Mr. Darcy, so I convinced her to allow us to sit in here. That way, if she calls for help, we will be available instantly."

"I am glad you were able to convince her, for that is the goal—to keep watch over them."

"Mrs. Darcy has lain down beside her husband. I think she may be asleep, but I am not certain. In any event, just listen for any sign that you are needed."

"I understand."

"I shall see you at dawn then. Be sure to summon me if anything changes. I am occupying the blue room tonight, just in case."

Mrs. Reynolds and Mrs. Fitzwilliam disappeared into the hallway. After a last squeeze of one another's hands, they separated, heading to their own beds.

Chapter 37

Pemberley

Morning, in shades of yellow and orange, flooded the world with a soft golden light, but most of Pemberley's occupants took no note of it, for grief covered the great house like a shroud. Servants walked about in silent disbelief that such a catastrophe could have happened to their master, a man known for his honesty and good works. Word of his injury had already spread through the greater part of the village of Lambton, and the vicar and his wife, Mr. and Mrs. Moody, arrived shortly after daylight. The elderly couple was immediately escorted upstairs and were the first allowed to see Mr. Darcy that morning.

Their arrival corresponded with the departure of the troops under Colonel North. Forced to go on to London, per his orders, the colonel had directed Sergeant Thaggart to stay behind at Pemberley to await Colonel Fitzwilliam. Never doubting that his colleague would come as soon as he got word, he felt there was no need for Thaggart to meet Richard along the road. Thus, with heartfelt wishes for Mr. Darcy's full recovery and gratitude for Pemberley's hospitality, the soldiers departed.

Upstairs, Mr. Camryn had risen early as well. Eager to find his friend alert, upon entering the bedroom he was disappointed to discover that William's condition had not changed. Frowning when the smelling salts again failed to elicit a reaction, he was filled with alarm. All his studies with regard to head injuries suggested that continued unconsciousness was indicative of an injury more serious in nature; thus, whilst re-inspecting his patient for signs of internal bleeding and other possible complications, Camryn mused in grave thought of what to say to Mrs. Darcy. Having asked the rest of the family to wait in the sitting room, Elizabeth stood at the foot of the bed, her eyes dilated with fear.

Mr. Camryn sighed deeply before speaking. "Mrs. Darcy, let us step into the sitting room, so that I may address everyone at once."

Elizabeth searched his face for a sign of what he might say. Finding none, she swallowed dryly. "Of course."

As they entered the room, all conversation halted. Camryn cleared his throat and focused on Olivia. Surmising what he wanted, she moved to stand by Elizabeth.

"I wish to be totally honest, so there are no misunderstandings. I had thought to find Mr. Darcy awake this morning. That he is not indicates that the injury to his head is much more severe than I had hoped."

A stifled cry brought every eye to Elizabeth, who turned into her aunt's arms. Georgiana had begun to cry silently, so Mrs. Reynolds handed her a handkerchief and patted her arm sympathetically.

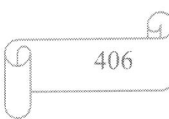

Uneasily, Mr. Camryn continued. "In my years as a physician, I have seen patients recover from this type of injury—often with miraculous results." He paused. "But, unfortunately, I have seen many who did not.

"Nevertheless, I am hopeful that Mr. Darcy will recover because he is young and in good health. If he were not, he would not have survived this long. And, since he is a good man, well-respected and generous to a fault, I have faith that Our Lord will consider this when we petition Him for a recovery."

Joseph replied, "Thank you for caring for my nephew and reminding us that while man is limited, God is not. Many prayers are being said on his behalf, and we trust that God will spare him."

"I pray for that as well," Camryn replied. "However, all we can do at this point is to keep him comfortable and carry on as normally as possible. Eat, even if you are not hungry, and rest as much as you are able. Be assured that you will be needed once he wakens, so keep up your strength. If you wish to help keep watch over him, do so in shifts, just as you did last night. No one can, or should, take full responsibility for his care." The last was said with a glance to Elizabeth, who still stood in Olivia's embrace. "Should you try, you will drain yourself and be of no use when he needs you the most."

When nothing more was said, Mrs. Reynolds spoke, "Cook arose early to feed Colonel North and his men, and the dining room is still filled with enough food to feed every soldier in England. I am certain that she would be pleased if you were to partake of the fare."

"I should be glad to," Camryn said, "and I urge everyone to do the same." As the room emptied, Elizabeth stepped out of her aunt's embrace, moving blindly toward the bedroom.

"You really need to eat something, Mrs. Darcy," Mr. Camryn said.

She stopped at the door, strangling a fierce tide of grief that welled up within her. "I... I am not hungry at present. Please enjoy your meal without me."

Joseph Fitzwilliam went to her then, grasping her forearms gently so she had to face him. "Elizabeth, dearest, I have no doubt that your appetite is lacking. I have none, either. Still, we must keep up our strength for Fitzwilliam's sake. I insist that you let me sit with him while you eat, for I ate with Colonel North and his men earlier."

Realising that she could not win the argument, Elizabeth said, "Give me just a moment, please."

At his nod, Elizabeth went into the bedroom and straight to William. Sitting on the side of the bed, she tried but could not stop the sense of panic that filled her heart. *Will he survive until I return?*

After kissing his lips, she tried to memorise the details of his face. His brows, black as coal, were now in stark contrast to his face, which was colourless. Equally dark eyelashes—eyelashes her mother had once declared were *too long to be wasted on a man*—fell upon his pale skin. Mesmerised, his handsome, straight nose drew her attention to a feature that she had always thought perfectly formed—the small indentation at the centre of his well-shaped lips. Longing to see his mouth loosen in an exultant smile as it had whenever he caught sight of her, she was lost in reminiscences when a cough broke the silence in the room.

Knowing that her time alone with her husband had come to an end, she said, "Uncle Joseph is going to stay with you, my darling, but only until I return. I will be back very soon, and I shall read to you then. I promise. I love you, Will."

Reluctantly, she allowed Olivia to take her hand and lead her toward the door, though her eyes locked on William until she could see him no longer.

The door to the main hallway closed with an ominous finality, and a great shuddering seized Elizabeth. Her carefully constructed facade crumbled as both hands covered her face and she sobbed. Guiding her into an empty guest room, Olivia embraced her, rocking her side to side as one would a child.

"There, there, dearest. Cry all you wish… let it out." Elizabeth wept for a long time, ultimately going silent because she was completely bereft of tears.

"As cruel as this may sound, I am relieved to see you cry," Olivia said. "You must let the pain escape; otherwise, you will make yourself sick. And since you may be with child, you must do all in your power to stay healthy."

Taking the handkerchief her aunt offered, Elizabeth sniffled as she dabbed her eyes and nose. "I feel so useless. There is nothing I can do to help Will."

"In situations like this, we have to put our loved one in God's hands and have faith in Him, just as Mr. Camryn said."

"But… " Elizabeth stuttered, "sometimes God does not give us what we ask, and I could not bear it if Will were to die."

"I do not believe that Fitzwilliam is going to die, Elizabeth. But whatever happens, we will face it together. For now, you know that your husband would want you to be strong for the baby."

The tumult in her heart subsided, and Elizabeth forced a faint, quivering smile. "I will try."

Love and sweet patience were in her aunt's look. "Come, then. We shall go to your dressing room so you may wash your face, and then we shall join the others."

"You are wise, as well as kind. Thank you for your encouragement, Aunt Olivia. I love you."

"With God's help, I have survived many hard lessons in my life. If I have any wisdom, it is only by His grace." She slid an arm around Elizabeth's waist, hugging her closer as they walked from the room. "And, I love you, too, Elizabeth. Very, very much."

Downstairs

Elizabeth ate very little, but it was apparently enough to satisfy Mr. Camryn. Once the meal had concluded, he went straight upstairs whilst the others filed into the foyer. The Moodys, who were needed at the foundlings' home, were leaving for Lambton with promises to keep William in their prayers as well as to come again the next day. Meanwhile, when a footman opened the huge entrance doors, the sombre atmosphere was broken by the

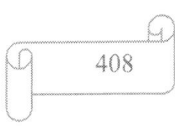

noise of a vehicle with matching pairs of greys, halting on the circular, gravel drive.

Elizabeth and Olivia walked towards the door. They both appeared stunned to see Lady Susan Hartley exit a carriage with Lord Attaway right behind her. Upon seeing Fitzwilliam's wife at the open door, Susan threw her head back, and with a frosty glare of defiance, began up the steps. Her companion scrambled to catch up. Astonished, Elizabeth stood like a statue as they passed her and Olivia and went into the house.

Inside, Georgiana was hurrying down the staircase. "Susan, I saw your arrival from my bedroom window," she declared. "I had no idea you would come so quickly."

"How could I delay after receiving your note about my dear Fitzwilliam," Lady Susan replied, now sniffing into a handkerchief as evidence of her grief. "I could not bear to stay away, knowing how near to death he lies. Please tell me that he has improved."

"I can say truthfully that he is no worse," Georgiana answered, linking their arms. "Come, I will take you to see him." Over her shoulder, she directed Mr. Walker, "Please show Lord Attaway to the library."

As they began up the stairs, Elizabeth stood her ground with the most perfect dignity. "No, Georgiana. Lady Susan is not welcome to see my husband. He is not to be disturbed."

Georgiana stopped and her lip curled with scorn. "My brother is unconscious. How can our presence disturb him?"

Elizabeth glared at the interloper. "After what happened in London, he expressly forbade Lady Susan from entering Pemberley ever again. Should he awaken to find that his wishes were ignored, he will be upset. And I will not have that."

If it were possible, Georgiana got angrier. "Fitzwilliam was stressed when he made that statement, of that I am certain. He would not begrudge her being here under the circumstances for, in spite of everything, Lady Susan has long been a beloved friend of his, as well as mine."

"Until he is able to speak for himself, I intend to follow his wishes."

Lord Attaway tried to intervene, saying condescendingly, "Surely you are not so resentful as to bar an old friend from seeing Fitzwilliam?"

Elizabeth turned around to face him, asking irritably, "Lord Attaway, what right have you to intrude in this conversation?"

He wilted under her steady gaze. "None, actually."

"Then may I suggest that you keep silent."

Flustered, Attaway apologised. "Excuse me. I meant no disrespect."

While this conversation was occurring, Mr. Walker had motioned three footmen forward. Seeing the men standing protectively behind her nemesis, Lady Susan decided that she would be unceremoniously tossed from the house if she kept to her plan.

"I did not come to cause turmoil, dearest Georgiana," she said, her scowl a silent rebuttal of her words. "Please keep me informed every minute of Fitzwilliam's progress. I can be here in less than a half-hour, if need be."

Georgiana proclaimed boldly, "You do not have to leave. This is my house too!"

Lady Susan patted her hand sympathetically. "It is best, for now, that I do."

As she walked past the woman who had stolen the man she desired, Lady Susan's eyes danced with malice. She said nothing more, though, as she marched out of the house with Attaway following timidly.

The closing of the front door signified that they were gone and brought Georgiana down the stairs to confront Elizabeth. "How dare you tell me whom I may invite to Pemberley?"

Suddenly, a disembodied voice declared, "You will not speak to your sister in that manner." Every eye flew to Joseph Fitzwilliam, who was now on the landing. As he came down the stairs, he added, "Furthermore, Georgiana, you will return to your room this instant and stay there until you can keep a civil tongue in your mouth."

"You cannot tell me what I can do," Georgiana replied, though she sounded hesitant.

"My nephew made it plain that he did not appreciate your disrespect of his wife. I intend to see that you respect Elizabeth while he is unable to make you do it himself."

Georgiana's eyes flicked about the room, meeting those of Mrs. Reynolds, Mr. Walker and several maids and footmen. Seeing that she was defeated, she began to climb the stairs. When she got to Joseph, she stopped. "We will see who is in charge once the earl arrives."

"Matlock is not master of this house, either," Joseph said matter-of-factly. "And all who serve here will obey Mrs. Darcy, not him."

Without another word, Georgiana fled to her rooms.

Elizabeth hurried up to meet him, asking, "Who is with Will?"

Smiling affectionately at her concern, Joseph answered, "Mr. Camryn had joined me in Fitzwilliam's room. I came down when I heard raised voices."

"Thank goodness." Her shoulders slumped with relief. "I do not want Will left alone."

"We will not let that happen."

"I appreciate your words, Uncle. I do not wish to be harsh with my sister, but I will not let Georgiana change what Fitzwilliam decreed just because he is unable to speak for himself."

"No thanks are necessary. I agree with you regarding Lady Susan, and I know my nephew would expect me to take your side against one and all."

"You know full well that Georgiana will be angry."

"She has been angry since Livy and I arrived. A little more anger will not hurt her," he teased.

Elizabeth's features softened to a quivering smile, and she nodded mutely before rushing up the stairs to her husband.

Descending the rest of the stairs, Joseph looked about to find that all the servants had disappeared. Gathering Olivia into his arms, he whispered, "Let us go into the garden so we may speak privately."

She nodded, and they walked in that direction. Once on the gravel path, they went straight to the garden containing the wooden swing. He helped her to sit down and then sat down beside her.

After a brief silence, he said, "I am sorry that it has come to this."

"It was not your fault. That Georgiana feels free, not only to attack Elizabeth, but to bring that woman here, is very alarming."

"I will not see Elizabeth treated disrespectfully."

"That makes me proud, dear. I do have to wonder, though, what the Earl of Matlock will say if he comes here." She sighed. "I remember how hateful he was the last time we were in his company."

"My brother can do nothing unless Fitzwilliam dies. If that were to happen, he could try to take charge, depending on how the will is written and how many men he still controls at court." Joseph heaved a sigh. "It is unfortunate that Elizabeth is not with child. An heir would make all the difference with regard to her future."

Olivia bit her lip and Joseph noticed the uneasy look on her face. "Clearly you know something that you have not shared with me, Livy."

"You know me too well." She breathed deeply. "I promised Elizabeth I would not tell anyone, yet I have had to confide in Mr. Camryn already. Please promise that you will not tell a soul."

His features softened, "I promise." Before she could explain, however, he added, "I assume from your reaction that my niece is with child."

"Elizabeth thinks she is, though she cannot be certain until she feels the quickening."

"How ironic—to feel such deep happiness and sadness at the same time. Our nephew would be ecstatic were he aware. Instead, he may never know how close he came to realising his dream of having a child."

"It is heartbreaking how everything can change in the blink of an eye." Tears filled his wife's eyes. "We learned that lesson well, did we not?"

He pulled her close. "Yes, we did, my love." Then seeking her eyes, he implored, "Try not to fret, Livy. Your delicate health causes me great concern."

"Do not worry. I mean to be here a long time, for whom else do Elizabeth or Fitzwilliam have?"

"It is my job to worry about you... and about Elizabeth and Fitzwilliam, too," Joseph said, placing a quick kiss on her nose. Over her shoulder, he saw Mr. Walker exit the back door and head in their direction.

"Walker, do you have need of me?"

"I hate to bother you, sir, but Mr. Coleridge and Mr. Harahan returned in the middle of the night and went directly to their rooms. Now that they are awake, they asked to see Mr. Darcy. I explained what has happened, and they seem eager to speak to you."

Joseph recalled Fitzwilliam mentioning the men, but he had never gone into detail about their employment. "Ask them to meet me in the library."

Walked nodded, hurrying back into the house.

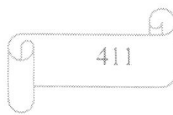

"After I meet with them, I think that you and I should stroll around the lake. My neck is stiff from the tension, and a walk would be just the remedy."

"Then I shall wait here and enjoy the sunlight."

Joseph leaned down to brush her lips with a kiss. "I shall return shortly."

Minutes later, Joseph Fitzwilliam passed a maid coming out of the library just as he was entering it. Coleridge and Harahan were seated on sofas, opposite each other, each holding a steaming cup of coffee and a plate containing a sweet roll. A nearby table held a tray with a pot of coffee. Both men started to stand when he entered the room, but he motioned for them to stay seated.

"My, that coffee smells incredible. I think I will join you in a cup." He stopped to fill an empty cup with the dark liquid and took a sip, closing his weary eyes. Then he walked over to them, stopping in between where they sat.

"I am Joseph Fitzwilliam, Mr. Darcy's uncle."

The bald-headed man answered, "Dale Coleridge, sir. And this is Patrick Harahan." He nodded to his red-haired co-hort. "We are former Bow Street Runners, employed by Mr. Darcy when he was in London."

"My nephew mentioned you, though he did not go into detail about your duties, other than to say that it involved keeping an eye on Andrew Darcy."

Harahan spoke. "We were shocked and saddened to learn of Mr. Darcy's misfortune."

"I note that you did not call it an accident," Joseph stated.

"From what we have heard, we do not believe it was," Harahan replied.

"No one else does, either; however, I have had too much on my mind to even consider investigating the incident. My nephew, Colonel Fitzwilliam, should be here any day, and I plan to leave that task in his capable hands. He had served as an investigator with His Majesty's army for many years and has many resources that a regular chap could not possibly imagine."

"We know Colonel Fitzwilliam well. It was he who recommended us to Mr. Darcy."

"I see. That is most fortunate, for he and Fitzwilliam are confidants, and he will know what should be done next. May I propose that until he arrives, you dress down and visit the local taverns—see what is being said about my nephew's calamity? Many may find their tongues if you buy them a drink."

"You sound as though you have done some investigating in your time," Coleridge ventured.

"I had to trace a deserter a time or two when I was with the navy. Please stay in touch if you do not return to Pemberley at night. That way Richard can locate you when he arrives. Do you need additional funds?"

"That will not be a problem. We will be staying at the Lambton Inn unless a lead takes us elsewhere. In that case, we will notify you straightaway. And, no, we are not in need of funds. Mr. Darcy was generous with his advance."

"Very well. Please finish your refreshments before you strike out again."

"We will. Thank you."

Joseph swallowed the last of his coffee, set the cup down and nodded to them as he left to return to Olivia.

"What is your impression of Darcy's uncle?" Coleridge asked a little later as he finished his second cup of coffee and placed the empty cup on the silver tray.

"Seems to me that he is a good man trying to hold everything together for his nephew's sake," Harahan replied. "I feel inclined to trust him."

"My thoughts exactly," Coleridge replied. "Well, are you ready to begin?"

Harahan came to his feet. "Yes, I could easily get used to living like this, and too much comfort tends to make me lazy."

Coleridge chuckled. "Well, let us change into our rags, smudge our faces with dirt and join the unwashed crowd at the local taverns. That should make you feel more at home."

"Very funny, old boy!" Harahan said, landing a punch on his friend's forearm. "I think we should, too, but only after we follow up on that lead regarding the farmhouse outside Lambton."

"So you are still set on finding Andrew Darcy?"

"I strongly believe that when we find that blackguard, we will learn that he is behind his cousin's *accident*."

"You are very untrusting, you know," Coleridge teased.

"I learned that from you."

Coleridge smiled widely. "So you did."

Sheffield
The Crown Inn

Andrew Darcy watched George Wickham primp in front of the mirror hanging over the dresser in their shared room. He could barely control his temper as Wickham turned from side to side, trying to see how his coat hung since he had had it pressed.

"I do not see how you can act so unconcerned!" Andrew said, throwing the newspaper that he had been perusing to the floor. "They could knock on our door any minute and arrest us for killing Fitz!"

Wickham rolled his eyes. "You have read too many novels, Andrew."

"I do not read novels. Nor would I have to in order to know that I am the prime suspect in my cousin's death. No wonder you do not care. They will put me under arrest for the crime, and you shall walk free."

"We do not even know that he is dead."

"He looked dead to me!"

Wickham sighed, running his hands through his hair to comb it. "Even if he is, how many times do I have to tell you that we have the perfect alibi? As far as anyone knows, we were here when the shooting occurred. Letty and Agnes will swear to it!"

"Letty and Agnes will sing like song birds if Darcy's cousin, Richard, gets a chance at them. You have never seen him question a suspect. He is tenacious!"

"And when have you seen him do that?"

"Once when I was a boy, Uncle George brought us all together—Fitz,

Richard and me—to settle who had let one of his prized hunting dogs escape. I had my uncle convinced that I knew nothing about it until Richard began asking questions. In the end, he got me so confused that I confessed."

"You are a man now. Besides, there will be no questions, for he will have no proof. He cannot arrest anyone on suppositions. So get dressed and join me. It will look better if we are seen at Lily's Pleasure Garden again tonight instead of hiding in this room as though we are thieves."

"Or murderers?"

Wickham smirked. "Not murderers—opportunists!"

Chapter 38

Pemberley
That same day

By evening, after there was no change in the master's condition, an air of deep and irredeemable gloom pervaded Pemberley. The fading light found Mr. Camryn going down the hall to check on his patient, and upon entering William's bedroom, he discovered Elizabeth still there. Sitting in a chair by the bed, she had laid her head on the counterpane next to William and was now fast asleep. Just as he started to wake her, Olivia and Joseph walked in the door. The three of them exchanged looks of frustration.

"I am beginning to worry about Mrs. Darcy's health," the physician said quietly, walking toward them. "She must be made to see reason."

"Let me try," Olivia answered. Going to her niece, she reached over and shook her shoulder gently. "Elizabeth, wake up."

Instantly, she sat up straight. "Wha... what? Is it Will?" Upon comprehending that he was no different than before, she looked about self-consciously. "I... I must have just fallen asleep."

"That is why I woke you, dearest," Olivia said. "You need to rest in your own bed. Taking naps will not replace restorative sleep."

"But I need—"

"You need to rest," Olivia interrupted her tenderly, placing a hand over her niece's. "Your uncle and I insist."

Elizabeth's heart fluttered with a vague terror. Glancing from Mr. Camryn, his arms folded and his face gravely authoritative, to the concerned mien of her uncle, she realised that to argue was futile; thus, leaning over to kiss William, Elizabeth whispered in his ear that she loved him, before standing unsteadily and allowing Olivia to guide her from the room.

Once Elizabeth was gone, the physician slid aside the chair she had been sitting in and sat down on the edge of the bed. He proceeded to listen to William's heart then pulled the covers down past the broken ribs that he had wrapped earlier so that he could press on his abdomen. Camryn continued to press across and down the abdomen, frowned perplexedly and covered William again.

"Is there no change?" Joseph Fitzwilliam asked, his voice sounding despondent for the first time.

"None visible to the eye," Camryn said, rising to his feet. "There is nothing I can do here, so I shall retire. Please wake me if there is any change."

When he got to the door, Georgiana was about to enter. She was followed by Mrs. Reynolds and Olivia, who had left Elizabeth in the capable hands of Mrs. O'Reilly. The maid's health had improved dramatically with the help of Mrs. Reynolds' draughts, and she had insisted on returning to her position to help her mistress.

"Is my brother… " One look at Camryn's face answered Georgiana's question, so her voice trailed off.

"I am sorry, Miss Darcy. There has been no change."

Just as she had nodded in silent acceptance, a loud moan filled the air. Realising what it meant, Mrs. Reynolds raced to fetch Elizabeth, while Camryn rushed to the bed with Georgiana on his heels. Olivia went to her husband, who had hurriedly grabbed a chamber candlestick and was holding it over William in order for the physician to have a better view.

"Mr. Darcy!" Mr. Camryn cried, his voice sounding almost frantic in its fervour. "Mr. Darcy, can you hear me?"

William's head began to roll side to side, so the physician grabbed the bottle of smelling salts still on the table, uncapped it, and held it under his nose, which wrinkled in protest. A raspy voice pleaded, "Stop!"

Mr. Camryn could not hold back a wide smile. In fact, his entire body seemed to uncoil with relief. Putting aside the salts, he said, "Can you open your eyes?"

William obliged, though just as quickly he closed them again. "Too bright," he murmured. As Camryn motioned for Joseph to move the candle aside, William croaked, "Water."

"Of course, you must be parched." Camryn motioned for Georgiana to pour a glass of water from the pitcher by the bed. While she did, he added, "We must lift you in order for you to drink. Your body will be quite sore, and you may experience pain on your left side, for I believe two ribs are broken. Tell me if you experience sharp pains elsewhere."

William did not cry out, but gritted his teeth as he was lifted and again afterward, when they placed several pillows behind his back. As soon as he was sitting upright, Camryn took the glass of water from Georgiana and held it for him to take several swallows.

"More?"

William shook his head and lay back against the pillows.

"We have moved the candle so that the room is not as bright. Will you try to open your eyes now?" They flickered open and Camryn held up two fingers right in front of his face. "How many fingers do you see?"

"Four… three?" William murmured. "It is a blur."

"That is not uncommon with a head injury. It should disappear with time."

William's voice full of confusion when he repeated, "Head injury?"

"You do not remember what happened?"

"No."

"You were thrown from a horse and hit your head on a large rock." William seemed to consider that, so Camryn continued. "Can you lift your left arm?" William grimaced as he tried. "Can you tell me whether it is your arm or your shoulder that hurt the most when you raised it?"

"I… I am not sure."

"Try the right arm." This time there was no corresponding grimace of pain as he complied. "What of your legs? Can you pull your knees up?" The effort

produced more groans.

"That is enough for the time being. Now, do you know who I am?"

With a bit of annoyance, William said, "I would know your voice even if I could not see you."

"Then indulge me. What is my name?"

"Camryn."

The physician pulled Georgiana forward, though he held a finger to his lips indicating she should not speak. "And who is this?"

William's eyes squinted. "My sister... Georgiana."

Feeling much relieved at this point, Camryn motioned Joseph and Olivia closer. "And do you recognise these two people?"

The longer William studied the couple, the more the level of anxiety in the room accelerated. Consequently, there was a common sigh of relief when he finally answered, "My aunt and uncle."

His next words, however, brought quite the opposite reaction. "I thought you were in Ireland."

Joseph looked surreptitiously at the others, before answering. "Olivia and I have been your guests at Pemberley for the last two months, Fitzwilliam."

"You have?"

Concerns for William's memory skyrocketed from the moment Elizabeth rushed into the room. Going straight to the end of the bed, her eyes filled with tears, she tented her hands over her mouth and stared unbelievingly, unable to speak. When at last she recovered, she hurried to sit on the bed next to William and reached for his hand.

"Oh, Will! Thank God, you are awake!" she sobbed. Then she began to place kisses over the back of his hand.

It was evident to all but Elizabeth that William regarded her with a perplexed expression. However, after she began to kiss his hand, that expression promptly changed to one of alarm.

"Do... do I know you, madam?"

After the initial gasps of disbelief, the silence in the room was deafening. As for Elizabeth, she stared at him, blinking uncomprehendingly, until the truth sank in. Then she collapsed onto the bed next to him.

Camryn hurried to Elizabeth, immediately taking her pulse. Then he announced what everyone already knew. "The stress was too much. She has fainted. We must get her to her bedroom. Please ring for a footman."

Joseph began gathering Elizabeth in his arms. "That will not be necessary."

As he carried his niece to the door, Camryn added, "Cool her forehead with a dampened washcloth. I shall be there shortly."

As Elizabeth was taken away, Olivia and Mrs. Reynolds hastened to follow. However, upon overhearing her nephew ask Georgiana a question, Olivia motioned for Mrs. Reynolds to go on, and she stepped back into the room.

"Who... who is she?" William asked, his eyes searching his sister's for the truth.

"No one of great import," Georgiana said matter-of-factly. "You need not concern yourself over her. You must use all your energy to get well."

The physician started to object, but before he could, Olivia stepped out of the shadows. "Georgiana!"

Whirling around to see her aunt, Georgiana lifted her chin in defiance. "Brother needs to focus on his recovery. He should not worry over what he cannot remember."

"At the expense of his wife's health?" Mr. Camryn said crossly. "The Fitzwilliam Darcy I know would never approve of such a thing."

Georgiana turned on him. "It seems that you, too, are determined to put my sister's welfare ahead of my brother's." Then she addressed William. "You will never know how relieved I am that you are awake, Brother. Some thought that they were in charge the moment you were injured." She leaned down to place a kiss on his forehead. "For now, I shall leave you to rest; however, you and I must talk tomorrow."

After Georgiana left the room, William said disbelievingly, "A wife? I cannot possibly have a wife."

Olivia stepped closer. "Oh, but you do, Fitzwilliam. You were married six weeks ago, right after Joseph and I came to Pemberley."

Mr. Camryn reached out to lay a comforting hand on his friend's shoulder. "Darcy, there is not a lot known about memory loss from head injuries; however, it appears that you do remember things in your past, just not the last few weeks or so. From what I have read, that is a good indicator that you will gain your memory completely at some point in the future. Most cases that I have studied involved a gradual process but, in a few instances, something triggered recollection all at once. The brain is a complex and awesome creation, and I am confident that your memory will eventually be restored completely."

Actually, Camryn was not certain, but he felt it best to always give his patients hope. "First, it is imperative that you get on your feet so pneumonia does not set in. To that end, you shall begin an exercise routine in the morning. Tonight, however, you should take some nourishment and continue to rest. A light broth would do well, in addition to plenty of liquids, so I shall send Mrs. Reynolds to the kitchen to procure that whilst I check on Mrs. Darcy."

At the bedroom door, the physician stopped to look back. He found William still observing him with a puzzled expression. "Try not to worry, if possible. That will only hinder your recovery, my friend." With those few words, he went to check on Elizabeth.

Olivia moved to stand by the bed. She longed to push a stray lock of hair from William's eyes but hesitated, unsure if he remembered how close they had become of late. "Oh, Fitzwilliam, you will never know how pleased I am to see you awake. Your uncle and I love you very much, and you gave us quite a scare."

It became apparent that his mind was elsewhere when he asked, "Was I... was I happy with—" His puzzled expression left Olivia to conclude that he did not remember Elizabeth's name.

"Elizabeth?" she said. William nodded. "Oh, yes, dear. Both of you were deliriously happy."

"Then why is Georgiana so dismissive of her?"

"When we arrived, you told us that Georgiana has been at odds with you over many things."

A heavy sigh escaped, as he said, "That much I do remember."

"Good. You will do well to keep that in mind if she talks ill of Elizabeth. She was against your marriage from the start and still is. Joseph and Richard will verify that."

William's voice had grown much weaker. "Richard? Is he here?"

"No. But he has been sent word of your injury, and I would not be surprised if he arrives at any moment."

William's eyes closed. "I am so weary."

"I know you are, dearest. Why not rest until the broth is brought up?"

His breathing got slower and steadier until he nodded off to sleep. At that point, Joseph returned, so she crossed the room to speak quietly to him.

"Is Elizabeth well? Should I go to her?"

"I do not think it necessary, Livy. She woke and is as well as can be expected after the shock. Just before I left, Mrs. O'Reilly was preparing a powder in a cup of tea—something Camryn ordered. The maid and Mrs. Reynolds plan to take turns staying with her tonight."

"My heart breaks for her," Olivia said, her voice cracking as she dabbed at her eyes with a handkerchief.

Joseph pulled his wife into his arms. "Now, Livy, she is in good hands."

"You are right." She sniffled, resting her head on his chest. "Are you planning to stay with Fitzwilliam?"

"No. Mr. Adams intends to watch our nephew tonight."

"That is for the best, I think. I fear that we shall both need clear heads if Georgiana continues to scheme tomorrow."

Joseph's brows knit. "Scheme? What has she done?"

Just then Mr. Adams returned, and they left him to his charge while they went on to their suite. As they did, Olivia quietly related what had happened after he left the room.

At their bedroom door, he escorted her inside before replying, "I see why you fear Georgiana. We must all be vigilant, so I shall seek Mrs. Reynolds' and Mr. Adams' help in keeping an eye on her." He began to fret. "If only Richard were here. He could speak for Elizabeth, for Fitzwilliam trusts him implicitly."

"I have a feeling that he will be here sooner than we ever thought possible."

"Would to God that your intuition is right."

Olivia reached out to take both his hands. "Let us pray, then, that it is."

⁂

The next day

The morning found the master fully awake, though still extremely confused, dizzy and unable to remember anything of the last few months. He consumed a meal of soft eggs and another cup of broth, despite complaints of occasional nausea. Later, he was helped to his feet and walked about his bedroom with the aid of a footman—howbeit, very unsteadily.

While most everyone was thrilled with his progress, Elizabeth was another matter. Still asleep, no doubt as a result of the powder the physician had ordered the night before, her sitting room had filled with concerned servants and family as the day progressed. They had been talking in hushed tones as Mr. Camryn entered the room. Instantly, he addressed Mrs. O'Reilly.

"Did the powder help Mrs. Darcy sleep?"

The maid nodded. "She did not move from one position all night."

"Have you tried to rouse her this morning?"

"No, sir. Usually, she hears me when I go into her dressing room to prepare for the day and she rises. Today she did not."

"Well, she should have awakened by now," Camryn declared gravely. "I fear that Mrs. Darcy must be roused, so I can determine her condition."

Everyone followed him into the room, standing inconspicuously out of sight, as he began to wake her. "Mrs. Darcy?" Camryn said, shaking her shoulder.

As Elizabeth began to rouse, her expression went from lethargic to puzzled, but in an instant, she recognised the physician. His presence brought back the events of the previous night, and Elizabeth's eyes filled with tears as her lips quivered. Olivia hurried to her side.

Sitting on the bed, Olivia smoothed a few unruly curls from her face saying, "Dearest, everything is going to be well—mark my words. Fitzwilliam is awake and will soon regain all his memory. Just give him time."

Elizabeth nodded, wiping tears from her face with the backs of her hands. Then with great effort to calm herself, she said, "I... I have to believe that, otherwise... " The sentence hung unfinished.

"Mrs. Darcy," Camryn broke in. "I know that you do not wish to create more problems for your family by getting sick, so I have several requests to make of you."

She studied him now, wide-eyed as a child. It reminded him of how young Elizabeth actually was, and he could not suppress a small smile. "I ask that you keep to your regular schedule of rising and sleeping. Eat, even if you do not feel hungry, and take a walk around the grounds every day. I have been told how much you love to walk, and you need to keep up your spirits by doing the things you love. Will you try to do that?"

"Yes, of course."

He patted her hand. "Excellent. I shall leave so that you may dress and eat. Whilst you do, I shall see how your husband is faring, now that I have him on his feet."

"On his feet? Is Will strong enough for that?"

"He is doing remarkably well, considering how severe his injury was, and it is important to get him out of bed. The blurry vision still exists, but I expect it to dissipate in time. When I left him this morning, he was walking with the

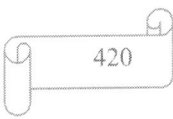

help of a footman. Of course, he was very unhappy that he could not walk unaided, and I tried to explain that his balance would improve as his vision does, but he was not convinced. You have a very stubborn husband, Mrs. Darcy."

For the first time in days, Elizabeth's frown softened to a quivering smile. "I cannot disagree with you on that point, Mr. Camryn."

"Not if you want to maintain your integrity," Camryn teased. "Now, I shall be off."

Camryn encountered Joseph near the door. "Mr. Fitzwilliam, can you spare me a few minutes of your time?" Joseph nodded and, with a tender smile for his wife and then his niece, he followed the physician. They were several feet down the main hallway before Camryn spoke.

"Is there a room on this floor where we may have a private word?"

"Certainly," Joseph answered, stopping abruptly to open a guest bedroom door. He motioned Camryn to go ahead and, following, closed the door soundly.

The physician wasted no time. "I have to call on a few of my other patients today. I will return this evening, or sooner, if I am needed. I shall leave a list with Mrs. Reynolds of whom I plan to visit so that you may locate me."

"That is kind of you. I can only imagine how many people rely on your expertise. I wish you to know that I—nay, all of us— realise that Fitzwilliam's condition has occupied most of your time lately, and we appreciate your dedication to his recovery."

"As well as being a friend, Mr. Darcy has been a great help to me in constructing a building for my practice, so no praise is necessary. If I can help him in any manner, I feel it a privilege to do so."

"Still, I wanted to make clear our gratitude. Call on your other patients with our heart-felt thanks. We will see after Fitzwilliam whilst you are elsewhere."

Camryn's expression became more sombre. "There is another reason I wanted to talk with you alone. If Mr. Darcy does not remember his wife, it may prove awkward for her to help with his recovery. He may be uncomfortable with her presence. Therefore, I feel I must rely on you and the others to note his symptoms and to send for me if certain ones appear."

Joseph said gravely, "What should we look for?"

"As a result of the concussion, Mr. Darcy is experiencing confusion, nausea, drowsiness and more headaches than usual. These symptoms, as well as some sporadic vomiting and, of course, the memory loss are commonly associated with these injuries. On the other hand, should he begin to exhibit more serious symptoms, you should send for me without delay. Unconsciousness, convulsions, muscle weakness, pupils that are not equal in size, repeated vomiting and unusual eye movements are considered dangerous. His balance issue should get better with exercise. If it does not, bring it to my attention."

"I shall put paper and ink on a table in the sitting room for all the caretakers to record their observations, as well as a list of the symptoms that warrant immediate concern."

The physician chuckled. "I see you know your nephew well, for Mr. Darcy would attempt to read it if it was in his bedroom."

"Exactly."

"Also, I realise it is not my place to say this, but I have noticed that Miss Darcy seems eager to discredit Mrs. Darcy."

"My wife told me what happened last night, so all of us plan to keep watch over Georgiana, especially when she is with Fitzwilliam."

"I think that is wise, under the circumstances."

Downstairs

Whilst the family and Mr. Camryn were upstairs, a large, black coach, pulled by matching sets of black stallions, traversed the long drive to the front of Pemberley. The Earl and Countess of Matlock had been at their country estate in Derbyshire and, upon receiving the express informing them of Darcy's injury, had struck out for their nephew's estate almost immediately. Worried sick about Fitzwilliam, the closer they got to their destination, the more Lady Matlock dreaded what might come. Fearful that her husband would not hold his tongue, she cautioned him one last time.

"Please remember, Edward, this is not our home, and you have no right to be unkind to Fitzwilliam's guests, even if you have had disputes with them in the past."

"Must you remind me again, Evelyn? I am not totally without good sense. If my nephew were not gravely injured, I would never have come with them here. But since I must, I will try to be civil. Let us hope that Joseph will do likewise."

"Thank you, dear." Pondering whether to voice what else she was thinking, Lady Matlock decided it could do no harm. "Have you considered that this is an opportune time to let bygones be bygones? We are not young anyone, and it may be the last time you see your brother."

"Do not start with that. I have too much on my mind to consider our broken relationship."

"Yes, dear."

Suddenly, the coach rocked to a stop and the door opened. As a footman let down the steps, the earl began his exit. Then he looked to the portico to see the front door open and Mr. Walker appear. After helping the countess to the ground, they turned to ascend the steps.

"Lord Matlock, Lady Matlock, it is a pleasure to see you again," Walker said.

"Thank you, Walker," the earl said. "I wish to see my nephew as soon as it is feasible. Is Mrs. Darcy available?"

"They are all upstairs at present," Walker said, busily accepting hats and cloaks and handing them to a maid. "If you do not mind waiting in the library, I shall be happy to locate Mrs. Darcy."

"That will not be necessary, we can—"

"We shall be happy to wait in the library," Lady Matlock interrupted, taking her husband's arm.

The earl gave her a scowl, but began to escort her in that direction. Breathing a sigh of relief, Walker rushed up the grand staircase to let the Fitzwilliams know that they had arrived. He soon found Joseph Fitzwilliam and Mr. Camryn, who had just exited Mr. Darcy's room.

"The Earl and Countess of Matlock have arrived," the butler announced. "Should I disturb Mrs. Darcy?"

Joseph took a deep breath. "Let me inform her." Then he said to the physician, "Might you be able to stay long enough to explain Fitzwilliam's condition to his aunt and uncle?"

"Certainly."

The library

Despite the length of time the earl and countess had been waiting, they had not been able to relax. Instead of being seated on one of many sofas or chairs, both had taken up positions on the far side of the room where floor-to-ceiling windows provided an excellent view of the gardens. Because the library was vast and the carpet thick, Lord and Lady Matlock were totally unaware when Joseph, Olivia, Elizabeth and Mr. Camryn quietly entered the room. Exchanging glances with her company, Elizabeth tilted her head and simultaneously raised her shoulders, as if to imply that she had no choice, and she walked toward her guests, whilst the others lingered behind.

"Aunt? Uncle?"

The earl and countess turned, immediately looking past her to the Fitzwilliams before their eyes settled again on Elizabeth. Lady Matlock went forward to hug her niece.

"Oh, Elizabeth, how sad it is to be drawn together by so terrible a circumstance."

Tears threatened when Elizabeth replied, "I… I am so sorry as well."

The earl stepped closer, asking tersely, "How is Fitzwilliam faring?"

Elizabeth turned to motion Camryn forward. "Mr. Camryn can explain better than I."

After the physician had gone over the details of William's injury and answered all their questions, he explained that he had to leave, and he made his exit. With his departure, Elizabeth joined the Fitzwilliams, standing between them and taking each by a hand.

"I could not have coped without the help of Uncle Joseph and Aunt Olivia. Uncle was instrumental in bringing Will back home and ever since has shared the burden of sitting up with him, just as Aunt Olivia has."

The earl and Joseph had locked eyes while she was speaking, and when she was finished, a strange thing happened. Lord Matlock offered a hand to his brother, which was immediately grasped. As they shook hands, the earl said, "Evelyn and I are indebted. Fitzwilliam means a great deal to us."

"Just as he does to Livy and me."

Suddenly Georgiana rushed into the room. "Aunt! Uncle! I was just informed that you were here." Kissing first one, then the other on the cheek,

she declared, "I am so relieved, for I have tried to make it clear that you would insist on taking Brother to London for treatment, but they will not listen. He cannot possibly receive the best care in Derbyshire when there are more learned physicians in Town."

Elizabeth spun around. "As I said before, Georgiana, Will is not going to be moved."

"But you used his unconsciousness as the excuse and now that he is awake—"

"Will loves Pemberley, and I know that he will recuperate faster here."

As Georgiana seethed, Elizabeth addressed Lord and Lady Matlock. "I have sent to London for Mr. Graham. Between him and Mr. Camryn, I believe my husband will be well served, and should he require any experts, I will send for them as well."

"Tell her that she is mistaken, Uncle! She must allow us to take Brother to Town."

The earl's brow knit at Georgiana's defiant stance. "Georgiana, you have evidently assumed that because I have disagreed with your brother regarding certain things that I will challenge his authority or Elizabeth's. You are badly mistaken. I will not allow you to challenge their authority, either. Elizabeth is the mistress at Pemberley, and decisions regarding Fitzwilliam's care fall to her."

Looking as though she had been slapped, Georgiana's face crimsoned, and her lips set in a thin line before she ran from the room.

Elizabeth began to speak. "I am sorry about—"

The earl held up a hand. "It is I who should apologise for letting Georgiana think she had my ear. Now, would it be possible to see my nephew?"

Chapter 39

Sheffield
The next day

Everything was wearing on Andrew Darcy's nerves of late—his cramped room at the Crown Inn, the dreadful food and even the mindless women at Lily's Pleasure Garden. George had spent yesterday evening there without him, for whilst Wickham had no trouble forgetting what had transpired in Derbyshire, he could not. Never doubting that Richard would know exactly who was to blame for Fitz's injury and with nothing to do but wait, the colonel came to mind more and more. So much so, that he had thought of Richard at a most inopportune time when he was last at Lily's. Unable to perform, he quickly decided to forego visiting the ladies, rather than chance being humiliated for a second time. All of this combined to keep Andrew's temper on edge.

"George, what were you thinking by bringing a whore to our room last night? I have not had a full night's sleep since Fitz was shot, and I had just fallen asleep when you roused me to go downstairs so that you could have the bed."

Carefully shaving himself at the mirror over the dresser, Wickham stopped to look at Andrew's reflection. "After leaving the brothel, I met a local woman who wanted to have a good time—so I obliged." Then he snickered. "You are just angry that the ladies like me better."

Though he had not shared his emasculating issues with George, the taunt was too close to home. "I can have any woman that I want," Andrew said with great vexation. "However, at present, I am too worried about safeguarding my life to pursue women every waking moment and, frankly, you should be more worried for yourself."

George splashed water on his face to remove the soap. Then he preened as he dried his face, examining his image closely. "I am never too worried to forego a bit of muslin."

At that instant there was a knock on the door and, for a moment, both stood immobilised. Then Andrew, who was nearest the door, cracked it open slightly. A small boy, one of the innkeeper's brood, stood without.

"What do you want?"

"This came for you, sir."

The boy held out a letter, and when Andrew took it, he kept his palm extended. Irritated, Andrew reached for a farthing lying on a table and tossed it to the lad, who promptly disappeared.

"What is it?"

As Andrew turned to show Wickham the missive, his hand trembled. "It is a letter from Susan." However, when he made no attempt to open it, it was snatched from his hand. "What are you doing? That is mine."

"And apparently you are too cowardly to open it, so I must."

Though furious, Andrew made no move to retrieve his property, and George ripped the seal open and began to read silently. When his expression darkened, however, Andrew could no longer suppress his curiosity.

"Wha… what does she have to say?"

"It seems that blasted fool is still alive."

"Bloody blazes! I *am* a dead man!" Andrew exclaimed. "Fitz will think it was I who shot him. Richard may already be on our trail, and if he finds me, it would be better to face the hangman's noose."

"Calm down! According to Susan, Georgiana says that Fitz cannot remember anything about how he was injured. This just alters our plans. That is all."

"What do you mean?"

"You are correct. If Fitzwilliam remembers you were there, Richard will have all the evidence he needs to hang you, therefore, it is imperative that you leave England. Since it is likely that I will be tied to the deed as well, I must go, too."

"You *should* be tied to it! *You* shot him, not me!"

"That is neither here nor there. The fact is that we both must leave England as quickly as possible. The only problem is a lack of funds. I do not want to sail with only the clothes on my back, and I do not think you do, either."

"It is too dangerous to resume robbing coaches with the extra lawmen watching the highways since the footman's death," Andrew replied.

"It would take too long to rob enough coaches, anyway. Given that we still have funds, all we need are jewels to sell once we reach our destination. They are easy to hide inside the linings of coats and luggage, unlike thousands of pounds would be."

"And where do you intend to get said jewellery?"

"Since we must do everything post-haste, I say that we stick to a pigeon that we know has a fortune in family jewels—*Fitzwilliam*." Having said that, Wickham immediately reached under the bed to fetch his bag and began filling it with items he had placed on the dresser and in the drawers.

Andrew noisily blew out a lungful of air. "And here I thought you were serious. Fitz would never hand over the Darcy jewels, and we cannot possibly slip into Pemberley unnoticed."

"Fitzwilliam will gladly hand them over if we take a member of his family and hold that person for ransom."

"You are mad! What you propose will only put us in more danger! I do not want to be any closer to Pemberley than we are at present."

"Nor do I, but I refuse to leave England a pauper. Do you have a better strategy?"

When Andrew did not answer, Wickham added indignantly, "I thought as much. Fine! Stay here and wait for Colonel Fitzwilliam to come for you. A portion of the ransom will convince Denny and the others to help me. By the time Fitzwilliam realises what has happened, I shall be in the Americas, whilst you are left to face him."

"You have me so befuddled, I cannot think rationally. What if, after exchanging the hostage for the ransom, we are arrested before our ship can sail?"

"That part is simple. We keep the location of the hostage a secret until after our vessel is underway. As long as Darcy's loved one is under our power, he will not dare bring the law down upon us. Right before we sail, a letter will be mailed detailing where the hostage can be found. Should Fitzwilliam attempt to track us later, at least we will have a substantial head start."

"Who would you take? Georgiana?"

"No. Since she has always been partial to you, Darcy would likely consider that a hoax. We shall take his new wife."

"Have you forgotten Fitz's loss of memory? He may be too confused to handle a ransom demand."

"That is why we must return to Derbyshire. Once there, we can monitor how he fares. Hopefully, he will have improved enough by the time everything is in place that we will be able to deal with him. If not, it shall fall to Colonel Fitzwilliam to follow our orders for the hostage's sake."

"But what if Richard is not at Pemberley?"

"I cannot believe you think that Richard would not rush to Pemberley after learning of Darcy's injury. After all, they are more brothers than cousins."

"And you think he will just step in and handle the exchange?"

"Richard projects a stern image, but he is much like his cousin in one area. He would think nothing of exchanging a few baubles to gain the freedom of a loved one."

"A few baubles? The Darcys have a fortune in diamonds alone. I know, for Uncle George once showed them to me." Andrew heaved a sigh. "I still do not like this idea, George. Richard is much more dangerous than my cousin."

"Then let us be glad that he does not scare me," Wickham boasted. "Now, get to packing. We are off to Lambton. We must be ready to pounce at a moment's notice."

"I would not be surprised if Pate's farm is already under surveillance."

"That will not matter. I have decided that Lady Susan must secrete us at Monthaven Manor until we complete our mission. Lord Concord has a hunting cabin that he abandoned after his accident. It will be the perfect hiding place."

"And if she does not want to help?"

"She will. She and I share a past that a lot of people would be interested in learning about."

"Am I allowed to know what it entails?"

"It is best that you do not. I will only say that if the details were known, it would put a hangman's noose around her pretty little neck."

"And your neck as well, I imagine."

"Yes. But what she desires is here in England, whereas I can be happy living anywhere in the world. I could leave the country and send the evidence back via post, if she declines to aid us. And she knows that I would."

"I feel it is best that I do not know the particulars, then."

"You see! You have gotten smarter just by being around me."

Pemberley
That evening

The presence of the earl and countess had only added to the tension at Pemberley. Though Lord Matlock was civil to his brother, he had ignored Olivia, which had not set well with her husband; thus, while the Matlocks visited with their nephew, the Fitzwilliams spent the day in the gardens, the library and their rooms. After the earl's rebuke, Georgiana had sulked in her own rooms, sending word that a tray should be sent to her at dinner, as she had no intention of coming downstairs. Unfortunately for her, this caused no great concern among the rest of her relations.

Having travelled that morning, Lord and Lady Matlock declined to come downstairs for dinner, and trays were sent to their rooms as well. Therefore, dinner found only Elizabeth, the Fitzwilliams and Mr. Camryn at the dining room table, which, if the truth were known, suited each one of them. Being sorely exhausted from days with nerves on edge and little sleep, conversation was sparse, leaving Elizabeth plenty of time to consider what she would do next.

While the earl and his wife had occupied William's time, Elizabeth stayed busy in her study, working on the coats for the children. Having made the decision earlier not to visit her husband until everyone was asleep, she prayed all day that William might recover at least a trace of his memory regarding her. Nevertheless, as the day progressed, feelings of grief and longing submerged her into a deep melancholy. She ached to see William, but was terrified of discovering the same blank stare that she encountered last night. Since consummating their marriage, his eyes never failed to light up the moment he saw her, and to see no recognition in them now broke her heart.

"Elizabeth?" Looking up from where she pushed the food about on her plate, she met her aunt's gaze. "Mr. Camryn asked if you have no appetite, dear."

She tried to smile reassuringly at the physician. "I beg your pardon, Mr. Camryn, I did not hear you. I believe I am too tired to eat. Once I am able to sleep, I am sure my appetite will return."

From Camryn's expression, he was not convinced. "Do you intend to visit your husband today?" he asked. "You have not seen him since... " The sentence was left unfinished.

"I will see him after everyone has retired. I wish to talk with him alone."

"After what happened last night, it would be wise if someone accompanied you. If you were to faint again with no one about to—"

"I will not faint," Elizabeth interrupted. Less adamantly, she added, "If it will ease your mind, Mrs. Reynolds can wait for me in the sitting room."

"If you are resolute to go in alone, I will not insist," Mr. Camryn said, rising wearily from his seat. "I am going to retire now, but do not hesitate to

wake me if I am needed. I do not think I have ever answered as many questions regarding a patient as I have today. The earl is certainly thorough."

"He has always been," Joseph volunteered.

With that, the physician excused himself and went directly to his room, leaving Joseph and Olivia alone with their niece.

"Are you sure you do not want one of us to accompany you when you visit Fitzwilliam? Adams says he is short-tempered since his injury, and you do not need to be overly stressed, my dear," Uncle Joseph said.

"I appreciate your concern, but I must talk to Will alone. Please try to understand."

His eyes flicked to his wife before resting on her again. Then he sighed in resignation. "Of course."

Standing, he began to help Olivia from her chair. "It is time that we retire as well, for it has been a long and trying day. Nonetheless, please do not hesitate to send for us if we are needed."

"I promise I will."

After they exited the room, Elizabeth quit all pretence of eating and left the dining room. Walking into the foyer, she met Mrs. Reynolds, who was coming from the direction of the kitchen with a small tray containing a pot of tea and a china cup with some type of powder inside it.

"Is that for Will?"

"Yes, Mrs. Darcy. Mr. Camryn ordered this powder to be taken at night, and it is best ingested with tea. I thought a fresh pot might make it more palatable."

"Please, let me take it in to him. I wish to speak with him, and the tea will be my purpose for being there."

"I would be glad to accompany you. Mr. Darcy is not in a very good mood today, though one can hardly blame him, what with all he has borne and continues to bear."

"I have been forewarned, but I had rather you not. If you wish to wait in the sitting room until I come out, Mr. Camryn will be pleased. He wanted assurances that I would not faint again with no one about to notice except Will."

"I shall be pleased to do so, ma'am."

Before long, they stood at the door separating the sitting room from William's bedroom. As Mrs. Reynolds handed her the tray, Elizabeth's heart began to pound. Watching as the housekeeper's hand inched toward the doorknob, she was taken aback when, out of the blue, a loud argument began behind the closed door. It seemed only a second before it flew open and Mr. Adams walked out. In his haste, he neglected to close the door securely.

Noting that the door was still slightly ajar, Mrs. Reynolds whispered anxiously, "What has happened?"

Looking a bit sheepish, Adams glanced nervously at the opening. "The more frustrated Mr. Darcy becomes, the more his temper flares. I merely offered to help him change his nightshirt and suddenly he was irate, declaring that he was not an invalid and ordering me out of his sight. Mr. Camryn said that this is to be expected, but it so unlike the master that I hardly knew how to react."

Before either woman could offer sympathy, he added. "Perhaps it is best if I give him some time alone, for I can certainly use a respite myself."

As he hurried away, Mrs. Reynolds asked Elizabeth, "Are you sure you want to go in by yourself?"

Elizabeth straightened her shoulders. "I am. Please close the door behind me." The elderly servant nodded and did as she was asked.

Entering noiselessly, the bedroom was brighter than Elizabeth expected, for more than one candle was burning. William stood in his nightshirt and robe at the end of the bed, his back to her. He appeared to be clinging to the bedpost for support, so she became alarmed. Setting the tray down on the dresser more soundly than she intended, the dishes rattled, alerting him to her presence. He reacted immediately.

"I told you to leave me alone for the night."

"I am not Mr. Adams. It is I, Will."

William's head swung around. It was evident that he had to squint in order to focus. "I apologise, madam."

"Elizabeth. Call me Elizabeth, please. And you need not apologise. I should have announced myself when I came into the room. It is just… you were angry, and I was not sure if my presence would be welcome."

He said nothing in reply, and the silence stretched on uncomfortably. As a result, Elizabeth busied herself by pouring tea in the cup and mixing it with the powder.

"I brought the powder that Mr. Camryn ordered for you at night. Mrs. Reynolds thought that some fresh tea might make it taste a little better, so she sent that as well."

"I do not think it possible to make it palatable."

Smiling at this pronouncement, she turned to face him. "Do you wish to climb back into bed before you take this?"

"I am tired of lying in bed, but when I stand, the room starts to spin. I have a constant headache, which lying about all day exacerbates."

"This powder is designed to help the headache, I am sure, but it will not do for you to hold a hot drink whilst standing. Would you like to sit in the chair next to the bed until you finish the tea?"

He did not answer or make any attempt to move. Elizabeth was beginning to wonder if he was going to ignore her when he spoke again. "On which side is the chair?"

She set the cup down and rushed to take his arm so that she could guide him. "It is on the side where you sleep. I had it moved next to the bed so I could sit there when I stayed overnight."

He made no objections as she guided him to the chair. Afterward, she retrieved the cup of tea, saying, "Be careful" as she handed it to him. Taking the cup, his hands trembled slightly, so she clasped his with her own.

"That is not necessary. I am perfectly able to hold the cup without spilling it."

Instantly, Elizabeth's hands dropped to her side, though she did not step away. After he had drunk the last drop, she took the cup and placed it on the tray. By the time she returned to William, his head had fallen back against the cushioned chair and his eyes were closed. Taking the opportunity to study the face she loved so dearly, her heart wrenched with longing.

"Do you... I mean to say... is all memory of me still lost?"

A deep intake of breath indicated that William had heard, though he did not answer immediately. At length he opened his eyes. "I am sorry, but I do not remember anything about you."

Her heart filled with speechless sorrow, and it was all she could do to murmur, "I see."

"I wish I could say that I do, but that would not be true. Still, you should know that I am grateful. Adams has told me how well you have cared for me since my accident."

"I took care of you because I love you, Will. If the circumstances were reversed, I am certain that you would have done the same for me."

He frowned, pinching the bridge of his nose as if that would dispatch his headache. "I cannot recall anyone ever calling me by that name."

A huge lump filled her throat. "That is why I chose to call you that."

"Your name is Elizabeth?" She nodded. "Did I call you Lizzy or perhaps Eliza?"

"No, you preferred Elizabeth."

He seemed to think about that several seconds before speaking again. "I am sorry for any pain my circumstances have caused you. However, I hope that you realise it may be some time before I recall the entirety of... of our relationship."

"What happened was not your fault, so please do not think you owe me an apology. I am well aware that it may take weeks or months for your memory to return. I shall try hard to be patient." William nodded, and she smiled wanly. "What you drank is supposed to make you very sleepy, so you really should get back into bed."

"No!" he answered, standing unsteadily once more. His reply was so abrupt that Elizabeth flinched, though he did not notice. "When I wish to go to bed, I shall, and I will not need anyone to tell me when or to help me."

Tears threatening, Elizabeth swallowed hard. "Then I shall leave you. Good night, Will."

"Good night, madam."

Entering the sitting room, the sight of Mrs. Reynolds' hopeful face caused her tightly held emotions to fall apart, and she began to weep; however, when the housekeeper tried to console her, Elizabeth refused.

"No. No. I am well, truly, I am. It is just so painful when he talks to me as though I am a stranger." She sniffled, using her hands to wipe the tears covering her cheeks and tried to smile. "Thank you for waiting up for me, Mrs. Reynolds. Please go to bed, for I know you must be as exhausted as I am."

"I shall as soon as Mr. Adams takes my place. He should be here shortly."

With mixed emotions, Mrs. Reynolds watched as her mistress entered the door leading to her bedroom. Part of her longed to go after Elizabeth and comfort her; the other knew that she was right. If she was going to survive this situation, she had to be strong.

Suddenly, Adams came into the room, and they exchanged a few words. Then she went across the hall to the blue room, where she had slept since Mr. Darcy's injury.

London
Gracechurch Street
The Gardiners' residence

Edward Gardiner and his wife sat in the small, fenced garden at the rear of their house, taking tea. Madeline's ankles swelled almost every day now, and their physician had advised that she forego any travel and keep her feet elevated as much as possible; thus, instead of trips to Colette's Confectionary in the afternoons, Edward would stop to buy some of her favourite items and bring them home. Afterwards, they would enjoy them in their garden while the maid stayed with the children.

As Edward reached for another biscuit, he noticed that his wife's expression had darkened as she read a letter she had received just moments before.

"What has you frowning, my dear?"

"My aunt writes to say that Fitzwilliam has met with a terrible accident."

"But we have heard nothing of an accident from Elizabeth?"

"No, but we could not expect her to write if his condition is critical."

"Tell me what she said."

After she related all that her aunt knew of the situation, they both sat in stunned silence. Finally, Madeline murmured, "I must go to her."

"No! Travelling could harm you and the baby. I shall go instead."

"But you have two shipments coming—one next week and one the week after. And with Mr. Clive off sick, there is no one to run the warehouse while you are away."

The reminder of his warehouse foreman's illness made Edward's frown deepen. He had other employees, but none capable of managing the warehouse like Mr. Clive.

"Then I shall send an express to Thomas. I know that he will leave for Pemberley the moment he learns of it. In fact, if he has already, it is likely that he is on his way as we speak."

"That is an excellent idea. Elizabeth needs her father. And Mr. Bingley will likely want to monitor the progress of his friend."

"You are right." Edward stood up. "Relax as much as possible, dear, while I write a short letter. I wish to post it today."

On the road to Pemberley

Pausing at a stream along the highway to water his horse, Colonel Richard Fitzwilliam dropped to his knees beside the creature. Filling his hat from the stream, he poured the contents over his head and shivered as the water ran

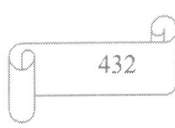

down his neck. *Maybe that will keep me alert.*

Colonel Franklin had unexpectedly returned to his job, prompting General Lassiter to approve Richard's request for a four-week leave. He was to take it before reporting to General Grier in York; thus, heading to Derbyshire sooner than expected, he encountered Colonel North at a post stop a day's ride from London. After hearing of his cousin's injury, nothing would do but to return to Pemberley faster than ever before. Riding as far as possible, daybreak to dark, he would accomplish his goal if the weather held.

Rocking back on his heels to allow Titan a few more minutes of rest, Richard tried to recall the last time he had been this fatigued, concluding that it was during his last campaign on foreign soil. Since being promoted to colonel, most of his time had been spent traversing the countryside as liaison for one general or another or escorting new recruits. Darcy had often teased him about his undemanding job, and the memory of it made him smile. In truth, these had been the most effortless years of his tenure in His Majesty's service, though he would never admit that to his cousin. Unbidden, an image of William lying near death came to mind and his smile vanished. Standing, he replaced his hat.

"Come, Titan. I promise you will rest for several weeks once we get to Pemberley, but today we must ride again as though our lives depend on it."

Mounting the stallion with the effortlessness of someone accustomed to being in the saddle, he kicked the animal into a trot and then in another hundred feet, urged him into a gallop.

Chapter 40

Longbourn

Early mornings at Longbourn had always been ruled by peace and quiet. It was then that Mrs. Bennet, Lydia and Kitty stayed abed far longer than the rest of the family, providing a welcome reprieve from their boisterousness and nerves. Being Mr. Bennet's favourite time of day, it always brought to mind his favourite daughter. For the greater part of her life, he would meet Lizzy in the kitchen upon waking, and, whilst Mrs. Hill busily prepared food, each would grab a roll and a piece of ham and steal off to sit together on a bench in the garden. There they would watch the sun rise, often sitting in pleasant companionship for long periods without speaking. Then while Lizzy took a walk about the countryside, Mr. Bennet would contemplate all he wished to discuss with those who managed Longbourn's stables, game and gardens. Since her marriage, Thomas still visited the garden most mornings, though now he mostly mulled over his daughter's new life. Had he done the right thing in persuading her to accept Mr. Darcy instead of Mr. Collins? Was she happy?

Regrettably, his routine had changed today out of necessity. Having twisted his knee the day before by leaping from the carriage to help a groom control an unruly horse, he could no longer walk. No bones had been broken, though his knee swelled so severely that donning his breeches was now impossible. Thus, he was reduced to wearing his nightshirt and robe all day long and keeping his leg elevated. In a stroke of genius, however, Mr. Bennet had insisted on being carried to the sofa in his study instead of to his bedroom, thus eliminating the need to go up and down the stairs. It also allowed him to avoid his wife and youngest girls by simply shutting the door, as was his habit.

"An express has just arrived, sir. The messenger is in the kitchen having something to eat."

Mrs. Hill's voice brought Mr. Bennet from his thoughts, and he found her coming towards him. Always anxious to receive a letter by so expensive a method, he winced as he took it and then glanced at the return address.

"It is from my Brother Gardiner." Suddenly remembering, he added, "If my wife did not see the express rider arrive, please do not mention it to her."

"As you wish, sir. Should I wait in case you wish to reply straightaway?"

"That would be wise."

Breaking the seal, he quickly scanned Edward Gardiner's note regarding his new son. Alas, his present condition would make it impossible for him to travel, but he had no doubt that Fanny would insist on going straight to Pemberley if she learned of the situation, with or without him. Suddenly Bingley came to mind.

"Bring me paper and pen from my desk, please. I shall send a note to Netherfield, asking Mr. Bingley to attend me as soon as possible."

As Mrs. Hill went toward the desk, a shrill voice could be heard coming from upstairs. Fanny was awake and calling for Lydia.

"Mrs. Hill?" The servant stopped. "Mrs. Bennet does not need to know that I have sent for Mr. Bingley. If I am fortunate, she will have left for Meryton before he arrives. In any case, have someone watch the front, and when he comes, send him directly to me."

Mrs. Hill handed him the paper and pen. "Yes, sir."

As he watched the servant leave the room, his thoughts flew to Darcy. *I hope Gardiner is mistaken, and Mr. Darcy's injury has been blown out of proportion.*

Somewhere between Monthaven and Pemberley

When Georgiana arrived at the meeting place she and Lord Attaway had used before, he was nowhere to be seen. Dismounting her horse, she tied him to the fence and with great frustration sank down on the grass under the huge tree that marked the spot. A half-hour later, her voice was full of hard-held temper as she declared out loud, "Is everyone destined to disappoint me?"

"Am I included in their number?"

Georgiana's head swung around. Attaway was walking toward her, leading his horse.

"My animal is favouring his right leg, so I walked him the last half-mile. Unfortunately, I shall have to walk him back to Monthaven as well. You should be grateful that I kept our appointment at all."

As he tied his horse to a low-hanging limb, Georgiana lifted her chin coldly. Then standing to her feet, she said, "Horses are replaceable. You should have ridden him rather than make me wait."

"I do not believe you think so little of any animal. You are just angry."

Georgiana tilted her head in a shrug. "You are correct, but I have every right to be angry. You have not bothered to contact me once since Elizabeth ordered you from Pemberley."

"Mrs. Darcy ordered my cousin from Pemberley, not me. I just happened to be with her. And as for contacting you, I felt it best if we did not meet until things calmed down. I did not wish to get you into further trouble on the chance you were caught meeting me."

"Humph! My sister is too focused on my brother at present to bother keeping up with me. I dare say she thinks I am in my rooms this very minute. I inhabit them most of the time now anyway and especially since the earl arrived."

"The Earl of Matlock?"

"One and the same."

"But I thought he and you were like-minded. Why would you want to avoid him?"

"I thought we were too, but that was before he sided with Elizabeth regarding my brother's course of treatment. In front of everyone, he stated that my opinion meant nothing. He practically got down on his knees to her!"

With this pronouncement Georgiana began to cry, so Attaway pulled her into his arms. "There, there. Did you not say that you would soon be married and away from your brother's control and, subsequently, his wife's? Just remember that whenever you feel upset."

"You are too kind to put up with my temper. I do not understand my uncle's change of heart, but I should not have gotten angry with you."

"I did not take it to heart." Attaway dropped to the ground, leaning back against the tree trunk and holding out his hand to Georgiana. "Sit back down so we may talk."

She took his hand, and he situated her so that she sat in front of him, the back of her head resting against his chest.

"Susan showed me the note, informing her that your brother was now awake. Is his health much improved?"

"I do not think it has. He still has difficulty seeing and gets off balance when he stands, but most shocking is the fact that he has completely forgotten the last few months, though he clearly remembers everything else in his past. He had no idea that the Fitzwilliams were staying at Pemberley and no recollection of his *dear* wife."

"He does not remember marrying?"

"He does not even remember meeting her! Is that not fortuitous? I do hope that part of his memory never returns, for it may aid my attempt to discredit Elizabeth."

"I would imagine it would. Have you told Susan this?"

"No. I was going to send her another note, but then I decided just to meet you and let you pass it along."

"I shall. Let me ask then, what have they decided regarding your brother's injury? Was it an accident or something more sinister?"

"What do you mean by sinister?"

Since hearing of Darcy's injury, Attaway had suspected Andrew's involvement. Of course, he had not voiced this fear to Susan, afraid of what his cousin would do if she remotely suspected Andrew was responsible for hurting Darcy. Sadly, she was too entwined with Andrew's mischief to switch alliances successfully, and he had no doubt that Fitzwilliam's cousin would bring her down if he were found out. Attaway's only worry at this point was how it might affect him, for what he was earning by doing Susan's bidding was enough to keep Grace Hill Park solvent for a long while; thus, he needed to know what was being discussed at Pemberley.

"I am only saying that there is always the possibility that it was not an accident."

"No one believes it was *not* an accident. Besides, I cannot think of anyone who might want to harm him."

"All men of your brother's rank have enemies. What about his dealings with your cousin, Andrew? Some might even point the finger in his direction, since they had argued recently."

Georgiana shrugged off the notion. "Susan said that Andrew is in

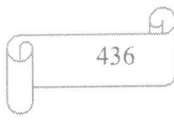

Sheffield. Besides, he would never hurt Brother; he is not that callous. Why, when I was a child, he often took me fishing, and he was so tender-hearted that he would put all the fish we caught back in the water."

"What of George Wickham? He had plenty to say about Fitzwilliam's fairness when he was tossed from Pemberley."

"That was when father died, and I was so young that I do not remember the particulars. But why would Wickham decide to do harm to Brother after all these years? It makes no sense."

Seeing her gullibility, Attaway changed the subject to his mission from Susan. "Perhaps you have the right of it. In any case, it is only conjecture on my part. Now, before I forget, I have a drawing that my cousin asked me to deliver."

Georgiana looked back at him. "A drawing, you say?"

"Yes. Sit up for a moment."

She did as he asked, and he reached into a pocket of his coat, bringing out the charcoal that resembled Elizabeth. Unfolding it, he handed it to Georgiana. As she took in the subject, her eyes went wide with shock.

"Andrew saw it in London at the shop of an artist he had befriended. He bought it to spare Darcy the embarrassment of having it fall into the wrong hands. When he asked Susan her opinion on whether he should show it to Darcy, she recognised the value of holding on to it for leverage and placed it in her safe. Now that Fitzwilliam is injured and Mrs. Darcy is in charge, she believes it is time for you to use it to your advantage."

"I… I cannot believe that prim and proper Elizabeth would pose like a… a common whore, though this proves my opinion of her. My brother would be mortified if he knew. Unfortunately, I cannot possibly present it to him now—not in his condition."

"That is not what my cousin meant. If Mrs. Darcy knows you have the drawing in your possession, it will likely be sufficient to control her temper. It may even be possible to get her to leave Pemberley before your brother recalls their marriage."

"I had not thought of that. Susan is brilliant! Tell her that I shall use it wisely, and once Brother is well, I shall have no qualms exposing Elizabeth for the harlot she is. "

Georgiana refolded the drawing and slipped it into her pocket. "I must return to Pemberley. Though my relations might not notice my absence, the servants may, and I do not want to raise suspicions among them."

Attaway stood then, helping her to her feet afterward. "I would not want that either." He leaned in to kiss her passionately. By the time he was finished, Georgiana's knees were buckling, and he steadied her to keep her from falling.

Kissing first her cheek, then across to her ear, he whispered, "When may I see you again?"

"Every day at this same time, unless I send word otherwise," she replied breathlessly.

"That makes me very happy. Rest assured that I shall not be late again."

Pemberley

The sun was no longer directly overhead and evening clouds were beginning to gather by the time Richard Fitzwilliam finally reached Pemberley. Every muscle he possessed ached as Titan traversed the last hundred feet of drive and he dearly wished to rest. His mind, however, was alive with questions regarding Darcy's injury—questions that he meant to have answered before the day was over.

When the stallion halted at the bottom of the steps, Richard dismounted without his usual vigour, for his muscles were uncharacteristically taut. Unable to conceal his discomfort once he stood on his feet, he said very little to the footman rushing to take his mount.

"Tell Mr. Miller to give Titan a good rub-down and extra oats. He deserves it after how hard I have ridden him the last few days."

"Yes, sir," the footman answered, taking the reins.

Richard watched him lead the horse away before turning to look up to the portico. Mr. Walker, who was waiting in the open door, gave him a nod and a slight smile. As he came up the steps, the butler greeted him.

"Colonel Fitzwilliam, we were expecting you, sir. It is good to have you here again, though I wish it were under different circumstances."

"As do I, Walker," Richard said, walking past him into the foyer. He doffed his greatcoat, hat and gloves as he went, handing them to the butler who followed his every step.

"I could not help but notice that you seem weary, Colonel. A hot bath will no doubt ease whatever ails you. Shall I order the water heated?"

"I have been looking forward to a bath for the last two days, but first things first. How is my cousin?"

"The good news is that Mr. Darcy woke three nights ago, but, unfortunately, he is now plagued by blurred vision, dizziness, headaches and memory loss, among a sundry of other maladies. Mr. Camryn will be able to explain better than I."

Richard nodded. He intended to question the physician extensively. "And Mrs. Darcy? How is she faring?"

Walker looked about and seeing no servants close by, replied in a low voice, "Mrs. Reynolds allows that the mistress is doing well under the circumstances."

"Under what circumstances?"

Again the butler perused the foyer, before answering. "It seems that Mr. Darcy does not remember anything of the last two months or so."

Richard stopped dead still, staring at the butler for a long moment. "Nothing?"

"Not even his marriage."

"That does not bode well."

"No, sir."

Just then a maid came down the hall from the direction of the kitchen carrying a tray. As she disappeared into the dining room, Richard enquired,

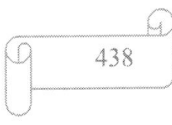

"Is tea ready? I could certainly use a cup to help keep me alert."

"You shall have your wish. Since Mr. Darcy's injury, Mrs. Darcy has arranged for Cook to keep her guests well fed, though some take tea in their rooms."

"I can certainly understand that. Is dinner still served at eight?"

"Yes. Mrs. Darcy, the Fitzwilliams and Mr. Camryn dine together each evening, unless one of them is with Mr. Darcy. Miss Darcy has been taking all her meals in her room, as have your parents."

"My parents are here?" Richard said with incredulity. Then he quickly added, "Of course, what was I thinking? Father would come if he thought he could make my aunt and uncle feel uncomfortable. Where is everyone at present?"

"Mrs. Darcy and Captain Fitzwilliam are walking around the lake. Miss Darcy is in the conservatory. Lord Matlock is in the master's bedroom and Lady Matlock is in the drawing room with Mrs. Fitzwilliam."

Richard looked alarmed. "My mother is with my aunt?" He swiftly walked in that direction, calling over his shoulder, "Do not tell a soul that I am here, Walker. I want it to be a surprise to one and all."

"Would you not rather have your bath first?"

"Have the water prepared. I shall bathe after I make sure that my aunt is well."

Walker watched him leave with mixed emotions, wondering whether the colonel's presence would be beneficial or cause even more tension. He feared the latter. Shrugging, he determined it was not for him to decide and went in search of Mrs. Reynolds. The least he could do was to alert her to Richard's presence, whether the colonel wished it or not.

The Library

When Olivia Fitzwilliam received the note from Lady Matlock asking to meet with her in the library, she was astonished. Since the earl and Lady Matlock's arrival, they had kept to themselves, even taking their meals in their rooms. Whatever the countess' motive, Joseph had been adamantly opposed to her meeting Lady Matlock alone. Still, Olivia had carried the argument, and, reluctantly, he had agreed to walk Elizabeth around the lake whilst she went to the library.

Thus, she found herself sitting in the elegantly appointed room, surreptitiously stealing glances over the rim of a delicately painted china cup at the countess, who was busily preparing a cup to her liking. When finished, Lady Matlock moved gracefully to sit on a sofa across from her. That was when Olivia realised how little her sister's outward appearance had changed over the years, for she was still slim of frame and very handsome. *Even her hair is not white like mine.*

They had been young when last they met and Joseph's father was still alive. Even then, however, Evelyn Fitzwilliam had been every inch a future countess, aloof and haughty. While Olivia pondered if she might have changed in that regard, Lady Matlock began to speak.

"I know that you wonder why I asked you here." Olivia stirred from her reflections, but not in time to reply before the countess continued. "I have been hoping that Edward and your husband might be reconciled before we leave for home tomorrow."

Olivia's brows furrowed just to consider such a thing.

"I know that it may sound strange for me to make such a remark, but I have accepted that some things are inevitable. In a few short years, those who make their fortunes in trade will travel in the highest circles—some do even now." She paused to take a sip of tea. "Most importantly, Fitzwilliam's marriage to Elizabeth has proven that station should matter far less than character, and his unfortunate injury has impressed upon me that concern for one's own flesh and blood should surpass any disagreement."

The countess gazed out the tall windows to her left for a moment as though she was carefully considering her next words. When she spoke again her voice was wistful.

"I have never said this to anyone, but Edward's father was wrong to ostracise the two of you from the family when you married. Edward and I were equally wrong to follow his lead, even holding to his dictates all these years since his death. For that, I am very sorry, and I apologize."

Olivia's mind was spinning. Unable to form a coherent thought, she stuttered, "You ... you are apologising?"

"I am. I ask your forgiveness as well as Joseph's. And though I cannot speak for my husband, I truly believe that Edward now wishes that things had been managed differently. Still, he struggles with the protocol that has governed his life since before he was born and with the opinion of his peers. Nonetheless, when he thanked your husband for taking care of Fitzwilliam, I feel certain that it opened a door that had long been shut. If nothing else, our mutual concern for that dear boy has united us."

"Indeed, we do have that in common," Olivia said sincerely. "And for myself, I am pleased to accept your apology. Knowing Joseph as I do, I am certain that he will say the same."

"That is very kind. My hope is that you and I can become friends and facilitate the reconciliation of our husbands—if not now, then in the near future."

"I am willing to do all that I can to make it possible," Olivia offered.

Suddenly, Richard came into the room, looking between the two of them with an anxious expression. Both stood to greet him, but, surprisingly, Lady Matlock rushed over to him.

"Richard, you are here, and you are safe!"

"Yes, Mother, I am. I am also filthy, so you may want to wait until I wash the dust off to greet me."

"I care not one whit if you are covered in dust. Since learning of Fitzwilliam's injury, I have dwelt on the fact that what happened to him could easily have befallen you, as well. After all, you travel the highways constantly, and your position requires you to track down deserters. You must make a lot of enemies."

While his mother embraced him, Richard covertly gave Olivia a wry smile over her shoulder. "Mother, I am hardly ever alone when I travel, and with my new position, I no longer track down deserters. So please do not worry for my sake."

"It is my lot as a mother to worry for my children," Lady Matlock declared. When Lady Matlock pulled back to take her measure of him, he addressed Olivia.

"Are you well, Aunt Olivia?"

"I am."

"When Walker told me that you and Mother were in the drawing room, I feared I would find a far different scene. Though I love her dearly, Mother can be almost as stubborn as Father."

"What a horrible thing to say, especially in my presence," Lady Matlock chided.

"I say it only because it is true." Richard kissed his mother's cheek, which seemed to mollify her. "Would I be correct in assuming that the two of you have reached a truce?"

Olivia answered. "Your mother and I wish to become better acquainted with the hope that it may influence our husbands to do likewise."

Richard's brows shot up. "I wish you every success. God knows it is past time for that to happen. Now, seeing that I was wrong and the two of you have not come to blows, I shall excuse myself. Before I look in on my cousin, I want to bathe and change clothes."

"Be prepared, Son," Lady Matlock said sombrely, "Fitzwilliam is struggling with many problems, and his temper is on edge. He is impatient with everyone."

"I understand that his memory is lacking, in particular, regarding his marriage."

"That is correct," Olivia replied. "It is destroying Elizabeth, though she tries hard not to show it."

"How ill-fated—finally grasping true happiness only to have it taken away in the blink of an eye," Richard said sombrely.

"Most unfortunate, indeed," Lady Matlock added. "Still, Mr. Camryn is hopeful that he will recall everything in time."

"Let us pray it is soon, for dear Elizabeth's sake," Olivia stated.

"And Darcy's," Richard added. "Now, if you will excuse me, I shall see you at dinner."

With that, Richard took his leave, disappearing from the room as quickly as he had appeared.

"I believe I shall find Joseph and see if the walk around the lake cheered Elizabeth," Olivia said.

"I hope she is being guarded, as well as the house, until we know more about what happened to my nephew."

"Oh, yes," Olivia answered. "Joseph saw to that as soon as Fitzwilliam was brought home. Many of the servants are standing watch covertly."

"Excellent. Still, I worry for Elizabeth's state of mind."

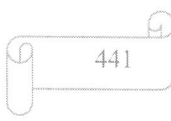

"As do I," Olivia said.

"Please advise me if there is anything I can do to assist her. For now, I shall find Edward and suggest he take a nap. If he does not, he will become even more irritable than usual. And I plan to insist that we dine with everyone else tonight."

"Then hopefully I shall see you at dinner," Olivia offered.

"If I am successful, you will see us both. If not, then I shall be there, in any case."

As she exited the drawing room, Olivia was nearly overcome with emotion. Going, in so short a time frame, from despair over Fitzwilliam to optimism for the reunion of Joseph's family was hard to grasp. And that Lady Matlock's apology was a result of their mutual love for Fitzwilliam was heart-rending. For just when he and Elizabeth had become separated by his injury, the rest of the family appeared to be reconciling.

Picking up her pace, Olivia was eager to find Joseph and tell him what had been discussed. And since the entire conversation had reminded her that no one was promised tomorrow, she wished to tell him again how dearly she loved him.

Later

Elizabeth ran across the joint sitting room and into her bedroom. Opening the door, she slipped inside and leaned back against it just as the tears that always hovered below the surface now began to roll down her cheeks. William's petulance was hard to suffer. In their few short weeks of marital bliss, she had become used to his kindness and the hunger in his eyes whenever he looked at her. To have him snap at her now and look at her as though she was a complete stranger was almost too much to bear. In fact, the sudden realisation that he might never again look at her with desire had caused her to be physically sick. Thus, out of necessity, she had excused herself and raced from his bedroom. In hindsight, she was relieved that Colonel Fitzwilliam had not as yet joined them, and only Mr. Adams was witness to her distress.

Totally unable to control her tears, she rushed to her huge bed. Flinging herself upon it, she sobbed into a pillow while grabbing another to cover her head in hopes of muffling the noise. It was not an easy task to hide when she cried, for her relations, her maid, and even the housekeeper had presumed it their duty to keep her company. Whilst she was grateful for their concern, the constant companionship left her little time to mourn the state of her marriage.

Thankfully, her sitting room was unoccupied, so no one knew of her discomposure today except Adams, and he was unlikely to mention it to anyone. If they were to check on her, they would find the doors locked and think she was taking a nap; thus, for a time, she was free to mourn her loss. Reaching under the counterpane on the other side of the bed, she brought out the nightshirt that William had left on the bed the morning he departed for Laughlin Manor. Since it held the scent of his cologne, she had kept it from the maid who collected the clothes to launder. Having it was the only way she could sleep with him gone. Bringing to her face the tangible reminder of the love they had shared only days ago, she took a deep breath. Then her hands slid down to the small swell of her stomach.

Chapter 41

Pemberley

Daylight found Richard slipping quietly down the grand staircase to meet with his uncle privately. Despite the exhaustion of having travelled at breakneck speed to get back to Pemberley, after seeing William last evening, he had done naught but stare at the fresco on the ceiling, waiting for the sun to rise. He had a decision to make, one that, if he followed his intuition, would most likely provoke his cousin to behave even worse than at present—at least in the beginning.

I am certain that I will not endear myself to him. Bloody blazes! I could have the entire family against me, but if he were one of my men, I would have acted already.

He was not unsympathetic to William's circumstances. On the contrary, after seeing the results of his injury, Richard worried that his cousin might never recover completely. Even so, he could not, in good conscience, watch William wallow in the self-pity that was currently manifesting itself in angry outbursts. He had seen the results of allowing William to brood. It had taken years to coax him from the despair that followed his father's death, and the prospect of that happening a second time frightened Richard much more than any discord he might create.

Everyone assumes Darcy will miraculously regain his good humour once he begins to heal. That proves they do not know you well at all, Cousin!

Confident of finding the dining room already laden with food, for Mrs. Lantrip always accommodated his early hours when he was in residence, Richard headed directly there. Fortuitously, the one he wished to talk with had preceded him and was pouring a cup of coffee as he entered the room.

"Good morning," Joseph Fitzwilliam greeted. Then noting Richard's blood-shot eyes, added, "My word, you look dreadful!"

Richard could not but smile at the declaration. "Has anyone ever told you that you are quite the flatterer, Uncle? I think not!" A yawn came so quickly that he barely managed to cover his mouth. "Excuse me. I suppose I must look a fright. I did not sleep a wink last night."

"Having my brother at the dinner table last evening was enough to keep me awake. What precipitated your insomnia?"

"Actually, that is what I wish to speak with you about; however, I refuse to do it on an empty stomach. As for Father, I can certainly sympathise, for he and I are like oil and water. It follows, then, that we are both fortunate, because my parents are leaving today." Richard began to pour his own cup of coffee. "Besides, while I pray Father is sincere, I do not trust his 'change of heart' concerning you just yet."

"Exactly," Joseph stated. "I am unable to decide between letting down my

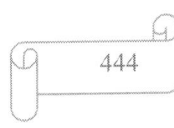

guard and keeping my powder dry."

"And well you should be." Shortly after, each had filled a plate with food, and as they took their places at the table, Richard added, "I will commend Father for thwarting Aunt Catherine's campaign to forcibly take Darcy to Rosings in order to oversee his recuperation."

"Catherine was always selfish, but I had no idea how evil she had become. Her scheme had nothing to do with Fitzwilliam. It was about tormenting Elizabeth for marrying the one she intended for Anne." Joseph stopped eating to consider a new idea. "I wonder if Georgiana had a part in letting my sister know of his injury, for Edward swore that he did not."

"Your suspicion makes me think that my cousin is being as contrary as usual."

"If anything, Fitzwilliam's injury has emboldened her." Joseph then related Georgiana's behaviour since William had lost all memory of Elizabeth. "It is difficult, but we try not to leave her alone with him."

"I will not allow Georgiana to undermine Mrs. Darcy. Even if my cousin does not show his wife the respect she deserves, he will appreciate our defence of her once he regains his senses."

Joseph nodded. Afterward, both ate in silence, each pondering what might happen if William never regained his memories of Elizabeth. Neither man dared to voice his misgivings however.

<hr />

After a while, Richard was too full to take another bite, so he began to explain to his uncle his rationale for not allowing William to continue his disagreeable behaviour. There was silence for a time after he finished, and he began to wonder if Joseph disagreed with his view. That was dispelled when his uncle finally spoke.

"Until recently, Fitzwilliam and I were scarcely in each other's company, so I may not be the best person to ask for an opinion. I will confess, though, that while Olivia and I are still extremely concerned for Fitzwilliam's health, we had begun to worry about his insensitivity with regard to those who are caring for him. Most especially, it breaks our hearts to see him respond so coldly to Elizabeth."

"I agree completely. I mentioned her last night—several times, actually, but he always changed the subject."

"With all you have shared, it appears that giving Fitzwilliam free rein to continue his rudeness will do more harm ultimately—not to mention the toll it is taking on my niece. He must be confronted, and who better to do the job than you? Being the best of friends, he cannot question your motivation."

"Oh, but he will! Never doubt that!" Richard said, letting go a hollow laugh. "Please understand, too, that while I am pleased you agree, I do not ask that you or my aunt take the same stiff posture."

"On the contrary, I think we all should," Joseph declared. "It will make more of an impression if none of us allow his petulance to go unchallenged. I do expect Georgiana to disagree, however."

"I will deal with her. After all, I am also her guardian, and I may just send her off to Matlock for a time."

"So you are. I had forgotten," Joseph said sombrely. "And there is Mr. Camryn to deal with. He advises us to ignore Fitzwilliam's rudeness, attributing his irritability to his maladies and concluding his amiability will return once he is healed."

"Camryn does not know Darcy as I do; he was not acquainted with him when Uncle George died. Besides, he comes once a day to examine my cousin now, so unless Darcy or Georgiana complains, Camryn may never be the wiser."

"I forgot to inform you that Elizabeth had me send for Mr. Graham. He is likely on his way here as we speak. In fact, I had hoped that you might meet him along the road."

"I was a day north of Town when I met Colonel North and was given the bad news. If Graham left Town immediately upon receipt of your letter, he could be here in another day or so. I am glad that he is coming, for, unlike Camryn, he completely understands Darcy's penchant for slipping into gloom."

Richard stood to his feet. "Well, I suppose all that commotion outside the door means Mother's trunks are amassing in the foyer, and it will not be long until they leave."

"They must eat before they depart."

"Exactly! And unless we wish to hear Father *hold forth* again this morning, we should vacate this room straightaway. Care to accompany me to locate Sergeant Thaggart?"

"I will if you wish it. Mr. Walker said Thaggart chose to stay in the grooms' quarters until your return."

"I am not surprised. That man enjoys the company of horses more than people. Unfortunately, it falls to me to inform him he is to attach himself to General Grier in York until my return to duty. He will not be pleased. He hates York."

"If you do not mind my asking, how long is your leave?"

"I requested four weeks, but that was before I learned of Darcy's illness. I intend to request another two weeks as soon as I have time to write General Lassiter in London."

"Hopefully, in that length of time my nephew shall be completely back to normal."

"Hopefully," Richard repeated. "By the way, after we are done with Thaggart, will you join me in bidding my parents adieu?"

"Safety in numbers?" Joseph teased.

"Could not hurt!"

Elizabeth's Study

Olivia was having no success finding Elizabeth. There was no question that she was still in the house, for she had promised not to leave the manor without informing Mrs. Reynolds; however, a search of her bedroom suite and all her favourite places downstairs had proved futile. Suddenly recalling where she should have looked in the first place, she made her way back up the grand staircase. Now standing at the door to Elizabeth's study, she hurriedly whispered a prayer. Before the tragedy, they had shared a bond that few women could boast—a marriage based on love—so Olivia knew exactly how she would feel if the situation was reversed.

Despite her best efforts, a tear slid down her cheek, and she swiftly wiped it away. Extracting a handkerchief from her pocket, Olivia dabbed at the corners of her eyes, replaced the handkerchief and took a deep breath. Knocking on the door, she called, "Elizabeth? Dearest, may I come in?"

There was no answer, so she tried the doorknob, and it turned effortlessly. Cautiously, she entered the study. Elizabeth was not behind her desk or at the large table used to assemble coats for the orphans and the tenants' children. One coat was lying on the table, unfinished—a poignant reminder of happier times spent with her niece. Upon closer inspection, though, she noted that the coat looked as if it had been abruptly abandoned, for a threaded needle was still stuck in the hem. In addition, scraps of cloth, scissors and thread lay scattered across the table where, normally, they would have been put away when work ceased.

As fortune would have it, when Olivia turned to leave, she caught sight of something passing the windows. *Elizabeth!* Recalling that there was a door in this room that opened onto the balcony, she walked to the wall of windows. There she discovered a door that looked like a window when it was closed. Opening it, she declared, "Elizabeth, I have been looking all over for you."

Elizabeth had been leaning against one of the posts along the balcony and quickly straightened. When she turned to face Olivia, it was with reddened eyes and a wan smile.

"I... I was working on a coat, but the sunlight was so beautiful that it beckoned me onto the balcony."

Olivia came forward to clasp her niece's hands and search her eyes for the truth. It was plain that each day without a change in Fitzwilliam had dimmed the hope that once burned brightly within them.

"I am pleased that you are getting some fresh air. You neglected your walk yesterday, and you have yet to walk out today."

"I was so busy that I forgot."

"Mrs. O'Reilly said that you went to visit Fitzwilliam and did not return afterward. Did he say something unkind to you again?"

Elizabeth's face crumpled and she struggled not to cry. "It seems that my presence only serves to make him ill at ease. He was in pain with his shoulder, and I offered to apply more of the salve. He snapped at me, and I began to cry. Then he said... he said... "

Her voice broke and she squeezed her eyes shut in an effort not to sob. "I am so, so sorry. I know I should not cry at every little thing he says or does."

Olivia cradled her face tenderly. "Do not apologise, Elizabeth. It is he who should apologise, not you. Now, tell me what he said."

Elizabeth stuttered a reply. "He said that he does not have the time or... or the strength to coddle me. He said he must have room to breathe if he is to recover and that my presence suffocates him." Having confessed, she broke down entirely, weeping as though her heart were breaking.

Olivia pulled her into her arms, patting her back sympathetically. "You poor child! I can only imagine the torment you suffer. Come, sit down." Olivia led her toward a nearby table surrounded by chairs. Elizabeth sat down tiredly.

"I shall step inside and ring for a maid. Then you and I shall share some tea and have a talk."

Olivia disappeared into the study and just as quickly returned, taking the chair beside Elizabeth and grasping one of her hands. "You are keeping your feelings inside again. That will not do. You must speak of your pain, or else it will destroy you."

"But there are expectations! I am the Mistress of Pemberley. I cannot be seen as weak or unstable."

"Believe me when I say that no one believes you are either. If anything, all of us, family and servant alike, admire your strength in dealing with my nephew. We marvel at how you have endured Fitzwilliam's curtness without being unkind in return."

"I try to remember that he is sick and lashes out from frustration. The man I love would never be unkind on purpose. And, when I am most upset, I think of the baby."

"Elizabeth. I would never discourage you, but you do realise that the shock of Fitzwilliam's injury could cause your courses to be late."

"They were late before he was injured. I *am* pregnant." Elizabeth brought her hands to her heart. "I know it in here."

"Then it is settled," Olivia said gently. "For, I, too, knew in my heart that I was expecting Arthur long before there was proof.

"I do have doubts, though."

"Tell me."

"I fear my strength will fail, and I shall be overcome. More and more, I find myself longing to escape to Longbourn, to fall into Jane's arms and to talk until I have no words left. Realistically, I know that if I did, my mother would make my life more miserable there than it is now."

"I had not thought of that! A trip could be the perfect solution." Elizabeth's brows knit in puzzlement. "A brief respite would do you a world of good. I am not speaking of returning to Longbourn," Olivia added. "Go to London. Madeline can invite Jane to her home without your mother becoming suspicious. In the bosom of your most beloved sister and the Gardiners, your strength will be renewed, I am certain."

For a moment, Elizabeth's mind wandered in a mist of blissful memories. "I love Will so much. I cannot comprehend ever willingly parting from him. His trip to Chesterfield was torture, even before I learned of his injury. How can I leave him when he needs me?"

"I appreciate how deeply you love him, Elizabeth, but Fitzwilliam has made it clear that he wants time apart. He will be well cared for. Joseph and I shall see to that. Perchance, if you are not here, he will realise how much he loves you."

Elizabeth sighed raggedly. "Or that he never loved me at all." She shook her head as though trying to rid herself of a thought too cruel to contemplate. "I fear my mind is too muddled at present to think clearly. I cannot decide."

"I understand perfectly. Still, you must know that Joseph and Richard had an important discussion this morning regarding Fitzwilliam's belligerence. And if Richard follows through on his proposal, your husband's temper could go from bad to worse before it improves."

Just then a maid appeared in the balcony door. "Please bring us some chamomile tea, and if there are any of those lovely scones left that Mrs. Lantrip served this morning, bring some of those as well."

The maid curtseyed and disappeared as quickly as she had come.

William's bedroom

Entering his cousin's bedroom, Richard was just as affected as he had been the evening before. It no longer resembled the manly retreat his cousin had employed to escape the cares of his station in the splendour of fine furnishings, good books and a comfortable bed. What furniture had not been removed entirely was now shoved against the walls. In addition, each tabletop held a tray. One contained a pot of tea and a few biscuits, but the majority held jars of cream, salves, herbal powders of every description and rolled bandages for use on William's broken ribs. All of this, plus a discarded nightshirt and the pungent smell of an herbal salve, put Richard in mind of a visit he had made to St. Bartholomew's Hospital a year past to console a comrade with a broken arm.

Last night's dinner conversation had consisted of how well William was progressing, but, observing him now, Richard was not impressed. Aided by Mr. Adams, William walked from the bedroom to the balcony and back repeatedly. Though his cousin nodded in Richard's direction when he first noticed him, William did not speak. That was satisfactory, for Richard was preoccupied with studying his cousin's balance, noting that whenever Adams let go of his arm, William staggered to the left or the right. However, each misstep was immediately followed by a loud oath, which was totally alien to his cousin's character. At length, Adams guided him to a chair by the bed, and William sat down wearily.

"Mr. Adams, would you excuse us, please? I would like to speak privately with my cousin," Richard requested.

Adams glanced tentatively to his employer. Finding no objection in the master's expression, he nodded to Richard and quickly escaped the room without saying a word.

William watched him leave with no little annoyance, though he did not speak until he was out of sight. "So, now that I am injured, you order my servants about as though they are yours?"

"Petulance does not become you, Darcy. I simply did not wish our conversation to be overheard." William removed the patch that now covered his right eye and rubbed both eyes tiredly. "Does the patch help?" Richard enquired.

"Sometimes I think it does, but do not change the subject. You should have asked if I was done with Adams."

"I suppose I could have, but I wished to address you while I was in complete control of my temper."

William shifted in his seat, narrowing his eyes in order to see his cousin clearly. "That sounds ominous. What is so important that you must be in control of your temper to speak of it?"

Richard took a quick breath and blew it out noisily. "I shall get straight to the point. You have been acting like an arse since you woke from your injury, snapping at everyone helping you and uttering oaths I never thought to hear you say."

"The oaths are aimed at myself... at my inability to improve."

"How can you expect those around you to know that? Besides, you should not swear at yourself, either. Contrary to what you have always believed, you are not in charge of everything! I know you are accustomed to giving orders and seeing them followed, but you are not in charge of your recovery—God is! You can only do your part, and trust Him to do the rest."

"According to you, my faults are many. But I am not dull! I realise that I may never be the man I once was!"

"That is rubbish! Obviously, you feel so sorry for yourself that you cannot think clearly."

William's face reddened, and he gripped the arms of the chair as his knuckles turned white. "Who are you to judge me?"

"I am the only one who will tell you when you act like a spoiled child! Everyone else fears hurting your feelings because you are obviously in pain. So they lick the wounds you inflict on them and stay silent. I, however, am not inclined to pamper a grown man."

"Every bone in *your* body does not ache when you move. *You* can walk without assistance, read whenever you wish and can see clearly, for God's sake! Perhaps if you were in my place, you might have more compassion."

"What is the true source of your anger, Cousin? If it is your physical maladies, why take it out on those who have done nothing but care for you?"

William looked somewhat ashamed but did not reply.

"Or are you angry because you are married and do not remember why you chose Mrs. Darcy? I was told that she has cared diligently for you, sitting with you for hours when you first came home—so much so, that she was utterly exhausted and forced to her bed by order of Mr. Camryn. Still, you treat her with indifference—nay, with coldness!"

"I thanked her for her care!"

"*Her?*" Richard began to pace about the room, his boots producing a loud thud with each step. "*Her* name is Elizabeth, though I have yet to hear you say it. I can only imagine how sincere your thanks sounded!"

"I cannot... " William swallowed hard. "I *do not* know what she expects. What if I am never more than *half* the man I was? I could not abide being married to a woman who pities me. She cries in my presence constantly, and I

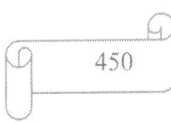

have no idea how to pacify her uncertainties, for I cannot alleviate my own. It takes all my strength just to get out of bed each day and walk without stumbling." He motioned to papers scattered about his bed. "I cannot even read my own correspondence, much less write a letter."

William passed a shaky hand over his face. "Pemberley could be in dire straits, and I would never know unless Mr. Sturgis informed me. Blast it, Richard! I cannot spend my energy on anything at this point save getting well!"

Richard walked over to place a hand on William's shoulder. "I am not unfeeling, Cousin. I realise how frightening your circumstances must be, for you have so many people depending on you; however, I care too deeply to stand idly by and see you sink into the abyss you occupied after Uncle George's death. Wallowing in your troubles will not help."

"I AM NOT wallowing," William said curtly. "And I will not be browbeaten by you, Richard. If my attitude bothers you so much, nothing is keeping you from rejoining your regiment."

"You will not be rid of me that easily."

"I am STILL master of this house, and I say who is to be a guest at Pemberley."

"When you are physically able to toss me from the house, we shall revisit that threat," Richard snarled.

Crossing the room, he stopped at the door to the balcony. Focusing on some horses grazing lazily in a distant pasture, Richard considered how ironic it was that Pemberley appeared the same outside the manor house, while turmoil reigned within.

Once he was composed, he addressed William again. "Darcy, all I ask is that you consider what your attitude is doing, not only to yourself, but to the woman who loves you. You say you have no memory of Mrs. Darcy, but believe me when I say that you were deeply in love with that woman. And I am not ashamed to add that I was greatly relieved that you had not chosen to marry a woman of the *ton*. In Elizabeth Bennet, you found a true companion in every sense of the word. If you do not play the hand you have been dealt wisely, you may lose everything you ever wanted in life. Just think on that."

Having had his say, Richard walked out of the bedroom and into the sitting room. As he closed the door, he turned to find his aunt waiting. The look on her face was evidence that she had heard some, if not all, of their argument.

"I suppose the entire house heard."

"Neither of you attempted to be quiet," Olivia said with a slight smile. "I think I should speak to him now."

"If you are brave enough, I will not stop you." Richard offered a wry smile. "Do you wish me to wait here in case you need reinforcements?"

"I am used to stubborn men," she said, stepping forward to smooth a lock of hair from Richard's forehead before patting his cheek. "That will not be necessary."

"Then I wish you luck." Richard said, saluting his aunt before he left the room.

Taking a deep breath, Olivia Fitzwilliam rose to her full height and opened the door to William's bedroom. As she entered, she noted that he looked away at the sight of her.

"May I have a word with you, Fitzwilliam?"

"Since Mrs. Darcy seems to have complained to everyone about my conduct, I imagine a line has formed of those wishing to have a word with me."

Walking toward him with a kindly expression, she said, "You are entirely wrong. Elizabeth never complains to anyone. In fact, I was concerned for her welfare and confronted her. It took quite a bit of prodding on my part to get her to admit that it was your words that wounded her. If others have noticed, it is simply because you do not try to hide your feelings."

William stood, managing to walk to the end of the bed. There, he clasped the bedpost to steady himself. He tried to focus on the sunlight playing across the balcony while he considered what to say.

"I never meant to hurt her. It is just... I do not know how to respond. My wife is a stranger to me, and I fear that she expects more affection than I am able to give."

Olivia hurried to his side, taking his hand. "Fitzwilliam, I know that Elizabeth would be content, for now, just to know you are not unhappy that she is your wife. If you would only force yourself to be affable, though you may have no tender feelings, it would do wonders for her melancholy."

William's brows knit. "She seems too intelligent to be convinced by merely a genial disposition."

"A woman in love wants to believe that her husband cares. And you may find that feigning affection leads to true affection." Then Olivia smiled, "It is telling, though, that you described Elizabeth as intelligent."

"Why is that?"

"Once I asked you what made you fall in love with her and you remarked that Elizabeth's intellect was what first attracted you and, afterwards, her eyes. You said they drew you like a moth to a flame."

William studied the floor as he considered her remark. "I do not remember saying that, but I suppose her intelligence would have been a draw. I have always despised the way most ladies of the *ton* scorn education."

"So you have."

He turned to face her. "I shall apologise to Mrs. Dar... to Elizabeth, though I fear it may be too late. She left here in tears earlier."

"It is never too late to apologise. Let me speak to her."

"Thank you, Aunt." William hesitated. "I have to say that you remind me of Mother. She would not have been happy with my attitude of late."

"Knowing Anne as well as I did, I have no doubt of it."

"If you do not mind, would you also ask Richard to return? I fear I owe him an apology, too."

"I will." Just then the valet came into the room and she addressed him. "I shall leave you to your duty, Mr. Adams."

Then she did something that she had wanted to do for several days—she

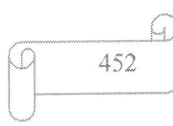

stood on tiptoes and kissed William on the cheek. "I am so pleased that you have come to this decision. And remember that I am always available should you need someone to listen."

As she quit the room, he stared after her, absently rubbing the place she had kissed. When finally he noticed the puzzled expression on his valet's face, he said, "I fear I owe you an apology, Adams."

⁕

Monthaven Manor
A drawing room

"What were they thinking coming here?" Lord Attaway exclaimed, waving the letter Lady Susan had just given him to read. "If Andrew and George are ever convicted of hurting Fitzwilliam, you could hang for hiding them on your property. Everyone knows you have run Monthaven Manor since your father's accident, so he will not be charged—you will."

"Be quiet," Lady Susan said, glancing to the door to see if any servants were nearby. "Andrew has done nothing wrong. He and George were in Sheffield when Fitzwilliam was assaulted."

"Richard will not believe that, and I am not sure that I do either."

"Do not talk nonsense. Andrew knows that I want to marry Darcy, so he would never do anything so foolish. But you are correct. Richard will presume Andrew to be guilty and George by association. So what choice do they have but to sail from England?"

"Sailing from England is not the problem. Kidnapping Mrs. Darcy is!" Attaway hissed under his breath. "I cannot believe that you are willing to go along with anything so utterly foolish!"

"If it means ridding Pemberley of Eliza Bennet, I am! And I shall insist that she not be set free. I want her to sail with them in payment for my assistance."

"I never agreed to be involved in a kidnapping. I will not risk hanging when they are caught, as they will be."

"YOU will do what I say, when I say, or I shall ruin you. Is that understood?"

Attaway's bravado ebbed. His cousin was a formidable foe when she was thwarted. "I understand. But I will only take food to them. That is all."

"That is all I need at present. Now, Mrs. Holden is downstairs filling a basket as we speak. Take it to the cabin straightaway and do not dawdle. It may look suspicious if you are not back in time for dinner."

"What have you told your father? You do realise that the groundskeeper may notice the cabin is occupied and say something to him."

"I have already explained to Father that some friends of yours from Liverpool are in Lambton on a fishing trip, and they asked about the area lakes. You enquired if they might fish in our lake, and I offered them the use of the cabin. If George and Andrew stay out of sight, no one will know who your friends are."

"And what of Georgiana? I cannot be in charge of both catering to Andrew and meeting her every day."

"I have already sent a note to Georgiana taking care of that problem."

"Well. I guess there is nothing more to discuss. I must leave if I am to get there and back before dark."

"Report to me when you return."

Andrew saluted insolently. "Aye, aye, Captain!" Then he marched from the room.

Susan watched him go with contempt. *You had best remember that I am YOUR superior in every way, Matthew!*

Hurriedly making her way back downstairs, Mrs. Holden prayed not to be seen by the other servants. She had no reason to be above stairs but had gone up and lingered just outside the drawing room while Lady Susan and Lord Attaway talked.

As she entered safely into the foyer without encountering anyone, she breathed a sigh of relief. What she had heard was very important, and she had to think of an excuse to go into Lambton tomorrow morning.

Chapter 42

Pemberley
One week later

Richard Fitzwilliam and Charles Bingley slowly made their way down the gravel path that led to the stables. Since Charles' arrival, they had begun each day with an early morning ride—a tradition Richard missed sharing with his cousin. As they neared the paddock, one of the under-grooms emerged from the barn leading Titan along with another stallion intended for Bingley.

"I see Mr. Miller has gotten used to our routine," Richard stated.

"Darcy certainly has excellent servants. I could use a coachman like Miller, but I suppose there is no need to hire one until I am ready to buy an estate in lieu of renting. At least then I could be certain of keeping him on. For now, I have a groom and an under-groom who suffice. Besides, it would not be fair to hire someone of that calibre, only to have to let them go because the estate did not suit."

"My cousin has taught you well."

Bingley smiled. "Yes, Darcy has passed along a great deal of information on how to manage servants and run an estate; otherwise, I would have been completely adrift. He became my mentor at Cambridge and has been ever since. He is like the brother I never had."

"I know what you mean. Darcy is more my brother than Edgar. By the way, Bingley, if I have neglected to tell you, I appreciate that you dropped everything to come to Pemberley to check on my cousin. Now that you are betrothed, it must be difficult to be separated from your fiancée, not to mention all the falderal that accompanies the preparations for that blessed state."

"To tell the truth, I do not miss the falderal, as you call it. Mrs. Bennet can be exhausting in her desire to impress her neighbours. I do not think there is a household in Meryton we have not visited twice since our engagement. Yet I confess that I do miss Jane keenly. So much so, that now that Darcy seems on his way to a full recovery I am thinking of leaving within the next few days."

"I assumed you might. I just wanted you to know that since your arrival my cousin's attitude has changed significantly, and for that, you have my gratitude."

Charles chuckled. "I can hardly take credit for Darcy's attitude. From what Captain Fitzwilliam told me, Darcy changed after you had a confrontation with him and that occurred before I came!"

"He needed a kick in the arse! Heaven knows the man was wallowing in self-pity. But I feel I was entirely wrong in one regard."

"Which was?"

"I assumed he was being curt to Mrs. Darcy because he had fallen into his old way of thinking—assuming she was too far beneath his station. I thought perhaps he could not come to terms with why he would have chosen her."

"And you believe you were wrong?"

"Yes. After our quarrel, when he apologised, it quickly became clear that that my poor cousin was acting out of fear, rather than disdain."

Charles stopped walking and turned to face Richard. "Darcy afraid? Of what?"

"Afraid he will never be the man he was before and utterly terrified that his wife, a woman he could not remember, might not be the kind to accept *half a man*, as he termed it. He even wondered aloud if she would pity him, declaring he could not abide that." Letting go a deep breath, Richard added, "I did my best to reassure him that the Elizabeth Darcy I had come to know is not the type of woman to abandon her vows, and she is certainly not capricious."

"Surely he believed you."

"While he realises that I spoke the truth about his melancholy, I cannot say he trusts my opinion of his wife. Regardless, my candour concerning his attitude did hurt his feelings. It may take a while for us to return to our prior camaraderie. You, on the other hand, have the uncanny ability to cheer him by your mere presence."

"I may cheer him, but I would never have had the nerve to challenge him; hence you are more useful than I."

"We could argue that point forever," Richard retorted. "But you will never know the burden that lifted from my shoulders when my grim cousin began to smile again. And he has steadily improved since."

"You cannot discount all that Mr. Graham has accomplished in the short time he has been in residence," Charles added. "I have seen great improvement in the few days I have been here."

"Yes, thank God that Graham thought to investigate the new treatments for head injuries espoused by his associates before he left Town. Between the latest techniques and medications and the eye exercises developed by Mr. Colpack, Darcy has showed immense improvement. He has not been plagued with double vision for days and can walk without stumbling."

"And he was able to toss away the eye patch," Bingley chuckled. "I tried to convince him that he looked dashing with it, but he said it put him in mind of the drawing of a pirate he once saw in a cheap novel he found in Georgiana's room."

Richard laughed. "I never said as much, but I thought he looked like a pirate, too. Seeing Darcy in his study this morning was like a tonic. For the first time, I had faith he would recover completely."

"I can only imagine Miss Eliz... err... Mrs. Darcy's relief!" Bingley declared. "Mr. Bennet told me that neither he nor the Gardiners received word of Darcy's injury directly from her. He assumed she was too distraught to think clearly enough to write."

"This is true. My aunt confided that in the first few days she was almost as worried for Mrs. Darcy as she was for my cousin. I will give him credit, though. After my lecture and my aunt's intervention, he made a conscious decision to be more considerate of his wife. As a consequence, her spirits have improved remarkably."

"That is good to hear. By the way, have you heard anything from the men investigating the ambush? Have they located Andrew Darcy yet?"

"Ambush is right! The more I learn about what happened, the more convinced I am that someone lay in wait for my cousin—to rob him, kill him, or both, I cannot say. The Bow Street Runners that Fitzwilliam hired as guards are following some clues, and I expect to hear from them shortly."

By then Richard, who now sat atop Titan, had cleared the paddock gate, with Charles riding right behind. "Shall we race to the far pasture again?" the colonel challenged. "Whoever first reaches the feed shed in the middle wins?"

"I am ready, if you are," Charles quipped.

"What say you if this time we wager a shilling on the outcome."

"Fair enough!"

Without warning Richard kicked the large, red horse into a gallop. "Excellent!" he shouted, racing away. "Titan can use the exercise, and I can use the money!"

Smiling at his antics, Charles kicked his own steed and quickly closed the gap. When he got close enough, he shouted, "Darcy warned me that you were not to be trusted when money rides on the outcome!"

"Darcy was wrong! As an officer I was trained NEVER to play fair, wager or no wager!"

With a loud guffaw, Richard surged ahead, leaving Bingley breathing his dust.

※

Monthaven Manor
That same morning

Hearing voices in the foyer, Lady Susan walked out of the library just in time to see Georgiana hand her cloak and gloves to the butler. Miffed that she now had to spend time with Fitzwilliam's whiny sister, she struggled to put a smile on her face as she walked toward her guest.

"Georgiana! What in the world are you doing here, and so early?"

Rushing to give her friend a peck on the cheek, Georgiana exclaimed with no little ire, "I am sorry I did not send word beforehand, but I could not take any more of the sweetness and light at Pemberley, so I left."

Seeing Mrs. Holden standing in a nearby doorway, Lady Susan ordered her to bring tea and refreshment to the drawing room and began to lead Georgiana in that direction. Once inside the room, Georgiana continued her rant.

"Now that Brother has gained some ground in his recovery, it seems that he and Elizabeth are getting reacquainted. I fear it is only a matter of time until they return to their previous worship of one another."

"You have the drawing. Why have you not used it?"

"I have come to believe that if I try to blackmail Elizabeth, I will fail. She has too much support from my aunt and uncle, Richard and now Mr. Bingley.

I do not doubt that if she confided in any of them about the drawing, it would be confiscated and destroyed, and Brother would never see it."

"Then why not show it to him yourself? He has sufficiently recovered to withstand the shock, has he not?"

"I am waiting for the right opportunity. With his progress, Brother has slipped back into his previous distrust of me, so I dare not bring it out until I am sure he can be convinced. Else, it would be fruitless. There is one good thing to report, though."

Lady Susan's eyebrows rose. "Oh?"

"They have relaxed their guard. They no longer watch to make sure that I am not left alone with Brother," Georgiana said enthusiastically. "So it should be easier to talk to him undetected when I decide to act."

Though wishing Georgiana would just get on with it, Susan could not say as much. "Then I suppose you are wise to wait."

"I am. I know I am." Georgiana glanced over Susan's shoulder. "Matthew... Lord Attaway, is he here?"

"No, I am afraid that he is on an errand for my father—I expect him back in an hour or so."

"That will be too late. I must get back to Pemberley before I am missed. Now that Richard has returned, he has taken an inordinate interest in what I do when I leave the house."

"I see that Richard is still a pest. When we were all young, he would run to Fitzwilliam whenever he caught me—" She stopped abruptly, realising what she was about to say. "Whenever he saw Andrew and me speaking privately, he would run to Fitzwilliam with some tale that we were devising a secret plan. One would have thought we were plotting to overthrow the king, the way he reacted."

"I know what you mean. I used to think Richard understood me; now I know that he only pretended to understand in order to gain my trust. He is just like Brother."

"Enough talk of that bore. What of Fitzwilliam? Does he treat Eliza as he did before the accident?"

"In my presence, he behaves as though she is only a friend, whereas before, he often acted like a lovesick—"

Susan interrupted. "I do not care to hear how besotted he was in the past. I only care that he NEVER acts that way again!"

Georgiana looked startled at Susan's outburst but murmured, "I agree." Then she stood suddenly. "I should return. I told the groom I would be riding in Pemberley's pastures."

"May I ask one other thing of you?"

"Of course. Anything."

"I need to know the minute you hear anything about Eliza going outside the grounds of Pemberley—even just a trip to Lambton. The very minute you know, you must send me word."

"You can count on me to do that."

Susan's frown relaxed and she pulled Georgiana into an embrace. "I know

I can, dear, just as you can always rely on me."

Pemberley
The hall outside of Elizabeth's study

Seeing Elizabeth about to enter her study, Olivia quickened her pace in the hallway, hoping to catch her before the door closed.

"I thought I might find you here. Were you intending to work on the coats, my dear?"

"No. Mr. Graham is examining Will now, so I came in search of a book— a poem actually. It is one my husband read to me during the weeks after we…" Elizabeth blushed, "after we were reconciled. My hope is that by reading it to him, it may strike a chord in his memory."

"What poem is that?"

"**The First Kiss of Love** by Lord Byron. [16] When age chills the blood, when our pleasures are past, for years fleet away with the wings of the dove–"

"The dearest remembrance will still be the last, our sweetest memorial, the first kiss of love," Olivia completed softly. "Joseph and I admire that poem as well. We read it often."

Elizabeth smiled, then noticed the item Olivia held in her hand. "Doll clothes?"

Holding up the miniature green gown with lavender trim, Olivia smiled. "I promised Mazie that I would make more clothes for her doll, but I have been remiss in keeping my word."

Sighing, Elizabeth added, "I fear that I have, too. I have not called on any of the tenants, not even the Beckers, since Will's injury."

"All of Pemberley's tenants understand why you have not been able to visit. They are just grateful that you take such good care of their master."

A wan smile was all the answer Olivia was to receive, so she hurried over to the sewing table. "Come! Help me complete the bows. I made one for the front of the doll's gown and a matching one for Mazie's hair, but I need a steady finger to hold them while I tie the knots."

As Elizabeth held a finger at the centre of each knot, Olivia noticed that she had changed wedding rings, but she said nothing and hurried to tack the smaller bow on the neckline of the doll's gown before holding it aloft. "There! All done! What do you think?"

"Mazie will adore it, and the matching bow for her hair will make her all the more proud."

"I hope she enjoys it as much as I enjoyed making it." Then Olivia reached out for Elizabeth's left hand, studying the ring once more. "This is not the ring that Fitzwilliam had crafted for you."

A deep sigh escaped as her niece pulled back the hand, covering it with her other. "No, I replaced it with Mrs. Darcy's ring—the one that I wore on my right hand." Elizabeth tugged on a small chain around her neck, causing the ring William had given her to slip from her décolletage. "I now wear his ring next to my heart."

"Will you tell me why?"

Elizabeth's countenance fell. "Each day Will is becoming more aware. I could not bear it if he asked... if he did not remember commissioning my ring. The sentiments expressed upon it are all I have left of my dear, sweet... " Her voice broke and it took a minute to compose herself. "I need him to remember having the ring designed for me. Only then can I be certain that he truly remembers all that we shared."

Olivia stood and pulled her into a tight hug. Then she pushed Elizabeth to arm's length. "I wish I could wave a magic wand and make everything between the two of you as it was."

"I fear our relationship will never be as it was."

"Has nothing improved?"

"While his words and actions are kinder, I can tell his heart is not engaged. I do not know which is worse—to have him snap at me or stare at me without emotion. The love that once danced in his eyes is no more. It is excruciatingly painful to be with him and more excruciating to be apart."

The conversation she had had with Mr. Camryn only minutes before weighed heavy on her heart. Olivia knew that, though it would only add to Elizabeth's distress, she had no option but to confess. After all, by failing to keep a promise she had made to her niece, she had created even more problems.

Praying for wisdom, she declared, "Oh my dear, I fear I have more bad news to share, and I would not blame you for being exceedingly angry with me after you hear what has happened."

Olivia watched as Elizabeth's brows knit in puzzlement. When her niece did not reply, she continued.

"When Fitzwilliam was so very ill, I confided about the baby to Mr. Camryn. I was beside myself with worry for your health and felt that I could not allow him to suggest potions for you without knowing that you could be with child.

"Only moments ago, as he was leaving, Camryn mentioned that he passed along that information to Mr. Graham, so that he might keep an eye on you as well. But when I asked if he told Graham that Fitzwilliam does not know, he said he had forgotten. Since Graham is with my nephew at this moment, he may mention the baby during the examination. Forgive me. If he does, it will be my fault for breaching your confidence."

Elizabeth looked stunned as she sank into one of the wooden chairs at the table. Studying the carpet as though the solution to her problem lay in the intricate design, when she finally looked at Olivia, she smiled wanly.

"I know that Fitzwilliam's injury has been as hard on you as on me. And I understand that you acted out of concern for my wellbeing, so there is nothing to forgive. I suppose it was impossible to hide for very long, and I need to tell him in any case. Before I return to his bedroom, however, I need time alone to decide exactly what I will say."

"I shall leave so that you may do just that." At the door Olivia paused. "If you need to talk to me before or after you speak to Fitzwilliam, please send a maid to fetch me."

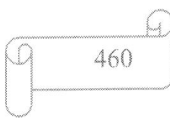

Elizabeth nodded. As she went out the door, closing it behind her, Olivia looked up to heaven. *Please let Fitzwilliam be thrilled at the news of his child.*

In the hallway outside the study

Having gone to retrieve a book for Georgiana from a small drawing room on the second floor, Florence was returning to her mistress when she heard voices coming from inside Elizabeth's study. Looking about to ascertain that no one was watching, she stopped to find that the door had not closed properly, leaving her free to eavesdrop. Clutching the book to her chest—ample evidence for being there—she felt safe, should Mrs. Reynolds turn the corner.

Once she overheard the news about the baby, she gave up her post, rushing down the hall in order to pass along the information as quickly as possible. That revelation would likely make her mistress angry, but it would earn her another cache of gowns in reward. She smiled. If she kept up her spying, she would soon have as grand a wardrobe as any privileged young lady. As fate would have it, as she turned the corner, she did encounter Mrs. Reynolds.

"What are you doing on this hall?" the housekeeper asked.

Florence held up the book as she lifted her chin in defiance. "Miss Darcy left this book in the green drawing room and I was sent to fetch it for her."

Mrs. Reynolds did not reply for a long moment, instead she stared at the maid for so long that it became plain that she did not trust her. Finally, she spoke. "Then be on your way."

Florence breathed a sigh of relief. While she was not afraid of Georgiana—after all, she could manipulate her—she feared the housekeeper, who she suspected knew whenever she lied. Pasting a false smile on her face, she replied, "Good day to you, Mrs. Reynolds."

As she hurried back down the next hall toward Georgiana's rooms, Mrs. Reynolds watched. *I may not know what she is up to, but I have no doubt that it is not good.*

Then sighing in resignation, she resumed her duties.

William's bedroom

Richard Fitzwilliam slipped into his cousin's bedroom just as Mr. Graham was finishing his examination. When the physician concluded, he nodded in his direction as he left the room, and the colonel walked to where William sat next to the bed.

"I did not hear all he had to say. Is Graham as pleased with your progress as his smile implied?"

William could not withhold a smile either. "So much so, that he intends to return to London soon. He allows that he will come back in three months for another examination, but feels that the injury to my shoulder is healing nicely, as are the broken ribs. And, if I follow the exercises for my eyes, my vision should steadily improve."

"Do you still have double vision?"

"Not for several days now."

"Excellent. And what about your memory?"

"Graham will not venture a guess as to when that might resolve, but I confided to him, and now to you, that last night I believe I dreamed about what happened."

Richard's expression changed, his brows knitting in concern, so William quickly cautioned, "Promise me that you will not mention this to anyone. I do not wish to raise Elizabeth's hopes. It could turn out to be just a dream and not a memory."

"You have my word. Now, tell me what you dreamed."

"I was riding Zeus through Mason's Pass, and I was aware that someone was ahead, waiting for me. Strangely, though, I did not seem fearful of whoever it was. Nonetheless, when I got to the bend where I would see his face, I woke up. When I went back to sleep, the dream did not return."

"I would wager a year's pay that you were remembering exactly what happened. That could mean that you will soon remember who tried to kill you."

"While I would like to know the circumstances of how I was injured, I am most anxious to remember my marriage." William walked over to the French doors and looked out. Richard noted that he fiddled with the signet ring on his little finger, a sure sign of anxiety. "I would give anything to remember why I was drawn to Elizabeth. Obviously, she is handsome, but I rejected many handsome women in my time. Why did I single her out?"

"I will tell you exactly what attracted you—she is a breath of fresh air. The exact opposite of the women you considered marrying before meeting her." Richard chuckled. "She is refreshingly unspoiled and honest."

He waited for William to reply but his cousin was weighing what he had said and did not speak. "With your abhorrence of all things deceitful, even I believed that you had found the perfect match."

"But, from what she has said of her family, she is far beneath our society."

"There is no shame in loving someone society claims is beneath you. The shame comes in letting society convince you otherwise. You were drawn to Elizabeth Bennet at first sight. In fact, the first time you told me of your admiration for her, you seemed almost in a trance. That was when I knew that she had stolen your heart. You would do well to give your heart to her again."

With those words, he patted William's back and slipped out of the study as quietly as he had come. William turned back to the window to ponder his cousin's advice.

As Richard entered the hallway from William's bedroom, Georgiana watched from the guest room one door down. Only minutes before, Florence had come to her with the dreadful news that Elizabeth was most likely pregnant; thus, she felt that she had to act now if she was to have any luck turning William against his wife.

Clutching the folded drawing, as soon as Richard cleared the hallway, she rushed toward her brother's bedroom. Once inside, Georgiana leaned back against the door, breathless with anticipation. Instantly, she realised that the room was empty and was cursing under her breath when she spied William on the balcony, leaning against a column. She hurried in that direction.

"Brother!" Noting that she had startled him, she apologised. "I... I am sorry. I did not mean to surprise you. I just wanted to talk to you while no one else was about."

William's expression darkened, his eyes narrowing in suspicion. "Oh? What is so private that no one else can hear?"

"I fear that you should sit down before I tell you."

"I do not believe that is necessary. I shall stand, thank you." When she hesitated, he added, "Get on with it, Georgiana; I have no times for games."

His impatience with her raised her ire. "Very well. I tried to prepare you for some disturbing news, but have it your way." She held out the paper to William. "Andrew saw this in the gallery of one of his friends in London. He purchased it so that it would not be left to bring shame upon our family."

Without taking her offering, William retorted, "I do not think Andrew capable of caring about shame brought upon our family. After all, is he not the author of most of it?"

"Perhaps you will change your mind about *who* has shamed our family when you see this," Georgiana replied, shoving the paper in his hand. "Look! That is, if you are not afraid of the truth!"

William took the drawing and unfolded it. Something inside assured him that he had seen a similar drawing before, though he could not remember the circumstances.

"I do not believe for one minute that this is Elizabeth, and I am disgusted that you would believe it is."

"Of course, it is! Look at it again!"

"I have no doubt that this... this forgery... was made only to discredit her. And since, by your own words, Andrew is involved, he likely concocted this sham. Once I am well, I shall prove it."

"I cannot believe that you would take *her* side over our cousin! He was only trying to save your good name, not that he should have bothered!"

"And I cannot believe that you still think Andrew is truthful. Now, as for this drawing, I forbid you to speak to Andrew henceforth or to mention the drawing to anyone. If I hear any mention of it, I shall know immediately the source of the gossip and you will be dealt with severely. Do you understand?"

Georgiana threw up her hands, beginning to pace the balcony. It was evident by the way her hands clenched and unclenched and the fire in her eyes that she was livid, but by the time she stopped to confront him again, her expression was completely maniacal. To William, it was reminiscent of the look on Lady Catherine's face when he had refused her order to marry Anne.

"No! I do not understand at all. You accuse Andrew of horrid acts—oh, do not think I have not heard you and Richard speak of illegitimate children and ruined women—but you are clearly just as guilty, if not more."

William's eyes darkened as he reached out to clutch Georgiana's arm. "What are you implying?"

"I am not implying, I am *saying* that you conceived a child—your heir—with Lady Susan, yet you pretend to be an innocent while condemning

Andrew for the same thing!"

"Where did you hear such lies?"

"Lies? Susan would never lie about something so important, and I have seen his likeness. He is the image of you! You made love to her before you left on your tour of Scotland, and she married Lord Hartley only because she discovered she was carrying your child whilst you were away. And, since you had sworn not to marry until you were thirty, she did not want to force your hand. Susan's son is your heir!"

"That is preposterous! I am not the father of that child, and it is definitely not MY HEIR! No court in England would hold that to be true! I have tried to be civil to her, but should she force my hand, I shall fight it in court until I prove she is not only a liar but also a woman with no morals."

"How dare you try to blame—"

"I dare because it is the truth! If you were not so blinded by hate, you would realise that Andrew and I favour each other. If the child looks similar, it is most likely another of his offspring for it certainly is not mine!"

"I cannot believe you would disavow your own flesh and blood. You deserve whatever that scheming wife of yours does in the future. And as for punishment, I had rather live in a convent than with someone who pretends to be honourable while acting like a rogue."

With that, Georgiana stormed off the balcony and out of William's bedroom via the hall door. Had she gone through the sitting room, she might have seen a small book of poems that had fallen to the floor. And if she had paused to pick it up, she could have heard the muffled sobs now emanating from her sister's bedroom. Instead, she was wholly unaware of the damage she had managed to inflict.

Chapter 43

That same evening

By the time Elizabeth had decided what she wanted to say to William about their child, it was growing late. Mr. Graham had already returned to his room to dress for dinner, according to a maid who had also informed her that Richard Fitzwilliam was now with her husband. Thus, Elizabeth returned to her bedroom to wait until William was alone. After several minutes, she heard the unmistakeable sound of the colonel's boots going down the hallway and waited for a few additional minutes to be sure that he was not going to return.

When she was satisfied, Elizabeth went through the sitting room and opened the door to her husband's bedroom. Stepping inside, she found it empty. Suddenly, an argument on the balcony caught her attention and she turned. It was plain that her husband was livid, though she was unable to see with whom he was arguing because of the curtains. Frozen in place, an angry rejoinder, uttered in William's unmistakeable baritone, dashed all her dreams and sent her racing from the room.

That is preposterous! I am not the father of that child, and it is definitely not MY HEIR! No court in England would hold that to be true! I have tried to be civil to her, but should she force my hand, I shall fight it in court until I prove she is not only a liar but also a woman with no morals.

Through blinding tears, Elizabeth stumbled to her bedroom, dropping the book of poetry on the sitting room floor without realising it.

The next day

When Elizabeth awakened, it was as though another woman had taken her place—one devoid of any emotion. William's tirade had crushed any expectation she had that he would ever again be the man with whom she had fallen in love. She knew that Aunt Olivia would urge her to discuss what she overheard with William, but she could not bring herself to do that for he was so different since the accident. Thus, a new Elizabeth had been forged—one with an entirely new perspective. It was no longer a matter of saving her marriage, but of saving her sanity and her child. She determined that she would leave Pemberley before William had an opportunity to confront her about the paternity of their child. That was the one thing she could not bear.

Sliding from the bed, she donned her slippers and walked silently into the darkness of the balcony. A brisk wind blew the wispy curls that had escaped her braids into her eyes. There was a chill in the air, and she rubbed her hands up and down her arms to keep warm. Dawn was just breaking, and Elizabeth could barely make out the silhouette of the stable and the shadows of the animals slowly making their way to the pastures. Suddenly realising that she would never see this sight again, her stomach lurched and her resolve wavered.

You know the misunderstandings that can result from eavesdropping. Perhaps he was not talking about your child. Elizabeth's brows knit as she tried to conceive of another explanation. Her heart sank with the realisation that she could not. *Stop it! YOUR Will is never coming back. Do you really think you can convince this stranger that the child is his? You must think of the baby.*

Fortuitously, a letter had arrived just before dinner last night, dropping the solution to the present quandary in her lap. Jane had written that she was on the way to visit the Gardiners in London, so Elizabeth had only to embellish the story and tell her husband and family that Jane was going to Town in order to help with the children because Madeline Gardiner had taken seriously ill. This untruth not only kept her from having to face them across the dinner table that evening, but also provided the perfect motive for her departure.

William could offer no objection to her wish to see her aunt straightaway, for his health had improved so significantly that no one dared object on those grounds. Moreover, upon hearing the news, Bingley had declared that he would go directly to London, instead of Netherfield, which meant he could be her escort. The fact that he was to leave today, in Elizabeth's estimation, had been wholly providential.

In truth, after last night, she had to wonder if William would not welcome her departure—if only to provide the opportunity for him to decide what to do next. As she was pondering these things, Mrs. O'Reilly entered her bedroom via the door to the sitting room carrying a chamber candlestick. The sudden light signalled her arrival, causing Elizabeth to return inside.

"There you are, Mrs. Darcy!" the maid declared as she studied her. "And where is your robe? You could catch your death of cold."

Elizabeth offered only a slight shrug in response, so O'Reilly's frown softened.

"I found this on the floor in the sitting room." She held out the book of poetry by Byron that Elizabeth had retrieved from her study yesterday. "In fact, I hit it with my toe and almost dropped the candle."

Elizabeth reached for the book. "How clumsy of me! I must have dropped it. I apologise."

"There was no real harm done."

Elizabeth laid the book on a table as the maid went to her closet. "Mrs. O'Reilly, I would like to wear my green muslin today—the one with the burgundy trim. It is comfortable and since I will be travelling, I prefer comfort over style."

"I know it is not my place to say, ma'am, but I worry about you travelling in your condition," O'Reilly said, giving her a concerned look. "You have endured so much since the master was incapacitated, and now that your aunt is sick, the strain may become unbearable. Are you sure I cannot accompany you?"

"The Gardiners have little room, and with Jane there already, the house

will be full. And, before you suggest it, I do not intend to have Darcy House opened. There is no need to open a house of that size for one person. Besides, Mrs. Reynolds said that one of the maids has asked for time off to visit her family on the outskirts of London. It seems her sister has been doing poorly since the birth of her child and she wishes to tend her. The maid can accompany me and travel on to her relations once we get to Town."

Left unspoken was the fact that she did not intend to return even if the maid did.

"Are you still resolute that you will not take any of your better gowns?"

"I am, and no satin slippers either. I will not be attending any soirées or making calls. Plain gowns and walking boots will suffice."

"If you are determined to go, you had better hurry if you intend to see Mr. Darcy before you leave. I passed Mr. Bingley going downstairs to break his fast, and he was telling Mr. Walker that he will be leaving very soon."

Elizabeth was relieved that her maid showed no distrust of her motive. Steeling herself for that encounter, as Mrs. O'Reilly finished fastening the last of her buttons, she said a prayer.

Please keep me calm, Lord. I have only to bypass William.

William's bedroom

Since Richard's lecture and William's apology, it had become Elizabeth's habit to visit her husband's bedroom at the beginning of each day. Once there, she would rub his shoulders with the salve she had concocted, a ritual performed not only to remind him that she was his wife, but also because it was the only time that she felt completely free to touch him. Afterward, with William clad in nothing save his shirt and breeches, they would sit on the balcony and drink cups of the coffee, delivered promptly at daylight. Then together they would watch Pemberley come to life whilst discussing mundane things—the weather, the grounds, last night's dinner—anything to avoid talking about the predicament in which they found themselves. A bit later, Adams would come in to help William finish dressing, and afterward, they would break their fast with the rest of the family.

Today, she had applied the salve hurriedly because William seemed particularly quiet and brooding. Afterward, whilst drinking their coffee on the balcony, their conversation had waned, and he stood and walked to the edge of the balcony to gaze into the distance. When she saw his face grow even more sombre, she feared he was about to talk about the baby, so Elizabeth offered an excuse to leave.

"If I am to travel with Charles, I should go down to eat now. Do you mind if I do not wait for you?"

He turned to study her and Elizabeth's breath caught. William's hair was dishevelled, his neck bare and his unbuttoned shirt was open, exposing the hard musculature of his chest. In the faint light of the rising sun, he looked as handsome as that night at the cottage when she had experienced the joys of married love for the first time. Transported to another place and time, his soft "No" barely penetrated her trance.

Nonetheless, with his next words, her attention was forced back to the present. "Are you sure you will not stay at Darcy House? It would be no imposition for the servants to open it for you; after all, you are their mistress."

"I would rather stay with my aunt and uncle. If circumstances change, I can always reconsider."

Her answer seemed to pacify him, and William once more was silent. Thinking he was finished, Elizabeth walked toward the door.

"Elizabeth?" She paused, looking over her shoulder. "Have I have done anything to upset you again?"

Has he seen through my lies? "Wh… why do you ask?" she stammered.

"It is just… you seem to be angry, as well as being upset about your aunt. If I have said or done anything that—"

"I am simply worried about Aunt Gardiner," she interrupted. "That is all."

He studied her as though looking for the truth. Then his head nodded ever so slightly. Elizabeth offered him a wan smile and rushed from the balcony.

Bewildered, William watched her leave. Yesterday, he would have sworn that they were making progress. While he still could not recall the circumstances of their marriage, he had begun to appreciate having chosen her for his wife. Elizabeth's wit and intelligence proved refreshing, and he was more affected by her beauty with each passing day.

Unbidden, the argument with Georgiana came to mind. Could Elizabeth have overheard? Just as quickly, he dismissed the idea. *Surely she would have told Aunt Olivia if she had overheard Georgiana's rants. And my aunt assured me that Elizabeth confessed nothing of the sort when she questioned her motivations for leaving.*

Adams' sudden entrance left William no alternative but to let go of his suspicions and finish dressing. In any case, it would not be long until his wife and Bingley left for London.

From the portico, the elegant black coach waiting below looked set to leave, for it was piled high with luggage and sported a smartly-dressed driver, an under-driver and two footmen, all wearing the Darcy colours. Though she was eager to leave, as Elizabeth began down the numerous steps on William's arm, she could not help but glance wistfully back at the home she had come to love. Recalling how utterly happy she had been at this place only weeks before, tears filled her eyes, though she refused to let them fall.

Facing the drive once more, she watched Charles Bingley help the young maid who was accompanying her into the coach and then turn to speak to the Fitzwilliams and Richard, who had come to the coach, despite having said farewell in the foyer. Once they reached the bottom step, however, William directed her to the back of the vehicle, away from the others. As he did, self-consciously Elizabeth glanced at the portico where the long-time housekeeper and butler stood. She offered them a wan smile and a small wave. They returned the wave, though neither could bring themselves to smile.

"Elizabeth."

The sound of her name caused her to look to William. She was amazed

when, despite all the witnesses, he placed a hand on either of her forearms and pulled her close. He studied her face for the longest time, and she was beginning to wonder if he meant to kiss her when, suddenly, his lips brushed ever so softly over her own. The kiss was torturously sweet, and when he drew back, the tears that had threatened previously rolled silently from the corners of her eyes. Immediately she wiped them away.

Believing the tears were evidence that she was not anxious to leave, William smiled ever so slightly. "Write to me as soon as possible, for I shall worry until I am assured that you are safe in London."

"I... I will," she murmured despite the large lump now in her throat.

Another small smile was all she was to receive before he helped her into the coach. "Take care of her, Charles," he instructed, though his eyes never left Elizabeth.

"You may rely on me," Bingley said more cheerily than the occasion dictated.

William closed the door, then slapped the top of the coach and stepped back. The coach lurched forward, and not one person watching it leave moved as it wound around the gravel circle before heading down the long, straight drive. Only when it was nearly out of sight did family and servants alike file back into the house. Once inside, William went wordlessly toward his study, too full of emotion to speak.

Richard hesitated only a moment before following.

Had any of those standing about the portico that day bothered to look up, they might have caught sight of Georgiana peering through the window of one of the guest rooms on that side of the manor. While she watched all that was happening below, her maid Florence entered the room and stood at another window.

Noting her arrival, Georgiana asked, "Did you get my message to Lady Susan?"

"Yes, ma'am. I put it in her hand first thing this morning," Florence said. "I even waited while she read it. She asked me to thank you for keeping her informed."

"I imagine she is as relieved as I am that my sister has left Pemberley. Perhaps now she will be able to visit my brother and convince him to do his duty."

"His duty?"

Recalling that she had said nothing to Florence about Susan's child and her brother, Georgiana lied. "Yes. As long as we have been neighbours, Brother is duty bound to forgive and forget whatever has made him angry and allow Lady Susan to visit me again at Pemberley."

Though she seemed sceptical that that was what Georgiana had meant by *duty*, Florence said, "I see your point. Perhaps you will be able to broker a truce between them."

"I hope so, for that would be what is best for Pemberley."

William's study

As Richard entered his cousin's study, he expected to see William sitting behind his desk. Instead, he found him standing at the windows overlooking the rose garden planted by his mother. Each of his hands gripped the side of a window frame while his head hung wearily.

"Seeing you like this only reinforces what I feared."

Startled, William straightened, quickly looking over his shoulder. Rolling his eyes at the sight of his cousin, he replied, "I do not wish to discuss this now, Richard. Otherwise, I would have asked you to join me."

"Better we discuss it now. You tend to let things fester."

William turned back to the window, so Richard continued. "Is there more to your wife's departure than meets the eye? I have not had the chance to talk to you since learning last night that Mrs. Darcy was leaving. So tell me, did you and she have another argument?"

William tilted his head towards the open door—a sign that he wanted the door closed. After he had done so, Richard found his cousin sitting behind his desk twisting his signet ring absently. Taking the chair in front of the desk, he waited for that to stop so that the discussion could begin. At length, it did.

"Elizabeth and I have had no arguments, no disagreements for that matter, since your reproof. I have tried to be very kind and considerate toward her since you pointed out the error of my ways. And, to be truthful, I have come to care deeply for her."

"I believe you."

"Before she left, I asked her outright if she was angry with me and she denied it. However, I cannot say for certain that there is nothing more to Elizabeth's departure than her aunt's illness. My intuition tells me something is wrong, though I am at a loss as to what that might be."

"What of Georgiana? Could she have said or done something to hurt her?"

"It is strange that you mention that, for Georgiana and I had an argument late yesterday regarding Elizabeth. However, I do not believe she knows anything about it. She had retired already, and Aunt Olivia assured me that she talked to Elizabeth, and the only reason she is going to London is to comfort her aunt. So I have no reason to refute that."

"What did you and Georgiana argue over?"

"For one thing, she accused me of being the father of Susan's child."

"Good Lord! Is she totally mad?"

"Apparently Lady Susan showed her a portrait of the boy and he looks just like me; thus, she was easily convinced. Besides, Georgiana is satisfied that I am a liar, and Andrew and Susan are saints."

"She is in for a rude awakening. Have I not told you all these years that Susan and Andrew are more than friends! If her son looks like you, he also looks like Andrew, and we both know that he is not yours!"

"Which is precisely what I told her!" William declared.

All the while he spoke, he searched the pockets of his coat and eventually brought out a paper, which he unfolded and studied.

"This is a nude drawing, purportedly of Elizabeth, that Georgiana had in

her possession. She boasted that Andrew bought it at a shop in London to keep my wife from disgracing the family."

"A lie if I ever heard one!"

"My sentiments exactly! Of course, Georgiana was livid when I said as much. Unsurprisingly, this drawing is so vile that I cannot bear to let even you look at it."

"Let me guess. It is a charcoal of a naked woman lying on a chaise, and it leaves nothing to the imagination."

William's forehead crinkled. "How did you know?"

"You may not remember, but when you first regained your senses, I began telling you about some of the things that had transpired since you first met Elizabeth—like the fire at Richmond."

"I do remember your mentioning the fire and the injury to my ankle."

"After the fire, Coleridge discovered that Andrew had an art studio in Town. Apparently, he has a talent for drawing nudes and was selling them to the men of the *ton* in order to pay his expenses. The drawings Coleridge found included several prominent women and a stack that looked as though they were finished except for the addition of a face. You wrote that you were going to keep them as evidence of his depravity in case you had to take him to court. If you look, you may find them in the satchel you always carry between here and London. If not, they may still be in your study in Town."

William immediately went to the door of a small closet and opened it. He extracted a large, leather satchel. Inside it were several rolled up canvases lying atop numerous business papers.

"I remember now!" William exclaimed. "Mr. Coleridge found that Andrew had leased a room over Poindexter's tailor shop, but still owed him months of rent. Thus, he paid off the rent in exchange for cleaning out the contents."

"Exactly! Poindexter was his landlord! Thank God, you are beginning to recall the past few months!"

William began eagerly sifting through the drawings. "There is no earthly way that Elizabeth posed in this manner, nor do I believe that the others did either. I should have run that blackguard through the last time I saw him."

"If I have my way, he will answer to you soon. I have not said much lately, but the search for Andrew and Wickham is ongoing and has been narrowed to Derbyshire now. They are evidently in hiding."

"Even if my sight has not returned to normal, I can still best him with the sword if necessary."

"The time will come. Just be patient," Richard advised. Then he smiled. "I am most pleased, though, that you had confidence in your wife's character, despite Georgiana's testimony."

"Even if you, my aunt, and my uncle had not vouched for Elizabeth's character, I had already realised that she is a lady in every respect."

"As opposed to those who carry the title but do not deserve it?"

"Precisely!"

"I have to wonder," Richard added, "how Georgiana came to possess one

of these drawings. When could she have gotten it from Andrew, unless he has been at Monthaven?"

"I am sure that Andrew has been there at some point since leaving London. In any case, I intend to forbid Georgiana from going to Monthaven ever again and to confront our *old friend* about her lies as soon as I can arrange a meeting. Would you accompany me as a witness?"

"I will, and I think you are wise to take me along. I would not put anything past Lady Susan if you arrive alone." Then Richard grew more solemn. "My Lord, Darcy, what did Georgiana think to gain by making these accusations?"

William sank despondently back into his desk chair. "She wants to drive Elizabeth away from me... away from Pemberley. She wishes to see me miserable."

Richard's brows knit. "Though Mrs. Darcy denied hearing the argument to our aunt, it is still possible that she did."

"I know. That is why I feel very uneasy about her leaving."

"Naturally, with her aunt so ill, you could not torture her with the fact that Georgiana is determined to destroy her character as well as your marriage."

"With all she has gone through of late, I could not subject her to more grief at this point. I shall tell her one day, but perhaps it is best that she is in London while I deal with Georgiana."

"And what will you do with Georgiana?"

"I wish to offer my sister a choice—either she can reside with your parents, if they concur, or at my estate in Scotland, under the supervision of Mrs. Donaldson, until she is one and twenty. At that point, I will arrange for her to marry a gentleman of good character. I did want to hear your opinion first, though."

"Mrs. Donaldson! Now, there is a woman who can keep a young woman in line. I remember when she supervised my cousin, Lady Louise, years ago. She was the only one able to rein in her foolishness."

"I tried to get her to supervise Georgiana after Lady Louise's marriage, but she was caring for her elderly parents. Later, after her parents passed, I employed her to run Dunston Manor. She has done an excellent job, and I feel certain she would agree to supervise Georgiana if I ask."

"I cannot disagree, Darcy. Mrs. Donaldson would do a credible job. Besides, Georgiana would be so far removed from the city that she would practically be living in a convent."

"Yes. Dunston is miles from any large cities. That is one reason I have kept it all these years. I love its solitude."

"You would." Richard chuckled. "Well, given those choices, I believe Georgiana will most likely agree to reside with my parents. Father knows how to take control of a headstrong girl, if it is needed. Believe me when I say he will be a lot stricter with her than you have been."

"It breaks my heart that it has come to this, but I cannot picture Georgiana ever being a sister to Elizabeth, for she no longer cares to be one to me."

"No, she does not. And you deserve happiness with a family of your own. Georgiana has made her choice and must live with it."

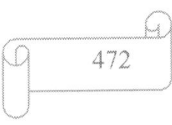

"I am pleased to hear that we are of the same opinion. Now, let us hope she accepts her fate without further drama."

"When do you plan to confront her?"

"Tomorrow."

In the coach

Elizabeth had worried until the minute the coach pulled away from Pemberley that she might be found out. Well aware that though she might have convinced everyone else to believe her lie, Aunt Olivia was not so easily persuaded. Her aunt had an uncanny ability to read between her words and had come to her bedroom after dinner the evening before to make sure that there was no other motive behind her decision to go.

Aunt Olivia had specifically asked if she had told William about the baby, which precipitated yet another lie—that Richard had stayed so long in William's room that she had retired without seeing him and that she had decided not to mention the baby unless he brought it up. Though Elizabeth loathed being untruthful to the woman she trusted above all others, she had resolutely held to both lies until she was able to leave.

Now that the coach was underway, however, Elizabeth had begun to relax and was having a pleasant conversation with Mr. Bingley. They talked cheerily for about a half-hour regarding Jane, and she rejoiced to note how effortlessly Bingley brightened at the mention of his fiancée. It was plain that he was truly in love with her sister, and for a brief time, Elizabeth envied Jane more than she could ever have imagined. Truth be known, she sorely missed the man who would forever reside in her heart and soul—the only man she would ever love.

"Mrs. Darcy?" Bingley's voice broke through her thoughts.

"Call me Elizabeth, please, for we will soon be family."

"If you will call me Charles."

"Agreed." She smiled.

"May I ask, since you have been with him continually, what you think of Darcy's progress? Even I could see improvement in his health in the short time I was a guest, but I cannot judge his memory, for I did not pry as to what he remembered, lest it cause him distress. So I ask you, do you believe his memory will gradually return as Mr. Camryn and Mr. Graham say?"

Elizabeth braced herself at the mention of her husband's name. "It pains me to say that, in my opinion, his memory has not improved—at least his memories of me have not."

Bingley was silent for a time before he replied. "I am so very sorry. I can imagine how awful it would be if suddenly Jane did not remember me."

"It is hard, Charles, very hard." Wishing to change the subject, she noticed that the maid was now fast asleep on the other end of the seat where she sat. Nodding in her direction, Elizabeth said, "I think I will follow Betsey's example and try to rest. After all, it is another two hours until we stop to change horses, is it not?"

"Yes, it is about that long. Rest, and I will wake you when we get to the

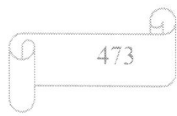

post inn."

Elizabeth smiled at her future brother, then leaned into the corner of the seat and closed her eyes. In only a few short minutes, she was asleep, too, for she had gotten little rest the night before.

At Pemberley

As soon as William and Richard retired to William's study, Joseph Fitzwilliam began to escort his wife up the stairs. Very attune to Olivia's moods, he was certain that she had more on her mind than Elizabeth's departure.

"I can see that you are disturbed, Livy. What are you thinking?"

"I cannot dismiss this niggling feeling that Elizabeth has not been completely truthful about her reason for going to London; however, having no evidence to the contrary, I could do naught but offer her my support. Now that she has departed, though, I am determined to know the truth. I will write directly to Madeline Gardiner to enquire about her health."

"Will Elizabeth not be hurt when she finds out?"

"Why should she? Madeline and I are friends, and friends enquire about one another, especially when one has been reported ill."

"This is true. In any event, will a letter not take too long to reach London and then receive a reply? Especially if you believe something is wrong?"

"I will pay to have it delivered by express, without letting either of my nephews be the wiser. Mrs. Reynolds will help me, of that I am certain."

"You two amaze me when it comes to keeping our dear niece and nephew from harm."

"And you are no different," she teased. "Now, let us go directly to our rooms. I shall write a short note and give it to Mrs. Reynolds while our nephews are yet occupied."

Later, with missive firmly in hand, she went in search of the housekeeper. If she was fortunate, Mrs. Reynolds could dispatch a footman to the post office in Lambton without drawing any notice, and an express rider could be sent to Town immediately. He might even pass the Darcy coach on the road today.

Perhaps I shall know the truth not long after Elizabeth reaches Town.

With that thought in mind, she stepped up her pace.

Chapter 44

On the road to London
That same day

A light mist had begun to fall by the time the Darcys' coach was an hour outside of Lambton. Within another half-hour, it began to rain in earnest, though the rain was not accompanied by thunder or lightning. The drivers and footmen accepted the weather with their usual forbearance, since the greatcoats provided by their employer kept them from getting soaked to the bone. Meanwhile, inside the vehicle, the occupants were completely unaware of the dull, grey fog that now blanketed everything outside, for each was nearly asleep, including Mr. Bingley.

It was the two on horseback, following the coach at a distance, who were most unfortunate. Having left Monthaven at a furious pace to catch up with Darcys' coach, neither George Wickham nor Andrew Darcy had the opportunity to retrieve their greatcoats from the cabin. Both were now soaking wet and miserable.

"I cannot believe that you insisted we leave straightaway. I shall be lucky if I do not catch my death of cold," Andrew grumbled, keeping his voice low for fear of being overheard by those ahead. "If I had had time to think, I would certainly have insisted on taking my greatcoat."

"Stop complaining!" George hissed angrily. "What is suffering a little rain when it means a fortune will soon be ours? Besides, there was no time to dawdle, since we only learned this morning that Mrs. Darcy was leaving."

"But we did not even have time to locate Pate and Duke."

"That is just as well. With my plan, we will not need them. With fewer people involved, our share will be greater."

"Do you still plan to drug all the Darcy servants before they retire?"

"I do—servants and gentry alike," Wickham replied, patting his coat. "I have the laudanum here in my pocket, and I know a pretty little wench who works at the inn the Darcys patronise. With a little flattery and a few coins, she will lace the servants' ale and Mrs. Darcy's and Bingley's tea. Then it will be only a matter of absconding with Darcy's wife after the inn settles down for the night. By the time anyone wakes, we shall be long gone."

"Easier said than done, I fear."

"Trust me. With the stairs at the rear of every floor, we shall be able to kidnap her with no one the wiser."

Suddenly, the sounds of the driver of the coach shouting for the horses to stop pierced the foggy landscape. Startled, George motioned for Andrew to follow as he darted into the trees on the side of the road.

Andrew whispered anxiously, "Have they noticed us?"

George craned his neck to see around a tree. "I do not think so. It appears there is something blocking the road."

Andrew stood in his stirrups to see over a limb that blocked his view. "Deuce take it! Now we shall have to sit here in the rain until they continue. I was right! I shall catch my death of cold!"

Andrew had no more gotten the words out of his mouth when something totally unexpected transpired that kept him and Wickham rooted to the spot, speechless.

Aboard Darcy's coach

Dark clouds and rain had reduced visibility dramatically, causing the driver of the coach not to see the wagon that lay across the road ahead until he was almost upon it. Briefly, he considered going to the left, but noted that two huge barrels lying on their sides now occupied that portion of the road. Therefore, having no choice, he summoned all his strength to stop the horses before they ploughed into the object blocking their way. He was successful; however, the momentum caused the dozing maid to grab hold of a hanging strap, while Elizabeth pitched toward Bingley. He barely had time to reach out in order to keep her from falling onto him.

"Pardon me, Elizabeth!"

Dazed, Elizabeth said, "Wha… what happened?"

"I have no idea, but I aim to find out." Despite the rain, Bingley opened the door to the coach, calling out, "What is the trouble?"

"A wagon has overturned and is blocking the road," was the driver's reply.

"I shall see if I can be of some assistance," Bingley assured Elizabeth as he donned his hat and grabbed his great coat, pulling it on as he exited the vehicle.

Once the coach door was closed, Bingley was instantly knocked unconscious by a highwayman wielding a club. He had targeted Bingley after incapacitating the footman who rode on the back of the coach. The driver and under-driver were so focused on the problem ahead, that they knew nothing of what was transpiring, and as they climbed off the coach, a group of highwaymen, with guns drawn and wearing masks, came out of the woods to surround the coach. Taken completely by surprise, they could do naught but raise their hands in surrender when ordered to do so.

Hearing the command to surrender, Elizabeth became aware of the drama taking place just outside, but before she could think of what to do, the door swung open, and a man dressed in all black stuck his head inside. He wore a black cowl that covered everything but his eyes.

"Stay calm and no one will get hurt!" the miscreant declared.

Visible through the open door was Bingley's body lying in the mud. The maid began to cry. Disregarding her own safety, Elizabeth tried to get past the man.

"What have you done to Mr. Bingley?" she demanded.

The thief restrained Elizabeth, motioning for his men to pick up Bingley. And, as they carried her future brother away, the blackguard addressed her concerns.

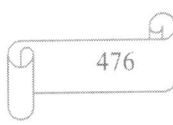

"He is not dead, nor will he die, as long as you cooperate. However, if you choose to be difficult, I cannot guarantee his safety or the safety of your servants. You decide, for all I need to accomplish my task is you. Do I kill all of the rest now for my convenience or let them live?"

The maid shrieked, causing Elizabeth's hair to stand on end. Not given any choice, she acquiesced. "I will cooperate if you promise not to harm anyone."

"You have my word. My master does not wish for you to be hurt, Mrs. Darcy. However, you are going to be his guest for a time, so I suggest that you try not to cause any trouble."

Elizabeth had innumerable questions, but having made his statement, the man backed out of the door and slammed it shut. There was the sound of something being put upon the roof and afterward, she heard him shout more orders. In what seemed only a short time, the coach began to move again. They had not travelled very far before the coach turned sharply to the left. Not lost to her was the fact that they were no longer heading toward London.

In the corner, the young maid was still weeping steadily, so Elizabeth reached out to pat her arm. "Do not cry. All will be well. They will demand a ransom for my release, and then we shall be set free."

The maid did not look convinced, but her tears did slow somewhat. For her part, Elizabeth began trying to calculate how far they were travelling in the new direction.

Where in the world can they be taking us? Her hand slid down to rest on her stomach. *Please keep us all safe, Lord.*

Pemberley

Later that same day, Olivia visited Elizabeth's study in the hope that Jane's letter to her niece might have been left there. Though she despised invading anyone's privacy, she felt it necessary in this case. Nonetheless, Jane's letter was nowhere to be found, and Olivia was just about to admit failure and leave, when Mrs. O'Reilly opened the door. In her arms she carried several books.

"I was not aware that you were in here, Mrs. Fitzwilliam," she said warmly. "Am I intruding?"

"Certainly not," Olivia said, smiling. "I was just leaving. I see you are returning some books."

"Yes, the mistress likes to keep several that interest her in the bookshelf behind her desk. In that way, she does not have to go downstairs to fetch them when she finds time to read. Invariably too many end up in her bedroom." With a chuckle she set the books on Elizabeth's desk. "I almost dropped a candle this morning on account of this one!"

"Oh? Why is that?"

"As I was going through the sitting room with only my candle and the light coming through the window to guide me, I happened to spy Mrs. Darcy's favourite shawl lying on the chair next to Mr. Darcy's bedroom. It is bright yellow and easily seen, so I decided to retrieve it. As I went to pick it up, I kicked this book and almost dropped the candle."

"The book was on the floor?"

"Yes. I remember thinking it odd, for since Mr. Darcy's injury, Mrs. Darcy never reads in the sitting room. There are just too many people coming in and out."

Olivia's brows knit. "Which book did you trip over?"

Mrs. O'Reilly held up the tome. "Lord Byron's poetry."

"And it was near my nephew's bedroom door?"

"One would have had to step over it to go into his bedroom." Mrs. O'Reilly replied. Then, noting the look on Olivia's face, she asked, "Is something wrong?"

"Nothing that I can be certain of," Olivia said quickly. "I suppose I am just worried about my niece's sudden departure."

"I understand entirely. I had a bad feeling about her going to London without me." Mrs. O'Reilly took a deep breath, letting it go noisily. "Oh well, there is nothing to be done about it now. The mistress asked me to visit the foundlings' home while she is away, and I must hurry if I wish a ride into town. Mrs. Reynolds is sending a maid to Lambton with food for a friend, so I shall accompany her."

"When you return, will you let me know how everyone is faring?"

"I shall be pleased to do so."

At the same time

Mrs. Reynolds was walking across the foyer when a knock at the front door sent her scurrying in that direction. As she approached, an express rider, bearing a large package was speaking to the footman who normally stood at the door. Accepting the bundle, she realised it was for Mr. Darcy from Mr. Curry, the Darcys' long-time portrait artist. A knowing smile crossed her face.

The sketches of Mrs. Darcy in her wedding gown! Maybe this will help him to remember.

As she approached William's study, she found Richard standing in the doorway. His back was to her, and he was speaking to his cousin. Suddenly, he turned and seeing her, reached for the package.

"Here let me help you with that, Mrs. Reynolds." Carrying it into the study, he added, "My word, this is lighter than I thought it would be. What is it?"

By then, William, who was equally curious, had stood. His expression grew more puzzled with Mrs. Reynolds' answer.

"I believe they are drawings from Mr. Curry." Then she said to William, "You were expecting them, sir."

"Curry?" Richard interjected. "Is that not the artist who paints your family's portraits?"

"Yes. He has done all of our portraits since I was a child, but I cannot fathom what he has sent."

"Begging your pardon, sir, but when you first returned from London, you said that he had sketched Mrs. Darcy in her wedding gown and that you expected the preliminary drawings to be delivered in a few weeks."

William's brows knit, though he made no attempt to take or open the bundle. Growing impatient, Richard said, "Well, are you going to open this package, or are we just to guess what it contains?"

Immediately, William began to clear his desk, and Richard set the package down there. Then the colonel took a knife from his boot and cut the numerous strings that bound the thick brown wrapping paper, before stepping aside to let his cousin do the rest. William removed layer after layer of paper and quilted batting, and when finished, at his fingertips were three poses of Elizabeth—a vision of loveliness sketched in coloured pencil. [17]

"My, my," said Mrs. Reynolds, who moved closer to get a look. "I have never seen a lovelier bride."

Richard, as was his inclination, was more enthusiastic. "Good heavens! What an excellent rendering of Mrs. Darcy! He has captured her perfectly."

William picked up the top drawing and stared at it tongue-tied. Seeing his discomposure, Richard's eyes met the housekeeper's, and he winked. This caused her to smile.

"I really should return to my duties," she said at last. And in no time at all, the cousins were alone again.

"Darcy?"

"Hmmm," William mumbled distractedly.

"Tell me what you are thinking?"

"I remember Elizabeth like this. She looked so very beautiful when she came down the aisle of the church that she literally took my breath away."

"Which church, Darcy?" Richard said, urging him on.

"The little white church at Meryton."

Richard continued prodding his memory. "Were the sketches done there… in Meryton?"

"No. Curry came to Darcy House."

"What do you remember about that day?"

"I… I remember trying to persuade Elizabeth to postpone the sitting because she had fainted earlier in the day."

"What had caused her to faint?"

Darcy's brow furrowed. "She had stood all morning for the modiste to take measurements and suggest fabrics. When she fainted, Mrs. Barnes pointed out that, by her own admission, Elizabeth had nothing to eat all day. And, she said that most likely my wife had not eaten much the previous day—which was our wedding day."

"Mrs. Barnes is a wise woman."

"She is. Except for her intervention, I would have sent for Mr. Graham to examine Elizabeth immediately. I was very frightened."

"You? Frightened? Whatever for?" Richard prodded.

"I feared for her because I was so in love, and I thought I had pushed her too hard," he whispered.

Richard walked over to grip his shoulder. "I knew that, given time, you would remember."

Shaken to the core at his recollections, William sank into his desk chair.

"There is more that I have not had the opportunity to tell you. Vivid scenes—recurring images, if you will—took control of my mind last night. What is more, I remember what I dreamt, which is rare. Normally, I do not remember any dreams."

"In all likelihood, your lost memories are surfacing while you sleep. Can you tell me what they were about?"

William sighed. "I suppose nothing is too personal if it will help me to remember, however, the meanings of the images in my dreams are unclear. For instance, in one I am at my mother's cottage, and I had opened the closet door to search the drawers of a chest inside there. Obviously, I am looking for something, but the dream always ends before I can remember what that may be. In another, I am wading in a shallow body of water, boots and all." William threw up his hands as though he had no idea what to make of it. "You, of all people, know that is not my nature. Then, from behind, someone begins splashing water on me. I know it is a woman, for I can hear her laughter, but when I turn to her, the dream ends." He was silent for a moment. "It could easily have been Georgiana when she was a young girl."

"But you believe it is Elizabeth, do you not?"

"I remember feeling incandescently happy and deeply in love with whomever it was. Could this be my mind playing tricks?"

"I think not! You have never mentioned more than three or four dreams that made enough of an impact that you felt it necessary to share them with me. May I make a suggestion?"

"Of course."

"If you did wade in the water in your boots, your valet should remember. Why not ask Adams? You might also go to your mother's cottage and see if that sparks any recollections."

"Will you accompany me? Now that Graham has returned to Town, Camryn agrees with him that I should not ride just yet."

"But, of course, you intend to ride as usual."

"I will when the need arises. If you accompany me and Camryn learns of it, it may pacify him to know that I was not alone."

"You can count on me, Darcy. Speaking of which, do you still wish to confront Georgiana tomorrow?"

"Yes. Tonight I shall warn my aunt and uncle that Georgiana's attitude could worsen after we talk to her. Then after we have eaten in the morning, we shall confront her. I do not relish talking to her on an empty stomach."

"My thoughts exactly. I am at your service. Just let me know when you wish to go to the cottage."

"Thank you, Richard. Have I said lately how much I appreciate our friendship and your consistent support?"

"That is not necessary, Cousin, for I know you do."

⁶⌒⌒⁹

After viewing the drawings and remembering the circumstances that surrounded them, William went to enquire of Adams if he had ever returned home with soaked boots. Adams allowed that he had indeed returned once after a picnic with his clothes and his boots wet. With mounting evidence that his dreams were actually memories, he found himself standing at the door to Elizabeth's bedroom. When he entered the quietness of her private sanctuary, the purpose of his intrusion became clear.

Perhaps something in here will prompt more memories.

For a long moment, he stood motionless, his eyes searching every inch of the bedroom for clues. Spying a small mahogany chest atop a dresser, he walked in that direction. Opening the box, he found two yellow flowers pressed between sheets of fine paper that were lying on top. Immediately, an image of Elizabeth wearing these flowers in her hair came to mind. *The flowers at the pond! I made a ring of them for a crown.*

Buoyant at that discovery, he laid the flowers aside to examine the rest of the box. A drawer at the bottom had not fully closed, so he pulled it open. Inside were several pressed flowers, some perhaps from years past. One in particular caught his eye though—a single white rose with a white ribbon. He smiled. *Her wedding bouquet!*

Expectantly, he went back to the main section again, finding some letters from Elizabeth's family tied with string. However, it was what lay beneath them that served as the catalyst to remind him of the love that he had once shared with Elizabeth.

Her ring!

His heartbeat quickened as he reached for the familiar velvet box. Inside it he found only the receipt: Blanchard's Jewellery – Gold wedding band, 18ct, engraved "First. Last. Only. Always." With four 1ct diamonds embedded between each word. Inscribe inside of band with April 28, 1812. One thousand pounds.

Tears pooled in his eyes. *Oh Elizabeth, my love, how I failed you! I should have remembered this, if nothing else. It is a miracle that you stayed after I awoke with no memories of us. Who could blame you for wanting to leave?*

Frantically, he searched the rest of the box, though all that was there was were more letters, an inexpensive ring with a matching brooch, a garnet necklace that he remembered her wearing at Netherfield and the pebbles she had collected at the pond.

Immediately, he checked the rest of the drawers in the dresser and those in a chest nearby. Finding nothing to indicate that she left for any reason other than her aunt's health, he was about to give up, when he spied her closet.

Opening the closet door, he scanned it until he discovered the small satchel she had carried to London lying on the floor at one end. Picking it up, its lightness established at once that it was empty. However, there was a book lying on the floor beneath it, so he stooped to pick it up. Realising straightaway that it was a diary, he debated opening it, but upon spying a letter stuck between the pages, he pulled the missive free. His first name was written on it, so he sat down on the side of the bed to read.

My husband,
Now that I know how foolish I have been, my heart is broken. Only after

Colonel Fitzwilliam revealed your true character on the trip to Pemberley did I realise how blind I had been to your worth and to my true feelings. Raised with better judgement, I allowed pride to overrule common sense and kept my own poor counsel.

Why would I do such a thing, you might ask? It is simple. My feelings were hurt when you began to avoid me at Netherfield. From that point on, I was inclined to think ill of you, no matter how many people sang your praises. Then, after seeing your kiss with Lady Susan in the garden and overhearing a conversation between you and Colonel Fitzwilliam, any restraint that I might have had was lost. I accused you of the most grievous of crimes—ruining maidens and fathering innocent children, in addition to being cruel to your cousin. Even now, I shudder to recall my hurtful words.

My heart cries out to make things right between us, but I fear that it is too late. If I mail this letter and you reject my apology, which you have every right to do, it would be more than I could bear. So, I shall not send it. Instead, I shall keep it as a reminder of my failings and my vow to be the best mistress possible for Pemberley and all your homes. Hopefully, one day you can forgive me and once more desire me as your wife in every sense of the word.

I fell in love with you the first time I saw you at Netherfield, and I know now that I will always love you.

   Your wife,
   Elizabeth

Tears rolled from the corners of his eyes, and he quickly wiped them away. He was still staring at the letter when his aunt peeked inside the still-open door.

"Fitzwilliam, I hate to bother you, but I must speak with you now."

William tried to put on a smile as he refolded the letter and placed it back into the diary, laying the book on the table by the bed. "Certainly. Shall we speak in here?"

His discomposure was not lost on his aunt. "Clearly, I have intruded because you are upset, but I cannot leave without knowing that you are well."

William heaved a sigh. It was impossible to keep a secret from his aunt. "I... I found this letter in Elizabeth's diary. I did not want to invade her privacy, so I did not read the diary, however, this letter was addressed to me, so I felt that it was not improper to read it."

"I agree. Would you like to talk about it?"

He stood and walked toward the two matching chairs near the door to the balcony. Motioning to them, he said, "Please, let us sit down." Olivia did as he asked and he followed suit, taking the chair opposite her.

He wasted no time in getting to the point. "Elizabeth wrote this letter after Richard talked with her on their journey to Pemberley. I asked him not to say anything, but you know Richard."

Olivia smiled. "I do."

"In the letter, Elizabeth allows that she was deeply sorry for misjudging

my character and not giving me any benefit of the doubt. She wrote that she hoped one day I would forgive her and want her as my wife again."

"I am not surprised, for she confessed the same thing to me a short while after she arrived. Why would this upset you? I would think it would please you to know that she realised her mistakes so soon."

"It makes me sad because, in hindsight, I see my own glaring mistakes. How arrogant I was to think she should blindly trust my character, though she hardly knew me; not to mention that she witnessed Susan kiss me at the Matlocks' ball. After her tongue-lashing, I was so focused on my own pain that I was blind to hers. I never explained anything to her, so she had every right to believe me a cad."

"I would not go so far as that, though I see her point of view as well as yours. She told me that the Gardiners vouched for your character, and since they are, by her own admission, like parents to Elizabeth, she should have trusted their judgement. And, as you say, you should have taken the time to explain to Elizabeth. So I believe there is plenty of blame to share. What matters now is what happens in the future."

Quivering with restrained grief, William said, "I pray there *is* a future. I have this curious feeling that something is wrong—that she left Pemberley for reasons other than her aunt's health."

"That is what I wished to speak to you about. I believe that quite possibly Elizabeth overheard something that sealed her determination to leave Pemberley."

William's expression darkened. "Why do you think that?"

Olivia held out a book. "Mrs. O'Reilly found this book on the floor of the sitting room just outside your door. I was with Elizabeth in her study when she found it. She said that she wanted to read a poem to you when she returned to your bedroom. That was yesterday evening."

William took the book. "Lord Byron's poetry. Yes, we often read these poems after we were reconciled."

"You remember that?"

"I do. In fact, I am beginning to remember a lot more."

"Thank the Lord!"

"May I ask what this book has to do with her leaving?"

"She had the book when she left her study and evidently dropped it just outside your door. Not realising that she had dropped something does not sound like the Elizabeth I know. If she was upset and trying to flee, it would make more sense."

"My Lord! She must have heard my argument with Georgiana!"

"What argument?"

"I have not had time to tell you, but after Richard and I talked yesterday, Georgiana slipped into my bedroom to confront me."

"What was the problem?"

William proceeded to explain all that had been taken place between the two of them. By the time he was finished, Olivia had paled considerably.

"Oh my goodness! Then it is possible that she overheard you tell

Georgiana that the child could not possibly be yours!"

"Why would that bother Elizabeth? After all, would she not be glad that Susan's child is not mine?"

"Fitzwilliam, you must prepare yourself for some unsettling news, for what I have to confess will come as a shock."

William stiffened. "What do you need to tell me, Aunt?"

An acute note of distress characterised Olivia's explanation. "Elizabeth may be pregnant—in fact, she is quite certain she is, though she has not felt the quickening yet. She confessed this to me when you were first brought home injured."

Stung by his regrets and impatient, a retort leaped to William's lips. "I cannot believe that she would keep something so important a secret from me." Then he looked to Olivia, "If you knew, why did you not tell me?"

"Your wife swore everyone that suspected to secrecy, saying she could not add to your worries while you were so ill. And, to be honest, when you awakened, you acted so coldly towards her that she was afraid to broach the subject."

He groaned, running his hands through his hair. "There, you see! It is my fault! I should have remembered our marriage vows, regardless of my injuries!"

Olivia stood and went to him, rubbing his shoulder sympathetically. "You cannot blame yourself. You were ill. If you could have chosen to remember, I have no doubt that you would have. It was a cruel twist of fate, nothing more."

"But to Elizabeth I must have appeared so callous—heartless even. In fact, I know I was, for I worried more about having been trapped into the marriage, than about how she felt."

"To your credit, you came around quickly."

"Not quickly enough. If not for Richard's lecture—" A river of shame washed over William, and he could no longer sit still. Standing, he began to pace. "Oh Aunt Olivia, if Elizabeth thinks I do not want our child, she may never come home." With a treacherous throb in his voice, he added, "What if she just disappears? I have to go after her."

"Now, now, Fitzwilliam, calm down. I have written to Madeline Gardiner to enquire of her health, and as soon as I receive her reply, we shall know if Elizabeth's excuse for leaving was valid. Besides, you have not been granted permission to travel as yet."

Aghast at his own helplessness William exclaimed, "A letter can take forever! I must see her now. I must explain!"

"I sent my letter by express, so it will not take long to hear from Mrs. Gardiner. Besides, Richard said that you were going to talk with Georgiana tomorrow, and I think it best that you deal with her before Elizabeth returns."

His heart sank. "If Elizabeth returns."

Olivia grasped his hand, affecting a tone of gayety. "She will. She loves you more than you will ever know."

A stifling sensation of pain caused him to stutter. "I... I pray you are right, for I have finally realised the depth of my love for Elizabeth. I ache to see

her—to hold her in my arms. And, while I appreciate your counsel, after I talk to Georgiana I will make plans to travel to London. I cannot just sit and wait while she wonders if I care. It will drive me mad."

"You are right and if Richard will accompany you, the trip may not be as taxing on your health. At least I know that he will make you get adequate rest along the way."

"Will I ever outgrow the need for your counsel?" William asked, with a wan smile.

Olivia stood on her tiptoes to give his cheek a kiss. "Not as long as I am alive."

Chapter 45

Briarwood Manor
The next day

The morning sun, peeking through a partially closed curtain, fell across Elizabeth's face, causing her to squint and then awaken. Sitting upright, she noted that she was still in the same gown she had worn when she left Pemberley. Suddenly, all that had happened since then came rushing back, and she glanced around the room for Betsey. Seeing that the maid was asleep on a large sofa next to the hearth, her thoughts flew immediately to Mr. Bingley, for the last she had seen of Charles, he was sprawled face-first on the ground.

Throwing aside the blanket covering her, she slid from the bed and rushed to one of the tall windows, pulling back a heavy curtain. It had rained so hard when they arrived that she had seen little of the estate as they were rushed inside and could make out nothing from the windows because of the downpour. As her forehead crinkled in examination of the few buildings that were visible, Betsey spoke.

"Not much to see," she murmured sleepily. "I tried to figure out if I could escape through a window, but there are no trees nearby, and the walls go straight down. The doors are locked, so it seems that we are imprisoned."

Elizabeth pushed open a window to peer at the ground below. "So it seems."

"I wonder if they have already sent Mr. Darcy a ransom demand."

Suddenly, the sound of a key in the lock gave notice that someone was about to enter the room. At length the door flew back, revealing a middle-aged woman, most likely the housekeeper as she wore a ring of keys at her waist, and a young maid. A footman stood behind them in the hallway.

As the young woman brought in a tray loaded with food and drink, the older woman said, "This will have to suffice for the both of you. You will be kept together for as long as you are here."

Elizabeth's courage rose. "And what is your name?"

The old servant's chin lifted bravely. "I am Mrs. Goode, the housekeeper."

"And just where are we being held?"

"That will be for the master to say, ma'am."

"Well, Mrs. Goode, I demand to see him this morning." The servants exchanged guarded looks. "Surely he is not afraid to meet with a mere woman?"

After a long silence, the housekeeper replied, "I shall tell the master that you wish to speak to him."

Elizabeth thanked the woman, and just as swiftly as they had appeared, they left the room. Elizabeth walked over to the table and began uncovering the dishes. Her stomach growled, and she realised she had not eaten anything the night before because she was too upset.

"It shall do neither of us any good to starve," she said to Betsey. "Please partake of whatever appeals to you."

Betsey seemed hesitant, and Elizabeth understood her reluctance was most likely due to the fact that she had always eaten in the servant's quarters at Pemberley.

"This is no time to adhere to tradition, Betsey. We must keep up our strength."

They had no more than finished eating when there was a knock at the door. As both women turned, it opened to reveal that Mrs. Goode had returned.

"The master will see you now. Follow me."

Elizabeth rose, and with a nod to Betsey, she followed the housekeeper out the door, which was immediately locked behind her. As she trailed the woman down several different hallways, Elizabeth noted that the house resembled Netherfield in many ways, though it was evident that it had seen better days. The walls were in grave need of a new coat of paint, and the rugs were worn in many places. Lost in trying to see every detail, Elizabeth was surprised when the housekeeper abruptly stopped, then entered an open door. Taking a deep breath, she followed her inside, just as she heard her name mentioned.

"Mrs. Darcy, your lordship," the old servant announced.

The room was dim, the curtains were closed, and there was only one candelabrum lit in the entire room. It took a moment for Elizabeth's eyes to adjust, but just as she made out the figure of a man sitting in a tall chair next to a window, he stood, startling her.

"Good morning, Mrs. Darcy," he said offhandedly. "Mrs. Goode said that you wished to speak to me. Is there something that you need?"

Though Elizabeth could not make out his face, the tone of his address caused her to seethe with anger. Sounding much braver than she felt, she retorted, "Do not speak to me as though I am a guest, sir. I am your prisoner! Hence I wished to confront the one who kidnapped me and my party."

"And so you have. You may call me Baron Acton."

"Do I know you?"

"No. But your husband knows me well. *That* is why you are here."

Elizabeth studied that assertion for a long moment, deciding not to question his allegation just yet. "I wish to see Mr. Bingley. I saw him brutally attacked on the road by your ruffians, and I would like to know that he is well."

"I am afraid that is not possible; however, I swear to you that Mr. Bingley is doing quite well, despite the knot on his head. He is being held in another wing of the house, along with all the men who were on the coach." Again he talked as though nothing was the matter, and Elizabeth was about to question his sanity when he spoke again, "Would you oblige me and come closer? I cannot see well."

Elizabeth took a few steps forward, pausing awkwardly when she could clearly see his features. He had ginger hair, long and extremely curly, pulled back in a queue and tied at the neck with a cord that did not do the job justice. His beard was equally unkempt. Nonetheless, it was the scar that crossed his forehead and cheek that held her spellbound, for it passed through what had been his left eye.

"I see that you have discovered my scar. I assure you that it makes me appear more fearsome than I actually am."

"You are fearsome enough, for kidnapping innocent people for profit is not the exploit of a gentleman."

"You are mistaken if you think I took you for monetary gain, though I admit that I will demand a ransom to see if Fitzwilliam cares enough about you to pay it."

Elizabeth's chin lifted in defiance, causing him to smile wryly.

"Whether you believe it or not, I took you for your own safety. My present condition is witness to how being acquainted with Fitzwilliam Darcy can be disadvantageous to your health. Now that you have left the safety of Pemberley, you have provided those that sought to kill me the perfect opportunity to do the same to you."

"I do not take your meaning. Who would want to harm me? Besides, how can you claim such familiarity with me when I do not know you?"

"You will understand everything soon enough. And, make no mistake, I know all about you, Elizabeth Bennet. I have been following you since you forced Fitzwilliam Darcy to marry you in Hertfordshire."

"Fitzwilliam married me of his own free will to protect my reputation and that of my family."

"That is not what the gossips said."

"I do not care what they said. I know the truth."

"It is admirable of you to defend him, especially since he claims no memory of you and in light of the fact that you have left him." The puzzled look on Elizabeth's face caused him to continue. "I have spies in his service and other venues, so I know all that has occurred since your marriage. I also know what Darcy claims happened to him—the injury that supposedly caused him to forget you—though I am not convinced that he did not deceive you there as well."

"His injury was genuine! I tended him for weeks afterward. It was hardly his fault that he could not remember everything once he regained consciousness. One thing I know for certain—no matter if he has no memories of me, my husband is not the kind of man to harm another person deliberately."

"Then why did you leave him when he is still not well? I do not believe your claim that you need to see to your aunt. The rumour among the servants is that you are with child. Do you fear that he will reject your child too?"

Elizabeth would not let him know of her quandary. "My circumstances are none of your business. William is not himself, and I will never hold his present words and actions against him. I love my husband very much, for the man I came to know and love is truly a good person."

"I have to say that your defence of him gives me pause. I have learned that you are not easily persuaded and have a mind of your own. I admire that very much. So, I have to wonder if I may have suspected the wrong man among the few that could be culpable."

"Suspect him of what?"

"You shall learn everything when I confront Fitzwilliam. For now, I would advise you to relax and enjoy your stay at Briarwood Manor."

"How can I relax? I am a prisoner, and I have no idea where I am, other than you call it Briarwood."

"You would be surprised how close to Pemberley we actually are, as the crow flies. Once Darcy gets my note, it should be less than a day's time before he comes to claim you… *if* he claims you. I am eager to see how he responds."

Her captor walked past her toward the door, stopping at the last moment to say, "We will both know the truth of my circumstances after I confront Fitzwilliam. If, after hearing his account, you decide he is not the honourable man you thought him to be, I will protect you."

"I can assure you that I will not need your protection."

"Wait until after you have heard everything to decide. Now, Mrs. Goode will escort you back to your rooms. If you need anything, just ask and she will see to it."

"But how will—"

He was out the door before she could finish her sentence. The housekeeper reappeared, and Elizabeth followed her back to the rooms that were to be her prison for now. As she walked, she considered all that he had said.

Will may not remember me, but I am well acquainted with his true character before this awful calamity took him away from me. The man I knew before his accident could never be so heartless as to harm another human being. Baron Acton is wrong!

Pemberley
The dining room

The dawn found William and Richard alone, and with no one else to overhear, they were free to strategize over possible arguments Georgiana might put forward when they confronted her. Having thoroughly discussed the matter, however, Richard was ready to change the subject.

"Do you wish to visit your mother's cottage after we talk to Georgiana?"

"I meant to tell you that that will not be necessary."

"Oh?" Richard asked with a puzzled expression.

"After we talked yesterday, I asked Adams about my boots, and he confirmed that I had come home wet from head-to-toe after a certain picnic with Elizabeth."

"I knew it!"

"After that discussion, I went to her bedroom, just to see if something there might stir more recollections."

"And did it work?"

"Greater than I ever imagined it would. I found the receipt from the establishment where I had commissioned her wedding ring and it unlocked scores of memories. When I recalled the felicity that we had shared before my injury, I was overwhelmed with love for Elizabeth."

"I am so pleased, Cousin."

"Unfortunately, I also recalled the pain that I inflicted. The despair in her eyes when I could not remember our marriage and how distrustful I was of her motives those first few days. I was incorrigible!"

"You were not yourself, Darcy. You were ill."

"Still, I should have treated her with more compassion. I would not blame her if she never forgave me." Torment filled his eyes. "You understand what this means, do you not? I have to find Elizabeth straightaway and tell her that I remember everything—that I love her ardently. I would like you to travel with me to London tomorrow."

"Are you sure? Riding horseback over Pemberley is a far cry from taking a coach all the way to London. Camryn will be livid when he hears you have disregarded his advice."

"Camryn is not my priority. Elizabeth is."

"If you are determined to go, then I shall accompany you."

"Good. Now let us find Georgiana and get this talk over with. With luck, our united front may cause her to accept the situation more readily."

"You do not believe that, do you?"

"No."

"Good. For a moment I thought you had lost your mind when you regained your memory."

William stood and dropped his serviette on the table with a frown. "That is not funny, Richard."

A short while later

Exiting their sitting room, Joseph and Olivia Fitzwilliam could hear the disagreement raging in Georgiana's suite two doors away. In fact, it was likely that most of Pemberley heard it as well. The few maids that were in the hallway dropped their heads as they passed them and hurried to the grand staircase where they descended as swiftly as they could without actually running.

"It seems our nephews are having that talk with Georgiana," Joseph whispered as they passed the scene of the confrontation.

"It is a shame that it had to come to this," Olivia added. "Fitzwilliam works so hard to please Georgiana, but she does not seem to care. I have never seen a more headstrong young woman."

"Come! Let us hurry on to the dining room. I would not want either of my nephews to think we were eavesdropping, or Georgiana, for that matter. She would resent it, I am certain."

"I agree."

When they reached the stairs, Joseph slowed his pace in order to help Olivia navigate the stairs. As he did, he ventured, "So, Fitzwilliam is

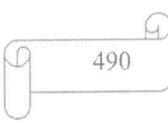

determined to go after Elizabeth as soon as possible."

"He is."

"Good for him!"

"But, he is not supposed to travel until the doctor agrees to it."

"Some things are more important than a doctor's orders, Livy—the love of a good woman, for one." With that he brought her hand up to his lips for a soft kiss. "Fitzwilliam is doing exactly what he should. He does not need to let another day pass with Elizabeth thinking he does not remember her."

"You are right. But, then you have always been a wise man, Joseph Fitzwilliam. You are your own man and have always taken control of your own destiny. I admire that. It is reassuring to know that one's husband is a man who can be trusted to do what is best—for himself and for you."

By then they had reached the foyer, and he leaned down to brush a kiss across her forehead. "I would not have had the courage without your support and love."

"Then we are a good match."

Another kiss followed—this one on her lips. "A match made in heaven."

"We should eat while everything is fresh. There is no need to wait for Fitzwilliam and Richard, for I imagine they ate before they went upstairs."

At that exact moment something crashed to the floor upstairs, and Georgiana's high-pitched cries of protest again filled the house. They hurriedly entered the dining room, letting the heavy door close behind them. Instantaneously, the drama playing out upstairs was relegated to muffled sounds.

Pate's farm
Outside of Lambton

As Wickham and Andrew travelled the overgrown trail toward the rundown farm, Pate's old hound rushed towards them sounding the alarm. He ran circles around them, baying continually until they reached the house. This was odd, for he was usually kept in the house. Also odd was that no one walked out on the porch to see who had arrived. Exchanging worried glances, they cautiously made their way to the stable, where they noted that the cow and Pate's horse were still inside. Even more vigilant now, they used the key hidden on a rail at the top of the porch to enter the house. The interior looked as it always had, dishevelled and dirty. Making their way to the kitchen, Andrew checked the pantry for food while Wickham went to the stove.

"Someone used the stove this morning," Wickham declared. "It is still warm."

"I do not like it, George," Andrew replied. "Pate never goes anywhere. Denny and Duke may leave for a time, but never Pate. His horse is here, so he should be here, too."

"I agree but we have no choice but to wait. We will need all the help we can get to take the ransom from whoever took Mrs. Darcy."

"How can you be certain he will demand a ransom?"

"I have faith in human nature," Wickham said sarcastically. "Let us hope

Pate shows soon. We must begin watching the estate where she is being held as quickly as possible. That is the only way we will know when the exchange is being made."

"Why do you think Darcy will do the deed himself? After all, he could send any number of servants or even Richard."

"Have you ever known Darcy to let anyone handle his business if he is capable?"

"No, but how do we know that he is capable at this point?"

"Did you not listen to what Susan said? Georgiana told her that your cousin has made great strides in his health, if not his memory. Let us hope he is too busy rescuing Mrs. Darcy to recollect what happened at Mason's Pass. For once he does, Colonel Fitzwilliam will not send Bow Street runners; he will come himself. Of this I *am* certain."

"What if Darcy brings too many men and we are outnumbered?"

"Think, Andrew! What would you do? I know how a fellow thief thinks, and he will tell Darcy to come alone, and your dutiful cousin will comply rather than take a chance on getting all of them killed."

"And you truly believe that we will be able to catch them unawares?"

"I do. They will be expecting Darcy, not us! It will be effortless if Pate, Duke and Denny help us. Of course, we will have to share with them, but part of a ransom is better than none at all."

"I think it will be harder than you imagine. Whoever took Mrs. Darcy had at least six men at the coach."

"Yes, but they have no idea that we saw them and are planning to take the ransom for ourselves. They will be concentrating on Darcy. They will be shocked when we appear to claim the prize."

"I do not know."

"I DO! Stop concocting problems! Listen to me and all shall be well!" Wickham declared in exasperation.

Just at that moment the back door flew open, and Pate walked in with his pistol drawn. Seeing who was there, he laid the weapon on the kitchen table. "I figured it was you, but I could not take the chance until I was certain."

"Certain of what?" Andrew asked.

"Just this week two Bow Street Runners were here asking questions about the two of you, and I do not think they believed a word I said."

"What did you tell them?"

"That you were both in London, as far as I knew."

Wickham stalked into the parlour, pulled back the curtain and looked out. "Do you think they could be watching the house now?"

"That is why I began to leave old Blue outside. He will let me know long before they reach the house that I have company. By the way, what brings you here? I thought you were going to remain at Monthaven until the uproar over Darcy's injury died down."

"We cannot afford to stay hidden any longer. There is a fortune at stake, and we need you, Denny, and Buck to help us secure it. Where are they now?"

"They are not far—in Lambton. We ran out of liquor, and they went to a pub to have a drink and bring a pint or two back here."

"Can you contact them and get them here quickly?"

"I can. Mind telling me what is going on, though?"

Wickham and Andrew told Pate what had happened, and afterward, he saddled his horse and rode into Lambton, knowing he would cause less notice than either of them. Finding the others just where he expected, they agreed to circle back to the farm via different routes just in case anyone might be watching.

Later, once everyone was assembled, it was decided that they would move to a location nearer the estate where Mrs. Darcy was being held. While Wickham and Andrew were spying on the estate, they had seen an old guard house, covered in vines and brush, near the entrance to the drive, and they believed it would do nicely for their purposes. They would each take a few days' rations and occupy the shack until Darcy came to claim his wife. Then they would make their move.

Pemberley
That afternoon

All of the family, except Georgiana, had gathered on the terrace outside the library for tea and biscuits. Since he and Richard were leaving early the next day for London, William wanted the Fitzwilliams to know what decision they had made regarding Georgiana and to leave them in charge until his return.

"So, Georgiana decided that she would rather live with the Matlocks," Joseph Fitzwilliam stated.

"Yes," Richard answered. "She has no idea how strict Father can be when he is confronted with a disobedient child." He chuckled. "I could have warned her, but it would have done little good in her present state. She is convinced that she is right regarding Elizabeth, Andrew, and Lady Susan, and that all the rest of us are wrong."

William stirred his cup of tea, staring absentmindedly at it. "I have written a letter to my aunt and uncle. If they accept the challenge of raising her, Georgiana will reside under their roof and their supervision. This is not what I wanted for her, but it seems my wishes have not been Georgiana's priority for some time. From this point on, I intend to concentrate on what constitutes my happiness."

"You must, Nephew," Olivia said. "You have sacrificed too many years already for Georgiana. You deserve contentment with a family of your own."

"I agree," Joseph declared. "As soon as you receive an answer from the earl, I shall forward it."

"There is no need, Uncle. I authorize you to open the letter, and if Lord Matlock agrees, you may send my sister on to them. Ideally, she will be gone before Elizabeth returns."

"If that is your wish."

"It is."

From a window above the terrace, Georgiana seethed as she whispered to

Florence.

"How dare Brother speak of my departure as though he is ridding Pemberley of a plague! I shall show him and Richard that I will not be forced to live with my aunt and uncle. They will be too busy chasing Elizabeth to give much thought to me, and I shall be married to Lord Attaway before anyone realises that I am missing."

"How will you accomplish that?" the maid asked. "Your brother gave strict orders that you were not to leave the house, even to ride, until he gets an answer from your uncle."

"But *you* are not restricted," Georgiana said with a smirk. "Just bring me one of your oldest gowns and bonnets. I will sneak out of the house tomorrow morning just as Brother and Richard are leaving for London. No one will notice me then."

"Should you send a note telling Lady Susan that you are coming?"

"There is no need. They will be pleased to see me, I am certain, and Lady Susan will help me escape to Gretna Green with Lord Attaway. She has often said that she wished me to be part of her family, and now I will be."

Florence pressed her lips together to thwart the smile that threatened. She had long recognised that Lady Susan had no love for Georgiana, but instead, used her for her own purposes. It was a trait they held in common. And, as for Lord Attaway, the way he looked at her when she delivered notes to Monthaven Manor, Florence was just as convinced that that gentleman had an eye for anything wearing a gown.

"Shall I accompany you tomorrow?"

"No. I need you to stay in my room and make some sounds—footsteps and such—so that they will think I am still there. By the time they realise it is you, it will be too late."

"Will they not punish me for fooling them?"

"For what? You have only to say that I asked you to wait there for me, and you had no idea where I went."

"I suppose you are right."

"I am. And, once I am married, I will send for you to be my lady's maid and give you a raise in pay for all your support."

"I shall look forward to that."

"So will I. Now, let us sneak back to my rooms through the servant's hall before anyone sees us."

Florence preceded Georgiana into the hall just in case they met any other servants along the way; however, they were fortunate not to be seen and were soon safely ensconced in the suite of rooms belonging to the master's sister.

On the terrace

After the Fitzwilliams retired to their rooms so that Olivia could rest before dinner, William announced that he was going to his study to finish some correspondence, since he would be leaving in the morning.

"I shall go with you," Richard declared. "I have some information that I wish you to know, but I did not want to speak of it in front of our aunt and further worry her. Your study will provide the privacy we need."

"Then by all means," William said, waving an arm for his cousin to go ahead of him to the study. In short order they were both inside the study with the door closed.

"Now, what important things have you to say?"

"The first thing is puzzling, if not verifiable. I hired Sergeant Woods, a retired friend, to investigate our late friend, Lord Hartley. He has just now sent me his report."

"Hartley? But he is dead. Why investigate him?"

"I felt that finding out what happened to Hartley would shine a light on Lady Susan's plans. At the time, you were trying to please Georgiana and were considering marriage to her, remember? I, however, was prepared to do whatever it took to dissuade you."

William shook his head slowly side to side. "I was out of my mind. I was running from my feelings for Elizabeth, for I feared she would wither under the disapproval of my family and the *ton* and had convinced myself that I had to marry a woman of my station. I began to think I should settle for the ▓▓▓ I know—"

"Instead of one you did not know," Richard finished.

"Precisely. Thank you for being bold enough to set me straight!"

"You are welcome."

"So, tell me, what did Woods discover?"

"According to my friend, rumours abound at Land's End that Hartley did not die after all."

"Is there any real evidence?"

"Nothing solid, but Hartley was great friends with the local fishermen since he grew up playing with them in the coves along the beach. Rumour has it that when he was shot he did not fall into the ocean, but instead landed on a ledge just below the cliff. One of his friends heard the shots and hurried to investigate. They say that he found Hartley gravely injured and secreted him to his cottage where a doctor was summoned to treat him."

"Did Woods talk to the fisherman?"

"He did, though the man would not admit to anything. From the answers the fisherman gave, Woods felt that he was trying to protect Hartley and was reluctant to admit that he was still alive."

"Is that all?"

"No. He found out that Lord Hartley had a godfather, Lord Montpier. Does that name sound familiar?"

"I think I remember hearing Father speak of him. Does he not live near here?"

"He lived in the southeast corner of the county until five years ago when he moved to Spain for his health. His estate was, for all intents and purposes, left idle except for a minimal staff. Then someone claiming to be Montpier's cousin moved in last year. He calls himself a baron, though little is known about the man, as locals say no one has seen him."

"And you suspect it is Hartley?"

"I think it is possible."

William rubbed his chin thoughtfully. "It is just conjecture."

"Admittedly, but I am of the opinion that I would like to meet this cousin of Montpier's, just to put to rest my suspicions."

"If it is Hartley, I doubt he would admit you."

"I shall just have to work out a plan. Oh, and in other business, Coleridge and Harahan returned while you were occupied with your steward earlier. I took their report and sent them on to their rooms, as they were clearly exhausted."

"I appreciate that you handled it. What did they have to say?"

"After greasing his palm with silver, the proprietor of Pig Whistle Inn north of Lambton proved most informative about Andrew and George. Apparently this Nate Burton said that they split their time of late between a farmhouse outside Lambton and a hunting cabin at Monthaven Manor."

"Monthaven? I imagine the whole county has heard by now that we are searching for them. Lord Concord would never let them stay there if he were still in charge, so why would Susan risk doing so?"

"Indeed, why would she—unless she is involved in the whole sordid mess?"

"After I retrieve my wife, I shall have an answer to that question."

"I look forward to being with you when you do. Also, Burton hinted that they were involved with a group of highwaymen."

"Nothing would surprise me at this point."

Richard stood up. "Nor I! Now I shall leave you to your work so that we can leave in the morning as planned."

"I will see you at dinner then."

"At dinner," Richard repeated. He went out the door and closed it soundly behind him.

William stared out the window absently. *If Hartley is not dead, why would he continue this pretence?* Sighing heavily, he concluded, *I suppose we shall know the answer to that question very soon if Richard has any say in the matter.*

Unfortunately, William had no way of knowing how quickly that would happen.

Chapter 46

Pemberley

The house was abuzz with servants running to follow instructions, as always seemed the case when the master was about to depart on a trip. Georgiana was counting on the chaos, for she had requested that food be sent to her bedroom in order that everyone would know that she was still keeping to herself. Still livid, she relied on this isolation to give her uninterrupted time to carry out her plans. Later, when Mrs. Reynolds accompanied the maid who brought the tray, her resentment rose even higher.

No doubt she is to be my jailer while Brother is occupied with going to London after his wife! None of the servants, save Florence, will take my side.

After the housekeeper and maid left, Georgiana found it a simple feat to slip out of the manor dressed as Florence, sporting a low brimmed bonnet that showed little of her face. She hurried down a rear staircase and out the back door without notice, quickly making her way to the woods at the end of the drive. There, she waited for one of the young grooms who was enamoured of Florence. He had been persuaded some time ago to bring a horse to that particular spot whenever Florence needed to deliver a message to Lady Susan. Never questioning the maid's need for secrecy, when he was notified that she would need a mount in the morning, he made sure to oblige her. He appeared shortly after Georgiana.

"I see you have another letter to deliver," he said with a smile.

Georgiana dropped her head. "Hmmm," was all she said in answer, for she worried that he might realise she was not Florence.

If he wondered why Florence did not reply to his friendly overtures with her usual lively banter, he kept it to himself as he helped her into the saddle. "There! You are ready to go."

"Thank you," Georgiana murmured so low that he could barely hear her before she hit the horse with her riding crop.

"You are welcome," the young man answered to no one in particular, since horse and rider were already too far from him to hear.

As he watched her kick the stallion into a gallop, however, he made a telling observation. *Florence has never ridden so effortlessly before.* Scratching his head in puzzlement, he made his way back to the stables.

So it was that while William and Richard were saying their goodbyes in the foyer, Georgiana was already galloping toward Monthaven Manor.

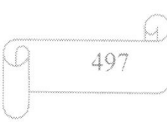

The foyer

"Please let us hear from you as soon as you reach London," Joseph Fitzwilliam cautioned, looking from one of his nephews to the other.

Olivia echoed his words. "We cannot help but be concerned, since you have not completely recovered from your ordeal, Fitzwilliam. Moreover, we will worry about Elizabeth until we know she, too, is well."

"Do not fret," Richard urged. "I will see that Darcy does not overtax himself."

Just then Mr. Walker came rushing towards them. "Sir!" he said loudly enough to interrupt their conversation. "A maid just found this note on your desk when she went in to clean the study."

Walker, who was by now as pale as a ghost, held the missive out to his employer with a shaky hand. Plainly visible on the outside, in large print, were the words: Private and Confidential, Fitzwilliam Darcy. Taking the paper, William observed that there was no return address and, though it was folded, it had not been sealed.

The butler declared, "It was not delivered with the regular post or by special messenger."

William realised that meant only one thing—someone in the household had to have placed it on his desk. He and Richard exchanged guarded looks.

William said louder than necessary, "I shall retire to my study." More quietly, he instructed the housekeeper and butler, "Will you please assemble all the servants in their dining room for a review of rules, or whatever subject you see fit. I want you to see if any are missing without them knowing what has happened."

As they rushed to gather all the servants below stairs, William motioned for his family to stay where they were. After a minute, starting with the rooms on the right, he peered into each door down the hallway. Realising what he was doing, Richard did the same on the other side. Eventually they returned to the foyer, and William tilted his head toward his study. Silently everyone filed into that room. When the door was closed, he even pulled the drapes.

"Please be seated," he said in a whisper. "In case anyone is listening, I suggest we converse quietly. It must appear that I have shared this letter with no one."

Everyone sat down as William opened the note and silently began to read. Almost immediately alarm filled his eyes, and he closed them tightly. When they opened again, he slammed a fist on the table causing everything to rattle. "Someone has taken Elizabeth, Charles and the servants."

Richard grabbed the missive from his fingers. "May I?" When there was no answer, he began to read the unsigned note aloud.

Mr. Darcy,
If you wish to see your wife, your friend and your servants again unharmed, you will follow these instructions to the letter. Gather all your family jewels in a small satchel, along with all the currency you have on hand. Do not try to deceive me. I am familiar with what should comprise the treasures of a family of such repute and the amount of money usually kept on hand at an estate the size of Pemberley.
I have enclosed a map showing where you are to bring the ransom. Come via horseback, alone and unarmed. Be forewarned, if you thwart me

by coming in force, your wife will be the first one killed.

Though he was attempting to appear calm for his aunt's sake, William shivered as fear gripped his heart.

Olivia's face had become completely devoid of colour. "Lord, help us all."

Joseph moved to stand beside his wife's chair, placing a hand on her shoulder to comfort her. "What are your thoughts, Fitzwilliam?"

"I... I must do as they say and go alone. I cannot risk anything happening to Elizabeth. I could never live with myself if she were harmed. Nor do I wish anything to happen to Charles or the servants."

"But there is no guarantee that this blackguard will not kill you all!" Richard declared a little too loudly before whispering. "Forgive me. I can barely keep quiet in the face of such evil." He examined the map. "Let me see if I can make sense of this."

Holding it up first one way then another, he whispered too loudly, "Whoever drew this is an amateur. The map has too little information. There are many small roads that are not shown between Lambton and the highway on which you are to turn east. I travelled that road and I do not recall an estate where indicated. How is one to find something so obscure?"

"I will find it, for I must."

"Well, I have no intention of letting you go alone, Darcy," Richard retorted. "Whoever is holding Elizabeth is obviously mad. Coleridge, Harahan and I will follow, though we will stay far enough behind that Mrs. Darcy's captor will think you have followed his orders."

"I would rather do this alone," William murmured. "I fear that whoever took Elizabeth would not hesitate to kill her if they suspect I was followed."

"You realise that Richard is correct, do you not?" his uncle said. "If this blackguard has no intentions of letting you or the hostages live, and I cannot think he would be so generous as to leave you alive to pursue him, you will need help. And, I should like to be a part of that."

Immediately Richard spoke up, "No, Uncle! I appreciate your willingness, but believe me when I say we risk being discovered if there are too many of us."

Wisely, Joseph acquiesced.

William took a deep breath and let it go. "I could not live with myself if anything happened to—"

"I promise that they will not suspect we are following," Richard broke in. "I shall have Mr. Miller use a distinct horseshoe on Zeus. Just make sure to keep to the mud along the road when possible and I shall be able to track you. I have trailed many an unsuspecting person during my time in the service," Richard stated with confidence.

William concurred reluctantly, and Richard asked, "When will you leave?"

"I do not want Elizabeth held a moment longer than necessary. I shall leave as soon as it can be arranged."

"Fine. I shall have Coleridge and Harahan leave now for the cemetery at Lambton. An hour later, I shall announce that I am riding into Lambton and will meet them there. I suggest you wait at least an hour after I leave before setting out. That will give us time to find a spot on the road toward London to wait for you. After you pass, we will follow you at a safe distance. With any luck, if the spy or spies are still at Pemberley, they will think that you are going to meet the assailant alone."

"How will I know that you are following?"

"That is not for you to worry about. Just trust me."

William was in a daze, for memories were busy at his heart—Elizabeth on their wedding day, delivering the Becker's child and giving herself to him at his mother's cottage. Richard reached out to grip his shoulder before giving it a squeeze.

"Do not be anxious, Cousin. Once you are captured, whoever has Elizabeth will be too busy to suspect that you were trailed at so great a distance. With the Lord's help, everyone will be freed unharmed."

Aunt Olivia stood and hurried over to embrace William, then pulled back to look him in the eye. "Remember 'Call upon Me in the day of trouble: I will deliver thee.' [18] God will not fail you if you trust in Him, Fitzwilliam."

"I shall cling to that promise," William replied sombrely. Then he crossed to a bookshelf against the wall, moved a book and pulled a lever. A panel in the bookshelves swung open. "Please leave through this passage which leads to the library. Richard will show you how to exit on the other end."

Everyone did as instructed, and soon William was alone. Steeling himself, he left the study to find his housekeeper and butler. As he walked he whispered a fervent prayer.

Dear God, all I ask is that you keep Elizabeth and the others safe. Give me another chance to be the husband that she deserves. Please!

※

Monthaven Manor

Going through the woods instead of the main road added several miles to Georgiana's journey. Nonetheless, rather than chance being seen by someone who might tell her brother, she was content with having taken the longer route. Smiling broadly when she reined the horse to a stop at the edge of a pasture where Monthaven Manor shone in the distance, she allowed herself to relax and take in the magnificent view.

She was just about to kick her mount into a trot again, however, when she realised that from this vantage point she could clearly see the back terrace. Several servants were scurrying in and out of the door, placing trays on a wrought-iron table where two people sat—Lady Susan and Lord Attaway! Instantly, an idea occurred to Georgiana.

Would it not be a great joke to suddenly appear whilst they are eating? They would never expect me to arrive so early, especially unannounced and dressed as Florence.

Certain that her plan would entertain, Georgiana dismounted and tied her mount to a tree. Picking her way first through a small orchard on the border of one of the gardens, she forced herself not to giggle with anticipation. When at last she entered the garden itself—one fashioned after an untamed wilderness—she easily stayed hidden behind the many shrubs and trees. At last standing at the edge of a manicured lawn that led to the terrace, she was stunned to realise that she could hear their conversation remarkably well. And, when her name was mentioned by Lord Attaway, she blushed.

"I do not care what Fitzwilliam says," he pronounced boldly, "I will marry Georgiana with his blessing or without it."

Her heart swelled at his declaration; yet, it fell just as quickly with his next words.

"I do not intend to let thirty thousand pounds slip through my fingers, even if I have to marry that foolish chit to get it!"

"If you had played your cards right, you would already be engaged to that whining child with his blessing. But, no, you had to insult him instead."

"I will not be browbeaten by Darcy! I shall retire my gambling debts with her dowry and then solicit his help to pay Gracehill Park's debts after our first child is born. I have no doubt that he will lend me whatever funds are necessary to keep the estate solvent after she delivers a child—if only to prevent his future niece or nephew from suffering along with me."

"You better hope that stupid girl agrees to marry you, otherwise, the money I promised will not be forthcoming."

"She will!" Attaway exclaimed. "You shall have no excuse to default on your pledge."

"I am still not certain that you have convinced her. I have seen very little support from her in my quest to secure Fitzwilliam!" Susan said equally as vociferous. Then she sighed heavily. "More to the point, if Andrew and George fail in this attempt to rid Pemberley of Eliza Bennet, I fear I may never be Mrs. Fitzwilliam Darcy, whether Georgiana supports me or not."

"Ridding Pemberley of Mrs. Darcy was not my task. Our bargain was that I have Georgiana fall in love with me and sway her towards your viewpoint," Matthew proclaimed as he stood. "I have done all that was asked of me, and I expect you to honour our agreement."

With that pronouncement, he threw his serviette down on the table and stalked back into the house. The back door slammed behind him just as a cup thrown by Lady Susan hit its mark. The china shattered when it hit the door, causing a maid to rush out to see what precipitated the noise. Surveying the damage, she returned inside to fetch a broom.

At first, Georgiana was too shocked to move, and it was only after their opinion of her began to sink in that her illusions crumbled. Collapsing to the ground, her constraint was excruciating. Holding back the threatening tears, all that she could think of was to get away.

Suddenly Lady Susan began shouting, and servants began to scamper in and out of the manor. The door continuously slammed in their hurry to comply with her wishes, and the racket gave Georgiana the opportunity to hurry back to her mount. Finding the stallion grazing just where she left him, she rode back into the wooded area she had emerged from only minutes before.

All the while that she galloped to Pemberley, the many lies that she had believed played over in her mind, and her tears would not stop. By the time she reached the manor house, she knew how foolish she had been to side with Lady Susan, especially against her brother. Leaving the horse where the groom could retrieve it, she found the house curiously empty of servants as she slipped back into her rooms. She had no way of knowing the drama that was playing out below in the servants' dining room and William's study.

Georgiana's Bedroom

When Georgiana entered her bedroom, she found Florence asleep in a chair. At her entrance, the maid jumped up, babbling almost senselessly.

"Oh, Miss Darcy, you startled me! I thought Mrs. Reynolds had come to check on you! What is the matter? Why have you returned? I though you would be halfway to Gretna Green by now."

"So Mrs. Reynolds does not know that I was missing?"

"No one knows." Noting the expression on her mistress' face, Florence became uneasy. "Are you well? You look as though you have seen a ghost."

Georgiana forced a faint, quivering smile. "I shall not be marrying Lord Attaway, after all." Then in an anguish of sharp and penetrating remorse, she broke down, sobbing, "Just today I learned that he is not trustworthy!"

Stony indifference marked Florence's attitude, for she was greatly disappointed. It had been her desire that Georgiana marry and take her away from Pemberley. Still, to cover her displeasure, she feigned sympathy by patting her back.

"Please do not despair. You are Georgiana Darcy! Lord Attaway is only the first in a long line of men who will offer for you. I dare say that you shall meet someone that you favour even more."

"I... I agree. I shall simply have to forget him and move on with my life."

"Forgive my curiosity, but will rejecting Lord Attaway mean breaking all ties with Lady Susan too?"

Georgiana lifted her chin resentfully, recalling how the woman she had once called her best friend had disparaged her. "It will, and I shall not miss her company one bit. I also learned today that she is just as untrustworthy as her cousin."

"I am so sorry that you were hurt by their deception," Florence murmured insincerely. "What are your plans now?"

"I... I have damaged my relationship with my brother, so I have no choice but to reside with my aunt and uncle, if they will have me."

Florence's demeanour darkened and she became silent. She had no wish to reside under Lady Matlock's scrutiny. Instantly, her mind flew to the prospect of finding another lady's maid position. Noticing that Florence had grown quiet, Georgiana reached out to take her hand.

"Do not worry, Florence. I shall always want you with me wherever I go."

Florence forced a smile. *Little consolation for all the trouble you have caused!* Aloud, she replied, "If I am not needed, I think I shall go to my room. I got little sleep while I waited to be discovered in your place."

"Of course," Georgiana answered. "You must be exhausted. I know that I

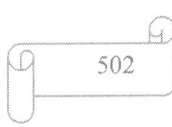

am. I intend to rest as well. Perhaps afterward I shall be able to think more clearly."

Both women tried to sleep, though neither found any rest because of all that played on their minds.

Outside of Briarwood Manor

The overgrowth of small trees and weeds around the former guard post proved a great help in disguising the presence of Wickham and his friends. However, it provided a hiding place for snakes, mice and bugs of all kind as well. Having been crammed into the small space for the better part of eight hours, tempers were beginning to flare amongst the group intent on capturing any ransom that Darcy might gather.

"If I get bitten by one more spider, I shall go back to Lambton and forget all about the money!" Pate growled. "I have not slept a wink since we got here, for I am afraid to lie down on the floor with all these creatures."

"You! Afraid of a few spiders?" George chided. "I thought you were tougher than that."

"Spiders I do not fear so much, though I hate being bitten, but snakes are another thing altogether. Besides, I have not seen you sleep on the ground either."

"No, and you will not. I do not intend to rest until this is over. Darcy should have been notified by now and knowing him as well as I do, he will not dally. He could appear at any time!"

"Let us hope he does," Andrew sighed. "I have to agree with Pate about the snakes, and it is hot as blazes in this godforsaken shack."

Duke spoke up. "Aye, it is hot. I have drunk all my water and half a bottle of wine already."

"You had better slow down," Denny declared. "None of us are leaving until this is finished."

Duke glared at him. "You cannot make us stay."

"I can make certain that you do not leave," Denny retorted. "You wanted to be part of this job, and you will see it finished. That has always been our rule."

Pate and Duke exchanged glances, but neither felt brave enough to answer. Seeing the tension that was mounting, Andrew reached into his sack.

"Here. Have some of my water, and sit on the bucket next to the wall. Rest until Darcy arrives."

Pate hesitated for only a second before grabbing the water and taking his place against the wall.

Pemberley
The stables

There was little fanfare when William left Pemberley to meet the rogue who had kidnapped Elizabeth. Exiting the front door, he walked resolutely down the steps to his waiting stallion. Only Mr. Walker came to see him off, for he carried the satchel that held almost every jewel the Darcy family had accumulated through the years, as well as nearly a thousand pounds that had been in the safe. As William took the bag from the butler and hung it over the saddle, he met the eyes of his faithful servant.

"Thank you, Walker," he called as he kicked Zeus into a trot and then a gallop when he reached the long drive.

As he rode toward Lambton, William recalled what Mrs. Reynolds and Mr. Walker had told him after the meeting with the servants. Two were missing, a footman named Barrows and a maid named Molly. Oddly enough, they had been under scrutiny for their propensity to talk privately in remote places in the house. Now, it appeared that they were the chief suspects.

While the notion that his servants may have been spying on his family sunk in, Mrs. Reynolds informed him of her suspicions regarding Georgiana's maid, Florence. Telling him what the other maids had witnessed and what she had seen for herself, she insisted that she had put off telling him when he was injured, resolving to share that information after he was much improved. Having no time or inclination to deal with Florence's behaviour at present, William declared that he would talk with her after Elizabeth and the others were safely home.

As he rode steadily toward the woman he loved with all his heart, it took all his strength not to crumble under the awareness that this whole debacle could turn out very badly. Remembering his aunt's admonition to trust God, he put his mind to work quoting all the promises in scriptures that he could remember.

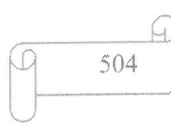

Briarwood Manor
Elizabeth's bedroom

A day as monotonous and colourless as the last greeted Elizabeth and Betsey upon awakening and an air of deep gloom still pervaded the room. When the housekeeper appeared to declare that the master wished Elizabeth to join him in the breakfast room, the request was met with coldness. She declined. When a tray was brought up later, she proceeded to eat with Betsey as usual, and everything seemed calm… for a while.

Nearing noon, though, the door to the bedroom flew open, slamming against the wall, as Baron Acton stepped inside. That he would invade their privacy without knocking was disquieting, though Elizabeth determined he would not see her cower. Betsey, however, could not help but shudder at first sight of their captor's disfigurement.

"Mrs. Darcy," Baron Acton said, demonstrating his displeasure by a contemptuous sneer. "I requested that you dine with me last evening and you refused. Then this morning you refused to join me to break your fast."

"I have no desire to dine with my jailer."

His reply was swift and caustic. "I explained why you are here!" Then his lips parted in a forced smile as his voice softened. "Allow me to begin again. Mrs. Darcy, would you care to join me in the dining room for tea and refreshments? I wish to explain what is to happen when your husband comes."

Elizabeth eyes danced with malice. "Do you not mean *if* my husband comes?"

"Quite right. I meant to say *if he comes*." He held out his arm as though expecting her to comply.

Her heart fluttering with a vague terror, Elizabeth placed her hand on his outstretched arm. "I do wish to know your plans."

"I thought you would."

Betsey watched as he escorted her mistress out of the room, and the door closed behind them. Releasing a deep breath, she prayed, *Lord, save us from this madman.*

Briarwood's dining room

The baron, in an attempt to make a good impression, displayed an overabundance of silver, china and crystal upon an intricately woven, Belgian lace tablecloth gracing a mahogany dining table. Plates of exotic fruits, bowls of nutmeats and an array of cakes and biscuits competed for space amongst a choice of beverages—tea, coffee and lemonade. Nevertheless, the fare was not the only thing meant to impress, for this room depicted the sheer opulence of a once grand estate.

The thick carpet, unlike the rest of the house, was new. It was a stunning shade of blue that complimented the gold, green and blue accents of the cream-coloured Chinese wallpaper. A magnificent chandelier glistened from its place over the centre of the table, while four enormous portraits of bucolic scenes were centred on each wall.

Elizabeth was lost in studying them when the baron spoke, his lips loosening into an exultant smile.

"I see you approve."

This caused her to divert her eyes, though it was apparent that he expected an answer.

"I admit to being surprised. This room is such a contrast to the others."

"I had this one updated to my taste. I intend to do the rest of the house as well." He hesitated before adding, "Only, of late, I began to think I might want to seek a woman's opinion. The right woman would have an unlimited allowance to renovate the house and grounds as she wished."

Forebodings of dread possessed her, and Elizabeth's throat constricted. She regarded him stonily. Was he insinuating that she could be that woman?

Still, he rattled on. "Until lately, I had no intention of ever caring for another woman. Knowing you has changed my mind."

"We do not know one another, sir."

"Oh, but I do know you from the numerous reports of my servants. I began to admire you for keeping your marriage vows in spite of your husband's indifference. Most women would not have."

"You eavesdropped on personal conversations, yet you seem to feel superior?"

"I did what I had to do—first, to find out the truth about my injury and second, to protect you when I began to believe you were also in danger."

"I say again that I do not need protection from Fitzwilliam."

"You may change your mind. In any event, I want you to know that I am

extremely wealthy, and soon I will step back into my rightful place. I will inherit all of my godfather's wealth very shortly, as he is not well. Should you decide to leave Darcy, I can take care of you."

Elizabeth stared at him as though he were insane, though her mind raced with questions. If he favoured her, would this madman let William live if she pleaded for his life?

"Am I to understand that you care not what society thinks? If I left Fitzwilliam it would bring scandal and, as you have stated, you are only just now stepping back into your *rightful place*. Would that not be a detriment to regaining your place?"

"When I refer to my place, I am speaking of my wealth and rank, not propriety! All propriety has gotten me was nearly killed. I care not if the *ton* receives me ever again."

"Know this, I could never befriend anyone who would do Fitzwilliam harm."

"Never say never, my dear. See what he has to say regarding my accusations first, for you may find yourself stunned at the depth of his depravity."

"I am certain that it is you who will be enlightened."

"We could argue that point forever, but that is not why you are here. I wish you to know what will occur if Fitzwilliam comes." She nodded mutely. "He will be ushered into the front drawing room—the one in which we first met. There is an alcove to the left side, where a pianoforte used to be placed. A curtain divides that part from the rest of the room, and you will be sitting behind it. From there you will be able to hear everything. Of course, I will need to make certain that you cannot speak or make your presence known until I am ready. For that I apologize."

"So you mean to gag me and tie me to a chair?"

"Only of necessity, I assure you. Once Fitzwilliam answers all my questions, the gag will be removed, and you will be free to speak."

"May I ask what your intentions are?"

"You mean, do I intend to kill him?"

She blinked back threatening tears, her voice catching involuntarily as she murmured, "Ye… yes."

"I can truthfully say that I have not decided. At one point, I would have done so without giving it a thought. Now, due to your faith in him, it will depend upon his answers."

"You have to believe me. William is a good man who would never harm anyone intentionally."

"I hope he can convince me as strongly as he has convinced you."

"You must give him a fair chance to do so."

For a long moment the baron seemed to consider that. "I am giving him a fairer chance than I was given."

Chapter 47

Briarwood Manor

As William approached the place where the map indicated he was to deliver the ransom, he realised that he might have ridden straight past the drive if he had not caught sight of recent coach tracks on the shoulder of the road. Clearly created during the recent rain, they had hardened in the sunlight afterward, a silent testament to the fact that an estate did indeed exist on that side of the road. Pulling Zeus to a stop, he studied the overgrowth of vines, brush, trees and weeds which almost hid a once magnificent wrought-iron gate about fifty feet away. It stood open in invitation to a road so overrun with vegetation that it, too, was concealed. Nonetheless, he nudged Zeus in that direction.

If he sought proof that the drive had recently accommodated a heavy vehicle, deep ruts in the little gravel left were convincing enough. Plainly, wheels had sunk deep into mud, while small trees, weeds and shrubs were flattened in a band down the middle. Taking a deep breath of air and whispering another prayer, William kicked Zeus forward. He had gone no more than thirty yards, when he heard a horse whinny and looked to the left where a dilapidated guard shack was barely visible underneath a layer of vines. He had no time to consider what that meant, for immediately, he heard horses' hooves pounding the ground, and that brought his attention back to the drive. Four men came galloping towards him, so he held his hands up in surrender. Once they surrounded him, one of the men seized Zeus' reins, and they headed back down the drive. After about a half-mile, a red-brick manor house came into view. It appeared to be as neglected as the rest of the estate, for it was in dire need of paint, and what shutters were not missing hung precariously by a single hinge. William shuddered to think what Elizabeth had endured inside this dilapidated prison.

As soon as they came to a halt, William was pulled from Zeus, and his hands were tied behind him. With a man on either side, he was marched into the house. Trying to remember everything he saw along the way, William found it difficult, for the inside of the house was very dark. Ushered down a long hallway, he was shoved into a room, causing him to lose his balance. He hit the floor hard on his injured left shoulder, which caused him to groan in spite of his best efforts. Ignoring the pain, he forced himself to get back on his knees and was abruptly pulled to his feet again. It was just in time to see the satchel he brought handed to a man sitting in a large chair facing the opposite direction. A single candelabrum was brought forward, and the stranger proceeded to pour the contents of the bag on a table. William watched as various pieces of jewellery were selected for inspection before being placed back into the satchel. Next the cash was counted. He was about to demand to see Elizabeth when the stranger spoke.

"I am surprised! In truth, I did not expect you to bring the Darcys' most prized pieces."

William bristled at the insult. "I would give everything I own for Elizabeth. I love her."

"Oh, really?" The gentleman stood and turned to him, though he kept his face hidden in the shadows. What William could see clearly, though, was the pistol in his hand. "Not according to what I have been told. I have had spies in your service for almost a year, Mr. Darcy, so I know everything that has transpired since you wed Elizabeth."

William bristled at the use of his wife's Christian name, but vowed not to lose his temper. "I have given you all that you demanded! Now, let me see my wife!"

"Not just yet," the black-clad figure said, coming closer. Then he laughed. "How does it feel not to be in control?"

"It is not my favourite position from which to bargain."

The man guffawed. "Still the same after all these years, I see. At least you are honest regarding that one thing."

With a cold gaze of curiosity, William ventured warily, "Do I know you?"

"At one time, I considered you a close friend."

Suddenly, William recognised the voice. "Fletcher?"

"Lord Hartley to you."

"But, I thought you were—"

"Dead." Hartley finished, stepping into the light. Reflexively, William gasped at his appearance.

"Are you disappointed? After all, I am sure that a good deal of money went toward planning my demise. As you can see, it was not money well spent."

"Wha… what happened?"

"I escaped with my life, but not intact, as you have noted. I lost an eye, and one leg is now a bit shorter than the other, but I shall not bore you with all the gruesome details. What I brought you here to learn is why you conspired with my wife to kill me? Who carried out the actual assault? Was it you?"

"I would never—" William sputtered, angry to be accused of such evil.

"Let me tell you why I believe you are lying," Hartley interrupted. "When I first met Lady Susan, I fell deeply in love with her. I realised at the time that she was not in love with me, but I felt that, given the opportunity, I might be able to win her heart. Imagine my surprise when the summer after you and I graduated from university, she began to notice me. Of course, it was only after you had left for Scotland, but all the ladies were trying to catch your eye then, so I thought nothing of it. It was barely a month later that she hinted she would accept an offer if I felt inclined to make one. I was deliriously happy, and we wed in a few short weeks.

"I was just as pleased when only two months later she informed me that she was with child. When she delivered a boy at seven months, I accepted her explanation that the child was early." Hartley walked over to a liquor cabinet, poured a glass of brandy and tossed the contents down his throat. "I suppose I could not accept what was right before my eyes, for he weighed as much as a full-term babe. Nonetheless, as he neared his first birthday, I could no longer pretend that he was mine; for, in fact, he is the spitting image of you!"

"I did not father that child! I swear that I never bedded Lady Susan."

"That is a bit hard to accept, given that it was your name she called in her sleep, not mine, and the fact that she insisted on naming the boy William. Do you see my dilemma?"

"Forgive me, but I must be blunt. It was no secret that Lady Susan expected to be the next mistress of Pemberley. Even when she was a mere girl, she told all who would listen that I would marry her. However, she never held any allure for me."

"Never? I find that hard to believe. After all, you are a man, and she is a beautiful woman."

"I could have had many beautiful women."

"How well I know."

"Beauty was never my measure for felicity. After you were presumed dead, she renewed her friendship with my sister, and they became very close. Georgiana hinted that if I married Susan, it would help to mend our broken relationship, so it crossed my mind. Nevertheless, I quickly abandoned the idea when my cousin reminded me of something important."

"Your cousin?"

"Colonel Fitzwilliam." Hartley nodded so William continued. "When I spoke to him about Lady Susan, he was quick to remind me that she had always shared a peculiarly close relationship with George Wickham and my cousin, Andrew, both of whom I never trusted. Had she severed those relationships after she became an adult, I might have seen their familiarity as a childish mistake. As it was, I could not disagree with my cousin."

"And you know for certain that she is still close to both?"

"Until recently, I spoke often with Andrew as I had to manage his inheritance. He boasted of being in her company often, with and without George Wickham. I think he believed it would upset me to know they were all still good friends."

"How do I know you are not lying to save yourself?"

"Think, Fletcher! You lived with her long enough to know Susan better than anyone, and you stated that she was a part of the attempt on your life. I am not the *only* man the child favours. If Susan is as evil as you believe, she would have no trouble bedding Andrew or, I would submit, Wickham as well."

Hartley said nothing, quietly listening, so William continued. "I presume that the boy is Andrew's. Not being able to seduce me, it would likely have been Susan's plan to ensure the child looked like me. She has already tried to convince Georgiana that he is mine, for my sister confronted me with that lie just days ago. I assured her that I am not the father of that child, he is not my heir, and no court in England would hold that to be true!"

A strange noise caused William to glance at a curtain covering one side of the room. Instantly, Hartley sought to distract him.

"Whoever shot me did so from a distance of a hundred yards or more. Andrew was never *that* good a shot."

"George Wickham is, and he will do anything for a price."

Having begun to harbour tender feelings for Elizabeth, Hartley had hoped that today's confrontation would discredit her husband. Thus, he was not pleased that William's answers made sense. Irritated, he began waving the pistol about, and spying a tall, ceramic statue on a table across the room, he tilted his head, squinted his remaining eye and aimed at it. For some time, he held steady before slowly swinging the barrel of the gun around so that it was aimed at William. Eyes locked, neither man deigned to blink. At length, Hartley slowly lowered the weapon, and William let go of the breath he had been holding.

"You were always very persuasive, Darcy. Even at university, you could best most of the professors with decisive arguments for your point of view, but it does not follow that you are telling the truth. Rest assured that you have not yet convinced me of your innocence. In fact, I have many other questions in need of answers."

"Ask me anything, and I shall tell you the truth!"

"I wonder why, knowing your repulsive behaviour toward Elizabeth, you came here today. My abduction would have been the perfect opportunity to rid yourself of someone who inadvertently got in the way of your plans."

"My plans? Of what are you accusing me?"

"It is my contention that you and Susan were planning to marry after a proper year of mourning but, unluckily, you were compromised in Meryton and forced to marry Elizabeth. That would explain why you and she have been at odds from the beginning and why you sent her on to Pemberley while you stayed in London. Afterward, a convenient injury allowed you to claim no memory of her."

"That is absurd! I never plotted anything with Lady Susan and, sadly, the assault on my person was as valid as your own. As for marrying Elizabeth, I had fallen in love with her earlier when I stayed at Netherfield."

Hartley stalked toward William, halting when their faces were inches apart. He growled, "I find that hard to swallow. She was of little consequence—no dowry to speak of, no connections and certainly not of your rank. I cannot fathom the heir of Pemberley lowering his standards so drastically, especially knowing what your family would think."

William's eyes turned black, and as he lashed out at Hartley, his voice rose with indignation. "I did not consider marriage to Elizabeth as lowering my standards and my family's wishes have never held much weight. As to why I am here, she is *my wife*."

With this reprisal, those holding William extracted several fierce grimaces and groans by harshly twisting his arms until Hartley nodded for them to halt. Half choked by a rising fit of rage, William would not remain silent.

"I would have come for her even if I had not recovered my memory because it is my duty to protect her. Nonetheless, I happened to receive the

drawings of her in her wedding gown the evening after she had left, and those sketches caused my suppressed memories to flood back like a river. I was so overcome that I made plans to follow her to London. I wished her to know as soon as possible that I remembered everything. Your ransom note changed those plans."

"Or perhaps, after she left, you heard the whispers among the servants that she might be with child. You would not be the first man to want his child, if not his wife. And I have no problem saying that I firmly believe she left Pemberley because she had concluded that you did not want her and subsequently would not want the child."

"Once Elizabeth left for London, my aunt started to question her motive for going. Then, and only then, did she inform me that Elizabeth suspected she was carrying my child. But you can rely on this—I am not the kind of man to forsake her or the child, even if I never remembered our marriage."

"I find that too preposterous to believe! What is more, I do not think you can convince her of it, either." William started to reply, but Hartley stopped him, saying, "Wait!" Then motioning to a servant to pull back the curtain, he evinced his displeasure with a contemptuous sneer. "Explain it to your wife, not me."

By then William was barely attending to Hartley's words, for as the curtain was removed, he was stunned to see Elizabeth sitting in a chair. Even more jolting, the rope secured about her waist excellently showcased her slightly protruding stomach.

While the scarf over her mouth was being untied, he exclaimed, "Elizabeth!" Longing to go to her, he fought to shake off his guards but was unable.

"I have found your wife to be very intelligent, and unless you have a more credible explanation, she cannot help but agree with me that you are lying to secure the child."

Her throat dry and voice hoarse from being gagged, Elizabeth asked the questions that had drummed in her head and heart day and night. "Oh, Will! Is it true? Do you remember?"

"I remember everything, my darling, but most especially I recall my horrible conduct toward you after I was injured. I am so ashamed of my coldness towards you." William spoke with hurried eagerness, his expression one of supplication. "Please believe me when I say that I love you ardently, and I am deliriously happy to see the evidence of our child."

Her gaze searched his face for the truth and, once she was certain, she nodded. Tears began to stream down her face.

A pang of jealously mingled with scorn marked Hartley's next words. "Enough honey-coated drivel!" he roared. "Tell Elizabeth something that will convince her that you truly remember her and are not lying to get your way."

William's lips curled into a smile as his eyes caressed her face. Murmuring in a tone filled with the deepest devotion, he said, "First... Last... Only... Always."

"That is all?" Hartley demanded incredulously. "Four little words?"

"I had those sentiments inscribed on her wedding band," William answered.

Hartley crossed to where Elizabeth sat. Cutting the ropes that bound her, he lifted her left hand to examine the ring she wore. A bit too triumphantly, he crowed, "There is no such inscription. Perhaps you confused Elizabeth's ring with one you gave another."

"He is right," Elizabeth interrupted, her eyes encouraging William. "This is his mother's ring." Reaching for the chain around her neck, she pulled William's ring from its hiding place and addressed him. "After you no longer recognised me, I began to wear your ring next to my heart. I could not have borne it if you never remembered what inspired you to have the words engraved on my ring."

Hartley was enraged at her ready acceptance of Darcy's proof. "Why would you acquiesce so readily, Elizabeth? Ask him for more proof. Has he not given you plenty of reasons to doubt his love?"

"I never doubted that he loved me—in his heart. That is why I prayed continually that his memory would soon discover what his heart already knew. Today I am persuaded that it has."

Seeing the expressions that passed between the couple—the kind of devotion he would gladly have given his fortune to gain—Lord Hartley's resolve began to crumble. Unmistakably, the woman he had hoped to influence believed that Fitzwilliam was telling the truth. More significantly, it was plain that she loved her husband wholeheartedly.

It was at that moment that Hartley realised that he had never stood a chance of winning Elizabeth. In addition, he was unable to dismiss the niggling feeling that his old friend was not only being truthful about his marriage, he was innocent of conspiring to kill him. Against his heart's desire, Hartley conceded defeat.

"Cut him loose!"

Instantly, Elizabeth rose to run to William. His hands were loosed just in time to catch her as she fell into his embrace. Bringing his mouth to hers, he clung to her as though never meaning to let her go. Oblivious to Hartley, they kissed as lovers separated far too long.

Despondent at the blatant display of felicity, Hartley hobbled over to a chair, sat down and let go a ragged sigh. "Jealousy can do strange things to a man, Fitzwilliam, and I admit to being jealous of you since the first time I heard Susan call your name while she dreamt. When the resemblance between you and the boy became impossible to ignore, I willingly believed that you had betrayed me. And, after I was shot… well, I would see no villain but you. I suppose I shall now have to focus my revenge on Wickham. What a pity, for I took great pleasure in believing the worst of you." He laughed hollowly then was silent for a moment.

"At any rate, I owe you an apology for accusing you of assaulting me and for absconding with your wife." Hartley motioned for a servant to pour him another brandy. After taking a few sips, he added, "You must know that I truly believed I was saving Mrs. Darcy from possible death, else I would never have seized the coach."

"I appreciate that you were only trying to protect her," William replied cautiously.

"How can I ever make amends? Will you at least accept my apology?"

"I accept your apology. And, no doubt, you appreciate my desire to take Elizabeth home immediately."

"I understand," Hartley said. "You must do what is best for—"

There was the sound of scuffling in the hall, and events took a more sinister turn. Instantly, two men burst into the room with pistols drawn.

"No one move!" Wickham declared, smiling gleefully as he and Andrew interrupted the discussion. "We have more men, so do not underestimate our strength." To Hartley and his servants, he ordered. "Lay your weapons on the floor." Andrew recovered the guns, slipping them into his belt.

As they complied, William could do absolutely naught to protect Elizabeth but step in front of her to face his childhood nemesis.

"Darcy, always the gentleman!" Wickham mocked, pushing him aside. "Sorry, but your beautiful wife will have to stay in my sight, too."

Wickham motioned to the closest servant, tossing him a rope he held in his other hand. "You! Tie up everyone, and do not be slow about it."

As the servant hurried to comply, Wickham could not resist boasting to Hartley, who he had not recognised. "I cannot believe how easy this job has been. Andrew and I were going to kidnap Mrs. Darcy for a ransom, but you snatched her first. All we had to do was follow your dim-witted servants here and wait until Darcy came with the ransom. They were so intent upon seizing him today, that they never saw us coming. Once we entered the house, the few not here with you were gathered at a table in the kitchen. They were having a drink in celebration." He guffawed. "Methinks they celebrated too soon!"

"I suppose my servants are not seasoned blackguards like you, George!"

At the mention of his name, Wickham studied the other man intently. "Hartley, is it really you, old man? I have to say that you look nothing like I remember. If not for your voice, I would not have recognised you at all. Oh, but why would I? After all, I did my best to kill you." George laughed wryly. "At your wife's bidding, I might add.

"How ill-fated it is that you survived my first attempt, only to come face-to-face with me again. This time I shall do a more credible job, I assure you. And, afterward, I shall spread the news that all those who died at Briarwood lost their lives as a result of a kidnapping gone awry—a kidnapping that *you* instigated. Forevermore you will be remembered as a murderer—a man who staged his own demise in order to kill the one who had seduced his wife."

"George, you never mentioned killing anyone," Andrew said nervously, finally finding his voice. "You said we would take the ransom and sail from England."

Wickham turned around, waving his gun wildly. "It is necessary if we are to escape! I did not mention killing Darcy at Mason's Pass either, but I acted after you proved too timid. Since I must do all the dirty work, I suggest that you keep your mouth shut, and do as I say."

Andrew held up his hands as though acquiescing, so George turned back to bark at the servant who had just finished tying up everyone. "Come over here!"

As he came forward, George told Andrew, "Tie him up."

As Andrew complied, Wickham ordered everyone to sit on the floor. Then he walked over to Darcy, now seated next to Elizabeth. "So, old friend, how does it feel to know that all your money cannot buy you another minute of life?"

"Your grievance is with me, George. Why not settle our differences like gentlemen."

"With a duel? Do you think me a dullard? You can best any man with a sword and most everyone else with a pistol. No, I am too close to getting what I rightfully deserve to take that chance."

"Untie me then, and we can fight without weapons."

"And ruin my pretty face? I think not."

"You are truly a coward," William retorted.

Wickham hit him with his fist, bloodying his lip and bruising his jaw, while Elizabeth screamed for him to stop.

"You dare refer to me as a gentleman, though you have looked down on me all my life! You were the heir! You got the best of everything, while I was the lowly steward's son. Still, you resented the fact that your father loved me! He would have wanted you to treat me much better than you have. So, you can consider today repayment for not doing it."

Wickham reached out to tip Elizabeth's chin up so he could look in her eyes. "Alas, I do not have time to show you what a real man is, Mrs. Darcy. This sorry excuse for a man could never have satisfied a woman like you."

"Take your hands off her!" William ordered, only to be beaten again. In a rage, Wickham brought the gun to William's forehead. Elizabeth screamed, but he ignored her, taunting his nemesis instead.

"I ought to kill you first, but I think it will be more painful for you to see your precious wife die right before your eyes while you can do nothing to save her. Then, after her, it shall be your turn to die."

When Wickham turned the gun on Elizabeth, Hartley cursed. Praying fervently that he could be quick enough, William attempted to throw his body in front of her.

A shot rang out just before he pushed her to the floor, and William's heart stopped beating. When he opened his eyes, however, Elizabeth was looking up at him, unharmed. Suddenly, Wickham fell to the floor next to them. He had been shot in the back. As William glanced at Andrew, he was tossing an empty pistol to the floor and drawing another from his waistband.

"Do not get the idea that you are saved, Fitz! I mean to have the ransom. I do not hold to murdering people of great consequence unless it is absolutely necessary, but I will kill anyone who tries to stop me."

He walked over to pull William to his feet. "I am afraid that you will have to come with me, Cousin. Richard will never risk trying to stop me if your life hangs in the balance."

"No!" Elizabeth pleaded as he dragged William toward the satchel, grabbed it and headed to the door. "Please, take me, not him."

William immediately objected and Andrew guffawed. "Seeing you so besotted, is too entertaining, Fitz." Then he addressed Elizabeth. "I apologise, Mrs. Darcy, but you are not as valuable a commodity as your husband. Do not worry, though. If he and Richard do as I say, he shall return to you unharmed in due time."

Straightaway, Andrew went out of the room with William, while those left behind tried to free themselves from the ropes. Suddenly, gunfire outside the house caused everyone to halt. From the number of shots, it was obvious that many weapons were involved. Elizabeth began to weep, terrified of what it meant for William.

Richard Fitzwilliam, Patrick Harahan and Dale Coleridge had found it a simple matter to follow William to Briarwood. They had watched as Wickham, Andrew and their associates followed him and his captors to the manor house. Though outnumbered, they were confident that they could make up for the deficit with their expertise—each being an expert marksman.

When they found Denny, Pate and Duke waiting at the front steps of Briarwood with a coach and extra horses, it was too good an opportunity to let pass. Each man took aim at a target chosen beforehand. Pate and Duke were killed outright while Denny, who was mortally wounded, tried to run. He fell before he could reach the coach. It was at that moment, that Andrew exited the house with William in tow and, seeing everyone dead, pulled his hostage back inside, hiding behind the entrance door.

Certain that Richard was behind the assault, Andrew shouted, "Stop shooting or I shall kill him, Richard! I swear it! Let me leave with Fitz, and I promise he will come to no harm. I shall let him go the day I sail for the Americas."

"You have yourself a bargain," Richard replied. "Do not hurt Darcy, and I shall see that you live to sail from England."

"Excellent! Come out where I can see you!" Richard nodded to the Bow Street Runners, and they all stepped into a clearing with guns in the air. "Throw down your weapons," Andrew ordered. Everyone hesitated, so he added, "Now!"

With Richard's nod of consent, the men did as he asked and watched powerlessly as Andrew came down the steps, pushing William ahead of him with the gun to his back.

"Back up," Andrew directed. Each man took a few steps back. "Do not play with me. Back up!"

Richard and his men complied, and as Darcy and his cousin reached the weapons, Andrew dropped all of the guns into the satchel. "Thank you, gentlemen," he exclaimed.

Now he motioned for William to mount a horse. Though his hands were tied, he easily took hold of the horse's mane, and with one fluid motion, was sitting on the animal. Andrew followed suit and, grabbing the reins of Darcy's horse, began to gallop down the drive.

"What are we to do now?" Coleridge asked.

"You and Harahan will stay here and see to Mrs. Darcy and the others," Richard replied, pulling a derringer from his boot. "I plan to go after Darcy alone. One man will be harder to spot."

"How do you know that Mrs. Darcy is still alive?"

"My cousin would give his life to protect Elizabeth. If he is alive, she is alive. Now, see to everyone else."

Richard was mounting Titan when a shot rang out. The sound of a rifle came from the direction William and Andrew had just taken, so he instantly raced down the drive. In no time at all, he reached the spot where his cousin still sat his horse, while Andrew lay on the ground. Jumping off his mount, Richard pulled William from his, shielding his body with his own as he guided him to the nearby cluster of trees for safety.

"Darcy? Are you injured?"

"I am not."

Reaching into his boot, Richard removed a knife, which he used to cut the ropes binding his cousin. Meanwhile, several men surrounded the scene, among them Lord Warren, who still held his hunting rifle. Seeing who it was, William and Richard stepped out.

"I apologise if I frightened you," Warren said. "I had a clear view of Andrew, and since it was apparent that he was holding Fitzwilliam hostage—his hands being tied while Andrew held the reins—I took the shot."

"What are you doing here?" Richard asked as he rolled Andrew over to discover that he had been shot between the eyes.

"I have been tracking Andrew for some time, and I realised that he was also being followed by others—Bow Street Runners, I had been told. I assumed Fitzwilliam had them on his trail and if I followed them, they would lead me to Andrew. Fortuitously, I was right."

"I just wish Andrew's choices had been different. He had all that he needed to succeed," William said.

"Yet he allowed jealousy and greed to rule his life," Richard declared.

"And this is the result," William added. Then he returned to his horse and, after mounting, addressed Lord Warren. "Whatever your reason for being here, I am indebted to you."

"I was determined to settle my family's business, hopefully, on a field of honour. However, finding Andrew in the midst of more evil, I am pleased to have settled it in this manner. At least today there is one less rogue left to prey on innocent young women."

"I cannot disagree with that," William answered sombrely. Then he tilted his head towards Briarwood Manor. "If you will excuse me, I must see to my wife."

"I am pleased to hear you say that, Darcy," Lord Warren exhorted. "A man's most valuable possessions are his wife and his children. My own dear father taught me that. They must come first for, without them, true happiness is unattainable."

"How well I know," William whispered.

Then he kicked his horse into a gallop, eager to return to the one who had taught him that truth.

On the road to Pemberley

Having spent the whole ordeal locked in a room at Briarwood, their legs and hands bound except when they ate, Bingley and Darcy's servants had continually feared for their lives. Their anxiety had increased substantially after the shot that killed Wickham echoed throughout the manor, and when a short while later footsteps came down the hall and stopped at their door, the tension became unbearable. Nonetheless, simultaneous sighs of relief were released once the door opened to reveal Coleridge and Harahan standing without. Afterward, they had joined Elizabeth and her maid in the dining room, while Hartley and what servants remained at the manor were secured in another room. There, the Bow Street Runners were on guard until it was decided what would be their lot.

Now that Bingley was on his way back to Pemberley in the Darcys' comfortable coach, he was painfully aware that if he and the maid were not present, his friend and future sister would likely be engaged in more pleasant pursuits. As it was, all William could do was pull his wife into his lap and hold her tightly to his chest while the coach raced home. The steady sway of the vehicle had finally lulled Elizabeth to sleep, leaving William free to kiss the top of her head, while his fingers slid softly back and forth across her back reassuringly.

Fully cognizant that he was intruding, Bingley had considered taking one of the horses back to Pemberley before remembering that Betsey would be occupying the coach as well. He glanced to the end of the seat where the maid was asleep and snoring softly. Looking back to William, a frown formed. The events of the last few days weighed heavily on his mind, and seeing that everyone else was sound asleep, Bingley took the opportunity to speak.

"I am sorry, Darcy."

William's eyes flicked from Elizabeth to Bingley. Noting his friend's strained expression, he said, "I fail to understand. There is no need to apologise."

"I should have protected Elizabeth. I should never have let us be taken."

"Charles, there was nothing you could have done to prevent what happened, as evidenced by the wound on the back of your head. Elizabeth said that she thought you were dead when she saw you lying in the mud."

"I should have realised we were under attack, but I did not. If I had been more observant—"

"Nonsense!" William declared a bit too loudly, making Elizabeth stir. More quietly he added, "Nothing would have changed if you had been aware from the beginning... except that you might have been killed." Then William smiled slightly. "I know that you would give your life to protect Elizabeth, and that is sufficient to satisfy me."

Bingley nodded, sank back into the comfortable seat and smiled. Darcy was right. He would have died protecting Elizabeth if it had come to that. Feeling much better, he leaned into the corner of the coach and closed his eyes. And, for the first time since they had been taken hostage, he slept.

Chapter 48

Pemberley
That same day

Midnight found William and Elizabeth wrapped in a sheet and lying in each other's arms on one of the upholstered chaises occupying their balcony. The heat created by their earlier activities, as well as the summer temperatures, had made staying in their bed insupportable. Thus, about an hour after they had retired, William gathered his wife in his arms and carried her out into the cooler night air where once more they engaged in the privileges of married love. Having relations on the balcony was nothing new, for they had often done so before his injury but, given all that had transpired, sharing love under the stars had proved magical.

Afterward, completely satiated and wide awake, they lay on their backs searching for Sirius amongst scores of luminous stars spread across the dark velvet expanse of sky. Elizabeth had suggested the search in hopes of keeping William from dwelling on the earlier events of the day.

Afterward, completely satiated and wide awake, they lay on their backs searching for Sirius amongst scores of luminous stars spread across the dark velvet expanse of sky. Elizabeth had suggested the search in hopes of keeping William from dwelling on the earlier events of the day.

"There it is!" she cried, pointing to the brightest star in the sky. "And there is the Plough of Ursa Major, which means the North Star is… here! I wager that I can locate another constellation before you do."

William could not hold back a chuckle, and it caused Elizabeth to tip her head back and look up at him. He was so devastatingly handsome that she smiled in spite of wanting to feign insult.

"What is so amusing? That I located it first?"

"Not at all. I am amused and amazed, *Mrs. Darcy*, to find that a young woman from the tiny village of Meryton knows so much about astronomy—not to mention literature, foreign languages, botany and heaven knows what else—all without the benefit of a governess."

"Did you and Caroline Bingley not discuss this very subject while I stayed at Netherfield?" William groaned, causing her to stifle a giggle. "If I remember correctly, in your opinion, an accomplished woman would likely know all of that and more."

"Must you remind me of my arrogance?"

This elicited a full-out laugh from Elizabeth. She teased, "Well, I must say that your superiority is still showing a tad."

"Why is that?"

"Because you pronounced amazement at the extent of my education. Having no son, my father took it upon himself to teach me all the subjects he would have taught an heir. Happily, I was a voracious reader, and I loved to learn. Howbeit, I did have my favourites—literature and astronomy."

"Alas, another reminder of my failure to see what was right before my eyes."

"I do not understand."

"Only months ago, I stood in this same spot, staring at the same stars and questioning God." He chuckled. "I am mortified to admit it now, but I was angry, and I demanded to know why He had not answered my prayers."

"What prayers were those?"

"After university, the majority of my friends were blessed to marry and start families. I envied them. Ever since then, I prayed that He would send a woman I could love—one I would be proud to have as the mother of my children. In hindsight," he added wistfully, "when God answered, I was too blind to see it. He sent you to Netherfield because you were the perfect match for me."

Elizabeth laughed. "I am far from perfect!"

"For me you are," William said. Then he leaned in to give her a gentle kiss.

Tenderly, she examined the bruises on his face and the split in the corner of his mouth, all inflicted by Wickham. "Does it hurt terribly?"

"Not enough to keep me from kissing you." He proceeded to demonstrate.

"I am glad," she sighed. Then she settled back into the crook of his arm and began anew to study the sky. "Now, let me see if I can best you again by finding Lyra first."

A strong breeze brought the scent of roses wafting up from the garden below, and William's thoughts flew to the one who had planted them—his mother. That brought to mind the night their marriage had begun in earnest at her cottage. At once, recently unearthed memories began to play across his mind as though scenes on a stage—delivering the tenant's child, picnicking at the pond, splashing in the water, and making love in the secret garden. Unfortunately, the events of the past few days intruded, reminding him that he had almost lost her. Incapable of focusing on the sky any longer, his gaze returned to Elizabeth.

Unaware of being examined, she looked perfectly angelic—her kissable lips having settled into an innocent pout as she searched the skies. Love flooded him, and he turned to her. Cupping her face with one hand, he murmured hoarsely, "I shall never be able to put into words how deeply I love you, Elizabeth."

At once his fingertips began a slow trickle from her face to her neck, across her décolletage and down to her breasts, before coming to rest on her abdomen. "Nor can I explain how overjoyed I am that you are carrying my child."

"I understand," Elizabeth murmured. "At times, our love is so overpowering that I am unable to find words to express it myself."

"I cannot believe that in all this tumult I failed to ask when our child will be born."

"If I have figured correctly, it will be the end of February or the beginning of March. According to Aunt Olivia, I shall know more precisely once I feel the quickening."

"My mother's birthday was the third day of March." His voice rose along with his excitement. "Mayhap the babe will wait until then!"

Elizabeth chuckled. "I believe that he will come when he is ready, birthday or no."

"He?"

"I am certain that I am having a boy."

His eyes twinkled as both dimples cut deeply into his face. "Are you a clairvoyant?"

"No," she said with a giggle. "But I listened often enough when Mrs. Harris explained the signs to expectant mothers—whether they were carrying a boy or a girl."

"Pray share them with me."

"Many signs will not be evident until later, such as how I carry the child—whether low or high. That being said, I have not felt sick at my stomach as most carrying girls do at this stage. I have had more headaches, my feet are colder than normal, and my hair is shinier whilst my skin is dryer. Not to mention that my stomach has already increased a little. There are more recorded in my notebook."

"I am astounded," William said. "But, know this. I care not whether our child is a boy or girl, only that it is healthy and, needless to say, that you are in good health during and after your confinement."

"Do you not wish for an heir?"

"God willing, an heir will come. But Pemberley is not entailed to the male line, so do not fret about birthing a son."

"That is good to know, but I assure you," Elizabeth patted her stomach, "this is a boy."

William slid down until he was able to lay his head on her stomach. "I cannot wait to meet you, little one."

In a flash, the desire to make love overruled his previous vow to let her rest. "Elizabeth, I long to love you again," he murmured, the tone of his voice now velvety with longing. "However, I would not overtax you. If you are too tired, just say—"

A finger against his lips halted his entreaty. Elizabeth's eyes were limpid, her beauty softened by an air of languor. "I want you, too."

His heart was pounding so hard that the blood thrumming though his ears made it difficult to hear her answer, but he was able to read her lips. He captured them eagerly, and Elizabeth responded with equal intensity, extracting a groan of pleasure from him. He murmured words of love and devotion as they joined, and what began as a slow rhythm progressed into lovemaking as feverishly as before, both reaching fulfilment swiftly. Breathless, William collapsed and quickly rolled onto his back.

Once he was able to speak, he gasped, "Sweetheart, you are the only woman who can make my heart stand still."

Smiling mischievously, Elizabeth ruffled his hair. "I think your heart has been standing still a great deal tonight."

"You minx!" he exclaimed, running his fingers across her ticklish abdomen. He stopped when she pleaded for him to and he kissed her tenderly.

As both recovered, Elizabeth began to chuckle. "Would you believe that I once told Jane that I would marry *only* for the deepest love, and for that reason I was likely to end up an old maid? I remember feeling so mature and clever. In hindsight, had I known of the bliss to be found in your arms, I would never have said such a thing."

William nuzzled her hair, placing a kiss there. "I once stunned Richard by saying that I had concluded that happiness in marriage was highly overrated. So you see, we are both guilty of speaking glibly about things of which we had no experience."

"I can only conclude that our marriage was truly a match made in heaven," Elizabeth declared, "for we made so many mistakes in the beginning."

"Given the gulf between us when we married, God's hand had to have been in it."

"That is a comforting thought."

"Very comforting."

They were both silent for a time before William spoke.

"Tomorrow will be another day filled with difficult decisions. So I propose that you close your eyes and try to sleep. I promise not to disturb you again."

"The question is whether you will be able to sleep? I know that your cousin's death weighs heavily on you, even if he brought it on himself."

"You know me well," William said. Taking a deep breath he let it go. "If I have learned one thing from you, it is to remember the past only as it gives me pleasure. So when those thoughts come, I shall replace them with memories of us."

Elizabeth brushed a soft kiss across his mouth. "I am glad. Sleep well, my darling husband."

"And you, my love."

Waiting until her breath began a rhythmic pattern, William tucked the sheet tighter about Elizabeth, drew her into his arms and closed his eyes. Given all that they experienced that day, it was not long until he drifted to sleep as well.

Tonight his dreams were of a different kind. He was chasing a small boy with dark curls and fine brown eyes through the gardens of Pemberley. Whenever he came close to capturing the child, Elizabeth would appear just ahead, and the boy would run into her arms. Then, amidst peals of laughter, the three of them would hug each other tightly.

Though the dream repeated throughout the night, William was oblivious to the fact that each time it did, he smiled in his sleep.

The next day
On the balcony

The sun was not yet up when William woke. Elizabeth was still soundly

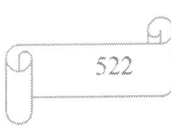

sleeping, so he carried her back into the bedroom, where he laid her on the bed and covered her with the counterpane. While he was accomplishing that, she roused slightly.

"Will?" she murmured groggily.

"Shhh, sweetheart," he said, planting a kiss on her forehead. "Try to go back to sleep. It is early, and you and the babe need rest. I shall be back in an hour or so, and we shall break our fast together."

"Come back," was all she managed to utter before slipping back into the arms of Morpheus.

Entering his dressing room, he found Adams already laying out his clothes. There was plenty of warm water in the basin, and William proceeded to wash and then dress for the day. Before long, he was on his way downstairs.

Mr. Walker was crossing the foyer when he spied the master descending the grand staircase. He waited at the bottom until William met him there.

"Sir, Colonel Fitzwilliam asked me to inform you that he is in the dining room."

"What time did he return last night?"

"It was after midnight. I waited up to be sure that he returned."

"Thank you for your diligence. You certainly did not have to trouble yourself."

"It was no trouble. I am quite fond of that young man."

William patted the elderly butler's shoulder. "I know."

"Besides, I was not without company. Captain Fitzwilliam stayed up too."

Shaking his head, William said, "That does not surprise me either." Then he glanced toward the dining room. "Is anyone else awake yet?"

"Not as far as I know, sir."

"Thank you. Carry on."

Walker went on his way while William walked to the dining room.

The second he entered the door, Richard exclaimed, "Darcy! With all that happened yesterday, I believed you would not come down until much later."

"I awoke and, with all that is on my mind, I could not go back to sleep."

William went straight to the sideboard and began filling a cup with coffee. Then he took his place at the end of the table on Richard's left.

"Are you not going to eat?"

"I promised Elizabeth that we would break our fast together in an hour, so this shall have to suffice for now."

"Is Elizabeth well?"

"Mr. Cameron said that she is."

"Perhaps it is not my place to mention what has not been discussed publicly, but is the child unharmed?"

A smile split William's face. "I suppose everyone suspected but me."

"It is hard to keep secrets from an officer trained in intelligence," Richard boasted.

"According to Cameron, it is full early to say with certainty, but he agrees that all signs indicate that she is with child. As for Elizabeth, she has no doubt and, yes, the child is fine."

"I would think a woman would know her own body better than anyone, so my money is on her." Richard said. Then he chuckled. "I am just relieved that I do not have to deal with such matters yet."

"Your time will come!" Then William's expression sobered. "I do regret that I forgot to have Cameron report back to me after he examined Bingley and the servants. I was focused entirely on my wife yesterday, and I have no idea what he found."

"Uncle told me last night that none of the servants were seriously injured, and as for Bingley, despite the lump on his head, he is in excellent shape and good spirits!" Then Richard guffawed. "In fact, this whole episode may have done him some good."

William took a sip of hot coffee before replying, "Why do you say that?"

"Because, after you and Elizabeth retired, Bingley told him and Aunt Olivia that he was not going to wait any longer to marry Jane Bennet. He said that his captivity gave him ample time to conclude that life is too uncertain to waste a moment of it. His intentions are to leave for London tomorrow, and as soon as a wedding can be arranged, they shall be man and wife. So, perhaps the knot on the head helped him to develop a stiffer spine."

William chuckled. "While I agree with Bingley regarding life's uncertainties, he will need more than a *stiffer spine* to change Mrs. Bennet's mind. Mark my words—that woman is determined to milk Miss Bennet's engagement for all it is worth. She will not be in favour of another hurried marriage."

"She may not be, but I would bet on Bingley getting his way. He is a driven man!"

"I am almost afraid to ask about the chaos I left behind at Briarwood? No! First, I should apologise for leaving you to deal with it while I came home."

"It was completely understandable, considering all that Elizabeth had endured, that you wished to get her home, not to mention Bingley and the others. Besides, I am used to handling such things."

"Still—"

Richard waved away his concerns. "As to the remains of George and Andrew, were it up to me, they would have rotted in the nearest ditch. But you are kinder than I, and you would take into consideration Uncle George's wishes. Therefore, I had their bodies transported to Lambton. Mr. Moody said that he would see to the interments. Also, he requested that you inform him right away if you wish to attend. I told him that I suspected that George will end up in the paupers' cemetery adjacent to the church, and he should consult you as to where Andrew will be buried."

"You know me well. Years ago, Wickham forfeited the right to be buried at Pemberley next to his father, a good and decent man. And, notwithstanding his horrible deeds, Father would want Andrew buried beside his father. I will not attend either service."

"I am glad." Seeing the brooding look now on William's face, Richard changed the subject. "Lord Warren sent a man to fetch the local constable, and he arrived shortly after you left. Clearly, that man is not qualified for the position, for Warren had to direct the investigation."

"I have met him, and I agree with your assessment."

"In any case, the constable intends to turn the entire matter over to the county sheriff—Farnsworth is the name he mentioned—as soon as that man returns from Sheffield. Lord Warren seemed very pleased to hear that, for it seems that the Farnsworths have a long history of service with his family. Years ago, Sheriff Farnsworth's grandfather was a valet for Warren's father."

"I suppose that means Lord Warren will not face any charges, not that he would have anyway."

"I agree. That man is so influential that it would be a mistake to lay any crime at his feet and, besides, he believed you to be in danger when he acted. As for Lord Hartley, he and his men are being held at Briarwood by order of the constable."

"What to do with Fletcher is another matter entirely," William said, fatigue in his voice. "If he were anyone else, I would gladly see him arrested and hanged. But, when I consider the similarities—but for the grace of God, I could have been badly impaired like him."

"Or dead! What I find hard to believe is that Susan did not have Wickham and Andrew skinned alive for what they did to you. If she was not aware of their plans, surely she thought of them when she heard the news. I know I did."

"It is apparent that she has controlled Wickham with money and possibly Andrew as well. As delusional as she is, I imagine it would be hard to convince her that they would go against her wishes."

"What are your plans regarding her?"

"I will deal with Susan after I decide what to do about Fletcher. Obviously, he is no longer sensible and, to his twisted way of thinking, his motive was to save Elizabeth, not harm her. I asked, and she assured me that she was not mistreated in any manner."

"I agree that fate dealt Hartley a harsh blow. Moreover, Lord Warren is convinced that his personality has changed completely, for he knew him well before he was assaulted. Keep in mind, too, that even if the episode at Briarwood is broadcast far and wide, Hartley could still garner the support of his former colleagues in the House of Lords to fight any charges. He may never be charged with a crime, unless you press the issue. Even then he might not be convicted in light of his present circumstances."

"I know. I will have to speak to Elizabeth and Bingley before I decide how I will proceed."

Just then Mrs. Reynolds rushed into the room, waving a letter. Seeing the anxious expression on her face, both men stood.

"Mr. Darcy, this just came from Monthaven Manor. A footman delivered it and is waiting for a reply. He seems to be very upset."

William took the missive, tore it open and began to read. The longer he read, the more his expression darkened.

"Mrs. Reynolds, please tell the footman not to wait for there will be no answer forthcoming." She nodded and quickly left to deliver the message.

As soon as she was out of the room, he addressed Richard. "It seems that Lord Hartley has saved me the trouble of deciding what to do about him or Lady Susan. According to this missive, he arrived at Monthaven at dawn and absconded with her against her will."

"Who sent the note? I do not think Lord Concord capable."

"It was Attaway," William replied. "He apparently knows that you are here and asks for your help, as well as mine, to recover his cousin. It seems Fletcher mentioned sailing to the West Indies, and Attaway fears that Lady Susan will be forced to accompany him."

"That blackguard can track her sorry arse down himself! I owe no allegiance to that family, and I have no intention of getting involved. In fact, I pray they do sail from England and neither is seen again. If Lord Attaway wants help, let him hire detectives just as anyone else would. Surely you have no plans to take part."

"No, I do not. Susan must face the she has created, and Attaway can see to his own relations."

"What if Georgiana pleads for you to help?"

"Alas, she will learn just how little influence she wields with me. Once I leave this room, I intend to call her into my study and tell her that her lady's maid will be leaving today with no references."

"The one that Mrs. Reynolds found so meddlesome? Florence, is it not?"

"One and the same."

"Until Georgiana leaves my supervision, she will make do with an upstairs maid to help her dress. Nothing more!"

"Oh, that should be a sight to behold—my cousin having to make do with a maid who cannot style her hair in the latest fashion."

"And if your parents agree to oversee her, I will suggest to Aunt Evelyn that she would do well to assign an older maid to Georgiana, one who will be loyal to her and not to my sister."

Richard relaxed, sitting back down. "That sounds like excellent advice. Do you wish me to attend that conversation?"

"If you wish to and have the time."

"I would not miss this for the world."

"Then, if you have finished eating, let us get started."

The sounds of chairs being pushed away from the table and footsteps crossing the polished hardwood floors gave warning to the servants waiting without that it was nearly time to clear the table. The instant that William and his cousin quit the room, maids and footmen rushed in from another door to do just that.

When they left a few minutes later, the table looked flawlessly set, whilst silver platters of food on the sideboard were covered with matching lids to keep everything warm.

Nearing the study, William and Richard spied Mrs. Reynolds coming down the hallway.

"Is my sister awake, Mrs. Reynolds?"

Not wishing for another servant to hear her reply, she approached them. "Yes, sir. I just came from Miss Darcy's bedroom. Per your instructions, I explained that she cannot send for a tray any longer but must eat in the dining room. She was getting dressed and indicated that she would come downstairs in a short while."

"Would you please ask her to come to my study first? Assure her that what I have to say will not take long. Moreover, once Georgiana is in my study, call Florence to your office and dismiss her, effective immediately. Tell her that we are aware of what she has been doing and, therefore, will provide no reference. Have several maids help her pack. I want her to be on her way before Georgiana finishes eating. Pay her for the entire month and have a groom drive her to the post station in Lambton. Send a trusted employee with them to purchase a ticket to any destination in England she chooses."

"I know it is not your custom to withhold references," Mrs. Reynolds replied, "but I am pleased with your decision. I could not, in good conscience, recommend her to another family."

William nodded. Then he and Richard walked into the study while the housekeeper hurried to do his bidding.

The Study

Twenty minutes later, William and Richard were still waiting for Georgiana to join them. Nerves on edge, Richard decided to have a glass of brandy. He was standing at the liquor cabinet, pouring himself a drink, when the door opened, and his cousin walked in unannounced. Instantly, he braced for the quarrel to come. Seeing his Darcy's posture stiffen as well, he poured another brandy and set the glass on the desk in front of William as he walked back to his seat.

"Brother," Georgiana said after Richard sat down. "Mrs. Reynolds said that you wanted to speak to me."

After William told Georgiana of his decision regarding Florence, she replied, "I cannot say that I blame you; however, I have something to say as well."

Instantly, foreboding filled the air, and William's eyes narrowed as he studied her. "Florence heard the news of what happened at Briarwood yesterday and told me. The reality of what occurred there has opened my eyes as nothing else could ever have done."

William and Richard exchanged suspicious glances.

"I will not deny that I was very saddened to learn of the deaths of Andrew and George. After all, one was a childhood friend and the other my cousin. Yet, once I heard that George meant to kill you and Elizabeth, I realised how wrong I had been to defend him." She took a deep breath and let it go. "I was also wrong to defend Andrew, especially after you told me of his drawings. It seems he was always a willing participant in George's plots. In hindsight, I know that my loyalty should have been to you, and I should have told you when Lady Susan began to talk of ridding Pemberley of Elizabeth."

William's brows knit before his face settled into a scowl. "Forgive me if I do not trust your abrupt change of heart."

Determined never to reveal her motivation—her abject humiliation by those she once considered her closest friends—Georgiana replied, "I understand why you would not trust me. Still, I am being truthful."

By his expression, William was not convinced. "Tell me this: Why would someone intent on doing Elizabeth harm share those plans with my sister?"

Nervously, she admitted, "I... Susan found in me a willing partner. Originally, it was I who suggested the kiss in the garden at our aunt's ball. I promised to provide witnesses to Lady Susan's compromise, so that you would be forced to offer for her. Once we learned that you had married, I insisted we carry on with the plan, only Elizabeth would be the one to discover you. I wrote the note to send you to the gazebo and I made sure that Elizabeth saw everything."

Slowly William shook his head side to side. "Did you also help plan Elizabeth's abduction—the one that Lord Hartley circumvented by taking her first?"

"No, though lately Susan spoke more stridently of shipping Elizabeth out of the country. I was, however, told to send word the moment she left Pemberley for any reason." Her next words were said in a whisper. "I sent Florence to Monthaven with a note the morning she left for London."

William slammed his unfinished glass of brandy on the desk, sending liquor flying across its polished surface. Looking up through her lashes, Georgiana could tell that he was livid.

"She... she was never supposed to be killed, mind you, only shipped to another continent under a different name."

William's voice sounded strangely void of emotion when he asked, "Did you know that she was pregnant when you sent the note to Monthaven?"

"Florence had told me that she might be but, at the time, I was convinced that you already had an heir in Susan's child."

"That boy is likely one of Andrew's throwaways!" William shouted, slamming his fist against the wall and sending a portrait crashing to the floor.

Trembling, Georgiana watched her brother stalk a path behind his desk. His hand clenched and unclenched until he stopped and addressed her again with thinly disguised revulsion.

"I realise that you never had any affection for Elizabeth and never gave her the slightest chance to be your sister, but disregarding that entirely, how is it that you never once considered what I wanted? Did you not think how I would suffer if Susan had succeeded? I love Elizabeth and our child. If she had been taken from—" His voice cracked, and he could not continue.

Richard had stood with William and was now a dividing wall between the two siblings. With William speechless, he took the opportunity to tell Georgiana exactly how he felt about all she had done.

"Georgiana, I am shocked—nay, I am astounded—at the evil you have just admitted. I would never have believed that you were so unfeeling. Is your conscience stripped entirely of the ability to determine right from wrong?"

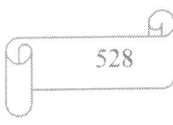

Her eyes filled with tears. Still, she did not cry. "I did not think any harm would come—"

"Spare me!" he interrupted angrily, causing her to shiver. "Do you actually believe Elizabeth would not have been harmed? It is obvious to me that Susan meant to have her killed from the start! Can you honestly say that you did not realise that?"

Richard walked toward his cousin, stopping with his face mere inches from hers. "I have watched Darcy sacrifice for you his entire life! I know how he has worried about your welfare and keeping Pemberley prosperous for your sake as well as for the servants and tenants who depend on it."

By now tears were rolling down Georgiana's cheeks, though she made not a sound.

"I cannot think of any plausible explanation for your selfishness. You have shown no love for the one who always put your needs above his own and nothing but disdain for a woman who has never done one thing to harm you."

"I… I can offer no excuse other than I have always been a selfish person, spoiled and used to having my way. When Fitzwilliam took on the duties of the estate, I resented him for letting responsibility come before amusing me. Later, I realised that Father had kept him in his study so often in order to impart all the knowledge that he could before he died. Unfair as it was, the more that Andrew, Susan and George included me in their pursuits, the more I was willing to agree with their lies about Brother."

Richard threw up his hands. "I can only agree. You have no excuse. Did it not once occur to you that perhaps he would have liked to shirk the responsibility of carrying so many people on his shoulders at such a tender age?"

Georgiana looked past him to where William had quit pacing and was listening. "It is true, Brother. I never thought of your feelings. And, on the rare occasion when my conscience reminded me that you were working for my sake, I dismissed every prompt. You see, I had to believe that I was right, or I would not fit in with my new coterie."

Georgiana glanced wistfully out the tall windows at the grand expanse of lawn that ran the length of the front drive. Realising for the first time how deeply she would miss her childhood home, she sighed. Then her eyes travelled back to William.

"Fitzwilliam, I am very, very sorry for my actions—most especially those since your marriage. I do love you, and I pray that in time you can find it in your heart to forgive me, and that Elizabeth will as well. Still, I heartily agree that it is best I live elsewhere. No couple should have to share their home with a sister who has acted so meanly towards them. Moreover, I humbly accept any punishment you feel is warranted for the part I played in this horror."

William sat down behind his desk and, for a short while, he stared silently at the portrait of his parents on the opposite wall. Continuously turning the ring on his little finger, it was obvious that he was considering how to respond. When at last he cleared his throat and faced Georgiana, his voice was filled with more regret than anger.

"I love you, too, Georgiana. I always will, for we are family. I am sorry if you felt neglected when I was forced to learn about and then manage Pemberley. Though it was certainly never my intention for my responsibilities to take precedent over time spent with you, I had little say in the matter."

He paused to look back at his parents again, as though seeking to find the right words. "You ask for forgiveness. Knowing Elizabeth as I do, she will forgive you at once and beg you to stay. I, however, insist that you go."

Georgiana's expression fell with this assertion, though she did not show any surprise.

"I forgive you. It is my Christian duty to forgive, but it will take time to come to terms with what almost happened to Elizabeth because you conspired against her. I will find it hard to forget that I could have lost her and our child."

"I understand. I will prove to you that I can be a better person. I promise."

"It will please me if you do."

Georgiana smiled slightly, and then her eyes rested on her cousin. "I love you, too, Richard, and I want to apologise to you as well. You have helped Brother care for me since father died, and I have shown you nothing but disrespect for all your trouble. I am sorry." Before Richard could reply, she added, "Now, please excuse me. I intend to break my fast and then go to my room and begin organising my things for the move."

She walked out the door and it closed silently behind her.

"Good lord!" Richard said. "Had I not heard it myself, I would not have believed Georgiana capable of doing such harm to another person. It simply boggles the mind."

"I had no idea," William said incredulously. "Am I so blind that I could not see that she was capable of harming Elizabeth? I shiver to think that they lived under the same roof all these weeks."

"You love Georgiana, as do I, so we did not want to see it."

William dropped his head. "You are right." Then he squared his shoulders. "I cannot focus on the past any longer. I have a wife who is going to have my child, and I intend to concentrate on her happiness."

"Then perhaps you had best return to Elizabeth," Richard teased, "It has been well over an hour since you came downstairs, and she is most likely starving."

"I am going now," William said. He opened the door, but paused. "Later, will you consider accompanying me to the rectory to confer with Mr. Moody? I would like to get the burials over as soon as may be."

Richard walked beside him. "I promised Bingley that I would ride out this morning. When we return, I shall gladly be of service."

William clasped his cousin on the shoulder. "I do not know what I would do without you, Richard."

"You might survive, but the rest of the world would sorely miss me. I am the only one who can keep the illustrious *Master of Pemberley* humble."

For the first time in many weeks both men laughed as though neither had a care in the world.

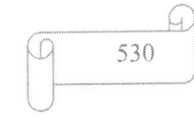

On a balcony

Joseph Fitzwilliam nuzzled Olivia's neck, pulling her tighter against his chest, as they stood wrapped in his robe against the morning chill. He had spied Olivia on the balcony earlier, clad only in her nightgown, and had hurried to embrace her, wrapping his robe about them both. Looking down at her feet, he smiled. *At least she remembered to don her slippers.*

The sun cast streaks of yellow and orange above a line of trees in the distance, causing the sky to change from the pearly grey of dawn to a soft golden hue. Suddenly, the silence was broken by the sound of a door closing somewhere below, signalling that Richard and Charles were leaving for their morning ride.

"Do you think that Fitzwilliam will resume riding with Richard when Mr. Bingley leaves?" Olivia asked, snuggling closer to Joseph.

"I suspect he may at some point in the future," Joseph said, "but not for a great while. He is too caught up with his bride to think of spending his mornings with his cousin."

Olivia laughed. "I hope he is always caught up in their love, for Elizabeth is the perfect woman for him. I am so pleased that she is home, the baby is well, and our dear boy has regained his joy."

"It would all be perfect were it not for Georgiana."

"Ah, yes, Georgiana. I cannot count the hours I have prayed for our niece since the day we arrived. It may take time, but she is intelligent, and I believe that eventually she will realize who truly loves her and wants what is best for her. When that happens, she will come to appreciate Fitzwilliam again."

Joseph hugged her tighter. "You are an optimist, so I am not surprised that you have hope for Georgiana. I must confess that I am more pragmatic. If I do not see signs of change right away, I tend to think a person is hopeless and give up."

"Sometimes it may take years, but prayers can change hearts. I have learned not to worry and to leave the outcome to God."

"You are a good woman, Olivia Angelina Fitzwilliam, and I am proud to have called you my wife these two and thirty years."

"If I have any good qualities, it is because of the Lord. He has blessed me richly. After all, He arranged for me to meet you, did He not?"

"That He did, Love! As I recall, it was at the parish of Kympton, after Sunday services, one beautiful, sunny day in April. A day I was supposed to be at Matlock with my family, not at Pemberley with Anne. Little did I know that in that small gathering was the woman with whom I was meant to spend my life."

Olivia laughed. "God works in mysterious ways."

"Yes, He does."

They kissed, tenderly at first, and then with a growing desire. This led to a return to their bedroom, where they affirmed their good fortune in marriage. By the time they went downstairs to break their fast, they were the only ones who had not done so.

Chapter 49

Meryton
Three months later

As they got closer to Meryton, William wished for the hundredth time that he had convinced Elizabeth not to make the journey. But Bingley had gotten his wish—the wedding being set for tomorrow—and Elizabeth was determined to stand up with Jane. Due to heavy rains, the route from Derbyshire had been fraught with teeth-jarring ruts, washed out roads, and swollen creeks. Thus, the trip had been painstakingly slow and much more difficult than he ever imagined. And, since Elizabeth was nearing her fifth month of pregnancy, he worried constantly for her health—so much so, that even Aunt Olivia had begun teasing him about being too watchful. If his aunt was hoping to ease his anxiety, she had not succeeded.

After all, he reasoned, *Elizabeth is my life—she and our child—and I am duty-bound to protect them in every possible way.*

One example of his increased vigilance was that this trip included four footmen, two drivers, and Mr. Coleridge and Mr. Harahan, who acted simultaneously as postillions and guards. All were expert shots, fully armed, with weapons in plain view. The display, something usual for the times, was meant to dissuade any prospective thieves or seasoned highwaymen from targeting this particular coach.

As another problem came to mind, William's expression darkened. What lay ahead of him at Longbourn, preventing Mrs. Bennet from belittling Elizabeth, would not be as simple as deterring a few blackguards. In his estimation though, a confrontation was long overdue. Not a week past he had stumbled upon Elizabeth on her balcony, clutching one of her mother's letters and sobbing. At his insistence, she had reluctantly handed it to him. It was full of demands that she tell Jane that she would not be her attendant at the wedding, though Jane expressly wanted Elizabeth.

In any case, Mrs. Bennet had written, *you are too far along to look presentable in whatever you wear. Besides, your condition will draw everyone's eyes away from Jane. It is not acceptable to take the attention away from your dear sister on her wedding day.*

Seeing his wife so distraught made up his mind. Mr. Bennet would hear from him once they reached Longbourn, and if that did not solve the problem, William would deal with Mrs. Bennet directly. He had a strategy planned. He would warn her that any future belittling of Elizabeth, as well as letting word slip of his intervention, would directly affect Mrs. Bennet to her detriment, should she ever be widowed. It was the perfect solution, he believed, and thinking of it now made him smile. At long last, Mrs. Bennet would realise her future security, at least on his part, depended upon how she treated

Elizabeth.

As all of this swirled in his head, William almost missed the sign that signified they were about to cross the bridge that led into the village of Meryton. In his opinion, of all the bridges in Hertfordshire, perhaps in all of England, this was the most unpleasant, for the majority of its boards were uneven or misshapen. Whether they had been so from the beginning, or if the weather had caused them to twist, he could not say. However, any vehicle unlucky enough to cross that bridge, even one as comfortable and well-sprung as his, would shake as though it was about to disintegrate into a thousand pieces. In addition, the noise created by the thumping of the wheels was sufficient to wake the dead.

Glancing to Elizabeth, who had thankfully fallen asleep earlier with her head resting on his chest, he longed for her to stay undisturbed. Thus, as they approached the familiar landmark, he laid a protective hand over the side of her face, covering her ear in an attempt to muffle the clatter. His efforts proved futile, however, for immediately upon taking the bridge, she sat up, yawning and rubbing her eyes.

"Are we here already?" she murmured sleepily, peering out a window. "I cannot believe it."

"Yes, dearest. We are almost in Meryton."

Suddenly she exclaimed, "Oh, no!"

Ever vigilant, William reacted by scanning her for signs of anything that might have caused her distress. "What it is, darling?"

Her hands flew to her hair. "I must look a fright! I cannot let Mama see me like this!" She looked about the coach. "Where is my bonnet?"

"Now, Elizabeth," William said soothingly as he reached for the offending item which was lying on his right side. "I laid it over here after we stopped to change horses. You know how I detest bonnets. I had rather see your beautiful locks."

"Beautiful?" Elizabeth cried, her lips forming a pout. "You know how easily my hair slips out of the pins. It is entirely too curly! Mama thinks me unladylike as it is."

Unable to resist, William leaned down to kiss her pout. "You forget that I requested Mrs. O'Reilly to fashion your hair in a French braid the day we left. In that style, it always stays beautiful for days on end. And, without the aid of any pins, I might add."

Elizabeth sighed, smiling crookedly. "I am still so sleepy that it completely slipped my mind." Then her expression grew concerned again. "Still, if I am not wearing a bonnet when—"

William stopped her protest with another quick kiss. "Do not upset yourself. I shall remind you to put it on once we enter the drive to Longbourn, but not a moment sooner."

Elizabeth's eyes twinkled. "One would think that you admire my hair more than me, *Mr. Darcy*."

William pulled her closer, laying his head atop hers. Then taking a deep breath to smell her lavender scented tresses, he said, "One would be wrong, sweetheart. Though, I do think every woman's hair should be her crowning glory." Lifting her face so that he could look into her eyes, he smiled roguishly. "Your hair is more, Elizabeth—so much more. Its beauty far surpasses that of any woman I have ever seen. The mere sight of those silky, ebony curls spilling over your soft shoulders makes my blood run hot."

"Goodness! Then I had better not let my hair down whilst we are here. Need I remind you that the walls of Longbourn are very thin, and we both know what happens when your blood runs hot?" Elizabeth replied mischievously.

William pulled her onto his lap, growling, "Suppose you remind me!"

One kiss led to another, each deeper and more urgent than the last, their tongues duelling in a quest to be satisfied. Even several townspeople who happened to peer in the coach windows as they passed through Meryton were shocked at the spectacle of the Darcys' amorous display. Still, they were nearly to Longbourn before William broke away, saying breathlessly, "If we do not quit now, my love, your family will be more than shocked when the coach door opens."

Elizabeth swallowed hard. Since she became pregnant, William's kisses could effortlessly prod her desire into a raging fire. "Would that we could drive to Netherfield first, as though it was planned. Then we would have the time to finish what we have started."

A deep, rumbling laugh emerged, and William broke into one of his devastating smiles. "You are truly insatiable, my love! Never would I have dreamt that being with child could create so passionate a lover." He nuzzled her neck. "Though I am not complaining. Never think that I do not want you just as ardently, but the driver was told to go to Longbourn, not Netherfield. I fear he and the others will surmise the reason for the change of plans, especially since Bingley is likely at Longbourn already."

Elizabeth took a deep breath, puffing out her cheeks before blowing the breath out slowly. "I apologise. It is just that Mama makes me so nervous, and being in your arms calms my nerves." As Longbourn came into view, she scowled, "Will you hand me my bonnet, please?"

Handing it to her, William lowered his voice seductively. "I will love you as often as you desire tonight, my love."

She fanned herself with the bonnet. "Oh, Will! When you say such things, it only makes matters worse!"

They shared one last bittersweet kiss as the coach slowed. It had not stopped completely when the door was flung open, and Mary peered inside to see them still kissing. Instantly, she jerked her head back.

"Reverend Fordyce," Mary declared primly, "writes that people ought never to show affection in public."

Kitty, who had been looking over Mary's shoulder, giggled. "They were not in public until you opened the door, Mary!"

Lydia clawed her way through both sisters. "What did you bring us, Lizzy? I hope it is something expensive. After all, you can afford anything in the world."

Looking back at William, Elizabeth shook her head wordlessly. Her pained expression spoke volumes about her inability to curb her sisters' bad manners. Also clear was a reluctance to face her mother again.

He squeezed her hand as he prepared to exit first, whispering, "Remember what we said, darling? We shall face your family as one."

Elizabeth broke into a relieved smile. "Yes, as one."

Longbourn
The parlour

Sitting on a settee next to Elizabeth, William was adrift in a sea of female conversation. To his way of thinking, it was remarkable that so few women could manage to produce such a sheer volume of noise. That was, he supposed, due in part to the fact that the Bennet women had help. Not only were all of them present, but also Mrs. Phillips had heard that the Darcys' coach had passed through Meryton and decided to call, bringing with her several neighbourhood ladies, many of whom he had never met. William had suffered through all the introductions, hoping he appeared to be appropriately interested, though he could not recall any of their names.

As he assessed the situation now, he knew why Mr. Bennet, shrewd man that he was, had slipped off to his study upon their arrival. If that was not bad enough, Bingley, who had been at Longbourn all day, looked as if he was about to desert him, too.

Sure enough, Charles stood and began to voice his remorse at having to leave so lively a group. William's heart sank, and he was totally unprepared for what Charles said next.

"Darcy, why do you not accompany me to Netherfield?" he asked innocently. "After I meet with my steward, we can play a few games of billiards. We will have plenty of time to return before dinner."

Not wishing to tell all those present why he could not, William walked over to his friend, placing an arm around his shoulder as he guided Charles out of the parlour door. "Since Elizabeth and I have only just arrived… "

Once in the hall, he went silent and did not speak again until only they stood on the portico. Then he quietly explained why he felt he had to stay.

"It is a shame that you must resort to guarding your wife from being insulted," Charles said sombrely. "Plainly, Mrs. Bennet is harder on Elizabeth than any of her other daughters. Nonetheless, what can you do or say that will not make her even more insufferable?"

William described his plan, and once he was finished, Charles mused, "It certainly sounds as though it might work. After all, she speaks often of how before you and Lizzy married, she feared being left a widow, living in the hedgerows."

"If it does not work, then I shall limit our contact with her. I think Mr. Bennet will understand, once he hears how it affects Elizabeth and how furious it makes me."

"Let us hope." Then Charles sheepishly confessed. "By the way, it is just as well that you are not accompanying me. Caroline has returned with the

Hursts to attend the wedding. And, while I will try to keep her in check, I cannot say wholeheartedly that she has learned her lesson."

"You should have told me earlier. I cannot deal with your sister as well as Mrs. Bennet during this visit."

"I am sorry I could not say anything. Jane wanted to break the news to Elizabeth privately. Louisa has been writing Jane, and apparently, Caroline is still quite enraged about your marriage, not to mention my wedding."

"I can only imagine."

"Well, Darcy," Charles said, donning his hat and patting the top. "Mrs. Bennet has been driving me mad all day, and this is my chance to escape. I am not going to waste it."

"Lucky you!"

They both chuckled. "See you at dinner," Charles exclaimed before entering his carriage.

William only nodded. Then he watched the carriage until it was out of sight. From somewhere inside the house, he heard Mrs. Bennet's cackling laugh. Shaking his head, he headed back to Elizabeth.

◈

After another insufferable hour in the parlour, the din in that small room brought to mind an incident from William's youth. Shortly after his ninth birthday, he had sneaked into one of Pemberley's chicken coups to obtain some eggs for his favourite hound, which relished the treat. While he was occupied, a fox suddenly appeared, pacing the fence outside the coup and stirring the frightened birds into turmoil. The racket became so unbearable that he decided he had rather face the fox. Much to his relief, a servant had heard the uproar and arrived, rifle in hand, to rout the animal just as he exited.

I doubt that I can depend on a servant with a rifle to dispatch this henhouse!

The image of the ladies running like frightened chickens caused a furtive smile to appear. A squeeze of his hand let him know that Elizabeth had seen and, glancing at her puzzled expression, he tilted his head in a shrug and brought her hand to his lips for a tender kiss. Satisfied, she went back to listening as one of the hens, *err ladies*, finished explaining her latest remedy for gout.

Happily, for those uninterested in the subject, the door suddenly opened and Mrs. Hill appeared with a tray of cakes, biscuits and sweets of every description. A maid followed with a tray containing a pot of tea and cups. After the trays were set on the largest table available, everyone rushed to partake of the food and drink—everyone except Elizabeth and William.

"Will, please do not think that you have to stay with me," she said so quietly that the others could not hear. "I know how you dislike listening to my mother and her friends, and Papa said he would welcome you in his study."

William took her hands in his. "Are you saying that you would rather not have my company?"

"Goodness, no! Your presence is what makes all of this bearable. I just do not want you to think—"

William's thumbs began making circles on the tops of her hands. With an expression of unconcealed adoration, he said, "If you do not hush, Elizabeth Darcy, I shall kiss you in front of all these witnesses."

Elizabeth's heart melted. "And if you keep looking at me like that, I shall let you."

Abruptly, an idea came to mind, and she addressed Mrs. Bennet. "Mama, the trip was tiring. I believe I should have a nap before dinner."

Mrs. Bennet's eyes lit up as she turned from putting cakes on her plate to face Elizabeth. "That is exactly the point I have been trying to make for months. Now that you are with child, it is likely that you will not have the stamina to stand throughout the entire wedding."

Then she began to pester Jane. "Lydia can be your attendant. I even had a new gown made especially for—"

Jane's posture stiffened, and she interrupted. "Mama, we have discussed this before. Lizzy will be my attendant and no one else."

With Jane's pronouncement, all activity in the room ceased in mid-air. Curious eyes darted between Mrs. Bennet and her two eldest daughters. Had they alighted on William instead, they would have seen that his eyes were locked on Elizabeth's mother in a lethal glare.

Oblivious to her new son's posture, the mistress of Longbourn's smile deflated, and her eyes flashed with anger aimed at Jane. "Then do not blame me if Lizzy faints at the altar and ruins everything."

A collective gasp escaped from the guests.

That William was furious became evident when he addressed her through clenched teeth. "Mrs. Bennet, my wife suffered through a very long trip in order to be here for her sister. I assure you that she was perfectly fine before we left Derbyshire, and she will be perfectly fine once she has rested."

Though she was still of a mind to argue, something in William's expression made Mrs. Bennet concede. "Any... anything you say, Mr. Darcy." Swallowing hard against the lump in her throat, she reached for a dangling rope. "I have rung for Hill. She arranged Lizzy's former bedroom for your comfort."

William began to escort Elizabeth from the room. "Mrs. Hill will not be needed. I am sure Elizabeth remembers which bedroom was hers."

"Yes... yes, of course she would," Mrs. Bennet stammered.

With that, he and Elizabeth went out the parlour door, closing it behind them. Mrs. Hill was coming toward them in the hall and was told she had been called in error.

The old servant nodded, then looked around before she spoke. "Miss Eliz... pardon me... *Mrs. Darcy*, I am so pleased to see you again, and to know that you are expecting your first child makes me very pleased."

Elizabeth could not resist giving the old housekeeper a hug. "I will always be Elizabeth to you, Hill. And you must know that I have missed your kindness and encouragement."

Over Elizabeth's shoulder, Hill fixed her eyes on William. "You chose to marry the best of the girls, in my opinion."

After another brief hug, she hurried back to the kitchen. Elizabeth watched her leave, teary-eyed. Two gentle fingers slipped under her chin to turn her head.

"I always knew that Mrs. Hill was a most perceptive woman."

This brought back a smile. "You are prejudiced!"

"On the contrary, I am very proud!"

Picking up Elizabeth, he began up the stairs to the second floor. And, once ensconced in the solitude of her old bedroom, they made the most of being alone.

Downstairs everyone was now eating and, as silence reigned, it became possible to hear certain sounds emanating from the second floor. Whilst an outsider might not recognise them straight off, Jane did. Lizzy's bed had always creaked, and that creaking was now being accompanied by an occasional thump, like a headboard hitting the wall. Jane was mortified that all present might recognise the cause and immediately launched into a louder than normal one-sided conversation with Mary who, momentarily befuddled at Jane's behaviour, never answered.

Seeing that that was not working, Jane changed strategies. "Mary, would you entertain us while we eat? I would love to hear the new music you have been practising all week."

Amidst loud groans of protestation from Lydia and Kitty, across the room, Mrs. Bennet's brows knit in suspicion. With her mouth full of cake, she was unable to thwart Jane's invitation, though she wondered at her motivation. After all, Jane was well aware of how ill her sister played.

"But, I have not practised very—" Mary began to protest.

"Then for heaven's sake!" Jane interrupted in frustration, "play something you know! Something lively! Play a jig!"

As Jane pleaded, she continually rolled her eyes toward the ceiling. At long last a particularly loud noise overhead led Mary to know what Jane was about. Blushing furiously, she hurried to the pianoforte.

"I think I know just the piece."

Pounding out a Scottish jig over and over, by the time Mary had played it through three times, all was quiet overhead. Looking over her shoulder at Jane, she was pleased to see her sister nod her approval. Hoping that another jig would not be needed, Mary again took the seat next to Jane. Both were blushing furiously and, glancing at each other, sighed in relief.

Jane's relief was short-lived, however, for instantly, she recalled that she was to be married in the morning. Having listened to her mother's version of the wedding night and then to her aunt's, she could not recall either of them speaking of marital duties being so... *spirited*. The realisation made her cheeks turn bright red. Subsequently, she settled on a plan. *I shall ask Lizzy tonight before she retires.*

Mrs. Bennet, who had watched it all, made a mental note to speak to both Jane and Mary after their guests departed. She suspected that something had occurred right under her nose, and she was not one to let sleeping dogs lie.

The wedding

The day of the ceremony dawned clear and sunny, and the wedding party looked handsome in their grand attire. The majority of the small village of Meryton turned out for the event, though, having been witness to Elizabeth's marriage to Mr. Darcy, this time they were not as surprised that a Bennet was marrying a man of great fortune. After all, Fanny Bennet had predicted that very outcome after her second daughter's stroke of luck.

Though Jane was undoubtedly a beautiful bride, William thought Elizabeth outshone her sister in every way. Wearing a simple gown of striped French gauze over a yellow satin slip, she looked every inch a princess in his eyes. He was surprised, though, to see in Elizabeth's hair some of the same yellow flowers he had fashioned into a crown at the pond. Not only had she managed to find the wildflowers in Meryton, she had kept them a secret until she had entered the church. The intimacy represented by the flowers made the ceremony seem more their own, and when Jane and Charles recited their vows, he and Elizabeth locked eyes, repeating them in their hearts.

Despite Mrs. Bennet's prediction, the ceremony concluded without any problems. Elizabeth performed her duties flawlessly, except perhaps for stealing a glance too often at the handsome man next to Charles. Whenever she did, she would blush anew. Whether those blushes resulted from the hurried love they had shared just before leaving for the church, or because she felt, as he had, a rush of emotions to realise that they had stood at this very altar a few scant months ago, William knew not.

Nonetheless, he had intentions of finding out as soon as they got back to Longbourn and were safely behind closed doors.

Netherfield
The wedding breakfast

Louisa Hurst had had no trouble convincing Mrs. Bennet to have the wedding breakfast at Netherfield, since it would accommodate more people. And, so long as she was completely in charge, Jane's mother was only too happy to take over that venue and its kitchen, not to mention their cooks. She had neighbours to impress, and she was determined not to fail. However, instead of using the large dining room as Louisa assumed, Fanny conscripted the ballroom. It was now bedecked with beautifully appointed tables, full of good things to eat, and there were smaller tables where guests were dining on that fare. Meryton had not seen so elaborate a display of wealth since Elizabeth's wedding breakfast, which had been much smaller due to the constraints of time.

Fanny was truly in her element now, flitting from table to table, flaunting her station as Mr. Bingley's new mother and spreading the news that for their honeymoon the Bingleys had decided to tour the Lake District after spending a week in London. Little did she know that they also planned to spend several weeks at Pemberley afterwards. All parties involved, especially Jane and Elizabeth, thought it best not to mention that detail, lest their mother assume that she, too, would be welcome at Pemberley while they were there. For, since the Darcys' arrival, she had hinted constantly that she expected to be invited to Elizabeth's home very soon.

The day had passed quickly, and though Charles and Jane had left for London, many of the guests were still at Netherfield. That was because Mrs. Bennet kept insisting at the top of her voice that everyone keep eating and, of course, drinking from Charles' extensive wine cellar. From his post at one of the double doors leading to the gardens, William followed her performance with disdain.

How that woman loves to be the centre of attention!

Determined that she would have no further opportunity to upset Elizabeth, who now sat between Lydia and Kitty at a table, his eyes flicked constantly between his wife and her mother. Looking dashingly handsome in his black suit, he drew the stares of many of the ladies still in attendance, and though he focused his attention solely on his wife, he could not help but notice who sat at the end of the table that Elizabeth occupied.

Caroline Bingley's attendance at the wedding had been calculated to put her in Mr. Darcy's company. Having resided in the country the entire time she stayed with the Hursts, she was willing to do anything to get back in Charles' good graces so that she could reside with him and Jane. Neither Louisa nor her husband cared much for Town, though that was precisely where she needed to be in order to find a husband. Only by living with Charles could she regain her position in Mr. Darcy's circle where real wealth was to be found.

Being too busy with his upcoming marriage, Charles had refused to meet with her before the wedding. So, today she decided to learn if Mr. Darcy was open to restoring their acquaintance if she asked forgiveness. If he forgave her, surely Charles would, too.

If it means acting as though I have changed my ways, grovelling to Brother and Jane, as well as being kind to Eliza Ben— she almost choked when she recalled Elizabeth's new name—*Eliza Darcy, then so be it.* She looked down at the plain, beige gown she was wearing. *I even made myself look dowdy to show that I have reformed. Surely that will count for something.*

Suddenly, Mrs. Bennet said very loudly, and to no one in particular, that she would return after she waited with two of her friends for their carriage to be brought around. As soon as she left the ballroom, Mr. Bennet went out the other set of double doors into the garden, and William followed shortly after.

Looking back just in time to see William go out the door, Caroline stood and hurried in his direction. William had gotten about halfway down the gravel path when suddenly he heard his name screeched in a high-pitched wail. The hair on the back of his neck stood on end, for only one woman of his acquaintance had ever sounded like that.

Without turning, he said, "Miss Bingley, why are you following me?"

"I… it is because I need to speak to you privately, Fitzwilliam."

He faced her now. "*Mr. Darcy* to you, and we have nothing to discuss. I suggest you go inside before someone sees you."

Caroline came closer, causing William to step back. "Please, you must listen to me. It is a matter of life and death."

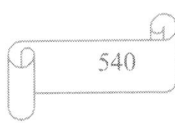

William's eyes narrowed. "Whose life or death?"

"My own."

When he did not reply, she added, "That is why I came for the wedding. I wish to... to apologise to you. I am so sorry for all that I said or did to hurt you."

Stifling a rising storm of words, he said evenly, "Do you not mean what you did to hurt *Mrs. Darcy?*"

She swallowed hard. "Yes, I meant to say Mrs. Darcy. My only excuse is that my expectations were dashed, and I lashed out at her because I was hurt."

William seemed to grow five inches taller as his jaw clenched. "If Elizabeth decides to forgive you, that is her prerogative. I am not of a mind to forgive or forget as easily as my wife. And, as for your expectations, I never gave you any reason to expect an offer from me. On the contrary, I always made it clear that I would never do that."

Caroline began to stutter. "I... I did not mean to infer that you had. I meant only that I had allowed myself to imagine expectations."

With his silence, she hurried on. "I tried to speak to Charles before the wedding, but he was too preoccupied. However, I need him to forgive me and let me live at his home. At least, on occasion, Charles and Jane will partake of decent society while Hurst and Louise care not if I ever make a respectable match."

"Madam, none of this is of concern to me."

"You are my brother's friend and my only hope. He will listen to you!"

"Then you have no hope, for I have no intention of speaking to Charles about you."

"But... but," Caroline sputtered incredulously. "It was not supposed to be this way. You are a gentleman. You are supposed to accept my apology and—"

Unbeknownst to William, Mr. Bennet had found a quiet place in the garden to occupy. As luck would have it, his respite was a bench on the opposite side of the tall shrubs where William had stopped. Deducing from the conversation between his son and Miss Bingley that he could be of help, in addition to teasing someone he disliked, Elizabeth's father stepped into view.

"Miss Bingley! What a delightful surprise finding you here!"

A small cry escaped her throat at the sight of him, and Caroline scurried back towards the house as though she had seen a ghost. Mr. Bennet chuckled for a long time before noticing that William was still scowling at her departing form.

"Do not let that sort of woman bother you, son. She is not the first, nor will she be the last, to approach you. For a fine looking chap like you, some may even sweeten the pot to gain your favour. Even so, your rebuff will sting far more if you act totally unaffected. And I would think that if word gets out, it will render others unlikely to bother you in the first place."

Not amused, William replied, "I shall never understand women like Miss Bingley or her ilk. I never paid her any attention or gave her reason to expect an offer from me. I have always treated her civilly because Charles is my friend, but after what she did to disparage Elizabeth, she is deranged if she thinks I would help her in any fashion."

"I think that is an apt description of Miss Bingley." All was eerily quiet for a moment, and Mr. Bennet cut his eyes to the side, studying William. "It has been a long day. I found a lovely spot to rest on a bench just behind these shrubs. Why not join me?" He chuckled aloud. "Surely you do not expect any more women to follow Miss Bingley?"

At this jest, William begrudgingly smiled and slowly shook his head side to side.

"Excellent! Then we may be able to enjoy a few minutes of peace before Mrs. Bennet returns to the ballroom and realizes I have escaped."

He began to walk away and William followed. They had no more than sat down on the bench when Elizabeth's father said, "I have not had the chance to say how pleased I am that my daughter is so blissfully happy. I know she is because she tells me so in her letters. At one point, I feared I might have done the wrong thing in encouraging her to marry you rather than Collins."

William glowered at him.

Mr. Bennet smiled wickedly. "That look will not silence me. Besides, I am only being truthful. When you were injured, Elizabeth's letters began to make me uneasy, for it was obvious that she was very unhappy. Then when she decided to go to London, and I got the letter from my Brother Gardiner saying that neither she nor Bingley had arrived—" He hesitated for a moment. "However, seeing the guards you brought on this trip, I know that will never happen again."

"Not if I can help it."

"It would appear that all is well between the two of you."

"It is. We love each other ardently."

"Good to hear."

William cleared his throat. "However, there is a matter concerning Elizabeth that I feel I must address."

Mr. Bennet's brows knit. "Does it concern Mrs. Bennet?"

"Perhaps we should walk further into the garden so that we cannot be overheard."

Since William ignored his question, it was obvious to Mr. Bennet what the subject would be.

"Then by all means let us walk."

The next day

When the Darcys' coach was ready to leave Longbourn the next morning, Elizabeth was astonished to have her mother lock arms with her and walk a few feet away from the others. William, who was speaking to Mr. Bennet, followed them with his eyes, causing her father to look in the same direction.

"I do not see why you cannot stay longer," Mrs. Bennet complained to her second born.

"We cannot for William has business in London that must be addressed."

In actuality, there was no business to attend, but she and William were eager to leave Meryton behind now that Jane and Charles had left.

Shrugging, her mother continued, "Lizzy, I want to apologise if I upset you regarding the matter of standing up with Jane."

"Mama, there is no need to discuss—"

"Yes, there is. I was entirely wrong, and you did an excellent job. Can you forgive me?"

Elizabeth was shocked. Never could she remember her mother apologising to her for anything. She stammered, "I... of course, I can. I mean, I do."

"Excellent!" Mrs. Bennet crowed. "Now, let us never mention it again. Be sure to write to me every week once you get to Pemberley. Tell me how you and the child are faring, for I shall worry if you do not."

"I... I will, Mama."

"Elizabeth?" Her husband's rich baritone broke through her bewilderment, and she looked back at William. He was holding a hand toward her.

"We must go, Mama."

With that, Mrs. Bennet grabbed Lizzy and hugged her so tightly she almost protested. "We shall miss you!"

Letting go of her daughter, she rushed to speak to William. "Please come back soon. There is always a place for you and Elizabeth at Longbourn."

William answered graciously. "Thank you. We shall, though it will not likely be until after the child is born."

When William turned back to bid Elizabeth's father goodbye, he found in his expression a question—was William satisfied with the results?

With a sly smile, William responded, "It looks as though it may have worked."

Unfortunately, Elizabeth heard. "What may have worked?"

Without missing a beat, he replied, "My prayers." Then he winked at Mr. Bennet. "It is not raining."

After they were ensconced in the vehicle and it began to roll down the drive, Elizabeth waved through the back window until the house was out of sight. Then she settled into the seat with a puzzled look.

"Are you not happy, my darling?" William asked, bringing her hand to his lips.

"I am, truly I am, but something strange seems to have happened to Mama."

"Oh?"

"I think she may have suffered an apoplexy of some sort."

William tried not to smile. "Why do you say that?"

"Because, today she acted entirely different—at least towards me. I hardly know what to make of it."

"Perhaps, with Jane's marriage, she was reminded of what the future will be like when no daughters are left to marry, and she decided to turn over a new leaf."

Elizabeth considered that theory. "Perhaps. I really have no idea, but I shall wait until Jane comes to Pemberley and see what she makes of it."

"That sounds like a logical thing to do." William pulled her into his lap.

"Now, Mrs. Darcy, since I have you alone, I believe we should seize the opportunity."

Elizabeth smiled mischievously. "I agree, sir. You shall never hear me complain," she said as she kissed him.

Chapter 50

**Pemberley
March 3, 1813
Late afternoon**

Although today was Lady Anne's birthday, it was given little thought by the occupants of Pemberley, for Elizabeth Darcy had been in labour since the evening before, and their focus was on her. As the hours passed, William, who was normally well mannered, had become increasingly irritable whenever he addressed Mr. Camryn. And, though the physician was pleased whenever a prospective father was supportive of his wife during childbirth, he had never encountered any man as *engaged* in the process as Fitzwilliam Darcy. Be that as it may, he did his best to stay unruffled amidst a steady barrage of questions and expressions of uncertainty from the father-to-be, even including lately, when due to the baby's reluctance to leave his current quarters, he had suggested that Mrs. Darcy walk the halls in a bid to hasten the child's birth.

Having been kept busy, Camryn had not eaten since breaking his fast that morning and was beginning to feel the effects of that omission. Thus, when Mrs. Reynolds brought a dinner tray upstairs and insisted that he sit down and eat, he acquiesced. Comfortably ensconced in Mrs. Darcy's sitting room, he had just finished his meal and was resting his eyes when the midwife who had accompanied him to Pemberley rushed into the room. Mrs. Posey, who was new to the profession, had come along to observe and learn, and her inexperience brought with it certain drawbacks.

"Mr. Camryn," Mrs. Posey said, glancing over her shoulder as if expecting the object of her report to appear. "Mr. Darcy said that I should tell you that the walking has not helped in the least. He said, in fact, that it has only served to make his wife exhausted."

Sighing heavily, he said, "Please tell Mr. Darcy that, other than walking, I can think of nothing to prod the child into being born sooner. I am certain the babe is in the proper position, so it will come when it is good and ready."

"But… but," the woman stuttered. "I dare not say that to Mr. Darcy. He is akin to a madman right now. Whenever I try to be helpful, he looks right through me with those piercing blue eyes. Perhaps I should wait here, and when he comes looking for me, you can tell him yourself."

Just then another cry echoed down the hallway outside. That Mrs. Darcy was in great pain was clear. She had endured the first half of her labour trying to be brave, possibly because she did not want to grieve her husband, for that gentleman winced with her every groan. However, since the labour had intensified, she had given up all pretence of serenity and now cried out whenever the pain overwhelmed her.

Being a compassionate man, his heart went out to her. "The first child is always the most difficult," Camryn said to no one in particular. Then addressing the midwife, he declared, "Please tell Mr. Darcy that I shall examine his wife again, Mrs. Posey. Perhaps the child has decided to be born now after all."

After a moment of cautious hesitation, the midwife left to do as asked. Camryn then glanced toward heaven, offering a silent entreaty.

Lord, would you consider helping this babe along? I fear that I shall have two patients to attend if Mrs. Darcy's labour lasts much longer.

Tossing his serviette down on the dinner tray, he walked through the door that led into Mrs. Darcy's bedroom. A maid was preparing the bed with layers of sheets and, upon seeing him, she nodded and went back to her work.

On a dresser sat a pitcher of steaming water, a bar of soap, a stack of towels and a bowl. Pouring some of the water into the bowl, he diligently washed his hands and dried them on a towel. As he was doing this, he caught sight of himself in a mirror hanging on the wall behind the dresser. Taking a deep breath, he silently spoke to the image in the mirror.

Do your best, trust God, and leave the outcome to Him.

The billiards room

Playing billiards alone, Richard was addressing the cue ball on another round when an even louder cry of pain echoed throughout the house. Consequently, he hit the ball too hard, causing the shot to go awry and sending one ball off the table entirely. Murmuring to himself, he got down on his knees and crawled under the table to fetch the errant ball.

Normally, Joseph Fitzwilliam would have found all of this very amusing and would have teased his nephew. Not today. At present he was too rattled by what was happening upstairs to find anything amusing. With the start of Elizabeth's labour, he had recalled his own feelings of helplessness when Olivia gave birth to Arthur and later Jenny, and that had occupied his mind ever since.

Richard ventured, "Do you suppose it would do any good to speak to Darcy again? If he would just let Aunt Olivia take over with Elizabeth for a time… just to get some rest, he—"

"Fitzwilliam has spent the last twenty-four hours encouraging Elizabeth and bolstering her spirits when she wanted to despair. I dare say, you cannot take his mind off her," Joseph cut in dryly. "You will have a better understanding of his frame of mind after your wife has birthed your first child."

"I think these last few hours have turned me against marriage completely or, at least, against the idea of having children," Richard replied glumly.

"And why is that?"

No longer able to act unflappable, Richard replaced his cue stick on the rack on the wall. "I may look as though I am not worried, but I am. Many women die during childbirth."

"Life is never certain, Son. Olivia and I have learned that. But marriage and children are what brings mankind the most happiness."

"Darcy is dearer to me than my own brother. I have no doubt that he would grieve himself to death if something were to happen to Elizabeth."

"I know. I have never seen a man so fiercely in love with a woman, with the exception of my love for Olivia." He could not hold back a smile with his last remark. "He must have gotten that trait from the Fitzwilliams."

At Richard's shocked look, he explained, "I should have said he got it from the good side of the Fitzwilliams!"

"It is hard to remember at times that there is a good side to our family; only you and Lady Anne hold that honour. My grandfather, my father, my brother and Lady Catherine have dominated the family for as long as I remember—one and all mean-spirited."

"I have to speak up for my brother, for I witnessed a definite change in his attitude after Fitzwilliam was hurt."

"Let us hope that the change is permanent," Richard said sombrely. "He and I were never close, and I doubt that will ever change. Still, I have always wished that he would drop the sword when it comes to you and Aunt Olivia."

"Olivia and I wish for that, too. Life is too short to hold grudges, especially against family, if it is possible to forgive."

"I agree."

Another anguished cry from the floor above brought both their eyes to the ceiling. Joseph pushed away from the wall he had been leaning against.

"I think I shall brave Fitzwilliam's temper to see how my niece is faring, and I should check on Olivia. She has been on her knees in prayer for the last hour." Tilting his head and smiling sheepishly, he added, "Perhaps this time she will not tell me to either join her in prayer or find some other useful employment. I fear I am no good at prayer in the midst of unfolding events. I do better before or afterward."

As Joseph headed to the door, Richard called, "If I can be of service, you know where to find me." His uncle nodded, though he never slowed his pace.

Knowing he was unlikely to be called upon, Richard went to Darcy's liquor cabinet and poured two fingers of his best brandy. Downing it in one swallow, he set the glass down and walked to the windows where he stared into the distance for a time.

Then he did something he rarely did in the light of day—with the exception of the times he had faced the enemy across a battlefield. He bowed his head and prayed.

When the physician examined Elizabeth again, he found that she was much closer to giving birth. At that point, he tried to convince William to wait in the sitting room; however, having stayed by her side the entire time, he was not about to leave his wife. Seeing that he was beaten, Camryn turned his attention to delivering the child, while William sat down beside Elizabeth on the bed, encircling her with his arms for support, so that she lay back against his chest.

"Mrs. Darcy, your baby has decided to make his appearance. In a moment,

I shall ask for your help. Whenever I say push, please do so with all your strength. It may take a while, but the end is in sight."

"But I... I have no strength left," Elizabeth said weakly.

William kissed the top of her head. "You have more courage than any woman I have ever known, Elizabeth Darcy, and I have no doubt you will find the strength within you."

Elizabeth took a shaky breath. "Help me, Will. Hold me up a bit more."

William did as she asked, and suddenly Mr. Camryn said, "It is time! Push, Mrs. Darcy!"

Elizabeth summoned all her strength to do as he asked, gripping William's arms as she bore down with all her might. Nonetheless, just as she collapsed from the exertion, he ordered her to repeat it. Time and again for close to an hour, Camryn insisted that she push. Consequently, when he went silent, the entire room seemed to still. Then suddenly, the wail of a newborn filled the hush.

As William helped his exhausted wife to lie back against some pillows, the physician exclaimed, "It is a boy!"

Holding the baby up for the parents to see, he added, "He is eight pounds if he is an ounce."

Elizabeth broke into waves of sobs, causing William's heart to stop.

"Elizabeth!" He looked back to Camryn. "Is she in pain?"

"No need to worry, Mr. Darcy. Your wife is doing very well," Camryn assured. After tying off the cord, he turned to hand the wailing child to Mrs. Posey. "Please wash the babe while I finish here."

Olivia, who had slipped into the room unnoticed, interrupted their exchange. "May I?" Beaming ear to ear, she added, "I am his grandmother."

"Of course, Mrs. Fitzwilliam."

Both parents' eyes looked on as Olivia took their crying child over to a table brought in for just this purpose. It was covered with stacks of towels and a large ceramic bowl that the midwife had already covered with a soft towel and filled with warm water. As Olivia began to gently wash the babe, however, the volume of his protests increased.

Elizabeth grasped her husband's arm. "Will, whenever you talked to the baby before he was born, he always quieted. I think hearing your voice may help to soothe him."

William placed a gentle kiss on Elizabeth's forehead and hurried to stand where the babe might see him. While Olivia continued the task of making him presentable, his father brushed a few wet curls from the baby's forehead. The realisation that this small person was his own child overwhelmed William and tears filled his eyes. Blinking to hold them back, he struggled to keep his voice from breaking when he spoke.

"There, there, Alexander. All will be well soon, Son."

Hearing his father's voice, Alexander ceased his frenzied wailing and seemed to focus on the large figure standing at the end of the table. Unable to hide the huge grin that spread over his face, William began to gently stroke one of the baby's velvety cheeks with two fingers. As he did, his tears refused to obey and slid from his eyes.

"You may find that you enjoy having a bath. And, that your grandmother is an excellent bather, if only you would calm down."

By now Alexander's fists were waving wildly, and William reached out to hold one. He was delighted when the fist opened and grasped one of his fingers. Swallowing the large lump in his throat, he continued. "And, surely you wonder who possesses the melodious voice that you have become used to—the one who has sung to you all these months. That lady is your beautiful mother. Surely you will want to be on your best behaviour when you greet her."

Though Alexander did not stop crying entirely, by the time Olivia was nearly finished with his bath, his cries were more sporadic. While all of this was transpiring, Mrs. Reynolds and Mrs. O'Reilly slipped quietly into the room with several maids. When Mrs. Reynolds went to the baby, the others lined one wall, waiting for Mr. Camryn to finish attending Elizabeth. As soon as he stood and nodded in their direction, O'Reilly motioned for them to begin.

Meanwhile, Mrs. Reynolds had stepped behind Olivia and peered over her shoulder. Seeing the housekeeper, William reached for her hand and pulled her to stand next to him. Tears filled the old servant's eyes as they looked at the baby.

She whispered, "I had despaired of living long enough to see another Darcy born at Pemberley. This is a landmark I shall never forget."

William slid an arm around her shoulder, giving it a slight squeeze. "Neither shall any of us."

Olivia, who was now busily drying Alexander with a towel, whispered, "He is just perfect."

Mr. Camryn walked over, still drying his hands on a towel. Laying it aside, he said, "Let me have a better look at this young man." He proceeded to examine the baby, nodding in satisfaction as he assessed the baby with different measures. When finished, he stepped back. "I agree, Mrs. Fitzwilliam. This is a perfectly healthy baby."

While the physician returned to the dresser where Mrs. Posey was washing his instruments, Olivia wrapped the child in a small blanket and handed him to his father. Immediately, William kissed his son then turned to look at Elizabeth. He found her surrounded by a veritable army of maids, three of whom were leaving with arms full of sheets.

The second Camryn had concluded his part in Elizabeth's care, the sheets had been removed, and Mrs. O'Reilly had begun to wash her mistress. Afterward, she had helped her into a fresh gown. Thus, by the time Alexander was ready to meet his mother, the lady's maid was tying a pink ribbon around her hair to keep it from her face.

"All done, ma'am," she said proudly.

"Thank you, Mrs. O'Reilly," Elizabeth murmured tiredly.

From across the room, William saw that Elizabeth was studying him, her face weary, yet absolutely radiant with joy. Hurrying to her side, he sat down beside her and peeled back the blanket. Immediately, she began to examine her child's feet and hands.

"Ten toes and ten fingers," William proclaimed proudly.

"Let me hold him."

"Are you sure, darling? He is not light and you must be exhausted."

"Yes. I need to hold him."

William passed the baby to her, grabbing a large pillow to stuff under her arm for support. Smiling through happy tears, Elizabeth smoothed the dark curls on Alexander's forehead and kissed him. Then running a finger gently over one of his chubby cheeks, she said, "He looks just like you—his eyes and hair."

"But his eyes are shaped like yours, and his hair is definitely curlier. His nose does not look like mine."

She tapped Alexander's button nose. "It is so small that I shall not make a judgement about that until later."

"If I remember correctly, my mother said that a baby's hair and eye colour could change months after they are born."

"I hope they do not. I wish him to look just like you."

William's heart melted. "Elizabeth, he is so precious. I have not the words to say how thankful I am that you and Alexander are in good health, nor how much I love you for giving him to me."

She quit studying the baby look at her husband. "I love you, too, Fitzwilliam, and I could say the same, for you have given me Alexander."

They shared a passionate kiss, causing their company to look away; however, the baby began whimpering, bringing his parents' attention back to him. Elizabeth cooed to him in between placing kisses over his face, which caused him to quiet.

"I would say without reservation that Alexander is much larger than the Becker's son," William offered.

"I agree."

Camryn appeared at the foot of the bed. Looking over the top of his spectacles, he said, "The Beckers? Do I know them?"

"They are our tenants," William replied. "Elizabeth was forced to deliver their son shortly after she came to Pemberley, and I was called upon to wash him."

"I heard about that, but I had completely forgotten," Camryn said. Then he declared to Mrs. Posey, "I suppose if I am not available, you may always call on the Darcys, should you ever need help with a birth."

The midwife looked aghast at the very thought, though William winked at Elizabeth. Not totally unexpected, Alexander soon began to cry in earnest. It was obvious that he wanted to be fed, so Aunt Olivia came forward, shooing the men away. William joined Camryn in a corner, quietly talking as the physician packed his instruments in a bag. Pulling the curtain part way around the bed, Olivia's voice was muffled as she offered Elizabeth her expertise. And, when the curtain was opened, it was clear that mother and son had caught on quickly. The baby's eyes were closed, and he was suckling robustly at his mother's breast.

William walked back to Elizabeth, settling beside her to watch Alexander nurse. At this point, she asked, "Have you forgotten something, Will?"

Brows furrowed in puzzlement. "Forgotten? I know not—"

Smiling crookedly, she interrupted. "Today is your mother's birthday."

His brows softened. "I thought of it yesterday, but today I was entirely focused on you and the baby. Now that my prayers for your safety have been answered, the fact that Alexander was born on Mother's birthday makes it all the sweeter. I know how proud she would have been of her grandson."

Mr. Camryn was weary and eager to return to his home. Nonetheless, he needed to issue instructions before he left. Donning his coat, he picked up his bag and walked over to the bed.

"Mrs. Darcy, because of the length of your labour, I am going to order you to rest in bed for at least two weeks."

Elizabeth wanted to protest, but before she could, William asked, "Do you intend for her to stay in bed the entire time?"

"No. There is nothing to keep her from sitting in a chair and walking a bit if she feels well enough. Of course, all meals must be served on a tray, as I do not want her taking the stairs."

"I am right here," Elizabeth reminded them. "Why do the two of you talk as though I cannot hear or comprehend what you are saying?"

Camryn tried to suppress a smile. Having dealt with his patient in the weeks after William was hurt, he was used to Mrs. Darcy's spirit. Biting his tongue, he motioned for Mrs. Posey to follow him from the room. Olivia and Mrs. Reynolds were right behind them.

"I am sorry, dearest. You are absolutely correct. I have been in a daze since Alexander's birth and I slipped back into my old ways."

"I understand, Will. And I respect that you have donned your protective husband and father manner. Still, we are a team, and I do not like being talked about as though I have no opinion."

It was just as well that the room had emptied, for Elizabeth might have been embarrassed had anyone heard William's next words.

"I shall try my best, Elizabeth, for we are, indeed, a team." A slight smirk played on the corners of his mouth. "After all, how else could Alexander have been conceived if not for *teamwork*?"

Instantly, a gleam of mischievousness filled her eyes, and William backed away from the bed with his hands raised in mock surrender. Elizabeth grabbed a small pillow and was poised to throw it.

"Just wait until I get on my feet, dear husband!" she said. Giggling, she tossed her weapon. "Being sorry will not save you then!"

In the sitting room, all those who had vacated Elizabeth's bedroom were in a circle talking when the sounds of laughter reached them. None could keep from smiling ear to ear.

At that moment Richard stuck his head in the door. "Uncle said that Elizabeth and Darcy have a boy. Are mother and child both well?"

"I am pleased to report that they are both in excellent health," Mr. Camryn replied.

"And Darcy?"

"Fitzwilliam is giddy with happiness," Olivia proclaimed.

Richard grinned. "I should like to see that."

"Sit down right here." Olivia took his hand and led him to a chair by the window. "As soon as Elizabeth is through feeding Alexander, I shall make certain that you have opportunity to do just that."

It was not twenty minutes later that his aunt kept her promise.

The birth of Fitzwilliam Alexander George Darcy, or Alex, as he was to be called, was officially announced the next morning. The news was greeted with great fanfare amongst Pemberley's tenants, the nearby village of Lambton, and the entirety of Derbyshire. Celebrations followed for days as word spread, for the prosperity of the inhabitants of those regions depended greatly upon a successful continuance of one generation of Darcys to the next.

Chapter 51

London
Four months later

Courtesy of a full moon, a muted, silvery hue bathed scores of carriages as they shuffled attendees of the Matlocks' dinner party back to their homes. Invitations to the soirée had been highly sought-after, and excitement was still running high amongst those who had attended, for they had been witness to the return of Mr. and Mrs. Fitzwilliam Darcy to London society. This august couple had not been seen in Town since shortly after their marriage more than a year before, and to be able to brag of having seen them was a feather in the cap of any lady of distinction. The residual excitement, however, did not extend to the occupants of one particular carriage.

"Will, if you are not careful, your face will freeze in that scowl," Elizabeth teased. "Then Alex will be as afraid of you as some I met tonight."

William could not hold back a smile at her contention. "Surely, you jest. Who could be frightened of me?"

"On the contrary, I am completely serious," Elizabeth replied with a wry grin. "You were perfectly amiable until after supper when that group of ladies stopped by our table. I shall never forget their fawning manner when you acknowledged them."

"Elizabeth." By the way William drew out the syllables of her name it was plain that he did not wish to discuss it. "I assure you that the women of the *ton* have never held any appeal for me."

"But some of them were extremely beautiful."

"And extremely dull. You are both beautiful and intelligent."

Elizabeth gave him a quick kiss in appreciation. "I love that you think so. Still, I am at a loss to comprehend their reason for acting so conspicuous. After all, you are now a married man."

"I presume it was curiosity. Most of those women were not at the ball after our marriage. And, since we arrived when the receiving line was nearly finished, they had no opportunity to get a close look at the woman who snatched the prize from under their noses."

"The prize?"

"Me, or rather, my wealth. That is all that marriage means to most of the *ton*."

"I do not happen to agree with that. For, after all, you are a very handsome man in addition to being rich." She laughed. "Having seen the eligible men in attendance tonight, I cannot blame them for envying me. It is sad, though, that they received such a scowl for their trouble."

"So, I looked fearsome, did I?"

"Oh, yes," Elizabeth retorted. "And you still do. I was almost afraid to interrupt your thoughts just now."

"I do not believe that." William leaned over to kiss her upturned face then settled back into the seat. "I have heard you say often enough that your courage rises with every attempt to intimidate you." He was silent for a long moment. "I do owe you an apology though, for I have been in a disagreeable mood ever since we left Pemberley. I would rather you had rested for another two months before making a trip of this duration—especially one to honour my sister."

"But Mr. Camryn declared that I have completely recovered."

His expression did not soften. "What does he know? I am with you every day. I have a clearer perspective of your health than he."

Placing a kiss on his cheek, she tried not to chuckle. "Yes, dear."

After a long moment of silence, she tried again. "But you must admit that coming to London was preferable to having my family visit us as they did in May. Mama settled in *too* eagerly at Pemberley, ordering our servants about as though they were her own. And it became obvious that she was jealous of my relationship with Aunt Olivia, not to mention how much Alexander adores her. In the end, I began to fear she would stay until she was certain that the baby favoured her over our aunt."

"That will never happen."

"I agree. A child knows when someone is sincere, and Mother's attentions to him are for display. Still, I was worried that she thought it a contest and would stay until she felt she had won."

"If not for your father, she would likely still be there," William said under his breath.

"I am sorry. I did not hear you."

"I said at least your father is sensible."

"It is a blessing that my family was scheduled to be in London this week. We can host them for dinner tomorrow and be free of obligations for months to come. And, as Aunt Evelyn pointed out, it was necessary that we attend Georgiana's engagement dinner to thwart the gossips. Besides, it was time you met her fiancé."

"I have been familiar with Georgiana's *fiancé* for many years. I did not relish meeting him."

"Why ever not?"

"Viscount Peabody often frequented White's after he completed Cambridge, and to say I was not impressed is an understatement."

"But you said nothing to me."

"Given Georgiana's spiteful conduct, I was determined that her circumstances not become your worry. You have your hands full being mistress of our homes and rearing our son. That is how it should be."

"I have forgiven her—you know that."

"I do. And I have forgiven her as well. But whenever I look at Alexander, I am reminded that she thought nothing of having you shipped from England knowing that you were carrying him. Perhaps, over time—"

He became silent, and again Elizabeth squeezed his hand, for she

understood his feelings all too well. Still, she wished to know more about Georgiana's tall, handsome and blond fiancé. "What worries you about Viscount Peabody?"

"The fact that he is your typical wealthy heir—spoiled and self-serving—chiefly known among men whose opinions I trust for his love of drink, his extravagant losses on the races, and his eye for the ladies."

"Will you inform Georgiana?"

"I wrote her about his reputation when I got word of their growing attachment. She responded that he has changed and, since they are engaged, it is obvious that she did not take my reservations seriously."

"Does Lord Matlock know?"

"Yes, but my uncle is a good friend of the young man's father; thus, he dismisses what I see as drawbacks. After all, most young men of the *ton* share these attributes. He does not see them as any reason to reject a legitimate offer and, as he pointed out, Georgiana seems determined to have him."

William stared out the window for a time before continuing. "If not for my aunt's plea, I would not have come tonight."

"Do you wish to hear my opinion?"

William chuckled. "I believe I am about to, regardless."

"I think that you are afraid that Georgiana is too immature to know her heart. You fear that she will marry in blissful ignorance."

"You know me well." He lifted Elizabeth's hand and placed a kiss thereon. "That is why when Lord Matlock consulted me about Peabody's offer I insisted that the engagement be for a full year. Though that still may not be enough time, Georgiana will be nineteen before they marry. Perhaps, by then she will have seen more of his character."

"I have no idea what has transpired since she went to live with the Matlocks, but I have to wonder if they see marriage as the only option to tame her."

"Both my aunt and uncle contend that she has been a model of decorum since she came to live with them."

"I pray that is so." Elizabeth considered how to continue. "Did you happen to notice when she approached me tonight? It was while you were dancing with your aunt?"

William stiffened. "Georgiana? No, I did not. What did she say?"

"She purchased a present for Alexander—Noah's ark with all the animals—and wanted to know if she could have it delivered to Darcy House. I suggested that she bring it in person and meet him. She declined."

"Did she give a reason?"

"She contended that Alexander deserves family about him who supported his birth from the beginning. I tried to argue the point, but Viscount Peabody came to claim her for another dance and the chance was lost."

"It is just as well. Let her decide if and when she is ready to meet our son."

Just then the carriage stopped in front of Darcy House, and the carriage door was instantly opened. A footman offered his hand, but William stepped out first and assisted Elizabeth to the pavement. Together they walked arm-in-arm up the steps to greet Mr. Barnes who stood in the open entrance.

The nursery
The next day

Already dressed for dinner, William entered the nursery and seeing that Alexander was awake, picked him up and kissed his forehead, followed by both cheeks. "How is Papa's fine boy?"

Turning, he caught the nanny suppressing a grin and assumed a more businesslike manner. "Mrs. Anderson, if you will follow me, you may wait in the kitchen until summoned to take Alexander back to the nursery."

Quickly he exited the room, and the servant had to hurry to catch up. "I shall have Mrs. Barnes fetch you just before we are called to dinner. I am praying that my son will behave until then."

"Master Alexander should do well, for he was fed within the hour and, unlike some children I have cared for, he is good natured."

William smiled at the compliment. Having reached the grand staircase with his child, he noticed that Mrs. Barnes was waiting at the bottom. Her eyes lit up upon seeing Alexander, and she smiled at the babe with a look reserved only for him, as father and child descended. Then patting the baby's hand affectionately, she relayed a message to her employer.

"Sir, Colonel Fitzwilliam has just arrived. He is waiting in the library."

"I wondered where he was. Please tell Mrs. Darcy that Alexander and I are in the library with my cousin. Oh, and Mrs. Anderson will wait in the kitchen to take Alex back to the nursery when you call us to dine."

"Very good, sir."

The library

When William entered, he was holding his look-alike son effortlessly. Naturally, Richard could not resist teasing him.

"I see you already have mastered fatherhood, Darcy. If you find it that simple, I should have no problem whatsoever."

"If it were only this simple," William answered, his mouth settling in a wry grin. "Wait until you are called upon for less agreeable duties."

"I do not intend to handle the *less agreeable* duties," Richard declared coming forward. "That is what nannies are hired to do!"

He stopped in front of William and the child, a ridiculous grin on his face. Reaching out to chuck Alexander under the chin, he said, "Do you remember me?"

Two amiable light blue eyes lit up and the baby smiled. That was all it took to provoke the colonel into making a series of silly faces and noises to accompany them. His efforts were successful in eliciting more smiles and that motivated William to demonstrate his own expertise.

"Watch this!" he ordered, holding his son at arms' length over his head. The instant he brought Alex down to bury his head in his stomach and blow on it, the child shrieked.

Richard laughed heartily. However, once he was able to catch his breath he warned, "Be careful, Cousin! Remember the Duke of Chichester's son—

the one that Edgar tossed about at Lady Alice's picnic! Children of that age are prone to spew the contents of their stomachs at the least provocation."

"Alex was fed some time ago, so there should be no danger. Still, lest my son make a liar of me, I shall abstain," he declared. "Elizabeth would be upset if he ruined his clothes before our guests arrive."

"And what of yours?"

William laughed. "She would say only that I got what I deserved!"

Richard looked about to make certain no one was in the room. "I was going to wait until tomorrow, but since we are alone, do you wish to hear what I learned of late regarding Lady Susan?"

William threw a small blanket over his shoulder and propped Alexander there as he sat down. Patting the child's back to occupy him, he said, "I would."

"According to my sources, Hartley and Susan are living in the West Indies, though Hartley travels between there and Spain. Seems a ship's captain confirmed that he met them on one of the smaller islands whilst unloading supplies and picking up merchandise. Invited to dinner, the captain said that Hartley had the only decent home there, though it is not much more than a larger version of the huts the natives occupy. And this is the best part! On this particular island there are only two other English speaking persons—both men of advanced age."

"I cannot imagine that Susan is content with no fine home, no shops to buy what her heart desires and no one to impress."

"You are correct. The captain also said that she tried to bribe him to take her along when he sailed. Seems he found that very amusing, for Lord Hartley's godfather owns the shipping line, though she has no idea. Moreover, she confessed to him that she had no access to money. All she could offer him as a bribe was a promise to pay once she arrived in England."

"I have to wonder if she will return one day. After all, if Hartley should die, what is to stop her? If those who can testify to her complicity in what happened to Fletcher or Elizabeth are gone or scattered, she could be in no danger of arrest."

"If she returns, it will be as a penniless woman. Hartley's solicitor is prone to drink, and during one drunken stint, he let it be known that Hartley changed his will before he sailed. He left Susan not a farthing and signed over daily governance of his properties here to a cousin from Wales. The only stipulation is that the cousin rears at Hartley Hall the boy that Susan bore and sends him to Eton and Cambridge. When her son reaches five and twenty he will receive half of Hartley's estate and at thirty, the remainder. For his service, the cousin will be given property in Wales and an income for life after the boy inherits."

"What would keep the cousin from doing away with the boy and keeping it all? Or the boy from helping his mother once he has control?"

"Apparently, the solicitor's law firm is executor of the will. If the child does not live to inherit, or the terms are broken in any manner, everything will pass to Hartley's godfather or to his descendents. As for the child helping Susan, I suppose it is possible. One can only hope that by the time he inherits, he will be married to a woman smart enough to manage Lady Susan should she suddenly reappear."

"Still, Susan will inherit Monthaven Manor."

"Do you not think it strange that Lord Concord's health improved after she was abducted? So much so, that his mind is now clear enough to manage the estate?"

"To be honest, I have been too busy enjoying my time with Elizabeth and Alexander to consider what was transpiring at Monthaven."

"Well, speculation is that Susan may have been tainting his food to muddle his mind. In any event, he has changed his will."

"The allegation against Susan does not surprise me. So who is to inherit Monthaven Manor? Not Lord Attaway, I hope."

"Good heavens, no! It is a great nephew—Lord Pearson of Wessex, if memory serves. I understand that he is four and twenty, newly graduated from Cambridge and already has a good head on his shoulders."

"Since he will be my neighbour in the future, let us hope that is true."

Suddenly, the knocker on the front door caught their attention. William sighed, standing to his feet with Alexander. "I should have known they would come early, and Elizabeth is not down yet."

"Yes, I am!"

Elizabeth swept into the room, breathtakingly beautiful with her dark hair swept up on the sides and held by pearl combs. Long curls were left to cascade down her back. She wore a teal blue, silk damask gown with skirts that made a swishing noise when she walked. William was instantly reminded of his mother and followed her progress with adoring eyes.

She hurried first to Richard and kissed his cheek, proclaiming, "I am so pleased to see you again, Cousin."

"And you," was his reply. She was already rushing toward William when Richard added, "Let me say that that gown is stunning on you."

Elizabeth suddenly stopped, turned and smiled. "Why, thank you, Richard. I shall have to remember to wear this colour more often."

Tickled to have received a jealous look from William, Richard smirked as Elizabeth hurried on to her husband. At last reaching William, she placed a quick kiss on his mouth and began to gather Alexander in her arms.

"Let me hold the baby, Will. The last time Mama greeted you, he was nearly crushed to death."

Acquiescing, William replied dryly, "How well I remember."

At his remark, mischievousness sparkled in her chocolate eyes. "Mama delights in greeting her *ten-thousand-a-year and half-of-Derbyshire* son with a generous hug. And, I would never suspend any pleasure of hers."

William threw up his hands in mock frustration. "Richard, do you see how cruel she has become since giving birth to Alexander?"

Richard retorted, "Her faults are vast indeed!"

At that exact moment Mr. Barnes appeared at the library door, followed by their company. "Sir, Mr. and Mrs. Ben—"

"Oh, Mr. Darcy," Fanny Bennet squealed, pushing past the startled butler

before he could finish. "It is so good to see you again!" She rushed to Darcy and embraced him. He stiffened with the gesture.

Mr. Barnes looked fit to be tied, so William addressed him. "Thank you, Barnes. You may return to your post." Glancing vexingly at Mrs. Bennet, the butler nodded and did as instructed, leaving the Gardiners and Bingleys to go unannounced.

Unperturbed, Elizabeth's mother continued her raptures. "I have been telling Mr. Bennet that we should stay here for the rest of our visit instead of in Cheapside. After all, you have so many rooms, and we can see more of our grandson if we are here."

A heavy sigh escaped Mr. Bennet, though he was not alone in his chagrin, for murmurings could be heard coming from the Gardiners as well. Fanny took no notice and, with no thought for her grandchild, stayed rooted to the spot with a hopeful expression on her face.

Elizabeth coughed. "Alexander is over here, Mama."

Mrs. Bennet looked in her direction. "So he is," she said unenthusiastically. Then remembering, in the blink of an eye, she assumed a grandmotherly smile, put on her former joviality, and approached the child. Ruffling Alexander's hair, she announced loudly, "Thank goodness he favours his father."

Realising what she had just said, she quickly added, "And my lovely daughter."

Mr. Bennet had been about to shake Darcy's hand when the last faux pas occurred. Rolling his eyes, he said quietly, "One cannot make a silk purse from a sow's ear overnight."

Sombrely, William nodded in agreement before welcoming the Gardiners and Bingleys.

During Dinner

"... and I told Lydia that she was certainly old enough to marry, but I insisted that she bide her time... reminding her that now that Lizzy has secured one of the wealthiest men in England, and Jane is married to a man with five thousand a year, she will be thrown into the company of many men with great fortunes. Of course, she insisted she would never marry a man who was not handsome, but I am sure that my Lydia's beauty will attract many a fine-looking gentleman... and there is truly no reason in the world that she cannot marry an earl, or even a duke, if she... "

Singlehandedly, Mrs. Bennet managed to ruin dinner. Except for a short period of time at the beginning of the meal when the Gardiners had responded to Elizabeth's inquiry about their new son, Bradley, the entire conversation had consisted of her mother's thoughts on securing rich husbands for Mary, Kitty and, especially, Lydia. After she had worn out that subject, she began to wax eloquently on how beautiful Jane's first child, due in the fall, would be.

"I just know it will be a boy, and I pray that he has Jane's blond hair... not to say that his father's hair is less handsome, but red-haired children are often teased unmercifully. You, of all people, should understand that, Mr. Bingley," she said, addressing Charles. "Surely you would not want your son to suffer the indignities you must have suffered all because you were born with ginger hair." Not waiting for a reply, she went on, "In any event, I know that he will be bright, for Jane is by far the most intelligent of my girls."

Darcy's expression instantly darkened, and she thought better of her last statement. "What I meant to say is that—in regards to following my advice—Jane is the most clever; whereas, Lizzy always listens to her father, not me."

For the thousandth time, Elizabeth thanked God that none of William's relations were present, save Colonel Fitzwilliam. However, knowing her new cousin's penchant for finding amusement in social gaffes, her mother's manners were all the more embarrassing for his presence. Nonetheless, when she glanced to the end of the table where Richard sat, she was surprised to find him examining her with a sombre expression. Then he offered a slight smile and shrug—perhaps a reminder that she should not take her mother too seriously. Elizabeth relaxed and smiled back.

Subsequently, she turned her attention to William, whose eyes had been locked on his plate during much of the meal. He was absently pushing his food about on the plate and eating little. The struggle for control of his temper was evident when he laid down his fork and brought a hand up to squeeze the bridge of his nose. This was a sure sign that he had a headache, and in that moment, Elizabeth wished that all their guests would simply vanish so that she could relieve his suffering. Smiling to herself at the thought of how she normally alleviated William's headaches, she was surprised to glance back to him and find that he was observing her. She smiled lovingly and gave him a wink.

Having seen their exchange, Richard could not resist. Grinning like a Cheshire cat, he tried his best to sound grave. "Darcy? Are you ill? I declare, you look as though you are suffering some sort of great pain."

Realising what his cousin was about, William said, "I assure you that I am in excellent health." Then he leaned toward him, saying so low that only Richard could hear, "If you wish to be welcome at Darcy House ever again, you will cease this very minute."

Undeterred, the colonel said loudly, "No need to thank me, Darcy. We are cousins, and it is only natural that I should worry about your welfare."

Following Richard's antics from her end of the table, Elizabeth was barely able to cover her mouth before she giggled. Mrs. Bennet stopped nattering and looked at her daughter.

"Are you well, Lizzy, dear? Remember one should never talk when one is eating."

The absurdity of that statement coming from someone who talked constantly— even whilst she ate—was not lost on the others, and many an eye rolled in response.

"I am well. But thank you for the advice, Mama."

Mrs. Bennet smiled exultantly, looking about the table. "It is not necessary to thank me. That is what mothers are supposed to do—impart wisdom to their children."

Elizabeth's eyes met Jane's, and they both looked away, pursing their lips to keep from laughing.

※

In a short while, William had doffed his clothes, donned his robe, and entered Elizabeth's bedroom. She was sitting on a sofa and stood upon seeing him. He came to a complete halt. For instead of wearing one of her cotton gowns, as her habit was of late, she wore a gown that her Aunt Gardiner had given her for their honeymoon. It was pale-pink and sleeveless, made of the thinnest, most delicate silk. The gown clung to her like a second skin, revealing all of her feminine attributes. In addition, her hair was loose, and it cascaded down in silky waves. Desire instantly stirred.

"Elizabeth, you look... stunning."

Without further hesitation, he went to her, gathering her into his embrace. Feeling the evidence of his desire against her abdomen, Elizabeth's longing grew stronger, and she slid her hands to his back, urging him closer.

"I wanted to look attractive for you," she murmured into his chest.

Kissing the tender skin of her shoulder, he feathered kisses to her ear where he whispered, "You are beautiful regardless of what you wear."

"Still, since Alexander's birth, I have practically lived in plain cotton gowns. And they are not meant to titillate."

"You excite me, sweetheart... only you."

"I am pleased to hear that," Elizabeth said dreamily. Then she pulled back to peer into his eyes. "Still, tonight I was reminded of how much you have endured because you love me. When I think of my mother's thoughtless chatter—"

"Do not forget the wickedness aimed at you by my own sister," William interrupted. "In my opinion, there is no comparison."

Kissing her tenderly, he enquired, "Are you sure that you are not too tired? Today has been so hectic and I will understand should you rather sleep."

Suddenly, his lips were captured with such passion that he almost took a step back. The fervour of Elizabeth's kiss stoked a rapidly increasing fire and William returned her kiss fiercely. Still, when he picked her up, he headed to the sofa instead of the bed, sitting down with her in his lap.

"Will? Are we not—"

Pleased by her eagerness, he brought a finger to her lips to silence her. "Patience, love. The sight of you in that gown almost caused me to forget what I wished to do before I ravish you." Laughing at her puzzled expression, he smoothed some loose curls from her face. "Do you remember the significance of this day?"

"It is neither your birthday nor mine, and since our anniversary was last month, I am afraid that I do not."

"We may have been married officially on the twenty-eighth of April, but our marriage did not begin in earnest until this day one year past."

Elizabeth's heart melted with the remembrance. "The night we spent in your mother's cottage."

"Exactly," William said triumphantly. "In my heart, our true anniversary will always be today."

"Does this mean I shall receive two anniversary presents each year?" she asked cheekily.

Reaching under one of the sofa cushions, William brought out a small black box. "Yes, you shall. And here is the second."

At once she looked remorseful. "I was only teasing, Will. Besides, I have nothing to give to you."

William smiled sensually. "Oh, but you do, my love. And I intend to thoroughly enjoy my gift in a few minutes."

"Mr. Darcy, you make me blush."

"It is my intention to make you do much more than blush, *Mrs. Darcy*."

"You are incorrigible!"

"When it comes to you, I am!" he declared, giving her a quick kiss. "Now, open your gift, for I wish to know if you like it."

As she took off the lid, Elizabeth said, "But I love the diamond brooch you gave me for our anniversary. And I certainly did not expect—"

Suddenly she became completely silent. Inside the box was a delicate, heart-shaped, gold locket engraved with the same sentiments as her wedding ring—First... Last... Only... Always—only this time the words were spelled using small rubies, and the perimeter of the heart was covered in diamonds, all matching in size and brilliancy.

"Oh, Will," she breathed. "It is lovely." Then hurriedly opening the lock, she found a miniature portrait of William. "You remembered!" she exclaimed.

When Mr. Curry brought the portrait of Elizabeth in her wedding gown to Pemberley, he had presented William with a miniature of his wife for his watchcase. Ever since then, Elizabeth had begged him to have a similar one painted for her use.

"I did."

"I cannot imagine when you found time to sit for it."

"I sat for a few sketches for Mr. Curry at Pemberley. Before he left, he promised to have it finished by the time we came to London for the dinner party. Now," William said, taking the locket from her hand and placing it back in the box. "If memory serves, I was about to partake of *my* present when I stopped to give you this."

Instantly William was kissing her and this passionate kiss intensified until he broke away, taking a deep breath of air. Then taking her in his arms, he strode quickly to the bed where he let her feet slip to the carpet and he pushed the straps of her gown off her shoulders. Watching with hungry eyes as the silky gown floated to the carpet, he was mesmerised by her nakedness and stood perfectly still while Elizabeth untied the belt of his robe and pushed it open. He heard her breath catch upon seeing the evidence of his desire, and when her hands began caressing the hard planes of his abdomen, he struggled to keep control. Once they slid to his muscular chest, raking over the fine hair there, he became consumed by need.

"Sweetheart, what you do to me," he growled, picking her up and laying her on the bed.

Shrugging off his robe and lying beside her, he initiated another searing kiss. Her fingers entwined in the longer hair at his neck, attempting to pull him even closer, while he spread kisses over every inch of her face, whispering, "I love you" in between each one.

Slowly kissing down the supple skin of her neck to her décolletage, he cradled one of her breasts in his hands, exciting it with his fingertips. Since Elizabeth was feeding Alexander, her breasts were tender, and he had to remind himself to be gentle. Even so, as he teased the taut nipple with his tongue, a low moan escaped her throat, and she writhed beneath him, murmuring her eagerness in his ear.

Having learned from experience that when Elizabeth became impatient, their couplings were more satisfying, he quickly complied. Joining with her, he began a steady rhythm, and it was not long until he felt her quiver deep within—a sign that her release had come. Restrained no longer, he thrust again and again until he was spent.

When he collapsed atop her and started to roll over, Elizabeth pleaded, "I want to stay as we are a while longer."

Framing her face with his palms, he kissed her ardently. "There are no words to describe—" He paused to think of how best to express what he felt, saying finally, "Sweetheart, you are an incredible lover!"

Still breathless from their lovemaking, she said softly, "I had a very good teacher."

They both chuckled. At length William rolled on his side, and Elizabeth did as well, so that she could face him. He traced the outline of her perfect jaw before pushing a stray curl behind one ear.

"I have a confession. This week I was reading from the journal covering my last year at Cambridge, and it dawned on me just what I had feared most in life—or at least until well after I met you."

Elizabeth looked puzzled. "I would never have thought you afraid of anything."

"Oh, but I was. From an early age my father told me of the lengths women would go to secure a husband. And I had seen firsthand the results of loveless marriages. I lived in fear of falling under the power of a woman. Only after our marriage did I discover that love could be my salvation and not my ruin."

Tears filled Elizabeth's eyes, and she reached out to caress his face. William turned his head to kiss her palm. Then he grew sombre. "Surely… you must know that you own me—heart, body and soul."

She leaned in, brushing a kiss across his lips. "I do. And I would never do anything to betray that trust, for I am entirely yours."

The next kiss they shared was exquisitely tender, and afterwards, Elizabeth settled into William's strong arms, her head nestled under his chin. Kissing her hair, he whispered, "Forever I shall love being yours."

Elizabeth sighed contentedly. "As I shall love being yours."

It was not long until both drifted into dreams of the future filled with boundless love, more babies and joy beyond measure.

Epilogue

As the years passed, Pemberley completely replaced Elizabeth's childhood home as her favourite place in the world. For though she retained fond memories of Longbourn, tramping through the meadows and being atop Oakham Mount, she experienced her greatest happiness at William's ancestral home. Life was kind, and though they did not escape the usual trials of life, she and William were abundantly blessed with love and good fortune. Consequently, with ample support from family, friends, devoted servants and tenants, they discovered the secrets of truly *becoming one* with one another and faced the future boldly together.

As Alexander grew, he not only proved to be as handsome as his father, but an exceptional young man in his own right. Although aware of his station and expectations from an early age, he was a precocious child with Elizabeth's outgoing personality and his father's watchful temperament. Extremely intelligent, as soon as he could ride, he spent hours with his father examining the length and breadth of Pemberley and learning firsthand the skills necessary to run the estate. And, as each of his siblings was born, Alexander became the perfect older brother, helping to guide them whenever their parents were not about. At least he was perfect as far as his sisters were concerned, though his younger brother was not convinced of that until both were well past the age of majority.

God blessed the Darcys with four more children in the next decade. A daughter, Olivia Elizabeth, was born two years after Alex. A beautiful child, she was identical to her mother in every aspect, except that her eyes were as light blue as her father's. Doted on by her namesake aunt as well as the rest of the family, she could often be found sitting in Olivia Fitzwilliam's lap in the garden swing, being read a book. Remarkably smart, by six years of age she began to beg her father to teach her estate matters alongside Alexander and, by the time she was grown, she was as qualified to run the estate as he.

Three years after Olivia, Joseph Richard Fitzwilliam was born. Named in honour of his uncle and cousin, as well as his father, he favoured Elizabeth more than William. In spite of inheriting the Darcy height, his hair was chocolate brown and his eyes finally settled into a serene dark blue, the same shade as Anne Darcy's. Blessed with an easy-going, charming personality, he was unimpressed with Alexander's attempts to make him a smaller version of himself and chafed against his efforts. It was not until after he began university that he and Alex became as close as brothers ought to be.

William was seven and thirty by the time the last of their children were born. Four years, almost to the day after Richard's birth, Elizabeth presented him with identical twins, Clair Jane and Rose Anne. Each sported hair as jet black as their father's and their mother's ebony eyes. William could not have been more pleased, for he had begun to think Richard was to be their last. Of course, the twins' arrival brought a good deal of liveliness to Pemberley, and the girls were thoroughly spoiled by everyone, including their older siblings.

By this point, William had built Pemberley into a formidable organization, and realising how quickly life was passing, he vowed to spend even more time with his wife and children. Anne Darcy's cottage continued to be a special place reserved for only himself and Elizabeth. Dear to their hearts for playing so prominent a role at the beginning of their marriage, they would frequently rendezvous there—at times for an afternoon but, more often than not, they would spend the night. The cottage provided the perfect opportunity to recommit themselves to each other, while the Darcy children grew up knowing that, from time to time, their parents needed time alone.

The family also enjoyed more frequent trips to the pond, for William had another small cottage erected there to facilitate overnight stays. After long summer days spent swimming and fishing, the entire family would retire to the cottage instead of making the long trek back to Pemberley. With no servants about, it became a welcome respite from the expectations of others and, in later years, the memories made at Lady Anne's cottage and the pond were what sustained the Darcys when their children began to leave home.

The firstborn Bingley, Penelope Jane, a miniature of her father, was so great a disappointment to Mrs. Bennet that her displays of frustration resulted in the Bingley's decision to move away from Meryton. Thus, not long after their daughter's birth, Charles and Jane purchased an estate in Derbyshire, Eastgate Manor, which was a mere twelve miles from Pemberley. The proximity suited Jane and Elizabeth immensely, and they visited often in the early years of their marriages. The move proved fortuitous, too, for just over a year later, the Bingleys' second child, Emma Elizabeth, was born. Reading of her mother's vexation for not having birthed a son on the second try, proved much more tolerable for Jane than suffering Fanny's lamentations in her own parlour. Sadly, when Jane delivered a son two years later, he lived for only a few hours. His death, however, managed to silence Mrs. Bennet on the subject of an heir forever. Thus, when Charles Bennet Bingley was born on their eighth wedding anniversary, Jane's mother was the model of decorum in her response to the news.

Over the years Elizabeth's younger sisters were not thrown into the company of rich men as often as Mrs. Bennet would have liked. Whether their boorish behaviour resulted in few invitations to the Darcys' homes or the fact that the Darcys did not entertain often, the true reason is uncertain. Still, Kitty was introduced to the second son of an earl who made her an offer the year she was twenty. She accepted and was surprisingly happy with her match.

Lydia, prodded by her mother, was bound and determined to charm an earl or a duke and *only a handsome one at that.* Learning far too late that while a nobleman might be entertained by her liveliness, an offer of marriage would not necessarily follow, she was five and twenty before she came to her senses. On the shelf and with her beauty fading, she accepted the hand of a retired officer in the militia—the third son of an earl who had inherited a small estate in Scotland from his grandmother. Already the father of three grown children,

Lieutenant Perkins made it plain that he wished only for companionship and not any more children. Relieved just to be under a man's protection, Lydia agreed to the marriage.

Other than Elizabeth, Mary was probably the most content with her life. At the age of nineteen, she married a newly appointed vicar in the next county, Mr. Cobb. She proved a great help to him with her knowledge of the Bible, and as she matured, she became less judgemental. A steadfast friend to all their parishioners, she was always ready with a hot meal, a new quilt, or a heart-felt prayer when one was needed. A good and humble man, Mr. Cobb was all that Mary had wished for in a mate. Their union produced four children, two boys and two girls, and though she never complained or sought help, Mary was often the recipient of the Darcys' good will. Among Elizabeth's kin, she and her family were most often invited to Pemberley, along with the Bingleys and Gardiners.

All of the Bennet girls were married and on their own by the time Mr. Bennet died. His death, the result of a heart condition, came ten years after Alexander's birth, though he was fortunate enough to live to see all of his grandchildren born. Over the years, he had often visited Pemberley by himself and loved getting lost in the library, where he could read for hours undisturbed. Yet as the grandchildren grew and began to follow him about, Thomas Bennet spent more time talking with them than reading, which delighted his favourite daughter. Often Elizabeth would find Alexander and Olivia sitting under the huge oak tree in the garden at her father's feet, listening raptly whist he regaled them with stories of his childhood. For Elizabeth, the blow of his death was softened only by the knowledge that he had spent many lovely summers with her before he was taken.

With her husband's death, Mrs. Bennet hinted that she wished to live with the Darcys, but Jane insisted that she live with them. To be fair, her mother's inability to control her tongue had improved considerably after the Bingley's first son died and, as it happened, her presence in their home proved to be more help than Jane could have imagined. The Bingleys' daughters were very fond of their grandmother, and Mrs. Bennet never tired of answering their questions or letting them play at styling her hair, which kept them entertained whilst Jane saw after young Charles. Surviving her husband by another two years, Fanny Bennet died peacefully in her sleep and was fondly remembered by all her children and grandchildren.

When the Earl of Matlock died approximately two years after Alexander's birth, the viscount began to drink even more. Edgar followed his father to the grave in less than a year. His demise, the result of a broken neck suffered while trying to take his stallion over a fence to win a bet, left Richard the Earl of Matlock. By that time, he was already in love with a young widow named Eugenie, who was left destitute when her husband, the Earl of Dunston, was killed in a gambling dispute. It was later revealed that he had lost everything on a bet. This red-haired, green-eyed beauty proved to be the love of Richard's life, and following their marriage, she gave birth to four children in close order—Richard Edward Harold, Joseph Darcy David, Eugenie Evelyn and Chloe Catherine.

Georgiana spent the years following her marriage regretting her unkindness to William and Elizabeth, though she was too proud to attempt reconciliation. Her husband, Viscount Peabody, proved to be as prolific a gambler and lover of the fair sex as William had warned. He joined the Four Horse Club [19] in order to place bets on the outcome of the races that sprung up between the members. During one such race, he insisted on driving a team when he was entirely too drunk and lost his life when the carriage collided with another and overturned. Though he was killed just after their fourth wedding anniversary, Georgiana was not as devastated as one might have imagined, for the viscount had long since vacated her bedroom in favour of his mistress' boudoir.

A childless widow at two and twenty, Georgiana found herself relegated to a small apartment, courtesy of her late husband's father. Her entire dowry, Georgiana discovered, had been gambled away, and though Elizabeth and William invited her to live with them, she refused. Instead, with Richard's permission, she made her home with her aunt, the Dowager Countess of Matlock, in the dowager's house on the Matlock estate. At the age of six and twenty, she met a baron many years her senior and accepted his offer of marriage. Moving to his home in Ireland, she was content to reside there until Baron Houston's death fifteen years later. At that time, his son took control of the estate, and she returned to England with what her husband had left her in his will.

She purchased a townhouse in Grosvenor Square and lived alone. Frequently invited to dine with William and Elizabeth when they were in London, she did so timidly at first. Over time, though, her nieces and nephews managed to break down the walls that divided them. Grateful to be treated as an esteemed aunt, Georgiana became the person she had long wished to be and spoiled her brother's children as though they were her own. Moreover, when she died unexpectedly at the age of nine and forty, she was sorely missed by all of her family.

The couple whom William and Elizabeth credited most with saving their marriage, Joseph and Olivia Fitzwilliam, resided at Pemberley until their deaths. Olivia, who was not expected to live long upon her return to England, defied the expectations of her doctor in Ireland and even outlived him. Having relished her role as a grandmother to all the Darcy children, she survived until the twins were almost three years of age. Speaking of Olivia fondly after her death, Mr. Camryn made the observation that the grandchildren were what kept her alive far longer than he had thought possible.

Heartbroken, Joseph Fitzwilliam poured himself into tutoring Alexander and Richard in all that he had learned during his service in the navy. Surviving another five years without his beloved Olivia, Joseph slipped away quietly one afternoon whilst sitting in their favourite spot—the swing in the garden. They found him with Olivia's shawl lying in his lap, his watch case in hand. The case was open to a miniature portrait of his wife painted the year they had married. With his death, a huge gap was left in the family, a fissure just as painful as the one Olivia's passing had generated. But, as life was meant to be, while the older generation slipped away, a new generation took its place.

The Darcy, Bingley and Fitzwilliam children were as close as their parents had been before them and spent copious amounts of time in each other's company. Moreover, as they matured, one estate or another would find itself host to various nieces and nephews with little or no warning. Thus, the next generations grew up as the best of friends, embraced by their fathers, mothers, aunts and uncles, who loved them beyond measure.

In the twilight of their lives, William and Elizabeth often spoke fondly of family long since passed, giving thanks for having had the guidance of those dearest to them when they were once the most unlikely couple in all of England.

As William observed, "We are forever indebted to those who loved us enough to set us straight."

He was right.

Finis

Footnotes

1. *Paradiso* is the third and final part of Dante's Divine Comedy following the Inferno and the Purgatorio. **Page 21**

2. *Kerseymere- A woollen fabric used for coats. Regency Encyclopedia.* http://www.reg-ency.com **Page 31**

3. Pride and Prejudice, Jane Austen, Author. Chapter 31. **Page 80**

4. *Romans 12:19 KJV of the Bible.* **Page 92**

5. *From 2005 Movie of Pride and Prejudice.* **Page 107**

6. *The Mint – Most notorious slum in London, a ten minute stroll from London Bridge and home to the most desperate thieves and beggars.* www.regencyassemblypress.com. **Page 111**

7. *Thruppence – Three pence (about $25). Shilling – Twelve pence (about $100). Ha-penny – Half a penny (about $4)* www.regencyassemblypress.com **Page 112**

8. *Countess Esterházy - wife of the Austrian ambassador Prince Paul Anton Esterházy; Princess Esterházy after 1833.* en.wikipedia.org/wiki/Almack's. **Page 120**

9. The Morning Post *was a newspaper that chronicled the doings of fashionable London.* www.regencyassemblypress.com. **Page 121**

10. *Miss Hannah Humphrey's shop, selling caricature prints, was located at 29 St. James's Street, next to Boodle's. I imagined Madam Bouvier's fictitious shop next door. The Regency Encyclopedia.* http://www.reg-ency.com **Page 155**

11. Newgate – *A prison situated in the heart of London. The Regency Encyclopedia.* http://www.reg-ency.com **Page 253**

12. George Lyon *(1761 – 22 April 1815), a gentleman highwayman in England, was 54 when he was executed in Lancaster by hanging for robbery, as the last Highwayman to be hanged there. Sentence was passed on Saturday 8 April 1815 along with two accomplices, Houghton and Bennett.* http://en.wikipedia.org/wiki/George_Lyon_(highwayman) **Page 254**

13. **Barbara Allen** - There are countless versions of Barbara Allen. AKA Barb'ry Ellen and Barbara Ellen. It is over three centuries old. Its origins are somewhere in the British Isles. Scotland and England both claim it. Versions are found as far afield as Italy and Scandinavia. **Page 295**

14. Chamber candlesticks - special candle holders for the purpose of lighting the way. They had a wide base to prevent wax from dripping on the hand or carpets, a handle for ease of carrying and sometimes an attached snuffer to make it easy to put out the candle. http://www.janeausten.co.uk/period-lighting-and-silhouette-making. **Page 312**

15. The German Waltz was introduced in England in 1811. The earliest waltzes were not as we think of them now, but more like the dance between Maria and Captain Von Trapp in The Sound of Music. "A waltz in Austen's novels refers to a tune and time signature for a country dance, which might have included a landler-like figure, in which the lady danced under her partner's raised arms."

The Regency Encyclopedia. For the purposes of this story I am referring to a waltz as we would know it. **Page 327**

16. Last verse of **The First Kiss of Love** - Lord Byron 1806
When age chills the blood, when our pleasures are past—
For years fleet away with the wings of the dove—
The dearest remembrance will still be the last,
Our sweetest memorial, the first kiss of love. **Page 459**

17. For the purpose of this story, I have coloured artistic pencils in use earlier than history allows. Graphite pencils, similar to the ones that are widely used today, date back to the 17th century, while colored pencils did not appear until the early 19th century. Early colored pencils were limited to a range of fifteen to twenty colors and were used mainly for utilitarian purposes. It wasn't until the early 20th century that colored pencils intended for artistic works were introduced. http://www.ehow.com/about_5371106_were-colored-pencils-first-made.html#ixzz34L8OHQHA **Page 479**

18. Psalms 50:15, King James Version of the Holy Bible. **Page 500**

19. The Four Horse Club - Originally one of the clubs frequented by the notorious Earl of Barrymore, the Four-Horse club had been a wild group of young men who enjoyed bribing coachmen to give them the reins to their vehicles and then driving them at break-neck speeds along the very poor British roads. Also called the Four-in-Hand Club, the Whip Club or the Barouche Club. http://www.janeausten.co.uk/well-hand-four-horse-club/ **Page 567**

Made in the USA
Lexington, KY
30 December 2014